Arthur Murphy

The works of Cornelius Tacitus

Volume 2

Arthur Murphy

The works of Cornelius Tacitus
Volume 2

ISBN/EAN: 9783742840332

Manufactured in Europe, USA, Canada, Australia, Japa

Cover: Foto ©Andreas Hilbeck / pixelio.de

Manufactured and distributed by brebook publishing software
(www.brebook.com)

Arthur Murphy

The works of Cornelius Tacitus

ASIA,
Designed for the Works of
TACITUS,
By Robert de Vaugondy,
Royal Geographer,
and Fellow of the Royal Academy at Nancy.
SCYTHIA
MARE PONTICUM
MARE CASPIUM
Aorsi
Siraci
Heniochi
IBERIA
ARMENIA
Pontus
Cappadocia
Caria
Pamphilia
Cilicia
Bithynia
THRACIA
MARE MEDITERRANEUM
SYRIA
Galilæa
Judæa
ARABES
ÆGYPTUS
Thebæ
Memphis
Nabathæi
SINUS ARABICUS
LIBYA
MEDIA
Elymai
Chaldæi
PERSÆ
CARMANIA
SINUS PERSICUS
MARE RUBRUM
BACTRI
Arii
Dahæ
Mardi
Millaria Romana

THE
WORKS

OF

CORNELIUS TACITUS;

BY

ÀRTHUR MURPHY, Esq.

WITH

AN ESSAY ON THE LIFE AND GENIUS OF TACITUS;

NOTES, SUPPLEMENTS, AND MAPS.

Præcipuum munus annalium reor, ne virtutes fileantur, utque pravis dictis factifque ex pofteritate et infamiâ metus fit.

Tacitus, Annals, iii. f. 65.

IN FOUR VOLUMES.
VOL. II.

LONDON:
PRINTED FOR G. G. J. AND J. ROBINSON, PATERNOSTER-ROW.
MDCCXCIII.

THE
ANNALS
OF
TACITUS.

BOOK XI.

CONTENTS of BOOK XI.

Novius

CONTENTS OF BOOK XI.

Novius detected with a dagger in the prince's presence: his fortitude on the rack. The first institution of the Roman quæstor: the history of that office in its progress. XXIII. Debates about filling the vacancies in the senate. The nobility of Gaul claim to be admitted. Speeches against that measure. The emperor's reply to the whole argument. The Gauls carry their point. Claudius refuses the title of Father of the Senate. XXVI. The frantic loves of Messalina and Silius. He proposes to marry the empress. She agrees: the nuptial ceremony, during the absence of Claudius, performed in the most public manner. XXIX. The freedmen bent on her destruction. Two courtesans, by the direction of Narcissus, inform the emperor. XXXI. Messalina diverts herself, and celebrates the autumnal season in the highest gaiety. Claudius returns from Ostia. Narcissus, his freedman, leads him to the camp. Silius and his confederates put to death. XXXVII. Claudius at a banquet wavers in favour of Messalina. Narcissus orders her execution. Her death in the gardens of Lucullus. The stupidity of Claudius. Narcissus obtains the ensigns of quæstorian rank.

These transactions include two years.

Years of Rome — of Chrift		Confuls
800	47	*Claudius, 4th time, Lucius Vitellius, 3d time.*
801	48	*Aulus Vitellius, L. Vipsanius.*

A N N A L S

O F

T A C I T U S.

B O O K XI.

I. MESSALINA was convinced that Poppæa had been for some time engaged in a course of adultery with Valerius Asiaticus, who had enjoyed the honour of two consulships. She had, besides, an eye to the elegant gardens, formerly the pride of Lucullus, which Asiaticus had improved in the highest taste and magnificence. Bent on the destruction of Poppæa and her lover, she suborned Suillius (a) to carry on the prosecution. Sosibius, the tutor of Britannicus, entered into the conspiracy. This man had the ear of Claudius. In secret whispers, and under a mask of friendship, he alarmed the emperor with the necessity of being on his guard against the machinations of his enemies. "Overgrown wealth," he said, "in

"the

" the hands of a private citizen, is always big with danger to
" the reigning prince. When Caligula fell, Afiaticus was the
" principal actor in that bloody tragedy. He owned the fact in
" a full affembly of the people, and claimed the glory of the
" deed (b). That bold exploit has made him popular at Rome;
" his fame is fpread through the provinces : and, even now, he
" meditates a vifit to the German armies. Born at Vienne (c),
" he has great family intereft and powerful connections in Gaul.
" A man thus fupported will be able to incite his countrymen
" to a revolt." The hint was enough for Claudius. Without
further enquiry, he difpatched Crifpinus, who commanded the
prætorian guards, with a band of foldiers. Their march refembled a body of troops going on a warlike expedition. Afiaticus was feized at Baiæ, and brought to Rome in chains.

II. He was not fuffered to appear before the fenate. The
caufe was heard in the emperor's chamber, in the prefence of
Meffalina. Suillius ftood forth as profecutor. He ftated the
corruption of the army, and accufed Afiaticus as the author of it.
By bribes, by largeffes, and by the practice of abominable vices,
the foldiers were feduced from their duty : they were prepared
for any enterprife, however atrocious. The crime of adultery
with Poppæa helped to fwell the charge ; and, to crown all, the
prifoner had unmanned himfelf by his unnatural paffions. . Stung
to the quick by this imputation, Afiaticus turned to the profecutor, " And afk your fons," he faid; " they will tell you that
" I am a man." He went into his defence in fuch a ftrain of
pathetic eloquence, that Claudius felt the ftrongeft emotions.
Even Meffalina dropped a tear. She left the room to wipe the
gufh of nature from her eyes, but firft charged Vitellius not to
fuffer the prifoner to efcape. In the mean time, fhe haftened
the deftruction of Poppæa. She fent her agents to alarm her

[with

with the horrors of a jail, and drive her, by that difmal profpect, to an act of defperation. Her malice was unknown to Claudius. He was fo little in the fecret, that, a few days afterwards, having invited Scipio as his gueft, he afked him, " Why his wife was " not of the party *(a)* ?" Scipio made anfwer, " She is dead."

III. CLAUDIUS was, for fome time, in fufpenfe. He was in-clined to favour Afiaticus, but Vitellius interpofed. With tears in his eyes, he talked of the friendfhip which had long fubfifted between the prifoner and himfelf; he mentioned their mutual habits at the court of Antonia, the emperor's mother; he ftated the public merit of Afiaticus; and, in particular, the glory of his late expedition into Britain : he omitted nothing that could excite compaffion, but, at laft, concluded (with a ftroke of treachery), that to allow him to choofe his mode of dying was an indul-gence due to fo diftinguifhed a character. This cruel fpecies of clemency was adopted by Claudius. The friends of Afiaticus recommended abftinence, as a mode of death eafy and gradual. He fcorned the pretended lenity, and betook himfelf to his ufual exercifes. He bathed and fupped with alacrity of mind. " To " die," he faid, " by the intrigues of an artful woman, or the " treachery of a debauched and profligate impoftor, fuch as Vi- " tellius, was an ignominious cataftrophe. He envied thofe who " perifhed by the fyftematic cruelty of Tiberius, or the headlong " fury of Caligula." Having declared thefe fentiments, he opened a vein, and bled to death. Before he gave himfelf the mortal wound, he had the fortitude to furvey his funeral pile. Perceiving that the flame might reach the branches of the trees, and hurt the fhade of his garden, he ordered it to be removed to a more diftant fpot. Such was the tranquillity with which he encountered death.

IV. The

IV. The senate was convened. Suillius followed his blow. He preferred an accusation against two Roman knights, of the name of Petra; both distinguished by their rank and character. The crime objected to them was, that they had made their house convenient to Poppæa, when she carried on her intrigue with Mnester. The charge against one of them imported, that, in a dream, his imagination presented to him the figure of Claudius crowned with a sheaf of corn, but the ears inverted downward. This vision was understood by the criminal as the prognostic of an approaching famine. Some will have it, that the wreath consisted of vine branches, with the leaves entirely faded; and this was deemed an omen of the emperor's death towards the end of the ensuing autumn. Whatever it might be, it is certain that it was held to be an act of treason. The two brothers died for a dream. . By a decree of the senate, Crispinus was rewarded with fifteen thousand sesterces, and the prætorian dignity. On the motion of Vitellius, a vote of ten thousand sesterces passed in favour of Sosibius, the preceptor of Britannicus, and the faithful adviser of the emperor. In the debate on this occasion, Scipio was called upon for his opinion: he rose, and said, " Since the conduct of my wife Poppæa must appear to me " in the same light that it does to this assembly, let me be " thought to concur with the general voice." A delicate stroke of prudence, yielding to the necessity of the times, yet not forgetting the ties of conjugal affection.

V. From this time, the rage of Suillius knew no bounds. A number of others followed in the same track, all rivals in iniquity. The constitution had been long since annihilated; the functions of the magistrates were wrested out of their hands; the will of the prince was the law; and, by consequence, the

crew

BOOK
XI.

A. U. C.
800.
A. D.
47.

crew of informers grew rich by injuftice and oppreffion. Their eloquence was put up to fale, like any other commodity at market. Samius, a Roman knight of diftinction, has left a memorable inftance. He had retained Suillius with a fee of ten thoufand crowns; but finding that his caufe was betrayed, he went to the houfe of the perfidious orator, and fell upon his own fword. To check this fatal mifchief, a motion was made in the fenate by Caius Silius, then conful elect. Of this man, his elevation, and his downfall, due notice will be taken hereafter. He reprefented, in ftrong colours, the avarice of the advocates. The fathers, with one voice, agreed to revive the Cincian law *(a)*, by which it was ordained in ancient times, that no advocate, for a fee, or gratuity of any kind, fhould proftitute his talents.

VI. The informers oppofed the motion. They faw that the blow was aimed at themfelves. Silius grew more eager. He was at open enmity with Suillius, and, for that reafon, preffed the bufinefs with his utmoft vigour. He cited the orators of ancient times, men of pure and upright principles, who confidered honeft fame, and the fair applaufe of pofterity, as the true reward of genius. " Eloquence," he. faid, " the firft of li-
" beral arts, if it condefcended to be let out for hire, was no
" better than a fordid trade. If it became mercenary, and fold
" itfelf to the higheft bidder, no truth can be expected; inte-
" grity is at an end. Take from venal oratory all its views of
" intereft, and the number of fuitors will, of courfe, be dimi-
" nifhed. In the reigning corruption of the modern forum,
" private feuds, mutual accufations, family quarrels, hatred, and
" animofity are kept alive. The practifers live by the paffions
" of mankind, as phyficians thrive by an epidemic diftemper.
" Call to mind Caius Afinius, Marcus Meffala, and, among the
" names of more recent date, remember the Arruntii and the

VOL. II.   C   " Æferini;

" Æferini ; men who never fet themfelves up to auction ; never
" made a bargain and fale of their talents, but rofe by their in-
" tegrity and their unbought eloquence to the higheft honours
" of the ftate." This fpeech from the conful elect was heard
with general approbation. The fathers were on the point of
declaring, by a decree, that all who took the wages of oratory
fhould be deemed guilty of extortion. Suillius and Coffutianus,
with many others who were confcious of their evil practices,
clearly faw, that if the decree paffed the fenate, it would be nothing lefs than a vote of pains and penalties againft themfelves.
To ward off the blow, they preffed round the emperor, praying
an indemnity for paft tranfactions. Claudius feeming by a nod
to affent to their petition, they took courage, and argued their
cafe as follows :

VII. " WHERE is the orator who can flatter himfelf that his
" name will reach pofterity ? The interefts of fociety require ad-
" vocates by profeffion, men verfed in queftions of right and
" wrong, and ready, as well as able, to protect the weak againft
" the proud and affluent. But eloquence is not a gratuitous gift;
" it is acquired by toil and induftry. To conduct the affairs of
" others, the orator neglects his own concerns. Life is varie-
" gated with different employments : fome betake themfelves to
" the profeffion of arms ; others to the arts of hufbandry : no
" man embraces a particular calling, without having beforehand
" made an eftimate of the profit. Afinius and Meffala have
" been cited : but it was eafy for men in their fituation, enriched
" as they were in the civil wars between Auguftus and Anthony,
" to forego all further views of emolument. It was eafy for the
" Arruntii and the Æferini, the heirs of great and opulent fa-
" milies, to act with an elevation of mind fuperior to the profits
" of the bar. And yet, we are not now to learn what prodi-
" gious

" gious fums Publius Clodius and Caius Curio received as the
" reward of their eloquence. As to ourfelves, we have not the
" advantages of fortune: in a time of profound tranquillity, it is
" but juft that we fhould be allowed to live by the arts of peace.
" The cafe of men defcended from plebeian families merits
" confideration. Without the career of eloquence, they have
" no way to emerge from obfcurity. Take from men the juft
" fruit of their ftudies, and learning will grow to feed." This
reafoning was far from honourable, but it had weight with
Claudius. He took a middle courfe, and fixed the legal per-
quifite at the fum of ten thoufand fefterces. All who prefumed
to tranfgrefs that line were to be deemed guilty of extortion, by
law compellable to refund.

VIII. About this time Mithridates, who, as has been mentioned, fwayed the fceptre of Armenia, and was brought in
chains to the tribunal of Caligula *(a)*, was releafed by the direction of Claudius. He fet out from Rome to take poffeffion
of his kingdom, relying on the fupport of his brother Pharafmanes, king of Iberia. By advices from that monarch, it appeared that the Parthian ftate was convulfed by internal divifions, and, while the regal diadem was at ftake, a people fo diftracted among themfelves would not have leifure to engage in
foreign wars. Gotarzes had feized the throne of Parthia, and
fpilt a deluge of blood. He had murdered his own brother
Artabanus, with his wife and fon, and by thefe, and other acts
of cruelty, gave his fubjects nothing to expect but flaughter and
defolation. Determined to fhake off the yoke, the people
planned a revolution in favour of Bardanes, the furviving brother of Gotarzes. This prince was by nature formed for enterprife. In two days he made a march of no lefs than three
thoufand furlongs. He took Gotarzes by furprife, attacked him

C 2

with

with sudden fury, and obliged him to consult his safety by flight. He pushed on with vigour to the adjacent provinces, and all, except Seleucia *(b)*, submitted without resistance. The inhabitants of that city shut their gates. Fired with indignation against a people, who had offered the same affront to his father, Bardanes yielded to the impulse of resentment, instead of pursuing the measures which prudence dictated. He staid to amuse himself with the siege of a place strong by nature, well fortified, amply provided with stores, and on one side defended by a rapid river *(c)*. Gotarzes, in the mean time, having obtained succours from the Dahans *(d)* and Hyrcanians, returned with a powerful army to renew the war. Bardanes was compelled to raise the siege of Seleucia. He retired to the plains of Bactria, and there pitched his camp.

IX. WHILE the east was thus thrown into convulsions, and the fate of Parthia hung on the doubtful event, Mithridates seized the opportunity to invade the kingdom of Armenia. The Roman legions and the Iberians supported the enterprise. By the former, all the forts and places of strength were levelled to the ground, and by the latter, the open country was laid waste. The Armenians, under the conduct of Demonax, at that time governor of the country, hazarded a battle, and, being defeated, were no longer able to make a stand. The new settlement, however, was for some time retarded by Cotys *(a)*, king of the lesser Armenia. A party of the nobles had declared in his favour; but, being intimidated by letters from Claudius, they abandoned their project. Mithridates mounted the throne of Armenia, with more ferocity than became a prince in the opening of a new reign. Meanwhile, the competitors for the Parthian monarchy, in the moment when they were going to try the issue of a decisive action, agreed on terms of peace. A conspiracy

had

had been formed against them both; but being detected by Gotarzes, the two brothers came to an interview. The meeting
was at first conducted with reserve on both sides. After balancing for some time, they embraced; and, taking each other by
the hand, bound themselves by an oath before the altar of the
gods, to join with their united force, in order to punish the treachery of their enemies, and, on equitable terms, to compromise
the war. The people declared for Bardanes. Gotarzes, accordingly, resigned his pretensions; and, to remove all cause
of jealousy, withdrew to the remotest parts of Hyrcania. Bardanes returned in triumph; and Seleucia threw open her gates,
after having, during a siege of seven years, stood at bay with the
whole power of the Parthian monarchy, to the disgrace of a
people, who, in such a length of time, were unable to reduce that
city to subjection.

X. BARDANES, without delay, made himself master of the
most important provinces. He intended to invade Armenia;
but Vibius Marsus, the governor of Syria, threatening to repel
him by force, he abandoned the project. Meanwhile, Gotarzes
had leisure to repent of his abdication. The Parthian nobility, who in peaceful times are always impatient of the yoke
of slavery, invited him to return. Roused by the call of the
people, he soon collected a powerful army. Bardanes marched
to meet him as far as the banks of the Erinde (a). The passage
over the river was warmly disputed. After many sharp engagements, Bardanes prevailed. He pushed his conquest with unin-
terrupted success as far as the river Sinden, which flows between
the Dahi and the territory of the Arians. His career of victory
ended at that place. Though flushed with the success of their
arms, the Parthians disliked a war in regions so far remote.
To mark, however, the progress of the victorious troops, and to

perpetuate

perpetuate the glory of having put under contribution so many distant nations, where the Arsacides had never penetrated, Bardanes raised a monument on the spot, and marched back to Parthia, proud of his exploits, more oppressive than ever, and, by consequence, more detested. A conspiracy was formed to cut him off; and accordingly, while the king on a hunting party, void of all suspicion, pursued the pleasures of the chase, his enemies fell upon him with sudden fury. Bardanes, in the prime and vigour of his days, expired under repeated blows. The glory of his reign, however short, would have eclipsed the few of his predecessors who enjoyed a length of days, if to gain the hearts of his people had been as much his ambition, as it was to render himself the terror of his enemies. By his death the kingdom was once more thrown into commotions. The choice of a successor divided the whole nation into factions. A large party adhered to Gotarzes; others declared for Meherdetes, a descendant of Phraates, at that time a hostage in the hands of the Romans. The interest of Gotarzes proved the strongest; but the people, in a short time, weary of his cruelty and wild profusion, sent a private embassy to Rome, requesting that the emperor would be graciously pleased to send Meherdetes to fill the throne of his ancestors.

XI. During the same consulship, in the year of Rome eight hundred, the secular games were celebrated, after an interval of sixty-four years since they were last solemnized in the reign of Augustus. The chronology observed by Augustus differed from the system of Claudius: but this is not the place for a discussion of that point. I have been sufficiently explicit on the subject in the history of Domitian (a), who likewise gave an exhibition of the secular games. Being at that time one of the college of fifteen, and invested with the office of prætor, it fell to my province

vince to regulate the ceremonies. Let it not be imagined that this is ſaid from motives of vanity. The fact is, in ancient times the buſineſs was conducted under the ſpecial directions of the quindecemviral order, while the chief magiſtrates officiated in the ſeveral ceremonies. Claudius thought proper to revive this public ſpectacle. He attended in the circus, and, in his preſence, the Trojan game *(b)* was performed by the youth of noble birth. Britannicus, the emperor's ſon, and Lucius Domitius, who by adoption took the name of Nero, and afterwards ſucceeded to the empire, appeared, with the reſt of the band, mounted on ſuperb horſes. Nero was received with acclamations, and that mark of popular favour was conſidered as an omen of his future grandeur. A ſtory, at that time current, gained credit with the populace. Nero in his infancy was ſaid to have been guarded by two ſerpents *(c)* ; but this idle tale held too much of that love of the marvellous which diſtinguiſhes foreign nations. The account given by the prince himſelf, who was ever unwilling to derogate from his own fame, differed from the common report. He talked of the prodigy, but graced his narrative with one ſerpent only.

XII. THE prejudice in favour of Nero roſe altogether from the eſteem in which the memory of Germanicus was held by the people at large. The only male heir of that admired commander was naturally an object of attention ; and the ſufferings of his mother Agrippina touched every heart with compaſſion. Meſſalina, it was well known, purſued her with unrelenting malice : ſhe was, even then, planning her ruin. Her ſuborned accuſers ſoon framed a liſt of crimes ; but the execution of her ſchemes was, for a time, ſuſpended. A new amour, little ſhort of phrenſy, claimed precedence of all other paſſions. Caius Silius *(o)* was the perſon for whom ſhe burned with all the

2

vehemence

vehemence of wild defire. The graces of his form and man‐
ner eclipfed all the Roman youth. That fhe might enjoy her
favourite without a rival, fhe obliged him to repudiate his wife,
Junia Silana, though defcended from illuftrious anceftors. Silius
was neither blind to the magnitude of the crime, nor to the
danger of not complying. If he refufed, a woman fcorned would
be fure to gratify her revenge; and, on the other hand, there
was a chance of deceiving the ftupidity of Claudius. The re‐
wards in view were bright and tempting. He refolved to ftand
the hazard of future confequences, and enjoy the prefent moment.
Meffalina gave a loofe to love. She fcorned to fave appearances.
She repeated her vifits, not in a private manner, but with all her
train. In public places fhe hung enamoured over him; fhe loaded
him with wealth and honours; and at length, as if the imperial
dignity had been already transferred to another houfe, the reti‐
nue of the prince, his flaves, his freedmen, and the whole fplen‐
dour of the court, adorned the manfion of her favourite.

XIII. CLAUDIUS, in the mean time, blind to the conduct of
his wife, and little fufpecting that his bed was difhonoured, gave
all his time to the duties of his cenforial office. He iffued an
edict to reprefs the licentioufnefs of the theatre. A dramatic
performance had been given to the ftage by Publius Pompo‐
nius *(a)*, a man of confular rank. On that occafion the author,
and feveral women of the firft condition, were treated by the
populace with infolence and vile fcurrility. This behaviour called
for the interpofition of the prince. To check the rapacity of
ufurers, a law was alfo paffed, prohibiting the loan of money to
young heirs, on the contingency of their father's death. The
waters, which have their fource on the Simbruine hills *(b)*, were
conveyed in aqueducts to Rome. Claudius, at the fame time,
invented the form of new letters, and added them to the Roman
alpha‐

alphabet, aware that the language of Greece, in its original state, could not boast of perfection, but received, at different periods, a variety of improvements.

XIV. THE Ægyptians were the first, who had the ingenuity to express by outward signs the ideas passing in the mind. Under the form of animals they gave a body and a figure to sentiment. Their hieroglyphics were wrought in stone, and are to be seen at this day, the most venerable monuments of human memory. The invention of letters *(a)* is also claimed by the Ægyptians. According to their account, the Phœnicians found legible characters in use throughout Ægypt, and, being much employed in navigation, carried them into Greece; importers of the art, but not intitled to the glory of the invention. The history of the matter, as related by the .Phœnicians, is, that Cadmus, with a fleet from their country, passed into Greece, and taught the art of writing to a rude and barbarous people. We are told by others, that Cecrops the Athenian, or Linus the Theban, or Palamedes the Argive, who flourished during the Trojan war, invented sixteen letters *(b)*: the honour of adding to the number, and making a complete alphabet, is ascribed to different authors, and, in particular, to Simonides. In Italy, Demaratus of Corinth, and Evander the Arcadian, introduced the arts of civilization: the former taught the Etrurians, and the latter, the aborigines, or natives of the country where he settled. The form of the Latin letters was the same as the characters of the ancient Greeks: but the Roman alphabet, like that of all other nations, was scanty in the beginning. In process of time, the original elements were increased. Claudius added three new letters, which, during the remainder of his reign, were frequently inserted, but after his death fell into disuse. In tables of brass, on which were engraved the ordinances of the people, and which remain to this day, hung up in the temples, and the forum, the shape of the three characters may still be traced.

XV. To regulate the college of augurs was the next care of Claudius. He referred the business to the confideration of the fenate, obferving to that affembly, " That an ancient and vene-
" rable inftitution ought not to be fuffered, for want of due atten-
" tion, to fink into oblivion. In times of danger, the common-
" wealth reforted to the foothfayers, and that order of men
" reftored the primitive ceremonies of religion. By the nobility
" of Etruria the fcience of future events was efteemed, and cul-
" tivated. The authority of the fenate gave additional fanctions,
" and thofe myfteries have ever fince remained in certain families,
" tranfmitted from father to fon. In the prefent decay of all
" liberal fcience, and the growth of foreign fuperftition, the
" facred myfteries are neglected, and, indeed, almoft extinguifhed.
" The empire, it is true, enjoys a ftate of perfect tranquillity;
" but, furely, for that bleffing, the people fhould bend in
" adoration to the gods, not forgetting, in the calm feafon of
" peace, thofe religious rites, which faved them in the hour of
" danger." A decree paffed the fenate, directing that the pontiffs fhould revife the whole fyftem, and retrench or ratify what
to them fhould feem proper.

XVI. In the courfe of this year, the Cherufcans applied to Rome for a king to reign over them. They had been diftracted by civil diffenfions, and in the wars that followed, the flower of their nobility was cut off. Of royal defcent there was only one furviving chief, by name Italicus, and he at that time refided at Rome. He was the fon of Flavius, the brother of Arminius; by the maternal line, grandfon to Catumer, the reigning king of the Cattians. He was comely in his perfon, expert in the

ufe

use of arms, and skilled in horsemanship, as well after the Roman manner, as the practice of the Germans. Claudius supplied him with money; appointed guards to escort him; and, by seasonable admonitions, endeavoured to inspire him with sentiments worthy of the elevation to which he was called. He desired him to go forth with courage, and ascend the throne of his ancestors with becoming dignity. He told him, that being born at Rome, and there entertained in freedom, not kept as a prisoner, he was the first, who went clothed with the character of a Roman citizen, to reign in Germany. The prince was received by his countrymen with demonstrations of joy. A stranger to the dissensions, which had for some time disturbed the public tranquillity, he had no party views to warp his conduct. The king of a people, not of a faction, he gained the esteem of all. His praise resounded in every quarter. By exercising the milder qualities of temperance and affability, and, at times, giving himself up to wine and gay carousals, which among Barbarians are esteemed national virtues, he endeared himself to all ranks of men. His fame reached the neighbouring states, and by degrees spread all over Germany.

His popularity, however, gave umbrage to the disaffected. The same turbulent spirits, who had before thrown every thing into confusion, and flourished in the distractions of their country, began to view the new king with a jealous eye. They represented to the adjacent nations, that "the rights of Germany, "transmitted to them by their forefathers, were now at the last "gasp. The grandeur of the Roman empire rises on the ruins "of public liberty. But is the Cheruscan nation at so low an "ebb, that a native, worthy of the supreme authority, cannot "be found amongst them? Is there no resource left, but that of "electing the son of Flavius, that ignominious spy, that traitor

D 2

"to

" to his country? It is in vain alleged in favour of Italicus, that
" he is nephew to Arminius. Were he the son of that gallant
" warrior, yet fostered, as he has been, in the arms, and in the
" bosom of Rome, he is, by that circumstance, unqualified to
" reign in Germany. From a young man, educated among our
" enemies, debased by servitude, and infected with foreign man-
" ners, foreign laws, and foreign sentiments, what have we to
" expect? And if this Roman king, this Italicus, inherits the
" spirit of his father; let it be remembered, that Flavius took the
" field against his kindred and the gods of Germany. In the
" whole course of that war, no man shewed a spirit so deter-
" mined; no man acted with such envenomed hostility against
" the liberties of his country."

XVII. By these, and such like incentives, the malecontents
inflamed the minds of the people, and soon collected a numerous
army. An equal number followed the standard of Italicus. " Their
" motives," they said, " were just and honourable: the young king
" did not come to usurp the crown; he was invited by the voice
" of a willing people. His birth was illustrious, and it was but
" fair, to make an experiment of his virtues. He might, per-
" haps, prove worthy of Arminius, his uncle, and of Catumer,
" his grandfather. Even for his father (a), the son had no rea-
" son to blush. If Flavius adhered with fidelity to the cause of
" Rome, he had bound himself by the obligation of an oath; and
" that oath was taken with the consent of the German nations.
" The sacred name of liberty was used in vain to varnish the guilt
" of pretended patriots; a set of men, in their private characters,
" void of honour; in their public conduct, destructive to the
" community; an unprincipled and profligate party, who, by
" fair and honest means having nothing to hope, looked for their
" private advantage in the disasters of their country." To this
reasoning

reafoning the multitude affented with fhouts of applaufe. The
Barbarians came to action. After an obftinate engagement,
victory declared for Italicus. Elate with fuccefs, he broke out
into acts of cruelty, and was foon obliged to fly the country.
The Langobards *(b)* reinftated him in his dominions. From
that time, Italicus continued to ftruggle with alternate viciffitudes
of fortune, in fuccefs no lefs than adverfity, the fcourge of the
Cherufcan nation.

XVIII. The Chaucians *(a)*, at this time free from domeftic
broils, began to turn their arms againft their neighbours. The
death of Sanquinius, who commanded the legions in the lower
Germany, furnifhed them with an opportunity to invade the
Roman provinces ; and as Corbulo, who was appointed to fucceed the deceafed general, was ftill on his way, they refolved to
ftrike their blow before his arrival. Gannafcus, born among the
Caninefates, headed the enterprife ; a bold adventurer, who
had formerly ferved among the auxiliaries in the Roman army.
Having deferted afterwards, he provided himfelf with light-built
fhallops, and followed the life of a roving freebooter, infefting
chiefly the Gallic fide of the Rhine *(b)*, where he knew the wealth
and the unwarlike genius of the people. Corbulo entered the
province. In his firft campaign he laid the foundation of that
prodigious fame, which afterwards raifed his character to the
higheft eminence. He ordered the ftrongeft galleys to fall down
the Rhine, and the fmall craft, according to their fize and fitnefs
for the fervice, to enter the æftuaries and the receffes of the
river. The boats and veffels of the enemy were funk or otherwife deftroyed. Gannafcus was obliged to fave himfelf by flight.

By thefe operations Corbulo reftored tranquillity throughout
the province. The re-eftablifhment of military difcipline was the

next

next object of his attention. He found the legions relaxed in sloth, attentive to plunder, and active for no other end. In order to make a thorough reform, he gave out in orders, that no man should presume to quit his post, or venture to attack the enemy, on any pretence, without the command of his superior officer. The soldiers at the advanced stations, the sentinels, and the whole army, performed every duty, both day and night, completely armed. Two of the men, it is said, were put to death, as an example to the rest; one, because he laboured at the trenches without his sword; and the other, for being armed with a dagger only; a severity, it must be acknowledged, strained too far, or, perhaps, not true in fact: but the rigid system, peculiar to Corbulo, might, with some colour of probability, give rise to the report. It may, however, be fairly inferred, that the commander, concerning whom a story like this could gain credit, was, in matters of moment, firm, decided, and inflexible.

XIX. By this plan of discipline, Corbulo struck a general terror through the army: but that terror had a twofold effect; it roused the Romans to a due sense of their duty, and repressed the ferocity of the Barbarians. The Frisians *(a)*, who, ever since their success against Lucius Apronius, remained in open or disguised hostility, thought it advisable, after giving hostages for their pacific temper, to accept a territory within the limits prescribed by Corbulo, and to submit to a mode of government, which he judged proper, consisting of an assembly in the nature of a senate, a body of magistrates, and a new code of laws. In order to bridle this people effectually, he built a fort in the heart of their country, and left it strongly garrisoned. In the mean time, he tried, by his emissaries, to draw over to his interest the leading chiefs of the Chaucian nation. Against Gannascus he did not scruple to act by stratagem. In the case of a deserter, who

had

B O O K
XI.
⌣
A. U. C.
800.
A. D.
47.

had violated all good faith, fraud and circumvention did not appear to him inconsistent with the dignity of the Roman name. Gannascus was cut off. His death inflamed the resentment of the Chaucians; nor was Corbulo unwilling to provoke a war. His conduct, however, though applauded at Rome by a great number, did not escape the censure of others. "Why enrage "the enemy? If he failed in his attempt, the commonwealth "must feel the calamity: if crowned with success, a general of "high renown, under a torpid and unwarlike prince, might "prove a powerful and a dangerous citizen." Claudius had no ambition to extend his dominions in Germany. He ordered the garrisons to be withdrawn, and the whole army to repass the Rhine.

XX. CORBULO had already marked out his camp in the enemy's country, when the emperor's letters came to hand. The contents were unexpected. A crowd of reflections occurred to the general: he dreaded the displeasure of the prince; he saw the legions exposed to the derision of the Barbarians, and in the opinion of the allies his own character degraded. He exclaimed with some emotion, "*Happy the commanders, who fought for the* "*old republic!*" Without a word more, he sounded a retreat. And now, to hinder his men from falling again into sluggish inactivity, he ordered a canal, three-and-twenty miles in length, to be carried on between the Meuse and the Rhine, as a channel to receive the influx of the sea, and hinder the country from being laid under water. Claudius, in the mean time, allowed him the honour of triumphal ornaments: he granted the reward of military service, but prevented the merit of deserving it.

In a short time afterwards, Curtius Rufus obtained the same distinction: the service of this man was the discovery of a mine

in

in the country of the Mattiaci *(a)*, in which was opened a vein of filver, of little profit, and foon exhaufted. The labour was feverely felt by the legions; they were obliged to dig a number of fluices, and in fubterraneous cavities to endure fatigues and hardfhips, fcarce fupportable in the open air. Weary of the labour, and finding that the fame rigorous fervices were extended to other provinces, they contrived, with fecrecy, to difpatch letters to the emperor, praying, that, when next he appointed a general, he would begin with granting him triumphal honours.

XXI. CURTIUS RUFUS *(a)*, according to fome, was the fon of a gladiator. For this I do not pretend to vouch. To fpeak of him with malignity is far from my intention, and to relate the truth is painful. He began the world in the train of a quæf- tor, whom he attended into Africa. In that ftation, while, to avoid the intenfe heat of the mid-day fun, he was fitting under a portico in the city of Adrumetum *(b)*, the form of a woman, large beyond the proportions of the human fhape *(c)*, appeared before him. A voice, at the fame time, pronounced, " You, " Rufus, are the favoured man, deftined to come hereafter into " this province with proconfular authority." Infpired by the vifion, he fet out for Rome, where, by the intereft of his friends, and his own intriguing genius, he firft obtained the quæftorfhip. In a fhort time after, he afpired to the dignity of prætor; and, though oppofed by competitors of diftinguifhed rank, he fuc- ceeded by the fuffrage of Tiberius. That emperor, to throw a veil over the mean extraction of his favourite candidate, fhrewdly faid, " *Curtius Rufus feems to be a man fprung from himfelf.*" He lived to an advanced old age, growing grey in the bafe arts of fervile adulation, to his fuperiors a fawning fycophant, to all be- neath him proud and arrogant, and with his equals, furly, rude, and impracticable. At a late period of his life, he obtained the

confular

consular and triumphal ornaments, and finally, to verify the prediction, went proconsul into Africa, where he finished his days.

XXII. About this time Cneius Novius, a man of equestrian rank, was seized in the circle at the emperor's court, with a dagger concealed under his robe: his motives were unknown at the time, and never since discovered. When he lay stretched on the rack, he avowed his own desperate purpose, but, touching his accomplices, not a syllable could be extorted from him. Whether his silence was wilful obstinacy, or proceeded from his having no secret to discover, remains uncertain. During the same consulship, Publius Dolabella proposed a new regulation, requiring that a public spectacle of gladiators should be exhibited annually, at the expence of such as obtained the office of quæstor. In the early ages of the commonwealth, that magistracy was considered as the reward of virtue. The honours of the state lay open to every citizen who relied on his fair endeavours, and the integrity of his character. The difference of age *(a)* created no incapacity. Men, in the prime of life, might be chosen consuls and dictators. The office of quæstor was instituted during the monarchy, as appears from the law CURIATA *(b)*, which was afterwards put in force by Lucius Junius Brutus. The right of election was vested in the consuls, till, at last, it centred in the people at large; and, accordingly, we find that about sixty-three years after the expulsion of the Tarquins, Valerius Potitus and Æmilius Mamercus were the first popular quæstors, created to attend the armies of the republic. The multiplicity of affairs increasing at Rome, two were added to act in a civil capacity. In process of time, when all Italy was reduced to subjection, and foreign provinces augmented the public revenue, the number of quæstors was doubled.

 Sylla

Sylla created twenty: he had transferred all judicial authority to the senate; and to fill that order with its proper complement was the object of his policy. The Roman knights, it is true, recovered their ancient jurisdiction; but even during those convulsions, and from that æra to the time we are speaking of, the quæstorship was either obtained by the merit and dignity of the candidates, or granted by the favour and free will of the people. It was reserved for Dolabella to make the election venal.

XXIII. Aulus Vitellius and Lucius Vipsanius were the next consuls. The mode of filling the vacancies in the senate became the subject of debate. The nobility of that part of Gaul styled Gallia Comata (a) had for some time enjoyed the privilege of Roman citizens: on this occasion they claimed a right to the magistracy and all civil honours. The demand became the topic of public discussion, and in the prince's cabinet met with a strong opposition. It was there contended, " That " Italy was not so barren of men, but she could well supply the " capital with fit and able senators. In former times, the mu- " nicipal towns and provinces were content to be governed by " their own native citizens. That system was long established, " and there was no reason to condemn the practice of the old " republic. The history of that period presents a school of " virtue. It is there that the models of true glory are to be " found ; those models that formed the Roman genius, and still " excite the emulation of posterity. Is it not enough that the " Venetians and Insubrians (b) have forced their way into the " senate? Are we to see a deluge of foreigners poured in upon " us, as if the city were taken by storm? What honours and " what titles of distinction will, in that case, remain for the an- " cient nobility, the true genuine stock of the Roman empire? " And for the indigent senator of Latium what means will then
" be

" be left to advance his fortune, and fupport his rank? All pofts
" of honour will be the property of wealthy intruders; a race
" of men, whofe anceftors waged war againft the very being of
" the republic; with fire and fword deftroyed her armies; and
" finally laid fiege to Julius Cæfar in the city of Alefia (c).
" But thefe are modern inftances: what fhall be faid of the
" Barbarians, who laid the walls of Rome in afhes, and dared to
" befiege the capitol and the temple of Jupiter? Let the prefent
" claimants, if it muft be fo, enjoy the titular dignity of Roman
" citizens: but let the fenatorian rank, and the honours of the
" magiftracy, be preferved, unmixed, untainted, and inviolate."

XXIV. These arguments made no impreffion on the mind
of Claudius: he replied on the fpot, and afterwards in the fenate
delivered himfelf to this effect (a): " To decide the queftion
" now depending, the annals of Rome afford a precedent;
" and a precedent of greater cogency, as it happened to the
" anceftors of my own family. Attus Claufus, by birth a Sabine,
" from whom I derive my pedigree, was admitted, on one and
" the fame day, to the freedom of Rome, and the patrician rank.
" Can I do better than adopt that rule of ancient wifdom? It is
" for the intereft of the commonwealth, that merit, wherever
" found, fhould be tranfplanted to Rome, and made our own.
" Need I obferve that to Alba we are indebted for the Julii, to
" Camerium for the Corruncani, and to Tufculum for the
" Portii? Without fearching the records of antiquity, we know
" that the nobles of Etruria, of Lucania, and, in fhort, of all
" Italy, have been incorporated with the Roman fenate. The
" Alps, in the courfe of time, were made the boundaries of the
" city: and by that extenfion of our privileges, not fimple indi-
" viduals, but whole nations were naturalized at once, and
" blended with the Roman name. In a period of profound

E 2

" peace,

" peace, the people beyond the Po were admitted to their free-
" dom. Under colour of planting colonies, we spread our le-
" gions over the face of the globe; and, by drawing into our
" civil union the flower of the several provinces, we recruited
" the strength of the mother country. The Balbi came from
" Spain, and others of equal eminence from the Narbon Gaul:
" of that accession to our numbers have we reason to repent?
" The descendants of those illustrious families are still in being:
" and can Rome boast of better citizens? Where do we see more
" generous ardour to promote her interest?

" The Spartans and the Athenians, without all question, ac-
" quired great renown in arms: to what shall we attribute their
" decline and total ruin? To what, but the injudicious policy of
" considering the vanquished as aliens to their country? The
" conduct of Romulus, the founder of Rome, was the very re-
" verse: with wisdom equal to his valour, he made those fellow
" citizens at night, who, in the morning, were his enemies in
" the field. Even foreign kings have reigned at Rome. To
" raise the descendants of freedmen to the honours of the state,
" is not, as some imagine, a modern innovation: it was the
" practice of the old republic. But the Senones waged war
" against us: and were the Volscians and the Æqui always our
" friends? The Gauls, we are told, well nigh overturned the
" capitol: and did not the Tuscans oblige us to deliver hostages?
" Did not the Samnites compel a Roman army to pass under
" the yoke(b)? Review the wars that Rome had upon her hands,
" and that with the Gauls will be found the shortest. From
" that time, a lasting and an honourable peace prevailed. Let
" them now, intermixed with the Roman people, united by ties
" of affinity, by arts, and congenial manners, be one people
" with us. Let them bring their wealth to Rome, rather than
                                                " hoard

" hoard it up for their own feparate ufe. The inftitutions of
" our anceftors, which we fo much and fo juftly revere at pre-
" fent, were, at one time, a novelty in the conftitution. The
" magiftrates were, at firft, patricians only ; the plebeians
" opened their way to honours ; and the Latins, in a fhort
" time, followed their example. In good time we embraced all
" Italy. The meafure which I now defend by examples will,
" at a future day, be another precedent. It is now a new re-
" gulation : in time it will be hiftory."

XXV. This fpeech was followed by a decree, in confequence
of which the Æduans, by way of diftinction, were, in the firft
inftance, declared capable of a feat in the fenate. Of all the
Gauls, they alone were ftyled the brethren of the Roman people,
and by their ftrict fidelity deferved the honour conferred upon
them. About the fame time, Claudius enrolled in the patrician
order fuch of the ancient fenators as ftood recommended by
their illuftrious birth, and the merit of their anceftors. The line
of thofe families, which were ftyled by Romulus the FIRST
CLASS OF NOBILITY, and by Brutus THE SECOND, was almoft
extinct. Even thofe of more recent date, created in the time
of Julius Cæfar by the CASSIAN LAW, and, under Auguftus,
by the SENIAN (a), were well nigh exhaufted. This new diftribution of honours was agreeable to the people, and this part
of his cenforial office Claudius performed with alacrity. A more
difficult bufinefs ftill remained. · Some of the fenators had
brought difhonour on their names ; and to expel them, according to the feverity of ancient ufage, was a painful tafk. He
chofe a milder method. " Let each man," he faid, " review
" his own life and manners ; and, if he fees reafon, let him
" apply for leave to erafe his name. Permiffion will of courfe
" be granted. The lift which he intended to make would
" contain,

" contain, without diſtinction, thoſe who retired of their own
" motion, and alſo ſuch as deſerved to be expelled. By that
" method, the diſgrace of being degraded would be avoided, or,
" at leaſt, alleviated."

For theſe ſeveral acts, Vipſanius the conſul moved that the
emperor ſhould be ſtyled THE FATHER OF THE SENATE.
The title, he ſaid, of FATHER OF HIS COUNTRY would be no
more than common ; but peculiar merit required a new diſtinction.   This ſtroke of flattery gave diſguſt to Claudius.   He
therefore over-ruled the motion.   He then cloſed the luſtre of
five years, and made a ſurvey of the people.   The number of
citizens amounted nearly to ſix millions (b).   From this time
the emperor no longer remained in ſtupid inſenſibility, blind to
the conduct of his wife.   He was ſoon reduced to the neceſſity
of hearing and puniſhing the enormity of her guilt : but the act
by which he vindicated his own honour, gave him an opportunity to ſully it by an inceſtuous marriage.

XXVI. MESSALINA had hitherto found ſo ready a compliance with her vicious paſſions, that the cheap delight was
grown inſipid.   To give a zeſt to pleaſure, ſhe had recourſe to
modes of gratification untried before.   Silius, at the ſame time,
intoxicated with ſucceſs, or, perhaps, thinking that the magnitude of his danger was to be encountered with equal courage,
made a propoſal altogether new and daring.   " They were not,"
he ſaid, " in a ſituation to wait, with patience, for the death of
" the prince.   Prudence and cautious meaſures were for the in-
" nocent only.   In caſes of flagrant guilt, a bold effort of cou-
" rage was the only remedy.   If they undertook with ſpirit,
" their accomplices, appriſed of their ſituation, would be ready
" to hazard all that was dear to them.   As to himſelf, he was
                                                    " divorced

" divorced from his wife ; he was a fingle man ; he had no
" children ; he was willing to marry Meffalina, and adopt Bri-
" tannicus for his fon.   After the nuptial ceremony, the power
" which Meffalina then enjoyed would ftill continue in her
" hands, unimpaired, and undiminifhed.   To infure their mu-
" tual fafety, nothing remained but to circumvent a fuperan-
" nuated emperor, when unprovoked, ftupid ; but when roufed
" from his lethargy, fudden, furious, and vindictive."   The
propofition was not relifhed by Meffalina.   Motives of conjugal
affection had no influence on her conduct ; but fhe beheld her
lover with a jealous eye.   Raifed to imperial dignity, he might
defpife an adulterefs, and their guilty joys.   Their mutual pleafures, endeared at prefent by the magnitude of the crime and
the danger, might, in the day of fecurity, appear in their native
colours, and pall the fated appetite.   The marriage, notwithftanding, had charms that pleafed her fancy.   It was a further
ftep in guilt and infamy ; and infamy, when beyond all meafure great, is the laft incentive of an abandoned mind.   She
clofed with the offer made by Silius, but deferred the carrying
of it into execution, till the emperor went to Oftia to affift at a
facrifice.   During his abfence, the nuptial ceremony was performed with pomp, and all the accuftomed rites.

XXVII. THE fact which I have ftated, it muft be acknowledged, carries with it an air of fable.   That fuch a degree of felf-delufion, in a populous city where every thing is
known and difcuffed in public, fhould infatuate the mind of any
perfon whatever, will hardly gain credit with pofterity.   Much
lefs will it be believed, that a conful elect, and the wife of an
emperor, on a day appointed, in the prefence of witneffes duly
fummoned, fhould dare to meet the public eye, and fign a contract with exprefs provifions for the iffue of an unlawful mar-

2.

riage.

riage. It will be a circumſtance ſtill more incredible, that the empreſs ſhould hear the marriage ceremony pronounced by the augur, and, in her turn, repeat the words; that ſhe ſhould join in a ſacrifice to the gods; take her place at the nuptial banquet; exchange careſſes and mutual endearments with the bridegroom, and retire with him to the conſummation of connubial joys. The whole muſt appear romantic; but to amuſe with fiction is not the deſign of this work. The facts here related are well atteſted by writers of that period, and by grave and elderly men, who lived at the time, and were informed of every circum-ſtance.

XXVIII. THE prince's family was thrown into conſternation. The favourites who ſtood high in power were alarmed for them-ſelves. Full of apprehenſions, and dreading a ſudden change, they diſcloſed their minds, not in ſecret murmurs, but openly, and in terms of indignation. " While a ſtage-player (a) en-" joyed the embraces of Meſſalina, the emperor's bed was diſ-" honoured, but the ſtate was not in danger. At preſent, what " had they not to fear from a young man of the firſt nobility, " endowed with talents and with vigour of mind, in his perſon " graceful, and, at that very time, deſigned for the conſulſhip? " Silius was preparing to open a new ſcene. The ſolemn farce " of a marriage has been performed, and the cataſtrophe, with " which they intend to conclude the piece, may be eaſily fore-" ſeen." Their fears were ſtill increaſed, when they conſidered the ſtupidity of Claudius, and the aſcendant which the empreſs had obtained over him, to ſuch a degree, that the beſt blood in Rome had been ſpilt to gratify her inſatiate vengeance. On the other hand, the imbecility of Claudius gave them hopes of ſucceſs. If they could once impreſs that torpid mind with an idea of Meſſalina's wickedneſs, ſhe might be condemned unheard,

heard, and, by the sudden violence of the emperor, hurried away to execution. The only danger was, that she might gain an audience. Her defence might satisfy the emperor ; and, even if she confessed her guilt, he might remain deaf to the truth, insensible of disgrace, weak, stupid, and uxorious.

XXIX. CALLISTUS *(a)*, who, as already mentioned, was a principal actor in the catastrophe of Caligula, held a meeting with Narcissus, the chief adviser of the murder of Appius, and with Pallas, the reigning favourite at the court of Claudius. Their first idea was, to address themselves at once to Messalina, and, without alluding to her other enormous practices, endeavour to break the connection between her and Silius. This plan was soon deserted. The danger of provoking the haughty spirit of Messalina operated on the fears of Pallas. Callistus knew his own interest too well : a politician formed by the maxims of the preceding reign, he was not then to learn that power at court is preserved by tame compliance, not by honest counsels. Narcissus was left to act from his own judgment. To ruin Messalina was his fixed resolution ; but the blow, he knew, must be struck before she could see the hand that aimed it. He laid his train with the deepest secrecy. Claudius continued loitering away the time at Ostia. Callistus employed the interval to the best advantage. He engaged in his plot two famous courtesans, at that time high in favour with the emperor. He allured them by presents and liberal promises. He convinced them both, that by the ruin of Messalina they might rise to power and influence. He represented their interest in the strongest colours, and, by those incentives, induced them to prefer an accusation against the empress.

XXX. THE plot being settled, one of the concubines (by

name Calpurnia) obtained a private interview with Claudius. Throwing herself at the emperor's feet, she told him that Meſſalina had diſhonoured him by a marriage with Silius. Cleopatra, the other actreſs in the ſcene, was near at hand to confirm the ſtory. Being aſked by the accuſer whether ſhe did not know the truth of the charge, her teſtimony confirmed the whole. Narciſſus was immediately ſummoned to the emperor's preſence. He began with an humble apology for the remiſſneſs of his conduct. " He had been ſilent as to Vectius and Plau-
" tius, whoſe criminal intrigues were too well known. Even
" in that very moment it was not his intention to urge the
" crime of adultery ; nor would he deſire reſtitution of the pa-
" lace, the houſehold train, and the ſplendours of the imperial
" houſe. Let Silius enjoy them all ; but let him reſtore the
" emperor's wife, and give up his marriage contract to be de-
" clared null and void. You are divorced, Cæſar, at this mo-
" ment divorced, and are you ignorant of it ? The people ſaw
" the marriage ceremony, the ſenate beheld it, and the ſoldiers
" know it. Act with vigour ; take a deciſive ſtep, or the adul-
" terer is maſter of Rome."

XXXI. CLAUDIUS called a council of his friends. Turranius, the ſuperintendant of the public ſtores, and Luſius Geta, the commander of the prætorian bands, acknowledged the whole of her flagitious conduct. The reſt of the courtiers crowded round the prince, with importunity urging him to go forth to the camp, and ſecure the prætorian guards. His own perſonal ſafety was the firſt conſideration. Vindictive meaſures might follow in good time. The alarm was too much for the faculties of ſo weak a man as Claudius. He ſtood in ſtupid amazement. He aſked ſeveral times, Am I emperor ? Is Silius ſtill a private man ?

Meſſalina,

Meſſalina, in the mean time, paſſed the hours in gay feſti-
vity, all on the wing of pleaſure and enjoyment. It was then
the latter end of autumn: in honour of the feaſon, an interlude,
repreſenting the vintage, was exhibited by her order at the palace. The wine-preſſes were ſet to work; the juice preſſed
from the grape flowed in copious ſtreams, and round the vats
a band of women, dreſſed after the Bacchanalian faſhion, with
the ſkins of tigers, danced in frolic meaſures, with the wild
tranſport uſual at the rites of Bacchus. In the midſt of the
revellers Meſſalina diſplayed the graces of her perſon, her hair
flowing with artful negligence, and a thyrſus waving in her
hand. Silius fluttered at her ſide; his temples crowned with
wreaths of ivy, his legs adorned with buſkins, and his head, with
languiſhing airs, moving in uniſon with the muſic, while a chorus
circled round the happy pair, with dance, and ſong, and laſci-
vious geſture animating the ſcene. There is a current tradition,
that Vectius Valens in a fit of ecſtaſy climbed up among the
branches of a tree, and being aſked what he ſaw, made anſwer,
" I ſee *a dreadful ſtorm* gathering at Oſtia." Whether the ſky
was then overcaſt, or the expreſſion fell by chance, it proved in
the end a true prediction.

XXXII. MEANWHILE, it became publicly known at Rome,
not by vague report, but by ſure intelligence brought by ſpecial
meſſengers, that Claudius, fully appriſed of all that paſſed, was
on his way, determined to do juſtice on the guilty. Meſſalina
withdrew to the gardens of Lucullus. Silius, endeavouring
under an air of gaiety to hide his fears, went towards the forum,
as if he had buſineſs to tranſact. The reſt of the party fled with
precipitation. The centurions purſued them. Several were
ſeized in the ſtreets, or in their lurking-places, and loaded with
fetters. In this reverſe of fortune, Meſſalina had no time for

                                              deli-

deliberation. She refolved to meet the emperor on his way, and, in a perfonal interview, to try that power over his affections which had fo often ferved her on former occafions. In order to excite compaffion, fhe ordered her children, Octavia and Britannicus, to fly to the embraces of their father. She prevailed on Vibidia, the eldeft of the veftal virgins, to addrefs the emperor as the fovereign pontiff, and wring from him, by the force of prayers, a pardon for his wife. She herfelf traverfed the city on foot, with only three attendants. Such, in the moment of adverfity, was the folitude in which fhe was left. She mounted into a tumbrel, ufually employed to carry off the refufe of the city-gardens, and in that vehicle proceeded on her way to Oftia. From the fpectators not a groan was heard; no fign of pity was feen. The enormity of her guilt fuppreffed every kind emotion of the heart.

XXXIII. CLAUDIUS, in the mean time, was thrown into violent agitations. Doubt and fear diftracted him. He had no reliance on Geta, who commanded the prætorian guards; a man at all times fluctuating between good and evil, and ready for any mifchief. Narciffus, feconded by his friends and affociates, fpoke his mind in terms plain and direct. He told the. emperor that all was loft, if the command of the camp were not, for that day, vefted in one of his freedmen. He offered himfelf for that important office; and left Claudius on the road to Rome fhould be induced, by the influence of Lucius Vitellius and Publius Largus Cæcina, to alter his refolution, he defired to be conveyed in the fame carriage with the prince. He mounted the vehicle, and took his place without further ceremony.

XXXIV. CLAUDIUS, as he proceeded towards the city, felt himfelf diftracted by contending paffions. He inveighed againft

2   his

his wife; he foftened into tendernefs, and felt for his children. During all that agitation of mind, Vitellius, we are told, contented himfelf with faying, " The vile iniquity! The infamous " crime!" Narciffus preffed him to be more explicit; but his anfwers were in the oracular ftyle, dark, ambiguous, and liable to be interpreted various ways. Cæcina followed his example. It was not long before Meffalina appeared in fight. Her fupplications were loud and vehement. " Hear your unhappy " wife," fhe faid; " hear the mother of Octavia and Britannicus." To prevent any impreffion of tendernefs, the accufer raifed his voice: he talked of Silius, and the wickednefs of the marriage; he produced a memorial, containing a full account of the whole proceeding, and, to draw the emperor's eyes from Meffalina, gave him the papers to read. As they entered Rome, Octavia and Britannicus prefented themfelves before the prince; but, by order of Narciffus, they were both removed. Vibidia claimed to be heard: in a pathetic tone fhe remonftrated, that to condemn his wife unheard, would be unjuft, and fhocking to humanity. She received for anfwer, that Meffalina would have her opportunity to make her defence; in the mean time, it became a veftal virgin to retire to the functions of her facred office..

XXXV. The filence of Claudius, during the whole of this fcene, was beheld with aftonifhment. Vitellius looked aghaft, affecting to underftand nothing. All directions were given by the freedman. He ordered the adulterer's houfe to be thrown open, and proceeded thither with the emperor. He fhewed him in the veftibule the ftatue of Silius the father, which the fenate had ordered to be deftroyed; he pointed to the fplendid ornaments, formerly the property of the Neros and the Drufi, now in the poffeffion of the adulterer; the reward of his profligacy.

B O O K
XI.
A. U. C.
801.
A. D.
48.

ligacy. Claudius was fired with indignation. Before he had time to cool, and while, with violent menaces, he was denouncing vengeance, Narciſſus took advantage of the moment, and conducted him to the camp. The ſoldiers were aſſembled in a body to receive him. Claudius, by the advice of his miniſters, delivered a ſhort harangue. On the ſubject of his diſgrace it was impoſſible to expatiate ; ſhame ſuppreſſed his voice. The camp reſounded with rage and clamour. The ſoldiers called aloud for the names of the guilty, threatening immediate vengeance. Silius was brought before the tribunal. He attempted no defence ; he aſked for no delay ; inſtant death was all he deſired. Several Roman knights followed his example, with equal firmneſs wiſhing to end their miſery. In the number were Titius Proculus, whom Silius had appointed to guard Meſſalina ; Vectius Valens, who confeſſed his guilt, and offered to give evidence againſt others ; Pompeius Urbicus, and Saufellus Trogus : by the emperor's order they were hurried to inſtant execution. The ſame fate attended Decius Calpurnianus, præfect of the night-watch ; Sulpicius Rufus, director of the public games ; and Juncus Virgilianus, a member of the ſenate.

XXXVI. Mnester was the only perſon, in whoſe favour Claudius was held in ſuſpenſe. This man, in agony, tore his garments, and " Behold," he ſaid, " behold a body ſeamed with " ſtripes. Remember your own words, Cæſar, the words, in " which you gave me ſtrict directions to obey the will and plea- " ſure of Meſſalina. The reſt acted for their reward ; they had " bright objects in view. If I have erred, I erred through neceſ- " ſity, not by inclination. Had Silius ſeized the reins of govern- " ment, I ſhould have been the firſt victim to his fury." Claudius heſitated : touched with compaſſion, he was on the point of granting the wretch his pardon ; but after executing ſo many
perſons

perfons of illuftrious rank, his freedmen told him, that the life
of a minftrel was of no value: whether the man offended from
inclination, or compulfion, was not worth a moment's paufe:
his cafe deferved no favour. The defence made by Traulus Montanus, a Roman knight, availed him nothing. In the prime of
youth, of ingenuous manners, and an elegant figure, he had
the misfortune to be diftinguifhed by Meffalina. She invited
him to her bed, and, after one night, difmiffed him from her fervice. Such was the caprice that ruled all her paffions: fhe loved
with fury, and was foon difgufted. A pardon was granted to
Suillius Cæfoninus and Plautius Lateranus: the laft, in confideration of the great merit of his uncle *(a)*, was faved from execution. Cæfoninus was protected by his vices. In that lewd
fociety, with whom he had been lately connected, he had been
obliged to fuffer unnatural indignities; and that difgrace was
deemed fufficient punifhment..

XXXVII. Messalina remained, during this whole time,.
in the gardens of Lucullus. She ftill entertained hopes of prolonging her days. She began to write to the emperor in a ftyle
of fupplication; her paffions fhifted, and fhe fpoke the language
of reproach: even in ruin, her pride was not abated. If Narciffus had not haftened the execution, there is no doubt but the
blow, aimed at her, would have recoiled upon himfelf. Claudius,
as foon as he returned to his palace, placed himfelf at his convivial table. Being refrefhed, and in a fhort time warm with wine,
he gave orders that a meffenger fhould be fent to tell the unhappy
woman (thofe were his words), that on the next day fhe fhould
be admitted to make her defence. Narciffus took the alarm: he
faw the refentments of his mafter ebbing faft away,. and his
former fondnefs flowing in upon him. Delay was big with
danger. The night, then coming on apace, might produce a
change of fentiment; and his very bed-chamber, the fcene of

all

all his happiness, might melt him into tenderness and conjugal
affection. Filled with these apprehensions, the freedman rushed
out of the banqueting-room, and, in the emperor's name, gave
orders to the centurions, and the tribune on duty, to do immediate
execution on Messalina. Evodus, one of the freedmen,
was sent to superintend the execution. This man made the best
of his way to the gardens. He found the empress stretched on
the ground, and Lepida, her mother, sitting by her. While
Messalina flourished in prosperity, the mother kept no terms
with her daughter. In her present distress, she felt the regret
and anguish of a parent. "Death," she told the unhappy criminal,
"was her only refuge. To linger for the stroke of the
" executioner were unworthy and ignoble. Life with her was
" over: she was in the last act, and nothing remained but to close
" the scene with dignity and a becoming spirit." But in a mind,
like that of Messalina, depraved by vicious passions, every virtue
was extinguished. She sunk under her afflictions, overwhelmed
with grief, dissolved in tears, and uttering vain complaints, when
the garden-gate was thrown open. The tribune presented himself
in sullen silence. Evodus, the freedman, discharged a
torrent of opprobrious language, with all the malice of a servile
spirit.

XXXVIII. Messalina was now, for the first time, sensible
of her condition. She saw that all was lost; she received a
poniard; she aimed it with a feeble effort at her throat; she
pointed it to her breast, irresolute, and clinging still to life. The
tribune dispatched her at one blow. Her body was left to be
disposed of by her mother. The emperor, in the mean time,
had not risen from table. He was told that Messalina was no
more; but whether she died by her own hand, or that of the
executioner, was not mentioned, nor did it occur to him to ask
the question. He called for wine, and pampered himself, as

usual

ufual, with the luxuries of the table. On the following days he appeared unmoved, unaltered, without a fymptom of anger, joy, or grief, or any one fenfation of the human heart. Even amidft the exultations of Meffalina's enemies, and the cries of her children, lamenting their unhappy mother, he remained funk in ftupid apathy. In order to blot her altogether from his memory, the fenate decreed, that her name fhould be effaced in all places, whether public or private, and that her images fhould be every where taken down. The enfigns of the quæftorian dignity were voted to Narciffus; a flender recompenfe, when it is confidered, that, though fecond in rank to Pallas and Calliftus, he was the chief advifer in the whole proceeding againft Meffalina. The punifhment inflicted, by his means, was undoubtedly juft; but it proved the fource of numberlefs crimes, and a long train of public calamity *(a)*.

BOOK XI. A. U. C. 801. A. D. 48.

END OF THE ELEVENTH BOOK.

THE
ANNALS
OF
TACITUS.

BOOK XII.

CONTENTS of BOOK XII.

CONTENTS OF BOOK XII.

tain. The work ill executed at first, and completed afterwards. Narcissus blamed by Agrippina. LVIII. Nero pleads for the inhabitants of Ilium, and other cities. LIX. Statilius Taurus accused by Tarquitius Priscus: the latter expelled the senate in spite of Agrippina. LX. The jurisdiction of the imperial procurators established in the provinces. Observations on that subject. LXI. An exemption from taxes granted to the isle of Coos, and to the city of Byzantium a remission of tribute for five years. LXIV. Portents and prodigies. Domitia Lepida, the aunt of Nero, for endeavouring to ingratiate herself with her nephew, accused by the artifice of Agrippina. Narcissus endeavours to save her, but in vain: she is condemned to die. LXVI. Claudius taken ill: he removes to Sinuessa. Agrippina prepares a plate of poisoned mushrooms. Xenophon, the physician, puts a poisoned feather down the emperor's throat, under pretence of making him vomit. LXVIII. Britannicus detained in the palace by Agrippina, while Nero is proclaimed emperor by the army. The senate approve, and decree divine honours to the memory of Claudius.

These transactions passed in six years.

Years of Rome—of Christ		Consuls
802	49	*Pomponius Longinus Gallus, Quintus Veranius.*
803	50	*Caius Antistius Vetus, M. Suillius Nervillianus.*
804	51	*Claudius, 5th time, S. Cornelius Orphitus.*
805	52	*{ P. Cornelius Sylla Faustus, L. Salvius Otho Titianus.*
806	53	*Decimus Junius Silanus, Q. Haterius Antoninus.*
807	54	*{ Marcus Asinius Marcellus, Manius Acilius Aviola.*

1. THE death of Meffalina threw the Imperial family into a ftate of diftraction. The freedmen were divided into contending factions. The emperor difliked a life of celibacy, and the uxorious difpofition of his nature made him liable to be governed by the partner of his bed. Which of the favourites fhould make the fortune of a future emprefs was the point in dif- pute. Nor was female ambition lefs excited. Several candi- dates afpired to the vacant throne, all depending on pretenfions, that gave to each a decided title; fuch as nobility of birth, fupe- rior beauty, immoderate riches, and, in fhort, every claim to that great elevation. The conteft, however, lay between Lollia Paulina, the daughter of Marcus Lollius the conful, and Agrip-

pina,

pina, the immediate issue of Germanicus. Pallas espoused the interest of Agrippina, and Lollia was supported by Callistus. There was still a third rival, namely Ælia Petina, descended from the family of the Tuberos. Narcissus declared in her favour. By the jarring counsels of the three favourites, Claudius was distracted in his choice; by turns inclined to each, persuaded always by the last, yet determined by none. At length, to weigh their different propositions, and the reasonings in support of them, he called his confidential ministers to an audience.

II. NARCISSUS urged in favour of Ælia Petina *(a)*, that she was formerly the wife of Claudius, and by him was the mother of Antonia. By joining her again in the bands of wedlock, no alteration would be made in the imperial family. A person, with whom the prince had already experienced the tenderest union, would be reinstated; and, since Octavia and Britannicus were so nearly allied to her daughter, she would embrace them both with sincere affection, free from the little jealousies of a step-mother. Callistus, on the contrary, was of opinion, that a woman, disgraced by a long divorce, and suddenly restored to favour, would bring with her the pride and arrogance of an actual conquest: but to Lollia no objection could be made: she had never been a mother, and, by consequence, her affections, not already engaged, would be reserved for the issue of the prince. Her whole stock of tenderness would be engrossed by Octavia and Britannicus. Pallas contended for Agrippina: by a match with her, the grandson of Germanicus would be transplanted into the imperial family, and that union would be an accession of strength to the Claudian line. Agrippina was still in the prime of life, of a constitution that promised a numerous issue; and to suffer a woman of her rank and dignity to carry the splendour of the Cæsarean line into another family, would be a measure highly impolitic.

III. THIS

III. This reasoning weighed with Claudius, and the beauty of Agrippina added force to the argument. She had, besides, the art of displaying her charms to the best advantage. The ties of consanguinity gave her free access to her uncle. She made use of her opportunities, and, in a short time, secured her conquest. Without waiting for the marriage rites, she was able to anticipate the splendour and authority of imperial grandeur. Sure of her triumph over her rival, she enlarged her views, and by a projected match between Domitius (*a*), her son by Cneius Ænobarbus, and Octavia, the emperor's daughter, began to plan the elevation of her family. The scene before her flattered her ambition, but without a stroke of iniquity could not be realized. The fact was, Octavia, with the consent of Claudius, was contracted to Lucius Silanus, a youth of noble descent, by triumphal honours rendered still more illustrious, and by a spectacle of gladiators, given in his name, endeared to the people. But to a woman of high ambition and a politic character it was not difficult to mould to her purposes a man like Claudius, void of sentiment, without a passion, and without a motive, except what was infused by the suggestion of others.

IV. Vitellius saw the tide running with a rapid current in favour of Agrippina. He resolved to ingratiate himself without delay. His office of censor gave him the power of executing the vilest purposes, and, at the same time, served as a veil to hide his iniquity. He made advances to Agrippina, and entered into all her measures. His first step was to frame an accusation against Silanus, whose sister, Junia Calvina, in her person elegant, but of a loose and lascivious character, had been, not long before, the daughter-in-law of Vitellius. He accused them both of an incestuous commerce. The charge, in truth, was without foundation; but the folly of a brother and sister, who were so unguarded as to give to natural affection an air of criminality, afforded colour for the imputation. Claudius liftened to the ftory. Inclined to protect his daughter, he was eafily incenfed againft an intended hufband, who had fhewn himfelf capable of fo foul a crime. Silanus was, at that time, prætor for the year. He little fufpected the treacherous arts, by which his character and his fortune were undermined. By an unexpected edict, iffued by Vitellius, he was expelled the fenate, though that affembly had been lately reviewed and regiftered by the cenfor. Claudius declared the marriage contract void; he renounced all ties of affinity with Silanus, and obliged him to abdicate the prætorfhip, though but a fingle day remained to complete the year. For that fhort interval, Eprius Marcellus was appointed to fill the vacant office.

V. In the confulfhip of Caius Pomponius Longinus and Quintus Veranius, the fond endearments, that paffed between the emperor and his niece, left no room to doubt but their criminal loves, moft probably indulged already, would foon be followed by the nuptial ceremony. But the marriage of an uncle with his brother's daughter, was, at that time, without a precedent. If they avowed an inceftuous marriage, the popular hatred might be inflamed againft them, and fome public calamity might befal the city of Rome. Claudius was held in fufpenfe. Vitellius undertook to remove every fcruple. He defired to know whether the emperor would make the fenfe of the people, and the authority of the fenate, the rule of his conduct. Claudius replied, that he was one of the people, an individual too weak to refift the public voice. Vitellius defired that he would remain in his palace, and went directly to the fenate. He began with affuring the fathers that he came on bufinefs of the firft importance, and, having obtained leave to fpeak out of his turn he proceeded as follows:

follows: " The office of fupreme magiftrate is at beft a ftate of pain-
" ful folicitude. The cares of a prince, who fuperintends the go-
" vernment of the world, requires domeftic comfort to fweeten
" anxiety, and leave him at leifure to think for the good of the
" whole. And where can he find a comfort fo fit, fo honourable,
" fo confiftent with his dignity, as in the arms of a wife, his
" partner in profperity, and in affliction the balm of all his
" cares? With a faithful affociate, he may unload his inmoft
" thoughts ; to her he may commit the management of his chil-
" dren ; and, in that tender union, unfeduced by pleafure, unde-
" bauched by riot and luxury, he may continue to fhew that
" reverence for the laws, which diftinguifhed the character of
" Claudius from his earlieft youth."

VI. AFTER this artful introduction, finding that he was heard
by the fathers with manifeft fymptoms of a complying fpirit, he
refumed his difcourfe. "Since it feems to be the prevailing
" opinion, that, to alleviate the cares of the emperor, an imperial
" confort is abfolutely neceffary, nothing remains but to recom-
" mend the choice of a perfon, diftinguifhed by her illuftrious
" birth, a fruitful womb, and the purity of her morals. This
" point may be foon decided. Agrippina muft, of courfe, pre-
" fent herfelf to every mind. Defcended from a noble ftock, fhe
" is the mother of children, and poffeffes, befides, all the virtues
" and all the graces of her fex. Nor is this all : by the fpecial
" care of the gods, a prince, who has known no lawlefs pleafures,
" who has fought the modeft enjoyments of connubial love, has
" now an opportunity of taking a widow to his arms, without
" injury to any private citizen, and without violating the rights
" of the marriage bed. By former emperors wives have been
" taken from the embraces of their hufbands : we have heard it
" from our fathers ; we have been eye-witneffes of the fact. But

BOOK
XII.
A. U. C.
802.
A. D.
49.

H 2

" thefe

"these acts of violence are now at an end.   A precedent may be
"established, to regulate the conduct of all future emperors.
"But it may be said, a marriage between the uncle and his niece
"is unknown to Roman manners.   To this the answer is ob-
"vious : it is the practice of foreign nations, and no law forbids
"it. By the rule of ancient times, cousin-germans were restrained
"from marrying; but the change of manners has introduced a
"different custom.   Such marriages are now grown familiar.
"Public convenience is the parent of all civil institutions : the
"marriage, which to-day seems an innovation, in future times
"will be the general practice."

VII. THIS speech was received with the general assent. Many
of the fathers rushed out of the house, declaring aloud, that if
the emperor hesitated, they knew how to enforce compliance.
The populace at the door echoed back the voice of the senate,
and, with violent uproar, called it the wish of the people. Claudius delayed no longer: he shewed himself in the forum, amidst
shouts and acclamations.   He proceeded to the senate, and there
desired that a decree might pass, declaring marriages between
the uncle and his niece legal for the future.   The law was
enacted, but little relished.   Titus Alledius Severus, a Roman
knight, was the only person willing to embrace such an alliance.   He married his niece, but, as was generally believed, with
a design to pay his court to Agrippina.   From this time a new
scene of affairs was opened.   The government of a woman
prevailed; but it was no longer a woman of loose and dissolute
manners like Messalina, who meant to mock the people with
a reign of lewdness and debauchery.   Agrippina established a
despotic system, and maintained it with the vigour of a manly
spirit : in her public conduct rigorous, and often arrogant, she
suffered no irregularity in her domestic management.   Vice,
when

when fubfervient to her fchemes of ambition, might be the
means, but never was her ruling paffion.   Her avarice knew no
bounds : but the fupport of government was her pretext.

VIII. On the day of the nuptial ceremony Silanus put an
end to his life.   Till that time he had nourifhed delufive hopes ;
or, it might be his intention to mark the day by a deed of horror.   His fifter Calvina was banifhed out of Italy.   Claudius,
to atone for her offence, revived the ancient law of Tullus, the
Roman king, and ordered a facrifice and expiations by the pontiffs to be made in the grove of Diana.   This provoked the
public ridicule.   It was obferved that the time for inflicting penalties, and performing folemn rites, was chofen with notable
judgment, when adultery was by law eftablifhed.   Agrippina
was not willing to be diftinguifhed by evil deeds alone : in order
to grace her character, fhe interceded for Annæus Seneca, who
had been driven into banifhment; and not only reftored him to
his country, but obtained for him the prætorian rank.   The
learning and brilliant genius of that philofopher, fhe had no
doubt, would render the meafure acceptable to the people ; and,
from the education of her fon Domitius under fuch a mafter, fhe
promifed herfelf great advantages.   She had ftill a deeper fcheme
in view: by the wifdom and advice of Seneca, fhe hoped to
make the road to empire fmooth and level for her fon.   Motives
of gratitude would have their influence on the mind of that eminent man, and fix him in her intereft, a faithful counfellor, and
her friend by fentiment; while a fenfe of former injuries would
make him the fecret enemy of Claudius.

IX. Having conceived this plan of ambition, fhe thought
her meafures could not be too foon concerted.   She contrived,
by large and generous promifes, to gain over to her purpofes
Memmius

Memmius Pollio, at that time conful elect. He moved in the fenate an addrefs to the emperor, requefting his confent to a contract of marriage between Domitius and Octavia. The match was fuited to the age of the parties Agrippina intended it as a prelude to greater fcenes, not yet difclofed. The fpeech of Pollio to the fathers was little more than a repetition of what had been urged by Vitellius. The motion fucceeded. Octavia was promifed to Domitius, and, by this additional tie, the young prince was raifed to higher fplendour. He was now confidered as the fon-in-law of the emperor. Supported by the intrigues of his mother, and not lefs by the enemies of Meffalina, who dreaded the vengeance of her fon, he began to vie with Britannicus, and even to difpute with him the point of precedence.

X. The deputies from Parthia fent, as has been related, to demand Meherdates for their king, were admitted to an audience before the fenate. They opened their commiffion in the following manner : " The alliance between Rome and Parthia,
" and the fubfifting treaties, are fully known to us ; nor is it a
" fpirit of difaffection to the family of the Arfacides that brings
" us to this affembly. We feek the fon of Vonones, the grand-
" fon of Phraates. In the prefent crifis, he is our only refuge,
" our fhield and beft protection from the tyranny of Gotarzes,
" who is juftly execrated by the whole Parthian nation. His
" reign is marked with blood. His brothers were the firft
" victims to his fury. His kindred have been fince cut off.
" No place is fafe from devaftation : neither age nor fex is
" fpared ; parents and their children perifh in one general maf-
" facre, and infants yet unborn are butchered in the mother's
" womb. Such are the exploits of Gotarzes ; in peace a tyrant,
" and in war difaftrous to his country. Cruelty, he hopes,
" will feem in the eyes of men a warlike fpirit. The treaties

" fubfifting

" fubfifting between Rome and Parthia are of ancient date :
" they have been the bafis of a lafting friendfhip; and to prove
" that friendfhip fincere, the fathers have now a fair oppor-
" tunity.. It is theirs to vindicate the rights of a nation, which,
" though not inferior in point of ftrength and numbers, yields
" to Rome from motives of refpect. For this reafon the fons
" of Parthian kings have been delivered up as hoftages. The
" principle of that acquiefcence is, that if domeftic tyranny
" fhould prove a galling yoke, the people may have recourfe to
" the emperor and the fenate. They now claim, at your hands,
" a king trained up in Roman manners, and, by confequence,
" likely to bring with him to his native country the beft notions
" of civil government."

XI. CLAUDIUS anfwered the ambaffadors in a ftyle of mag--
nificence. He fet forth the grandeur of the Roman name,
and the deference due from the Parthian nation. He placed
himfelf on a level with Auguftus, who, in like manner, had received the applications of a whole people ; but he made no mention of Tiberius (a), though that emperor had dealt out fceptres,
and placed foreign kings on the throne of Parthia. After this
brilliant harangue, he turned to Meherdates, then prefent in the
fenate, and in a ferious ftrain admonifhed him to remember
that he was going forth, not the lord of flaves, but the governor
of men ; not the tyrant, but the chief magiftrate of his fellow
citizens. He advifed him to practife the virtues of juftice and
moderation ; virtues, he faid, unknown to favage life, but for
that reafon more likely to charm by their novelty. From the
prince he turned to the Parthian ambaffadors, and, in handfome
terms, commended to their care the pupil of Rome ; a young
prince of ingenuous manners, and no ftranger to the liberal arts.
He added, that the Parthians would do well to temporife with
the

the genius of their kings, and to overlook the failings of human nature. Frequent revolutions could give no folid advantage. Rome was at the higheft point of grandeur. Enough of glory had been gained by the progrefs of her arms; fhe therefore put a period to her victories, and the tranquillity of foreign nations was now the object of her care. Meherdates was committed to the Parthian deputies; and Caius Caffius, the governor of Syria, had it in command to conduct him to the banks of the Euphrates.

XII. CASSIUS, at that period, was the moft eminent man of the age for his profound knowledge of the laws. In times of peace, the military fcience falls into neglect. Between the warlike genius and the inactive fluggard no diftinction remains. And yet the ardent mind of Caffius could not languifh in a ftate of ftupid indolence. Though there was no war upon his hands to roufe the fpirit of the legions, he refolved, by every method in his power, to maintain the rigour of ancient difcipline. He kept the foldiers in conftant exercife; he eftablifhed new regulations, and practifed every duty with as much zeal as if the enemy were actually in arms againft him. This feverity, he thought, became a man who had before his eyes the bright example of his anceftors, and, above all, the fame of the celebrated Caffius, which was diffufed through all the eaftern nations. Having pitched his camp near Zeugma, a city where the paffage over the Euphrates is moft practicable, he waited for a convention of the Parthian chiefs, who had made their application to Rome. As foon as they arrived, and with them Abgarus, king of the Arabs (a), he delivered Meherdates into their hands, having previoufly reminded the prince, that among Barbarians the firft impulfe of their zeal is violent, but apt to relax, and end in treachery. His intereft, therefore, called for

vigorous

vigorous meafures. By the artifice of Abgarus that advice was rendered abortive. The prince, as yet without experience, fufpecting no deceit, and weak enough to think that royalty confifts in luxury and riot, was feduced to the city of Edeffa, and there detained feveral days, the dupe of the wily Arabian. Carrhenes, in the mean time, preffed Meherdates to advance with expedition. By his meffengers he promifed certain fuccefs, if no time was loft in frivolous delay. All was ineffectual. Though Mefopotamia was at hand, they never entered that country, but, taking a wider circuit, marched towards Armenia, where the rigour of the winter was already begun.

XIII. After a toilfome march over craggy mountains covered with a wafte of fnow, they defcended at laft into the open country. Carrhenes joined them at the head of his forces. Thus reinforced, the army paffed over the Tigris, and penetrated into the country of the Adiabenians *(a)*. Izates, king of that people, in outward fhew favoured Meherdates, but in his heart inclined to Gotarzes. In the courfe of their march, they made themfelves mafters of the city of Ninos *(b)*, formerly the feat of the Affyrian monarchy. They alfo took the caftle of Arbela, memorable in ftory for the laft battle between Darius and Alexander, by which the fate of the Perfian monarchy was decided. Gotarzes, in the mean time, took poft on the heights of mount Sambulos *(c)*. He there offered up a facrifice to the deities of the place, and chiefly to Hercules, the leading god. At ftated periods, according to an ancient legend, Hercules infpired the dreams of the priefts, and, in a vifion, gave his orders, " That a " fet of horfes, ready for the chafe, fhould be ftationed near the " temple. The hunters, accordingly, are drawn out, well " equipped with quivers and a ftore of arrows." Thus caparifoned, they ftretch at full fpeed through the woods, and, at the clofe of day, return to the temple without an arrow left, weary, and panting for breath. The god appears again, in a midnight vifion, to tell the priefts the tracts of the foreft where he purfued his game. After this information, diligent fearch is made, and a large quantity of game, killed in the chafe, is found in the woods.

XIV. GOTARZES had not as yet affembled all his forces, and the iffue of a battle was what he wifhed to avoid. The river Corma ferved to cover him from the affaults of the enemy. He there ftood at bay, devifing various delays, encamping, and fhifting his ground; and though provoked by various infults, and even by meffengers challenged to the conflict, he contrived, notwithftanding, to protract the war, while his agents were bufy in the adverfe camp, by gifts and promifes feducing the friends of Meherdates. Izates, king of the Adiabenians, was the firft to withdraw with all his forces. Abgarus, the Arabian, followed his example, both difplaying the fickle difpofition and the venality of Barbarians. To fue for kings at the hands of Rome was their frequent cuftom; but experience fhews that they petitioned only to betray. Weakened by defertion, and fufpecting further treachery, Meherdates refolved to try the iffue of a battle. Nor was Gotarzes difpofed to decline the conflict. A fierce engagement followed, with great flaughter on both fides. The victory was long held in fufpenfe, till Carrhenes, having broke the enemy's lines, purfued his advantage with too much ardour. He was attacked in the rear by a body of referve, and hemmed in on every fide. Meherdates faw nothing but impending ruin. In his diftrefs he trufted to the advice of Parrhaces, one of his father's freedmen. By that traitor he was thrown into fetters, and delivered up to the conqueror. Gotarzes behaved with the pride and infolence of victory. He

4

reviled

reviled his captive as a ftranger to the blood of the Arfacides, a man of foreign extraction, and a flave to Rome. He ordered his ears to be cut off, and left him, in that condition, a wretched proof of Parthian clemency, and a living difgrace to the Romans. Gotarzes was foon after carried off by a fit of illnefs. Vonones, at that time governor of Media, mounted the vacant throne. Of this prince, either in his diftreffes or his profperity, nothing remains worthy of a place in hiftory. After a fhort and inglorious reign, he left the Parthian diadem to his fon Vologefes.

XV. DURING thefe tranfactions, a new alarm was raifed by Mithridates *(a)*, king of Bofphorus, who had been lately driven out of his dominions. He continued, ever fince his expulfion, wandering from place to place, forlorn and helplefs. He learned, at length, that Didius, the Roman general, retired with the flower of his army, leaving the kingdom of Thrace in the hands of Cotys, a prince without experience, fcarcely fettled on the throne, and depending on the flender fupport of a few cohorts, under the command of Julius Aquila, a Roman knight. The news infpired Mithridates with fudden courage. He roufed the neighbouring nations, drew together a body of deferters, and, putting himfelf at the head of his tumultuary levies, fell with impetuous fury on the king of the Dandarides *(b)*, and made himfelf mafter of his dominions. The invafion of Bofphorus was expected to be his next attempt. Cotys and Aquila did not think themfelves in force to refift the attack ; and Zorfines, king of the Siracians *(c)*, commencing hoftilities in that critical juncture, added greatly to their fears. In this diftrefs, they looked round to the neighbouring ftates for affiftance, and by their ambaffadors invited Eunones, king of the Adorfians, to join the Roman arms. In a war between a powerful nation and a ruined difmantled

BOOK
XII.

A. U. C.
802.
A. D.
49.

I 2

king,

king, it was not difficult to form a new confederacy. The plan of their operations was soon settled. Eunones was to ravage the open country with his cavalry. The Romans undertook to lay siege to the towns and places of strength.

XVI. The combined forces took the field. On their march the Adorsians *(a)* led the van, and also brought up the rear. The centre consisted of the cohorts and the succours collected in Bosphorus, armed after the Roman manner. The enemy not daring to look them in the face, they marched, without opposition, to the town of Soza *(b)*, in the country of the Dardanides. Finding the place abandoned by Mithridates, they took possession, and, to guard against the treachery of the inhabitants, left it strongly garrisoned. They penetrated next into the country of the Siracians, and, having crossed the river Panda *(c)*, invested the city of Uspes, situated on an eminence, and defended by walls and a fosse. The walls, indeed, not being constructed with stone, but with earth thrown up and bound with hurdles, could not long resist the operations of a siege. Towers of considerable height were advanced against the works, and from that elevation darts and flaming brands were thrown into the town with such incessant fury, that, if the approach of night had not prevented a general assault, the siege had been begun and ended in a single day.

XVII. The besieged, next morning, sent a deputation with offers of an immediate surrender, and no less than ten thousand slaves, on condition that the free-born should remain unhurt. The terms were rejected. After a capitulation, to put the inhabitants to the sword would be an act of inhumanity, and a violation of all the laws of war. On the other hand, to bridle such a number, an adequate force could not be spared from a

scanty

scanty army. The besiegers, therefore, returned for answer, that every thing must be left to the decision of the sword. The soldiers scaled the walls, and the signal was given for a general slaughter. The city was levelled to the ground. The adjacent nations saw that neither arms, nor lines of circumvallation, nor places almost inaccessible, defended by nature and by rapid rivers, could withstand the vigour of the Roman arms. In this general consternation, Zorsines, the Siracian king, began to waver. He now considered whether it were best to adhere to Mithridates, or to provide in time for the security of his own dominions. Self-interest prevailed. He gave hostages, and humbled himself before the image of Claudius. Nothing could be more honourable to the Roman army. Victorious without the loss of blood, they traversed a vast tract of country, and were within three days of the Tanais *(a)*. Their return was not so prosperous. They went back by sea, and some of the ships were thrown by adverse winds on the coast of Taurus *(b)*. The Barbarians poured down to the shore, and with savage fury murdered a considerable number, with the præfect of a cohort, and most of the centurions.

XVIII. MEANWHILE Mithridates, undone and hopeless, began to consider where he might implore compassion. His brother Cotys had at first betrayed him, and then became an open enemy: on him no reliance could be had. If he surrendered to the Romans, there was not in the territory of Bosphorus any one officer of weight and\ authority to ensure the performance of his promises. In this distress, the unhappy monarch turned his thoughts to Eunones. That prince had no motive for personal animosity, and his late alliance with Rome gave him no small degree of influence. Mithridates resolved to apply at that court. With a dejected mien, and a garb that

spoke

spoke his wretchedness, he entered the palace, and falling prostrate at the feet of the king, "Behold," he said, "behold the
" man, who for years has grappled with the whole power of
" Rome. Mithridates humbles himself before you; the perse-
" cuted Mithridates, whom the Romans have pursued by sea and
" land. My fate is in your hands; use your discretion: treat,
" as you shall think best, a prince descended from the great
" Achæmenes (*a*). The honour of that high lineage is all my
" enemies have left me."

XIX. The appearance of a man so distinguished, the turns
of fortune that attended him, and, even in ruin, the affliction that
softened, but could not subdue his spirit, touched Eunones with
generous sympathy. He raised the royal suppliant from the
ground. He praised the magnanimity with which he threw
himself into the power of the Adorsian nation, and, with pleasure, undertook to be mediator between Rome and the unfortunate monarch. He dispatched messengers to Claudius with
letters to the following effect : " In all treaties between the Ro-
" man people and foreign nations, similitude of fortune was the
" basis of their alliance. The present union between Claudius
" and the Adorsians was founded on a participation of victory;
" and victory is then most honourable when mercy spares the
" vanquished. Of this truth Zorsines is a recent instance. He
" still retains his former possessions. But equal terms could not
" be expected in the case of Mithridates. His offence was of a
" more grievous nature. To restore him to his throne and king-
" dom is not the object of this application. Spare his life, and
" let him not walk in fetters, a public spectacle to grace the
" victor's triumph."

XX. Claudius was, at all times, disposed to act with mode-

ration

ration towards the nobility of foreign nations. In the present conjuncture, he doubted which were moſt expedient, to receive the royal priſoner under a promiſe of pardon, or to take him by force of arms. Reſentment and the love of revenge were ſtrong incentives; but ſtill there were reaſons of policy in the oppoſite ſcale. "A war muſt be commenced in a diſtant region, where "the roads were difficult, and the ſea had neither harbours nor "ſtations for ſhipping; where the ſtruggle would be with fierce "and warlike kings, and a people by their wandering life inured "to fatigue; where the ſoil was unproductive, and an army, of "courſe, would be diſtreſſed for proviſions. Campaigns drawn "out into length would diſpirit the ſoldiers; ſudden operations "might be attended with hazard; from victory no glory could "redound to the Roman name, and to be defeated were inde-"lible diſgrace." For theſe reaſons, it was judged adviſable to accept the proffered terms. Mithridates, in that caſe, would remain a wandering exile, poor, diſtreſſed, and wretched. To protract his days were to protract his miſery. Claudius returned an anſwer to Eunones: "Mithridates," he obſerved, "had merited the utmoſt rigour, and the vengeance of Rome "was able to reach him. But to ſubdue the proud, and ſpare "the ſuppliant, had ever been a Roman virtue. It was by "curbing the pride of kings, and by conquering an entire people, "that Rome acquired renown in arms. Then, and then only, "ſhe had reaſon to triumph."

XXI. In conſequence of theſe diſpatches, Mithridates was delivered up to Julius Cilo, at that time imperial procurator of Pontus. He brought with him to Rome a mind unbroken by his misfortunes. In his language to Claudius he towered above his helpleſs condition. One ſentence that fell from him was celebrated at the time. "In me you ſee a man, not taken pri-
"ſoner,

" foner, but willing to furrender: I came of my own accord;
" if you doubt the fact, fet me at liberty, and retake me if you
" are able."   He was conducted under a guard to the roftrum,
and there prefented as a fpectacle to the people.   He ftood unmoved, with his natural ferocity pictured in his countenance.
Cilo and Aquila were rewarded for their fervices; the former
with confular ornaments, and the latter with the enfigns of prætorian dignity.

XXII. DURING the fame confulfhip, the hatred of Agrippina,
deep and implacable, broke out with gathered rage againft Lollia,
who had been guilty of the crime of contending for the imperial
bed. An accufation was foon contrived, and a profecutor fuborned.
The fubftance of the charge was, " That in the late conteft for
" the emperor's choice, Lollia held confultations with Chaldæan
" feers; that fhe employed magicians, and fent to confult the
" Clarian Apollo." She was condemned unheard.   Claudius
addreffed the fenate on the occafion.   He mentioned the nobility of her birth; by the maternal line fhe was niece to Lucius
Volufius, grand niece to Cotta Meffalinus, and formerly the wife
of Memmius Regulus.   He faid nothing of her marriage with
Caligula (a).   Having made that flourifhing preface, he changed
his tone, imputing to her dark defigns againft the ftate.   To
defeat her pernicious views, nothing remained but to confif-
cate her eftates, and banifh her out of Italy.   The fenate complied.   Out of her immoderate wealth fhe was allowed to retain
no more than five millions of fefterces.   Calpurnia, another woman of high rank, was obnoxious to the refentments of Agrippina.   It happened that Claudius, in accidental difcourfe, without a wifh to enjoy. her perfon, praifed the elegance of her
figure.   This gave jealoufy to the emprefs.   She confidered,
however, that the mere crime of beauty did not deferve to

I   be

be punifhed with death. She fent a tribune to Lollia, with orders
to make her put an end to her days. Cadius Rufus, at the fame
time, was found guilty of extortion at the fuit of the Bithy-
nians.

BOOK
XII.

A. U. C.
802.
A. D.
49.

XXIII. As a mark of favour to the province of Narbon
Gaul, and to reward the veneration in which the authority of
the fenate had ever been held by the people of that country, it was
fettled by a decree, that fuch of the natives as were Roman fenators fhould be at liberty, without a fpecial licence from the
emperor, to vifit their eftates in their native province, with as
full and ample privileges as had been granted to the Sicilian
fenators. Sohemus and Agrippa, kings of Ituria *(a)* and Judæa,
being both dead, their refpective territories were annexed to the
province of Syria. An order was alfo made, that the auguries,
relating to the public fafety, which had lain dormant for five-
and-twenty years, fhould be revived, and never again be fuffered to fall into difufe. The limits *(b)* of the city were enlarged by Claudius. The right of directing that bufinefs was,
by ancient ufage, vefted in all fuch as extended the boundaries
of the empire. The right, however, had not been exercifed by
any of the Roman commanders (Sylla and Auguftus excepted),
though remote and powerful nations had been fubdued by their
victorious arms.

XXIV. What was done in early times by the ambition or
the public virtue of the Roman kings, cannot now be feen
through the mift that hangs over diftant ages. It may, however, be matter of fome curiofity to mark out the foundation of
the city, and the boundaries affigned by Romulus. The firft
outline began at the ox-market, where ftill is to be feen the
brazen ftatue of a bull, that animal being commonly employed at

Vol. II.   K   the

BOOK
XII.
⏜
A. U. C.
8..
A. D.
49.

the plough. From that place a furrow was carried on of fuffi-cient dimenfions to include the great altar of Hercules. By boundary-ftones, fixed at proper diftances, the circuit was con-tinued along the foot of mount Palatine to the altar of Consus, extending thence to the old Curiæ, next to the chapel of the Lares, and finally to the great Roman forum. The capitol, it is generally thought, was added, not by Romulus, but by Titus Tatius. From that period the city grew with the growth of the empire. With regard to the enlargement made by Clau-dius, the curious may be eafily fatisfied, as the public records contain an exact defcription.

A. U. C.
8o2.
A. D.
5o.

XXV. In the confulfhip of Caius Antiftius and Marcus Suil-lius, the adoption of Domitius was hurried on by the credit and influence of Pallas. Connected with Agrippina, whom he had raifed to imperial fplendour, by ties of mutual intereft, and ftill more fo by the indulgence of criminal paffions, this favourite advifed his mafter to provide for the public fafety, and, in aid to the tender years of Britannicus, to raife collateral branches in the Cæfarean line. For this meafure Auguftus had left a pre-cedent. That emperor adopted the iffue of his wife, though he had, in that very juncture, grand children to reprefent him. Tiberius copied the example, and to his own immediate offspring united Germanicus. It would therefore become the wifdom of Claudius to embrace, as his own, a young man who would in time be able to relieve the fovereign, and lighten the cares of government. Convinced by this reafoning, Claudius gave the precedence to Domitius, though but two years older than his own fon. On this fubject he made a fpeech to the fenate, content to be the organ of what his freedman had fuggefted. It was obferved by men verfed in the hiftory of their country, that this was the firft adoption into the Claudian family; an old

patrician

patrician line, which, from the days of Atta Claufus *(a)*, had
continued, without any mixture of foreign blood, in one regular
courfe of defcent.

XXVI. THE fenate paffed a vote of thanks to the emperor;
but in a ftyle of exquifite flattery their court was chiefly paid to
Domitius.   A law was alfo enacted, by virtue of which the
young prince, under the name of Nero, was naturalized into the
Claudian family.   Agrippina was dignified with the title of AU-
GUSTA.   During thefe tranfactions, there was not a man fo
void of fentiment, as not to behold the cafe of Britannicus with
an eye of compaffion.   His very flaves were taken from him.
His ftep-mother interpofed with officious civility.   The young
prince laughed at her kindnefs, aware of the underplot, which
fhe was carrying on againft him.   Want of difcernment was
not among his faults.   It has been faid that he was by nature
penetrating : that, perhaps, was his true character; or, it may
be, that men were willing to give him credit for talents, without
waiting to make the experiment.

XXVII. AGRIPPINA had now the ambition to difplay her
weight and influence to the eyes of foreign nations.   To this
end fhe caufed a body of veterans to be fent to the capital city
of the Ubians, the place of her nativity, to be eftablifhed there
as a colony, called after her own name *(a)*.   When that people
firft paffed over the Rhine, it happened that Agrippa, her grandfather, was the Roman general, who received them as the allies
of Rome.   In the prefent juncture, when the new colony was
to be fettled, a fudden alarm broke out in the Upper Germany,
occafioned by an irruption of the Cattians *(b)*, who iffued forth
from their hive in queft of plunder.   To check their progrefs,
Lucius Pomponius difpatched a body of auxiliary troops, com-

K 2

pofed

pofed of the Vangiones *(c)* and Nemetæans, with a fquadron of light horfe, to make a forced march, and, if they could not attack the front line of the Barbarians, to fall upon the rear. The ardour of the foldiers was not inferior to the fkill of the general. They formed two divifions: one marched to the left, and came up with the freebooters, who had been committing depredations, and lay funk in fleep and wine. The victory was cheap, but enhanced by the joy with which the conquering foldiers relcafed, at the end of forty years, fome of the prifoners who were taken in the maffacre of Varus and his legions.

XXVIII. The fecond divifion, which had marched to the right, and by a fhorter road, met with greater fuccefs. The Barbarians ventured to give battle, and were defeated with prodigious flaughter. Elate with fuccefs, and loaded with fpoils, the conquerors marched back to mount Taunus *(a)*, where Pomponius, at the head of his legions, lay in wait, expecting that the Cattians, prompted by a fpirit of revenge, would return to the charge. But the Barbarians, dreading the Romans on one fide, and on the other, their conftant enemies, the Cherufcans, fent a deputation to Rome, with hoftages to fecure a pacification. Triumphal honours were decreed to Pomponius; but military fame is the leaft part of the eftimation in which he is held by pofterity. He excelled in elegant compofition, and the character of the general is now eclipfed by the genius of the poet.

XXIX. Vannius *(a)*, who had been formerly raifed by Drufus to reign over the Suevians, was, about this time, driven from his kingdom. His reign, at firft, was mild and popular; but the habit of commanding had corrupted his nature. Pride and arrogance had taken root in his heart. Domeftic factions confpired againft him, and the neighbouring nations declared

open

open hoſtility. Vibillius, king of the Hermundurians, conducted
the enterprife. He was joined by Vangio and Sido, the nephews of Vannius by a ſiſter. In this quarrel Claudius was
determined not to interfere. Though often preſſed to take a
decided part, he obſerved a ſtrict neutrality, content with pro-
miſing the Suevian king a ſafe retreat from the rage of his enemies. In his diſpatches to Publius Atellius Hiſter, who had
the command in Pannonia, his orders were, that the legion and
the troops of the province ſhould be held in readineſs on the
banks of the Danube, to ſuccour the vanquiſhed, and repel the
incurſions of the Barbarians, if they attempted to invade the
frontier. A powerful confederacy was then actually formed by
the nations of Germany. The Ligians *(b)*, and other ſtates,
were up in arms, attracted by the fame of an opulent kingdom,
which Vannius, during a ſpace of thirty years, had made ſtill
richer by plunder and depredations. To make head againſt the
forces combined againſt him was not in the power of the Suevian king. The natural ſtrength of his kingdom conſiſted of
infantry only : the Iazigians *(c)*, a people of Sarmatia, ſupplied
him with a body of horſe. Notwithſtanding this reinforcement,
Vannius felt his inferiority. He reſolved to keep within the
ſtrong holds and ſaſtneſſes of the country, and draw the war into
a lingering length.

XXX. The Iazigians were not of a temper to endure the
ſlow operations of a ſiege. They ſpread themſelves, in their
deſultory manner, round the country, and by their raſhneſs
brought on a general engagement. The Ligians and Hermundurians fell in with their roving parties. Vannius was obliged
to ſally out to the aſſiſtance of his friends. He gave battle, and
was totally overthrown. But the praiſe of valour could not be
withheld from him. Covered with honourable wounds, he

eſcaped

escaped to his fleet, which lay in the Danube. His partisans followed him, and, with a proper allotment of lands, were settled in Pannonia. The dominions of the depofed king were divided between his two nephews Vangio and Sido, both, from that time, diftinguished by their fidelity to Rome. In the beginning of their reign, they flourished in the affections of the people; honoured by all, while they ftruggled for power; when they obtained it, defpifed and hated. Their own mifconduct was, perhaps, the caufe; perhaps, the fickle temper of the people; or, it may be, that in the nature and genius of fervitude, there is a tendency to innovation, always difcontented, fullen, and unquiet.

XXXI. PUBLIUS OSTORIUS was appointed governor of Britain, in the character of propraetor. On his arrival he found the province in commotion. A new commander, with an army wholly unknown to him, the Barbarians imagined would not venture to open a winter campaign. Fierce with this idea, they made an irruption into the territory of the ftates in alliance with Rome, and carried devaftation through the country. Oftorius, knowing how much depends on the firft operations of war, put himfelf at the head of the light cohorts, and, by rapid marches, advanced againft the enemy. The Britons were taken by furprife. All who refifted were put to the fword. The fugitives were purfued with prodigious flaughter. The rout was fo complete, that there was no reafon to apprehend a junction of their forces; but peace on thofe terms, the general knew, would be no better than difguifed hoftility. The legions would ftill be fubject to perpetual alarms from a fierce and infidious enemy. He therefore refolved to difarm all who were fufpected, and, by extending a chain of forts between the Nen and the Severn (a), to confine the malecontents between thofe two rivers.

To

To counteract this defign, the Icenians *(b)* took up arms ; a brave and warlike people, who, at their own requeft, had lived in friendfhip with the Romans, and were, by confequence, un-impaired by the calamities of war. They formed a league with the adjacent ftates, and chofe their ground for a decifive action. The place was inclofed with a rampart thrown up with fod, leaving an entrance in one part only, and that fo difficult of accefs, that the Roman cavalry would not be able to force their way. Oftorius refolved to ftorm the place. Though unfupported by the legions, he relied on the valour of the allied forces, and, having formed his difpofition for the attack, ordered his cavalry to difmount, and act with the foot foldiers. The fignal being given, the affault began, and the rampart was carried by affault. The Britons, inclofed by their own fortifications, and preffed on every fide, were thrown into the utmoft confufion. Yet even in that diftrefs, confcious of the guilt of rebellion, and feeing no way to efcape, they fought to the laft, and gave fignal proofs of heroic bravery. In this engagement Marcus Oftorius, the general's fon, faved the life of a Roman, and obtained the civic crown.

XXXII. The defeat of the Icenians drew after it important confequences. The neighbouring nations, no longer balancing between peace and war, laid down their arms. Oftorius led his army againft the Cangians *(a)*, and laid wafte their country. The foldiers carried off a confiderable booty, the enemy never daring to make head againft them. Wherever they attempted to annoy the army by fudden fkirmifhes, they paid for their rafh-nefs. The fea, that lies between Britain and Ireland, was within a fhort march, when Oftorius received intelligence of an infur-rection among the Brigantes *(b)*. The news obliged him to return with expedition. Till every thing was fecured in his

rear,

rear, it was his maxim not to pufh on his conquefts. The Brigantes were foon reduced to fubjection. Such as refifted were
cut to pieces, and a free pardon was granted to the reft. The
Silures *(c)* were not fo eafily quelled : neither lenity nor rigorous
meafures could induce them to fubmit. To bridle the infolence
of that warlike race, Oftorius judged it expedient to form a camp
for the legions in the heart of their country. For this purpofe
a colony, fupported by a ftrong body of veterans, was ftationed
at Camalodunum *(d)*, on the lands conquered from the enemy.
From this meafure a twofold effect was expected : the garrifon
would be able to overawe the infurgents, and give to the allied
ftates a fpecimen of law and civil policy.

XXXIII. These arrangements fettled, Oftorius marched
againft the Silures. To their natural ferocity that people added
the courage which they now derived from the prefence of Caractacus *(a)*. Renowned for his valour, and for various turns
of good and evil fortune, that heroic chief had fpread his fame
through the ifland. His knowledge of the country, and his fkill
in all the wiles and ftratagems of favage warfare, gave him many
advantages ; but he could not hope with inferior numbers to
make a ftand againft a well-difciplined army. He therefore
marched into the territory of the Ordovicians *(b)*. Having there
drawn to his ftandard all who confidered peace with Rome as
another name for flavery, he determined to try the iffue of a
battle. For this purpofe he chofe a fpot *(c)* where the approach
and the retreat were difficult to the enemy, and to himfelf every
way advantageous. He took poft in a fituation defended by
fteep and craggy hills. In fome places where the mountains
opened, and the acclivity afforded an eafy afcent, he fortified the
fpot with maffy ftones, heaped together in the form of a rampart.
A river, with fords and fhallows of uncertain depth, wafhed the

extremity

extremity of the plain.   On the outfide of his fortifications, a vaft
body of troops fhewed themfelves in force, and in order of
battle.

XXXIV. THE chieftains of the various nations were bufy in
every quarter.   They rufhed along the ranks ; they exhorted their
men ; they roufed the timid ; they confirmed the brave ; and,
by hopes, by promifes, by every generous motive, inflamed the
ardour of their troops.   Caractacus was feen in every part of the
field ; he darted along the lines ; he exclaimed aloud, " This
" day, my fellow-warriors, this very day decides the fate of Bri-
" tain.   The æra of liberty, or eternal bondage, begins from this
" hour.   Remember your brave and warlike anceftors, who met
" Julius Cæfar in open combat, and chafed him from the coaft of
" Britain.   They were the men who freed their country from a
" foreign yoke ; who delivered the land from taxations, impofed
" at the will of a mafter ; who banifhed from your fight the fafces
" and the Roman axes ; and, above all, who refcued your wives
" and daughters from violation."   The foldiers received this
fpeech with fhouts of applaufe.   With a fpirit of enthufiaftic valour, each individual bound himfelf by the form of oath peculiar
to his nation, to brave every danger, and prefer death to flavery.

XXXV. THE intrepid countenance of the Britons, and the
fpirit that animated their whole army, ftruck Oftorius with aftonifhment.   He faw a river (a) to be paffed ; a palifade to be
forced ; a fteep hill to be furmounted ; and the feveral pofts defended by a prodigious multitude.   The foldiers, notwithftanding,
burned with impatience for the onfet.   All things give way to
valour, was the general cry.   The tribunes and other officers feconded the ardour of the men.   Oftorius reconnoitred the ground,
and having marked where the defiles were impenetrable, or eafy

of approach, gave the signal for the attack. The river was passed with little difficulty. The Romans advanced to the parapet. The struggle there was obstinate, and, as long as it was fought with missive weapons, the Britons had the advantage. Ostorius ordered his men to advance under a military shell, and level the pile of stones, that served as a fence to the enemy. A close engagement followed. The Britons abandoned their ranks, and fled with precipitation to the ridge of the hills. The Romans pursued with eagerness. Not only the light troops, but even the legionary soldiers, forced their way to the summit of the hills, under a heavy shower of darts. The Britons, having neither breastplates nor helmets, were not able to maintain the conflict. The legions, sword in hand, or with their javelins, bore down all before them. The auxiliaries, with their spears and sabres, made prodigious havoc. The victory was decisive. The wife and daughter of Caractacus were taken prisoners. His brother surrendered at discretion.

XXXVI. Caractacus fled for protection to Cartismandua, queen of the Brigantes. But adversity has no friends. By that princess he was loaded with irons, and delivered up to the conqueror. He had waged war with the Romans during the last nine years (a). His fame was not confined to his native island; it passed into the provinces, and spread all over Italy. Curiosity was eager to behold the heroic chieftain, who, for such a length of time, made head against a great and powerful empire. Even at Rome the name of Caractacus was in high celebrity. The emperor, willing to magnify the glory of the conquest, bestowed the highest praise on the valour of the vanquished king. He assembled the people to behold a spectacle worthy of their view. In the field before the camp the praetorian bands were drawn up

under

under arms. The followers of the Britifh chief walked in proceffion. The military accoutrements, the harnefs and rich collars,
which he had gained in various battles, were difplayed with pomp.
The wife of Caractacus, his daughter, and his brother, followed
next: he himfelf clofed the melancholy train.   The reft of the
prifoners, ftruck with terror, defcended to mean and abject fupplications.   Caractacus alone was fuperior to misfortune.   With a
countenance ftill unaltered, not a fymptom of fear appearing, no
forrow, no condefcenfion, he behaved with dignity even in ruin.
Being placed before the tribunal, he delivered himfelf in the following manner :

XXXVII. " If to the nobility of my birth, and the fplendour of
" exalted ftation, I had united the virtues of moderation, Rome
" had beheld me, not in captivity, but a royal vifitor, and a friend.
" The alliance of a prince, defcended from an illuftrious line of
" anceftors ; a prince, whofe fway extended over many nations,
" would not have been unworthy of your choice.   A reverfe of
" fortune is now the lot of Caractacus.   The event to you is glo-
" rious, and to me humiliating.   I had arms, and men, and
" horfes ; I had wealth in abundance : can you wonder that I
" was unwilling to lofe them ? The ambition of Rome afpires to
" univerfal dominion : and muft mankind, by confequence, ftretch
" their necks to the yoke ? I ftood at bay for years : had I acted
" otherwife, where, on your part, had been the glory of con-
" queft, and where, on mine, the honour of a brave refiftance ? I
" am now in your power : if you are bent on vengeance, execute
" your purpofe ; the bloody fcene will foon be over, and the
" name of Caractacus will fink into oblivion.   Preferve my life,
" and I fhall be, to late pofterity, a monument of Roman cle-
" mency.' " Claudius granted him a free pardon, and the fame to
his wife, his daughter, and his brother.   Releafed from their fet-

ters,

ters, they advanced to another tribunal near at hand, where Agrippina fhewed herfelf in ftate. They returned thanks to her, and paid their veneration in the fame ftyle as they had before addreffed to the emperor. The fight was altogether new. A woman, ftationed amidft the enfigns and the armies of Rome, prefented a fpectacle unknown to the old republic: but in an empire, acquired by the valour of her anceftors, Agrippina claimed an equal fhare.

XXXVIII. At the next meeting of the fenate, the victory over Caractacus was mentioned with the higheft applaufe, as an event no way inferior to what had been feen in ancient times, when Publius Scipio brought Syphax in chains to Rome; when Lucius Paulus led Perfes in captivity; and when other commanders exhibited to the Roman people kings and princes at their chariot wheels. Triumphal ornaments were decreed to Oftorius. That officer had hitherto feen his operations crowned with fuccefs. He began foon after to experience the viciffitudes of fortune. Perhaps the war, by the overthrow of Caractacus, was thought to be at an end, and, in that perfuafion, military difcipline was relaxed; perhaps the enemy, enraged by the lofs of that gallant chief, fought with inflamed refentment. A camp had been formed in the country of the Silures, and a chain of forts was to be erected. The Britons in a body furrounded the officer who commanded the legionary cohorts, and, if fuccours had not arrived in time from the neighbouring garrifons, the whole corps had been cut to pieces. The præfect of the camp, with eight centurions and the braveft of the foldiers, were killed on the fpot. A foraging party, and the detachment fent to fupport them, were foon after attacked, and put to the rout.

XXXIX. Ostorius, on the firft alarm, ordered the light
armed

armed cohorts to advance against the enemy. That reinforcement
was infufficient, till the legionary foldiers marched to their fupport.
The battle was renewed, at firft on equal terms, but, in the end, to
the difadvantage of the Britons. But their lofs was inconfiderable.
The approach of night prevented a purfuit. From that time the
Britons kept up a conftant alarm. Frequent battles, or rather
fkirmifhes, were fought with their detached parties, roving in
queft of plunder. They met in fudden encounters, as chance directed, or valour prompted ; in the fens, in the woods, in the narrow defiles ; the men, on fome occafions, led on by their chiefs,
and frequently without their knowledge, as refentment, or the
love of booty, happened to incite their fury. Of all the Britons,
the Silures were the moft determined. They fought with obftinacy, with inveterate hatred. It feems the Roman general had
declared, that the very name of the Silures muft be extirpated,
like that of the Sigambrians, formerly driven out of Germany, and
tranfplanted into Gaul. That expreffion reached the Silures, and
roufed their fierceft paffions. Two auxiliary cohorts, whom the
avarice of their officers fent in queft of plunder, were intercepted
by that ferocious people, and all made prifoners. A fair diftribution of the fpoils and the captives drew the neighbouring ftates
into the confederacy. Oftorius, at this time, was worn out with
anxiety. He funk under the fatigue, and expired, to the great
joy of the Britons, who faw a great and able commander, not, indeed, flain in battle, but overcome by the war.

XL. The death of Oftorius being known at Rome, the emperor, aware that a province of fo much importance ought not to
remain without a governor, fent Aulus Didius to take upon him
the command. That officer fet out with all poffible expedition ;
but on his arrival found the ifland in a ftate of diftraction. The
legion under Manlius Valens had rifked a battle, and fuffered a
defeat.

defeat. In order to imprefs with terror the new commander, the Britons took care to fwell the fame of their victory. Didius, on his part, was willing to magnify the lofs. The merit of the general, he knew, would rife in proportion to the danger furmounted; and if he failed, the difficulty would be an apology for his conduct. In the defeat of Valens, it was the nation of the Silures that ftruck the blow. Emboldened by fuccefs, they continued their prædatory war, till the arrival of Didius checked their operations. In this juncture Venufius was the Britifh chieftain; a man, as already mentioned, born in the city of the Jugantes, and, fince the lofs of Caractacus, the firft in fame for valour and military experience. He had married Cartifmandua, the queen of the Brigantes; and while they lived on good terms, his fidelity to Rome remained inviolate. Being afterwards driven from her throne and bed, he purfued his revenge by open hoftilities, and even dared to wage war againft the Romans.

The quarrel was at firft a civil war amongft themfelves. Cartifmandua contrived to feize, by ftratagem, the brother of Venufius, with the reft of his kindred. The Britons by that event were fired with indignation. They fcorned to fubmit to a female government *(a)*, and, with the flower of their youth, attacked Cartifmandua in the heart of her territories. The infurrection was forefeen, and a detachment from the cohorts was fent in time to counteract the motions of the enemy. An engagement followed, at firft with doubtful fuccefs; but after a ftruggle, victory inclined to the fide of the Romans. In another part of the country, the legion under the command of Cefius Nafica fought with equal fuccefs. Didius did not expofe his perfon in any of thefe engagements. Impaired by years, and loaded with accumulated honours, he was content to act by his inferior officers; and while the enemy was kept in check, the honour of doing it was not his paffion.

I

Thefe

Thefe tranfactions, which happened in the courfe of different years, under the conduct of Oftorius and Didius, are here related in one connected feries, to avoid breaking the thread of the narration.   I now return to the order of time.

B O O K
XII.
⎴
A. U. C.
803.
A. D.
50.

XLI. In the fifth confulfhip of Claudius, and the firft of his colleague, Servius Cornelius Orphitus, the manly gown was affigned to Nero, before his time, that, though ftill under age, he might appear qualified to take upon him a fhare in public bufinefs. The fenate, in a fit of adulation, refolved that the young prince fhould be declared capable of the confulfhip at the age of twenty, and be confidered, in the mean time, as conful elect, with proconfular authority out of the city, and the additional title of prince of the Roman youth.   Claudius not only affented to thofe flattering decrees, but, in the name of Nero, gave a largefs to the people, and a donative to the army.   To conciliate the affections of the people, the Circenfian games were likewife exhibited.   During that fpectacle, Britannicus and Nero paffed in review; the former clad in the prætexta, or the drefs of his boyifh days; the latter, with the triumphal ornaments of a Roman general.   So glaring a difference ftruck the fpectators, as a certain prelude of their future fortunes.   Among the centurions and tribunes there were men of principle, who beheld the cafe of Britannicus with an eye of compaffion.   All fuch were removed from court; fome under pretence of advancing them to higher offices, and the reft for plaufible reafons.   The policy was extended even to the freedmen. In that clafs, whoever was found to be above corruption, was difmiffed from his place.

A. U. C.
804.
A. D.
51.

The two young princes met by accident.   Nero faluted Britannicus by name, and in return was familiarly called DOMITIUS.

This

This incident gave umbrage to Agrippina. She flew to the emperor with her complaint: " Contempt," she said, " was thrown " on the adoption of Nero ; what the senate decreed, and the voice " of the people ratified, was repealed with contumacy in the very " palace. If the men, who taught those dangerous lessons, were " not repressed, the mischief would increase, and, perhaps, prove " fatal to the commonwealth." Claudius was easily alarmed. He considered what was no more than bare surmise, as a crime then actually committed, and, accordingly, either sent into banishment, or put to death the best and ablest of his son's tutors. New men were appointed to superintend the prince's education, and the choice was left to the stepmother.

XLII. AGRIPPINA had still greater objects in view, but Lusius Geta and Rufius Crispinus were first to be removed from the command of the prætorian bands. They were both under obligations to Messalina, and, by sentiment, attached to her children. Men of their disposition might obstruct her measures. She represented to the emperor, that, under two rival commanders, the soldiers would be divided into factions ; but if that important office centered in one person, all would act with a principle of union, and strict attention to military discipline. Claudius concurred in the same opinion. The command was given to Afranius Burrhus ; an officer of great experience and a warlike character, but disposed to remember the friend that raised him to that elevation. Having succeeded in these arrangements, Agrippina thought it time to act without reserve : she claimed a right to be conveyed in her carriage to the capitol ; a right, by ancient usage, allowed only to the sacerdotal order, the vestal virgins, and the statues of the gods. Being now communicated to Agrippina, it could not fail to raise the veneration of the people for a princess, in whom they saw the

daughter

daughter *(a)*, fifter, wife, and mother of an emperor; a combination of illuftrious titles never, before that time, united in one perfon.

In this juncture, Vitellius, the active leader of Agrippina's faction, after having ftood high in the efteem of Claudius, was at laft, in an advanced age, involved in a profecution, fet on foot againft him by Junius Lupus, a member of the fenate. Such is the inftability of human grandeur! The charge imported violated majefty, and a defign to feize the reins of government. Claudius was willing to liften to the ftory; but, by the interpofition of Agrippina, who fcorned to defcend to prayers and fupplications, the blow recoiled upon the profecutor. He was interdicted from fire and water. To ftretch refentment further was not the wifh of Vitellius.

XLIII. In the courfe of this year, the people were kept in a conftant alarm by a fucceffion of portents and prodigies. Birds of evil omen infefted the capitol; earthquakes were felt; houfes were laid in ruin, and while the multitude, in a general panic, preffed forward to make their efcape, the feeble and infirm were trampled under foot. A dearth of corn brought on a famine: this too was deemed a prodigy. The people were not content to murmur their difcontents; they crowded to the tribunal, and gathering round the emperor, then fitting in judgment, they forced him from his feat, and pufhed him to the extremity of the forum. The guards came to his affiftance, and Claudius made his way through the crowd. Fifteen days fubfiftence was the moft that Rome had then in ftore. The winter, providentially, was mild and favourable to navigation: diftrefs and mifery muft, otherwife, have been the confequence. In former times the cafe. was very different. Italy was the granary that fupplied foreign markets. Even at this hour, the prolific vigour of the foil is not

worn out; but to depend on Egypt and Africa is the prevailing
fyftem.   The lives of the people are, by choice, committed to
the caprice of winds and waves.

XLIV. In the fame year the flame of war broke out between
the Armenians and Iberians.   The Romans and the Parthians
were, by confequence, involved in the quarrel.   The fceptre of
Parthia was at that time fwayed by Vologefes, with the confent of
his brothers, though his mother, by birth a Greek, was no higher
than a concubine.   Pharafmanes reigned in Iberia, confirmed on
his throne by long poffeffion.   His brother, Mithridates, received the regal diadem of Armenia from the power of Rome.
The former had a fon named Rhadamiftus, of a tall and graceful
ftature, remarkable for bodily vigour, and an underftanding perfectly trained in the political fchool of his father.   His talents
were high in the efteem of all the neighbouring ftates.   He faw,
with impatience, the old age of his father protracted to a length of
years.   To difguife his ambition was no part of his character.   He
expreffed his difcontent in a manner that alarmed Pharafmanes.
That monarch faw the afpiring genius of his fon; and, being in
the decline of life, he dreaded the enterprifing fpirit of a young
man, who had conciliated to himfelf the affections of the people.
To change the tide of his paffions, and find employment for him
elfewhere, he held forth the kingdom of Armenia as a dazzling
and inviting object: he himfelf, he faid, expelled the Parthians,
and placed Mithridates on the throne.   Pharafmanes added, that
it would not be advifable to proceed with open force.   Covert
ftratagem might deceive Mithridates, and enfure fuccefs.

Rhadamiftus made the beft of his way to his uncle's court, as
to a place of fhelter from the difpleafure of his father, and the tyranny of a ftep-mother.   He met with a gracious reception.   Mithridates

thridates treated him as his own fon, with all the tendernefs of a
father. The young prince, in the mean time, drew to his intereft the nobility of the country ; and, while his uncle loaded him
with favours, he was bufy in forming a confpiracy againft the
crown and life of his benefactor.

B O O K
XII.
A. U. C.
804.
A. D.
51.

XLV. HAVING concerted his meafures, he returned, under
colour of a family-reconciliation, to his father's court. He there
explained the progrefs of his treachery, the fnares that were prepared, and the neceffity of giving the finifhing blow by force of
arms. To find oftenfible reafons for open hoftility, was not difficult to a politic genius like that of Pharafmanes. He alleged, that
in the war between himfelf and the king of the Albanians, his application to the Romans, for a reinforcement, was defeated by the
practices of Mithridates ; and an injury of fo heinous a nature
could not be expiated by any thing lefs than the ruin of the man
who did the mifchief. To this end, he gave the command of his
forces to his fon, who entered Armenia at the head of a numerous
army. An invafion fo unexpected filled Mithridates with confternation. He fled the field, and, leaving the enemy in poffeffion of his
camp, threw himfelf into the fort of Gorneas (a) ; a place ftrong
by nature, and defended by a Roman garrifon, under the command of Cælius Pollio, the præfect, and Cafperius, a centurion.
The machinations of a fiege, and the ufe of warlike engines, are
things unknown to favage nations : the Romans have reduced that
branch of the military art to a regular fyftem. Rhadamiftus attempted to carry the works by affault, but without effect, and
with confiderable lofs. He formed a blockade, and, in the mean
time, made his approaches to the avarice of the governor. By
bribes and prefents he bargained with that officer to betray his
truft. The centurion protefted againft fo foul a treachery, declaring, in a tone of firmnefs, that he would neither agree to give

M 2

up

up a confederate prince, nor to barter away the kingdom of Armenia, which had been affigned to Mithridates by the Roman people.

Pollio, the commander in chief, affected to dread the fuperior force of the enemy; and Rhadamiftus, pleading the orders of his father, ftill urged on the fiege. In this diftrefs, Cafperius, the centurion, ftipulated a ceffation of arms, and left the garrifon, in order to have an interview with Pharafmanes, and deter him from profecuting the war. If his endeavours failed, he refolved to proceed with expedition to Ummidius Quadratus, who commanded in Syria, in order to make that governor acquainted with the ftate of affairs, and the iniquity of the whole proceeding.

XLVI. The centurion had no fooner left the place, than Pollio felt himfelf at liberty to act without controul. He advifed Mithridates to compromife the quarrel, and end the war by a regular treaty. He urged the ties of natural affection between brothers, and the rights of feniority, which preponderated in favour of Pharafmanes. He added, that " Mithridates was, in " fact, the fon-in-law of his brother, and, at the fame time, " uncle, and father-in-law to Rhadamiftus. The Iberians were " fuperior in number, and yet willing to accede to terms of pa- " cification. The perfidy of the Armenians was become prover- " bial. Pent up in a fortrefs, ill fupplied with provifions, he " could not hope to hold out much longer. In that diftrefs, " what room was left for deliberation? Peace, on reafonable " terms, was preferable to a deftructive war."

Such were the arguments urged by Cælius Pollio; but Mithridates fufpected the counfels of a man, who had feduced one of the royal concubines, and fhewn himfelf a venal tool, ready at
the

the beck of the higheft bidder, to commit any crime however
atrocious.   Meanwhile, Cafperius reached the court of Pharafmanes.. He expoftulated with that monarch, and preffed him to
raife the fiege.   The politic king amufed the centurion with
plaufible anfwers.   He talked in equivocal terms, and drew the
bufinefs into a negociation, while his fecret difpatches urged
Rhadamiftus, by any means, and without delay, to make himfelf
mafter of the place.   Pollio raifed the price of his treachery, and
Rhadamiftus complied with his terms.   In confequence of their
bargain, the governor, by corrupt practices, contrived to make
the foldiers demand a capitulation, and, if not granted, to threaten
one and all to abandon the place.   Mithridates, in that extremity, fixed the time and place for a congrefs, and went out of the
garrifon.

XLVII. RHADAMISTUS advanced to meet him. He rufhed to
the king's embrace; he offered every mark of duty and refpect
to his uncle and his father-in-law; and, by a folemn oath, affured
him that he would not at any time employ either fword or
poifon againft his life.   He decoyed Mithridates into a neighbouring wood, where he faid a facrifice was prepared, to ratify
the treaty in the prefence of the gods.   Among the eaftern kings,
whenever they enter into mutual engagements, a peculiar cuftom
prevails: the contracting parties take each other by the right
hand, and with a ligature bind their thumbs together, till the
blood is forced to the extremities, and with a flight puncture
finds a vent.   As it gufhes forth, the kings apply their mouths
to the orifice, and fuck each other's blood.   The treaty, in this
manner, receives the higheft fanction, figned, as it were, with
the blood of the parties.   On the prefent occafion, the perfon,
whofe office it was to tie the knot, pretending to have made a
falfe ftep, fell at the feet of Mithridates, and laying hold of his
                                                              knees.

knees, brought him to the ground. A crowd rushed in and bound the prostrate king with fetters. A chain was fastened to his foot, and in that condition (esteemed by those nations the highest disgrace) he was dragged along with brutal violence. The populace, resenting the grievances which they had suffered under an oppressive and despotic reign, insulted him with vulgar scurrility, and even with blows. Thinking men beheld the sad reverse with compassion. The wife of the unhappy monarch followed with her children, and filled the place with shrieks and lamentations. They were all secured in covered carriages, apart from each other, till the pleasure of Pharasmanes should be known. Lust of power was the passion of that prince. For a brother and a daughter not one tender sentiment remained. He ordered them to be put to death; but, though inured to crimes, not in his sight. Rhadamistus observed his oath with a pious fraud, that added to his guilt. He had bound himself not to use either sword or poison; but he smothered his uncle under a load of clothes, and by that evasion satisfied the religion of a murderer. The children of the unhappy monarch bewailed the loss of their father, and, for that crime, were massacred.

XLVIII. This act of treachery, and the murders that followed it, were soon made known to Quadratus. He called a council of war, and, after stating that the enemies of the deceased king were in possession of his dominions, the point which he submitted to consideration was, Whether, in that conjuncture, vindictive measures were advisable. Few at the meeting retained a sense of public honour. Maxims of policy and self-interest weighed with the majority. " The guilt," they said, " of " foreign nations gave a solid advantage to the empire, and for " that reason ought to be a source of joy. To foment divisions " among the enemies of Rome was the truest wisdom; and,

" with

" with that view, the crown of Armenia had been often, with
" a fhow of generofity, dealt out by the emperor as the fpecial
" gift of the Roman people.   Let Rhadamiftus hold his ill-
" gotten power; he will hold it with infamy, and the execration
" of mankind : while he owes his elevation to his crimes, he
" will effectually ferve the interefts of Rome."   This reafoning
prevailed.   The council, however, wifhed to fave appearances.
That they might not be thought to countenance a foul tranfaction, which might afterwards provoke the emperor to iffue
contrary orders, it was agreed to fend difpatches to Pharafmanes,
requiring him forthwith to evacuate Armenia, and recall his
fon.

B O O K
XII.
A. U. C.
804.
A. D.
51.

XLIX. In that juncture Julius Pelignus, with the title of
procurator, commanded in Cappadocia; a man, whom all orders
of the people beheld with contempt and derifion.   The de-
formity of his perfon excited ridicule, and the qualities of his
mind correfponded with his outward figure.   He had lived,
notwithftanding, in the clofeft intimacy with Claudius, at the
time when that prince, as yet a private man, paffed the hours of
a ftupid and liftlefs life in the company of buffoons. Pelignus, in a
fit of vain-glory, undertook to recover Armenia.   Having drawn
together the auxiliaries of the province, he marched at the head
of his forces, and, in his route, plundered the allies, as if the war
was with them, inftead of the Iberians.   Haraffed by the
fudden incurfions of the barbarians, and deferted by his followers, he was left without refource.   In that diftrefs, he fled to
Rhadamiftus.   Bribery foon purchafed a man of his defcription.
He advifed the prince to affume the regal diadem, and affifted,
under arms, at the coronation, at once the author of the meafure,
and the foldier to fupport it.   A proceeding fo vile and infamous could not be long unknown to the eaftern nations.   The
character

character of the Roman generals might, by confequence, fink into contempt; and therefore, to wipe off the difgrace, Helvidius Prifcus was fent at the head of a legion, with orders to act as exigencies might require. That officer preffed forward with expedition. He paffed mount Taurus, and, in the courfe of his march, reftored the public tranquillity, not fo much by the terror of his arms as by the wifdom and moderation of his councils. There was reafon, however, to fear that his approach would give jealoufy to the Parthians. To avoid a rupture with that people, Helvidius was ordered to return with his army into Syria.

L. Vologeses thought it a fair opportunity to recover the kingdom of Armenia. His anceftors had fwayed the fceptre of that country, and now a foreign invader, by guilt and treachery, ufurped the crown. The Parthian king faw his own brother Tiridates deprived of power. His pride could not brook that any part of his family fhould be left in that humble condition. Determined to dethrone the ufurper, and inveft his brother Tiridates with the regal diadem, he put himfelf at the head of a powerful army. The Iberians, without hazarding a battle, fled before the Parthian monarch. Artaxata and Tigranocerta, the two principal cities of Armenia, opened their gates to the invader. The inclemency of the winter feafon, and the want of due attention to provide for the fubfiftence of an army, brought on a famine, and, by confequence, an epidemic difeafe. Vologefes was obliged to abandon his enterprife. Armenia was once more left defencelefs. Rhadamiftus feized his opportunity, and returned to his dominions, elate with pride, and fired with refentment againft a people who had already betrayed him, and with their national inconftancy were ready on the firft occafion to repeat their treachery. He mounted the throne;

but

but the people, though inured to fervitude, grew impatient of
the yoke. They refolved to depofe the ufurper, and in a body
rufhed forward, fword in hand, to inveft the palace.

LI. RHADAMISTUS was obliged to confult his fafety by
flight. He efcaped with his wife, and both owed their lives
to the fpeed of their horfes. The queen was far advanced in
her pregnancy. Her dread of the enemy, confpiring with conjugal affection, ferved to animate her in the firft hurry of their
flight. She bore the fatigue with wonderful refolution. Her
condition, however, was too feeble for the violence of fo rapid
a motion. Seized with pains in her womb, and unable to hold
out longer, fhe intreated her hufband to end her mifery, and, by
an honourable death, prevent the infults of impending bondage.
Rhadamiftus was diftracted by the violence of contending paffions; he clafped her in his arms; he fupported her drooping
fpirits, and, by every tender perfuafion, exhorted her to per-
fevere. Her virtue charmed him, and the idea of leaving her to
the embraces of another, pierced him to the quick. In a fit of
defpair and love, he drew his fcymitar, and, with a hand already
imbrued in blood, wounded the idol of his heart. In that condition he dragged her to the margin of the Araxes, and dafhed
her into the river, that her body might be carried away by the
current, and never fall into the hands of his enemies. Having
thus difpofed of his wife, he fled towards Iberia, and purfued
his way to his father's court.

Meanwhile, Zenobia (fo the princefs was named), floating
gently down the ftream, was feen by the fhepherds on the
fmooth furface of the water, ftruggling in diftrefs, and ftill with
manifeft figns of life. The elegance and dignity of her form
announced a perfon of illuftrious rank. They bound up her

wounds, and gave her the physic of the field. Having soon after learned her name, and the story of her sufferings, they conveyed her to the city of Artaxata. From that place she was conducted, at the public expence, to the court of Tiridates, where she was graciously received, and treated with all the marks of royalty.

LII. During the consulship of Fauſtus Sylla and Salvius Otho, an accuſation was ſet on foot againſt Furius Scribonianus. He was charged with having conſulted the Chaldæans about the length of the emperor's reign, and condemned to baniſhment. Junia his mother, who had been formerly driven into exile, was accuſed of harbouring reſentment, and ſtill feeling with indignation the ſeverity of her fate. Her huſband Camillus, the father of Scribonianus, had levied war in Dalmatia, and obtained his pardon. From that circumſtance, and, in the preſent caſe, from a ſecond inſtance of clemency to a diſaffected family, Claudius took occaſion to boaſt of his moderation. The unhappy exile did not long ſurvive his ſentence; but whether he died by poiſon, or a natural death, cannot now be known. Reports were various at the time. The aſtrologers and mathematicians were baniſhed out of Italy, by a decree of the ſenate, full of rigour, but ending in nothing. In a ſpeech to the fathers Claudius beſtowed great commendation on ſuch of the members of that aſſembly as abdicated their rank on account of their narrow circumſtances. Some were unwilling to withdraw their names, but they were all degraded as obſtinate men, who to their poverty added pride and inſolence.

LIII. During theſe tranſactions, a motion was made in the ſenate for a law to inflict certain penalties on ſuch women as ſhould diſparage themſelves by intermarrying with ſlaves. The

ſenate

fenate decreed, that all who defcended to fo mean an act, without the confent of the mafter of the flave, fhould be confidered
as perfons who had forfeited their rank, and paffed into a ftate
of flavery; if the mafter confented, his approbation fhould operate as a manumiffion only. The honour of this regulation
the emperor afcribed to Pallas, and thereupon Barea Soranus,
conful elect, moved, that the author of fo wife a meafure fhould
be rewarded with prætorian ornaments, and a fum of fifteen
million of fefterces. By way of amendment to the motion,
Cornelius Scipio propofed that public thanks fhould be given to
a man, who derived his origin from the ancient kings of Arcadia,
and, notwithftanding the dignity of his rank, condefcended to be
claffed among the minifters of the emperor. Claudius informed
the fenate, that. Pallas was content with honours, and felt no
ambition to emerge from his ftate of poverty. A decree was
engraved on brafs *(a)*, exhibiting to the public eye a panegyric
on the moderation of a manumitted flave, who had amaffed no
lefs than three hundred million of fefterces, and, with that fum
in his pocket, could give fo ftriking an example of ancient parfimony.

LIV. PALLAS had a brother known by the name of Felix,
who had been for fome time governor of Judæa. This man did
not think it neceffary to prefcribe any reftraint to his own defires. He confidered his connection with the emperor's favourite as a licenfe for the worft of crimes. The Jews, it is
true, with a fpirit little fhort of open rebellion, had refufed, in
the reign of Caligula, to place the ftatue of that emperor in the
temple. Intelligence of his death arrived foon after; but even
that event was not fufficient to allay the ferment. Future princes
might have the fame ambition, and the dread of a fimilar order
kept the province in agitation. Felix inflamed the difcontents

of

of the people by improper remedies; and Ventidius Cumanus, to whom a part of the province was committed, was ready to co-operate in any wicked project. The Galilæans were under the controul of Cumanus; Felix governed the Samaritans. Those two nations, always fierce and turbulent, were at variance with each other, and now, when they despised their governors, their animosity broke out with redoubled fury.

They waged a predatory war; laid waste each others lands, rushed from their ambuscade to sudden encounters, and, at times, tried their strength in regular engagements. The plunder of the war was given up to their rapacious governors, who, therefore, connived at the mischief. The disorders of the province grew to an alarming height, insomuch that the two governors were forced, at last, to have recourse to arms in order to quell the tumult. The Jews resisted, and numbers of the Roman soldiers were massacred in the fray. Quadratus, who commanded in Syria, saw the danger of an impending war, and, to restore the public tranquillity, advanced at the head of his forces. The insurgents, who rose in arms against the Roman soldiers, were punished with death. That measure was soon decided; but the conduct of Felix and Cumanus held the general in suspense. Claudius, duly apprised of the rebellion, and the causes from which it sprung, sent a commission directing an inquiry, with power to try and pronounce judgment on the two provincial ministers. To make an end of all difficulties, Quadratus placed Felix on the tribunal among the judges, and, by that measure, sheltered him from his enemies. Cumanus was found guilty of the crimes committed by both, and in this manner the peace of the province was restored.

LV. CILICIA was soon after thrown into convulsions. The
peasants

peafants of that country, known by the name of the Clitæans *(a)*, a wild and favage race, inured to plunder and fudden commotions, aſſembled under Trofobor, a warlike chief, and pitched their camp on the fummit of a mountain, fteep, craggy, and almoſt inacceſſible. From their faſtneſſes they came ruſhing down on the plain, and, ftretching along the coaſt, attacked the neighbouring cities. They plundered the people, robbed the merchants, and utterly ruined navigation and commerce. They laid fiege to the city of Anemurium, and difperfed a body of horfe, fent from Syria, under Curtius Severus, to the relief of the place. With that detachment the freebooters dared to hazard battle. The ground being rugged, difadvantageous to cavalry, and convenient only to foot foldiers, the Romans were totally routed. At length Antiochus, the reigning king of the country, appeafed the infurrection. By popular arts he gained the good will of the multitude, and proceeded by ftratagem againſt their leader. The confederates being ruined by difunion among themfelves, Trofobor, with his principal adherents, was put to death. By conciliating meafures the reft were brought to a fenfe of their duty.

LVI. It was about this time, that between the lake Fucinus and the river Liris *(a)*, a paſſage was cut through a mountain. That a work of fuch magnificence *(b)* fhould be feen to advantage, Claudius exhibited on the lake a naval engagement, in imitation of Auguſtus, who formed an artificial bafon on the banks of the Tiber, and gave a fpectacle of the fame kind, but with lighter veſſels, and an inferior number of mariners. Ships of three and even four ranks of oars were equipped by Claudius, with no lefs than nineteen thoufand armed men on board. To prevent a deviation from the fight, the lake was fenced round with rafts of timber *(c)*, leaving the intermediate fpace wide

enough

enough to give free play to the oars; ample room for the pilots to diſplay their ſkill, and, in the attack, to exhibit the various operations of a ſea fight. The prætorian guards ſtood on the rafts of timber, ranged in their ſeveral companies. In their front redoubts were raiſed, with proper engines for throwing up maſſy ſtones and all kinds of miſſive weapons. The reſt of the lake was aſſigned to the ſhips. The mariners and combatants filled the decks. An incredible multitude of ſpectators from the neighbouring towns, and even from Rome, attracted by the ſpectacle, or with a view to pay their court to the emperor, crowded round the borders of the lake. The banks, the riſing ground, the ridge of the adjacent hills, preſented to the eye a magnificent ſcene, in the form of an amphitheatre. Claudius and Agrippina preſided at the ſhow; the prince in a ſuperb coat of mail, and the empreſs in a ſplendid mantle, which was a com-plete tiſſue of entire gold *(d)*. The fleet was manned with malefactors; but the battle, nevertheleſs, was fought with heroic bravery. After many wounds, and a great effuſion of blood, to favour a ſet of men who had performed feats of valour, the ſurvivors were excuſed from fighting to deſtruction.

LVII. THE whole of this magnificent ſpectacle being con-cluded, the channel through which the waters flowed was laid open, and then it appeared with what little ſkill the work was executed. The bed was not ſunk deep enough to gain a level either with the middle or the extremities of the lake. It was found neceſſary to clear away the ground, and give the current a freer courſe. The work was finiſhed with expedition, and, to attract a multitude of ſpectators, bridges were thrown over the lake, ſo conſtructed as to admit a foot engagement. On this prodigious platform a ſhow of gladiators was exhibited. Near the mouth of the lake a ſumptuous banquet was prepared; but

the

the fpot was ill-chofen.   The weight of a vaft body of water
rufhing down with irrefiftible force, carried away the contiguous
parts of the works, and fhook the whole fabric.   Confufion and
uproar filled the place.   The roar of the torrent, and the noife
of materials tumbling in, fpread a general alarm.   Claudius ftood
in aftonifhment.   Agrippina feized the moment to accufe Narciffus, who had the direction of the whole.   She imputed the
mifchief to his avarice.   The favourite made reprifals on the
character of Agrippina, condemning, without referve, the impo-
tence of a female fpirit, her overbearing pride, and boundlefs
ambition.

LVIII. Decimus Junius and Quintus Haterius fucceeded
to the confulfhip.   In the courfe of the year Nero, who had
attained the age of fixteen, was joined in marriage to Octavia,
the emperor's daughter.   To grace his character with the fame
of liberal fcience and the powers of eloquence, he undertook the
caufe of the inhabitants of Ilium.   The young orator began with
a deduction of the Roman people from a Trojan origin.   Æneas,
the founder of the Julian family, and other paffages drawn from
antiquity, but in their nature fabulous, ferved to embellifh his
difcourfe.   He fucceeded for his clients, and obtained an entire
exemption from impofts of every kind.   He was advocate alfo
for the colony of the Bolognians, who had lately fuffered by fire.
By the rhetoric of their pleader they obtained a grant of one
hundred thoufand fefterces.   The Rhodians, in like manner,
were obliged to his talents.   That people, after many viciffitudes,
fometimes in full poffeffion of their privileges, and occafionally
deprived of all, as they happened to be friendly or adverfe to the
Roman arms, had their rights confirmed in the ampleft manner.
The city of Apamea, which had been damaged by an earth-

quake,

A. U. C.
8 6.
A D.
53.

quake, owed to the eloquence of their advocate a fufpenfion of all dues for the term of five years.

LIX. In a fhort time after, the conduct of Claudius, under the management of the wife, prefented a contraft of cruelty to all thefe acts of benevolence. Agrippina panted for the gardens of Statilius Taurus. He had been proconful of Africa, and pof-feffed a brilliant fortune. Tarquitius Prifcus had ferved under him as his lieutenant. At the inftigation of Agrippina, this man preferred a charge againft his fuperior officer, founded on fome articles of extortion, but refting chiefly on the practice of magic arts. Taurus was fired with indignation at the perfidy of his colleague. Seeing himfelf devoted to deftruction, he re-folved not to wait the final fentence, and with his own hand delivered himfelf from the malice of his enemies. The profe-cutor was expelled the fenate. The members of that affembly, detefting the treachery of this vile informer, carried their point, in fpite of the arts and fecret influence of Agrippina.

LX. In the courfe of this year, the emperor gave to his fa-vourite political maxim the force of a law. He had been often heard to fay, " that the judicial refolutions of the imperial pro-" curators ought to be, in their feveral provinces, of as high " authority as if they had been pronounced by himfelf." To fhew that this was not fpoken in vain, the doctrine was con-firmed by a decree that carried the principle to a greater extent than ever. By a regulation made by Auguftus, the Roman knights, who ruled the provinces of Ægypt, were empowered, in all cafes, to hear and determine with as full authority as the magiftrates of Rome. The rule was afterwards extended to other provinces, and, even at Rome, the jurifdiction of the knights embraced a variety of queftions, which till then were

                                                            cognizable

cognizable by the prætor only. Claudius enlarged the powers of
his favourites, and finally vested in that body the judicial authority, which had been for ages the cause of civil commotions; for
which the people had shed their blood; and which, in those
memorable struggles, was given by the Sempronian law *(a)* to the
equestrian order, till, in some time afterwards, the Servilian law
restored it to the senate. In the wars between Marius and Sylla
this was the cause of that fierce contention; but, in those turbulent
times, the different orders of the state were engaged in factions
against each other. The party that prevailed, called itself the Public, and made laws in the name of the commonwealth. Caius
Oppius and Cornelius Balbus, supported by Augustus, were the
first who decided the rights of war and peace. To mention,
after them, the names of Matius, Vedius, and others of the
equestrian order, seems now entirely needless; since we find the
enfranchised slaves of Claudius, men no higher than mere domestic servants, raised to a level with the prince, and armed with
the authority of the laws.

LXI. A GRANT to the people of Coos*(a)*, of a general immu-
nity from taxes, was the next measure proposed by the emperor.
He introduced the question with a splendid account of their ancient origin. "The Argives, or, at least, Cœus, the father of
"Latona, first settled on the island. Æsculapius arrived soon
"after, and carried with him the invention of medicine. That
"useful science continued in his family through a long line of
"descendants." He mentioned by name the several persons in regular succession, and the period of time in which they flourished.
He added, that Zenophon, his own physician, was descended from
that illustrious family. The exemption, therefore, now requested
by a man of such distinguished eminence, ought to be granted, in
favour of an island so famous in story, to the end that the inha-

bitants, free from every burthen, might dedicate themfelves altogether to the worfhip of their God. A more fubftantial plea of merit might have been urged in their favour. They could boaft,
with truth, of fingular fervices done to the Romans, and could
fet forth the victories obtained by their affiftance; but Claudius,
with his ufual facility, chofe to gratify the wifhes of an individual,
and, in his opinion, the favour which he conferred ought not to
be varnifhed with confiderations of a public nature.

LXII. The deputies from Byzantium *(a)* were admitted to
an audience before the fenate. They prayed to be relieved from
the heavy rates and duties under which they laboured. They relied on the merit of having been, for a length of time, the faithful
allies of Rome. They traced the hiftory of their fervices from
the war in Macedonia, when the king of that country, on account
of his degenerate character, was called Pfeudophilippus, or Philip
the Falfe *(b)*. They alleged, moreover, the fuccours which
they fent againft Antiochus *(c)*; againft Perfes, and Ariftonicus;
the affiftance, which they gave to Anthony *(d)* in the piratic war,
and, afterwards, to Sylla, to Lucullus, and Pompey. Nor did they
omit their zeal for the Cæfars at the time when they entered Byzantium, and found not only a free paffage for their fleets and armies, but likewife a fafe conveyance for their provifions and military ftores.

LXIII. Byzantium, it is well known, ftands at the extremity of Europe, on the narrow ftrait that feparates Europe from
Afia. The city was built by the Greeks, who were led to the
fpot by the Pythian Apollo. They confulted that oracle about
the proper place for a new city, and received for anfwer, that they
fhould choofe a foundation directly oppofite to the territory of the
blind. The advice, though dark and myfterious, pointed the
people

people of Chalcedon *(a)*, the firſt adventurers in that part of the
world, who had their opportunity to ſeize the beſt ſituation, and,
through want of diſcernment, choſe the worſt.   Byzantium enjoys many advantages : the ſoil is fertile, and the ſea abounds with
fiſh, occaſioned by the prodigious ſhoals, that pour down from the
Pontic ſea, and, to avoid the rocks which lurk beneath the waves
on the Chalcedonian coaſt, make directly to the oppoſite ſhore,
and fall into the bay of Byzantium.   The fiſhery was at firſt a
great branch of commerce.   In proceſs of time, the trade was
cramped by exceſſive impoſitions; and to be relieved, either by a
total extinction, or, at leaſt, a reduction of the duties, was now the
prayer of their petition.   Claudius was inclined to favour their
cauſe : in the late wars in Thrace and Boſphorus, they had ſuffered heavy loſſes ; and it was, therefore, proper to grant them a
compenſation.   They were accordingly freed from all duties for
the term of five years.

LXIV. In the conſulſhip of Marcus Aſinius and Manius Acilius, a ſucceſſion of prodigies kept the minds of men in conſtant
dread of ſome violent convulſion in the ſtate.   The tents and en-
ſigns of the ſoldiers were ſet on fire by a flaſh of lightning; a
ſwarm of bees ſettled on the capitol ; women were delivered of
monſtrous births; and a pig, as ſoon as farrowed, had the talons of
a hawk.   It happened, at this time, that every order of the magiſtracy was ſhort of its proper number, the public having loſt by
death, within a few months, a quæſtor, an ædile, a tribune, a prætor, and a conſul.   This was reckoned among the prodigies.
Amidſt the conſternation that covered the whole city, no perſon
whatever was ſo ſeriouſly alarmed as Agrippina.   Claudius, it
ſeems, had ſaid in converſation, that, by ſome fatality, it had been
his conſtant lot to bear, for a time, the irregularities of his wives,
and in the end to puniſh them.   The expreſſion fell from him in

O 2

his

B O O K
X II.

A. U. C.
806.
A. D.
53.

A. U. C.
807.
A. D.
54.

his liquor. Agrippina knew the force of it, and refolved to take her meafures beforehand. But Domitia Lepida, whom fhe hated for female reafons, was to be the firft devoted victim. She was the daughter of the younger Antonia, great niece to Auguftus, and fifter to Cneius Domitius *(a)*, the firft hufband of the emprefs. Proud of thefe advantages, Lepida confidered herfelf no way inferior to the imperial confort. Their age, their beauty, and their riches were nearly on a level; both of diffolute manners, proud, fierce, lafcivious, and in their vices, no lefs than their views of ambition, determined rivals. Which of them fhould have entire dominion over the mind of Nero, the aunt or the mother, was the point in difpute between them. Lepida made her approaches to the young prince by affability and foftnefs of manners. Her liberality and endearing tendernefs gained the affections of the prince. Agrippina behaved with the authority of a mother, eager to grafp the imperial dignity for her fon, and, when fhe gained it, unwilling to own him for her fovereign.

LXV. A charge was framed againft Lepida, importing, "That " by magic arts fhe afpired to the emperor's bed, and, by neg- " lecting to bridle the infolence of her numerous flaves in Cala- " bria, fhe fhewed herfelf an enemy to the peace of Italy." She was condemned to die. Narciffus endeavoured to avert the fentence; but his efforts were ineffectual. That minifter had for fome time beheld Agrippina with deep miftruft. He faw through her defigns, and, to his felect friends, did not fcruple to declare, " That whatever became of the fucceffion, whether it devolved on " Nero or Britannicus, the dilemma would either way be fatal to " himfelf. He was bound, however, to the emperor by ties of " gratitude, and in his fervice was ready to lay down his life. It " was by his counfels that Silius and Meffalina were both undone. " Should Nero feize the fovereignty, the crimes of his mother

7   " might

" might bring forward the fame cataſtrophe ; and if Britannicus
" ſucceeded to the empire, with that prince he had no claim of
" merit.   At preſent, a ſtep-mother plans the ruin of the imperial
" houſe.   To look on in ſilence, and yield to her towering am-
" bition, were a more flagitious crime, than to have connived at
" the vices of the emperor's former wife.   But the vices of the
" former wife are now renewed by Agrippina.   Her adulterous
" commerce with Pallas is too well known ; and it is equally
" known, that her modeſty, her fame, her honour, and even her
" perſon, all are ſubſervient to her ambition."   Such was the
language of Narciſſus.   In the warmth of his emotions he embraced Britannicus ; he hoped to ſee him grow up to man's
eſtate ; he fixed his eyes on the prince ; he lifted up his hands to
the gods, devoutly praying that he might live to cruſh the enemies
of his father, even though all, who took an active part againſt
his mother, ſhould be doomed to periſh with them.

LXVI. In the midſt of theſe diſtractions, Claudius was attacked by a fit of illneſs.   For the recovery of his health he ſet
out for Sinueſſa (a), to try the effect of a milder air, and the ſa-
lúbrious waters of the place. Agrippina thought ſhe had now an
opportunity to execute the black deſign which ſhe had long
ſince harboured in her breaſt.   Inſtruments of guilt were ready at
her beck, but the choice of the poiſon was ſtill to be conſidered :
if quick and ſudden in its operation, the treachery would be ma-
nifeſt : a ſlow corroſive would bring on a lingering death.   In
that caſe, the danger was, that the conſpiracy might, in the interval, be detected, or, in the weakneſs and decay of nature, the
affections of a father might return, and plead in favour of Britannicus.   She reſolved to try a compound of new and exqui-
ſite ingredients, ſuch as would make directly to the brain, yet not
bring on an immediate diſſolution.   A perſon of well-known
ſkill.

skill in the trade of poisoning was chosen for the business. This was the famous Locusta; a woman lately condemned as a dealer in clandestine practices, but reserved among the instruments of state to serve the purposes of dark ambition. By this tool of iniquity the mixture was prepared. The hand to administer it was that of Halotus, the eunuch, whose business it was to serve the emperor's table, and taste the viands for his master.

LXVII. THE particulars of this black conspiracy transpired in some time after, and found their way into the memoirs of the age. We are told by the writers of that day, that a palatable dish of mushrooms was the vehicle of the poison. The effect was not soon perceived. Through excess of wine or the stupidity of his nature, perhaps the strength of his constitution, Claudius remained insensible. An effort of nature followed, and gave him some relief. Agrippina trembled for herself. To dare boldly was now her best expedient. Regardless of her fame, and all that report could spread abroad, she had recourse to Zenophon, the physician, whom she had seduced to her interest. Under pretence of assisting Claudius to unload his stomach, this man, it is said, made use of a feather tinged with the most subtle poison, and with that instrument searched the emperor's throat. With the true spirit of an assassin he knew, that, in atrocious deeds, a feeble attempt serves only to confound the guilty, while the deed, executed with courage, consummates all, and is sure to earn the wages of iniquity.

LXVIII. MEANWHILE, the senate was convened, and, though the emperor had breathed his last, the consuls and the pontiffs joined in vows and supplications for his recovery. Medical preparations were still applied to a lifeless body, and the farce of attending the sick was continued, till proper measures were taken for the succes-

sion

fion of Nero. Agrippina, with a dejected mien, affected to fink under the weight of affliction. She looked round for confolation, and feeing Britannicus, fhe folded him in her arms, and called him, with expreffions of tendernefs, the image of his father. She detained him with fond careffes, and never fuffered him to leave the apartment. With the fame deceitful arts fhe contrived to decoy his two fifters, Antonia and Octavia. The avenues of the palace were clofely guarded, and, at intervals, favourable accounts of the emperor were iffued, the better to keep every thing in fufpenfe, and amufe the hopes and fears of the foldiers, till the arrival of the propitious moment, promifed by the Chaldæan aftrologers.

LXIX. At length, on the third day before the ides of October *(a)*, about noon, the palace gates were thrown open. A præ-torian cohort, as ufual, was drawn up under arms. Nero, at-tended by Burrhus, made his appearance, and, on a fignal given by the commanding officer, the foldiers received him with fhouts and acclamations. He was immediately put into a litter. Some of the foldiers, we are told, even in that fcene of joy and uproar, looked around for Britannicus, and afked in vain for that unfortunate prince. None of his party appearing, they yielded to the impulfe of the moment. Nero was conveyed to the camp. He addreffed the foldiers in a fpeech fuited to the occa-fion, and promifed a donative, equal to the liberality of his de-ceafed father. He was proclaimed Emperor of Rome. The voice of the army was confirmed by the fenate. The provinces acquiefced without reluctance. Divine honours were decreed to the memory of Claudius, and funeral ceremonies, not inferior to the magnificence that attended the remains of Auguftus. In this article, Agrippina was willing to vie with the pomp difplayed by her great-grandmother Livia. The will of the deceafed em-

peror

B O O K
XII.

A. U. C.
807.
A. D.
54.

BOOK
XII.

A. U. C.
807.
A. D.
54.

peror was not read in public. The preference given to the son of his wife, in prejudice to the rights of his own immediate issue, might raise a spirit of discontent, and alienate the affections of the people.

END OF THE TWELFTH BOOK.

THE ANNALS OF TACITUS

BOOK XIII.

CONTENTS of BOOK XIII.

4

CONTENTS OF BOOK XIII.

*to ſolicit the emperor. Their behaviour in Pompey's theatre.
By Nero's order the Friſians exterminated. The Anſibarians,
under Boiocalus, make the ſame attempt, and with no better ſucceſs. The ſpirited anſwer of Boiocalus to the Roman general.*
LVII. *War between the Hermundurians and the Cattians: both
nations entertain ſuperſtitious notions about a river that produces
ſalt; their quarrel on that account more fierce and violent. The
Hermundurians conquer, and the Cattians almoſt cut to pieces.*
LVIII. *The Ruminal tree, that gave ſhade to Romulus and
Remus, begins to decay; this was deemed an ill omen, till the
branches once more diſplayed their leaves.*

Theſe tranſactions paſſed in four years.

Years of Rome—of Chriſt		Conſuls
808	55	*The emperor Nero, L. Antiſtius Vetus.*
809	56	*Q. Voluſius Saturninus, P. Cornelius Scipio.*
810	57	*Nero, 2d time, L. Calpurnius Piſo.*
811	58	*Nero, 3d time, Valerius Meſſala.*

THE

ANNALS

OF

TACITUS.

BOOK XIII.

I. THE new reign opened with the murder of Junius Sila-nus *(a)*, proconful of Afia. The deed was perpetrated, by the contrivance of Agrippina, without the knowledge of Nero. In the character and conduct of Silanus there was nothing that could provoke his fate. Under the preceding emperors he had led a life fo inactive, that he fell into contempt, and was called by Caligula, "The Golden Calf." But Agrippina had cut off his brother Lucius Silanus, and lived in fear of the vengeance due to her crime. Her fon Nero, not yet arrived at years of dif-cretion, was raifed by her treacherous arts to the fovereign power, and, in oppofition to that meafure, the public voice was loud in favour of Silanus, a man every way qualified, of an un-

derftand-

derftanding matured by years, an unblemifhed character, by his birth illuftrious, and (what was then of great importance) defcended from the houfe of Cæfar. Silanus, in fact, was the great grandfon of Auguftus. Thefe circumftances confpired to work his ruin. The actors in this dark tranfaction were Publius Celer, a Roman knight, and Helius, an enfranchifed flave; both employed in Afia to collect the revenues of the prince. At a public feaft thofe two confpirators adminiftered a dofe of poifon to the proconful with fo little precaution, that fecrefy did not feem to be worth their care. The murder of Narciffus, the freedman of Claudius, was difpatched with as little ceremony. The quarrel between him and Agrippina (b) has been already ftated. He was thrown into prifon, and there confined in clofe and rigorous cuftody, till, driven to the extremity of want, he put an end to his mifery with his own hand. Nero wifhed to prolong his days. The fecret vices of the prince, though they had not then broke out into action, inclined him, by a wonderful bias of nature, to favour a man in whofe avarice and prodigality he faw the counterpart of himfelf.

II. A NUMBER of other victims were marked for deftruction; and Rome would have been a theatre of blood, had not Afranius Burrhus and Annæus Seneca prevented the impending danger. The education of the emperor had been committed to thofe two minifters; both high in power, and yet (uncommon as it is) free from jealoufy; poffeffing different talents, united by fentiment, and each, in his peculiar province, of great confideration. Burrhus gave the prince inftructions in the military fcience, and the aufterity of his manners added weight to his precepts. Seneca taught the principles of eloquence, and charmed by the fuavity of his manners. The two preceptors exerted their joint endeavours to fix in the prince's mind the principles of virtue, or,

if

if that could not be, to reftrain his youthful paffions, and, by
moderate indulgence, infufe into his mind a tafte for elegant, if
not innocent pleafures.

Agrippina threw difficulties in their way.   Fierce with all the
paffions that attend inordinate ambition, fhe was fupported, in
her worft defigns, by Pallas, that pernicious favourite, who incited Claudius to an inceftuous marriage, and advifed the adoption of Nero; two fatal meafures, by which that emperor was
precipitated to his ruin.   But it was not in the temper or genius
of Nero to bend to the politics of a freedman; on the other
hand, the arrogance of Pallas, who afpired above himfelf, gave
difguft to the prince.   Public honours, in the mean time, were
beftowed with a lavifh hand on the emperor's mother.   To a
tribune, who, according to the military practice, afked for the
word, Nero gave " THE BEST OF MOTHERS."   Two lictors,
by a decree of the fenate, were ordered to attend her perfon.
She was, at the fame time, declared the prieftefs of Claudius.
The funeral of that prince was performed with all the pomp of
cenforial obfequies.   He was, afterwards, added to the number
of the gods.

III. NERO pronounced the funeral oration.   He reprefented,
in the brighteft colours, the illuftrious birth of the deceafed emperor, the number of his confulfhips, and the triumphal honours
of his anceftors.   On thofe topics he dwelt with propriety, and
commanded attention.   The tafte of Claudius for the liberal arts,
and the undifturbed tranquillity that prevailed throughout his
reign, afforded ample room for panegyric, and the orator was
heard with pleafure.   But when the judgment and political wifdom of Claudius were mentioned with praife and decorations of
language, the ridicule was too ftrong, and none could refrain
                                                          from

from laughter. And yet the speech was written by Seneca, in a style of elegance peculiar to that amiable writer, who possessed a vein of wit and fancy, that charmed the taste of the age in which he lived. It was observed, on this occasion, by men advanced in life, who love, at leisure, to compare the past with the present times, that of all the emperors, Nero was the first, who was content to be the organ of another's eloquence. In Cæsar the dictator the most eminent orators found an illustrious rival. Augustus had a flow of language, easy, clear, and copious, well suited to the dignity of a prince. Precision was the talent of Tiberius; and if his meaning was sometimes obscure, it was when he chose to be dark and impenetrable. The confused and turbulent genius of Caligula did not transfuse itself into his discourse. Even in Claudius, when he came with a speech prepared and studied, there was no want of elegance. Nero, in the prime of life, took a different turn, and, with lively parts, applied himself to other objects. Engraving *(a)*, painting, music, and horsemanship were his favourite pursuits. At intervals he was fond of poetry, and his verses shewed that he had, at least, a tincture of letters.

IV. HAVING played the part of a public mourner, Nero made his appearance in the senate. He began with a florid compliment to the authority of the fathers, and the concurrent suffrages of the army, which raised him to the imperial dignity. He added, " that he had many bright examples to excite emu-
" lation, and in his councils superior wisdom to direct his con-
" duct. His youth had not been engaged in civil commotions,
" and to the rage of contending factions he was, by consequence,
" an utter stranger. He brought with him no private animo-
" sity, no sense of injuries, no motives to inspire revenge. He
" explained the system of government, which he intended to
" pursue;

" purfue ; the abufes which occafioned difcontent and murmur-
" ings in the former reign, were to be reformed altogether ; and,
" in particular, the decifion of caufes, he was determined, fhould
" no longer depend on the authority of the prince. The
" practice of hearing in a chamber of the palace *(a)* the accufer
" and the accufed, and thereby fubjecting the lives and fortunes
" of men to the influence of a few favourites, was to be abo-
" lifhed. In his palace nothing fhould be venal ; nothing car-
" ried by intrigue, by bribery, or fecret influence. The revenues
" of the prince, and the public treafure, fhould be diftinct and
" feparate rights. The fenate might retain the full exercife of
" the powers vefted in that affembly by the fpirit of the con-
" ftitution. Italy and the provinces might, in all cafes, addrefs
" themfelves to the tribunal of the confuls, and, through that
" channel, find their way to the fenate. The executive power
" over the army was his peculiar province, and he claimed no
" more *(b)*."

V. THE promife was fair, and for fome time regularly obferved. The fathers of their own authority made feveral regulations, and among other things ordained, that no advocate
fhould hire out his talents in any caufe whatever. The law requiring *(a)* a fpectacle of gladiators from fuch as were chofen to
the office of quæftor, was entirely abrogated. To thefe refolutions,
tending, in effect, to repeal the acts of Claudius, Agrippina
made a ftrong oppofition. In order to carry her point, fhe
caufed the fenate to be convened in the palace, where, at a convenient ftation at the door behind the arras, fhe might conceal
her perfon, and overhear the debate. The fathers acted with
a fpirit of independance, and a decree was paffed accordingly.
On a fubfequent occafion the ambaffadors of Armenia were admitted to an audience before the prince. Agrippina advanced

to the tribunal to take her feat, and preside with joint authority. All who beheld the scene were struck with terror and amazement, when Seneca, in the general confusion, had the presence of mind to bid the emperor step forward to meet his mother. Under an appearance of filial piety, the honour of the state was saved.

VI. TOWARDS the end of the year, a report prevailed that the Parthians had once more invaded Armenia, and that Rhadamistus, tired of a kingdom so often taken and retaken, declined to end the dispute by force of arms. At Rome, where public affairs were discussed with freedom, the popular opinion was, " that Nero, young in life, just out of his seventeenth " year, would not be equal to a conjuncture so arduous and im- " portant. What dependance could· be had on the flexibility " of a boy, still under the government of his mother? He had " tutors, indeed; but would they undertake the command of " armies, the conduct of sieges, and all the various operations " of war?" It was argued on the other hand, " that the situa- " tion of affairs was better than it could have been under a " prince like Claudius, worn out with·age, and sunk in sloth, " the willing dupe of his favourite freedmen. Burrhus and· " Seneca were men of experience: and, with such advisers, why " conclude that Nero, bordering on the season of manly vigour, " was unequal to the task? Pompey, at the age of eighteen, and· " Octavianus Cæsar, having barely passed his nineteenthyear, were· " both at the head of armies, in times big with danger, amidst· " the distractions of a civil war. It is by the wisdom of their· " councils, and not by personal valour, that princes are crowned· " with glory. Whether the cabinet of Nero was filled with evil· " counsellors, or with men of talents and integrity, would soon " be evident. If the emperor, without regarding party con-·

nections

" nections and court intrigue, chofe a general, not on account
" of his wealth and intereft, but for his military character, the
" queftion would be then fairly decided."

VII. While thefe different opinions kept the public mind
in agitation, Nero ordered levies to be made in the eaftern nations, and the legions, thus recruited, to take poft on the confines of Armenia. He defired, at the fame time, that Agrippa *(a)*
and Antiochus, two oriental kings, fhould hold their forces in
readinefs to enter the territory of the Parthians. For the convenience of his armies bridges were thrown over the Euphrates.
The leffer Armenia *(b)* was committed to Ariftobulus, and the
country called Sophenes *(c)* to Sohemus: both princes were
allowed to affume the enfigns of royalty. In this crifis a for-
tunate circumftance gave a fudden turn in favour of Rome.
Vardanes, the fon of Vologefes, became a competitor for the
crown in oppofition to his father. The Parthians were, by
confequence, obliged to recall their armies, and under colour of
deferring, not of abandoning the war, Armenia was evacuated.

VIII. The fathers extolled thefe tranfactions with their ufual
ftrain of flattery. They voted that prayers and public thankf-
givings fhould be offered to the gods, and that during the folemnity Nero, adorned with a triumphal robe, fhould enter the
city with all the fplendour of an ovation. It was farther refolved, that in the temple of Mars the Avenger a ftatue fhould be
erected to the prince, in form and dimenfion equal to that of
the god. Amidft this fervile adulation, the appointment of
Domitius Corbulo to the command of the army in Armenia,
gave univerfal fatisfaction. The road to preferment, men
began to hope, would, from that time, be open to talents
and fuperior merit. By the arrangement which was fettled

in

in the eaft, part of the auxiliaries, with two legions, were
ftationed in Syria, under the command of Ummidius Quadratus,
the governor of that province. An equal number of legionary
foldiers and allies, befides the cohorts and light troops that
wintered in Cappadocia, were affigned to Corbulo. The kings
in alliance with Rome had directions to co-operate with thofe
generals, as the events of war fhould happen to require. Corbulo was high in favour with the princes of the eaft. Aware
that fame, in the beginning of all military operations, makes a
deep impreffion, that general advanced by rapid journeys, and
at Ægea *(a)*, a city of Cilicia, met Quadratus, who chofe an interview at that place, rather than wait till Corbulo fhewed himfelf at the head of his army in the province of Syria, where he
had reafon to fear that the eyes of the people would be fixed on
his rival in command. The fact was, Corbulo poffeffed many
advantages: in his perfon manly, of a remarkable ftature, and
in his difcourfe magnificent, he united with experience and
confummate wifdom thofe exterior accomplifhments, which,
though in themfelves of no real value, give an air of elegance
even to trifles.

IX. THE two commanders fent a joint meffage to Vologefes,
warning him to prefer the fweets of peace to the calamities of
war, and, by fending hoftages, to mark his refpect for the Roman name. The Parthian monarch, intending to wait for a
more favourable opportunity, or, perhaps, wifhing to remove
from his court his moft dangerous enemies, gave up as hoftages
the moft diftinguifhed of the line of the Arfacides. Hifterius,
a centurion, fent by Quadratus with orders to travel with expedition, received the hoftages under his care; but Corbulo,
apprifed of this artful project, difpatched Arrius Varus, the commander of a cohort, to claim the care and cuftody of the Parthian

thian nobles. The centurion refifted. A warm difpute enfued
between the two officers, till, at length, that they might not
exhibit a ridiculous fcene to foreign nations, the matter was referred to the decifion of the hoftages themfelves, and the ambaffadors who accompanied them. The Parthians, ftruck with
the recent fame of the commander in chief, and, as often happens
even among enemies, conceiving the higheft refpect for his perfon, gave the preference to Corbulo. Hence a new fource of
difcord between the two generals. Quadratus complained, that
the honour which he had acquired was unfairly wrefted from
him. Corbulo maintained his right, infifting that the idea of
delivering up hoftages had never occurred to Vologefes, till fuch
time as his hopes were humbled by the name of the fuperior
officer who had the conduct of the war. To appeafe their jealoufy, Nero iffued an order, that on account of the profperous
events achieved by the conduct of both generals, the imperial
fafces under each of them fhould be decorated with wreaths of
laurel. Thefe tranfactions happened in different years; but,
for the fake of perfpicuity, they are here related in one connected feries.

X. In the courfe of the fame year, Nero defired that by a
decree of the fenate a ftatue might be erected to his father
Cneius Domitius Ænobarbus, and that Afconius Labeo, his
former tutor, might be honoured with the confular ornaments.
The fenate propofed, that ftatues of folid gold or filver fhould be
erected in honour of the prince; but Nero had the modefty to
reject the offer. A law was alfo in agitation, by which the year
was to begin from December, the month in which Nero was
born. This too was over-ruled. The emperor refolved to
continue the old ftyle, dating the year from the calends of January; a day rendered facred by the eftablifhed religion of the
Romans.

Romans. An attempt was made to arraign Carinas Celer, a member of the senate, and Julius Densus, of the equestrian order. The first was accused by his slave; the crime objected to the latter was his attachment to Britannicus. Both prosecutions were suppressed by order of the emperor.

XI. NERO and Lucius Antistius were the next consuls. During the solemnity of swearing the magistrates, according to custom, on the acts of the emperor, Antistius had it in command not to include in his oath the acts of the reigning prince; an instance of modesty and self-denial, which the fathers thought could not be too highly commended. They were lavish of praise, in hopes that the sense of honest fame, even in matters of little moment, implanted early in the mind of a young man, might shoot up to a principle of honour, and the love of solid glory. In a short time after, Nero distinguished himself by an act of clemency in the case of Plautius Lateranus *(a)*, who, for his criminal intrigues with Messalina, had been expelled the senate. The emperor restored him to his rank. He even bound himself to observe throughout his reign the virtues of humanity. This promise he renewed in several speeches prepared for him by the pen of Seneca, and probably written to display the moral lessons which the philosopher taught, or to shew the brilliant talents of that lively writer.

XII. THE authority of Agrippina was now on the decline. An enfranchised female slave of the name of ACTE *(a)* had gained an entire ascendant over the affections of the prince. To conduct this intrigue, Nero chose Otho *(b)* and Claudius Senecio for his confidential friends; the former descended from a family of consular rank; the latter, the son of a freedman belonging to the late emperor. They were both elegant in their persons.

Their

Their tafte for debauchery and clandeftine vices introduced them to the notice of the prince. Their firft approaches to his friendfhip were unperceived by Agrippina: fhe endeavoured afterwards to remove them from his prefence, but her efforts were without effect. The emperor's friends, though famed for wifdom and the feverity of their manners, made no oppofition to his new intrigue. A courtefan, who gratified the ardour of a young man's paffion, without injury to any perfon whatever, was thought an object of no importance. Nero, it is true, was married to Octavia; but neither the nobility of her birth, nor her unfpotted virtue, could fecure his affections. By fome fatality, or, perhaps, by the fecret charm of forbidden pleafures, his heart was alienated from his wife. The connection with his favourite concubine ferved to reftrain the prince from other purfuits; and there was reafon to fear, that, detached from her, he might riot in fcenes of higher life, and deftroy the peace and honour of the nobleft families.

XIII. AGRIPPINA was fired with indignation. She complained aloud that an enfranchifed flave was put in competition with the emperor's mother, and a wretch of mean extraction was to be treated as her daughter-in-law. She ftormed with all the rage of female pride, never reflecting that the prince might fee his error, or that fatiety and cold indifference might, in time, fucceed to the vehemence of youthful paffion. The haughty fpirit of the mother ferved only to inflame the ardour of her fon. He gave a loofe to love, and threw off all regard for his mother, determined, for the future, to yield to no authority but that of Seneca. Among the friends of that minifter was a man of the name of Annæus Serenus (a), who pretended to admire the perfon of Acte, and, to throw a veil over the growing paffion of Nero, conveyed to her, in his own name, the prefents sent by the secret gallantry of the prince. Agrippina thought it time to abate from her ferocity. She had recourse to art, and hoped by gentle methods to regain her influence. Her own apartment was now at her son's service. Love, at his time of life, was natural, and his superior rank demanded some indulgence. Under the care and management of his mother he might enjoy his secret pleasures. She apologized for the warmth with which she broke out at first, and even made an offer of all her treasure, little inferior to imperial riches. Her conduct was always in extremes; violent in the beginning, and in the end too complying.

A transition so sudden did not escape the observation of Nero. His confidential friends were alarmed. Dreading nothing so much as the return of Agrippina's influence, they cautioned the prince not to be the dupe of a woman, who, in reality, abated nothing from the pride and arrogance of her character, though now she played an humble, but insidious part. It happened at this time that Nero examined a rich wardrobe, appropriated to the use of the mothers and wives of the emperors. He selected a splendid dress and a considerable quantity of jewels. These he ordered to be presented to Agrippina. The things were gay and magnificent, the kind of ornaments that please the taste and vanity of women, and, being unasked and unexpected, they were sent with a better grace. Agrippina construed this civility into an affront. The design, she said, was not to adorn her person, but to deprive her of the rest of those valuable effects. Her son affected to divide with his mother what he owed entirely to her protection. Her words were reported to the emperor with additional malice.

XIV. In order, by a sudden blow, to humble Agrippina and

her

her party, Nero difmiffed Pallas *(a)* from all his employments. By the favour of Claudius this man had been raifed to a degree of power that made him affume the air and importance of firft minifter, and fovereign arbiter of the empire. As he withdrew from court with his train of followers, Nero pleafantly faid, "Pallas is going to abdicate." Before he retired, it is certain that he had bargained for himfelf. It was agreed that no inquiry fhould be had into his conduct, and that all accounts between him and the public fhould be confidered as clofed and balanced. The indignation of Agrippina was not to be reftrained: in a tone of menace fhe endeavoured to intimidate her enemies; even in the emperor's hearing, fhe exclaimed aloud, "Britan-"nicus is grown up, the genuine iffue of Claudius, and every "way worthy of the fucceffion to his father. The fovereignty "has been wrefted from him by an intruder, who owes his title "to adoption only, and now prefumes to trample on the rights "of a mother, who gave him all. But every thing fhall be "brought to light: the misfortunes which fhe herfelf had caufed "in the imperial family, her inceftuous marriage with her un-"cle, and the poifon that put an end to his life; all fhall be "difclofed, all laid open to the world. By the favour of the "gods Britannicus is ftill alive: that refource ftill remains. "With that young prince fhe would join the army: in the "camp fhould be heard the daughter of Germanicus; Burrhus, "and Seneca, the famous exile, might prefent themfelves before "the prætorian foldiers; the firft with his maimed hand, and "the fecond, armed with his tropes and flowers of rhetoric; "both worthy minifters, fit, in their own opinion, to govern "the Roman world." In this ftrain fhe raved with vehemence, brandifhing her hands, and pouring out a torrent of invective. She appealed to the deified Claudius; fhe invoked the manes of the murdered Silani, and of others who perifhed by her

BOOK XIII.

A. U. C. 808.
A. D. 55.

guilt, though now, in return for all, she met with nothing but treachery and ingratitude.

XV. THESE violent declarations made a deep impreſſion on the mind of Nero. The birth-day of Britannicus, when that prince was to enter on his fifteenth year, was near at hand. This gave riſe to a number of reflections. The turbulent ſpirit of Agrippina, and the character of the prince, filled him with apprehenſions. On a late occaſion Britannicus had given a ſpecimen of early acuteneſs, ſlight, indeed, in itſelf, but ſuch as diſpoſed the people in his favour. It happened, during the Saturnalian feſtival (a), that, among the diverſions uſual among young people, the play, " WHO SHALL BE KING (b), became part of the amuſement at court. The lot fell to Nero: he impoſed his commands on the company, in no inſtance aiming at ridicule or inconvenience, till he came to Britannicus. He ordered the young prince to ſtand in the middle of the room, and ſing a ſong to the company. By this deviſe he hoped that a ſtripling, not yet accuſtomed even to ſober converſation, much leſs to revelry and the joys of wine, would be expoſed to deriſion. Britannicus performed his part without embaraſſment. His ſong (c) alluded to his own caſe, expreſſing the ſituation of a prince excluded from the throne of his anceſtors. The whole company felt a touch of compaſſion, and, in the moment of gaiety, when wine and the midnight hour had thrown off all diſſimulation, they expreſſed their feelings without diſguiſe. Nero found that his pleaſantry recoiled upon himſelf. Hatred, from that moment, took poſſeſſion of his heart. The furious and implacable ſpirit of Agrippina kept him in a conſtant alarm. No crime could be alleged againſt Britannicus, and, by conſequence, there was no colour to juſtify a public execution.

Nero reſolved to act by covert ſtratagem. A preparation of
poiſon

poifon was ordered, and Julius Pollio, a tribune of the prætorian cohorts, was called in as an accomplice. This man had in his cuftody the famous Locufta, a woman guilty of various crimes, and then under fentence for the practice of adminiftering poifon. She was made an inftrument in the confpiracy. For fome time before, care had been taken to admit none to the prefence of Britannicus, but fuch as had long fince renounced every principle of honour and of virtue. The firft potion was given to Britannicus by his tutors; but being weak, or injudicioully qualified, it paffed without effect. The flow progrefs of guilt did not fuit the genius of Nero. He threatened the tribune, and was on the point of ordering the forcerefs to be put to death. He railed at both as two cowards in vice, who wiflhed to fave appearances, and concert a defence for themfelves, while they left a dreadful interval, big with fear and danger. To appeafe his wrath, they promifed to prepare a dofe as fure and deadly as the affaffin's knife. In a room adjoining to the apartment of the emperor they mixed a draught, compounded of ingredients, whofe fure and rapid quality they had already experienced.

XVI. ACCORDING to the cuftom at that time eftablifhed at court, the children of the imperial family dined, in a fitting pofture, with the nobility of their own age, in fight of their relations, at a table fet apart, and ferved with due frugality. Whenever Britannicus was, in this manner, feated at his meal, it was a fettled rule that an attendant fhould tafte his food and liquor. To preferve this cuftom, and prevent detection by the death of both, an innocent beverage, without any infufion that could hurt, was tried by the proper officer, and prefented to the prince. He found it too hot, and returned it. Cold water, in which the poifon had been mixed, was immediately poured into

B O O K
XIII.

A. U. C.
809.
A. D.
55.

R 2

the

the cup. Britannicus drank freely; the effect was violent, and, in an inftant, it feized the powers of life: his limbs were palfied, his breath was fuppreffed, and his utterance failed. The company were thrown into confternation. Some rufhed out of the room, while others, who had more difcernment, ftaid, but in aftonifhment, with their eyes fixed on Nero, who lay ftretched at eafe on his couch, with an air of innocence, and without emotion. He contented himfelf with calmly faying, " This is " one of the epileptic fits to which Britannicus has been fubject " from his infancy. The diforder will go off, and he will foon " recover his fenfes." Agrippina was ftruck with horror. She endeavoured to fupprefs her feelings; but the inward emotions were too ftrong; they fpoke in every feature, plainly fhewing that fhe was as innocent as Octavia, the fifter of Britannicus. By this horrible act the emperor's mother faw all her hopes at once cut off, and from fo daring a ftep, fhe could even then forefee that her fon would wade in blood, and add to his crimes the horror of parricide. Octavia, though ftill of tender years, had feen enough of courts to teach her the policy of fmothering her grief, her tendernefs, and every fentiment of the heart. In this manner the feene of diftraction ended, and the pleafures of the table were renewed.

XVII. One and the fame night faw the murder of Britannicus and his funeral. Both were preconcerted. Without expence, or any kind of pomp, the prince's remains were interred in the Field of Mars, under a fhower of rain, which fell with fuch violence, that it paffed with the multitude as the fure forerunner of divine vengeance on the authors of fo foul a deed; a deed, notwithftanding all its horrors, which many were inclined to think of with lefs feverity, when they confidered that, from the earlieft times, a fpirit of jealoufy always fubfifted be-

6

tween

tween brothers, and that the nature of fovereign power is fuch, as not to endure a rival. From the writers of that period there is reafon to conclude, that Nero, on various occafions, had taken advantage of the tender years of Britannicus, and offered vile indignities to his perfon. If the anecdote be founded in truth, the death, which delivered a defcendant of the Claudian line from foul difgrace, cannot be deemed premature or cruel. The prince, it is true, died in the hour of hofpitality, without warning, without time allowed to his fifter to take the laft farewell; and his mortal enemy faw him in the pangs of death. After all his fufferings, the poifoned cup was mercy. The hurry with which the funeral was performed, was juftified by Nero in a proclamation, ftating the practice of the ancient Romans, who ordained with wifdom, " That the bodies of fuch as died in the " prime of life fhould, as foon as poffible, be removed from " the public eye, without waiting for funeral orations, and the " flow parade of pomp and ceremony. For himfelf, deprived as " he was of the affiftance of a brother, he depended altogether " on the affections of the people, in full perfuafion, that the fe- " nate, and all orders of men, would exert their beft endeavours " to fupport a prince, who now remained the only branch of a " family born to rule the empire of the world." After this public declaration, his next care was, by large donations, to fecure in his intereft all his moft powerful friends.

XVIII. THE conduct of fuch as were moft diftinguifhed by the munificence of the emperor, did not pafs uncenfured. They were men who profeffed integrity, and yet did not blufh to take palaces (a), country-feats, and extenfive lands, all equally willing to have fhare of the plunder. By their apologifts it was argued, that they could not avoid fubmitting to the will of a prince, who knew the horror of his crimes, and hoped by his liberality

to

to soften the public resentment. Agrippina continued implacable. Indignation like hers was not to be appeased by presents. She cherished Octavia with the tenderest regard; she had frequent meetings with the leaders of her party; and, with more than her natural avarice, she collected money in all quarters; she courted the tribunes and centurions; and to the thin nobility, which then remained, she paid every mark of respect, dwelling with pleasure on their names, applauding their virtues, with a view to strengthen her interest by a coalition of the first men in Rome. Nero was apprised of all that passed. By his orders the sentinels who guarded her gates (as had been done in the time of Claudius, and since his decease) were all withdrawn. The German soldiers, who had been added by way of doing honour to the emperor's mother, were likewise dismissed from her service. Nor did the matter rest here. To retrench the number of her adherents and visitors, Nero resolved to hold a separate court. He assigned to his mother the mansion formerly occupied by Antonia. He visited her in her new situation, but his visits were a state farce: he went with a train of attendants, and, after a short salute, took his leave with cold civility.

XIX. In the mass of human affairs there is nothing so vain and transitory as the fancied pre-eminence which depends on popular opinion, without a solid foundation to support it. Of this truth Agrippina is a melancholy proof. Her house was deserted; no friend to comfort her; no courtier to flutter at her levee; and none to visit her, except a few women who frequented her house, perhaps with a good intention, or, more probably, with the little motives of female triumph. In the number was Junia Silana, formerly divorced, as has been mentioned, from Caius Silius, at the instigation of Messalina.. Since that time, she became the intimate friend of Agrippina; by her birth
illustrious,

illuſtrious, diſtinguiſhed by her beauty, and not leſs ſo by her laſ-
civious conduct.   Her friendſhip for Agrippina, ſoured afterwards by contentions between themſelves, turned to bitter hatred.
A treaty of marriage between Silana and Sextius Africanus, a citizen of illuſtrious rank, was rendered abortive by the ill offices
of Agrippina.   She told the lover, that his miſtreſs, though no
longer in the prime of life, was of a diſſolute character, and ſtill
abandoned to her vicious pleaſures.   In this act of hoſtility love
had no kind of ſhare.   Agrippina had not ſo much as a wiſh for
the perſon of Africanus ; but Silana enjoyed large poſſeſſions,
and being a widow without children, her whole fortune might
devolve to the huſband.

Silana, from that moment, was ſtung with reſentment.   The
ſeaſon for revenge ſhe thought was now arrived, and, for that purpoſe, ſhe employed Iturius and Calviſius, two of her creatures,
to frame an accuſation againſt Agrippina, not on the ground of
the old and threadbare ſtory about her grief for Britannicus, and
her zeal for Octavia ; but with a deeper intent, that revenge
might have its full blow.   The head of the accuſation was, That
Agrippina had conſpired with Rubellius Plautus, a deſcendant of
Auguſtus, by the maternal line in the ſame degree as Nero, to
bring about a revolution, and, in that event, to marry the uſurper,
and once more invade the commonwealth.   With this charge,
drawn up in form, Iturius and Calviſius ſought Atimetus, one
of the freedmen of Domitia, the emperor's aunt.   A fitter perſon
could not be choſen : he knew the enmity that ſubſiſted between
his miſtreſs and Agrippina, and, for that reaſon, liſtened eagerly
to the information.   Having heard the particulars, he employed
Paris the comedian (who had likewiſe received his freedom from
Domitia), and, by him, conveyed the whiſper to the emperor,
with circumſtances of aggravation.

XX. The

XX. THE night was far advanced, and Nero paffed the time in riot and gay caroufal, when Paris entered the apartment. In the prince's parties he had always been a pimp of pleafure; but now, a meffenger of ill news, he appeared with an air of dejection. He laid open the particulars of the charge. Nero heard him with difmay and terror. In the firft agitations of his mind he refolved to difpatch his mother, and Plautus, her accomplice. Burrhus was no longer to command the prætorian bands: he was the creature of Agrippina, raifed at firft by her influence, and in his heart a fecret friend to her and her intereft. If we may credit Fabius Rufticus, a commiffion was actually made out, and fent to Cæcina Tufcus; but recalled, at the requeft of Seneca, who interpofed to fave his friend from difgrace. According to Cluvius and Pliny, the honour of Burrhus was never called in queftion. To fay the truth, the authority of Fabius Rufticus is not free from fufpicion. He flourifhed under the protection of Seneca, and the gratitude of the writer embraces every opportunity to adorn the character of his patron.

The hiftorical evidence is fairly before the reader, agreeably to the defign of this work, which profeffes to depend, at all times, on the teftimony of authors, when they agree among themfelves; and, when they differ, to ftate the points in difpute, with the reafons on each fide. Nero was diftracted with doubt and fear. In the tumult of his thoughts, he determined to difpatch his mother without delay. Nor was his fury to be reftrained till Burrhus pledged himfelf, if the charge was verified, to fee execution done upon her; but to be heard in anfwer to the accufation, he faid, was the right of the meaneft perfon, much more fo of a mother. In the prefent cafe, no charge was made in form; no profecutor appeared; the whole was nothing but the whifper of a bufy tale-bearer, who brought intelligence from
the

the houfe of an enemy; but the time chofen for the difcovery makes the whole improbable. Paris the informer came in the dead of night; and after many hours fpent in caroufing, what can be expected, but confufion, ignorance, and fatal temerity?

XXI. NERO was pacified by this reafoning. At the dawn of day, proper perfons were fent to Agrippina, to inform her of the allegations againft her, and to hear her defence. The commiffion was executed by Burrhus in the prefence of Seneca, and a number of freedmen, who were fent to watch the whole proceeding. Burrhus ftated the charge; he named the informers, and, in a tone of feverity, enforced every circumftance. Agrippina heard him undifmayed, and, with the pride and fpirit of her character, replied as follows: " That Silana, who has " never known the labours of child-bed, fhould be a ftranger to " the affections of a mother, cannot be matter of furprife. " A woman of profligate manners may change her adulterers, but " a mother cannot renounce her children. If Iturius and Cal- " vifius, two bankrupts in fame as well as fortune, have fold " themfelves to an old woman, is it of courfe that I muft be " guilty of a crime which they have fabricated? And muft my " fon, at the inftigation of two fuch mifcreants, commit a parri- " cide? Let Domitia fhew her kindnefs to my fon; let her vie " with tendernefs like mine, and I will forgive her malice; I " will even thank her for it. But fhe is in league with Atime- " tus, who is known to be her paramour: Paris, the ftage- " player, lends his aid: the talents that figured in the theatre, " he hopes, will be able to plan a real tragedy.

" At the time when my cares were bufy to make Nero the " adopted fon of Claudius; to inveft him with proconfular digni- " ty, and declare him conful elect; when I was labouring to open

VOL. II.S" to

BOOK XIII.

A. U. C.
808.
A. D.
55.

" to my fon the road to empire, where was **Domitia** then? Her
" ponds and lakes at Baiæ engroffed all her attention. Stand
" forth the man, who can prove that I tampered with the city-
" guards; that I feduced the provinces from their allegiance, or
" endeavoured to corrupt the flaves and freedmen of the em-
" peror. Had Britannicus obtained the imperial dignity, could
" I have hoped to live in fafety? And if Rubellius Plautus, or
" any other perfon, had feized the reins of government, can
" it be fuppofed that my enemies would not have feized their op-
" portunity to exhibit their charge, not for intemperate words,
" thrown out in the warmth of paffion, the effufion of a mo-
" ther's jealoufy, but for real crimes, and thofe of fo deep a dye,
" that no man can forgive them, except a fon, for whom they
" were committed." Such was the language of Agrippina. The
warmth and energy with which fhe delivered herfelf, made an impreffion on all who heard her. They endeavoured to foften affliction, and mitigate the violence of her feelings. She demanded
an interview with her fon, and the meeting was granted. In his
prefence fhe fcorned to enter into a vindication of herfelf. To
anfwer the charge might betray too much diffidence: nor did
fhe dwell on the fervices which fhe had rendered to her fon; that
were to tax him with ingratitude. Her object was to punifh her
accufers, and reward her friends. She fucceeded in both.

XXII. THE fuperintendance of corn and grain was granted to
Fænius Rufus. The public fpectacles, then intended by the emperor, were committed to the care of Arruntius Stella. The
province of Ægypt was affigned to Caius Balbillus *(a)*, and that
of Syria to Publius Anteius. But the laft was the bubble of
promifes, and never fuffered to proceed to his government. Silana
was fent into exile. Calvifius and Iturius *(b)* fhared the fame
fate. Atimetus was punifhed with death. Paris, the comedian,

was

was of too much confequence: he had the art of miniftering to
the pleafures of the prince: his vices faved him. Rubellius
Plautus was, for the prefent, paffed by in filence.

XXIII. Soon after this tranfaction, Pallas and Burrhus were
charged with a confpiracy to raife Cornelius Sylla to the imperial
feat, in confideration of his illuftrious birth, and the affinity
which he bore to Claudius, being, by his marriage with Antonia, the fon-in-law of that emperor. In this bufinefs, a man of
the name of Pætus was the profecutor ; a bufy pragmatical fellow,
notorious for haraffing his fellow-citizens with confifcations to the
treafury, and on the prefent occafion a manifeft impoftor. To
find Pallas innocent would not have been unpleafant to the fathers, if the arrogance of the man had not given difguft to all.
In the courfe of the trial, fome of his freedmen being mentioned
as accomplices in the plot, he thought proper to anfwer, " That
" among his domeftics he never condefcended to fpeak: he fig-
" nified his pleafure by a nod, or a motion of his hand. If the
" bufinefs required fpecial directions, he committed his mind to
" paper, unwilling to mix in difcourfe with people fo much be-
" neath his notice." Burrhus, though involved in the profecution, took his feat on the bench with the judges, and pronounced
his opinion. Pætus was condemned to banifhment, and all his
papers, which he preferved as documents to be ufed in the revival
of treafury-fuits, were committed to the flames.

XXIV. Towards the clofe of the year, the cuftom of having
a cohort on duty, at the exhibition of the public fpectacles, was
entirely laid afide. By this meafure the people were amufed
with a fhew of liberty ; and the foldiers, being thus removed
from the licentioufnefs of the theatre, were no longer in danger of
tainting the difcipline of the army with the vices of the city.

From

BOOK
XIII.

A. U. C.
808.
A. D.
55.

From this experiment it was to be further seen, whether the populace, freed from the control of the military, would be observant of decency and good order. The temples of Jupiter and Minerva being struck with lightning, the emperor, by the advice of the soothsayers, ordered a solemn lustration to purify the city.

A. U. C.
809.
A. D.
56.

XXV. The consulship of Quintus Volusius and Publius Scipio was remarkable for the tranquillity that prevailed in all parts of the empire, and the corruption of manners that disgraced the city of Rome. Of all the worst enormities Nero was the author. In the garb of a slave, he roved through the streets, visited the brothels, and rambled through all by-places, attended by a band of rioters, who seized the wares and merchandize exposed to sale, and offered violence to all that fell in their way. In these frolics, Nero was so little suspected to be a party, that he was roughly handled in several frays. He received wounds on some occasions, and his face was disfigured with a scar. It was not long, however, before it transpired that the emperor was become a night-brawler. The mischief from that moment grew more alarming. Men of rank were insulted, and women of the first condition suffered gross indignities. The example of the prince brought midnight riots into fashion. Private persons took their opportunity, with a band of loose companions, to annoy the public streets. Every quarter was filled with tumult and disorder, insomuch that Rome, at night, resembled a city taken by storm. In one of these wild adventures, Julius Montanus, of senatorian rank, but not yet advanced to the magistracy, happened to encounter the emperor and his party. Being attacked with force, he made a resolute defence; and finding, afterwards, that Nero was the person whom he discomfited in the fray, he endeavoured to soften resentment by apologies for his behaviour: but the

5   excuse

excufe was confidered as a reflection on the prince, and Montanus was compelled to die.

Nero perfifted in this courfe of debauchery, and, for the fafety of his perfon, took with him a party of foldiers, and a gang of gladiators. Thefe men, in flight and accidental fkirmifhes, kept aloof from the fray; but if warm and active fpirits made a ftout refiftance, they became parties in the quarrel, and cut their way fword in hand. The theatre, at the fame time, was a fcene of uproar, and violent contention. The partifans of the players waged a kind of civil war. Nero encouraged them, not only with impunity, but with ample rewards. He was often a fecret fpectator of the tumult; and, at length, did not blufh to appear in the face of the public. Thefe difturbances were fo frequent, that, from a people divided into factions, there was reafon to apprehend fome dreadful convulfion: the only remedy left, was to banifh the players out of Italy, and once more make the foldiers mount guard at the theatre.

XXVI. About this time, the enfranchifed flaves, by the infolence of their behaviour to the patrons who had given them their freedom, provoked a debate in the fenate. It was propofed to pafs a law, empowering the patron to reclaim his right over fuch as made an improper ufe of their liberty. The fathers were willing to adopt the meafure, but the confuls did not choofe to put the queftion before due notice was given to the emperor. They reported the cafe, and the fubftance of the debate, requefting to know whether the prince would, of his own authority, enact a law that had but few to oppofe it. In fupport of the motion, it had been argued, that the freedmen were leagued in a faction againft their patrons, and had the infolence to think them anfwerable for their conduct in the fenate. They went fo far as to threaten violence to their perfons; they raifed their hands against their benefactors, and, with audacious contumacy, prefumed to hinder them from feeking redrefs in due courfe of law. The patron, it is true, has peculiar privileges: but in what do they confift? In the empty power of banifhing the freedman, who proves unworthy of the favour beftowed upon him, to the diftance of twenty miles from Rome; that is, to fend him, by way of punifhment, to the delightful plains of Campania. In every other point of view, the freedman is on a level with the higheft citizen. He enjoys equal privileges. It were, therefore, a prudent meafure to arm the patron with coercive authority, effectual for the purpofe, and of force not to be eluded. The manumitted flave fhould " be taught to prolong the enjoyment of his liberty " by the fame behaviour that obtained it at firft. Nor could " this be deemed an oppreffive law; fince, as often as the freed- " men fhewed no fenfe of duty or fubordination, to reduce them " to their primitive fervitude, would be the foundeft policy. " When gratitude has no effect, coercion is the proper remedy."

XXVII. In anfwer to this reafoning, it was contended by the oppofite party, " That, in all cafes of partial mifchief, punifhment " fhould fall on the guilty only. For the delinquency of a few, " the rights of all ought not to be taken away. The freedmen " were a large and numerous body. From them the number of " the tribes was completed, the magistrates were fupplied with " inferior officers, the facerdotal orders with affiftants, and the " prætorian cohorts with recruits. Many of the Roman knights, " and even the fenators had no other origin. Deduct the men " whofe fathers were enfranchifed, and the number of freeborn " citizens will dwindle into nothing. When the ranks of fo- " ciety were eftablifhed at Rome, it was the wifdom of the old " republic to make liberty the common right of all, not the pre-
7
" rogative

" rogative of a few. The power of conferring freedom was alfo
" regulated, and two different modes *(a)* were eftablifhed, to the
" end that the patron, if he faw reafon for it, might either revoke
" his grant, or confirm it by additional bounty. The man en-
" franchifed, without proper ceremonies before the prætor, was
" liable to be claimed again by his mafter. But it is the bufinefs
" of the patron to confider well the character of his flave; till
" he knows the merit of the man, let him withhold his generofity;
" but when freedom is fairly beftowed, there ought to be no
" refumption of the grant." To this laft opinion Nero acceded.
He fignified his pleafure to the fenate, that, in all caufes between the patron and his freedman, they fhould decide on the
particular circumftances of the cafe, without derogating from the
rights of the body at large. Soon after this regulation, Paris,
who had received his freedom from Domitia, the emperor's
aunt, was removed from her domeftic train, and declared to be
a freeborn citizen *(b)*. The colour of law was given to this proceeding; but the judgment was known to be dictated by the
prince, and the infamy, therefore, was all his own.

XXVIII. THERE remained, notwithftanding, even at this
juncture, an image of ancient liberty. A proof of this occurred
in a conteft that took place between Vibullius, the prætor, and
Antiftius, tribune of the people. Certain partifans of the players
had been, for their tumultuous behaviour, committed to jail by
the prætor. The tribune interpofed his authority, and releafed
the prifoners. This conduct was condemned by the fenate, as
extrajudicial and illegal. A decree paffed, ordaining that the
tribunes fhould not prefume to counteract the jurifdiction of the
prætor, or the confuls; nor to fummon to their own tribunal
men, who refided in different parts of Italy, and were amenable
to the municipal laws of the colony. It was further fettled, on
                                                          the

the motion of Lucius Pifo, conful elect, that it fhould not be competent to the tribunes to fit in judgment at their own houfes; and that the fines, impofed by their authority, fhould not be entered by the quæftor in the regifters of the treafury, before the end of four months from the day of the fentence, that, in the mean time, the party aggrieved might have the benefit of an appeal to the confuls. The jurifdiction of the ædiles, patrician as well as plebeian, was defined and limited; the fureties which they might demand were ftated with precifion; and the penalties to be impofed by their authority were reduced to a certain fum. In confequence of thefe regulations, Helvidius Prifcus, tribune of the people, feized the opportunity to proceed againft Obultronius Sabinus, a quæftor of the treafury. He charged him with haraffing the poor with unreafonable confifcations, and unmercifully feizing their effects to be fold by auction. To redrefs the grievance, Nero removed the regifter out of the hands of the quæftor, and left that bufinefs to the care of præfects commiffioned for the purpofe.

XXIX. In this department of the treafury various changes had been made, but no fettled form (a) was eftablifhed. In the reign of Auguftus, the præfects of the treafury were chofen by the fenate; but there being reafon to fufpect that intrigue and private views had too much influence, thofe officers were drawn by lot out of the lift of the prætors. This mode was foon found to be defective. Chance decided, and too often wandered to men unqualified for the employment. Claudius reftored the quæftors, and, to encourage them to act with vigour, promifed to place them above the neceffity of foliciting the fuffrages of the people, and, by his own authority, to raife them to the higher magiftracies. But the quæftorfhip being the firft civil office that men could undertake, maturity of underftanding was not to be expected. Nero,

for

for that reason, chose from the prætorian rank, a set of new com-
missioners of known experience and tried ability.

XXX. During the same consulship, Vipsanius Lænas was found guilty of rapacity in his government of Sardinia. Cestius Proculus was prosecuted for extortion; but his accusers giving up the point, he was acquitted. Clodius Quirinalis, who had the command of the fleet at Ravenna, and by his profligate manners and various vices harassed the people in that part of Italy, with a degree of insolence not to be endured by the most abject nation, was brought to his trial on a charge of rapine and oppression. To prevent the final sentence, he dispatched himself by poison. About the same time, Caninius Rebilus, a man distinguished by his knowledge of the laws, and his ample riches, determined to deliver himself from the miseries of old age and a broken constitution. He opened a vein, and bled to death. The event was matter of surprise to all. The fortitude, that could voluntarily rush on death, was not expected from a man softened by voluptuous enjoyments, and infamous for his effeminate manners. Lucius Volusius, who died in the same year, left a very different character. He had lived, in splendid affluence, to the age of ninety-three, esteemed for the honest arts by which he acquired immense wealth, under a succession of despotic emperors, yet never exposed to danger. He found the art of being rich and virtuous with impunity.

XXXI. Nero, with Lucius Piso for his colleague, entered on his second consulship. In this year we look in vain for transactions worthy of the historian's pen. The vast foundation of a new amphitheatre (a), built by Nero in the Field of Mars, and the massy timbers employed in that magnificent structure, might swell a volume; but descriptions of that kind may be left to grace

Vol. II.   T   the

the pages of a city-journal. The dignity of the Roman people requires that thefe annals fhould not defcend to a detail fo minute and uninterefting. It will be proper to mention here, that Capua and Nuceria, two Roman colonies, were augmented by a body of veterans tranfplanted to thofe places. A largefs of two hundred finall fefterces to each man was diftributed to the populace, and, to fupport the credit of the ftate, the fum of four hundred thoufand great fefterces was depofited in the treafury. The twenty-fifth penny *(b)*, impofed as a tax on the purchafe of flaves, was remitted, with an appearance of moderation, but, in fact, without any folid advantage to the public. The payment of the duty was only fhifted to the vendor, and he, to indemnify himfelf, raifed his price on the purchafer. The emperor iffued a proclamation forbidding the magiftrates and imperial procurators to exhibit, in any of the provinces, a fhow of gladiators, wild beafts, or any other public fpectacle. The practice of amufing the people with grand exhibitions had been as fore a grievance as even the grafping hand of avarice. The governors plundered the people, and by difplays of magnificence hoped to difguife, or, in fome degree, to make atonement for their crimes.

XXXII. A DECREE paffed the fenate to protect, by additional terrors of law, the life of the patron from the malice of his flaves. With this view, it was enacted, that, in the cafe of a mafter flain by his domeftics, execution fhould be done, not only on fuch as remained in a ftate of actual fervitude, but likewife on all, who, by the will of the deceafed, obtained their freedom, but continued to live under his roof at the time when the murder was committed. Lucius Varius, who had been degraded for rapacious avarice, was reftored to his confular rank, and his feat in the fenate. Pomponia Græcina, a woman of illuftrious birth, and

the

the wife of Plautius *(a)*, who, on his return from Britain, entered the city with the pomp of an ovation, was accufed of embracing the rites of a foreign fuperftition *(b)*. The matter was
referred to the jurifdiction of her hufband. Plautius, in con-
formity to ancient ufage, called together a number of her relations, and, in their prefence, fat in judgment on the conduct of
his wife. He pronounced her innocent. She lived to a great
age, in one continued train of affliction. From the time when
Julia, the daughter of Drufus, was brought to a tragical end by
the wicked arts of Meffalina *(c)*, fhe never laid afide her mourning weeds, but pined in grief during a fpace of forty years, inconfolable for the lofs of her friend. During the reign of Claudius
nothing could alleviate her forrow, nor was her perfeverance imputed to her as a crime: in the end, it was the glory of her
character.

XXXIII. This year produced a number of criminal accufations. Publius Celer was profecuted by the province of Afia.
The weight of evidence preffed fo hard, that Nero, unable to
acquit him, drew the caufe into a tedious length. During that
ftate of fufpenfe, the criminal died of old age. Celer, the reader
will remember, was an inftrument in the murder of Silanus *(a)*,
the proconful. The magnitude of his guilt on that occafion
fo far furpaffed the reft of his flagitious deeds, that nothing elfe
was deemed worthy of notice. The enormity of one atrocious crime fkreened him from punifhment.

The Cilicians demanded juftice againft Coffutianus Capito, a
man of an abandoned character, who at Rome had fet the laws
at defiance, and thought, that, with equal impunity, he might
commit the fame exceffes in the government of his province.

T 2

The

The profecution was carried on with fuch unremitting vigour, that he abandoned his defence. He was condemned to make reftitution. A fuit of the fame nature was commenced againft Eprius Marcellus by the people of Lycia, but with different fuccefs. A powerful faction combined to fupport him. The confequence was, that fome of the profecutors were banifhed for a confpiracy againft an innocent man.

XXXIV. Nero entered on his third confulfhip, having for his colleague Valerius Meffala, the great grandfon of Corvinus Meffala (a), the celebrated orator, who, in the memory of a few furviving old men, had been affociated in the confulfhip with Auguftus, the great grandfather of Nero's mother, Agrippina. The prince granted to his colleague an annual penfion of fifteen hundred thoufand fefterces, and with that income Meffala, who had fallen into blamelefs poverty, was able to fupport the dignity of his rank and character. Yearly ftipends were alfo granted to Aurelius Cotta, and Haterius Antoninus, though they were both, by diffipation, the authors of their own diftrefs.

In the beginning of this year, the war between the Romans and the Parthians, hitherto flow in its operations, grew warm and active on both fides. The poffeffion of Armenia was the point ftill in difpute. Vologefes faw with indignation the crown, which he had fettled on his brother Tiridates, withheld by force, and, to let him receive it as the gift of a foreign power, was a degree of humiliation to which his pride could not fubmit. On the other hand, to recover the conquefts formerly made by Lucullus and Pompey, was in Corbulo's judgment worthy of the Roman name. The Armenians balanced between the powers at war, and in their turn invited each. Their natural bias inclined them to the Parthians. Neighbours by fituation, congenial

nial

nial in their manners, and by frequent intermarriages clofely allied, they were willing to favour the enemies of Rome, and even inclined to fubmit to a Parthian mafter. Inured by habit to a ftate of fervitude, they neither underftood, nor wifhed for civil liberty.

XXXV. CORBULO had to ftruggle with the flothful difpo-fition of his army; a mifchief more embarraffing than the wily arts of the enemy. The legions from Syria joined his camp, but fo enervated by the languor of peace, that they could fcarce fupport the labours of a campaign. It is certain, that there were amongft them veterans who had feen no fervice; who had never been on duty at a midnight poft; who never mounted guard, and were fuch total ftrangers to a foffe and a palifade, that they gazed at both as at a novelty. They had ferved the term prefcribed in garrifon-towns, without helmets, and without breaft-plates, fpruce and trim in their attire, by profeffion fol-diers, yet thinking of nothing but the means of enriching them-felves. Having difmiffed all fuch as were by age and infirmity rendered unfit for the fervice, Corbulo ordered new levies to be made in Galatia and Cappadocia. To thefe he added a legion from Germany, with fome troops of horfe, and a detachment of infantry from the cohorts. Thus reinforced, his army kept the field, though the froft was fo intenfe, that, without digging through the ice, it was impoffible to pitch their tents. By the inclemency of the feafon many loft the ufe of their limbs, and it often happened that the fentinel died on his poft. The cafe of one foldier deferves to be mentioned. He was employed in carrying a load of wood: his hands, nipt by the froft, and cleav-ing to the faggot, dropt from his arms, and fell to the ground.

The general, during the feverity of the weather, gave an example

ample of ſtrenuous exertion; he was buſy in every quarter, thinly clad, his head uncovered, in the ranks, at the works, commending the brave, relieving the weak, and by his own active vigour exciting the emulation of the men. But the rigour of the ſeaſon, and the hardſhip of the ſervice, were more than the ſoldiers could endure. The army ſuffered by deſertion. This required an immediate remedy. The practice of lenity towards the firſt or ſecond offence, which often prevailed in other armies, would have been attended with dangerous conſequences. He who quitted his colours ſuffered death as ſoon as taken; and this ſeverity proved more ſalutary than weak compaſſion. The number of deſerters, from that time, fell ſhort of what happens in other camps, where too much indulgence is the practice.

XXXVI. HAVING reſolved to wait the return of ſpring, Corbulo kept his men within their entrenchments during the reſt of the winter. The auxiliary cohorts were ſtationed at proper poſts, under the command of Pactius Orphitus, who had ſerved as principal centurion. The orders given to this officer were, that the advanced poſts ſhould by no means hazard an engagement. Orphitus ſent to inform the general, that the Barbarians ſpread themſelves round the country with ſo little caution, that advantage might be taken of their imprudence. Corbulo renewed his orders, that the troops ſhould keep within the lines, and wait for a reinforcement. Orphitus paid no regard to the command of his ſuperior officer. A few troops of horſe, from the adjacent caſtles, came up to join him, and, through inexperience, demanded to be led againſt the enemy. Orphitus riſked a battle, and was totally routed. The forces poſted near at hand, whoſe duty it was to march to the aſſiſtance of the broken ranks, fled in confuſion to their entrenchments. Corbulo no ſooner received intelligence of this defeat,

than

than he refolved to pafs the fevereft cenfure on the difobedience
of his officer.   He ordered him, his fubalterns, and his men, to
march out of the entrenchments *(a)*, and there left them in difgrace, till, at the interceffion of the whole army, he gave them
leave to return within the lines.

XXXVII. MEANWHILE Tiridates, at the head of his vaffals
and followers, with a ftrong reinforcement fent by his brother
Vologefes, invaded Armenia, not, as before, by fudden incurfions, but with open hoftility.   Wherever the people were in the
interefts of Rome, he laid wafte their lands; if an armed force
advanced againft him, he fhifted his quarters, and, by the velocity of his flight, eluded the attack.   He moved with rapidity
from place to place, and, by the terror of a wild and defultory
war, more than by the fuccefs of his arms, kept the country in
a conftant alarm.   Corbulo endeavoured, but without effect, to
bring him to an engagement.   He determined, therefore, to
adopt the plan of the enemy, and, for that purpofe, fpread his
forces round the country, under the conduct of his lieutenants
and other fubordinate officers.   At the fame time he caufed a
diverfion to be made by Antiochus, king of Syria, in the provinces of Armenia that lay contiguous to his dominions.   Pharafmanes, king of Iberia, was willing, in this juncture, to co-
operate with the Roman arms.   He had put his fon Rhadamiftus to death for imputed treafon, and, to make terms with
Rome, while, in fact, he gratified his rooted averfion to the
Armenians, he pretended to enter into the war with the zeal and
ardour of a friend to the caufe.   The Ifichians *(a)* alfo declared
for Corbulo.   That people were now, for the firft time, the
allies of Rome.   They made incurfions into the wild and defert
tracts of Armenia, and by a defultory rambling war diftracted
the operations of the enemy.

Tiridates,

BOOK
XIII.

A. U. C.
811.
A. D.
58.

Tiridates, finding himfelf counteracted on every fide, fent ambaffadors to expoftulate, as well in the name of the Parthians, as
for himfelf. " After hoftages fo lately delivered, and a renewal
" of friendfhip, that promifed mutual advantages, why was his
" expulfion from the kingdom of Armenia the fixed, the avowed
" intention of the Roman army? If Vologefes was not as yet
" in motion with the whole ftrength of his kingdom, it was be-
" caufe he wifhed to prevail by the juftice of his caufe, and not
" by force of arms. If the fword muft be drawn, the event
" would fhew that the Arfacides had not forgot that warlike
" fpirit which, on former occafions, had been fatal to the Roman
" name." Corbulo heard this magnificent language; but, being
informed, by fure intelligence, that the revolt of the Hyrcanians (b) found employment for Vologefes, he returned for
anfwer, that the wifeft meafure Tiridates could purfue, would be
to addrefs himfelf in a fuppliant ftyle to the emperor of Rome.
The kingdom of Armenia, fettled on a folid bafis, might be his
without the effufion of blood, and the havoc of a deftructive
war, if to diftant and chimerical hopes he preferred moderate
meafures and prefent fecurity.

XXXVIII. From this time the bufinefs fell into a train of
negociation. Frequent difpatches paffed between both armies;
but no progrefs being made towards a conclufive treaty, it was
at length agreed that, at a fixed time and place, the two chiefs
fhould come to an interview. Tiridates gave notice that he
fhould bring with him a guard of a thoufand horfe: the number which Corbulo might choofe for his own perfon, he did not
take upon him to prefcribe; all he defired was, that they fhould
come with a pacific difpofition, and advance to the congrefs
without their breaft-plates and their helmets. This ftroke of
eaftern perfidy was not fo fine, but even the dulleft capacity, not

to mention an experienced general, might perceive the latent fraud. The number limited on one side, and to the opposite party left indefinite, carried with it a specious appearance; but the lurking treachery was too apparent. The Parthian cavalry excelled in the dexterity of managing the bow and arrow ; and, without defensive armour, what would be the use of superior numbers? Aware of the design, but choosing to disguise his sentiments, Corbulo calmly answered, that the business being of a public nature, the discussion of it ought to be in the presence of both armies. For the convention he appointed a place inclosed on one side by a soft acclivity of gently rifing hills, where the infantry might be posted to advantage, with a vale beneath, stretching to an extent that gave ample space for the cavalry. On the stated day Corbulo advanced to the meeting, with his forces in regular order. In the wings were stationed the allies and the auxiliaries sent by the kings in friendship with Rome. The sixth legion formed the centre, strengthened by a reinforcement of three thousand men from the third legion, drafted in the night from the neighbouring camp. Being embodied under one eagle, they presented the appearance of a single legion. Towards the close of day, Tiridates occupied a distant ground, visible indeed, but never within hearing. Not being able to obtain a conference, the Roman general ordered his men to file off to their respective quarters.

XXXIX. Tiridates left the field with precipitation, alarmed at the various movements of the Roman army, and fearing the danger of an ambuscade, or, perhaps, intending to cut off the supplies of provisions then on the way from the city of Trebizonde *(a)* and the Pontic sea. But the supplies were conveyed over the mountains, where a chain of posts was formed, to secure the passes. A slow and lingering war was now to be apprehended:

Vol. II. U to

to bring it to a fpeedy iffue, and compel the Armenians to act on the defenfive, Corbulo refolved to level their caftles to the ground. The ftrongeft fort in that quarter was known by the name of VOLANDUM *(b)*: the demolition of that place he referved for himfelf, and againft the towns of inferior note he fent Cornelius Flaccus, a lieutenant general, and Infteius Capito, præfect of the camp. Having reconnoitred the works, and prepared for the affault, he harangued his men in effect as follows: " You have now to do with a daftardly and fugitive enemy ; a " vagabond race, always roving in prædatory bands, betraying " at once their unwarlike fpirit and their perfidy ; impatient of " peace, and cowards in war. The time is arrived, when the " whole nation may be exterminated : by one brave exploit " you may gain both fame and booty to reward your valour." Having thus inflamed the fpirit of his men, he arranged them in four divifions ; one clofe embodied under their fhields, forming a military fhell, to fap the foundation of the ramparts ; a fecond party advanced with ladders to fcale the walls ; a third with their warlike engines threw into the place a fhower of darts and miffive fire ; while the flingers and archers, pofted at a convenient diftance, difcharged a volley of metal and huge maffy ftones.

To keep the enemy employed in every quarter, the attack was made on all fides at once. In lefs than four hours the Barbarians were driven from their ftations ; the ramparts were left defencelefs, the gates were forced, and the works taken by fcalade. A dreadful flaughter followed. All who were capable of carrying arms were put to the fword. On the part of the Romans only one man was killed ; the number of wounded was inconfiderable. The women and children were fold to flavery : the reft was left to be plundered by the foldiers. The operations

tions of Flaccus and Capito were attended with equal fuccefs. In one day three caftles were taken by ftorm. A general panic overfpread the country. From motives of fear or treachery the inhabitants furrendered at difcretion. Encouraged by thefe profperous events, Corbulo was now refolved to lay fiege in form to Artaxata *(c)*, the capital of the kingdom. He did not, however, think it advifable to march the neareft way. The river Araxes *(d)* wafhes the walls of the city: the legions would have found it neceffary to conftruct the neceffary bridges in fight of the enemy, expofed to their darts and miffive weapons. They took a wider circuit, and forded over where the current was broad and fhallow.

XL. TIRIDATES was thrown into the utmoft diftrefs. Shame and fear took poffeffion of him by turns. If he fuffered a block-ade to be formed, his weak condition would be too apparent; if he attempted to raife the fiege, his cavalry might be fur-rounded in the narrow defiles. He refolved to fhew himfelf towards the clofe of day in order of battle, and, next morning, either to attack the Romans, or, by a fudden retreat, to draw them into an ambufcade. With this intent he made a fudden movement, and furrounded the legions. The attempt gave no alarm to Corbulo: prepared for all events, he had marfhalled his men either for action, or a march. The third legion took poft in the right wing; the fixth advanced on the left; and a felect detachment from the tenth formed the centre. The baggage was fecured between the ranks: a body of a thoufand horfe brought up the rear, with orders to face the enemy whenever an attack was made, but never to purfue them. The foot archers, and the reft of the cavalry, were diftributed in the wings. The left extended their ranks towards the foot of the hills, in order, if the Barbarians advanced on that fide, to hem them in between

he

the front lines and the centre of the army. Tiridates contented himself with vain parade, shifting his ground with celerity, yet never within the throw of a dart, advancing, retreating, and, by every stratagem, trying to make the Romans open their ranks, and leave themselves liable to be attacked in scattered parties. His efforts were without effect: one officer, who commanded a troop of horse, advanced from his post, and fell under a volley of darts. His temerity restrained the rest of the army. Towards the close of day, Tiridates, seeing his wiles defeated, withdrew with all his forces.

XLI. Corbulo encamped on the spot. Having reason to imagine that Tiridates would throw himself into the city of Artaxata, he debated whether it would not be best, without loss of time, to push forward by rapid marches, and lay siege to the place. While he remained in suspense, intelligence was brought by the scouts that the prince set off at full speed towards some distant region, but whether to Media or Albania, was uncertain. He resolved, therefore, to wait the return of day, and in the mean time dispatched the light armed cohorts, with orders to invest the city, and begin their attack at a proper distance. The inhabitants threw open their gates, and surrendered at discretion. Their lives were saved, but the town was reduced to ashes. No other measure could be adopted: the walls were of wide extent, and a sufficient garrison could not be spared, at a time when it was necessary to prosecute the war with vigour; and if the city were left unhurt, the advantage, as well as glory of the conquest, would be lost. To these reasons was added an extraordinary appearance in the heavens. It happened that the sun-beams played with brilliant lustre on the adjacent country, making the whole circumference a scene of splendour, while the precinct of the town was covered with the darkest gloom, at in-

tervals

tervals rendered ftill more awful by flafhes of lightning, that ferved
to fhew the impending horror. This phænomenon was believed to
be the wrath of the gods denouncing the deftruction of the city.

B O O K
XIII.

A. U. C.
811.
A. D.
58.

For thefe tranfactions Nero was faluted IMPERATOR. The
fenate decreed a folemn thankfgiving. Statues and triumphal
arches were erected, and the prince was declared perpetual conful. The day on which the victory was gained, and alfo that
on which the news arrived at Rome, and the report was made
to the fenate, were by a decree to be obferved as annual feftivals.
Many other votes were paffed with the fame fpirit of adulation,
all in their tendency fo exceffive, that Caius Caffius, who had
concurred with every motion, obferved at laft, that if, for the
benignity of the gods to the Roman people, due thanks were to
be voted, acts of religion would engrofs the whole year ; and,
therefore, care fhould be taken to fix the days of devotion at
proper intervals, that they might not encroach too much on the
bufinefs of civil life.

XLII. ABOUT this time, a man who had fuffered various
revolutions of fortune, and by his vices had brought on himfelf
the public deteftation, was cited to anfwer a charge exhibited
againft him before the fenate. He was condemned, but not
without fixing a ftain on the character of Seneca. Suillius *(a)*
was the perfon : in the reign of Claudius he had been the fcourge
and terror of his fellow-citizens ; a venal orator, and an informer by profeffion. In the late changes of government he
had been much reduced, but not low enough to gratify the refentment of his enemies. His fpirit was ftill unconquered:
Rather than defcend to humble fupplications, he preferred the
character of a convicted malefactor. To come at this man, a
late decree of the fenate, reviving the pains and penalties of the

Cincian

Cincian law *(b)* againft fuch advocates as received a price for their eloquence, was thought to have been framed by the advice of Seneca. Suillius exclaimed againft the proceeding. At his time of life he had little to fear. To the natural ferocity of his temper he now added a contempt of danger.

He poured out a torrent of invective, and in particular railed with acrimony againft Seneca. "The philofopher," he faid, "was an enemy to the friends of Claudius. He had been ba- "niſhed by that emperor, and the difgrace was not inflicted "without juft reafon. He is now grown old in the purfuit of "frivolous literature, a vain retailer of rhetoric to raw and inex- "perienced boys. He beholds with an eye of envy all, who, in "the defence of their fellow-citizens, exert a pure, a found, a "manly eloquence. That Suillius lived with reputation in the "fervice of Germanicus, is a fact well known. He was quæf- "tor under that prince, while Seneca corrupted the morals "of his daughter, and diſhonoured the family. If it be a "crime to receive from a client the reward of honeft induftry, "what ſhall be faid of him, who fteals into the chamber of a "princefs to debauch her virtue *(c)* ? By what fyftem of ethics, "and by what rules of philofophy, has this profeffor warped "into the favour of the emperor, and, in lefs than four years, "amaffed three hundred million of fefterces ? Through the city "of Rome his fnares are fpread ; laft wills and teftaments are "his quarry ; and the rich, who have no children, are his prey. "By exorbitant ufury *(d)* he has overwhelmed all Italy ; the "provinces are exhaufted, and he is ftill infatiate. The wealth of "Suillius cannot be counted great ; but it is the fruit of honeft "induftry. He is now determined to bid defiance to his ene- "mies, and hazard all confequences, rather than derogate from

" his

" his rank and the glory of his life, by poorly yielding to a new
" man ; an upſtart in the ſtate ; a ſudden child of fortune."

XLIII. By a ſet of officious tale-bearers, who love to carry intelligence, and inflame it with the addition of their own malevo-
lence, theſe bitter invectives were conveyed to Seneca.   The enemies of Suillius were ſet to work: they charged him with rapine
and peculation during his government in Aſia.   To ſubſtantiate
theſe allegations, twelve months were allowed to the proſecutors :
but that put off their vengeance to a diſtant day..   To ſhorten their
work, they choſe to proceed upon a new charge, without going
out of Rome for witneſſes.   The accuſation ſtated, " That by a
" virulent proſecution he had driven Quintus Pomponius (a) into
" open rebellion ; that by his pernicious arts Julia, the daughter
" of Druſus, and Poppæa Sabina, were forced to put a period to
" their lives ; that Valerius Aſiaticus, Luſius Saturninus, and
" Cornelius Lupus, with a long liſt of Roman knights, were all
" cut off by his villany ; and, in ſhort, every act of cruelty in
" the reign of Claudius was imputed to him."   To theſe charges
Suillus anſwered, That he acted always under the immediate
orders of the prince, and never of his own motion.   Nero over-
ruled that defence, averring, that he had inſpected all the papers
of the late emperor, and from thoſe vouchers it plainly appeared,
that not one proſecution was ſet on foot by the order of Claudius.
The criminal reſorted to the commands of Meſſalina ; but, by
ſhifting his ground, his cauſe grew weaker.   Why, it was argued, was he the only perſon who lent himſelf to the wicked
deſigns of that pernicious proſtitute? Shall the perpetrator of
evil deeds, who has received his hire, be allowed to transfer his
guilt to the perſon who paid him the wages of his iniquity ?

Suillius was condemned, and his effects were confiſcated,

6

except

except a part allowed to his fon and grandaughter, in addition to what was left to them under the will of their mother, and their grandmother. He was banifhed to the iflands called the Baleares *(b)*. During the whole of the trial, he behaved with undaunted firmnefs, and even after the fentence his fpirit was ftill unbroken. He is faid to have lived in his lone retreat, not only at eafe, but in voluptuous affluence. His enemies intended to wreak their malice on his fon Nerulinus, and, with that view, charged him with extortion. Nero checked the profecution; the ends of juftice being, as he thought, fufficiently anfwered.

XLIV. It happened, at this time, that Octavius Sagitta, tribune of the people, fell in love to diftraction with a married woman of the name of Pontia. By prefents and unbounded generofity he feduced her to his embraces, and, afterwards by a promife of marriage, engaged her confent to a divorce from her hufband. Pontia was no fooner free from the nuptial tie, than her imagination opened to her other profpects. She affected delays; her father made objections; fhe had hopes of a better match, and finally fhe refufed to perform her contract. Octavius expoftulated; he complained; he threatened; his reputation fuffered, and his fortune was ruined. His life was all that he had left, and that he was ready to facrifice at her command. His fuit, however earneft, made no impreffion. In defpair, he begged one night only; that fmall indulgence would affuage his forrows, and take the fting from difappointment. The affignation was made. Pontia ordered her fervant, who was privy to the intrigue, to watch her bed-chamber. The lover went to his appointment. He carried with him one of his freedmen, and a poniard under his robe. The fcene which ufually occurs, when love is flung to jealoufy, was acted between the parties; reproaches,

proaches, fond endearments, rage, and tendernefs, war and peace took their turn *(a)*.

Part of the night was paffed in mutual enjoyment. At length, Octavius, in the moment of foft fecurity, when the unhappy victim thought all violence at an end, feized his dagger, and fheathed it in her heart. The maid rufhed in to affift her miftrefs. Octavius wounded her, and made his efcape. On the following day, the murder was reported abroad; and the hand that gave the blow was ftrongly fufpected. Octavius, it was certain, had paffed the night with the deceafed; but his freedman boldly ftood forth, and took the crime upon himfelf. It was his deed; an act of juftice due to an injured mafter. This generous fortitude from the mouth of an affaffin was heard with aftonifhment, and for fome time gained credit, till the maid, who had recovered from her wound, difclofed the particulars of the whole tranfaction. Pontia's father appealed to the tribunal of the confuls, and Octavius, as foon as his office of tribune ceafed, was condemned to fuffer the penalties of the Cornelian law againft affaffins *(b)*.

XLV. In the courfe of the fame year, another fcene of libidinous paffion was brought forward, more important than that which we have related, and, in the end, the caufe of public calamity. Sabina Poppæa, at that time, lived at Rome in a ftyle of tafte and elegance. She was the daughter of Titus Ollius, but fhe took her name from Poppæus Sabinus *(a)*, her grandfather by the maternal line. Her father Ollius was, at one time, rifing to the higheft honours; but, being a friend to Sejanus, he was involved in the ruin of that minifter. The grandfather had figured on the ftage of public bufinefs. He was of confular rank, and obtained the honour of a triumph. To be the known

Vol. II.   X   defcendant

descendant of a man so distinguished flattered the vanity of Poppæa. Virtue excepted, she possessed all the qualities that adorn
the female character. Her mother *(b)* was the reigning beauty of
her time. From her the daughter inherited nobility of birth,
with all the graces of an elegant form. Her fortune was equal
to her rank; her conversation had every winning art; her talents were cultivated, and her wit refined. She knew how to
assume an air of modesty, and yet pursue lascivious pleasures; in
her deportment, decent; in her heart, a libertine. When she
appeared in public, which was but seldom, she wore a veil, that
shaded, or seemed to shade her face; perhaps intending, that
her beauty should not wear out and tarnish to the eye; or because that style of dress was most becoming. To the voice of
fame she paid no regard: her husband and her adulterer were
equally welcome to her embraces. Love, with her, was not an
affair of the heart. Knowing no attachment herself, she required none from others. Where she saw her interest, there she
bestowed her favours; a politician even in her pleasures. She
was married to Rufius Crispinus, a Roman knight, and was by
him the mother of a son *(c)*; but Otho, a youth of expectation,
luxurious, prodigal, and high in favour with Nero, attracted her
regard. She yielded to his addresses, and, in a short time, married the adulterer.

XLVI. Otho, in company with the emperor, grew lavish
in her praise. Her beauty and her elegant manners were his
constant theme. He talked, perhaps, with the warmth and
indiscretion of a lover; perhaps, with a design to inflame the
passions of Nero, and from their mutual relish of the same enjoyments to derive new strength to support his interest. Rising
from Nero's table, he was often heard to say, " I am going to the
" arms of her, who possesses every amiable accomplishment; by

" her

" her birth ennobled; endeared by beauty; the wifh of all be-
" holders, and to the favoured man the fource of true delight."
Nero became enamoured. No time was loft. Poppæa received
his vifits. At the firft interview fhe called forth all her charms,
and enfured her conqueft. She admired the dignity of the prince.
His air, his manner, and his looks were irrefiftible. By this well-
acted fondnefs fhe gained entire dominion over his affections.
Proud of her fuccefs, fhe thought it time to act her part with
female airs and coy reluctance. If Nero wifhed to detain her
more than a night or two, fhe could not think of complying;
fhe was married to a man whom fhe loved. She could not
rifk the lofs of a fituation fo perfectly happy. Otho led a life of
tafte and elegance, unrivalled in his pleafures. Under his roof
fhe faw nothing but magnificence, in a ftyle worthy of the higheft
ftation. She objected to Nero that he had contracted different
habits. He lived in clofe connection with Acté, a low-born
flave; and from fo mean a commerce, what could be expected but
fordid manners and degenerate fentiment! From that moment,
Otho loft his intereft with the prince: he had orders neither to
frequent the palace, nor to fhew himfelf in the train of attendants. At length, to remove a rival, Nero made him governor of
Lufitania. Otho quitted Rome, and, till the breaking out of the
civil wars, continued in the adminiftration of his province, a firm
and upright magiftrate, in this inftance exhibiting to the world
that wonderful union of repugnant qualities which marked the
man; in private life, luxurious, profligate, and prone to every
vice; in his public capacity, prudent, juft, and temperate in the
ufe of power.

XLVII. It was in this juncture that Nero firft threw off the
mafk. He had hitherto cloked the vices of his nature. The
perfon whom he dreaded moft, was Cornelius Sylla; a man, in

X 2

fact,

fact, of a dull and sluggish underſtanding; but his ſtupidity paſſed with Nero for profound thinking, and the deep reſerve of a dangerous politician. In this idea he was confirmed by the malignity of one Graptus, a man enfranchiſed by the emperor, and from the reign of Tiberius hackneyed in the practice of courts. He framed an artful ſtory. The Milvian *(a)* bridge was, at that time, the faſhionable ſcene of midnight revelry : being out of the limits of Rome, the emperor thought that he might riot, at that place, with unbounded freedom. Graptus told him, that a conſpiracy had been formed againſt his life, and the vil‑ lains lay in ambuſh on the Flaminian way ; but as fortune would have it, the prince, by paſſing through the Salluſtian *(b)* gardens, eſcaped the ſnare. To give colour to this invented tale, he al‑ leged the following circumſtance : In one of the riots, which were common in thoſe diſſolute times, a ſet of young men fell into a ſkirmiſh with the attendants of the emperor. This, he ſaid, was a concerted plot, and Sylla was the author of it, though not ſo much as one of his clients, nor even a ſlave of his, was found to have been of the party. Sylla, in fact, had neither capacity, nor ſpirit for an undertaking ſo big with danger ; and yet, on the ſuggeſtion of Graptus, which was received as poſitive proof, he was obliged to quit his country, and reſide, for the future, in the city of Marſeilles.

XLVIII. DURING the ſame conſulſhip, the ſenate gave au‑ dience to the deputies from the magiſtrates and the people of Puteoli *(a)*. The former complained of the licentiouſneſs of the populace, and the latter retaliated, in bitter terms, againſt the pride and avarice of the nobles. It appeared that the mob roſe in a tumultuous body, diſcharging volleys of ſtones, and threaten‑ ing to ſet fire to the houſes. A general maſſacre was likely to be the conſequence. Caius Caſſius was diſpatched to quell

the

the infurrection. His meafures, too harfh and violent for the
occafion, ferved only to irritate the people. He was recalled, at
his own requeft, and the two Scribonii were fent to fupply his
place. They took with them a prætorian cohort. By the terror
of a military force, and the execution of a few ringleaders, the
public tranquillity was reftored.

XLIX. A DECREE of the fenate, which had no higher object
than to authorife the people of Syracufe to exceed, in their public fpectacles, the number of gladiators limited by law, would·be
matter too trite, and unworthy of notice, if the oppofition, made
by Pætus Thrafea, had not excited againft that excellent man a
number of enemies. They feized the opportunity to traduce
his character. " If he is, as he pretends to be, ferioufly of
" opinion, that the public good requires liberty of fpeech and
" freedom of debate, why defcend to things fo frivolous in their
" nature? Are peace and war of no importance? When laws
" are in queftion; when tributes and impofts are the fubject
" before the fathers, and, when points of the firft importance
" are in agitation, where is his eloquence then? Every fenator,
" who rifes in his place, has the privilege of moving what-
" ever he conceives to be conducive to the public welfare; and
" what he moves, he has a right to difcufs, to debate, and put
" to the vote. And yet to regulate the amphitheatre of Syracufe
" is the fole bufinefs of a profefled and zealous patriot. Is the
" adminiftration in all its parts fo fair and perfect, that even
" Thrafea himfelf, if he held the reins of government, could
" find nothing to reform? If he fuffers matters of the firft
" importance to pafs in filence, why amufe us with a mock
" debate on queftions, wherein no man finds himfelf in-
" terefted."

BOOK
XIII.
A. U. C.
811.
A. D.
58.

The

The friends of Thrafea defired an explanation of his conduct : his anfwer was as follows: When he rofe to make his objections to the law in queftion, he was not ignorant of the mifmanagement that prevailed in all departments of the government; but the principle on which he acted, had in view the honour of the fenate. When matters of little moment drew the attention of the fathers, men would fee that affairs of importance could not efcape a body of men, who thought nothing that concerned the public beneath their notice.

L. THE complaints of the people, in the courfe of this year, againft the oppreffions practifed by the collectors (a) of the revenue, were fo loud and violent, that Nero was inclined to abolifh the whole fyftem of duties and taxes, thereby to ferve the interefts of humanity, and beftow on mankind the greateft bleffing in his power. To this generous fentiment the fathers gave the higheft applaufe ; but the defign, they faid, however noble, was altogether impracticable. To abrogate all taxes, were to cut off the refources of government, and diffolve the commonwealth. Repeal the impofts on trade, and what would be the confequence ? The tribute paid by the provinces muft, in like manner, be remitted. The feveral companies that farmed the revenue were eftablifhed by the confuls and tribunes of Rome, in the period of liberty, when the old republic flourifhed in all its glory. The revenue fyftem, which has fince grown up, was formed on a fair eftimate, proportioned to the demands of government. It would, indeed, be highly proper to reftrain within due bounds the conduct of the collectors, that the feveral duties, which were fanctioned by the acquiefcence of ages, might not, by oppreffion and rapacity, be converted into a grievance too rigorous to be endured.

LI. NERO

LI. Nero iffued a proclamation, directing that the revenue laws *(a)*, till that time kept among the myfteries of ftate, fhould be drawn up in form, and entered on the public tables for the infpection of all degrees and ranks of men. It was alfo made a rule, that no arrear of more than a year's ftanding fhould be recovered by the tax-gatherers, and, in all cafes of complaint againft thofe officers, the fame fhould be heard and. decided in a fummary way, by the prætor at Rome, and in the provinces by the proprætors or proconfuls. To the foldiers all former privileges and immunities were preferved, with an exception of the duties on merchandize, if they entered into trade. Many other regulations were added, all juft and equitable, and, for fome time, ftrictly obferved, but fuffered afterwards to fall into difufe. The abolition, however, of the fortieth and the fiftieth penny, with many other exactions, invented by the avarice of the publicans, ftill continues in force. The exportation of corn, from the provinces beyond fea, was alfo put under proper regulations ; the impofts were diminifhed ; the fhipping employed in commerce was not to be rated in the eftimate of the merchants effects, and, of courfe, ftood exempted from all duties.

LII. Sulpicius Camerinus *(a)* and Pomponius Silvanus, who had governed in Africa with proconfular authority, were both accufed of mal-adminiftration, and acquitted by the emperor. The accufers of Camerinus were few in number, and their allegations were private acts of cruelty to individuals, not rapine or extortion, or any charge of a public nature. Silvanus was befet by powerful enemies. They prayed time to produce their witneffes : the defendant preffed for an immediate hearing. He was rich, advanced in years, and had no children ; the confequence was, that a ftrong party efpoufed his intereft. He triumphed over his enemies and his friends went unrewarded.

They

They hoped by their services to merit his estate, but he survived them all.

LIII. DURING this whole period, a settled calm prevailed in Germany. The commanders, in that quarter, plainly saw that triumphal ornaments, granted, as they had been, on every trifling occasion, were no longer an honour. To preserve the peace of the provinces they thought their truest glory. Paulinus Pompeius and Lucius Vetus were then at the head of the legions. That the soldiery, however, might not languish in a state of inaction, Paulinus finished the great work of a bank, to prevent the inundations of the Rhine; a project begun by Drusus sixty-three years before *(a)*. Vetus had conceived a vast design: he had in contemplation a canal, by which the waters of the Moselle *(b)* and the Arar were to be communicated, to the end that the Roman forces might be able, for the future, to enter the Rhone from the Mediterranean, and passing thence into the Arar, proceed through the new channel into the Moselle, and sail down the Rhine into the German Ocean. This plan was on a great scale: fatiguing marches over a long tract of land would be no longer necessary, and a commodious navigation would be opened between the western and the northern seas.

Ælius Gracilis, who commanded in the Belgic Gaul, heard of this magnificent plan with the jealousy of a little mind. He gave notice to Vetus, that he and his legions must not think of entering the province of another officer. Such a step, he said, would have the appearance of a design to gain the affections of the people of Gaul, and, by consequence, might give umbrage to the emperor. In this manner, as often happens, the danger of having too much merit laid aside a project of great importance to the public.

LIV. THE Barbarians, having seen the long inactivity of
the

the Roman armies, conceived a notion, that the generals had it
in command not to march against the enemy. In this perfuafion,
the Frifians *(a)*, having ordered the weak, through fex or age, to
be conveyed acrofs the lakes, marched with the flower of their
young men through woods and moraffes towards the banks of
the Rhine, where they took poffeffion of a large tract, vacant,
indeed, at the time, but in fact appropriated to the ufe of the
Roman foldiers. In this emigration, the leading chiefs were
Verritus and Malorix, both of them fovereign princes, if fovereign power may be faid to exift in Germany. They had already
fixed their habitations ; they began to cultivate the foil, and the
lands were fown in as full fecurity as if they occupied their native
foil ; when Vibius Avitus, who fucceeded Paulinus in the government of the province, threatened to attack them with his
whole force, if they did not evacuate the country, or obtain a
fettlement from the emperor. Intimidated by thefe menaces, the
German chiefs fet out for Rome. Being there obliged to wait
till Nero was at leifure from other bufinefs, they employed their
time in feeing fuch curiofities as are ufually fhewn to ftrangers.
They were conducted to Pompey's theatre *(b)*, where the grandeur
of the people, in one vaft affembly, could not fail to make an impreffion. Rude minds have no tafte for the exhibitions of the
theatre *(c)*. They gazed at every thing with a face of wonder:
the place for the populace, and the different feats affigned to the
feveral orders of the ftate, engaged their attention. Curiofity
was excited : they enquired which were the Roman knights, and
which the fenators? Among the laft they perceived a few, who,
by their exotic drefs, were known to be foreigners. They foon
learned that they were ambaffadors from different ftates, and that
the privilege of mixing with the fathers was granted by way of diftinction, to do honour to men, who by their courage and fidelity
furpaffed the reft of the world. The anfwer gave offence to the

Vol. II.   Y   two

two chieftains. In point of valour and integrity, the Germans, they faid, were fecond to no people upon earth. With this ftroke of national pride, they rofe abruptly, and took their feats among the fenators. Their rough, but honeft fimplicity diffufed a general pleafure through the audience. It was confidered as the fudden impulfe of liberty; a glow of generous emulation. Nero granted to the two chiefs the privilege of Roman citizens, but, at the fame time, declared, that the Frifians muft depart from the lands which they had prefumed to occupy. The Barbarians refufed to fubmit. A detachment of the auxiliary horfe was fent forward, with orders to diflodge them. The attack was made with vigour, and all who refifted, were either taken prifoners, or put to the fword.

LV. ANOTHER irruption was foon after made in the fame quarter by the Anfibarians *(a)*, a people refpected for their own internal ftrength, and ftill more formidable, on account of the general fympathy with which the neighbouring ftates beheld their fufferings. They had been driven by the Chaucians from their native land, and having no place which they could call their country, they roamed about in queft of fome retreat, where they might dwell in peace, although in exile. Boiocalus, a warlike chief, was at the head of this wandering nation. He had gained renown in arms, and diftinguifhed himfelf by his faithful attachment to the interefts of Rome. He urged, in vindication of his conduct, that, in the revolt of the Cherufcans *(b)*, he had been loaded with irons by the order of Arminius. Since that time, he had ferved in the Roman armies; at firft under Tiberius, and afterwards under Germanicus; and now, at the end of fifty years, he was willing to add to his paft fervices the merit of fubmitting himfelf and his people to the protection of the Romans. "The country in difpute," he faid, "was of wide

"extent; and under colour of referving it for the ufe of the
"legions, whole tracts of land remained unoccupied, wafte, and
"defolate. Let the Roman foldiers depafture their cattle; let
"them retain lands for that purpofe; but let them not, while
"they feed their horfes, reduce mankind to the neceffity of
"perifhing by famine. Let them not prefer a dreary folitude
"to the interefts of humanity. The affections of a people,
"willing to live in friendfhip with them, are preferable to a wide
"wafte of barren lands. The exclufive poffeffion of the country
"in queftion was by no means a novelty. It had been occu-
"pied, firft by the Chamavians (c); after them, by the Tuban-
"tes; and, finally, by the Ufipians. The firmament over our
"heads is the manfion of the gods; the earth was given to
"man; and what remains unoccupied, lies in common for all."
At thefe words, he looked up to the fun, and appealing to the
whole planetary fyftem, afked with a fpirit of enthufiafm, as
if the heavenly luminaries were actually prefent, whether an un-
cultivated defert, the defolation of nature, gave a profpect fit
for them to furvey? Would they not rather let loofe the
ocean, to overwhelm in a fudden deluge a race of men, who
made it their trade to carry devaftation through the nations,
and make the world a wildernefs?

LVI. Avitus anfwered in a decifive tone, that the law of the
ftrongeft muft prevail. "The gods, whom Boiocalus invoked,
"had fo ordained. By their high will, the Romans were in-
"vefted with fupreme authority: to give, or take away was
"their prerogative; they were the fovereign arbiters, and would
"admit no other judges." Such was the anfwer given in public to the Anfibarians. To Boiocalus, in confideration of his
former merit, an allotment of lands was privately offered. The
German confidered it as the price of treachery, and rejected it

Y 2   with

with difdain : " The earth," he faid, " may not afford a fpot " where we may dwell in peace ; a place where we may die we " can never want." The interview ended here. Both fides departed with mutual animofity. The Anfibarians prepared for war. They endeavoured to roufe the Brutterians *(a)*, the Tencterians, and other nations ftill more remote. Avitus fent difpatches to Curtilius Mancia, the commander in chief on the Upper Rhine, with inftruttions to crofs the river, and fhew himfelf in the rear of the enemy. In the mean time, he put himfelf at the head of his legions, and entered the country of the Tentterians *(b)*, threatening to carry fword and fire through their territories, if they did not forthwith renounce the confederacy. The Barbarians laid down their arms. The Brutterians in a panic followed their example. Terror and confternation fpread through the country. In the caufe of others none were willing to encounter certain danger.

In this diftrefs, the Anfibarians, abandoned by all, retreated to the Ufipians and Tubantes. Being there rejetted, they fought protettion from the Cattians, and afterwards from the Cherufcans. In the end, worn out with long and painful marches, no where received as friends, in moft places repulfed as enemies, and wanting every thing in a foreign land, the whole nation perifhed. The young, and fuch as were able to carry arms, were put to the fword ; the reft were fold to flavery.

LVII. In the courfe of the fame fummer, a battle was fought, with great rage and flaughter, between the Hermundurians and the Cattians *(a)*. The exclufive property of a river, which flowed between both nations, impregnated with ftores of falt *(b)*, was the caufe of their mutual animofity. To the natural fiercenefs of Barbarians, who know no decifion but that of the fword, they

added

added the gloomy motives of fuperftition. According to the creed of thofe favage nations, that part of the world lay in the vicinity of the heavens, and thence the prayers of men were wafted to the ear of the gods. The whole region was, by con-fequence, peculiarly favoured; and to that circumftance it was to be afcribed, that the river and the adjacent woods teemed with quantities of falt *(c)*, not, as in other places, a concretion on the fea-fhore, formed by the foaming of the waves, but produced by the fimple act of throwing the water from the ftream on a pile of burning wood, where, by the conflict of oppofite ele-ments, the fubftance was engendered. For this falt a bloody battle was fought. Victory declared in favour of the Her-mundurians. The event was the more deftructive to the Cat-tians, as both armies, with their ufual ferocity, had devoted the vanquifhed as a facrifice to Mars and Mercury. By that horrible vow, men and horfes, with whatever belonged to the routed army, were doomed to deftruction. The vengeance meditated by the Cattians fell with redoubled fury on themfelves.

About the fame time, a dreadful and unforefeen difafter befel the Ubians, a people in alliance with Rome. By a fudden eruption of fubterraneous fire, their farms, their villages, their cities, and their habitations were all involved in one general con-flagration. The flames extended far and wide, and well nigh reached the Roman colony, lately founded in that part of Ger-many. The fire raged with fuch violence, that neither the rain from the heavens, nor the river-waters could extinguifh it. Every remedy failed, till the peafants, driven to defperation, threw in heaps of ftones, and checked the fury of the flames. The mifchief beginning to fubfide, they advanced with clubs, as if to attack a troop of wild beafts. Having beat down the fire, they ftripped off their cloaths, and throwing them, wet and

befmeared

befmeared with filth, upon the flames, extinguifhed the conflagration.

LVIII. THIS year the tree, called RUMINALIS *(a)*, which
ftood in the place affigned for public elections, and eight hundred
and forty years before *(b)* had given fhelter to the infancy of
Romulus and Remus, began to wither in all its branches. The
fapless trunk feemed to threaten a total decay. This was confidered as a dreadful prognoftic, till new buds expanding into
leaf, the tree recovered its former verdure.

END OF THE THIRTEENTH BOOK.

ANNALS

TACITUS.

BOOK XIV.

CONTENTS of BOOK XIV.

tonius Paulinus sent to command the army. He takes the isle of Mona (now Anglesey), and destroys the religious groves. During his absence in those parts, a general massacre of the Romans. The province almost lost, but recovered by Suetonius, who defeats Boadicea with prodigious slaughter. XL. The governor, or præfect of Rome, murdered by one of his slaves. Debates in the senate about the punishment of all slaves in the house at the time of a murder committed on the master. XLVI. Tarquitius Priscus condemned. Death of Memmius Regulus: his character. Nero dedicates a school for athletic exercises. The law of majesty revived. Antistius, the prætor, prosecuted for a satyrical poem on the emperor. The senate willing to inflict a capital punishment: Pætus Thrasea opposes the motion: the majority vote on his side. LI. Burrhus dies universally lamented. LII. Attempts against Seneca: his enemies undermine him with the prince. His interview with Nero: his speech, and the prince's answer. LVII. Tigellinus in high favour: by his advice Sylla murdered at Marseilles, and Plautus in Asia. LX. Nero repudiates his wife Octavia, and marries Poppæa. An insurrection of the populace. Anicetus suborned by Nero to confess himself guilty of adultery with Octavia. She is banished by Nero to the isle of Pandatavia, and soon after murdered.

These transactions include near four years.

Years of Rome—of Christ		Consuls
812	59	*Caius Vipstanus Apronianus, Lucius Fonteius Capito.*
813	60	*Nero, 4th time, Cossus Cornelius Lentulus.*
814	61	*Cæsonius Pætus, Petronius Turpilianus.*
815	62	*P. Marius Celsus, L. Asinius Gallus.*

B O O K   XIV.

I. CAIUS VIPSTANUS and Lucius Fontelus fucceeded to the confulfhip. Nero was determined no longer to defer the black defign which had lain for fome time foftered in his heart. He had gained in four years a tafte of power, and was now grown fanguine enough to think that he might hazard a daring ftride in guilt. His love for Poppæa kindled every day to higher ardour. To be the imperial wife was the ambition of that afpiring beauty; but while Agrippina lived, fhe could not hope to fee Octavia divorced from the emperor. She began, by whifpered calumny, to undermine the emperor's mother, and, at times, in a vein of pleafantry, to alarm the pride and jealoufy of Nero. With an air of raillery fhe called him a pupil, ftill under

Z 2

tuition;

tuition; a dependant on the will of others, in fancy guiding the reins of government, but, in reality, deprived of perfonal liberty. "For what other reafon was her marriage fo long deferred? "Had her perfon already loft the power of pleafing? Were "the triumphal honours obtained by her anceftors a bar to her "preferment? Or, was it fuppofed that fhe was not of a fruitful "conftitution, capable of bearing children? Perhaps the fincerity "of her love was called in queftion. No; the voice of a wife "might be heard, and the pride and avarice with which an im- "perious mother infulted the fenate and oppreffed the people, "might be expofed in open day. If, however, it was a fettled "point with Agrippina, that no one but the bofom plague of "the emperor fhould be her daughter-in-law, Poppæa could "return to the embraces of Otho *(a)*; with him fhe could re- "tire to fome remote corner of the world, where fhe might hear, "indeed, of the emperor's difgrace, but at a diftance, with the "confolation of neither being a fpectatrefs of the fcene, nor a "fharer in his afflictions." By thefe and fuch like fuggeftions, intermixed with tears and female artifice, fhe enfnared the heart of Nero. No one attempted to weaken her influence. To fee the pride of Agrippina humbled was the wifh of all; but that the fon would renounce the ties of natural affection, and imbrue his hands in the blood of his mother, was what never entered the imagination of any man.

II. In the hiftory of thofe times tranfmitted to us by Cluvius, we read, that Agrippina, in her rage for power, did not fcruple to meet the emperor about the middle of the day, as he rofe from table, high in blood, and warm with wine. Having adorned her perfon to the beft advantage, fhe hoped, in thefe moments, to incite defire, and allure him to the unnatural union. Wanton play and amorous dalliance were feen by the confi-

2

dential

dential attendants, and deemed a certain prelude to the act of criminal gratification. Againſt the artifices of one woman Seneca reſolved to play off the charms of another, and Acté *(a)* was accordingly employed. The jealouſy of the concubine was eaſily alarmed: ſhe ſaw her own danger, and the infamy that awaited the prince. Being taught her leſſon, ſhe gave notice to Nero that he was publicly charged with inceſt, while his mother gloried in the crime. The army, ſhe ſaid, would revolt from a man plunged in vice of ſo deep a dye. Fabius Ruſticus differs from this account. If we believe that author, Agrippina did not ſeek this vile pollution. It was the unnatural paſſion of Nero, and Acté had the addreſs to wean him from it. Cluvius, however, is confirmed by the teſtimony of other writers. The report of common fame is alſo on his ſide. Men were willing to believe the worſt of Agrippina. If ſhe was not, in fact, guilty of a deſign ſo deteſtable, a new inclination, however ſhocking to nature, ſeemed probable in a woman of her character; who, in the prime of her youth, from motives of ambition, reſigned her perſon to Lepidus *(b)*; who afterwards, with the ſame view, deſcended to be the proſtitute of Pallas, and, to crown the whole, by an inceſtuous marriage with her uncle, avowed herſelf capable of the worſt of crimes.

III. From this time Nero ſhunned the preſence of his mother. Whenever ſhe went to her gardens, or to either of her ſeats at Tuſculum *(a)* or Antium, he commended her taſte for the pleaſures of retirement. At length, deteſting her whereever ſhe was, he determined to diſpatch her at once. How to execute his purpoſe, whether by poiſon, or the poniard, was the only difficulty. The former ſeemed the moſt adviſable; but to adminiſter it at his own table might be dangerous, ſince the fate of Britannicus was too well known. To tamper with her do-

meſtics

mestics was equally unsafe. A woman of her cast, practised in guilt, and inured to evil deeds, would be upon her guard; and besides, by the habit of using antidotes, she was fortified against every kind of poison. To assassinate her, and yet conceal the murder, was impracticable. Nero had no settled plan, nor was there among his creatures a single person in whom he could confide.

In this embarrassment Anicetus offered his assistance. This man had a genius for the worst iniquity. From the rank of an enfranchised slave he rose to the command of the fleet that lay at Misenum. He had been tutor to Nero in his infancy, and always at variance with Agrippina. Mutual hostility produced mutual hatred. He proposed the model of a ship upon a new construction, formed in such a manner that, in the open sea, part might give way at once, and plunge Agrippina to the bottom. The ocean, he said, was the element of disasters; and if the vessel foundered, malignity itself could not convert into a crime what would appear to be the effect of adverse winds and boisterous waves. After her decease the prince would have nothing to do but to raise a temple to her memory. Altars and public monuments would be proofs of filial piety.

IV. NERO approved of the stratagem, and the circumstances of the time conspired to favour it. The court was then at Baiæ, to celebrate, during five days, the festival called the QUIN-QUATRUA (a). Agrippina was invited to be of the party. To tempt her thither Nero changed his tone. "The humours of " parent claimed indulgence; for sudden starts of passion " allowance ought to be made, and petty resentments could not " ....d too soon." By this artifice he hoped to circulate an " ... his entire reconciliation, and Agrippina, he had no doubt,

doubt, with the eaſy credulity of her ſex, would be the dupe of a report that flattered her wiſhes. She ſailed from Antium to attend the feſtival. The prince went to the ſea-coaſt to receive her. He gave her his hand; he embraced her tenderly, and conduſted her to a villa called Bauli *(b)*, in a pleaſant ſituation, waſhed by the ſea, where it forms a bay between the cape of Miſenum and the gulph of Baiæ. Among the veſſels that lay at anchor, one in particular, more ſuperb than the reſt, ſeemed intended by its decorations to do honour to the emperor's mother. Agrippina was fond of ſailing parties. She frequently made coaſting voyages in a galley with three ranks of oars, and mariners ſelected from the fleet. The banquet, of which ſhe was to partake, was fixed at a late hour, that the darkneſs of the night might favour the perpetration of an atrocious deed.

But the ſecret tranſpired: on the firſt intelligence, Agrippina, it is ſaid, could ſcarce give credit to ſo black a ſtory. She choſe, however, to be conveyed to Baiæ in a land carriage. Her fears, as ſoon as ſhe arrived, were diſſipated by the polite addreſs of her ſon. He gave her the moſt gracious reception, and placed her at table above himſelf. He talked with frankneſs, and, by intermixing ſallies of youthful vivacity with more ſedate converſation, had the ſkill to blend the gay, the airy, and the ſerious. He protracted the pleaſures of the ſocial meeting to a late hour, when Agrippina thought it time to retire. The prince attended her to the ſhore; he exchanged a thouſand fond endearments, and, claſping her to his boſom, fixed his eyes upon her with ardent affection, perhaps intending, under the appearance of filial piety, to diſguiſe his purpoſe; or, it might be, that the ſight of a mother doomed to deſtruction, might make even a heart like his yield, for a moment, to the touch of nature.

V. That

176

V. THAT this iniquitous scene should not be wrapped in darkness, the care of Providence seems to have interposed. The night was calm and serene; the stars shot forth their brightest lustre, and the sea presented a smooth expanse. Agrippina went on board, attended by only two of her domestic train. One of them, Crepereius Gallus, took his place near the steerage; the other, a female attendant, by name Acerronia, stretched herself at the foot of the bed where her mistress lay, and in the fullness of her heart expressed her joy to see the son awakened to a sense of his duty, and the mother restored to his good graces. The vessel had made but little way, when, on a signal given, the deck over Agrippina's cabbin fell in at once. Being loaded with lead, Crepereius was crushed under the weight. The props of the bed-room, happening to be of a solid structure, bore up the load, and saved both Agrippina and her servant. Nor did the vessel, as was intended, fall to pieces at once. Consternation, hurry, and confusion followed. The innocent, in a panic, bustled to and fro, embarrassing and confounding such as were in the plot. To heave the ship on one side, and sink her at once, was the design of the accomplices: but not acting in concert, and the rest making contrary efforts, the vessel went down by slow degrees. This gave the passengers an opportunity of escaping from the wreck, and trusting to the mercy of the waves.

Acerronia, in her fright, called herself Agrippina, and, with pathetic accents, implored the mariners to save the emperor's mother. The assassins fell upon her with their oars, with their poles, and with whatever instruments they could seize. She died under repeated blows. Agrippina hushed her fears; not a word escaping from her, she passed undistinguished by the murderers, without any other damage than a wound on her shoulder.

fhoulder. She dafhed into the fea, and, by ftruggling with all her efforts, kept herfelf above water till the fmall barks put off from the fhore, and, coming in good time to her affiftance, conveyed her up the Lucrine lake *(a)* to her own villa.

VI. SHE was now at leifure to reflect on the mifery of her fituation. The treachery of her fon's letter, conceived in terms of affection, and his mock civility, were too apparent. Without a guft of wind, and without touching a rock, at a fmall diftance from the fhore, the veffel broke down from the upper deck, like a piece of mechanifm conftructed for the purpofe. The death of Acerronia, and the wound which fhe herfelf received, were decifive circumftances. But even in that juncture fhe thought it beft to temporife. Againft powerful enemies not to fee too much is the fafeft policy. She fent her freedman Agerinus to inform her fon that, by the favour of the gods, and the good aufpices of the emperor, fhe had efcaped from a fhipwreck. The news, fhe had no doubt, would affect her fon, but, for the prefent, fhe wifhed he would forbear to vifit her. In her fituation, reft was all fhe wanted. Having difpatched her meffenger, fhe affumed an air of courage; fhe got her wound dreffed, and ufed all proper applications. With an air of cafe fhe called for the laft will of Acerronia, and, having ordered an inventory to be made of her effects, fecured every thing under her own feal; acting in this fingle article without diffimulation.

VII. NERO, in the mean time, expected, with impatience, an account of his mother's death. Intelligence at laft was brought that fhe ftill furvived, wounded, indeed, and knowing from what quarter the blow was aimed. The prince heard the news with terror and aftonifhment. In the hurry of his imagination he faw his mother already at hand, fierce with indignation, calling

VOL. II.   A a   aloud

aloud for vengeance, and rouſing her ſlaves to an inſurrection. She might have recourſe to the army, and ſtir up a rebellion; ſhe might open the whole dark tranſaction to the ſenate; ſhe might carry her complaints to the ear of the people. Her wound, the wreck, the murder of her friends, every circumſtance would inflame reſentment. What courſe remained for him? Where was Seneca? and where was Burrhus? He had ſent for them on the firſt alarm: they came with expedition, but whether ſtrangers to the plot, remains uncertain. They ſtood, for ſome time, fixed in ſilence. To diſſuade the emperor from his fell deſign, they knew was not in their power; and, in the preſent dilemma, they ſaw, perhaps, that Agrippina muſt fall, or Nero periſh. Seneca, though on all other occaſions ready to take the lead, fixed his eyes on Burrhus. After a pauſe, he deſired to know whether it were adviſable to order the ſoldiers to complete the buſineſs? Burrhus was of opinion, that the prætorian ſoldiers, devoted to the houſe of Cæſar, and ſtill reſpecting the memory of Germanicus, would not be willing to ſpill the blood of his daughter. It was for Anicetus to finiſh the laſt act of the tragedy.

That bold aſſaſſin undertook the buſineſs. He deſired to have the 'cataſtrophe in his own hands. Nero revived at the ſound. From that day, he ſaid, the imperial dignity would be his, and that mighty benefit would be conferred by an enfranchiſed ſlave. " Haſte, fly," he cried; " take with you men fit for your pur- " poſe, and conſummate all." Anicetus heard that a meſſage was ſent by Agrippina, and that Agerinus was actually arrived. His ready invention planned a new ſcene of villany. While the meſſenger was in the act of addreſſing the prince, he dropped a poniard between his legs, and inſtantly, as if he had diſcovered a treaſonable deſign, ſeized the man, and loaded him with irons,

from

from that circumſtance taking colour to charge Agrippina with
a plot againſt the life of her ſon. When ſhe was diſpoſed of,
a report that, in deſpair, ſhe put an end to her life, would be
an apt addition to the fable.

VIII. MEANWHILE, the news of Agrippina's danger ſpread
an alarm round the country. The general cry imputed it to
accident. The people ruſhed in crowds to the ſea-ſhore; they
went on the piers that projected into the ſea: they filled the
boats; they waded as far as they could venture; ſtretching
forth their hands, and calling aloud for help: the bay reſounded
with ſhrieks and lamentations, with diſtracting queſtions, diſſo-
nant anſwers, and a wild confuſion of voices. Amidſt the uproar, numbers came with lighted torches. Finding that Agrippina was ſafe, they preſſed forward to offer their congratulations,
when a body of armed ſoldiers, threatening violence, obliged the
whole crowd to diſperſe. Anicetus planted a guard round the
manſion of Agrippina, and having burſt open the gates, he
ſeized the ſlaves, and forced his way to her apartment.

A few domeſtics remained at the door to guard the entrance;
fear had diſperſed the reſt. In the room, the pale glimmer of a
feeble light was ſeen, and only one maid in waiting. Before the
ruffians broke in, Agrippina paſſed the moments in dreadful
agitation: ſhe wondered that no meſſenger arrived from her ſon.
What detained Agerinus? She liſtened, and on the coaſt where,
not long before, the whole was tumult, noiſe, and confuſion, a
diſmal ſilence prevailed, broken, at intervals, by a ſudden uproar, that added to the horror of the ſcene. Agrippina trembled
for herſelf. Her ſervant was leaving the room: ſhe called to
her, "And do you too deſert me?" In that inſtant ſhe ſaw
Anicetus entering the chamber. Herculeus, who had the com-

A a 2

mand

mand of a galley, and Oloaritus, a marine centurion, followed him. " If you come," faid Agrippina, " from the prince, tell " him I am well; if your intents are murderous, you are not " fent by my fon: the guilt of parricide is foreign to his heart." The ruffians furrounded her bed. The centurion of the marines was drawing his fword: at the fight Agrippina prefented her perfon, " And here," fhe faid, " PLUNGE YOUR SWORD " IN MY WOMB." Herculeus, in that moment, gave the firft blow with a club, and wounded her on the head. She expired under a number of mortal wounds.

IX. THE facts here related ftand confirmed by the concurrent teftimony of hiftorians. It is added, but not with equal authority, that Nero beheld his mother ftretched in death, and praifed the elegance of her form. This, however, is denied by other writers. The body was laid out on a common couch, fuch as is ufed at meals, and, without any other ceremony, burnt that very night During the life of Nero, no honour was offered to her remains; no tomb was erected to tell where fhe lay: nor was there fo much as a mound of earth to inclofe the place. After fome time an humble monument *(a)* was raifed by her domeftics on the road to Mifenum, near the villa *(b)* of Cæfar the Dictator, which, from an eminence, commands a beautiful profpect of the fea and the bays along the coaft. Mnefter, one of the enfranchifed flaves of Agrippina, attended the funeral. As foon as the pile was lighted, this man, unwilling to furvive his miftrefs, or, perhaps, dreading the malice of her enemies, difpatched himfelf with his own fword. Of her own dreadful cataftrophe Agrippina had warning many years before, when confulting the Chaldæans about the future lot of her fon, fhe was told, that he would reign at Rome, and

I   kill

kill his mother. " Let him," she said, " let him kill me, but
" let him reign."

X. THIS dreadful parricide was no sooner executed, than
Nero began to feel the horrors of his guilt. He lay, during the
rest of the night, on the rack of his own mind; silent, pensive,
starting up with sudden fear, wild and distracted. He lifted his
eyes in quest of day-light, yet dreaded its approach. The tribunes and centurions, by the advice of Burrhus, were the first
to administer consolation. The flattery of these men raised
him from despair. They grasped his hand, congratulating him
on his escape from the dark designs of his mother. His friends
crowded to the temples to offer up their thanks to the gods.
The neighbouring cities of Campania followed their example.
They offered victims, and sent addresses to the prince. Nero
played a different part: he appeared with a dejected mien,
weary of life, and inconsolable for the loss of his mother. But
the face of a country cannot, like the features of man, assume
a new appearance. The sea and the adjacent coast presented
to his eyes a scene of guilt and horror. It was reported at the
time that the sound of trumpets was distinctly heard along the
ridge of the hills, and groans and shrieks issued from Agrippina's
grave. Nero removed to Naples, and from that place dispatched
letters to the senate, in substance as follows:

XI. " AGERINUS, the freedman of Agrippina, and of all her
" creatures the highest in her confidence, was found armed with
" a poniard; and the blow being prevented, with the same spirit
" that planned the murder of her son, she dispatched herself."
The letter proceeded to state a number of past transactions:
" Her ambition aimed at a share in the supreme power, and
" the prætorian bands were obliged to take an oath of fidelity
" to

" to her. The senate and the people were to submit to the same
" indignity, and bear the yoke of female tyranny. Seeing her
" schemes defeated, she became an enemy to the fathers, to the
" soldiers, and the whole community; she neither suffered a
" donative to be distributed to the army, nor a largess to the
" populace. At her instigation prosecutions were set on foot
" against the best and most illustrious men in Rome. If she
" did not enter the senate, and give audience to the ambassa-
" dors of foreign nations *(a)*, all would remember how that
" disgrace was prevented." The reign of Claudius did not escape his animadversion; but whatever were the enormities of
that period, Agrippina, he said, was the cause of all. Her death
was an event in which the good fortune of the empire was sig-
nally displayed. He gave a circumstantial account of the ship-
wreck: but what man existed, so absurd and stupid, as to believe it the effect of chance? Was it probable that a woman,
who had just escaped from the fury of the waves, would send a
single ruffian to attempt the life of a prince, surrounded by his
guards and his naval officers? The indignation of the public
was not confined to Nero: with regard to him, who had
plunged in guilt beyond all example, it was useless to complain.
Censure was lost in mute astonishment. The popular odium
fell on Seneca: his pen was seen in the prince's letters, and the
attempt to gloss and varnish so vile a deed, was considered as
the avowal of an accomplice.

XII. THE voice of the people did not restrain the adulation
of the senate. Several decrees were passed in a strain of servile
flattery; such as supplications and solemn vows at all the altars
throughout the city of Rome; the festival called the Quin-
quatrua (during which the late conspiracy was detected) were
to be celebrated, for the future, with the addition of public
games;

games; the ſtatue of Minerva, wrought in gold, to be placed in
the ſenate-houſe, with that of the emperor near it; and finally,
the anniverſary of Agrippina's birth-day to be unhallowed in
the calendar.   Pætus Thraſea had been often preſent, when
the fathers deſcended to acts of meanneſs, and he did not riſe in
oppoſition; but, upon this occaſion, he left his ſeat, and walked
out of the houſe, by his virtue provoking future vengeance, yet
doing no ſervice to the cauſe of liberty.

There happened, about this time, a number of prodigies, all
deemed ſtriking prognoſtics, but no conſequences followed.   A
woman was delivered of a ſerpent: another died in the embrace
of her huſband, by a ſtroke of thunder.   The ſun ſuffered an
eclipſe (a), and the fourteen quarters of Rome were ſtruck with
lightning.   In theſe extraordinary appearances the hand of providence, it is evident, did not interpoſe; ſince the vices and tyranny of Nero continued to haraſs mankind for ſeveral years.
The policy of the prince had now two objects in view; the firſt
to blacken the memory of his mother; and the ſecond, to amuſe
the people with a ſhow of his own clemency, when left, without
controul, to the bent of his own inclination.   To this end, he
recalled from baniſhment, to which they had been condemned
by the vindictive ſpirit of Agrippina, two illuſtrious women,
namely, Junia (b) and Calpurnia, together with Valerius Capito, and Licinius Gabolus, both of prætorian rank.   He permitted the aſhes of Lollia Paulina (c) to be brought to Rome,
and a mauſoleum to be erected to her memory.   To Iturius
and Calviſius (d), whom his own violence had driven into exile,
he granted a free pardon.   Silana (e) had paid her debt to nature.
Towards the end of Agrippina's life, when the power of that
princeſs began to decline, or her reſentment to be appeaſed, ſhe

7

had

had obtained leave to return from her diftant exile as far as Tarentum.   At that place fhe clofed her days.

XIII. Nero loitered in the towns of Campania, full of doubt and perplexity, unable to determine how he fhould enter the city of Rome.   Would the fenate receive him with a fub-miffive and complying fpirit?   Could he rely on the temper of the people?   Thefe were points that made him anxious and irre-folute.   The vile advifers of his court (and never court abounded with fo pernicious a race) interfered to animate his drooping fpirit.   They affured him, with confidence, that the name of Agrippina was held in deteftation, and, fince her death, the affections of the people for the perfon of the emperor knew no bounds.   He had only to fhew himfelf, and it would be feen that he reigned in the hearts of the multitude.   To prepare the way, they defired leave to enter the city of Rome before him.

On their arrival, they found all things favourable beyond their hopes; they faw the feveral tribes going forth in proceffion to meet the prince; the fenate in their robes of ftate; whole crowds of women, with their children, ranged in claffes according to their refpective ages, in the ftreets through which Nero was to pafs; rows of fcaffolding built up, and an amphitheatre of fpectators, as if a triumph were to enter the city.   Nero made his entry, fluthed with the pride of victory over the minds of willing flaves, and proceeded, amidft the acclamations of gazing mul-titudes, to the capitol, where he offered thanks to the gods. From that moment he threw off all reftraint.   The authority of his mother, feeble as it was, had hitherto curbed the violence of his paffions: but that check being now removed, he broke out at once, and gave a full difplay of his character.

XIV. To

XIV. To acquire the fame of a charioteer, and to figure in the race with a curricle and four horfes, had been long the favourite paffion of Nero. He had befides another frivolous talent: he could play on the harp, and fing to his own performance. With this pitiful ambition he had been often the minftrel of convivial parties. He juftified his tafte by obferving, that " in ancient " times, it had been the practice of heroes and of kings. The " names of illuftrious perfons, who confecrated their talents to " the honour of the gods, were preferved in immortal verfe. " Apollo was the tutelar deity of melody and fong ; and, though " invefted with the higher attributes of infpiration and prophecy, " he was reprefented, not only in the cities of Greece, but alfo " in the Roman temples, with a lyre in his hand, and the drefs " of a mufical performer." The rage of Nero for thefe amufe-ments was not to be controuled. Seneca and Burrhus en-deavoured to prevent the ridicule, to which a prince might expofe himfelf by exhibiting his talents to the multitude. By their direction, a wide fpace, in the vale at the foot of the Vatican (u), was inclofed for the ufe of the emperor, that he might there manage the reins, and practife all his fkill, without being a fpectacle for the public eye. But his love of fame was not to be confined within thofe narrow bounds. He invited the multitude. They extolled, with raptures, the abilities of a prince, who gratified their darling paffion for public diverfions.

The two governors were in hopes that their pupil, as foon as he had his frolic, would be fenfible of the difgrace ; but the effect was otherwife. The applaufe of the populace in-fpired him with frefh ardour. To keep himfelf in countenance, he conceived, if he could bring the practice into fafhion, that his own infamy would be loft in the difgrace of others. With this view, he caft his eye on the defcendants of families once illuftrious, but at that time fallen to decay. From that clafs of men he felected the moft neceffitous, fuch as would be eafily tempted to let themfelves out for hire. He retained them as actors, and produced them on the public ftage. Their names I forbear to mention: though they are now no more, the honour of their anceftors claims refpect. The difgrace recoils on him, who chofe to employ his treafure, not for the noble end of preventing fcandal, but to procure it. Nor was he willing to ftop here: by vaft rewards he bribed feveral Roman knights to defcend into the Arena, and prefent a fhow to the people. The fituation of thefe unhappy men deferves our pity: for what are the bribes of an abfolute prince, but the commands of him who has power to compel?

XV. NERO was not as yet hardy enough to expofe his perfon on a public ftage. To gratify his paffion for fcenic amufements, and at the fame time to fave appearances, he eftablifhed an entertainment, called the JUVENILE SPORTS. To promote this inftitution, numbers of the firft diftinction enrolled their names. Neither rank, nor age, nor civil honours were an exemption. All degrees embraced the theatrical art, and, with emulation, became the rivals of Greek and Roman mimickry; proud to languifh at the foft cadence of effeminate notes, and to catch the graces of wanton deportment. Women of rank *(a)* ftudied the moft lafcivious characters. In the grove planted round the lake, where Auguftus gave his naval engagement, booths and places of recreation were erected, to pamper luxury, and inflame defire. By the prince's orders fums of money were diftributed. Good men, through motives of fear, accepted the donation; and to the profligate, whatever miniftered to fenfuality, was fure to be acceptable. Luxury and corruption triumphed.

The

The manners, it is true, had, long before this time, fallen into
degeneracy; but in thefe new affemblies a torrent of vice bore
down every thing, beyond the example of former ages.   Even
in better days, when fcience and the liberal arts-had not entirely
loft their influence, virtue and modefty could fcarce maintain
their poft; but in an age, that openly profcffcd every fpecies of de-
pravity, what ftand could be made by truth, by innocence, or by
modeft merit? The general corruption encouraged Nero to throw
off all reftraint.   He mounted the ftage, and became a public
performer for the amufement of the people.   With his harp in
his hand, he entered the fcene; he tuned the chords with a
graceful air, and with delicate flourifhes gave a prelude to his
art.   He ftood in a circle of his friends, a prætorian cohort on
guard, and the tribunes and centurions near his perfon.   Burrhus
was alfo prefent, pleafure in his countenance, and anguifh at his
heart.   He grieved, while he applauded.   At this time was inftituted a company of Roman knights under the title of THE
AUGUSTAN SOCIETY *(b)*, confifting of young men in the prime
of life, fome of them libertines from inclination, and others
hoping by their profligacy to gain preferment.   They attended,
night and day, to applaud the prince; they admired the graces
of his perfon, and, in the various notes of that exquifite voice,
they heard the melody of the gods, who were all excelled by
the enchanting talents of the prince.   The tribe of fycophants
affumed airs of grandeur, fwelling with felf-importance, as if they
were all rifing to preferment by their genius and their virtue.

XVI. THEATRICAL fame was not fufficient for the ambition
of Nero : he wifhed to excel in poetry.   All, who poffeffed the
art of verfification, were affembled to affift his ftudies.   In this
fociety of wits, young men, not yet qualified by their years to
figure in the world, difplayed the firft effays of their genius.

B b 2

They

They met in the dearest intimacy. Scraps of poetry, by different hands *(a)*, were brought to the meeting, or compofed on the fpot; and thofe fragments, however unconnected, they endeavoured to weave into a regular poem, taking care to infert the words and phrafes of the emperor, as the moft brilliant ornaments of the piece. That this was their method, appears from a perufal of the feveral compofitions, in which we fee rhapfody without genius, verfe without poetry, and nothing like the work of one creative fancy. Nor was philofophy difregarded by the emperor. At ftated hours, when his convivial joys were finifhed, the profeffors of wifdom were admitted. Various fyftems were dogmatically fupported; and to fee the followers of different fects quarrel about an hypothefis was the amufement of Nero. He faw befides, among the venerable fages, fome with formal mien and looks of aufterity, who under an air of coynefs plainly fhewed that they relifhed the pleafures of a court.

XVII. ABOUT this time a dreadful fray broke out between the inhabitants of Nuceria *(a)* and Pompeii, two Italian colonies. The difpute, flight in the beginning, foon rofe to violence, and terminated in blood. It happened that Livinieus Regulus *(b)*, who, as already mentioned, had been expelled the fenate, gave a fpectacle of gladiators. At this meeting jefts and raillery, and the rough wit of country towns, flew about among the populace; abufe and fcurrility followed; altercation excited anger; anger rofe to fury; ftones were thrown, and finally they had recourfe to arms. The people of Pompeium, where the fpectacle was given, were too ftrong for their adverfaries. The Nucerians fuffered in the conflict. Numbers of their friends, covered with wounds, were fent to Rome. Sons wept for their parents, and parents for their children. The fenate, to whom the matter was referred by the prince, directed an enquiry before

I   the

the confuls, and, upon their report, paffed a decree, prohibiting, for the fpace of ten years, the like affemblies at Pompeium, and, moreover, diffolving certain focieties eftablifhed in that city, and incorporated contrary to law. Livineius and others, who appeared to be ring-leaders in the riot, were ordered into banifhment.

BOOK XIV.

A. U. C.
812.
A. D.
59.

XVIII. At the fuit of the Cyrenians, Pedius Blæfus *(a)* was expelled the fenate. The charge againft him was, that he had pillaged the facred treafure of Æfculapius, and, in the bufinefs of lifting foldiers, had been guilty of receiving bribes, and committing various acts of grofs partiality. A complaint was preferred by the fame people againft Acilius Strabo, a man of prætorian rank, who had been fent a commiffioner by the emperor Claudius, with powers to afcertain the boundaries of the lands which formerly belonged to king Apion *(b)*, and were by him bequeathed, with the reft of his dominions, to the Roman people. Various intruders had entered on the vacant poffeffion, and from occupancy and length of time hoped to derive a legal title. The people, difappointed in their expectations, appealed from the fentence of Strabo. The fenate, profeffing to know nothing of the commiffion granted by Claudius, referred the bufinefs to the decifion of the prince. Nero ratified the award made by Strabo ; but, to fhew a mark of good will to the allies of Rome, he reftored the lands in queftion to the perfons, who had been difpoffeffed.

XIX. In a fhort time after died Domitius Afer and Marcus Servilius, two illuftrious citizens, eminent for the civil honours which they attained, and not lefs diftinguifhed by their eloqence. Afer had been a fhining ornament of the bar : Servilius entered the fame career, but having left the forum, gave a fignal proof of his genius by a well digefted hiftory of Roman affairs.

affairs.   Elegant in his life and manners, he formed a contrast to the rough character of Afer, to whom in point of genius he was every way equal, in probity and morals his superior *(a)*.

XX. NERO entered on his fourth consulship, with Cornelius Cossus for his colleague.   On the model of the Greek olympics, he instituted public games to be celebrated every fifth year, and, for that reason, called quinquennial *(a)*.   In this, as in all cases of innovation, the opinions of men were much at variance.   By such as disliked the measure, it was observed, " that even " Pompey, by building a permanent theatre *(b)*, gave offence to " the thinking men of that day.   Before that period, an oc- " casional theatre, with scenery and benches to serve the purpose, " was deemed sufficient ; and, if the enquiry were carried back " to ancient times, it would be found that the spectators were " obliged to stand during the whole representation.   The reason " was, that the people, accommodated with seats, might be " tempted to waste whole days in idle amusements.   Public " spectacles were, indeed, of ancient origin, and, if still left to " the direction of the prætor, might be exhibited with good " order and propriety.   But the new mode of pressing the citi- " zens of Rome into the service of the stage had ruined all de- " corum.   The manners had long since degenerated, and now, " to work their total subversion, luxury was called in from every " quarter of the globe ; foreign nations were ransacked for the " incentives of vice ; and, whatever was in itself corrupt, or " capable of diffusing corruption, was to be found at Rome. " Exotic customs and a foreign taste infected the young men of " the time ; dissipation, gymnastic arts, and infamous intrigues " were the fashion, encouraged by the prince and the senate, and " not only encouraged, but established by their sanction, en- " forced by their authority.

" Under

" Under colour of promoting poetry and eloquence, the patri-
" cians of Rome difgraced themfelves on the public ftage. What
" further ftep remained ? Nothing, but to bare their bodies ; to
" anoint their limbs ; to come forth naked in the lifts ; to wield
" the cæftus, and, throwing afide their military weapons, fight
" prizes for the entertainment of the rabble. Will the fanctity
" of the augur's office, or the judicial character *(c)* of the Roman
" knights, edify by the manners now in vogue ? Will the former
" be held in higher reverence, becaufe he has been lately taught
" to thrill with ecftafy at the foft airs of an effeminate fong ?
" And will the judge decide with greater ability, becaufe he
" affects to have a tafte, and to pronounce on mufic ? Vice
" goes on increafing ; the night is added to the day ; and, in
" mixed affemblies, the profligate libertine, under covert of the
" dark, may fafely gratify the bafe defires, which his imagina-
" tion formed in the courfe of the day."

XXI. Licentious pleafure had a number of advocates ; all
of them the apologifts of vice difguifed under fpecious names.
By thefe men it was argued, " that the citizens of Rome, in the
" earlieft period, were addicted to public fhows, and the expence
" kept pace with the wealth of the times. Pantomime players *(a)*
" were brought from Tufcany, and horfe-races *(b)* from Thu-
" rium. When Greece and Afia were reduced to fubjection,
" the public games were exhibited with greater pomp ; though
" it muft be acknowledged, that in two hundred years (the time
" that elapfed from the triumph of Lucius Mummius *(c)*, who
" firft introduced theatrical reprefentations) not one Roman
" citizen of rank or family was known to degrade himfelf by
" lifting in a troop of comedians. But it is alfo true, that, by
" erecting a permanent theatre, a great annual expence was
" avoided. The magiftrate is now no longer obliged to ruin his
" private

" private fortune for the diverſion of the public. The whole
" expenditure is transferred to the ſtate, and, without encumber-
" ing a ſingle individual, the people may enjoy the games of
" Greece. The conteſts between poets and orators would raiſe
" a ſpirit of emulation, and promote the cauſe of literature.
" Nor will the judge be diſgraced, if he lends an ear to the
" productions of genius, and ſhares the pleaſures of a liberal
" mind. In the quinquennial feſtival, lately inſtituted, a few
" nights, every fifth year, would be dedicated, not to criminal
" gratifications, but to ſocial gaiety, in a place fitted for a large
" aſſembly, and illuminated with ſuch a glare of light, that
" clandeſtine vice would by conſequence be excluded."

Such was the argument of the advocates for diſſipation. It
is but fair to acknowledge, that the celebration of the new
feſtival was conducted without any offence againſt decency or
good manners. Nor did the rage of the people for theatrical
entertainments break out into any kind of exceſs. The pantomime performers, though reſtored to the theatre, were ſtill excluded from ſuch exhibitions as were held to be of a ſacred
nature. The prize of eloquence was not adjudged to any of
the candidates ; but it was thought a fit compliment to the emperor, to pronounce him conqueror. The Grecian garb, which
was much in vogue during the feſtival, gave diſguſt, and from
that time fell into diſuſe.

XXII. A comet having appeared, in this juncture, that
phænomenon, according to the popular opinion, announced that
governments were to be changed, and kings dethroned. In the
imaginations of men Nero was already depoſed, and who ſhould
be his ſucceſſor was the queſtion. The name of Rubellius
Plautus reſounded in every quarter. By the maternal line this
eminent

eminent citizen was of the Julian houfe. A ftrict obferver of
ancient manners, he maintained a rigid aufterity of character.
Reclufe and virtuous in his family, he lived remote from danger,
but his fame from the fhade of obfcurity fhone forth with
brighter luftre. The report of his elevation was confirmed by an
accident, flight in itfelf, but by vulgar error received as a fure
prognoftic. While Nero was at table at a villa called SUBLA-
QUEUM (a), on the borders of the Simbruine lakes, it happened
that the victuals, which had been ferved up, received a ftroke of
lightning, and the banquet was overturned. The place was on
the confines of Tivoli, where the anceftors of Plautus by his
father's fide derived their origin. The omen, for that reafon,
made a deeper impreffion, and the current opinion was, that
Plautus was intended for imperial fway. The men, whom bold,
but often mifguided, ambition leads to take an active part in revolutions of government, were all on his fide. To fupprefs a
rumour fo important, and big with danger, Nero fent a letter to
Plautus, advifing him " to confult the public tranquillity, and
" withdraw himfelf from the reach of calumny. He had pa-
" trimonial lands in Afia, where he might pafs his youth, re-
" mote from enemies, and undifturbed by faction." Plautus
underftood the hint, and with his wife, Antiftia, and a few
friends, embarked for Afia.

In a fhort time after, Nero, by his rage for new gratifications,
put his life in danger, and drew on himfelf a load of obloquy.
He chofe to bathe at the fountain-head of the Marcian waters (b),
which had been brought to Rome in an aqueduct of ancient
ftructure. By this act of impurity he was thought to have
polluted the facred ftream, and to have profaned the fanctity of
the place. A fit of illnefs, which followed this frolic, left no

doubt in the minds of the populace. The gods, they thought, purfued with vengeance the author of fo vile a facrilege.

XXIII. WE left Corbulo employed in the demolition of Artaxata *(a)*. That city being reduced to afhes, he judged it right, while the confternation of the people was ftill recent, to turn his arms againft Tigranocerta *(b)*. The deftruction of that city would fpread a general panic ; or, if he fuffered it to remain unhurt, the fame of his clemency would add new laurels to the conqueror, He began his march, and, that the Barbarians might not be driven to defpair, preferved every appearance of a pacific difpofition, ftill maintaining difcipline with the ftricteft rigour. He knew, by experience, that he had to do with a people prone to change ; cowards in the hour of danger, but, if occafion offered, prepared, by their natural genius, for a ftroke of perfidy. At the fight of the Roman eagles the Armenians were varioufly affected. They fubmitted with humble fupplications ; they fled from their villages ; they took fhelter in their woods ; and numbers, carrying off all that was dear to them, fought a retreat in their dens and caverns. To thefe different movements the Roman general adapted his meafures ; to the fubmiffive he behaved with mercy ; he ordered the fugitives to be purfued with vigour, but for fuch as lay hid in fubterraneous places he felt no compaffion. Having filled the entrances, and every vent of the caverns, with bufhes and faggots, he fet fire to the heap. The Barbarians perifhed in the flames. His march lay on the frontier of the Mardians *(c)*, a race of freebooters, who lived by depredation, fecure on their hills and mountains from the affaults of the enemy. They poured down from their faftneffes, and infulted the Roman army. Corbulo fent a detachment of the Iberians to lay wafte their country, and thus

thus at the expence of foreign auxiliaries, without fpilling a drop of Roman blood, he punifhed the infolence of the enemy.

XXIV. CORBULO had fuffered no lofs in the field of battle; but his men, exhaufted by continual toil, and forced, for want of grain and vegetables, to fubfift altogether on animal food, began to fink under their fatigue. The heat of the fummer was intenfe; no water to allay their thirft; long and laborious marches ftill remained; and nothing to animate the drooping fpirits of the army but the example of their general, who endured more than even the common foldiers. They reached, at length, a well cultivated country, and carried off a plentiful crop. The Armenians fled for fhelter to two ftrong caftles. One of them was taken by ftorm; the other, after refifting the firft affault, was by a clofe blockade obliged to furrender. The army marched into the territories of the Tauranitians (a). In that country Corbulo narrowly efcaped a fnare laid for his life. A Barbarian, of high diftinction among his people, was found lurking with a concealed dagger near the general's tent. He was inftantly feized, and, being put to the rack, not only confeffed himfelf the author of the plot, but difcovered his accomplices. The villains, who, under a mafk of friendfhip, meditated a foul affaffination, were on examination found guilty of the treachery, and put to death. Ambaffadors arrived foon after from Tigranocerta, with intelligence, that their gates ftood open to receive the Roman army, and the inhabitants were ready to fubmit at difcretion. As an earneft of hofpitality and friendfhip they prefented a golden crown. Corbulo received it with all marks of honour. To conciliate the affections of the people, he did no damage to their city, and left the natives in full poffeffion of their effects.

C c 2

XXV. THE

XXV. THE royal citadel, which was confidered as the ftrong hold of the Armenian kings, did not immediately furrender. A band of ftout and refolute young men threw themfelves into the place, determined to hold out to the laft. They had the fpirit to fally out, but, after a battle under the walls, were driven back within their lines, and, the Romans entering fword in hand, the garrifon laid down their arms. This tide of fuccefs, however rapid, was in a great meafure forwarded by the war, that kept the Parthians engaged in Hyrcania. From the laft-mentioned country ambaffadors had been fent to Rome, foliciting the alliance of the emperor, and, as an inducement, urging, that, in confequence of their rupture with Vologefes, they had made a powerful diverfion in favour of the Roman army : the deputies, on their way back to their own country, had an interview with Corbulo. The general received them with marks of friendfhip, and fearing, if they paffed over the Euphrates, that they might fall in with detached parties of the Parthian army, he ordered them to be efcorted, under a military guard, as far as the margin of the Red-fea *(a)*. From that place, their road was at a diftance from the Parthian frontier.

XXVI. MEANWHILE, Tiridates *(a)*, after a march through the territory of the Medians, was hovering on the extremities of Armenia, intending from that quarter to invade the country. To counteract his motions, Corbulo difpatched Verulanus with the auxiliary forces, and, to fupport him, made a forced march at the head of the legions. Tiridates retired with precipitation, and, in defpair, abandoned the war. The Roman general proceeded with feverity againft all who were known to be difaffected : he carried fire and fword through their country, and took upon himfelf the government of Armenia. The whole kingdom

dom was reduced to subjection, when Tigranes arrived from
Rome, by the appointment of Nero, to assume the regal
diadem.

The new monarch was by birth a Cappadocian, of high nobility in that country, and grandson to king Archilaus *(b)*; but
the length of time which he had passed at Rome in the condition of a hostage broke the vigour of his mind, and sunk him
to the meanest servility. He was not received with the consent
of the nation. A strong party still retained their old affection
for the line of the Arsacides ; but an inveterate antipathy
to the Parthians, on account of their pride and arrogance,
inclined the majority to accept a king from Rome. Corbulo
placed Tigranes on the throne, and assigned him a body-guard,
consisting of a thousand legionary soldiers, three cohorts from
the allied forces, and two squadrons of horse. That his new
kingdom might not prove unwieldy, parts of the country, as
they happened to lie contiguous to the neighbouring princes,
were parcelled out to Pharasmanes *(c)*, to Polemon, Aristobulus,
and Antiochus. Having made these arrangements, Corbulo
marched back into Syria, to take upon him the administration of
that province, vacant by the death of Ummidius Quadratus *(d)*,
the late governor.

XXVII. In the course of the same year *(a)*, Laodicea, a
celebrated city in Asia, was destroyed by an earthquake, and
though Rome in so great a calamity contributed no kind of aid,
it was soon rebuilt, and, by the internal resources of the inhabitants, recovered its former splendour. In Italy, the ancient
city of Puteoli received new privileges, with the title of the Ne-
ronian colony. The veteran soldiers, entitled to their discharge
from the service, were incorporated with the citizens of Tarentum,

and

and Antium ; but the meafure did not increafe population in thofe deferted places. The foldiers rambled back to the provinces, where they had formerly ferved, and, by the habits of a military life, being little inclined to conjugal cares and the education of children, the greateft part mouldered away without iffue. The old fyftem of colonifation was at this time greatly altered. Entire legions were not, as had been the practice, fettled together, with their tribunes, their centurions, and foldiers, in one regular body, forming a fociety of men known to each other, and by fentiments of mutual affection inclined to act with a fpirit of union. A colony, at the time we fpeak of, w s no more than a motley mixture, drawn together from different armies, without a chief at their head, without a principle to unite them, and, in fact, no better than a mere conflux of people from diftant parts of the globe ; a wild heterogeneous multitude, but not a colony.

XXVIII. The election of prætors had been hitherto fubject to the difcretion of the fenate ; but the fpirit of competition breaking out with unufual violence, Nero interpofed his authority. He found three candidates more than ufual. By giving to each the command of a legion *(a)* he allayed the ferment. He alfo made a confiderable addition to the dignity of the fenate by an ordinance, requiring that, in all appeals from an inferior judicature to that affembly, a fum equal *(b)* to what was cuftomary in like cafes before the emperor, fhould be depofited by the appellant, to wait the final determination. Before this rule was eftablifhed, an appeal to the fathers was open to all, without being fubject to cofts, or any kind of penalty. Towards the end of the year, Vibius Secundus, a Roman knight, was accufed by the Moors *(c)* of rapine and extortion, and, being found guilty of the charge, was banifhed out of Italy. For fo mild a fentence

he

he was indebted to the weight and influence of his brother, Vibius Crifpus *(d)*.

XXIX. During the confulfhip of Cæfonius Pætus and Petronius Turpilianus *(a)*, a dreadful calamity befel the army in Britain. Aulus Didius *(b)*, as has been mentioned, aimed at no extenfion of territory, content with maintaining the conqueft already made. Veranius, who fucceeded him, did little more : he made a few incurfions into the country of the Silures *(c)*, and was hindered by death from profecuting the war with vigour. He had been refpected, during his life, for the feverity of his manners ; in his end, the mafk fell off, and his laft will difcovered the low ambition of a fervile flatterer, who, in thofe moments, could offer incenfe to Nero, and add, with vain oftentation, that, if he lived two years, it was his defign to make the whole ifland obedient to the authority of the prince. Paulinus Suetonius fucceeded to the command ; an officer of diftinguifhed merit. To be compared with Corbulo was his ambition. His military talents gave him pretenfions, and the voice of the people, who never leave exalted merit without a rival, raifed him to the higheft eminence. By fubduing the mutinous fpirit of the Britons he hoped to equal the brilliant fuccefs of Corbulo in Armenia. With this view, he refolved to fubdue the ifle of Mona *(d)* ; a place inhabited by a warlike people, and a common refuge for all the difcontented Britons. In order to facilitate his approach to a difficult and deceitful fhore, he ordered a number of flat-bottomed boats to be conftructed. In thefe he wafted over the infantry, while the cavalry, partly by fording over the fhallows, and partly by fwimming their horfes, advanced to gain a footing on the ifland.

XXX. On the oppofite fhore ftood the Britons, clofe embodied,

bodied, and prepared for action.   Women were feen rufhing through the ranks in wild diforder ; their apparel funereal ; their hair loofe to the wind, in their hands flaming torches, and their whole appearance refembling the frantic rage of the furies.   The Druids (a) were ranged in order, with hands uplifted, invoking the gods, and pouring forth horrible imprecations. . The novelty of the fight ftruck the Romans with awe and terror.   They ftood in ftupid amazement, as if their limbs were benumbed, rivetted to one fpot, a mark for the enemy.   The exhortations of the general diffufed new vigour through the ranks, and the men, by mutual reproaches, inflamed each other to deeds of valour.   They felt the difgrace of yielding to a troop of women, and a band of fanatic priefts ; they advanced their ftandards, and rufhed on to the attack with impetuous fury.   The Britons perifhed in the flames, which they themfelves had kindled.   The ifland fell, and a garrifon was eftablifhed to retain it in fub-jection.   The religious groves, dedicated to fuperftition and barbarous rites, were levelled to the ground.   In thofe recelfes, the natives imbrued their altars with the blood of their prifoners, and in the entrails of men explored the will of the gods.   While Suetonius was employed in making his arrangements to fecure the ifland, he received intelligence that Britain had revolted, and that the whole province was up in arms,

XXXI. Prasutacus (a), the late king of the Icenians, in the courfe of a long reign had amaffed confiderable wealth. By his will he left the whole to his two daughters and the em-peror in equal fhares, conceiving, by that ftroke of policy, that he fhould provide at once for the tranquillity of his king-dom and his family.   The event was otherwife.   His dominions were ravaged by the centurions ; the flaves pillaged his houfe, and his effects were feized as lawful plunder.   His wife,

Boadicea,

Boadicea, was difgraced with cruel ftripes; her daughters were
ravifhed, and the moft illuftrious of the Icenians were, by force,
deprived of the poffeffions which had been tranfmitted to them
by their anceftors.   The whole country was confidered as a
legacy bequeathed to the plunderers.   The relations of the deceafed king were reduced to flavery.   Exafperated by thefe acts
of violence, and dreading worfe calamities, the Icenians had recourfe to arms.   The Trinobantians joined in the revolt.   The
neighbouring ftates, not as yet taught to crouch in bondage,
pledged themfelves, in fecret councils, to ftand forth in the caufe
of liberty.   What chiefly fired their indignation was the conduct of the veterans, lately planted as a colony at Camalodunum.
Thefe men treated the Britons with cruelty and oppreffion;
they drove the natives from their habitations, and calling them
by the opprobrious names of flaves and captives, added infult to
their tyranny.   In thefe acts of oppreffion, the veterans were
fupported by the common foldiers; a fet of men, by their habits
of life, trained to licentioufnefs, and, in their turn, expecting
to reap the fame advantages.   The temple built in honour of
Claudius was another caufe of difcontent.   In the eye of the
Britons it feemed the citadel of eternal flavery.   The priefts,
appointed to officiate at the altars, with a pretended zeal for
religion, devoured the whole fubftance of the country.   To
over-run a colony, which lay quite naked and expofed, without
a fingle fortification to defend it, did not appear to the incenfed
and angry Britons an enterprife that threatened either danger
or difficulty.   The fact was, the Roman generals attended to
improvements of tafte and elegance, but neglected the ufeful.
They embellifhed the province, and took no care to defend it.

XXXII.   WHILE the Britons were preparing to throw off the
yoke, the ftatue of victory, erected at Camalodunum, fell from

its bafe, without any apparent caufe, and lay extended on the ground with its face averted, as if the goddefs yielded to the enemies of Rome.   Women in reftlefs ecftafy rufhed among the people, and with frantic fcreams denounced impending ruin. In the council-chamber of the Romans (a) hideous clamours were heard in a foreign accent; favage howlings filled the theatre, and near the mouth of the Thames the image of a colony (b) in ruins was feen in the tranfparent water; the fea was purpled with blood, and, at the tide of ebb, the figures of human bodies were traced on the fand.   By thefe appearances the Romans were funk in defpair, while the Britons anticipated a glorious victory.   Suetonius, in the mean time, was detained in the ifle of Mona.   In this alarming crifis, the veterans fent to Catus Decianus, the procurator of the province, for a rein- forcement.   Two hundred men, and thofe not completely armed, were all that officer could fpare.   The colony had but a handful of foldiers.   Their temple was ftrongly fortified, and there they hoped to make a ftand.   But even for the defence of that place no meafures were concerted.   Secret enemies mixed in all their deliberations.   No foffe was made; no palifade thrown up; nor were the women, and fuch as were difabled by age or in- firmity, fent out of the garrifon.   Unguarded and unprepared, they were taken by furprife, and, in the moment of profound peace, overpowered by the Barbarians in one general affault. The colony was laid wafte with fire and fword.

The temple held out, but, after a fiege of two days, was taken by ftorm. Petilius Cerealis, who commanded the ninth legion, marched to the relief of the place.   The Britons, flufhed with fuccefs, advanced to give him battle.   The legion was put to the rout, and the infantry cut to pieces.   Cerealis efcaped with the cavalry to his entrenchments.   Catus Decianus, the pro-

curator

curator of the province, alarmed at the scene of carnage which
he beheld on every side, and further dreading the indignation
of a people, whom by rapine and oppression he had driven to
despair, betook himself to flight, and crossed over into Gaul.

XXXIII. Suetonius, undismayed by this disaster, marched
through the heart of the country as far as London *(a)*; a place
not dignified with the name of a colony, but the chief residence
of merchants, and the great mart of trade and commerce. At
that place he meant to fix the seat of war; but reflecting on the
scanty numbers of his little army, and the fatal rashness of Cerealis, he resolved to quit that station, and, by giving up one
post, secure the rest of the province. Neither supplications, nor
the tears of the inhabitants could induce him to change his plan.
The signal for the march was given. All who chose to follow
his banners were taken under his protection. Of all who, on
account of their advanced age, the weakness of their sex, or the
attractions of the situation, thought proper to remain behind, not
one escaped the rage of the Barbarians. The inhabitants of
Verulamium *(b)*, a municipal town, were in like manner put to
the sword. The genius of a savage people leads them always in
quest of plunder ; and, accordingly, the Britons left behind them
all places of strength. Wherever they expected feeble resistance,
and considerable booty, there they were sure to attack with the
fiercest rage. Military skill was not the talent of Barbarians.
The number massacred in the places which have been mentioned, amounted to no less than seventy thousand, all citizens
or allies of Rome. To make prisoners, and reserve them for
slavery, or to exchange them, was not in the idea of a people,
who despised all the laws of war. The halter and the gibbet,
slaughter and desolation, fire and sword, were the marks of savage valour. Aware that vengeance would overtake them, they

D d 2

were

were refolved to make fure of their revenge, and glut themfelves with the blood of their enemies.

XXXIV. The fourteenth legion, with the veterans of the twentieth, and the auxiliaries from the adjacent ftations, having joined Suetonius, his army amounted to little lefs than ten thou-fand men. Thus reinforced, he refolved, without lofs of time, to bring on a decifive action. For this purpofe he chofe a fpot encircled with woods, narrow at the entrance, and fheltered in the rear by a thick foreft. In that fituation he had no fear of an ambufcade. The enemy, he knew, had no approach but in front. An open plain lay before him. He drew up his men in the following order: the legions in clofe array formed the centre; the light armed troops were ftationed at hand to ferve as occafion might require: the cavalry took poft in the wings. The Britons brought into the field an incredible multitude. They formed no regular line of battle. Detached parties and loofe battalions difplayed their numbers, in frantic tranfport bounding with exultation, and fo fure of victory, that they placed their wives in waggons at the extremity of the plain, where they might furvey the fcene of action, and behold the wonders of Britifh valour.

XXXV. Boadicea (a), in a warlike car, with her two daughters before her, drove through the ranks. She harangued the different nations in their turn: " This," fhe faid, " is not " the firft time that the Britons have been led to battle by a " woman. But now fhe did not come to boaft the pride of a " long line of anceftry, nor even to recover her kingdom and " the plundered wealth of her family. She took the field, like " the meaneft among them, to affert the caufe of public liberty, " and to feek revenge for her body fcarred with ignominious
" ftripes,

B O O K
XIV.
⏜
A. U. C.
814
A. D.
61.

" ftripes, and her two daughters infamoufly ravifhed. From the
" pride and arrogance of the Romans nothing is facred ; all are
" fubject to violation ; the old endure the fcourge, and the vir-
" gins are deflowered. But the vindictive gods are now at
" hand. A Roman legion dared to face the warlike Britons :
" with their lives they paid for their rafhnefs ; thofe who fur-
" vived the carnage of that day, lie poorly hid behind their en-
" trenchments, meditating nothing but how to fave themfelves
" by an ignominious flight. From the din of preparation, and
" the fhouts of the Britifh army, the Romans, even now, fhrink
" back with terror. What will be their cafe when the affault
" begins? Look round, and view your numbers. Behold the
" proud difplay of warlike fpirits, and confider the motives for
" which we draw the avenging fword. On this fpot we muft
" either conquer, or die with glory. There is no alternative.
" Though a woman, my refolution is fixed : the men, if they
" pleafe, may furvive with infamy, and live in bondage."

XXXVI. SUETONIUS, in a moment of fuch importance, did
not remain filent. He expected every thing from the valour
of his men, and yet urged every topic that could infpire and
animate them to the attack. " Defpife," he faid, " the favage
" uproar, the yells and fhouts of undifciplined Barbarians. In
" that mixed multitude, the women out-number the men. Void
" of fpirit, unprovided with arms, they are not foldiers who come
" to offer battle ; they are daftards, runaways, the refufe of your
" fwords, who have often fled before you, and will again betake
" themfelves to flight when they fee the conqueror flaming in
" the ranks of war. In all engagements it is the valour of a
" few that turns the fortune of the day. It will be your im-
" mortal glory, that with a fcanty number you can equal the
" exploits of a great and powerful army. Keep your ranks ;

5

" difcharge

" difcharge your javelins; rufh forward to a clofe attack; bear
" down all with your bucklers, and hew a paffage with your
" fwords.   Purfue the vanquifhed, and never think of fpoil
" and plunder.   Conquer, and victory gives you every thing."
This fpeech was received with warlike acclamations.   The foldiers burned with impatience for the onfet, the veterans bran-
difhed their javelins, and the ranks difplayed fuch an intrepid
countenance, that Suetonius, anticipating the victory, gave the
fignal for the charge.

XXXVII.   The engagement began.   The Roman legion
prefented a clofe embodied line.   The narrow defile gave them
the fhelter of a rampart.   The Britons advanced with ferocity,
and difcharged their darts at random.   In that inftant, the Romans rufhed forward in the form of a wedge.   The auxiliaries
followed with equal ardour.   The cavalry, at the fame time,
bore down upon the enemy, and, with their pikes, overpowered all who dared to make a ftand.   The Britons betook themfelves to flight, but their waggons in the rear obftructed their
paffage.   A dreadful flaughter followed.   Neither fex nor age
was fpared.   The cattle, falling in one promifcuous carnage,
added to the heaps of flain.   The glory of the day was equal to
the moft fplendid victory of ancient times.   According to fome
writers, not lefs than eighty thoufand Britons were put to the
fword.   The Romans loft about four hundred men, and the
wounded did not exceed that number.   Boadicea, by a dofe of
poifon, put a period to her life.   Pænius Pofthumus, præfect in
the camp (a) of the fecond legion, as foon as he heard of the
brave exploits of the fourteenth and twentieth legions, felt the
difgrace of having, in difobedience to the orders of his general,
robbed the foldiers under his command of their fhare in fo complete

plete a victory. Stung with remorse, he fell upon his sword, and expired on the spot.

BOOK XIV.
A. U. C. 814.
A. D. 61.

XXXVIII. SUETONIUS called in all his forces, and, having ordered them to pitch their tents, kept the field in readiness for new emergencies, intending not to close the campaign till he put an end to the war. By directions from the emperor a reinforcement of two thousand legionary soldiers, eight auxiliary cohorts *(a)*, and a thousand horse, arrived from Germany. By this accession of strength the ninth legion was completed. The cohorts and cavalry were sent into new quarters, and the country round, wherever the people had declared open hostility, or were suspected of treachery, was laid waste with fire and sword. Famine was the evil that chiefly distressed the enemy: employed in warlike preparations, they had neglected the cultivation of their lands, depending altogether on the success of their arms, and the booty which they hoped to seize from the Romans. Fierce and determined in the cause of liberty, they were rendered still more obstinate by the misunderstanding that subsisted between the Roman generals. Julius Classicianus had succeeded to the post vacant by the sudden flight of Catus Decianus. Being at variance with Suetonius, he did not scruple to sacrifice the public good to private animosity. He spread a report, that another commander in chief might be soon expected, and in him the Britons would find a man, who would bring with him neither ill will to the natives, nor the pride of victory. The vanquished would, by consequence, meet with moderation and humanity. Classicianus did not stop here: in his dispatches to Rome, he pressed the necessity of recalling Suetonius. The war would, otherwise, never be brought to a conclusion by an officer, who owed all his disasters to his own want of conduct, and his success to the good fortune of the empire.

XXXIX. In

XXXIX. In confequence of thefe complaints, Polycletus, one of the emperor's freedmen, was fent from Rome to inquire into the ftate of Britain. The weight and authority of fuch a mef-fenger, Nero flattered himfelf, would produce a reconciliation between the hoftile generals, and difpofe the Britons to a more pacific temper. Polycletus fet out with a large retinue, and, on his journey through Italy and Gaul, made his grandeur a burthen to the people. On his arrival in Britain he overawed the Roman foldiers; but his magnificent airs and affumed im-portance met with nothing from the Britons but contempt and derifion. Notwithftanding the misfortunes of the natives, the flame of liberty was not extinguifhed. The exorbitant power of a manumitted flave was a novelty which thofe ferocious iflanders could not digeft. They faw an army that fought with valour, and a general who led them on to victory; but both were ob-liged to wait the nod of a wretched bondfman. In the report made by this man the ftate of affairs was fuch as gave no jealoufy to Nero. Suetonius, therefore, was continued in his govern-ment. It happened, in a fhort time afterwards, that a few fhips were wrecked on the coaft, and all on board perifhed in the waves. This was confidered as a calamity of war, and, on that account, Suetonius was recalled. Petronius Turpilianus, whofe confulfhip had juft then expired, fucceeded to the command. Under him a languid ftate of tranquillity followed. The ge-neral faw the paffive difpofition of the Britons, and not to pro-voke hoftilities was the rule of his conduct. He remained in-active, content to decorate his want of enterprife with the name of peace.

XL. This year was remarkable for two atrocious crimes; one, the act of a fenator, and the other perpetrated by the daring fpirit of a flave. Domitius Balbus, of prætorian rank, was, at that

time,

time, far advanced in years. His wealth, and his want of
iffue, made him obnoxious to the arts of ill-defigning men. His
relation, Valerius Fabianus, a man high in rank, and likely to
obtain the firft honours of the ftate, forged his will. To give colour
to the fraud, he drew into his plot Vincius Rufinus and Terentius Lentinus, two Roman knights, who chofe to act in concert
with Antonius Primus *(a)* and Afinius Marcellus. Antonius was
a prompt and daring fpirit, ready for any mifchief. Marcellus
was grandfon to the renowned Afinius Pollio: his character was,
till that time, without a ftain; but his favourite maxim was,
that poverty *(b)* is the worft of evils. In the prefence of thofe
confpirators, and other witneffes of inferior note, Fabianus
fealed the will. The fraud being brought to light before the
fenate, the author of it, with three of his accomplices, namely,
Antonius, Rufinus, and Terentius, were condemned to fuffer
the penalties of the Cornelian law *(c)*. Marcellus found in
the favour of the prince, and the dignity of his anceftors, a
powerful protection. He was faved from punifhment, not from
infamy.

XLI. The fame day was fatal to two others of rank and diftinction. Pompeius Ælianus, a young man who had already
paffed with honour through the office of quæftor, was charged
as an acceffary in the guilt of Fabianus. He was banifhed, not
only from Italy, but from Spain, the place of his birth. Valerius Ponticus met with equal feverity. The crime alleged againft
him was, that, with a defign to elude the jurifdiction of the
præfect of Rome, he had accufed feveral delinquents before the
prætor; intending, in the firft inftance, under colour of a legal
procefs, and afterwards, by abandoning the profecution, to defeat
the ends of juftice. The fathers added a claufe to their decree,
whereby all perfons concerned either in procuring or conducting

for hire a collufive action, were to be treated as public prevari-
cators *(a)*, and to fuffer the pains and penalties inflicted by the
law on fuch as ftood convicted of a falfe and calumnious accufation.

XLII. The fecond daring crime that marked the year, as
mentioned above, was the act of a flave. This man murdered
his mafter, Pedanius Secundus, at that time præfect of the city.
His motive for this defperate act was either becaufe his liberty,
after a bargain made *(a)*, was ftill withheld, or being enamoured
of a foreign pathic, he could not endure his mafter as his rival.
Every flave in the family where the murder was committed,
was by ancient ufage fubject to capital punifhment; but the populace, touched with compaffion for fo many innocent men, oppofed the execution with rage and tumult little fhort of a feditious infurrection. In the fenate many of the fathers embraced
the popular fide, but the majority declared for the rigour of the
law without innovation. In the debate on this occafion *(b)*,
Caius Caffius fpoke to the following effect:

XLIII. " I have been often prefent, confcript fathers, when
" motions have been made in this affembly for new decrees,
" repugnant of the laws in being, and utterly fubverfive of all
" ancient eftablifhments. To thofe meafures I made no oppo-
" fition, though well convinced, that the regulations made by
" our anceftors were the beft, the wifeft, the moft conducive
" to the public good. To change that fyftem is to change for
" the worfe. This has ever been my fettled opinion; but I
" forbore to take a part in your debates, that I might not be
" thought bigoted either to antiquity, or to my own way of
" thinking. I had another reafon for my conduct. The weight
" and influence which I flattered myfelf I had acquired in this
                                                  " affembly,

" affembly, might, by frequently troubling you, lofe its effect.
" I determined, therefore, to referve myfelf for fome important
" conjuncture, when my feeble voice might be of ufe. That
" conjuncture occurs this very day. A man of confular rank,
" without a friend to affift him, without any one perfon to op-
" pofe the ruffian's blow, no notice given, no difcovery made,
" has been in his own houfe barbaroufly murdered. The law
" which dooms every flave under the roof to execution, is ftill
" in force. Repeal that law, and, if you will, let this horrible
" deed pafs with impunity ; but when you have done it, which
" of us can think himfelf fafe ? Who can depend on his rank
" or dignity, when the firft magiftrate of your city dies under
" the affaffin's ftroke ? Who can hope to live in fecurity amongft
" his flaves, when fo large a number as four hundred could not
" defend Pedanius Secundus ? Will our domeftics affift us in
" the hour of need, when we fee, in the inftance before us, that
" neither their own danger nor the terrors of the law could
" induce them to protect their mafter ? Will it be faid that the
" murderer ftruck his blow to revenge a perfonal injury ? What
" was the injury ? The paternal eftate of a ruffian, perhaps, was
" in danger ; or the foreign pathic, whom they were going to
" ravifh from him, defcended to him from his anceftors. If
" that be fo, the deed was lawful, and, by confequence, we,
" confcript fathers, ought to pronounce it juftifiable homicide.

XLIV. " But let me afk you ; are we, at this time of day,
" to fupport by argument, what has been long fettled by the
" wifdom of ages ? Suppofe the point in difpute were a new
" queftion, to be now decided for the firft time : can we ima-
" gine that a ruffian, who had formed a black defign to murder
" his mafter, kept the whole fo clofely locked up in his breaft,
" that, in the agitations of a guilty mind, nothing efcaped from

E e 2
" him ?

" him? Not a menace, not fo much as a rafh word to give the
" alarm? Nothing, we are told, of this fort happened; we are
" to believe that the affaffin brooded over his horrible purpofe
" in fullen filence; that he prepared his dagger unfeen by every
" eye, and that his fellow-flaves knew nothing of it. Be it fo:
" did he pafs unfeen through the train of attendants that guarded
" the bed-chamber? Did he open the door unperceived by all?
" Did he enter with a light, and ftrike the mortal blow, without
" the knowledge of any perfon whatever?

" Between the firft defign, and the final execution of evil deeds,
" fymptoms of guilt are often feen. If our flaves are faithful,
" if they give timely intelligence, we may live fecure in our
" houfes; or if we muft fall by the murderer's dagger, it is a
" fatisfaction to know, that juftice will overtake the guilty.
" The mind and temper of the flave, though born on the
" mafter's eftate, or even in his houfe, imbibing with his firft
" milk affection and gratitude to the family, were always fuf-
" pected by our anceftors. At prefent, we have in our fervice
" whole nations of flaves; the fcum of mankind, collected from
" all quarters of the globe; a race of men, who bring with them
" foreign rites, and the religion of their country, or, probably,
" no religion at all. In fuch a conflux, if the laws are filent,
" what protection remains for the mafter? But, it is faid, the
" innocent may fuffer with the guilty. To this I anfwer, when
" an army, feized with a general panic, turns its back on the
" enemy, and, to reftore military difcipline, the men are drawn
" out and decimated; what diftinction is then made between
" the gallant foldier and the coward, who fled from his poft? In
" political juftice there is often fomething not ftrictly right:
" but partial evil is counterbalanced by the good of the
" whole."

XLV. To

XLV. To this reasoning no reply was made, and yet a murmur of disapprobation ran through the assembly. The number doomed to suffer, their age, their sex, and the undoubted innocence of the greatest part, awakened sentiments of compassion; but the majority was for letting the law *(a)* take its course. Their opinion prevailed. The popular cry was still for mercy. The rabble rose in a tumultuous body, and with stones and firebrands stopped the execution. To quell their fury, Nero issued a proclamation, and by his order the streets were lined with soldiers under arms. The unhappy victims suffered death. Cingonius Varro moved, that even the freedmen, who were actually in the house at the time of the murder, should, by a decree of the senate, be banished out of Italy. To this Nero answered, that, since mercy was not allowed to mitigate the system of ancient laws, to increase their rigour by new pains and penalties, would be an act of cruelty.

XLVI. During the same consulship, Tarquitius Priscus, at the suit of the people of Bithynia, was convicted of extortion, and condemned to make restitution. The senate remembered the violence of this man in the prosecution against Statilius Taurus *(a)*, his own proconsul in Africa, and now retaliated with a vindictive spirit. The people in both the Gauls were reviewed and rated by Quintus Volusius, Sextius Africanus, and Trebellius Maximus. The two former, elate with family-pride, passed their time in mutual jealousy, thwarting each other, and struggling for pre-eminence. They looked down with contempt on Trebellius; but their petty animosities served only to degrade themselves, and give to their colleague a decided superiority.

XLVII. In the course of this year died Memmius Regulus, distinguished by his virtues, and his unblemished character.

Admired!

Admired for his conftancy and unfhaken firmnefs, he rofe to as high a pitch of credit and authority, as can be attained under a government, where the grandeur of the prince throws a fhade over the merit of every private citizen. As a proof of this, we have the following anecdote. Nero being confined with a fit of illnefs, the tribe of fycophants, fluttering about his perfon, poured forth the anguifh of their hearts, and, " if any thing happened " to the emperor, the day," they faid, " that put a period to his " life, would be the laft of the empire." " No," replied the prince, " a pillar of the ftate will ftill remain." The courtiers ftood at gaze, wondering who that perfon could be; Nero told them, " Memmius Regulus is the man." Strange as it may feem, Regulus furvived that opinion of his virtue. In his love of retirement he found a retreat from danger. A man, whofe family had lately rifen to honours, gave no alarm; and his fortune raifed no envy. It was in the fame year that Nero dedicated a gymnafium *(a)*, or public fchool for athletic exercifes, and, with the obliging facility of Greek manners, gave orders that the fenators and Roman knights, without any expence on their part, fhould be provided with oil, to prepare their limbs for that elegant exhibition.

XLVIII. During the confulfhip of Publius Marius and Lucius Afinius, a profecution was fet on foot againft Antiftius, then invefted with the office of prætor. The conduct of this man, when tribune of the people *(a)*, has been already mentioned. The charge againft him was, that being the author of farcaftic verfes againft the emperor, he produced his poem to a large company at the table of Oftorius Scapula. For this libel he was arraigned on the law of majefty. The caufe was conducted by Coffutianus Capito *(b)*, who had been lately raifed, by the intereft of Tigellinus, his father-in-law, to the fenatorian order. The

                                                                    law

law of majesty had fallen into disuse, and was now revived, for the first time in the reign of Nero, not, as was imagined, to make Antistius feel its severity, but, in fact, to give the emperor an opportunity, after judgment of death was passed, to interpose his tribunitian *(c)* authority, and, by preventing the execution, add new lustre to his name. Ostorius Scapula was called as a witness. He remembered nothing of the verses in question. The evidence of others was believed, and, thereupon, Junius Marcellus, consul elect, moved, that the criminal, divested in the first instance of his prætorship, should suffer death according to the laws in force *(d)*, and the practice under former emperors. The rest of the senate concurring in the same opinion, Pætus Thrasea rose to oppose the motion. He began with honourable mention of the prince, nor did he take upon him to defend the conduct of Antistius. On the contrary, he blamed the licentious spirit of the man in terms of severity ; but under a virtuous emperor, and, in a senate left to act with independance, the question, he said, was not the magnitude of the crime, nor what punishment the rigour of the law would warrant. The executioner, the gibbet, and the halter were, for some time, unknown at Rome. Other pains and penalties were provided by law, and those might be inflicted, without branding the judges with cruelty, and the age with infamy. Antistius may be condemned to banishment ; his effects may be confiscated. Let him pass the remainder of his days in one of the islands. His life, in that situation, will be protracted misery. He will there continue to languish in exile, a burthen to himself, yet a living monument of the equity and moderation of the times.

XLIX. The firmness with which Thrasea delivered his sentiments inspired the senate with the same ardour. The consul put the question, and the fathers divided *(a)*. The majority voted with Thrasea. The dissentients were but a small number.

Amongst

Amongſt them was Aulus Vitellius *(b)*, of all the flattering crew, the moſt corrupt and ſervile; fluent in invective; eager to attack the moſt eminent characters, and ever ſure, with the confuſion of a little mind, to ſhrink from the reply. He heard his adverſary with ſilent patience. The conſuls, however, did not preſume to cloſe the buſineſs by a decree in form: they choſe to make their report to the emperor, and wait his pleaſure. Nero, for ſome time, balanced between ſhame and reſentment. At length, his anſwer was, " That Antiſtius, without provocation, " or any cauſe of complaint, had diſtilled the venom of his pen " on the name and character of his ſovereign. The matter had " been referred to the ſenate, and juſtice required a puniſhment " adequate to the crime. Nevertheleſs, as it had been from the " firſt his reſolution to mitigate a rigorous ſentence, he would " not now controul the moderation of the fathers. They might " determine, as to their wiſdom ſhould ſeem meet. They were " even at liberty to acquit the criminal altogether." From this anſwer it was evident, that the conduct of the ſenate had given offence at court. The conſuls, however, were not inclined to alter their report. Thraſea maintained his former opinion, and all who had voted with him followed his example. Some were unwilling, by a change of ſentiment, to expoſe the prince to the popular odium; others thought themſelves ſafe in a large majority; and Thraſea, with his uſual elevation of mind, would not recede from the dignity of his character.

1. On a charge of the ſame complexion as the former, Fabricius Veiento *(a)* was involved in ſimilar danger. In certain writings, which he called the LAST WILLS of perſons deceaſed, he had inſerted ſtrokes of ſatire reflecting on ſeveral members of the ſenate, and others of the ſacerdotal order. Talius Geminus was the proſecutor. He added another allegation, charging, that the criminal

ninal abufed his credit at court, and difpofed of the favours of
the prince, and the honours of the ftate, by bargain and fale, for
his own private emolument. This laft article roufed the refentment of Nero; he removed the caufe to his own tribunal. Veiento
was banifhed out of Italy. His books were condemned to the
flames, but eagerly fought, and univerfally read. Men perufed
with avidity what was procured with danger. When no longer
prohibited, the work funk into oblivion.

LI. MEANWHILE, the public grievances went on with increafing violence, and the means of redrefs diminifhed every day.
Burrhus died at this time, whether in the courfe of nature, or by
poifon, cannot now be known. The general opinion afcribed
his death to a fit of illnefs. He was feized with a diforder in the
throat, and the inflammation in the glands fwelling to a prodigious fize, fuffocation followed. There was, however, a current
report, that, under a pretence of adminiftering a proper gargle,
poifon was mixed in the medicine, by order of Nero, and that
Burrhus, having difcovered the villany, as foon as he perceived
the prince entering his room, turned from him with averfion,
and to all enquiries fhortly anfwered, "I am well at prefent."
He died univerfally lamented. His virtues were long remembered, and long regretted. Nor was the public grief alleviated
by the two perfons, who fucceeded to his employments, namely
Fenius Rufus and Sofonius Tigellinus (a), the former a man of
undoubted innocence, but the innocence that proceeds from
want of fpirit. Tigellinus ftood diftinguifhed by a life of debauchery, and the infamy of his character. Rufus owed his
advancement to the voice of the people, who were pleafed with
his upright management of the public ftores. Tigellinus was a
favourite of the emperor. The early vices of the man recommended him to notice. The command of the prætorian guards,

which had been entrusted to Burrhus only, was granted to those two by a joint commission. The impression, which they had given of their characters, was confirmed by their conduct in office. Tigellinus gained an absolute ascendant over the mind of a debauched and profligate emperor. In all scenes of revelry he was a constant companion. Rufus obtained the good-will of the soldiers and the people, but his merit ruined him with the prince.

LII. By the death of Burrhus, Seneca lost the chief support of his power. The friend of upright measures was snatched away, and virtue could no longer make head against the corruption of a court, governed altogether by the vile and profligate. By that set of men Seneca was undermined. They blackened his character, and loaded him with various imputations. "His wealth
" was exorbitant, above the condition of a private citizen ; and
" yet his unappeasable avarice went on without intermission,
" every day grasping at more. His rage for popularity was no
" less violent. He courted the affections of the people, and by
" the grandeur of his villas, and the beauty of his gardens, hoped
" to vie with imperial splendour. In matters of taste and genius
" he allows no rival. He claims the whole province of eloquence
" as his own ; and since Nero shewed his taste for poetry, from
" that moment Seneca began to court the muse (a), and he too
" has his copy of verses.

" To the other diversions of the prince he is an avowed, an
" open enemy. The skill of the charioteer provokes his raillery ;
" he sneers at the management of horses ; and the melody of the
" prince's voice is a subject for his wit and ridicule. In all this
" what is his drift ? Why truly, that, in the whole extent of the
" empire, there should be nothing worthy of praise but what
" flows from his superior talents. But Nero is no longer the pu-
" pil

" pil of this subtle philosopher ; he has attained the prime season
" of manhood, and may now discard his tutor. He has before
" his eyes the brightest model for his conduct, the example of
" his own illustrious ancestors."

LIII. These insidious arts were not unknown to Seneca. There
were still at court a few in the interests of virtue, and from such
men he received intelligence of all that passed. Finding that the
prince had withdrawn his friendship, and no longer admitted him
to his conversation, he demanded an audience, and spoke to the
following effect : " It is now, Cæsar, the fourteenth year, since
" I was placed near your person ; of your reign it is the eighth.
" In that space of time you have lavished upon me both wealth
" and honours, with so liberal an hand, that to complete my
" happiness nothing now is necessary but moderation and con-
" tentment. In the humble request, which I presume to make,
" I shall take the liberty to cite a few examples, far, indeed, above
" my condition, but worthy of you. Augustus, your illustrious
" ancestor, permitted Marcus Agrippa to retire to Mitylene (a) ;
" he allowed Mæcenas to live almost a stranger in Rome, and in
" the heart of the city (b) to dwell as it were in solitude. The
" former of those illustrious men had been the companion of his
" wars ; the latter supported the weight of his administration :
" both, it is true, received ample rewards, but rewards fairly
" earned by great and eminent services. For myself, if you ex-
" cept some attainments in literature, the fruit of studies pursued
" in the shade of retirement, what merit can I assume ? My feeble
" talents are supposed to have seasoned your mind with the first
" tincture of letters, and that honour is beyond all recompense.

  " But your liberality knows no bounds. You have loaded me
" with favours, and with riches. When I reflect on your gene-
F f 2
" rosity,

" rofity, I fay to myfelf, Shall a man of my level, without family
" pretenfions, the fon of a fimple knight, born in a diftant pro-
" vince (c), prefume to rank with the grandees of Rome? My
" name, the name of a new man, figures among thofe who boaft
" a long and fplendid line of anceftors.   Where is now the mind,
" which long fince knew, that to be content with little is true happi-
" nefs? The philofopher is employed in laying out gardens (d),
" and improving pleafure-grounds.   He delights in the extent of
" ample villas; he enjoys a large rent-roll, and has fums of
" money (e) laid out at intereft.   I have but one apology; your
" munificence was a command, and it was not for me to
" refift.

LIV. " But the meafure of generofity on your part, and fub-
" miffion on mine, is now complete. What a prince could give, you
" have beftowed: what a friend could take, I have received. More
" will only ferve to irritate envy, and inflame the malice of my
" enemies.   You indeed tower above the paffions of ill defigning
" men; I am open to their attacks; I ftand in need of protection.
" In a campaign, or on a march, if I found myfelf fatigued and
" worn out with toil, I fhould not hefitate to fue for fome indul-
" gence.   Life is a ftate of warfare; it is a long campaign, in
" which a man in years, finking under a load of cares, and even
" by his riches made obnoxious, may crave leave to retire.   I am
" willing to refign my wealth: let the auditors of the imperial
" revenue take the account, and let the whole return to its foun-
" tain-head.   By this act of felf-denial I fhall not be reduced to
" poverty; I fhall part with that fuperfluity which glitters in
" the eyes of my enemies; and for the reft, the time, which is
" fpent in the improving of gardens, and the embellifhing of
" villas, I fhall transfer to myfelf, and for the future lay it out in
" the cultivation of my mind.   You are in the vigour of your
                                        " days;

"days; a long train of years lies before you. In full poffeffion of
"the fovereign power you have learned the art of reigning. Old
"age may be permitted to feek repofe. It will, hereafter, be
"your glory, that you knew how to choofe men of moderation,
"who could defcend from the fummit of fortune, to dwell with
"peace and humble content in the vale of life."

LV. Nero replied as follows: "If I give an immediate anfwer
"to a fpeech of prepared eloquence, the power of doing it I derive
"from you. The faculty of fpeaking, not only when the matter
"has been premeditated, but alfo on fudden occafions, I poffefs
"(if I do poffefs it) by your care and inftruction. Auguftus, it
"is true, releafed Agrippa and Mæcenas from the fatigue of bufi-
"nefs; but he did it, at a time, when his authority was eftablifhed
"on the firmeft bafis, and his own experience was equal to the
"cares of government. He did not, however, refume the grants
"which he had made. What thofe eminent citizens obtained,
"they deferved in war and civil commotions; for in thofe bufy
"fcenes Auguftus paffed his youth. Had my lot been the fame,
"your fword would not have been idle. What the conjuncture
"demanded, you fupplied; you formed my mind to fcience, and
"you affifted me with your wifdom and advice. The advan-
"tages which I derive from you are not of a perifhable nature;
"they will cleave to me through life. As to the favours which
"it was in my power to grant, fuch as houfes, gardens, and fums
"of money, they are precarious gifts, fubject to accidents and
"the caprice of fortune. Prefents of that kind may feem magni-
"ficent; but they fall fhort of what I have beftowed on others,
"who had neither your accomplifhments, nor your merit. I
"could mention freedmen, who flourifh in higher fplendour;
"but I blufh to name them. I blufh, that you, who are the firft

"in

" in my efteem, fhould net, at the fame time, be the firft man
" in my dominions.

LVI. " I GRANT that you are advanced in years, but the vi-
" gour of your conftitution is ftill unbroken. You are equal to
" bufinefs, and the fruit of your labours you can ftill enjoy. My
" reign is but juft begun; and what has been my liberality? Vi-
" tellius was three times conful (*a*), and Claudius was his friend:
" are you to be deemed inferior to the former? and muft I, in
" point of munificence, yield to the latter? Volufius (*b*), by a
" long life of parfimony, raifed an immoderate fortune; and fhall
" not my generofity put you on a level with a man of that de-
" fcription? The impetuofity of youth may hurry me beyond the
" bounds of prudence: it will then be yours to recal my wander-
" ing fteps, and lead me to the paths of honour. You helped to
" form my youthful underftanding, and to what you polifhed
" you ftill can give life and energy. If you refign your wealth,
" can you fuppofe that your moderation will be deemed the
" caufe? If you defert your prince, will your love of quiet be
" thought the motive? Far otherwife: my avarice will be ar-
" raigned; my cruelty will be the general topic. The praife,
" indeed, of wifdom may purfue you in your retreat; but will it
" be generous to build your fame on the difgrace and ruin of
" your friend?"

To this flattering fpeech Nero added fond embraces, and all the
external marks of affection. Inclined by nature to difguife his
fentiments, and by habit exercifed in the arts of diffimulation,
he knew how to hide under the furface of friendfhip the fecret
malice of his heart. Seneca anfwered in a fubmiffive tone. He
returned his beft thanks, the ufual clofe of every conference in
the

the cabinet of the prince. He refolved, however, to change his mode of living: he refigned his power, and retained no appearance of his former fplendour; the crowd of vifitors no longer frequented his houfe; he difmiffed his train of followers, and but rarely appeared abroad, willing to be confidered as an infirm old man, obliged to take care of his health at home, or a philofopher, abforbed in abftract fpeculations.

LVII. SENECA's influence was now in its wane. To ruin the credit of Fenius Rufus was the next object. In this his enemies found no difficulty. The crime of being attached to Agrippina was fufficient. Tigellinus, in the mean time, rofe to the higheft pitch of credit and influence at court. Poffeffing a genius for every mifchief, and having no other talents, he refolved to draw the prince into a confederacy in guilt. Congenial vices, he had no doubt, would render him ftill more dear to his mafter. With this view he began to watch the paffions of Nero, and to explore the fecrets of his heart. He found that the two perfons whom the emperor dreaded moft were Plautus (a) and Sylla; both lately removed out of Italy; the former into Afia, and the latter to Narbon Gaul. Tigellinus began his fecret hoftilities againft them both. He talked of their rank and high defcent. Plautus, he obferved, was not far diftant from the armies in the eaft; and Sylla was near the legions in Germany. For himfelf, he had not, like Burrhus, the art of managing parties for his own private advantage. The welfare of his fovereign was his only object. At Rome, he could enfure the fafety of the prince. If plots were formed, by vigilance and activity they might be crufhed in the bud. But for diftant provinces who could anfwer? The name of Sylla, rendered famous by the celebrated dictator of that name, would roufe and animate the people of Gaul. In Afia the grandfon of Drufus (b) would

have

have a number of adherents, and might, by confequence, excite the nations to a revolt. Sylla, indeed, was indigent and diftreffed: but his very poverty would be a fource of courage, a motive for vigorous enterprife; and though he feemed to languifh in repofe and indolence, his love of eafe was a cloak to cover his ambition. He waited for an opportunity to avow his dark defigns.

Plautus, on the other hand, poffeffed immoderate wealth. To lead a fluggifh life was not in his temper or his character: he did not even affect it. He copied, with emulation, the manners of the ancient Romans, and to his aufterity added the maxims of the ftoic fect: a fect at all times fond of public commotions, proud, fierce, and turbulent. By this reafoning Nero was convinced. No delay intervened. Affaffins were difpatched. On the fixth day they landed at Marfeilles, where, without notice, or fo much as a hint to alarm him, Sylla was taken by furprife at his own table, and inftantly murdered. His head was conveyed to Rome. Nero amufed himfelf with the fight; he faw that the hairs were grown grey before their time, and in that circumftance found a fubject for mirth and brutal raillery.

LVIII. The murder of Plautus could not be executed with equal fecrecy. His friends were numerous, and his life was valuable to many. The place lay remote; a voyage was to be performed, and, in the mean time, the plot began to tranfpire. A report prevailed at Rome, that Plautus had put himfelf under the protection of Corbulo, who was then at the head of powerful armies; a man, in that evil period, when merit and innocence were capital crimes, likely to fall a devoted victim. The rumour further added, that in favour of Plautus all Afia was up in arms, and that the ruffians fent from Rome had either

failed

failed in their refolution, or, not finding themfelves in force, had
gone over to the oppofite party. The whole ftory was without
foundation ; but, according to cuftom, credulity fwallowed it, and
idle men added from their own invention. Plautus, in the mean
time, received intelligence of the defign againft his life by one
of his freedmen, who, having the advantage of a fair wind, got
the ftart of the centurions difpatched by Nero. This faithful
fervant was fent by Lucius Antiftius, his mafter's father-in-law,
with advice, that no time was to be loft. In fuch a crifis, floth
would ill become a man whofe life was in danger. To fall a
tame and paffive victim were to die an ignominious death. He
had but to exert his moft ftrenuous efforts, and good men,
touched with compaffion, would efpoufe his caufe. The bold
and turbulent would be fure to join him. Nothing fhould be
left untried. It was only neceffary to defeat fixty men (for that
was the number employed in this bloody tragedy): before Nero
could receive intelligence, and difpatch another band of ruffians,
there would be time to concert bold and vigorous meafures.
The flame of war might be kindled all over Afia, and, by this
refolute conduct, he might fave his life. At the worft, by daring
bravely, his cafe would not be more defperate. Courage might
fuffer, but it could not fuffer more than cowardice.

LIX. This fpirited advice had no effect on Plautus. Banifhed from his country, without arms, or any means of defence,
he faw no gleam of hope, and was, therefore, unwilling to be the
dupe of vifionary fchemes. Perhaps his affection for his wife
and children foftened and difarmed his mind. The emperor,
if not exafperated by refiftance, he imagined, would act with
lenity towards his unhappy family. According to fome hiftorians, the advice fent by Antiftius was of a different tendency,
importing that there was no danger to alarm him. We are

further told, that, by the exhortations of two philofophers, by name Cæranus (a), a Greek by birth, and Mufonius, of Tufcan origin, he had been taught that, though life is a feries of toil, and danger, and calamity, to wait with patience till the ftroke of death delivered him from a fcene of mifery, would be heroic fortitude. Thus much is certain, he was furprifed by the affaffins in the middle of the day, difarmed and naked, attending to the refrefhment and exercife of his body.

In that condition a centurion difpatched him, while Pelagon, one of the eunuchs, ftood a fpectator of the tragic fcene. This wretch was fent by Nero to fuperintend the ruffians, like the minifter of a defpotic prince, placed over the guards and tools of iniquity to fee his mafter's orders ftrictly executed. The head of the deceafed was carried to Rome. At the fight of the difmal object the emperor cried out (I give his very words), " Nero, now you may fafely marry Poppæa. What obftacle " remains to defer a match, long intended, and often deferred on " account of this very Plautus, and men of his defcription ? " Octavia may be divorced without delay: her conduct, it is " true, has been blamelefs, but the imperial name of her fa- " ther (b), and the efteem of the people, have made her in my " eyes an object of terror and deteftation." Having thus forti- fied his mind, he difpatched a letter to the fenate, written in guarded terms, without fo much as glancing at the murder of Sylla and Plautus. He mentioned them both, charging them with feditious machinations, by which he himfelf was kept in a con- ftant alarm, left fome dreadful convulfion fhould, by their means, fhake the empire to its foundation. The fathers decreed public vows and fupplications to the gods. Sylla and Plautus, though no longer in being, were expelled the fenate ; and with this
mockery,

mockery, to every good mind more grievous than the worſt oppreſſion, the people were amuſed and inſulted.

LX. NERO finding, by the ſlaviſh tenor of the decree, that the fathers were willing to transform his vices into virtues, reſolved to balance no longer. He repudiated Octavia, alleging her ſterility for his reaſon, and immediately married Poppæa. This woman, ſome time the concubine of the emperor, and now his wife, continued to govern him with unbounded ſway. Not content with her new dignity, ſhe ſuborned a domeſtic ſervant of Octavia to charge his miſtreſs with a diſhonourable intrigue with one of her ſlaves. For this purpoſe they choſe for the pretended adulterer a man of the name of Eucerus, a native of Alexandria, remarkable for his ſkill on the flute. The female ſervants were put to the torture. Some of them, overcome by pain and agony, confeſſed whatever was demanded of them; but the greateſt part perſevered, with conſtancy, to vindicate the honour of their miſtreſs. Tigellinus ſtood near at hand, preſſing them with queſtions. One of them had the ſpirit to anſwer, " The perſon of Octavia is freer from pollution than your " mouth." Sentence was pronounced againſt Octavia. With no more ceremony than what is uſual among citizens of ordinary rank, ſhe was diſmiſſed from the palace. The houſe of Burrhus, and the eſtates of Plautus, two fatal preſents ! were allotted for her ſeparate uſe. She was ſoon after baniſhed to Campania, under a military guard. Murmurs of diſcontent were heard in every quarter of Rome. The common people ſpoke out without reſerve. To rules of caution and political wiſdom their rough manners made them ſtrangers, and the meanneſs of their condition left them nothing to fear. Their clamours were ſo loud and violent, that Nero gave orders to recall Octavia, but without affection, and without remorſe.

G g 2

LXI. THE

LXI. The populace, tranfported with joy by this event, preffed in crowds to the capitol, to offer up their thanks to the gods. The ftatues of Poppæa were dafhed to the ground, while thofe of Octavia, adorned with wreaths of flowers, were carried in triumph on men's fhoulders, and placed in the forum and in the temples. The multitude went in a tumultuous body to greet the emperor; they furrounded his palace; they defired him to come forth and receive their congratulations. A band of foldiers rufhed forth fword in hand, and obliged the crowd to difperfe. Whatever was pulled down during the riot, was reftored to its place, and the ftatues of Poppæa were once more erected. But her malice to Octavia was not to be appeafed. To inveterate hatred fhe added her dread of a popular infurrection, in confequence of which, Nero might be compelled to renounce his paffion for her perfon.

She threw herfelf at his feet: "I am not now," fhe faid, "in a fituation to contend for our nuptial union, though dearer "to me than life itfelf. But my life is in danger. The flaves "and followers of Octavia, calling their own clamour the voice "of the people, have committed, in a time of profound peace, "public outrages little fhort of open rebellion. They are in "arms againft their fovereign. They want nothing but a leader, "and, in civil commotions, that want is foon fupplied. What "has Octavia now to do, but to leave her retreat in Campania, "and fhew herfelf to the people of Rome? She, who in her "abfence can raife a tumult fo fierce and violent, will foon dif- "cover the extent of her power. But what is my crime? What "have I committed? Whom have I offended? The people "may fee me the mother of legitimate heirs to the houfe of "Cæfar; but, perhaps, they would fain referve the imperial "dignity for the iffue of an Ægyptian minftrel (a). Submit to
                                                    "Octavia,

" Octavia, since your interest will have it so: recall her to your
" embrace, but do it voluntarily, that the rabble may not give
" the law to their sovereign.   You must either adopt that mea-
" sure, or, by just vengeance on the guilty, provide for your
" own safety and the public peace.   The first alarm was easily
" quelled ; a second insurrection may prove fatal.   Should the
" mob have reason to despair of seeing Octavia the partner of
" Nero's bed, they may, in their wisdom, find for her another
" husband."

B O O K
XIV.
A. U. C.
815.
A. D.
62.

LXII. This artful speech, tending at once to inflame the
prince with resentment, and alarm his fears, had its effect.   Nero
heard the whole with mixed emotions of rage and terror.   That
Octavia was guilty with one of her slaves, was a device of which
men could be no longer made the dupes.   The firmness of her
servants on the rack removed even the shadow of suspicion.
A new stratagem was now to be tried.   A man was to be found
who would dare to confess the guilt; and if the same person
could, with some colour of probability, be charged with a conspiracy against the state, the plot would lie the deeper.   For
this dark design, no one so fit as Anicetus (a), the commander
of the fleet at Misenum, and the murderer of the prince's mother.   This officer, for some time after that atrocious deed, enjoyed the smiles of the emperor, but soon experienced the common fate of all pernicious miscreants : he was favoured at first,
and detested afterwards.   It is the nature of great men, when
their turn is served, to consider their tools as a living reproach,
and standing witnesses against themselves.   Nero summoned
Anicetus to his presence : he thanked him for services already
performed.   " By you," he said, " I was delivered from the
" snares of an ambitious mother.   A deed of greater moment
" still remains.   Set me free from the furious spirit of an im-

" perious

5

" perious wife. To effect this you need not fo much as raife
" your hand. Neither fword nor dagger will be wanted. Con-
" fefs yourfelf guilty of adultery with Octavia ; I afk no more."
He concluded with a promife of ample rewards, to be managed,
indeed, with fecrecy, but without bound or meafure, and, in
the end, a fafe retreat in fome delightful country. " And now,"
he faid, " accept the offers which I have made, or certain death
" awaits you."

Anicetus undertook the bufinefs. Practifed in guilt, and
by the fuccefs of his former crimes infpired with courage, he
went even beyond his commiffion. In the prefence of certain
chofen perfons, whom Nero fummoned to a fecret council, he
told his ftory with circumftances that fhewed he had no need of
a prompter. He was banifhed to the ifland of Sardinia. At
that place he continued to live in affluence, and died, at laft, in
the courfe of nature.

LXIII. NERO iffued a proclamation, declaring the guilt of
Octavia, and, in exprefs terms, averring, that, to obtain the command of the fleet at Mifenum, fhe had proftituted her perfon to
Anicetus. He added, that, by the ufe of medicines to procure
abortion, fhe had thrown a veil over her adulterous commerce.
In this public declaration, the objection on account of fterility, fo
lately urged, was no more remembered. The facts, however,
were faid to be clearly proved. She was banifhed to the ifle of
Pandataria (a). The public mind was never fo deeply touched
with compaffion. The banifhment of Agrippina, by order of
Tiberius, was remembered by many ; and that of Julia (b), in
the reign of Claudius, was ftill more frefh in the memory of all :
but thofe two unfortunate exiles had attained the vigour of their
days, and were, by confequence, better enabled to endure the
                                                         ftroke

ſtroke of adverſity. They had known ſcenes of happineſs, and, in the recollection of better times, could loſe, or, at leaſt, aſſuage the ſenſe of preſent evils. To Octavia the celebration of her nuptials was little different from a funeral ceremony. She was led to an houſe, where ſhe could diſcover nothing but memorials of affliction; her father carried off by poiſon *(c)*, and her brother, in a ſhort time afterwards, deſtroyed by the ſame deteſtable machination. She ſaw herſelf ſuperſeded by the allurements of a female ſlave; ſhe ſaw the affections of her huſband alienated from herſelf, and a marriage, by which her ruin was completed, openly celebrated with Poppæa. Above all, ſhe underwent a cruel accuſation, to an ingenuous mind worſe than death. At the time when the ſtorm burſt upon her, ſhe was only in the twentieth year of her age, and even then, in the bloom of life, delivered to the cuſtody of centurions and ſoldiers. Her preſent afflictions, ſhe plainly ſaw, were a prelude to her impending fate. She was cut off from all the comforts of life; but the tranquillity of the grave was ſtill denied to her.

LXIV. In a few days afterwards ſhe received a mandate, commanding her to end her days. Alarmed and terrified, ſhe deſcended to ſupplications; ſhe admitted herſelf to be a widow; ſhe claimed no higher title than that of the emperor's ſiſter *(a)*; ſhe invoked the race of Germanicus, the common anceſtors of Nero and herſelf, and, in the anguiſh of her heart, regretted even Agrippina, during whoſe life, ſhe ſaid, her marriage would have been a ſtate of wretchedneſs, but would not have brought her to an untimely end. Amidſt theſe effuſions of ſorrow, the ruffians ſeized her, and, having bound her limbs, opened her veins. Her blood was chilled with fear, and did not iſſue at the wound. The aſſaſſins carried her to a bath of intenſe heat, where ſhe was ſuffocated by the vapour. To complete the horror of this barbarous

tragedy,

BOOK XIV.

A. U. C. 815. A. D. 62.

tragedy, her head was cut off, and fent to Rome, to glut the eyes of Poppæa.

Such were the tranfactions, for which the fathers decreed oblations to the gods. I mention the fact in this place, that the reader of this, or any other hiftory of thofe difaftrous times, may know, once for all, that as often as banifhment, or a bloody execution was ordered, the fenate never failed to thank the gods for their bounty. Thofe folemn acts, which, in the earlier periods of Rome, were the pious gratitude of the people for increafing happinefs, were now profanely and abominably converted to memorials of horror and public mifery. This may be received as a general truth ; and yet, whenever a decree occurs, remarkable either for a new ftrain of adulation, or the bafe fervility of the times, it is my intention not to pafs it by in filence.

LXV. In the courfe of this year, Nero is faid to have deftroyed by poifon the moft confiderable of his freedmen. Among thefe, Doryphorus had oppofed the marriage with Poppæa, and for that crime loft his life. Pallas was in poffeffion of exorbitant wealth ; but, living to a great age, he delayed the eager avarice of the emperor. He was murdered for his riches *(a)*. Romanus, another of the freedmen, endeavoured, by clandeftine calumny, to accomplifh the ruin of Seneca. He charged the philofopher with being an accomplice in the machinations of Caius Pifo ; but the blow, warded off by Seneca, recoiled upon the accufer. By this incident Pifo was alarmed for his own fafety *(b)*. A dark confpiracy followed, big with danger to Nero, but abortive in the end.

THE END OF THE FOURTEENTH BOOK.

THE
ANNALS
OF
TACITUS.

BOOK XV.

CONTENTS of BOOK XV.

H h 2

lace.

lace. *The christians accused of being the incendiaries, and, though innocent, put to death with cruel barbarity.* XLVII. *A variety of extraordinary omens.* XLVIII. *A conspiracy against Nero in favour of Caius Piso. A number of Roman knights and senators engaged in the plot. The first mover of it unknown. Subrius Flavius a forward leader. Epicharis, an enfranchised slave, endeavours to animate the conspirators. By her imprudence, and the information of Milichus, a freedman, the conspiracy is detected.* LVI. *The conspirators betray their accomplices. Lucan the poet accuses his mother.* LVII. *The fortitude of Epicharis on the rack. Fenius Rufus, though engaged in the plot, acts with vehemence against the rest of the accomplices. Several illustrious men put to death.* LX. *Seneca accused, and a tribune sent to him with the particulars of the information. His answer. He receives orders to die. His wife, Pompeia Paulina, saved by order of Nero. Seneca dies in the bath.* LXVI. *Fenius Rufus accused by the rest of the conspirators* LXVII. *The firm behaviour of Subrius Flavius, his intrepid answer to Nero, and his death.* LXVIII. *Vestinus, the consul, though innocent, commanded by a tribune to open his veins.* LXX. *Lucan the poet dies, repeating his own verses.* LXXII. *Nero distributes a largess among the soldiers. The senate convened. Their base and servile flattery. Oblations decreed to the gods. The month of April styled by the name Nero.*

These transactions passed in little more than three years.

Years of Rome—of Christ		Consuls
815	62, *continued.*	*Marius Celsus, Asinius Gallus.*
816	63	*Memmius Regulus, Verginius Rufus.*
817	64	*C. Læcanius Bassus, M. Licinius Crassus.*
818	65	*Licinius Nerva Silianus, M. Vestinus Atticus.*

BOOK XV.

I. **D**URING thefe tranfactions, Vologefes, king of the Parthians, began to raife new commotions in the Eaft. The fuccefs of Corbulo alarmed his jealoufy; he faw, with wounded pride, the defeat of his brother, Tiridates; and, in his room, Tigranes, an alien prince (*a*), feated on the throne of Armenia. The honour of the Arfacides was tarnifhed by thefe events, and he was determined to reftore its former luftre. But the ftruggle was to be with a great and powerful empire. Treaties of alliance, long in force and long refpected by the two nations, held him in fufpenfe. By nature anxious and irrefolute, he formed no fettled plan. He was at variance with the Hyrcanians, and, after a long and obftinate conflict, that brave and powerful nation

ftill

BOOK
XV.
A. U. C.
815.
A. D.
62.

ftill made head againft him. While he continued wavering, frefh intelligence fired him with indignation. Tigranes marched his army into the territory of the Adiabenians, a people bordering on Armenia, and laid wafte their country. The enterprife did not refemble the fudden incurfion of Barbarians roving in queft of prey: a regular war feemed to be declared in form. The chiefs of the Adiabenians faw, with refentment, their lands made a fcene of defolation, not by a Roman army, but by a foreigner, a defpicable hoftage, who for years had lived at Rome undiftinguifhed from the common flaves.

Monobazus, the fovereign of the province, inflamed the difcontents of the people, and, at the fame time, roufed the pride of Vologefes by frequent meffages, importing, that he knew not which way to turn, nor from what quarter to expect relief. Armenia, he faid, was loft, and the neighbouring ftates, if not reinforced by the Parthians, muft be all involved in the fame calamity, perhaps, with the confent of the people, as Rome, it was well known, made a diftinction between the nations that fell by conqueft, and thofe that fubmitted at difcretion. Tiridates, by his behaviour, added force to thefe complaints. Driven from his throne, he appeared with all the filent dignity of diftrefs, or, if he fpoke occafionally, his words were few, fhort, and fententious. " Mighty kingdoms," he faid, " are not fupported by in-" activity. Men and arms, and warlike preparations are ne-" ceffary. The conqueror has always juftice on his fide. In a " private ftation, to defend their property is the virtue of indivi-" duals; but to invade the poffeffions of others is the preroga-" tive and the glory of kings."

II. Roused by thefe incentives, Vologefes fummoned a council, and, feating Tiridates next himfelf, fpoke in fubftance as follows:
I
" You

"You fee before you a prince defcended from the fame father
"with myfelf. Acknowledging the right of primogeniture, he
"ceded to me the diadem of Parthia : in return I placed him on
"the throne of Armenia, the third kingdom among the eaftern
"nations. Media, in fact, is the fecond, and Pacorus, at that
"time, was in poffeffion. By this arrangement, I provided for
"my family, and, by the meafure, extinguifhed for ever thofe
"unnatural jealoufies, which formerly envenomed brothers againft
"brothers. This fyftem, it feems, has given umbrage to the
"Romans; they declare againft it ; and though they never
"broke with Parthia without paying dearly for their temerity,
"they now are willing to provoke a war, and rufh on their
"own deftruction. Thus much I am willing to declare; the
"poffeffions, which have defcended to me from my anceftors,
"fhall never be difmembered ; but I had rather maintain them
"by the juftice of my caufe, than by the decifion of the fword.
"I avow the principle, and if, in confequence of it, I have been
"too much inclined to pacific meafures, the vigour of my future
"conduct fhall make atonement. The national honour, in the
"mean time, has fuffered no diminution. Your glory is unim-
"paired, and I have added to it the virtues of moderation ;
"virtues, which the gods approve, and which no fovereign, how-
"ever great and flourifhing, ought to defpife."

Having thus delivered his fentiments, he placed the regal
diadem on the head of Tiridates, and, at the fame time, gave to
Monefes, an officer of diftinguifhed rank, the command of the
cavalry, which, by eftablifhed ufage, is always appointed to
attend the perfon of the monarch. He added the auxiliaries
fent by the Adiabenians, and, with that force, ordered him to
march againft Tigranes, in order to exterminate the ufurper from
the throne of Armenia. In the mean time, he propofed to compromife

BOOK
XV.
A U. C.
815.
A. D.
62.

promife the war with the Hyrcanians, and fall with the whole weight of his kingdom on the Roman provinces.

III. CORBULO was no fooner apprifed of thefe tranfactions, than he difpatched, to fupport Tigranes, two legions, under the command of Verulanus Severus and Vettius Bolanus.   In their private inftructions thofe officers had it in command, to proceed with caution, and act on the defenfive, without pufhing on their operations with too much vigour.   A decifive campaign was not Corbulo's plan.   He wifhed to protract the war, and, in the mean time, ftated, in his letters to the emperor, the neceffity of appointing a commander, with a fpecial commiffion to protect Armenia, as he forefaw a ftorm gathering in the province of Syria.   If Vologefes made an irruption in that quarter, a powerful army would be wanted to repel the invader.   With the reft of his legions he formed a chain of pofts along the banks of the Euphrates, and, having made a powerful levy of provincial forces, he fecured all the paffes againft the inroads of the enemy.   In order to make fure of water in a country not well fupplied by nature, he erected ftrong caftles near the fprings and fountains; and, where the ftations were inconvenient, he choaked up a number of rivulets with heaps of fand, with intent to conceal their fource from the Parthian army.

IV. WHILE Corbulo was thus concerting meafures for the defence of Syria, Monefes advanced by rapid marches, and with all his forces entered Armenia.   He hoped to outftrip the fame that flies before an enterprifing general, and to fall upon Tigranes by furprife.   That prince, aware of the defign, had thrown himfelf into the city of Tigranocerta, a place furrounded by high walls *(a)*, and defended by a numerous garrifon.   The river Nicephorius *(b)*, with a current fuf-

2

ficiently

ficiently broad, waſhes a conſiderable part of the walls. A
deep trench incloſed the reſt. There was a competent number
of ſoldiers to man the works, and proviſions had been laid
in with due precaution. Some of the foraging parties having
raſhly ventured too far were ſurrounded by the enemy. This
check, however, inſtead of diſheartening the garriſon, ſerved
only to inſpire them with a ſpirit of revenge. The operations of a ſiege are ill ſuited to the genius of the Parthians,
whoſe courage always fails in a cloſe engagement. A few arrows
thrown at random made no impreſſion on men ſheltered by their
fortifications. The beſiegers could only amuſe themſelves with
a feeble attack. An attempt was made by the Adiabenians to
carry the works by aſſault. They advanced their ſcaling ladders
and other military engines, but were ſoon repulſed, and, the
garriſon ſallying out, the whole corps was cut to pieces.

V. Corbulo was not of a temper to be elated with ſuccefs.
He choſe to act with moderation in proſperity, and, accordingly,
diſpatched an embaſſy to expoſtulate with Vologeſes on the violence with which he had invaded a Roman province, and not
only beſieged the cohorts of the empire, but alſo a king in alliance
with Rome. If the Parthian prince did not raiſe the ſiege, he
threatened to advance with the ſtrength of his army, and encamp
in the heart of the country. Caſperius, a centurion, was charged
with this commiſſion. He met the king in the city of Niſibis (a),
diſtant about ſeven and thirty miles from Tigranocerta, and
there delivered his orders in a tone of firmneſs. To avoid a war
with Rome had been for ſome time the fixed reſolution of Vologeſes, and the ſucceſs of the preſent enterpriſe gave him no reaſon to alter his ſentiments.

The ſiege promiſed no kind of advantage; Tigranes poſſeſſed

Vol. II.   I i   a ſtrong

a ſtrong hold, well garriſoned, and provided with ample ſupplies; the forces, that attempted to ſtorm the works, met with a total overthrow; the Roman legions were in poſſeſſion of Armenia, and others were in readineſs, not only to cover the province of Syria, but to puſh the war into the Parthian territories: his cavalry ſuffered for want of forage, and, all vegetation being deſtroyed by a ſwarm of locuſts, neither graſs nor foliage could be found. Determined by theſe conſiderations, yet diſguiſing his fear, Vologeſes, with the ſpecious appearance of a pacific diſpoſition, returned for anſwer to Caſperius, that he ſhould ſend ambaſſadors to Rome, with inſtructions to ſolicit the ceſſion of Armenia, and the re-eſtabliſhment of peace between the two nations. Meanwhile, he ſent diſpatches to Moneſes, with orders to abandon the ſiege of Tigranocerta, and, without farther delay, returned to his capital.

VI. THESE events, aſcribed by the general voice to the conduct of the general, and the terror impreſſed on the mind of Vologeſes, were extolled in terms of the higheſt commendation. And yet malignity was at work. Some would have it, " That " there was at the bottom a ſecret compact to make an end of the " war. According to their ſiniſter interpretation, it was ſtipu- " lated, that Vologeſes ſhould return to his own dominions, and " that Armenia ſhould be evacuated by Tigranes. With what " other view were the Roman ſoldiers withdrawn from Tigra- " nocerta? Why give up, by an ill-judged peace, what had " been ſo well defended in time of war? Could the army find, " at the extremity of Cappadocia, in huts ſuddenly thrown up, " better winter-quarters, than in the capital of a kingdom, " which had been preſerved by force of arms? Peace is held " forth; but it is, in fact, no more than a truce, a ſuſpenſion " of arms, that Vologeſes may have to contend with another ge-
" neral,

" neral, and that Corbulo fhould not be obliged to hazard the
" great renown, which he had acquired during a fervice of fo
" many years."

The fact was, Corbulo, as we have ftated, required a new
commander for the fpecial purpofe of defending Armenia, and
the nomination of Cæfennius Pætus was already announced.
That officer arrived in a fhort time. A divifion of the forces
was allotted to each commander. The fourth and twelfth legions,
with the fifth lately arrived from Mæfia, and a body of auxiliaries from Pontus, from Galatia and Cappadocia, were put under the command of Pætus. The third, the fixth, and tenth
legions, with the forces of Syria, were affigned to Corbulo. Both
commanders were to act in concert, or to pufh the war in different quarters, as the occafion might require. But the fpirit of
Corbulo could not brook a rival, and Pætus, though to be fecond
in command under fuch a general would have been his higheft
glory, began to afpire above himfelf. He defpifed the fame acquired by Corbulo, declaring all his beft exploits to be no better
than boafted victories, without bloodfhed, and without booty;
mere pretended fieges, in which not a fingle place was carried by
affault. For himfelf, he was refolved to carry on the war for more
fubftantial purpofes. By impofing tributes and taxes on the
vanquifhed, he meant to reduce them to fubjection, and, for the
fhadow of an oriental king, he would eftablifh the rights of conqueft, and the authority of the Roman name.

VII. In this juncture, the ambaffadors, who had been fent by
Vologefes to treat with Nero, returned back to their own country.
Their negotiation was unfuccefsful, and the Parthians declared
war. Pætus embraced the opportunity to fignalife his valour.
He entered Armenia at the head of two legions; the fourth,

I i 2

commanded

B O O K
XV.

A. U. C.
81c.
A. D.
6:.

commanded by Funifulanus Vettonianus, and the twelfth by Ca-lavius Sabinus. His firft approach was attended with unpro-pitious omens. In paffing over a bridge, which lay acrofs the Euphrates, the horfe that carried the confular ornaments, taking fright without any apparent caufe, broke from the ranks, and fled at full fpeed. A victim, likewife, intended for facrifice, ftanding near the unfinifhed fortifications of the winter camp, efcaped out of the entrenchments. Nor was this all : the ja-velins, in the hands of the foldiers, emitted fudden flafhes of fire ; and this prodigy was the more alarming as the Parthians brandifh the fame weapon.

VIII. PORTENTS and prodigies had no effect on Pætus. Without waiting to fortify his winter encampment, and with-out providing a fufficient ftore of grain, he marched his army over Mount Taurus, determined, as he gave out, to recover Tigranocerta, and lay wafte the country through which Cor-bulo had paffed with vain parade. In his progrefs fome forts and caftles were ftormed, and it is certain that his fhare of glory and of booty would have been confiderable, if to enjoy the former with moderation, and to fecure the latter, had been his talent. He over-ran by rapid marches vaft tracts of country, where no conqueft could be maintained. His provifions, in the mean time, went to decay, and, the winter feafon ap-proaching faft, he was obliged to return with his army. His difpatches to Nero were in a ftyle as grand as if he had ended the war, high founding, pompous, full of vain glory, but with-out any folid advantage.

IX. IN the mean time Corbulo never neglected the banks of the Euphrates. To his former chain of pofts he added new ftations ; and left the enemy, who fhewed themfelves in de-tached

tached parties on the oppofite plains, fhould be able to ob-
ftruct the building of a bridge over the river, he ordered a number of veffels of large fize to be braced together with great
beams, and on that foundation raifed a fuperftructure of towers
armed with flings and warlike engines. From this floating bat_
tery he annoyed the enemy with a difcharge of ftones and javelins, thrown to fuch a length, that the Parthians could not
retaliate with their darts. Under this fhelter the bridge was
finifhed. The allied cohorts paffed over to the oppofite hills.
The legions followed, and pitched their camp. The whole of
thefe operations was executed with fuch rapidity, and fo formidable a difplay of ftrength, that the Parthians abandoned their
enterprife, and, without attempting any thing againft the Syrians,
drew off their forces to the invafion of Armenia.

X. PÆTUS had fixed his head-quarters in that country, little
aware of the ftorm ready to burft upon him, and fo much off his
guard, that he fuffered the fifth legion to remain in Pontus, at a
confiderable diftance, while he ftill weakened his numbers by
granting leave of abfence to his foldiers without referve. In
this fituation he received intelligence of the approach of Vologefes
with a powerful army. He called the twelfth legion to his affiftance, and, by the neceffity of that reinforcement, betrayed to the
enemy the feeble condition of his army. He was, notwithftanding, fufficiently ftrong to maintain his poft, and baffle all the
efforts of the Parthians, had it been in the genius of the man
to purfue with firmnefs either his own idea, or the counfel of
others. But in preffing exigencies, he no fooner embraced the
plan recommended by officers of known experience, than his little
fpirit was ftung with jealoufy, and, left he fhould be thought to
ftand in need of advice, he was fure to adopt very different meafures, always changing for the worfe.

On

BOOK
XV.

A. U. C.
815.
A. D.
62.

On the firſt approach of the Parthians, he ſallied out of his en-trenchments, determined to hazard a battle. Ditches and ramparts, he ſaid, were not given to him in commiſſion, nor had he any need of that defence: the ſoldier and the ſword were all he wanted. In this vapouring ſtrain he led his legions to the field; but a centurion, and a few ſoldiers, who had been ſent to reconnoitre the enemy, being cut off, his courage failed, and he ſounded a retreat. He was no ſooner in his camp, than, perceiving that Vologeſes had not preſſed on the rear, he once more grew bold, and, in a fit of valour, ordered three thouſand of his beſt infantry to take poſt on the next eminence of Mount Taurus, to diſpute the paſs with the Parthian king. The Pannonians, who formed the ſtrength of his cavalry, were drawn up on the open plain. He placed his wife and her infant ſon in a caſtle, called Arſamoſata (a), and left a cohort to defend the place. In this manner he contrived to divide an army, which, acting with united force, would have been able to repel the attack of a wild and deſultory enemy. When preſſed by Vologeſes, we are told it was with difficulty that he could ſubmit to acquaint Corbulo with his ſituation. That officer did not hurry to his aſſiſtance. To augment the glory of delivering him, he was willing to let the danger increaſe. In the mean time, he ordered a detachment of a thouſand men, drafted from each of his three legions, and a body of eight hundred horſe, with an equal number from the cohorts, to hold themſelves in readineſs for a ſudden enterpriſe.

XI. Vologeses knew from his ſcouts that his paſſage over Mount Taurus was obſtructed by the Roman infantry, and that the plain was occupied by the Pannonian horſe; but the news did not deter him from purſuing his march. He fell with impetuous fury on the cavalry, who fled with precipitation. The

legionary

legionary foldiers, in like manner, abandoned their poft. A
tower, commanded by Tarquitius Crefcus, a centurion, was the
only place that held out. That officer made feveral fallies with
fuccefs, routing fuch of the enemy as dared to approach the
walls, and purfuing the run-aways with great flaughter ; till by
a volley of combuftibles, thrown in by the befiegers, the works
were fet on fire. The gallant centurion perifhed in the flames.
Some of the garrifon efcaped unhurt, and made the beft of their
way to diftant wilds. The wounded returned to the camp, and
there related wonders, magnifying, beyond all bounds, the valour
of the Parthian king, the number of his troops, and their ferocity
in battle. A panic pervaded the army. Men, who feared for
themfelves, fwallowed all that was faid with eafy credulity.
Pætus felt the preffure of his misfortunes. He feemed to refign
the command, unable to ftruggle with adverfity. He fent again
to Corbulo, with earneft prayers entreating him to fave the Roman eagles, with the ftandards of an unfortunate army, and the
army itfelf, from impending ruin. In the mean time, he and his
men would hold out to the laft, determined to live or die in the
fervice of their country.

XII. Corbulo, as ufual, firm and collected in the moment of
danger, prepared for the expedition. Having left a fufficient force to
guard his pofts on the banks of the Euphrates, he moved forward
towards Armenia, taking the fhorteft route through Commagena,
and next through Cappadocia, both fertile countries, and capable
of furnifhing fupplies for his army. Befides the ufual train attending on a march, he took with him a number of camels,
loaded with grain, to anfwer the double purpofe of preventing the want of provifions, and of ftriking the enemy with the
terror of an unufual appearance. Pactius, a centurion of principal rank *(a)*, was the firft from the vanquifhed army that encountered.

countered Corbulo on his march.   The common men came up
foon after, all endeavouring by various excufes to palliate their
difgrace.   The general ordered them to join their colours, and
try to gain their pardon from Pætus.   The merciful difpofition
of that officer might incline him to forgive; but, for himfelf, he
favoured none but fuch as conquered by their valour.   He then ad-
drefled his own legions, vifiting the ranks, and infpiring all with
zeal and ardour.   He called to mind their paft exploits, and
opened to their view a new field of glory.   " It is not," he
faid, " the towns and villages of Armenia that now demand
" our fwords: a Roman camp invokes our aid, and two legions
" look to us for relief.   Their delivery from the Barbarians will
" be the reward of victory.   If to a private foldier the civic
" crown (b), delivered by the hand of his general, is the brighteft
" recompenfe for the life of a citizen faved; how much greater
" will be the glory of the prefent enterprife, in which the num-
" ber of the diftreffed is equal to thofe who bring relief, and, by
" confequence, every foldier in this army may fave his man !"
By this difcourfe one general fpirit was diffufed through the
ranks.   The men had private motives to inflame their courage;
they felt for their brothers; they wifhed to fuccour their relations, and, without halting night or day, purfued their march
with alacrity and vigour.

XIII. MEANWHILE Vologefes prefled on the fiege.   He
affaulted the entrenchments; he endeavoured to ftorm a caftle,
where the weaker fex, the aged, and infirm were lodged for
fecurity.   In thefe feveral attacks, he came to a clofer engagement than ufually confifts with the military genius of his
country.   By a fhow of temerity he hoped to bring on a decifive
action.   The Romans remained clofe in their tents, content with
a fafe poft within their entrenchments; fome in deference to the
orders

orders of their general; others, through want of ſpirit, tamely waiting to be relieved by Corbulo. If, in the mean time, the enemy overpowered them, they called to mind, by way of conſolation, the example of two Roman armies that paſſed under the yoke; one at Caudium *(a)*, and the other at Numantia. By thoſe two events ſubmiſſion, in their preſent diſtreſs, would be fully juſtified, ſince neither the Samnites, nor the Carthaginians, thoſe famous rivals of the Roman republic, could be compared with the extenſive power of the Parthian empire: and, moreover, the boaſted virtue of the ancient Romans, however decorated by the praiſes of poſterity, was always pliant in misfortune, and willing to make terms with the conqueror. By this unwarlike ſpirit of his army Pætus was driven to deſpair. He wrote to Vologeſes. His letter was more in the ſtyle of reproach than the language of a ſuppliant. "Hoſtilities," he ſaid, " were com-
" menced by the Parthians to wreſt the kingdom of Armenia
" from the Romans; a kingdom always in the power of the
" emperor, or governed by kings inveſted by him with the regal
" diadem. Peace is equally the intereſt of both nations. From the
" preſent juncture no concluſion can be drawn, ſince the whole
" weight of Parthia is employed againſt two legions, and Rome
" has it ſtill in her power to arm in her cauſe the remaining na-
" tions of the world."

XIV. VOLOGESES, without entering into the queſtion of right, returned for anſwer, " That he muſt wait for his two brothers,
" Pacorus and Tiridates: when they arrived, a convention
" might be held, and there the rights of Armenia would be ad-
" juſted. The gods would then decide the fate of the Roman
" legions." Pætus ſent another embaſſy, requeſting an interview. The king ſent Vaſaces, his general of the cavalry, to act in the royal name. At that meeting Pætus cited a number of an-

cient

A. U. C.
815.
A. D.
62.

cient precedents. He talked of Lucullus, Pompey, and the emperors of Rome, who had dealt out the sceptre of Armenia. Vasaces coolly answered, that some shadow of right must be allowed to have been claimed by the Romans; but the substantial power was always vested in the Parthian kings. After much debate, it was agreed, that on the next day, Monobazus, the Adiabenian, should attend as a witness to the compact. In his presence it was agreed that, the siege being raised, the Roman legions should forthwith evacuate Armenia; that the strong holds, with their stores and magazines, should be delivered up to the Parthians; and, these conditions duly performed, Vologeses was to be at liberty, by his ambassadors, to negociate with Nero.

XV. These preliminaries being settled, Pætus ordered a bridge to be built over the Arsanias (a), a river that flowed by the side of his camp. For this work his pretext was, that it would be convenient to his army, when the march began: but the fact was, the Parthians, knowing the utility of a bridge, had made it an article of the treaty, intending, at the same time, that it should remain a monument of their victory. The Roman troops, instead of using the bridge, filed off another way. A report (b) was spread abroad, that the legions had passed under the yoke, and, in addition to that disgrace, suffered all the humiliating circumstances, which usually attend the overthrow of an army. The Armenians gave some colour to the report. Before the Romans marched out, they entered the entrenchments, and formed a line on each side, in order to fix on the slaves and beasts of burthen that formerly belonged to themselves. Not content with seizing what they called their own property, they laid violent hands on the apparel of the soldiers, who yielded, with fear and trembling, to avoid a new cause of quarrel.

Vologeses,

Vologeſes, as a monument of his victory, raiſed a pile of
dead bodies, and arms taken from the enemy; but declined to
be a ſpectator of the legions in their flight. He firſt indulged
his pride, and then ſought the fame of moderation. He waded
acroſs the Arſanias, mounted on an elephant, while his train
and his near relations followed him on horſeback. The reaſon
was, a report prevailed, that, by the fraudulent contrivance of the
builders, the whole fabric of the bridge would give way at once;
but by thoſe, who made the experiment, it was found to be a
firm and ſolid ſtructure.

XVI. The beſieged, it is now clear, were provided with grain
in ſuch abundance, that, on their departure, they burned their
magazines; and, on the other hand, by the account given by
Corbulo, it appears, that the Parthians, having conſumed their
whole ſtock of proviſions, were on the point of raiſing the ſiege,
at the very time when he was within three days march of the
place. Upon the ſame authority it may be averred as a fact, that
Pætus, under the ſanction of a ſolemn oath, ſworn under the eagles,
and in the preſence of witneſſes ſent by Vologeſes, took upon
him to engage, that no Roman ſhould ſet his foot within the
territories of Armenia, till Nero's pleaſure touching the terms of
the treaty ſhould arrive from Rome. Theſe aſſertions, it may be
ſaid, were ſuggeſted by malignity, to aggravate the infamy of an
unwarlike officer; but it is now known, beyond the poſſibility
of a doubt, that Pætus made a forced march of no leſs than forty
miles in one day; leaving behind him the ſick and wounded, and
flying, with as much diſorder and confuſion, as if he had been
routed in the field of battle. Corbulo met the fugitives on the
banks of the Euphrates. He received them without parade, and
without that diſplay of military pomp which might ſeem a triumph over the fate of the vanquiſhed. His men beheld with

K k 2

regret

regret the difgrace of their fellow-foldiers, and tears gufhed from every eye. The ufual forms of military falutation were fuppreffed by the general condolence. The pride of courage and the fenfe of glory, which, in the day of profperity, are natural paffions, were now converted into grief and fympathy. The lower the condition of the foldier, the more fincere his forrow. In that clafs of men the honeft emotions of the heart appeared without difguife.

XVII. THE conference between the two commanders was fhort, and without ceremony. Corbulo complained that all his labours were rendered abortive, whereas the war might have been terminated by the total overthrow of the Parthians. Pætus obferved in reply, that all things were ftill in the fame condition. He propofed to turn the eagles againft the enemy, and, fince Vologefes had withdrawn his forces, by their joint force Armenia would be eafily reduced. Corbulo rejected the offer. He had no fuch orders from the emperor. It was the danger, in which the legions were involved that drew him out of his province, and, fince it was uncertain where the Parthians would make their next attempt, he was determined to return into Syria with his army ; and if his infantry, haraffed out with fatiguing marches, could keep pace with the Parthian cavalry, who with their ufual velocity could traverfe the open plains, he fhould hold himfelf indebted to his own good fortune for fo fignal an event. Pætus fixed his winter-quarters in Cappadocia. Vologefes fent difpatches to Corbulo, requiring, that the ftrong holds and fortreffes on the banks of the Euphrates fhould be rafed to the ground, and the river left, as heretofore, the common boundary of the two empires. Corbulo had no objection, provided both parties withdrew their garrifons, and left Armenia a free and independant country. The Parthian monarch, after fome hefitation,

acceded

acceded to the terms. The caftles erected, by Corbulo's order, on the banks of the Euphrates, were all demolithed, and the Armenians were left to their natural liberty.

XVIII. MEANWHILE trophies of victory were erected at Rome, and triumphal arches on the mount of the capitol. This was ordered by the fenate, while the war was ftill depending; nor was the work difcontinued, when the event was known. The public eye was amufed at the expence of truth. To add to the impofition, and to appear free from all folicitude about foreign affairs, Nero ordered all the damaged grain, that lay in the public ftores, to be thrown into the Tiber. By this act of oftentation an idea of great abundance was to be impreffed on the minds of the people. Nor did he fuffer the price of corn to be raifed, though near two hundred veffels, loaded with grain, were loft in the harbour by the violence of a ftorm, and a hundred more, working their way up the Tiber, were deftroyed by the accident of fire. At the fame time Nero committed the care of the public impofts to three men of confular rank, namely, Lucius Pifo, Ducennius Geminus, and Pompeius Paullinus. In making this arrangement he animadverted with feverity on the conduct of former emperors, whofe extravagance made heavy anticipations of the revenue; whereas he himfelf, by his frugality, paid annually into the treafury, for the exigencies of the ftate, fix millions of fefterces.

XIX. A CUSTOM, highly unjuft and prejudicial to the rights of others, was, at this time, in general vogue. When the time drew near for the election of magiftrates, or the allotment of provinces, it was the practice of men, who had no iffue (a), to become fathers by adoption. Having ferved their turn in a conteft with real parents for the prætorfhip, and the adminiftration of provinces, they emancipated their pretended fons, and refumed their former ftate. Againft this abufe warm remonftrances were made to the fenate. The complainants urged the rights of nature, the care and expence of rearing children, while the compenfation by law eftablifhed (b) was wrefted from them by fraud, by artifice, and the facility of feigned adoptions. It was furely a fufficient advantage to fuch as had no children, that they could live free from all charge and folicitude, without leaving the road to favour, to preferment, and honours open to them in common with men who are of fervice to the community. Real parents are taught by the laws to expect the reward due to ufeful members of the community; but the laws are eluded, and the promifed reward is fnatched away, if fuch, as have raifed no heirs to themfelves, are allowed to become parents without paternal affection, and childlefs again without regret. The deception of a moment ferves to counterbalance whole years of expectation, and the true father fees all his hopes defeated. The fenate paffed a decree, by which it was provided, that in all cafes, either of election to the magiftracy, or fucceffion by teftament, no regard fhould be paid to adoptions merely colourable.

XX. CLAUDIUS TIMARCHUS, a native of Crete, was cited to anfwer a profecution commenced againft him. Befides the allegations ufually laid to the charge of fuch as rife in the provinces to overgrown wealth, and become the oppreffors of their inferior neighbours, an expreffion, that fell from him, excited the indignation of the fenate. This man, it feems, had made it his boaft, that addreffes of public thanks to the proconfular governors of Crete depended entirely on his weight and influence. Pætus Thrafea feized this opportunity to convert the incident to the public good. He gave his opinion that the offender ought to be banifhed from the ifle of Crete, and proceeded as follows: " Ex-
2
" perience

" perience has taught us, confcript fathers, that the wifeft laws
" and the beft examples of virtue owe their origin to the actual
" commiffion of crimes and mifdemeanours. Men of integrity
" make it their ftudy, on fuch occafions, to deduce good from
" evil. To the corrupt practices of public orators we are in-
" debted for the Cincian law *(a)*, and for the Julian to the intrigues
" and open bribery of the candidates for public honours. The
" Calpurnian regulations *(b)* were produced by the avarice and
" rapacity of the magiftrates. Guilt muft precede the punifh-
" ment, and reformation grows out of abufe. We have now before
" us the pride and infolence of petty tyrants in the provinces. To
" check the mifchief, let us come to a refolution, confiftent with
" good faith, and worthy of the Roman name. Protection is due
" to our allies ; but let us remember, that, to adorn our names,
" we are not to depend on the voice of foreign nations. Our
". fellow-citizens are the beft judges of our conduct.

XXI. " THE old republic was not content with fending prae-
" tors and confuls to adminifter the provinces. Men who fuf-
" tained no public character were often commiffioned to vifit the
" remoteft colonies, in order to report the condition of each, and
" the temper with which the people fubmitted to the authority of
" government. By the judgment of individuals whole nations
" were kept in awe. What is our practice now? We pay court
" to the colonies ; we flatter the provinces, and, by the influence
" of fome powerful leader, we receive public thanks for our ad-
" miniftration. In like manner, accufations are framed at the
" will and pleafure of fome overgrown provincial. Let the right
" of complaining ftill remain ; and, by exercifing that right, let
" the provinces fhew their importance ; but let them not, by falfe
" encomiums, impofe upon our judgment. The praife, that fprings
" from cabal and faction, is more pernicious than even malice or
" cruelty,

" cruelty. Let both be fuppreffed. More mifchief is done by
" the governor who wifhes to oblige, than by him who fhews
" himfelf not afraid of offending. It is the misfortune of certain
" virtues to provoke ill will. In that clafs may be reckoned in-
" flexible feverity, and the firmnefs that never yields to intrigue,
" or the arts of defigning men. Hence it happens, that every
" new governor opens a promifing fcene, but the laft act feldom
" correfponds with the outfet. In the end we fee an humble can-
" didate for the fuffrages of the province. Remove the evil, and
" government, in every quarter, will be more upright, more juft,
" more uniform. By profecutions avarice and rapine have re-
" ceived a check. Abolifh the cuftom of giving public thanks,
" and you fupprefs the pitiful ambition which, for vain applaufe,
" can ftoop to mean compliances."

XXII. This fpeech was received with the unanimous affent
of the fathers. The propofition, notwithftanding, could not be
formed into a decree, the confuls refufing to make their report.
The prince interpofed in the bufinefs, and, with his authority, a
law was paffed, forbidding any perfon whatever to move in a
provincial affembly *(a)* for a vote of thanks to the proconful or
prætor, or to fend a deputation to Rome for that purpofe. During the fame confulfhip, the gymnafium, or place of athletic
exercifes, was ftruck with lightning, and burnt to the ground.
The ftatue of Nero was found in the ruins, melted down to a
fhapelefs mafs. The celebrated city of Pompeii *(b)* in Campania
was overthrown by an earthquake, and well nigh demolifhed.
Lælia, the veftal virgin, departed this life; and Cornelia, defcended
from the family of the Coffi, fucceeded to the vacant office.

XXIII. During the confulfhip of Memmius Regulus and
Verginius Rufus, Poppæa was delivered of a daughter. The ex-

ultation

ultation of Nero was beyond all mortal joy.   He called the new-
born infant Augufta, and gave the fame title to her mother.   The
child was brought into the world at Antium, where Nero himfelf was born.   The fenate, before the birth, had offered vows to
the gods for the fafe delivery of Poppæa.   They fulfilled their
obligations, and voted additional honours.   Days of fupplication
were appointed: a temple was voted to the goddefs of fecundity;
athletic fports were inftituted on the model of the religious games
practifed at Antium; golden ftatues to the two goddeffes of fortune *(a)* were to be erected on the throne of Jupiter Capitolinus;
and in honour of the Claudian and Domitian families *(b)* Circenfian games were to be celebrated at Antium, in imitation of the
public fpectacles exhibited at Bovillæ to commemorate the Julian
race.   But thefe honours were of fhort duration: the infant died
in lefs than four months, and the monuments of human vanity
faded away.   But new modes of flattery were foon difplayed:
the child was canonized for a goddefs; a temple was decreed to
her, with an altar, a bed of ftate, a prieft, and religious ceremonies.

Nero's grief, like his joy at the birth, was without bounds or
meafure.   At the time when the fenate went in crowds to Antium, to congratulate the prince on the delivery of Poppæa, a
circumftance occurred worthy of notice.   Pætus Thrafea was ordered by Nero not to appear upon that occafion.   The affront
was deemed a prelude to the ruin of that eminent citizen.   He
received the mandate with his ufual firmnefs, calm and undifmayed.   A report prevailed foon after, that Nero, in converfation
with Seneca, made it his boaft, that he was reconciled to Thrafea,
and in return the philofopher wifhed him joy.   In confequence
of this incident the glory of thofe excellent men rofe to the higheft
pitch; but their danger kept pace with their glory.

XXIV. In the beginning of the spring ambassadors from Vologeses arrived at Rome, with letters from the king, their master, in substance declaring, " that he would not revive the question " of right, so often urged and fully discussed, since the gods, the " sovereign arbiters of nations, had delivered Armenia into the " hands of the Parthians, not without disgrace to the Roman " name. Tigranes had been hemmed in by a close blockade; " Pætus and his legions were enveloped in the like distress, and, " in the moment when destruction hung over them, the whole " army was suffered to decamp. The Parthians displayed at " once their superior valour and their moderation. But even in " the present juncture Tiridates had no objection to a long " journey to Rome, in order to be there invested with the so- " vereignty; but, being of the order of the Magi, the duties of " the sacerdotal function *(a)* required his personal attendance. " He was willing, however, to proceed tot he Roman camp, and " there receive the regal diadem under the eagles, and the images of " the emperor, in the presence of the legions."

XXV. The style of this letter differed essentially from the account transmitted by Pætus, who represented the affairs of the east in a flourishing situation. To ascertain the truth, a centurion, who had travelled with the ambassadors, was interrogated concerning the state of Armenia. The Romans, he replied, have evacuated the country. Nero felt the insulting mockery of being asked to yield what the Barbarians had seized by force. He summoned a council of the leading men at Rome, to determine, by their advice, which was most eligible, a difficult and laborious war, or an ignominious peace. All declared for war. The conduct of it was committed to Corbulo, who, by the experience of so many years, knew both the temper of the Roman army, and the genius of the enemy. The misconduct of Pætus had brought

disgrace

difgrace on the Roman name; and to hazard the fame calamities
from the incapacity of another officer, was not advifable.

The Parthian deputies received their anfwer, but were difmiffed
with handfome prefents, leaving them room to infer from the mild
behaviour of the emperor, that Tiridates, if he made the requeft
in perfon, might fucceed to the extent of his wifhes. The civil
adminiftration of Syria was committed to Ceftius, but the whole
military authority was affigned to Corbulo. The fifteenth legion,
then in Pannonia under the command of Marius Celfus, was
ordered to join the army. Directions were alfo given to the
kings and tetrarchs of the eaft, as alfo to the governors and imperial procurators of the feveral provinces in thofe parts, to fubmit
in every thing to the commander in chief. Corbulo was now
invefted with powers little fhort of what the Roman people committed to Pompey (a) in the war againft the pirates. Pætus, in
the mean time, returned to Rome, not without apprehenfions
of being called to a fevere account. Nero appeafed his fears,
content with a few fallies of mirth and ridicule. His words were,
" I make hafte to pardon you, left a ftate of fufpenfe fhould
" injure a man of your fenfibility. Since you are fo apt to take
" fright, delay on my part might hurt your nerves, and bring on
" a fit of illnefs."

XXVI. CORBULO expected no advantage to the fervice from
the fourth and twelfth legions, the braveft of their men being all
cut off, and the furvivors ftill remaining covered with confternation. He removed them into Syria; and, in exchange, reinforced himfelf with the fixth legion, and the third; both in full
vigour, inured to hardfhip, and no lefs diftinguifhed by their
fuccefs than by their valour. To thefe he added the fifth legion,
which happened to be quartered in Pontus, and, by confequence,

L l 2

had

had not suffered in the late defeat. The fifteenth legion had lately joined the army, as also a body of select troops from Illyricum and Ægypt, with the cavalry, the cohorts, and auxiliaries sent by the confederate kings. The whole force assembled at Melitene *(a)*, where Corbulo proposed to cross the Euphrates. His first care was to purify his army by a solemn lustration *(b)*. Those rites performed, he called his men to a meeting, and in a spirited harangue painted forth the auspicious government of the reigning prince; he mentioned his own exploits, and imputed to the imbecility of Pætus all the disasters that happened. The whole of his discourse was delivered in a style of authority, the true eloquence of a soldier.

XXVII. He began his march without delay, and chose the road formerly traversed by Lucullus *(a)*, having first given orders to his men to open the passes, and remove the obstructions, with which time and long disuse had choaked up part of the way. He heard that ambassadors from Tiridates and Vologeses were advancing with overtures of peace, and having no inclination to treat them with disdain, he sent forward some chosen centurions, with instructions neither harsh nor arrogant, in substance stating, " that the misunderstanding between the two nations might still " be compromised, without proceeding to the decision of the " sword. Both armies had fought with alternate vicissitudes of " fortune, in some instances favourable to the Romans, in others " to the Parthians; and from those events both sides might derive " a lesson against the pride and insolence of victory. It was the " interest of Tiridates to receive, at the hands of the Roman emperor, a kingdom in a flourishing state, before hostile armies " laid a scene of desolation; and Vologeses would consult his own " advantage, as well as that of his people, by preferring the friend- " ship of Rome to wild ambition and the havoc of a destructive
                                                    " war.

" war. The internal diffenfions that diftract the kingdom of
" Parthia are too well known. It is alfo known, that Vologefes
" has for his fubjects fierce and barbarous nations, whom no law
" can check, no government can controul. Nero, on the con-
" trary, fees a fettled calm throughout the Roman world, and,
" except the rupture with Parthia, has no other war upon his
" hands." Such was Corbulo's anfwer. To give it weight, he
added the terrors of the fword. The grandees of Armenia, who
had been the firft to revolt, were driven out of their poffeffions,
and their caftles were levelled to the ground. Between the
weak, who made no refiftance, and the brave and refolute, no
diftinction was made. All were involved in one common danger ;
no place was fafe ; hills and mountains no lefs than the open
plain were filled with confternation.

XXVIII. THE name of Corbulo was not, as is ufual among
adverfe nations, hated by the enemy. He was, on the contrary,
held in high efteem, and, by confequence, his advice had great
weight with the Barbarians. Vologefes did not wifh for a
general war. He defired a truce in favour of fome particular
provinces. Tiridates propofed an interview with the Roman
general. An early day was appointed. The place for the congrefs was chofen by the prince on the very fpot where Pætus
and his legions were invefted. The fcene of their late victory
flattered the pride of the Barbarians. Corbulo did not decline the
meeting. The face of things he knew was changed, and the
reverfe of fortune was glorious to himfelf. The difgrace of Pætus
gave him no anxiety. Having refolved to pay the laft funeral
rites to the flaughtered foldiers, whofe bodies lay weltering on
the field, he chofe, for that purpofe, the fon of the vanquifhed
general, then a military tribune, and ordered him to march at
the head of the companies appointed to perform that melancholy
duty.

duty. On the day fixed for the convention *(a)*, Tiberius Alexander, a Roman knight, who had been sent by Nero to superintend the operations of the campaign, and with him Vivianus Annius, son-in-law to Corbulo, but not yet of senatorian age *(b)*, though, in the absence of his superior officer, he was appointed to command the fifth legion, arrived in the camp of Tiridates, in the character of hostages, chosen, not only to remove from the mind of the prince all suspicion, but at the same time to do him honour. The Parthian and the Roman general proceeded to the interview, each attended by twenty horsemen. As soon as they drew near, Tiridates leaped from his horse. Corbulo returned the compliment. They advanced on foot, and took each other by the hand.

XXIX. The Roman general addressed the prince. He praised the judgment of a young man, who had the moderation to prefer pacific measures to the calamities of war. Tiridates expatiated on the splendour of his illustrious line, and then taking a milder tone, agreed to set out on a journey to Rome. In a juncture when the affairs of Parthia were in a flourishing state, a prince, descended from the Arsacides humbling himself before the emperor, would present to the Roman people a new scene of glory. It was then settled as a preliminary article, that Tiridates should lay down the regal diadem at the foot of Nero's statue, and never again resume it, till delivered to him by the hand of the emperor. The parties embraced each other, and the convention ended.

In a few days afterwards the two armies were drawn out with great military pomp. On one side stood the Parthian cavalry, ranged in battalions, with all the pride of eastern magnificence. The Roman legions appeared on the opposite ground, the eagles glittering to the eye, the banners displayed, and the images of

the

the gods, in regular order, forming a kind of temple. In the
centre stood a tribunal, and upon it a currule chair supporting
the statue of Nero. Tiridates approached. Having immolated
victims with the usual rites, he took the diadem from his brow,
and laid it at the foot of the statue. The spectators gazed with
earnest ardour, and every bosom heaved with mixed emotions.
The place where the legions were besieged and forced to capitulate was before the eye, and the same spot exhibited a reverse
of fortune. They saw Tiridates on the point of setting out for
Rome, a spectacle to the nations through which he was to pass,
and to exhibit, in the presence of Nero, the humble condition of
a suppliant prince; how little better than a captive!

XXX. To the glory resulting from these events Corbulo added
the graceful qualities of affability and condescension. He invited
Tiridates to a banquet. The prince was struck with the novelty
of Roman manners. Every object awakened his curiosity. He
desired to know the reason of all that he observed. When the
watch *(a)* was stationed, why was it announced by a centurion?
Why did the company, when the banquet closed, rise from
table at the sound of a trumpet? And why was the fire on
the augural altar lighted with a torch? The Roman general answered all enquiries, not without partiality for his country. He
aggrandized every thing, and gave the Parthian the noblest idea
of the manners and institutions of the ancient Romans. On the
following day Tiridates desired reasonable time to prepare for so
long a journey, and, before he undertook it, desired that he might
be at liberty to visit his mother and his brothers. His request
was granted. The prince delivered up his daughter, as a hostage,
and dispatched letters to Nero in terms of submission.

XXXI. He met his two brothers, Pacorus in Media, and
Vologeses

B O O K
XV.
A. U. C.
816.
A. D.
63.

Vologeses at Ecbatana *(a)*. The Parthian king was not inattentive to the interest of Tiridates. He had already sent dispatches to Corbulo, requesting that his brother should not be disgraced by any circumstance that looked like a badge of slavery; that he should not be obliged to surrender his sword; that the honour of embracing the governors *(b)* of the several provinces should not be denied to him; that he should not undergo the humiliating affront of waiting at their gates, or in their antichambers; and that at Rome he should be treated with all the marks of distinction usually paid to the consuls. The truth is, the Parthian king, trained up in all the pride of despotism, knew but little of the Romans. He was not informed, that it is the character and policy of that people to maintain, with zeal, the substantial interests of the empire, without any regard to petty formalities, the mere shadow of dominion.

XXXII. In the course of the year Nero granted the rights and privileges of Latium to the maritime nations *(a)* at the foot of the Alps. He likewise assigned to the Roman knights distinct seats in the circus, advancing them before the ·space allotted to the populace. Till this regulation took place, the knights were mixed indiscriminately with the multitude, the Roscian law *(b)* extending to no more than fourteen rows of the theatre. A spectacle of gladiators was exhibited this year, in nothing inferior to the magnificence displayed on former occasions; but a number of senators, and women of illustrious rank, descended into the arena *(c)*, and, by exhibiting their persons in the lists, brought disgrace on themselves and their families.

XXXIII. In the consulship of Caius Læcanius and Marcus Licinius, Nero's passion for theatrical fame broke out with a degree of vehemence not to be resisted. He had hitherto performed

in

in private only, during the sports of the Roman youth, called
the JUVENALIA ; but, upon those occasions, he was confined to
his own palace or his gardens; a sphere too limited for such
bright ambition, and so fine a voice.   He glowed with impatience to present himself before the public eye, but had not yet
the courage to make his first appearance at Rome.   Naples was
deemed a Greek city, and, for that reason, a proper place to
begin his career of glory.   With the laurels, which he was there
to acquire, he might pass over into Greece, and after gaining,
by victory in song, the glorious crown which antiquity considered as a sacred prize, he might return to Rome, with his honours blooming round him, and by his celebrity inflame the
curiosity of the populace.   With this idea he pursued his plan.
The theatre at Naples was crowded with spectators.   Not only
the inhabitants of the city, but a prodigious multitude from all
the municipal towns and colonies in the neighbourhood, flocked
together, attracted by the novelty of a spectacle so very extraordinary.   All who followed the prince, to pay their court, or
as persons belonging to his train, attended on the occasion.   The
menial servants, and even the common soldiers, were admitted
to enjoy the pleasures of the day.

XXXIV. THE theatre, of course, was crowded.   An accident
happened, which men in general considered as an evil omen:
with the emperor it passed for a certain sign of the favour and
protection of the gods.   As soon as the audience dispersed, the
theatre tumbled to pieces.   No other mischief followed.   Nero
seized the opportunity to compose hymns of gratitude.   He sung
them himself, celebrating with melodious airs his happy escape
from the ruin.   Being now determined to cross the Adriatic, he
stopt at Beneventum.   At that place Vatinius entertained him
with a shew of gladiators.   Of all the detestable characters that

difgraced the court of Nero, this man was the moft pernicious. He was bred up in a fhoe-maker's ftall.   Deformed in his perfon, he poffeffed a vein of ribaldry and vulgar humour, which qualified him to fucceed as buffoon.   In the character of a jefter he recommended himfelf to notice, but foon forfook his fcurrility for the trade of an informer; and having by the ruin of the worthieft citizens arrived at eminence in guilt, he rofe to wealth and power, the moft dangerous mifcreant of that evil period!

XXXV. NERO was a conftant fpectator of the fports exhibited at Beneventum; but even amidft his diverfions his heart knew no paufe from cruelty.   He compelled Torquatus Silanus to put an end to his life, for no other reafon, than becaufe he united to the fplendor of the Junian family the honour of being great grandfon to Auguftus (a).   The profecutors, fuborned for the bufinefs, alleged againft him, that, having prodigally wafted his fortune in gifts and largeffes, he had no refource left but war and civil commotion.   With that defign he retained about his perfon men of rank and diftinction, employed in various offices: he had his fecretaries, his treafurers, and paymafters, all in the ftyle of imperial dignity, even then anticipating what his ambition aimed at.   This charge being made in form, fuch of his freedmen as were known to be in the confidence of their mafter were feized, and loaded with fetters.   Silanus faw that his doom was impending, and, to prevent the fentence of condemnation, opened the veins of both his arms.   Nero, according to his cuftom, expreffed himfelf in terms of lenity. "The guilt of Silanus," he faid, "was manifeft; and, though, by an act of defpair, he "fhewed that his crimes admitted no defence, his life would "have been fpared, had he thought proper to truft to the cle "mency of his judge."

XXXVI. IN

XXXVI. In a short time after, Nero, for reasons not sufficiently explained, resolved to defer his expedition into Greece. He
returned to Rome, cherishing in imagination a new design to
visit the eastern nations, and Ægypt in particular. This project
had been for some time settled in his mind. He announced it
by a proclamation, in which he assured the people, that his
absence would be of short duration, and, in the interval, the
peace and good order of the commonwealth would be in no kind
of danger. For the success of his voyage he went to offer up
prayers in the capitol. He proceeded thence to the temple of
Vesta. Being there seized with a sudden tremor in every joint,
arising either from a superstitious fear of the goddess, or from a
troubled conscience, which never ceased to goad and persecute
him, he renounced his enterprise altogether, artfully pretending
that the love of his country, which he felt warm at his heart, was
dearer to him than all other considerations. "I have seen," he
said, "the dejected looks of the people; I have heard the mur-
"murs of complaint: the idea of so long a voyage afflicts the
"citizens; and, indeed, how should it be otherwise, when the
"shortest excursion I could make was always sure to depress
"their spirits? The sight of their prince has, at all times, been
"their comfort and their best support. In private families the
"pleges of natural affection can soften the resolutions of a father,
"and mould him to their purpose: the people of Rome have the
"same ascendant over the mind of their sovereign. I feel their
"influence; I yield to their wishes." With these and such like
expressions he amused the multitude. Their love of public spectacles made them eager for his presence, and, above all, they
dreaded, if he left the capitol, a dearth of provisions. The senate
and the leading men looked on with indifference, unable to decide which was most to be dreaded, his presence in the city, or
his tyranny at a distance. They agreed at length (as in alarm-

BOOK
XV.

A. U. C.
817.
A. D.
64.

M m 2

ing

ing cafes fear is always in hafte to conclude) that what happened was the worft evil that could befall them.

XXXVII. NERO wifhed it to be believed that Rome was the place in which he moft delighted. To diffufe this opinion, he eftablifhed convivial meetings in all the fquares and public places *(a)*. The whole city feemed to be his houfe. Of the various feafts given upon this occafion, that, which was prepared for the prince by Tigellinus, exceeded in profufion and luxury every thing of the kind. I fhall here give a defcription of this celebrated entertainment, that the reader, from one example, may form his idea of the prodigality of the times, and that hiftory may not be encumbered with a repetition of the fame enormities. Tigellinus gave his banquet on the lake of Agrippa *(b)*, on a platform of prodigious fize *(c)*, built for the reception of the guefts.

To move this magnificent edifice to and fro on the water, he prepared a number of boats fuperbly decorated with gold and ivory. The rowers were a band of Pathics. Each had his ftation, according to his age, or his fkill in the fcience of debauchery. The country round was ranfacked for game and animals of the chafe. Fifh was brought from every fea, and even from the ocean *(b)*. On the borders of the lake brothels were erected, and filled with women of illuftrious rank. On the oppofite bank was feen a band of harlots, who made no fecret of their vices, or their perfons. In wanton dance and lafcivious attitudes they difplayed their naked charms. When night came on, a fudden illumination from the adjacent groves and buildings blazed over the lake. A concert of mufic, vocal and inftrumental, enlivened the fcene. Nero rioted in all kinds of lafcivious pleafure. Between lawful and unlawful gratifications he made no diftinction. Cor-

ruption

ruption feemed to be at a ftand, if, at the end of a few days, he had not devifed a new abomination to fill the meafure of his crimes. He perfonated a woman, and in that character was given in marriage to one of his infamous herd, a Pathic, named Pythagoras *(d)*. The emperor of Rome, with the affected airs of female delicacy, put on the nuptial veil. The augurs affifted at the ceremony; the portion of the bride was openly paid *(e)* ; the genial bed was difplayed to view; nuptial torches were lighted up; the whole was public, not even excepting the endearments which, in a natural marriage, decency referves for the fhades of night.

XXXVIII. A DREADFUL calamity followed in a fhort time after, by fome afcribed to chance, and by others *(a)* to the execrable wickednefs of Nero. The authority of hiftorians is on both fides, and which preponderates it is not eafy to determine. It is, however, certain, that of all the difafters that ever befel the city of Rome from the rage of fire, this was the worft, the moft violent, and deftructive. The flame broke out in that part of the circus which adjoins, on one fide, to mount Palatine, and, on the other, to mount Cælius. It caught a number of fhops ftored with combuftible goods, and, gathering force from the winds, fpread with rapidity from one end of the circus to the other. Neither the thick walls of houfes, nor the inclofure of temples, nor any other building, could check the rapid progrefs of the flames. A dreadful conflagration followed. The level parts of the city were deftroyed. The fire communicated to the higher buildings, and, again laying hold of inferior places, fpread with a degree of velocity that nothing could refift. The form of the ftreets, long and narrow, with frequent windings, and no regular opening, according to the plan of ancient Rome *(b)*, contributed

to

to increafe the mifchief. The fhrieks and lamentations of women, the infirmities of age, and the weaknefs of the young and tender, added mifery to the dreadful fcene. Some endeavoured to provide for themfelves, others to fave their friends, in one part dragging along the lame and impotent, in another waiting to receive the tardy, or expecting relief themfelves; they hurried, they lingered, they obftructed one another; they looked behind, and the fire broke out in front; they efcaped from the flames, and in their place of refuge found no fafety; the fire raged in every quarter; all were involved in one general conflagration.

The unhappy wretches fled to places remote, and thought themfelves fecure, but foon perceived the flames raging round them. Which way to turn, what to avoid, or what to feek, no one could tell. They crowded the ftreets; they fell proftrate on the ground; they lay ftretched in the fields, in confternation and difmay refigned to their fate. Numbers loft their whole fub-ftance, even the tools and implements by which they gained their livelihood, and, in that diftrefs, did not wifh to furvive. Others, wild with affliction for their friends and relations whom they could not fave, embraced a voluntary death, and perifhed in the flames. During the whole of this difmal fcene no man dared to attempt any thing that might check the violence of the dreadful calamity. A crew of incendiaries ftood near at hand denouncing vengeance on all who offered to interfere. Some were fo abandoned as to heap fuel on the flames. They threw in firebrands and flaming torches, proclaiming aloud, that they had authority for what they did. Whether, in fact, they had received fuch horrible orders, or, under that device, meant to plunder with greater licentioufnefs, cannot now be known.

XXXIX. DURING the whole of this terrible conflagration
Nero

Nero remained at Antium, without a thought of returning to the city, till the fire approached the building by which he had communicated the gardens of Mæcenas *(a)* with the imperial palace. All help, however, was too late. The palace, the contiguous edifices, and every houfe adjoining, were laid in ruins. To relieve the unhappy people, wandering in diftrefs without a place of fhelter, he opened the field of Mars, as alfo the magnificent buildings raifed by Agrippa *(b)*, and even his own imperial gardens *(c)*. He ordered a number of fheds to be thrown up with all poffible difpatch, for the ufe of the populace. Houfehold utenfils and all kinds of neceffary implements were brought from Oftia, and other cities in the neighbourhood. The price of grain was reduced to three fefterces. For acts like thefe, munificent and well-timed, Nero might hope for a return of popular favour; but his expectations were in vain; no man was touched with gratitude. A report prevailed *(d)* that, while the city was in a blaze, Nero went to his own theatre, and there, mounting the ftage, fung the deftruction of Troy, as a happy allufion to the prefent misfortune.

XL. On the fixth day the fire was fubdued at the foot of mount Efquiline. This was effected, by demolifhing a number of buildings, and thereby leaving a void fpace, where for want of materials the flame expired. The minds of men had fcarce begun to recover from their confternation, when the fire broke out a fecond time with no lefs fury than before. This happened, however, in a more open quarter, where fewer lives were loft; but the temples of the gods, the porticos, and buildings raifed for the decoration of the city, were levelled to the ground. The popular odium was now more inflamed than ever, as this fecond alarm began in the houfe of Tigellinus, formerly the manfion of Æmilius. A fufpicion prevailed, that to build a new city, and give it his own name, was the ambition of Nero. Of the four-

teen

teen quarters, into which Rome was divided, four only were left entire, three were reduced to afhes, and the remaining feven prefented nothing better than a heap of fhattered houfes, half in ruins.

XLI. The number of houfes, temples, and infulated manfions deftroyed by the fire cannot be afcertained. But the moft venerable monuments of antiquity, which the worfhip of ages had rendered facred, were laid in ruins: amongft thefe were the temple dedicated to the moon by Servius Tullius; the fane and the great altar confecrated by Evander, the Arcadian, to Hercules, his vifitor and his gueft *(a)*; the chapel of Jupiter Stator *(b)*, built by Romulus; the palace of Numa, and the temple of Vefta *(c)*, with the tutelar gods of Rome. With thefe were confumed the trophies of fo many victories, the inimitable works of the Grecian artifts, with the precious monuments of literature and ancient genius, all at prefent remembered by men advanced in years, but irrecoverably loft. Not even the fplendour, with which the new city rofe out of the ruins of the old, could compenfate for that lamented difafter. It did not efcape obfervation, that the fire broke out on the fourteenth before the calends of July *(d)*, a day remarkable for the conflagration kindled by the Senones, when thofe Barbarians took the city of Rome by ftorm, and burnt it to the ground. Men of reflection, who refined on every thing with minute curiofity, calculated the number of years, months and days, from the foundation of Rome to the firing of it by the Gauls; and from that calamity to the prefent they found the interval of time precifely the fame.

XLII. Nero did not blufh to convert to his own ufe the public ruins of his country. He built a magnificent palace *(a)*, in which the objects that excited admiration were neither gold

nor

nor precious ftones. Thofe decorations, long fince introduced by luxury, were grown ftale, and hackneyed to the eye. A different fpecies of magnificence was now confulted: expanfive lakes and fields of vaft extent were intermixed with pleafing variety; woods and forefts ftretched to an immeafurable length, prefenting gloom and folitude amidft fcenes of open fpace, where the eye wandered with furprife over an unbounded profpect. This prodigious plan was carried on under the direction of two furveyors, whofe names were Severus and Celer. Bold and original in their projects, thefe men undertook to conquer nature, and to perform wonders even beyond the imagination and the riches of the prince. They promifed to form a navigable canal from the lake Avernus *(b)* to the mouth of the Tiber. The experiment, like the genius of the men, was bold and grand; but it was to be carried over a long tract of barren land, and, in fome places, through oppofing mountains. The country round was parched and dry, without one humid fpot, except the Pomptinian marfh *(c)*, from which water could be expected. A fcheme fo vaft could not be accomplifhed without immoderate labour, and, if practicable, the end was in no proportion to the expence and labour. But the prodigious and almoft impoffible had charms for the enterprifing fpirit of Nero. He began to hew a paffage through the hills that furround the lake Avernus, and fome traces of his deluded hopes are vifible at this day.

XLIII. THE ground, which, after marking out his own domain, Nero left to the public, was not laid out for the new city in a hurry and without judgment, as was the cafe after the irruption of the Gauls. A regular plan was formed; the ftreets were made wide and long; the elevation *(a)* of the houfes was defined, with an open area before the doors, and porticos *(b)* to fecure and adorn the front. The expence of the porticos Nero under-

<table>
<tr><td>VOL. II.</td><td>N n</td><td>took</td></tr>
</table>

took to defray out of his own revenue. He promifed, befides, as foon as the work was finifhed, to clear the ground, and leave a clear fpace to every houfe, without any charge to the occupier. In order to excite a fpirit of induftry and emulation, he held forth rewards proportioned to the rank of each individual, provided the buildings were finifhed in a limited time. The rubbifh, by his order, was removed to the marfhes of Oftia, and the fhips that brought corn up the river were to return loaded with the refufe of the workmen. Add to all this, the feveral houfes, built on a new principle, were to be raifed to a certain elevation, without beams or wood work, on arches of ftone from the quarries of (c) Alba or Gabii ; thofe materials being impervious, and of a nature to refift the force of fire. The fprings of water, which had been before that time intercepted by individuals for their feparate ufe, were no longer fuffered to be diverted from their channel, but left to the care of commiffioners, that the public might be properly fupplied, and, in cafe of fire, have a refervoir at hand to ftop the progrefs of the mifchief.

It was alfo fettled, that the houfes fhould no longer be conti-guous, with flight party-walls to divide them (d) ; but every houfe was to ftand detached, furrounded and infulated by its own inclofure. Thefe regulations, it muft be admitted, were of pub-lic utility, and added much to the embellifhment of the new city.. But ftill the old plan of Rome was not without its advocates. It was thought more conducive to the health (c) of the inhabitants.. The narrownefs of the ftreets and the elevation of the buildings ferved to exclude the rays of the fun ; whereas the more open fpace, having neither fhade nor fhelter, left men expofed to the intenfe heat of the day.

XLIV. THESE feveral regulations were, no doubt, the beft
that

that human wifdom could fuggeft. The next care was to propitiate the gods. The Sibylline books were confulted, and the confequence was that fupplications were decreed to Vulcan, to Ceres, and Proferpine. A band of matrons offered their prayers and facrifices to Juno, firft in the capitol, and next on the neareft margin of the fea, where they fupplied themfelves with water, to fprinkle the temple and the ftatue of the goddefs. A felect number of women, who had hufbands actually living, laid the deities on their facred beds *(a)*, and kept midnight vigils with the ufual folemnity. But neither thefe religious ceremonies, nor the liberal donations of the prince, could efface from the minds of men the prevailing opinion, that Rome was fet on fire by his own orders. The infamy of that horrible tranfaction ftill adhered to him. In order, if poffible, to remove the imputation, he determined to transfer the guilt to others. For this purpofe he punifhed, with exquifite torture, a race of men detefted for their evil practices *(b)*, by vulgar appellation commonly called Chriftians.

The name was derived from Chrift, who, in the reign of Tiberius, fuffered under Pontius Pilate, the procurator of Judæa. By that event the fect, of which he was the founder, received a blow, which, for a time, checked the growth of a dangerous fuperftition *(c)*; but it revived foon after, and fpread with recruited vigour, not only in Judæa, the foil that gave it birth, but even in the city of Rome, the common fink into which every thing infamous and abominable flows like a torrent from all quarters of the world. Nero proceeded with his ufual artifice. He found a fet of profligate and abandoned wretches, who were induced to confefs themfelves guilty, and, on the evidence of fuch men, a number of Chriftians were convicted, not, indeed, upon clear evidence of their having fet the city on fire, but rather on account of their fullen hatred of the whole human race *(d)*. They were put

N n 2

to

to death with exquisite cruelty, and to their sufferings Nero added mockery and derision. Some were covered with the skins of wild beasts, and left to be devoured by dogs ; others were nailed to the cross ; numbers were burnt alive ; and many, covered over with inflammable matter, were lighted up, when the day declined, to serve as torches during the night *(e)*.

For the convenience of seeing this tragic spectacle, the emperor lent his own gardens. He added the sports of the circus, and assisted in person, sometimes driving a curricle, and occasionally mixing with the rabble in his coachman's dress. At length the cruelty of these proceedings filled every breast with compassion. Humanity relented in favour of the Christians. The manners of that people were, no doubt, of a pernicious tendency, and their crimes called for the hand of justice : but it was evident, that they fell a sacrifice, not for the public good, but to glut the rage and cruelty of one man only.

XLV. Meanwhile, to supply the unbounded prodigality of the prince, all Italy was ravaged ; the provinces were plundered ; and the allies of Rome, with the several places that enjoyed the title of free cities, were put under contribution. The very gods were taxed. Their temples in the city were rifled of their treasures, and heaps of massy gold, which, through a series of ages, the virtue of the Roman people, either returning thanks for victories, or, performing their vows made in the hour of distress, had dedicated to religious uses, were now produced to answer the demands of riot and extravagance. In Greece and Asia rapacity was not content with seizing the votive offerings that adorned the temples, but even the very statues of the gods were deemed lawful prey. To carry this impious robbery into execution, Acratus and Secundus Carinas were sent with a special commission ; the

former,

former, one of Nero's freedmen, of a genius ready for any black
defign; the latter, a man of literature, with the Greek philofophy
fluent in his mouth, and not one virtue at his heart. It was a
report current at the time, that Seneca, wifhing to throw from
himfelf all refponfibility for thefe impious acts, defired leave to
retire to fome part of Italy. Not being able to fucceed in his
requeft, he feigned a nervous diforder, and never ftirred out of
his room. If credit be due to fome writers, a dofe of poifon was
prepared for him by Cleonicus, one of his freedmen, by the inftigation of Nero. The philofopher, however, warned by the fame
fervant, whofe courage failed him, or, perhaps, fhielded from
danger by his own wary difpofition, efcaped the fnare. He lived
at that very time on the moft fimple diet: wild apples, that grew
in the woods, were his food; and water from the clear purling
ftream ferved to quench his thirft.

XLVI. About the fame time a body of gladiators, detained
in cuftody at Prænefte *(a)*, made an attempt to recover their
liberty. The military guard was called out, and the tumult died
away. The incident, notwithftanding, revived the memory of
Spartacus *(b)*. The calamities, that followed the daring enterprife of that adventurer, became the general topic, and filled the
minds of all with dreadful apprehenfions. Such is the genius of
the populace, ever prone to fudden innovations, yet terrified at
the approach of danger. In a few days after, advice was received,
that the fleet had fuffered by a violent ftorm. This was not an
event of war, for there never was a period of fuch profound tranquillity; but Nero had ordered the fhips, on a ftated day, to
affemble on the coaft of Campania. The dangers of the fea
never entered into his confideration. His orders were peremptory.
The pilots, to mark their zeal, fet fail in tempeftuous weather
from the port of Formia *(c)*. While they were endeavouring to

double.

double the cape of Mifenum, a fquall of wind from the fouth threw them on the coaft of Cuma, where a number of the larger gallies, and almoft all the fmaller veffels, were dafhed to pieces.

XLVII. Towards the clofe of the year omens and prodigies filled the minds of the people with apprehenfions of impending mifchief. Such dreadful peals of thunder were never known. A comet appeared, and that phænomenon was a certain prelude to fome bloody act to be committed by Nero. Monftrous births, fuch as men and beafts with double heads, were feen in the ftreets and public ways; and in the midft of facrifices, which required victims big with young, the like conceptions fell from the entrails of animals flain at the altar. In the territory of Placentia *(a)* a calf was dropped with its head growing at the extreme part of the leg. The conftruction of the foothfayers was, that another head was preparing for the government of the world, but would prove weak, infufficient, and be foon detected, like the monftrous productions, which did not reft concealed in the womb, but came before their time, and lay expofed to public view near the high road.

XLVIII. Silius Nerva and Atticus Veftinus entered on their confulfhip. In that juncture a deep confpiracy was formed, and carried on with fuch a fpirit of enterprife, that in the moment of its birth it was almoft ripe for execution. Senators, Roman knights, military men, and even women gave in their names with emulation, all incited by their zeal for Caius Pifo, and their deteftation of Nero. Pifo was defcended from the houfe of Calpurnius, by his paternal line related to the firft families in Rome. His virtues, or his amiable qualities that refembled virtues, made him the idol of the people. An orator of high diftinction, he employed his eloquence in the defence of his fellow citizens;

poffeffed of great wealth, he was generous to his friends; by nature courteous, he was affable and polite to all. To thefe accomplifhments he united a graceful figure and an engaging countenance. In his moral conduct neither ftrict nor regular, he led a life of voluptuous eafe, fond of pomp and fplendour, and, at times, free and luxurious in his pleafures. His irregularities ferved to grace his character. At a time when vice had charms for all orders of men, it was not expected, that the fovereign fhould lead a life of aufterity and felf-denial.

XLIX. THE confpiracy did not originate from the ambition of Pifo. Among fo many bold and generous fpirits it is not eafy to name the perfon who firft fet the whole in motion. Subrius Flavius, a tribune of the prætorian guards, and Sulpicius Afper, were the active leaders. The firmnefs with which they afterwards met their fate fufficiently marks their characters. Annæus Lucan, the celebrated poet, and Plautius Lateranus, conful elect, entered into the plot with ardour and inflamed refentment. Lucan had perfonal provocations : Nero was an enemy to his rifing fame: not being able to vie with that eminent genius, he ordered him not to make his verfes public, determined to filence what he vainly ftrove to emulate. Lateranus brought with him no private animofity : he acted on nobler principles ; the love of his country infpired him, and he knew no other motive. Flavius Scevinus and Afranius Quinctianus, both of fenatorian rank, ftood forward to guide the enterprife with a degree of fpirit little expected from the tenour of their lives. Scevinus, addicted to his pleafures, paffed his days in luxury, floth, and languor. Quinctianus was decried for the effeminacy of his manners. Nero had lampooned him in a copy of defamatory verfes, and to revenge the injury Quinctianus became a patriot.

L. THE

L. THE confpirators had frequent meetings. They inveighed againft the vices of Nero; they painted forth in glaring colours all his atrocious deeds, by which the empire was brought to the brink of ruin; they urged the neceffity of choofing a fucceffor equal to the tafk of reftoring a diftreffed and tottering ftate, and, in the interval, enlifted in their confederacy feveral Roman knights, namely, Tullius Senecio, Cervarius Proculus, Vulcatius Araricus, Julius Tugurinus, Munatius Gratus, Antonius Natalis, and Martius Feftus. Senecio, the firft in the lift, had lived in the clofeft intimacy with the prince, and, being ftill obliged to wear the mafk, he found the interval big with anxiety, miftruft, and danger. Antonius Natalis was the bofom-friend and confidential agent of Pifo: the reft had their feparate views, and in a revolution hoped to find their private advantage. There were, befides Subrius Flavius and Sulpicius Afper already mentioned, a number of military men ready to draw their fwords in the caufe. In this clafs were Granius Silvanus and Statius Proximus, both tribunes of the prætorian bands; Maximus Scaurus and Venetus Paullus, two centurions. But the main ftrength and pillar of the party was Fenius Rufus *(a)*, commander in chief of the Prætorian guards; a man of principle, and for the integrity of his conduct efteemed and honoured by the people. But Tigellinus ftood in higher favour with the prince, and by his cruel devices no lefs than by his tafte for riot and debauchery, fo ingratiated himfelf, that he was able to fupplant the prætorian præfect, and by fecret accufations to endanger his life. He reprefented him to Nero as the favoured lover of Agrippina *(b)*, ftill cherifhing a regard for her memory, and lying in wait for an opportunity to revenge her wrongs.

Rufus inclined to the difcontented party, and, at length, declared

clared himfelf willing to affift their enterprife. Encouraged by this acceffion of ftrength, the confpirators began to think of the decifive blow, and to deliberate about the time and place. We are told that Subrius Flavius refolved to take to himfelf the glory of the deed. Two different fchemes occurred to him. One was, while the prince was finging on the ftage, to difpatch him in fight of the whole theatre. His fecond project was, while Nero was rambling abroad in his midnight frolics, to fet fire to the palace, and, in the tumult, to take him by furprife, unattended by his guards. The laft feemed to be the fafeft meafure. The tyrant, unfeen and unaffifted, would fall a devoted victim, and die in folitude. On the other hand, the idea of a brave exploit, performed in the prefence of applauding numbers, fired the generous ardour of that heroic mind. But prudential confiderations had too much weight. He wifhed to gain immortal fame, and he thought of his own perfonal fafety; a tame reflection, always adverfe to every great and noble enterprife.

LI. WHILE the confpirators lingered in fufpenfe, prolonging the awful period of their hopes and fears, a woman, of the name of Epicharis, apprifed of the plot (by what means is ftill a myftery), began to animate their drooping fpirit, and to blame their cold delay. What made her conduct fingular on this occafion was, that, before this time, not one great or honourable fentiment was ever known to have entered her heart. Seeing the bufinefs languifh, fhe retired in difguft, and went into Campania. But a fpirit like hers could not be at reft. She endeavoured to feduce the officers of the fleet then lying at Mifenum. She began her approaches to Volufius Proculus, an officer who had under his command a thoufand marines. He was one of the affaffins employed in the tragic cataftrophe of Nero's mother. His reward, he thought, was in no proportion to the magnitude of the

VOL. II.   O o   crime.

crime. Being known to Epicharis, or having then contracted a recent friendſhip, he began to diſcloſe the ſecrets of his heart. He enumerated his exploits in Nero's ſervice, and complained of the ingratitude with which he was ill requited ; avowing, at the ſame time, a fixed reſolution to revenge himſelf, whenever an opportunity offered. The woman, from this diſcourſe, conceived hopes of gaining a proſelyte, and by his means a number of others. She ſaw that a revolt in the fleet would be of the greateſt moment. Nero was fond of ſailing parties on the coaſt of Miſenum and Putcoli, and would, by conſequence, put himſelf in the power of the mariners.

Epicharis entered into cloſe conference with Proculus ; ſhe recapitulated the various acts of cruelty committed by Nero. The fathers, ſhe ſaid, had no doubt remaining; they were of one mind; all agreed, that a tyrant, who overturned the laws and conſtitution of his country, ought to fall a ſacrifice to an injured people. She added, that Proculus would do well to co-operate with the friends of liberty. If he kindled the ſame ſpirit in the minds of the ſoldiers, a ſure reward would wait him. In the fervour of her zeal, ſhe had the prudence to conceal the names of the conſpirators. That precaution ſerved to ſcreen her afterwards, when the marine officer turned informer, and betrayed the whole to Nero. She was cited to anſwer, and confronted with her accuſer ; but the charge, reſting entirely on the evidence of one man, without a circumſtance to ſupport it, was eaſily eluded. Epicharis, notwithſtanding, was detained in cuſtody. Nero's ſuſpicions were not to be removed. The accuſation was deſtitute of proof, but he was not the leſs inclined to believe the worſt.

LII. The undaunted firmneſs of Epicharis did not quiet the apprehenſions of the conſpirators. Dreading a diſcovery, they

deter-

determined to execute their purpofe without delay. The place
they fixed upon was a villa belonging to Pifo, in the neighbourhood of Baiæ, where the emperor, attracted by the beauties of
that delightful fpot, was ufed to enjoy the pleafure of bathing,
and his convivial parties, divefted of his guards, and unincum-
bered by the parade of ftate. Pifo objected to the meafure.
" What would the world fay, if his table were imbrued with
" blood, and the gods of hofpitality violated by the murder of a
" prince, however detefted for his atrocious deeds ? Rome was
" the proper theatre for fuch a cataftrophe. The fcene fhould be
" in his own palace, that haughty manfion built with the fpoils
" of plundered citizens. The blow for liberty would be ftill
" more noble before an affembly of the people. The actions of
" men, who dared nobly for the public, fhould be feen by the
" public eye."

Such were the objections advanced by Pifo in the prefence of
the confpirators : in his heart he had other reafons. He dreaded
Lucius Silanus (a), knowing his high defcent, and the rare accomplifhments which he had acquired under the care of Caius Caffius (b), who had trained him from his youth, and formed his mind
to every thing great and honourable. A man thus diftinguifhed
might afpire to the imperial dignity. All who ftood aloof from
the confpiracy would be ready to fecond his ambition, and, moft
probably, would be joined by others, whom the fate of a devoted
prince, cut off by treachery, might touch with compaffion. Pifo
was fuppofed to have another fecret motive : he knew the genius
and the ardent fpirit of Veftinus, the conful. A man of his character might think of reftoring the old republic, or be for choofing
another emperor, to fhew mankind that the fovereign power was
a gift to be difpofed of according to his will and pleafure. Veftinus, in fact, had no fhare in the confpiracy, though he was

after-

afterwards charged as an accomplice, and, under that pretence, doomed to death by the unappeasable malice and the cruelty of Nero.

LIII. At length the conspirators fixed their day. They chose the time of the public games, which were soon to be performed in the circus, according to established usage, in honour of Ceres. During that festival, the emperor, who rarely shewed himself to the people, but remained sequestered in his palace or his gardens, would not fail to attend his favourite diversions; and, in that scene of gaiety, access to his person would not be difficult. The assault was to be made in the following manner. Lateranus, a man of undaunted resolution, and an athletic form, was to approach the prince, with an humble air of supplication, as if to entreat relief for himself and family; and, in the act of falling at his feet, to overthrow him by some sudden exertion, and by his weight keep him stretched on the ground. In that condition the tribunes, the centurions, and the rest of the conspirators, as the opportunity offered, and as courage prompted, were to fall on, and sacrifice their victim to the just resentments of the people.

Scevinus claimed the honour of being the first to strike. For this purpose, he had taken a dagger from the temple of Health, in Etruria, or, as some writers will have it, from the temple of Fortune, in the city of Ferentum. This instrument he carried constantly about him, as a sacred weapon, dedicated to the cause of liberty. It was further settled, that, during the tumult, Piso was to take his post in the temple of Ceres, and there remain till such time as Fenius and his confederates should call him forth, and conduct him to the camp. To conciliate the favour of the people, Antonia, the daughter of the late emperor, was to appear in the cavalcade.

This

BOOK
XV.

A. U. C.
818.
A. D.
65.

This laſt circumſtance, ſince it is related by Pliny, muſt reſt upon his authority. If it came from a leſs reſpectable quarter, I ſhould not think myſelf at liberty to ſuppreſs it ; but it may be proper to aſk, Is it probable that Antonia would hazard her reputation, and even her life, in a project ſo uncertain, and·ſo big with danger ? Is it probable that Piſo, diſtinguiſhed by his conjugal affection, could agree at once to abandon a wife whom he loved, and marry another to gratify his own wild ambition? But it may be ſaid, of all the paſſions that inflame the human mind, ambition is the moſt fierce and ardent, of power to extinguiſh every other ſentiment.

LIV. In a conſpiracy like the preſent, ſo widely diffuſed among perſons of different ages, rank, ſex, and condition, ſome of them poor, and others rich, it may well be matter of wonder, that nothing tranſpired, till the diſcovery burſt out at once from the houſe of Scevinus. This active partiſan, on the day preceding the intended execution of the plot, had a long conference with Antonius Natalis ; after which he returned home, and, having ſealed his will, unſheathed his ſacred dagger, already mentioned. Finding it blunted by long diſuſe, he gave it to Milichus, his freedman, to be well whetted, and ſharpened at the point. In the mean time, he went to his meal, more ſumptuouſly ſerved than had been his cuſtom. To his favourite ſlaves he granted their freedom, and among the reſt diſtributed ſums of money. He affected an air of gaiety ; he talked of indifferent things, with counterfeited cheerfulneſs; but a cloud hung over him, and too plainly ſhewed, that ſome grand deſign was labouring in his breaſt. He deſired the ſame Milichus to prepare bandages for the bracing of wounds, and applications to ſtop the effuſion of blood. If this man was, before that time, appriſed of the plot, he had till then acted with integrity ; but

the

the more probable opinion is, that he was never trufted, and now from all the circumftances drew his own conclufion.

The reward of treachery no fooner prefented itfelf to the fervile mind of an enfranchifed flave, than he faw wealth and power inviting him to betray his mafter. The temptation was bright and dazzling ; every principle gave way ; the life of his patron was fet at nought ; and for the gift of freedom no fenfe of gratitude remained. He advifed with his wife, and female advice was the worft he could take. The woman, with all the art and malice of her fex, alarmed his fears. Other flaves, fhe faid, and other freedmen had an eye on all that paffed. The filence of one could be of no ufe. The whole would be brought to light ; and he, who firft made the difcovery, would be entitled to the reward.

LV. At the dawn of day Milichus made the beft of his way to the gardens of Servilius. Being refufed admittance, he declared that he had bufinefs of the firft importance, nothing lefs than the difcovery of a dark and dangerous confpiracy. The porter conducted him to Epaphroditus, one of Nero's freedmen, who introduced him to the prefence of his mafter. Milichus informed the emperor of his danger, and laid open the machinations of his enemies, with all that he knew and all that he conjectured. He produced the dagger, deftined to give the mortal ftab, and defired to be confronted with the criminal.

Scevinus was feized by the foldiers, and dragged in cuftody to anfwer the charge. " The dagger," he faid, " was a facred re" lic, left to him by his anceftors. He had preferved it with " veneration, and kept it fafe in his chamber, till the perfidy of " a flave furreptitioufly conveyed it away. As to his will, he
" had

" had often changed it, often figned and fealed a new one, with-
" out any diftinction of days. He had been always generous to
" his domeftics; nor was it now for the firft time that he had
" given freedom to fome, and to others liberal donations. If in
" the laft inftance his bounty exceeded the former meafure, the
" reafon was, that being reduced in his circumftances, and preffed
" by his debts, he was afraid that his will would be declared void
" in favour of his creditors. With regard to his table, it was well
" known that his ftyle of living had ever been elegant, and even
" profufe, to a degree that drew upon him the cenfure of rigid
" moralifts. To the preparation of bandages and ftyptics he was
" an utter ftranger. None were made by his order. The whole
" was the invention of a vile informer, who found himfelf defti-
" tute of proof, and, to prop his infamous calumny, dared to
" fabricate a new charge, at once the author and the witnefs of
" a lie." This defence was uttered by Scevinus in a tone of
firmnefs, and the intrepidity of his manner gave it ftrength and
credit. He pronounced the informer a notorious profligate, and,
by confequence, an incompetent witnefs. This he urged with
fuch an air of confidence, and with fo much energy, that the information would have fallen to the ground, if the wife of Milichus had not obferved, in the prefence of her hufband, that a long
and fecret interview had taken place between the prifoner and
Natalis, both connected in the clofeft friendfhip with Caius Pifo.

LVI. NATALIS was cited to appear. Scevinus and he were
examined apart, touching their late meeting. What was their
bufinefs? and what was the converfation that paffed between
them? Their anfwers did not agree. Frefh fufpicions arofe, and
both were loaded with irons. At the fight of the rack, their
refolution failed. Natalis was the firft to confefs the guilt. He
knew all the particulars of the confpiracy, and was, by confequence,

quence, able to fupport his information. He named Caius Pifo, and proceeded next to Seneca. He had, probably, been employed as a meffenger between Seneca and Pifo; or, knowing the inveterate rancour with which Nero fought the deftruction of his tutor, he intended by that charge, however falfe, to make terms for himfelf. Scevinus, as foon as he heard that Natalis had made a difcovery, faw the inutility of remaining filent. Thinking the whole confpiracy detected, he yielded to his fears; and, following a mean example of pufillanimity, difcovered his accomplices. Three of the number, namely, Lucan, Quinctianus, and Senecio, perfifted for fome time to deny the whole with undaunted firmnefs, till induced, at length, by a promife of pardon, they thought they could not do enough to atone for their obftinacy. Lucan did not fcruple to impeach *(a)* his own mother, whofe name was Acilia. Quinctianus gave information againft Glicius Gallus, his deareft friend; and Senecio, in like manner, betrayed Annius Pollio.

LVII. Nero did not forget that Epicharis was ftill detained in cuftody, on the evidence of Volufius Proculus. The weaknefs of a female frame, he imagined, would not be able to endure the pangs of the rack. He therefore ordered her to be put to the moft exquifite torture. But neither ftripes, nor fire, nor the brutal rage of the executioners, who were determined not to be baffled by a woman, could fubdue a mind like hers, firm, conftant, and undaunted to the laft. Not a word was extorted from her. Her mifery ended for that day. On the next, the fame cruelty was prepared. Epicharis had no ftrength left. Her limbs were rent and diflocated. The executioners provided a chair to convey her to the place of torture. While they were conducting her, fhe took from her breaft the girdle that braced her garment, and, having faftened one end of it to the top of the chair, made

a noofe

a noofe for her neck, and, throwing herfelf from her feat, hung
fufpended with the whole weight of her body. In her mangled
condition the remains of life were foon extinguifhed.

Such was the fate of this magnanimous woman. She left behind her a glorious example of truth and conftancy, the more
ftriking, as this generous part was acted by an enfranchifed flave,
to fave the lives of men, in no degree related to her, and almoft
unknown. With heroic fortitude fhe endured the worft that
malice could inflict, at a time when men of illuftrious birth,
when officers, Roman knights and fenators, untried by the pangs
of torture, betrayed, with a kind of emulation, their friends, their
relations, and all that was dear to them. Quinctianus, Senecio,
and even Lucan continued to give in the names of the confpirators. Every new difcovery filled Nero with confternation,
though he had doubled his guard and taken every precaution to
fecure his perfon.

LVIII. PARTIES of foldiers under arms were flationed in
every quarter, on the walls of Rome, on the fea-coaft, and along
the banks of the Tiber. The city prefented the appearance of a
garrifoned town. The forum and the open fquares were filled
with cohorts of horfe and foot. The neighbouring villages and
the country round were invefted. Even private houfes were
fecured. The German foldiers, ordered out on duty, mixed with
the reft of the army. Being foreigners, Nero depended on their
fidelity. The confpirators were led forth in a long proceffion to
the tribunal of the prince. They ftood in crowds at his garden-
gate, waiting their turn to be fummoned before him. In regular
fucceffion they were admitted to an audience, and every trifle was
magnified into a crime. A fmile, a look, a whifper, a cafual
meeting at a convivial party, or a public fhow, was evidence of

treafon. Nor was it fufficient that Nero and Tigellinus were keen and vehement in their enquiries: Fenius Rufus took an active part. Having hitherto efcaped detection, he thought that violence againft his accomplices would be the beft way to fkreen himfelf. While he was eagerly preffing them with queftions, Subrius Flavius, the prætorian tribune, by figns and tokens, fignified to him his intention to cut off the tyrant in the midft of the examination. He had his hand on the hilt of his fword, when Rufus checked the brave defign.

LIX. On the firft detection of the plot, while Milichus was giving his evidence, and Scevinus was ftill wavering and irrefolute, fome of the confpirators exhorted Pifo to fhew himfelf in the camp, or to mount the public roftra, in order to gain the affections of the army and the people. " Let your friends," they faid, " affemble in a body; let them ftand forth in your caufe, " and they will be joined by numbers. The fame of an impend— " ing revolution would excite a general fpirit; and fame in great " undertakings has been often known to decide the event. Nero " will be taken by furprife; on his part no meafures are con- " certed. In fudden commotions the braveft are often ftruck " with terror; and if courage may be thus overpowered, what " will be the cafe of a theatrical emperor, a fcenic performer, a " vile comedian, affifted by Tigellinus and his band of harlots? " In all great enterprifes the attempt appears impracticable to little " minds; but the brave and valiant know that to dare is to " conquer. In a plot, in which numbers were embarked, the " filence of all could not be expected. The mind will waver, " and the body will fhrink from pain. There is no fecret fo " deeply laid but bribery will draw it forth, or cruelty can ex- " tort it. The guards in a fhort time might feize Pifo himfelf, " and drag him to an ignominious death. How much more glo-
" rious

" rious to fall bravely in the caufe of liberty! to die fword in
" hand, vindicating the rights of freeborn men, and roufing the
" army and the people to their own juft defence! The foldiers
" may refufe to join, and the people may be guilty of treachery
" to themfelves; but, even in that cafe, how noble to clofe the
" fcene with a fpirit worthy of your anceftors, bleft with the
" wifhes of the prefent age and the applaufe of all pofterity!"

BOOK XV.
A. U. C.
8,8.
A. D.
65.

Thefe exhortations made no impreffion on Pifo. He retired
to his own houfe, and there fortified his mind againft the worft
that could happen. A band of foldiers broke in upon him, all
felected from the recruits lately raifed, undifciplined, and new to
the fervice, but preferred by Nero to the veterans, whom he fufpected of difaffection. Pifo ordered the veins of both his arms to be
opened, and expired: his will was a difgrace to his memory. It was
written in a ftrain of fulfome flattery to the prince. He was betrayed into that act of meannefs by his affection for his wife, a
woman deftitute of merit, who had great elegance of form, and
nothing elfe to recommend her. Her name was Arria Galla.
She had been married to Domitius Silius, and from him feduced
by Pifo. The paffive fpirit of the injured hufband and the wanton character of the wife confpired to fix an indelible ftain on
the name of Pifo.

LX. PLAUTIUS LATERANUS, conful elect, was the next
victim. He was feized, and dragged to inftant death; no time
allowed to take the laft farewell of his children, nor even the
ufual liberty of choofing his own mode of dying. He was hurried
to the place of execution ufually allotted to flaves, and there difpatched by the hand of Statius, a military tribune. He met his
fate with a noble and determined filence, not fo much as con-

P p 2

defcending

defcending to tax the executioner with his fhare in the con-fpiracy.

The next exploit of Nero was the death of Seneca. Againft that eminent man no proof of guilt appeared; but the emperor thirfted for his blood, and what poifon had not accomplifhed he was determined to finifh by the fword. Natalis was the only perfon who had mentioned his name. The chief head of his accufation was, "That he himfelf had been fent on a vifit to Seneca, then " confined by illnefs, with inftructions to mention to him, that " Pifo often called at his houfe, but never could gain admittance, " though it was the intereft of both to live on terms of mutual " friendfhip." To this Seneca made anfwer, "That private in-" terviews could be of no fervice to either; but ftill his happinefs " was grafted on the fafety of Pifo." Granius Silvanus, a tribune of the prætorian guards, was difpatched to Seneca, with direc-tions to let him know what was alleged againft him, and to enquire, whether he admitted the converfation ftated by Natalis, with the anfwers given by himfelf. Seneca, by defign or acci-dent, was that very day on his return from Campania. He ftopt at a villa of his own (a) about four miles from Rome. Towards the clofe of day the tribune arrived, and befet the houfe with a band of foldiers. Seneca was at fupper with his wife Pompeia' Paulina, and two of his friends, when Silvanus entered the room, and reported the orders of the emperor.

LXI. SENECA did not hefitate to acknowledge that Natalis had been at his houfe, with a complaint that Pifo's vifits were not received. His apology, he faid, imported no more than want of health, the love of eafe, and the neceffity of attending to a weak and crazy conftitution. "That he fhould prefer the
" intereft

" intereſt of a private citizen to his own ſafety, was too abſurd
" to be believed.   He had no motives to induce him to pay ſuch
" a compliment to any man : adulation was no part of his cha-
" racter.   This is a truth well known to Nero himſelf: he can
" tell you that, on various occaſions, he found in Seneca a man,
" who ſpoke his mind with freedom, and diſdained the arts of
" ſervile flattery."   Silvanus returned to Rome.   He found the
prince in company with Poppæa and Tigellinus, who, as often
as cruelty was in agitation, formed the cabinet-council.   In their
preſence the meſſenger reported his anſwer.   Nero aſked, "Does
" Seneca prepare to end his days by a voluntary death?"   "He
" ſhewed," ſaid the tribune, "no ſymptom of fear, no token of ſorrow,
" no dejected paſſion : his words and looks beſpoke a mind ſerene,
" erect and firm."   "Return," ſaid Nero, " and tell him, he muſt
" reſolve to die." Silvanus, according to the account of Fabius
Ruſticus, choſe to go back by a different road. He went through a
private way to Fenius Rufus, to adviſe with that officer, whether he ſhould execute the emperor's orders.   Rufus told him
that he muſt obey.   Such was the degenerate ſpirit of the times.
A general panic took poſſeſſion of every mind.   This very Silvanus was one of the conſpirators, and yet was baſe enough to
be an inſtrument of the cruelty which he had combined to revenge.   He had, however, the decency to avoid the ſhock of
ſeeing Seneca, and of delivering in perſon the fatal meſſage.   He
ſent a centurion to perform that office for him.

LXII. Seneca heard the meſſage with calm compoſure.   He
called for his will, and being deprived of that right of a Roman
citizen by the centurion, he turned to his friends, and " You ſee,"
he ſaid, " that I am not at liberty to requite your ſervices with
" the laſt marks of my eſteem. One thing, however, ſtill remains.
" I leave you the example of my life, the beſt and moſt precious

" legacy

"legacy now in my power. Cherish it in your memory, and
"you will gain at once the applause due to virtue, and the fame
"of a sincere and generous friendship." All who were present
melted into tears. He endeavoured to assuage their sorrows;
he offered his advice with mild persuasion; he used the tone of
authority. "Where," he said, "are the precepts of philosophy,
"and where the words of wisdom, which for years have taught
"us to meet the calamities of life with firmness and a well pre-
"pared spirit? Was the cruelty of Nero unknown to any of us?
"He murdered his mother; he destroyed his brother; and, after
"those deeds of horror, what remains to fill the measure of his
"guilt but the death of his guardian and his tutor?"

LXIII. Having delivered himself in these pathetic terms, he
directed his attention to his wife. He clasped her in his arms,
and in that fond embrace yielded for a while to the tenderness of
his nature. Recovering his resolution, he entreated her to ap-
pease her grief, and bear in mind that his life was spent in a constant course of honour and of virtue. That consideration would
serve to heal affliction, and sweeten all her sorrows. Paulina
was still inconsolable. She was determined to die with her hufband; she invoked the aid of the executioners, and begged to
end her wretched being. Seneca saw that she was animated by
the love of glory, and that generous principle he thought ought
not to be restrained. The idea of leaving a beloved object exposed to the insults of the world, and the malice of her enemies,
pierced him to the quick. "It has been my care," he said, "to
"instruct you in that best philosophy, the art of mitigating the
"ills of life; but you prefer an honourable death. I will not
"envy you the vast renown that must attend your fall. Since
"you will have it so, we will die together. We will leave behind
"us an example of equal constancy; but the glory will be all
"your own."

These

Thefe words were no fooner uttered, than the veins of both their arms were opened. At Seneca's time of life the blood was flow and languid. The decay of nature, and the impoverifhing diet *(a)* to which he had ufed himfelf, left him in a feeble condition. He ordered the veffels of his legs and joints to be punctured. After that operation, he began to labour with excruciating pains. Left his fufferings fhould overpower the conftancy of his wife, or the fight of her afflictions prove too much for his own fenfibility, he perfuaded her to retire into another room. His eloquence ftill continued to flow with its ufual purity. He called for his fecretaries, and dictated, while life was ebbing away, that farewell difcourfe, which has been publifhed, and is in every body's hands. I will not injure his laft words by giving the fubftance in another form.

LXIV. NERO had conceived no antipathy to Paulina. If fhe perifhed with her hufband, he began to dread the public execration. That he might not multiply the horrors of his prefent cruelty, he fent orders to exempt Paulina from the ftroke of death. The flaves and freedmen, by the direction of the foldiers, bound up her arm, and ftopped the effufion of blood. This, it is faid, was done without her knowledge, as fhe lay in a ftate of languor. The fact, however, cannot be known with certainty. Vulgar malignity, which is ever ready to detract from exalted virtue, fpread a report, that, as long as fhe had reafon to think that the rage of Nero was implacable, fhe had the ambition to fhare the glory of her hufband's fate; but a milder profpect being unexpectedly prefented, the charms of life gained admiffion to her heart, and triumphed over her conftancy. She lived a few years longer, in fond regret, to the end of her days, revering the memory of her hufband. The weaknefs of her whole frame,

and

and the fickly languor of her countenance, plainly fhewed that fhe had been reduced to the laft extremity.

Seneca lingered in pain. The approach of death was flow, and he wifhed for his diffolution. Fatigued with pain, worn out and exhaufted, he requefted his friend, Statius Annæus, whofe fidelity and medical fkill he had often experienced, to admi-nifter a draught of that fwift-fpeeding poifon (a), ufually given at Athens to the criminals adjudged to death. He fwallowed the potion, but without any immediate effect. His limbs were chilled: the veffels of his body were clofed, and the ingredients, though keen and fubtle, could not arreft the principles of life. He defired to be placed in a warm bath. Being conveyed according to his defire, he fprinkled his flaves with the water, and "Thus," he faid, " I MAKE LIBATION TO JUPITER THE DELIVERER." The va-pour foon overpowered him, and he breathed his laft. His body, without any funeral pomp, was committed to the flames. He had given directions for that purpofe in his laft will, made at a time when he was in the zenith of power, and even then looked for-ward to the clofe of his days.

LXV. A REPORT was at that time current at Rome, that Subrius Flavius and feveral centurions held a private meeting, with the knowledge and confent of Seneca, and there refolved to open a new and unexpected fcene. The blow for liberty was to be ftruck in the name of Pifo, and as foon as the world was freed from the tyranny of Nero, Pifo was to be the next victim, in order to make way for Seneca, who, for his virtues, was to be raifed to the higheft elevation, with an air of innocence, and of a man unconfcious of the plot. The very words of Flavius were reported among the people. He is fuppofed to have faid, " What " good end will it anfwer to depofe a MINSTREL, if we place a

" TRA-

" TRAGEDIAN in his room ?" The fact was, Nero played on his guitar, and Pifo trod the ftage in the bufkin of tragedy.

LXVI. THE part, which the military men had taken in the confpiracy, did not long remain a fecret. The double game played by Fenius Rufus, at firft a confederate in the plot, and then a judge pronouncing fentence on his accomplices, provoked the indignation of all. In the examination of Scevinus that officer preffed his interrogatories with over-acted zeal, and by menaces endeavoured to extort a confeffion. Scevinus anfwered with a fmile, " No man knows the particulars better than your-" felf. You now may fhew your gratitude to fo good a prince." Rufus was covered with confufion. To fpeak was not in his power, and to remain filent was dangerous. He trembled, faul-tered, and hefitated an anfwer. His embarraffment betrayed his guilt. The reft of the confpirators, with Cervarius Proculus, a Roman knight, at their head, were eager to depofe againft him. At length a foldier of the name of Caffius, remarkable for his robuft ftature, and for that reafon ordered to attend, laid hold of Rufus by the emperor's order, and loaded him with irons.

LXVII. THE fame witneffes gave evidence againft Subrius Flavius. In anfwer to the charge, he relied much on his courfe of life, and the diffimilitude of manners between himfelf and his accufers. " Was it probable that a foldier, inured to the profeffion " of arms, would affociate with an effeminate fet of men, ftrang-" ers to danger and to manly enterprife !" Finding himfelf preffed by the weight of evidence, he changed his tone, and with heroic fortitude avowed the part he had acted. Being afked by Nero, what could induce him to forget the folemn ob-ligation of his oath ? " Becaufe," he faid, " I hated, I detefted " you. There was a time when no foldier in your army was

" more

" more devoted to your fervice, and that was as long as you
" deferved the efteem of mankind.   I began to hate you when
" you was guilty of parricide; when you murdered your
" mother, and deftroyed your wife; when you became a coach-
" man, a comedian, and an incendiary."   I have given the very
words of this intrepid confpirator, becaufe they were not, like
thofe of Seneca, publifhed to the world; and the rough fentiments
of a foldier, in his own plain, but vigorous language, merit the
attention of pofterity.

In the whole difcovery of the plot nothing made fo deep an
impreffion on the mind of Nero.   Though his heart never knew
remorfe for the worft of crimes, his ear, unaccuftomed to the
voice of truth, fhrunk from the found of freedom, and ftartled at
reproach.   Flavius was ordered for execution.   Veianius Niger,
one of the tribunes, led him to the next field, and there directed
a trench to be opened.   The prifoner furveyed the fpot, and,
finding it neither wide nor deep enough, turned with a fmile to
the foldiers, and " This," he faid, "fhews no military fkill."   Niger
defired him to extend his neck with courage: " Strike," faid
Flavius, " and prove your courage equal to mine."   The tribune was feized with a tremor in every joint.   He fevered the
head at two blows, and made a merit of it with Nero, giving
the name of cruelty to his want of firmnefs.   He made it his
boaft, that, by repeating the ftroke, he made him die twice.

LXVIII. Sulpicius Asper, the centurion, gave the next
example of magnanimity.   Being afked by Nero, why he confpired againft his life? he anfwered fhortly, " I knew no other
" relief from your flagitious deeds."   He was inftantly put to
death.   The reft of the centurions underwent their fate, and all
died worthy of their characters.   Fenius Rufus had not equal
                                                        conftancy.

conftancy.   He betrayed an abject fpirit, and even in his will
was weak enough to bewail his unhappy fate.   Nero lived in
hopes of feeing Veftinus, the conful, charged as a criminal. He
knew the character of the man ; an intrepid daring fpirit, ambitious, and fufpected of difaffection.   The confpirators, however, had no communication of counfels with that active magiftrate.   Some declined him on account of former animofities,
and others, becaufe they thought him rafh and impetuous. Nero's
rancour grew out of a clofe and intimate friendfhip.   In that
familiar intercourfe Veftinus faw into the very heart of the
prince, and defpifed him for his vices.   Nero fhrunk from a
man, who had the fpirit to fpeak his mind with freedom, and,
in his farcaftic vein, had often made the prince the fubject of his
raillery ; and raillery, when feafoned with truth, never fails to
leave a fting that fefters in the memory.   A recent incident gave
an edge to Nero's refentment.   Veftinus married Statilia Meffalina *(a)*, though he knew that the prince was one of her lovers.

LXIX. No witnefs appeared againft Veftinus ; no crime was
laid to his charge, and, by confequence, no proceeding could be
had in due form of law.   But the will of the tyrant ftill remained.
He fent Gerelanus, one of the tribunes, at the head of a cohort,
with orders fo to take his meafures, that the conful might not be
able to ftand on the defenfive, and, for that purpofe, to inveft
his houfe, which, like a proud citadel, overlooked the forum,
and contained a numerous train of young and hardy flaves, in
the nature of a garrifon.   Veftinus had that very day difcharged
all the functions of his confular office.   He was at table with his
friends, free from apprehenfion, or, it may be, affecting an air of
gaiety, when the foldiers entered, and informed him that the tribune had important bufinefs with him.   He rofe and left the
room.   The fcene of death was inftantly laid.   He was fhut up

in a chamber; a phyſician attended; his veins were opened; he was conducted to a warm bath, and, being put into the water, expired without a complaint, and without a groan. His gueſts, in the mean time, remained in the banqueting room, impriſoned by the guards. It was late at night before they were releaſed. Nero heard the account with pleaſure. He ſaw, in the ſport of his imagination, a ſet of men aſſembled at a convivial party, and every moment expecting their final doom. He laughed at their diſtreſs, and ſaid facetiouſly, " They have paid for their conſular " ſupper."

LXX. Lucan, the famous poet, was the next ſacrifice to the vengeance of Nero. His blood flowed freely from him, and being ſoon well nigh exhauſted, he perceived that the vital heat had left the extremities of his limbs. His hands and feet were chilled, but, the warmth retiring to his heart, he ſtill retained his ſenſes and the vigour of his mind. The lines in his poem, which deſcribe a ſoldier dying in the ſame condition (a), occurred to his memory. He repeated the paſſage, and expired. His own verſes were the laſt words he uttered. Senecio, Quinctianus, and Scevinus, ſuffered in a ſhort time after. The diſſolute ſoftneſs of their lives did not diſgrace them in their end. They met their fate with reſolution. The reſt of the conſpirators were led to execution. In their deaths there was nothing that merits particular notice.

LXXI. While the city preſented a ſcene of blood, and funerals darkened all the ſtreets, the altars of the capitol ſmoked with victims ſlaughtered on the occaſion. One had loſt a ſon; another was deprived of his brother, his friend, or his near relation; and yet, ſtifling every ſentiment of the heart, all concurred in offering thanks to the gods; they adorned the prince's houſe
with

with laurel *(a)*; they fell at the tyrant's feet; they clasped his
knees, and printed kisses on his hand.   Nero received this vile
adulation as the token of real joy.   In order to make sure of the
people, he shewed his clemency to Antonius Natalis and Cervarius Proculus, whose merit consisted altogether in their treachery
to their friends.   To Milichus he granted a rich and ample recompense, and moreover added the honourable appellation of a
Greek name, importing the CONSERVATOR.   Granius Silvanus,
one of the tribunes engaged in the conspiracy, received a free
pardon; but, disdaining to enjoy it, he died by his own hand. Statius Proximus had the vanity to follow his example.   Pompeius,
Cornelius Martialis, Flavius Nepos, and Statius Domitius were
all degraded from their tribunitian rank, not as men condemned,
but suspected of disaffection.   Novius Priscus, Glitius Gallus, and
Annius Pollio were ordered into exile; the first on account of
his known intimacy with Seneca; and the two last, to disgrace
them, though not convicted of any crime.   Antonia Flaccilla,
the wife of Novius Priscus, followed her husband into banishment.
Egnatia Maximilla, at that time possessed of great wealth, had
the spirit, in like manner, to adhere to Glitius Gallus.   Her
fortune was soon after taken from her by the hand of power.
Her conduct, both in affluence and poverty, did honour to her
character.

Rufius Crispinus was likewise banished: the conspiracy fur-
nished a pretext, but his having been married to Poppæa was the
crime that brought on his ruin.   Verginius *(b)* and Musonius
Rufus *(c)* owed their banishment to the celebrity of their names :
the former trained the Roman youth to eloquence, and the latter
formed their minds by his lectures on wisdom and philosophy.
At one sweep, Cluvidienus Quietus, Julius Agrippa, Blitius Ca-
tulinus, Petronius Priscus, and Julius Altinus, like a colony of
criminals,

criminals, were sent to islands in the Ægean sea. Cadicia, the wife of Scevinus, and Cæsonius Maximus were ordered out of Italy, without being heard in their defence. The sentence of condemnation was the first notice of any crime alleged against them. Acilia, the mother of Lucan, was neither pardoned, nor condemned. She was suffered to live in silent obscurity.

LXXII. HAVING performed these dreadful exploits, Nero called an assembly of the soldiers, and, after a specious harangue, ordered a largess of a thousand sesterces to be paid to each man, and the corn, which they had been used to purchase at the market-price, to be distributed as the bounty of the prince. He then ordered the senate to be convened, with as much importance as if the events of war and splendid victories occasioned the meeting. He granted triumphal ornaments to Petronius Turpilianus *(a)*, of consular rank, to Cocceius Nerva *(b)*, prætor elect, and Tigellinus, commander of the prætorian guards. The two last were mentioned by him in strains of the highest commendation. Not content with erecting their statues in the forum, adorned with triumphal decorations, he placed them also in the imperial palace. Nymphidius *(c)* was honoured with the ensigns of consular dignity Of this man, who now occurs for the first time, since he is to figure hereafter on the stage of public business, it may be proper in this place to say a few words.

He was the son of an enfranchised female slave, distinguished by her beauty, and the ease with which she granted her favours to the slaves as well as the freedmen about the court. Nymphidius, however, pretended to be of higher origin. He called himself the son of Caligula. His large stature, and the stern cast of his countenance, bore some resemblance to that emperor ; and, in fact, as Caligula was never delicate in the choice of his mistresses,

tresses,

treſſes, but was known to ſhare the embraces of common harlots, it is poſſible that he might, on ſome occaſion, indulge his paſſion with the mother of Nymphidius.

LXXIII. The ſenate being aſſembled, Nero delivered a ſpeech on the ſubject of the late tranſactions, and, for the information of the people, iſſued a proclamation, with a ſtatement of the evidence againſt the conſpirators, and their own confeſſion. The clamours of the public made this expedient neceſſary.. While the executions were going on, the public voice was loud and violent againſt Nero, the inſatiate tyrant, who was daily ſacrificing to his cruelty, or his fears, the lives of innocent and illuſtrious men.. That a plot was actually formed; that it was conducted with reſolution, and in the end was totally defeated,. no man, who made it his buſineſs to inveſtigate the truth, entertained a doubt at the time; and ſince the death of Nero, the acknowledgment of all, who returned from baniſhment, eſtabliſhed the fact beyond a controverſy. Nero was received by the ſenate with the baſeſt flattery. In that aſſembly, the men, who had the greateſt reaſon to be overwhelmed with grief, were the moſt forward to offer incenſe to the emperor. Junius Gallio (a), the brother of Seneca, was, by the loſs of that excellent man, ſo ſtruck with ter_ ror, that to ſave his own life he deſcended to humble ſupplications. Salienus Clemens roſe to oppoſe him, as a parricide and an enemy to the ſtate. He continued his invective till the fathers checked his violence. It was not now, they ſaid, a time to gratify perſonal animoſity, under an appearance of zeal for the public good; nor would it become any man to open again the wounds which the clemency of the prince had cloſed for ever.

LXXIV. Oblations and public thankſgivings were decreed to all the gods, and particularly to the Sun, in whoſe temple,

ſituated

fituated in the forum, the murder was to have been perpetrated, if that god had not difpelled the clouds that hung over the machinations of evil minded men, and brought their dark proceedings into open day-light.   It was further ordered, that the fports of the circus, in honour of Ceres, fhould be celebrated with an additional number of chariot-races ; that the month of April *(a)* fhould be ftyled after the name of Nero ; and that, on the fpot, where Scevinus furnifhed himfelf with a dagger, a temple fhould be erected to the GODDESS OF SAFETY.   The dagger itfelf was dedicated in the capitol, with an infcription to the avenging god, called JUPITER VINDEX.   The infcription, at that time, had no equivocal meaning ; but foon after, when JULIUS VINDEX *(b)* excited a revolt in Gaul, it was confidered as an omen of impending vengeance.

In the journals of the fenate I find an entry, by which it appears, that Cerealis Anicius, conful elect, moved in his place, that a temple fhould be raifed, at the public expence, to the DEIFIED NERO, who, in his opinion, had rifen above the condition of human nature, and was, therefore, entitled to religious worfhip. This motion was afterwards underftood to portend nothing lefs than the death of Nero ; fince it was a fettled rule, that divine honours fhould never be paid to the emperor, till he ceafed to be mortal *(c)*.

THE END OF THE FIFTEENTH BOOK.

THE

ANNALS

OF

TACITUS.

———

BOOK   XVI.

CONTENTS of BOOK XVI.

it

These transactions passed, partly in the former consulship, and in the following year.

Years of Rome—of Christ		Consuls
818	65	*Silius Nerva, Atticus Vestrinus.*
819	66	{ *Caius Suetonius Paulinus, Caius Lucius Telesinus.*

A N N A L S

O F

T A C I T U S.

B O O K   XVI.

1. NERO, in confequence of his own credulity, became in a fhort time afterwards the fport of fortune, and a fubject of public derifion. He believed the vifionary fchemes of Cefellius Baffus, a native of Carthage, of a crazed imagination, who relied on whatever occurred to him in his diftempered dreams. This man arrived at Rome, and, by the influence of money well applied, gained admiffion to the prefence of the emperor. The fecret, which he had to communicate, was, that on his own eftate he had found a cavern of aftonifhing depth, in which were contained immenfe ftores of gold, not wrought into the form of coin, but in rude and fhapelefs ingots, fuch as were in ufe in the early ages of the world. In one part of the cave

were

B O O K
XVI.

A. U. C.
818.
A. D.
65.

were to be seen vaft maffy heaps, and in other places columns of gold towering to a prodigious height; the whole an immenfe treafure, referved in obfcurity to add to the fplendour of Nero's reign.   To give probability to his ftory, he pretended, that Dido, the Phœnician *(a)*, when fhe fled from Tyre, and founded the city of Carthage, depofited her whole ftock in the bowels of the earth, that fo much wealth might neither prove the bane of a new colony, nor excite the avarice of the Numidian princes *(b)*, of themfelves already hoftile to her infant ftate.

II. NERO neither weighed the character of the man, nor the circumftances of fo wild a report.   He had not even the precaution to fend commiffioners to inform themfelves on the fpot.   He helped to fpread the report; he began to count his riches, and difpatched his agents to tranfport the treafure to Rome.   The light galleys were equipped with expedition, and a chofen band of mariners fent on board.   Rome, in the mean time, was diftracted with hope and fear, with doubt and expectation.   No other fubject was talked of.   The common people, with their ufual facility, believed every thing; while men of reflection argued in a different manner.   It happened that the quinquennial games *(a)* were to clofe the fecond luftre of five years.   During that feftival, the expected treafure was the fubject on which the orators expatiated, and the poets exhaufted their invention.   In their flights of fancy, the earth was no longer content with pouring forth fruit and grain, and producing metals intermixed with veins of precious ore; the prefent fecundity fhewed that the gods were working miracles to blefs the reign of Nero.   Thefe were the bright conceits, which flattery difplayed with rapture, and eloquence adorned with her richeft colouring.   While the paffions of Nero ftood ready to receive every new device, fiction

G   paffed

paſſed for truth, and nothing was too hyperbolical for the credulity of the prince.

III. WITH ſuch immoderate riches in view, no wonder that
Nero launched out into greater profuſion than ever. Deluded
by his hopes, and ſure of a ſupply for years to come, he exhauſted his treaſury *(a)*, and began to anticipate his imaginary
funds. He made aſſignments on the property, and granted with
generoſity what was not in his poſſeſſion. The expectation of
enormous wealth made him the bubble of a madman, and im-
poveriſhed the public. In the mean time Baſſus, the grand pro-
jector, arrived at Carthage. In the preſence of a number of
ſoldiers, and a large body of peaſants employed as labourers, he
dug up his grounds, and made his experiment in the adjacent
fields, diſappointed in one place, ſure of ſucceſs in another, ſtill
confident, and ſtill miſcarrying; till at length, finding no ſubter-
raneous cave, and weary of the fruitleſs ſearch, he abandoned
his chimerical hopes, coming gradually to his ſenſes, yet wondering, that, of all his dreams, the laſt ſhould be the only one that
deceived him. Covered with ſhame, and dreading the reſentment of the emperor, he delivered himſelf from all his troubles
by a voluntary death. According to ſome writers, he was inſtantly ſeized, and loaded with irons, till Nero ordered him to
be releaſed, but ſeized his effects, determined to enjoy the fortunes of a wild adventurer, ſince he could not obtain the wealth
of Dido.

IV. THE time of contending for the prizes in the quinquennial games being near at hand, the ſenate, with intent to ward
off from the emperor *(a)* the diſgrace of being a candidate, offered to adjudge, in his favour, the victory in ſong, and the
crown of eloquence. The fathers hoped, that honours freely

granted

BOOK
XVI.

A. U. C.
813.
A. D.
65.

granted would fatisfy the prince, and prevent a ridiculous difplay of theatrical talents. Nero returned for anfwer, that he ftood in no need of favour or protection. He depended on himfelf alone, and would fairly enter the lifts with his competitors. The equity of the judges was to decide, and by that teft he was willing to ftand or fall. With that fpirit he entered the fcene, and recited a poem of his own compofition. The people, with earneft entreaty, prayed that he would let them tafte the fupreme delight of hearing and enjoying all his divine accomplifhments. Such was the language of the populace. In compliance with their wifhes, he mounted the public ftage, conforming in all things to the rules of the orcheftra, where no performer was to fit down, nor to wipe the fweat from his face with any thing but his own garment, and never to fpit or clear his noftrils in fight of the audience. Having exhibited his fkill, he went down on his knee, and ftretching forth his hands with pretended agitations of hope and fear, waited in that humble pofture for the decifion of the judges. The populace, accuftomed to applaud the notes and gefticulations of the common players, paid their tribute of admiration to the prince, with meafured cadence, in one regular chorus of applaufe. You would have thought their joy fincere, and, perhaps, it was fo in fact: the rabble wifhed to be diverted at any rate, and for the difgrace that befel the ftate vulgar minds felt no concern.

V. THINKING men were affected in a very different manner. All who came from the municipal towns, or the more remote parts of Italy, where fome tincture of ancient manners ftill remained; and a confiderable number, befides, who arrived from the provinces on public bufinefs, or their own private affairs, as yet ftrangers to vice, and undebauched by luxury, beheld the fcene with heavinefs of heart. A fpectacle, in which the prince

expofed

expofed his frivolous talents, gave them the higheft difguft. They thought the applaufe difhoneft, but they were obliged to concur with the reft. They acted their part with warm, but aukward zeal. Their unpractifed hands were eafily tired; they were not able to keep time in the grand concert, and, exerting themfelves without fkill, they difturbed the general harmony. For every blunder they were chaftifed by the foldiers, who were ftationed at their pofts, with orders to take care, that the applaufe fhould be kept up with fpirit, without an interval of reft, or filence. It is a certain fact, that feveral Roman knights, endeavouring to make their way through the crowd, were crufhed to death in the narrow paffes *(a)*; and that others, who kept their feats in the theatre day and night, fell dangeroufly ill. The dread of being abfent from fuch a performance was more alarming than the worft ficknefs that could happen. Befides the foldiers ftationed in the theatre to fuperintend the audience, it is well known that a number of fpies lay in ambufh, to take down the names of the fpectators, to watch their countenances, and note every fymptom of difguft or pleafure. Offenders of mean condition were punifhed on the fpot. Men of diftinction were overlooked with an air of calm neglect, but refentment was only fmothered for a time, to break out afterwards with deadly hate. We are told, that Vefpafian, for the crime of being ready to fall afleep, was obliged to endure the infulting language of one Phœbus, an imperial freedman, and was faved from harfher treatment by the interceffion of men of rank and influence. The offence, however, was not entirely forgotten; it remained in ftore for future vengeance; but Vefpafian was referved, by his fuperior deftiny, for the higheft elevation.

VI. The public games were followed by the death of Poppæa *(a)*. She died of a kick on her womb, which Nero gave

BOOK
XVI.

A. U. C.
818.
A. D.
65.

her in a fudden paffion, though fhe was then advanced in her pregnancy. Some writers will have it that fhe was carried off by a dofe of poifon; but they affert it with more fpleen than truth. Nero was defirous of having iffue, and he loved his wife with fincere affection. Her body was not, according to the Roman cuftom (b), committed to the funeral pile, but, after the manner of the eaftern kings, embalmed with precious fpices (c), and depofited in the monument of the Julian family. The ceremony was performed with great pomp, and Nero pronounced the funeral oration. He was lavifh in praife of her beauty; and the peculiar happinefs of being the mother of an infant (d) enrolled among the gods, was a topic on which he dwelt with pleafure. By enlarging on that and other accidental circumftances, he made a panegyric, in which not one virtue could find a place.

VII. THE death of Poppæa occafioned a general face of mourning, but no real grief. Men remembered her loofe incontinence, and, having felt her cruelty, rejoiced in fecret at an event that freed the world from a woman of a detefted character. Nero laboured under a load of reproach, and the public refentment rofe ftill higher, when it was known that, by his orders, Caffius did not attend the funeral. That illuftrious Roman underftood the imperial mandate as the fignal of his approaching ruin. In fact, his doom was fixed in a fhort time after, and Silanus was devoted with him. The crime of Caffius (a) was the fplendid fortune which he inherited from his anceftors, and the aufterity of his manners. Silanus offended by the nobility of his birth, and his modeft merit. Nero fent a letter to the fenate, ftating in ftrong terms the neceffity of removing them both from all civil offices. To Caffius he objected, that, among the images of his anceftors he preferved, with veneration, the picture of the famous Caius Caffius, with this infcription: THE

LEADER OF THE PARTY. That circumftance plainly fhewed the fullen fpirit of a man brooding mifchief; a fierce republican, who meditated another civil war, and a revolt from the houfe of Cæfar. But to revive the name of a daring factious chief was not fufficient for the purpofes of a turbulent incendiary: he was charged with feducing Lucius Silanus, a youth defcended from an illuftrious line, bold, ambitious, enterprifing, and in the hands of ill defigning men a fit tool to fpread the flame of rebellion.

VIII. SILANUS *(a)* was no lefs an object of Nero's hatred. It was urged againft him, as had been formerly done in the cafe of his uncle Torquatus, that he affected the ftyle of imperial dignity, and had in his houfehold train his mock-treafurers, his auditors of accounts, and his fecretaries of ftate. Nothing could be more deftitute of all foundation. Silanus faw the tyranny of thofe difaftrous times, and from the fate of his uncle received a leffon of prudence. Lepida *(b)*, the wife of Caffius, and aunt of Silanus, was alfo doomed to fall a facrifice to the unrelenting fury of the prince. Informers were fuborned to accufe her of inceft with her nephew; and, to fwell the charge, they imputed to her impious facrifices, magic rites, and horrible incantations. Vulcatius Tullinus, and Marcellus Cornelius *(c)*, of fenatorian rank, with Calpurnius Fabatus, a Roman knight, were involved in the profecution. They appealed to the tribunal of the emperor, and, by removing the caufe, prevented a final fentence. Nero was, at that time, brooding over crimes of the deepeft dye, and having nobler game in view, he difdained to ftoop to an inferior quarry. The three laft were faved by their want of importance.

IX. CASSIUS and Silanus were banifhed by a decree of the fenate. The cafe of Lepida was referred to the prince. Caffius, in a fhort time after, was tranfported to the ifland of Sardinia,

S s 2

where

where Nero was content to leave him to old age and the decay of nature. Silanus was conveyed to Oftia, there, as was pretended, to embark for the ifle of Naxos. He never reached that place. Barium *(a)*, a municipal city of Apulia, was the laft ftage of his journey. He there fupported life with a temper that gave dignity to undeferved misfortune, till a centurion, employed to commit the murder, rufhed upon him abruptly. That officer advifed him to open his veins. " Death," faid Silanus, " has been familiar to my thoughts, but the honour of " preferibing to me I fhall not allow to a ruffian and a murderer." The centurion, feeing that he had to do with a man, unarmed indeed, but robuft and vigorous, not a fymptom of fear in his countenance,- but, on the contrary, an eye that fparkled with indignation, gave orders to his foldiers to feize their prifoner. Silanus ftood on the defenfive: what man could do without a weapon he bravely dared, ftruggling, and dealing his blows about him, till he fell by the fword of the centurion, like a gallant officer, receiving honourable wounds, and facing his enemy to the laft.

X. Lucius Vetus, and Sextia his mother-in-law, with Pollutia his daughter, died with equal fortitude. Nero thought them a living reproach to himfelf for the murder of Rubellius Plautus *(a)*, the fon-in-law of Lucius Vetus. The root of bitternefs rankled in Nero's heart, till Fortunatus, one of the manumitted flaves of Vetus, gave him an opportunity to wreak his vengeance on the whole family. The freedman had been employed by Vetus in the management of his affairs, and having defrauded his mafter, he thought it time to add treachery to peculation, and give evidence againft his patron. In this black defign he affociated with himfelf one Claudius Demianus, a fellow of an abandoned character, who had been charged in Afia, while

7

Vetus

Vetus was proconful of the province, with various crimes, and
fent to Rome in fetters. To forward the profecution, Nero fet
him at liberty.

B O O K
XVI.
A. U. C.
818.
A. D.
65.

Vetus heard, with indignation, that the evidence of a freedman
was received againft the life of his patron, and retired to his coun-
try-feat in the neighbourhood of Formiæ. A band of foldiers
followed him, and befet his houfe. His daughter was then with
him. A fenfe of former injuries was ftill frefh in her mind. She
had feen her hufband, Rubellius Plautus, maffacred by a band of
ruffians. Upon that occafion fhe oppofed her perfon to the
affaffins ftroke: fhe clung to her hufband's bleeding neck, and
preferved the garment ftained with his blood. From that time
nothing could affuage her forrows: fhe remained a widow, a prey
to grief, inconfolable, loathing all food, except what was neceffary for the fupport of nature. In the prefent diftrefs, by her
father's advice, fhe fet off for Naples, where Nero then refided.
Not being admitted to his prefence, fhe watched the palace-gates,
and, as foon as he came forth, fhe cried aloud, " Hear my fa-
" ther, hear an innocent man; he was your colleague *(b)* in the
" confulfhip; extend your mercy, nor let him fall a facrifice to
" the pernicious arts of a vile abandoned flave." She perfifted,
as often as Nero paffed, to renew her application, fometimes in
tears and mifery of heart; often in a tone of vehemence, roufed
by her fufferings above the weaknefs of her fex. But neither tears
nor reproaches had any effect on the cruelty of Nero: infenfible
to both, and heedlefs of the popular hatred, he remained obdurate and implacable.

XI. POLLUTIA returned to her father, and, fince not a ray
of hope was left, exhorted him to meet his fate with a becoming
fpirit. Intelligence arrived at the fame time, that preparations

for

for the trial were going on with rapidity, and that the fenate fhewed a difpofition to pronounce the fevereft fentence. Among the friends of Caffius fome were of opinion, that the fureft way to fecure part of his fortune for his grand-children, would be by making the emperor heir in chief. He rejected that advice as unworthy of his character. Having lived his days with a fpirit of independance, he refolved to die with honour. He diftributed the money then in his poffeffion among his flaves, and ordered them to remove for their own ufe all the effects that could be carried off, with an exception of three couches, to ferve as funeral beds for himfelf and his family.

They retired to die together. In the fame chamber, and with the fame inftrument, the father, the mother-in-law, and the daughter opened their veins, and, without any other covering, than fuch as decency required, were conducted to a warm bath; the father with his eyes fixed upon his daughter; the grandmother gazing on the fame object; and fhe, in return, looking with tender affection on both her parents; each of them wifhing to avoid the pain of feeing the others in the pangs of death, and praying to be releafed. Nature purfued her own courfe. They died in the order of their refpective ages, the oldeft firft. After their deceafe, a profecution was carried on in due form of law, and all three were adjudged to capital punifhment. Nero fo far oppofed the fentence, as to give them the liberty of choofing their mode of dying. When the tragedy was already performed, fuch was the farce that followed.

XII. Publius Gallus, a Roman knight, for no other crime than his intimacy with Fenius Rufus (a), and fome connection with Vetus, was interdicted from fire and water. The freedman of Vetus, who betrayed his mafter, and the accufer,

who

who undertook the conduct of the profecution, obtained, to reward their villany, a feat in the theatre among the officers who follow in the train of the tribunes. The month of April was already ftyled by the name of Nero *(b)*, and, in like manner, May was changed to that of Claudius, and June to Germanicus. Cornelius Orfitus was the author of this innovation. His reafon for the laft was, becaufe the two Torquati *(c)* fuffered in the month of June, and that inaufpicious name ought, therefore, to be abolifhed from the calendar.

XIII. To the blood and horror, that made this year for ever memorable, we may add the vengeance of Heaven, declared in ftorms and tempefts, and epidemic diforders. A violent hurricane made the country of Campania a fcene of defolation ; whole villages were overthrown ; plantations were torn up by the roots, and the hopes of the year deftroyed. The fury of the ftorm was felt in the neighbourhood of Rome, where, without any apparent caufe in the atmofphere, a contagious diftemper broke out, and fwept away a vaft number of the inhabitants. The houfes were filled with dead bodies, and the ftreets with funeral proceffions. Neither fex nor age efcaped. Slaves and men of ingenuous birth were carried off, without diftinction, amidft the fhrieks and lamentations of their wives and children. Numbers, while they affifted their expiring friends, or bewailed their lofs, were fuddenly feized, and burnt on the fame funeral pile. The Roman knights and fenators fuffered the common lot of mortality ; but death delivered them from the power of the tyrant, and, for that reafon, they were not regretted.

In the courfe of the year new levies were made in Narbon Gaul, and likewife in Afia and Africa, in order to recruit the legions in Illyricum, at that time much reduced by the difcharge

of

of such as by age or infirmity were rendered unfit for service. The city of Lyons having before this time suffered a dreadful disaster *(a)*, Nero, to relieve the inhabitants, ordered a remittance of forty thousand sesterces, being the amount of what that city granted *(b)* to the treasury of Rome in a period of distraction and public distress.

XIV. Caius Suetonius and Lucius Telesinus entered on the consulship. During their administration, Antistius Sosianus, formerly banished *(a)*, as has been mentioned, for a satirical poem against Nero, began to think of regaining his liberty. He heard of the high estimation in which informers were held at Rome, and the bias of Nero's nature to acts of cruelty. A bold and restless spirit like his was ready for any project, and he possessed a promptitude of mind that quickly saw how to seize his opportunity. There was, at that time, an exile in the same place, famous for his skill in the arts of Chaldean astrology, and, on that account, intimate with several families. His name was Pammenes. Antistius entered into a league of friendship with him. Their mutual sufferings endeared them to each other. The astrologer had frequent consultations, and messengers were every day crowding to his house. Antistius judged that such a concourse could not be without reasons of important consequence. He found that Pammenes received an annual pension from Anteius; a man, on account of his attachment to Agrippina, obnoxious to the emperor, and by his riches likely to tempt the avarice of a prince, who had already cut off some of the most opulent and illustrious men in Rome.

Antistius kept a watchful eye upon his new friend. He intercepted letters from Anteius, and gained access to other secret papers, in which was contained a calculation of the nativity of

Anteius,

Anteius, with many particulars relating to the birth and future
fortune of Oſtorius Scapula *(b)*. Armed with theſe materials,
he repreſented, by letters to Nero, that he had diſcoveries of the
firſt importance, involving even the ſafety of the prince, and, if
he might reviſit Rome for a few days, the whole ſhould be
brought to light, with all the machinations of Anteius and Oſtorius Scapula, who, beyond all doubt, were engaged in a treaſonable
deſign, and had been prying into their own deſtiny, and that of
the imperial houſe. In conſequence of theſe letters, a light galley
was diſpatched, and Antiſtius was conveyed to Rome. His
arrival, and the buſineſs on which he came, were no ſooner
known, than Anteius and Oſtorius were conſidered as devoted
victims, inſomuch that the former could not find a friend bold
enough to be a witneſs to his will *(c)*, till Tigellinus adviſed him
to ſettle his affairs without loſs of time. Anteius ſwallowed a
doſe of poiſon ; but finding the operation flow and tedious, he
opened his veins, and put a period to his exiſtence.

XV. Oſtorius, at this time, was at a diſtance from Rome,
amuſing himſelf on his own eſtate near the confines of Liguria.
A centurion was ſent with orders to diſpatch him. Nero had
his reaſons for deſiring this buſineſs to be done with expedition.
He knew the military character of Oſtorius, and the high reputation, with which he had gained the civic crown in Britain *(a)*.
He dreaded a man renowned in arms, remarkable for his bodily
vigour, and a thorough maſter of the art of war. From a
general of his experience he lived in fear of a ſudden attack, and
the late conſpiracy kept him in a conſtant alarm. The centurion
obeyed his orders, and having firſt ſecured all the avenues round
the houſe, communicated the emperor's orders. Oſtorius turned
againſt himſelf that courage which had often made the enemy
fly before him. He opened his veins, but, though the inciſion

<table><tr><td>Vol. II.</td><td>T t</td><td>was</td></tr></table>

was large, the blood flowed with languor.   He called a flave
to his affiftance, and having directed him to hold a poniard with
a firm and fteady hand, he laid hold of the man's arm, and ap-
plying his throat to the point, rufhed on certain death.

XVI. If the narrative, in which I am engaged, prefented a
detail of foreign wars, and a regifter of men, who died with
honour in the fervice of their country, even in that cafe, a continued train of diafters, crowding faft upon one another, would
fatigue the writer, and make the reader turn, with difguft, from
fo many tragic iffues, honourable indeed, but dark, melancholy,
and too much of a colour.   How much more muft the uni-
formity of the prefent fubject be found irkfome, and even re-
pulfive ! We have nothing before us but tame fervility, and a
deluge of blood fpilt by a tyrant in the hour of peace.   The
heart recoils from the difmal ftory.   But let it be remembered
by thofe, who may hereafter think thefe events worthy of their
notice, that I have difcharged the duty of an hiftorian, and if,
in relating the fate of fo many eminent citizens, who refigned
their lives to the will of one man, I mingle tears with indignation,
let me be aliowed to feel for the unhappy.   The truth is, the
wrath of Heaven was bent againft the Roman ftate.   The calamities that followed cannot, like the flaughter of an army, or
the facking of a city, be painted forth in one general draught.
Repeated murders muft be given in fucceffion ; and, if the remains of illuftrious men are diftinguifhed by their funeral obfequies from the mafs of the people, may it not be confidered as a
tribute due to their memory, that, in like manner, their deaths
fhould be fnatched from oblivion, and that hiftory, in defcribing
the laft act of their lives, fhould give to each his diftinct and
proper character, for the information of pofterity ?

XVII. I pro-

XVII. I proceed to add to the lift of murdered citizens, Annæus Mela, Cerealis Anicius, Rufius Crifpinus, and Petronius. In the compafs of a few days they were all cut off, as it were at one blow. Mela and Crifpinus were no higher than Roman knights; but in fame and dignity of character equal to the moft diftinguifhed fenators. Crifpinus, at one time, commanded the prætorian bands; he was afterwards invefted with the confular ornaments, but lately charged as an accomplice in the confpiracy, and banifhed to the ifland of Sardinia (a). At that place he received the emperor's mandate, and died by his own hand. Mela (b) was brother to Seneca and Gallio. He abftained through life from the purfuit of civil honours, vainly flattering himfelf, that a fimple knight could rife to the higheft fplendour, and tower above the confular dignity. By remaining in his rank, he was qualified to act in the adminiftration of the imperial revenue, and that employment he thought the fhorteft road to immoderate riches. He was the father of Lucan, the poet, and from fuch a fon (c) derived additional luftre. When Lucan was no more, Mela endeavoured to recover the whole of his property (d); but proceeding with too much eagernefs, he provoked the enmity of Fabius Romanus, one of the poet's intimate friends. This man framed a charge againft the father. He accufed him of being engaged with his fon in the late confpiracy, and, for that purpofe, forged feveral letters in the name of Lucan.

Nero was eager to feize his prey: he panted for his riches, and with that view fent the letters as evidence of his guilt. Mela had recourfe to the mode of death, at that time deemed the eafieft, and, for that reafon, moft in vogue. He opened his veins, and expired. By his will he bequeathed a large fum to Tigellinus, and to his fon-in-law, Coffutianus Capito, hoping by that bequeft to fecure the remainder for his family. A claufe, it has been

T t 2

faid,

said, was added to the will, afferting the innocence of the deceafed, and the flagrant injuftice of cutting him off, while fuch men as Rufius Crifpinus and Anicius Cerealis were fuffered to live in fecurity, though they were both envenomed enemies of the prince. The claufe, however, was thought to be fabricated, with a view to juftify the murder of Crifpinus, which was already perpetrated, and to haften the fentence then in agitation againft Cerealis, who, in a few days afterwards, difpatched himfelf. He fell unlamented. The public remembered that he formerly difcovered a confpiracy *(c)* to Caligula, and, for that reafon, no man regretted him in his end.

XVIII. WITH regard to Caius Petronius *(a)*, his character, his courfe of life, and the fingularity of his manners feem to merit particular attention. He paffed his days in fleep, and his nights in bufinefs, or in joy and revelry. Indolence was at once his paffion, and his road to fame. What others did by vigour and induftry, he accomplifhed by his love of pleafure and luxurious eafe. Unlike the men who profefs to underftand focial enjoyment, and ruin their fortunes, he led a life of expence, without profufion; an epicure, yet not a prodigal; addicted to his appetites, but with tafte and judgment; a refined and elegant voluptuary. Gay and airy in his converfation, he charmed by a certain graceful negligence, the more engaging as it flowed from the natural franknefs of his difpofition. With all this delicacy, and carelefs eafe, he fhewed, when he was governor of Bithynia, and, afterwards, in the year of his confulfhip, that vigour of mind and foftnefs of manners may well unite in the fame perfon. With his love of fenfuality he poffeffed talents for bufinefs. From his public ftation he returned to his ufual gratifications, fond of vice, or of pleafures that bordered upon it. His gaiety recommended him to the notice of the prince. Being

in

in favour at court, and cherifhed as the companion of Nero in
all his felect parties, he was allowed to be the arbiter of tafte and
elegance.   Without the fanction of Petronius nothing was exquifite, nothing rare or delicious.

Hence the jealoufy of Tigellinus, who dreaded a rival, in the
good graces of the emperor almoft his equal; in the fcience of
luxury his fuperior.   Tigellinus determined to work his downfall; and, accordingly, addreffed himfelf to the cruelty of the
prince; that mafter-paffion, to which all other affections and
every motive were fure to give way.   He charged Petronius with
having lived in clofe intimacy with Scevinus *(b)*, the confpirator; and, to give colour to that affertion, he bribed a flave to
turn informer againft his mafter.   The reft of the domeftics were
loaded with irons.   Nor was Petronius fuffered to make his
defence.

XIX.   Nero, at that time, happened to be on one of his ex-
curfions into Campania.   Petronius had followed him as far as
Cuma, but was not allowed to proceed further than that place.
He fcorned to linger in doubt and fear, and yet was not in a
hurry to leave a world which he loved.   He opened his veins,
and clofed them again, at intervals lofing a fmall quantity of
blood, then binding up the orifice, as his own inclination prompted.
He converfed during the whole time with his ufual gaiety, never
changing his habitual manner, nor talking fentences to fhew his
contempt of death.   He liftened to his friends, who endeavoured
to entertain him, not with grave difcourfes on the immortality
of the foul, or the moral wifdom of philofophers, but with ftrains
of poetry, and verfes of a gay and natural turn.   He diftributed
prefents to fome of his fervants, and ordered others to be chaftifed.
He walked out for his amufement, and even lay down to fleep.

In

In this laſt ſcene of his life he acted with ſuch calm tranquillity, that his death, though an act of neceſſity, ſeemed no more than the decline of nature. In his will he ſcorned to follow the example of others, who, like himſelf, died under the tyrant's ſtroke: he neither flattered the emperor, nor Tigellinus, nor any of the creatures of the court; but having written, under the fictitious names of profligate men and women, a narrative of Nero's debauchery, and his new modes of vice *(a)*, he had the ſpirit to ſend to the emperor that ſatirical romance, ſealed with his own ſeal, which he took care to break, that, after his death, it might not be uſed for the deſtruction of any perſon whatever.

XX. NERO ſaw, with ſurpriſe, his clandeſtine paſſions, and the ſecrets of his midnight revels, laid open to the world. To whom the diſcovery was to be imputed ſtill remained a doubt. Amidſt his conjectures, Silia, who by her marriage with a ſenator had riſen into notice, occurred to his memory. This woman had often procured for the libidinous pleaſures of the prince, and lived, beſides, in cloſe intimacy with Petronius. Nero concluded that ſhe had betrayed him, and for that offence ordered her into baniſhment. Having made that ſacrifice to his own reſentment, he gave another victim to glut the rage of Tigellinus, namely, Numicius Thermus, a man of prætorian rank. An accuſation preferred againſt the favourite, by a ſlave enfranchiſed by Thermus, was the cauſe that provoked the vengeance of Tigellinus. For that daring attempt againſt a man in power the informer ſuffered on the rack, and his patron, who had no concern in the buſineſs, was put to death.

XXI. NERO had not yet ſatiated his vindictive fury. He had ſpilt the beſt blood in Rome, and now, in the perſons of Pætus Thraſea and Bareas Soranus, he hoped to deſtroy virtue
itſelf.

itfelf. His rancour to thofe two illuftrious citizens had been long working in his heart. Thrafea, in particular, was the devoted object, and various motives confpired againft him. When the bufinefs of Agrippina *(a)* was brought before the fenate, it will be in the memory of the reader, that Thrafea withdrew from the debate. Afterwards, in the youthful fports, called JUVENALES, he feldom attended, and never with the alacrity which was expected. This cold indifference was the more grating to the prince, as Thrafea, at Padua, his native city, not only affifted at the games of the CESTUS, originally inftituted by Antenor, the fugitive from Troy, but alfo performed in the habit of a tragedian. It was further remembered, that, when Antiftius, the prætor, was in danger of being capitally condemned for his verfes levelled at Nero, Thrafea was the author of a milder fentence *(b)*. There was ftill another circumftance: when divine honours were decreed to Poppæa, he wilfully abfented himfelf, nor did he afterwards attend her funeral. Thefe offences were not fuffered to fink into oblivion. The whole was treafured up by Coffutianus Capito *(c)*, a man, who to a bad heart and talents for every fpecies of iniquity united motives of perfonal ill-will to Thrafea, which he nourifhed in fecret, ever fince the victory obtained over him in a charge of extortion conducted by the deputies from Cilicia, and fupported with all the credit and eloquence of Thrafea.

XXII. THE fertile genius of the profecutor was not at a lofs for new allegations. The heads of his charge were, " That " Thrafea made it a point to avoid renewing the oath of fidelity " ufual at the beginning of the year *(a)*, and, though a member " of the quindecemviral college, he never affifted at the cere- " mony of offering vows for the fafety of the prince, and the " prefervation of that melodious voice. A magiftrate formerly

" of.

" of unremitting affiduity, he took a part in every debate, fup-
" porting or oppofing the moft trifling motions; and now what
" is his conduct? For three years together he has not fo much
" as entered the fenate *(b)*. Even on a late occafion, when the
" bufinefs relating to Silanus and Vetus drew the fathers to a
" crowded meeting, Thrafea was not at leifure; the affairs of
" his clients engroffed his attention, and the patriot was detained
" from the fenate by his own petty concerns. What is this but
" a public feceffion! He is at the head of a faction, and if his
" partifans take fire from his example, a civil war muft be the
" confequence. Cæfar and Cato were the names that formerly
" kept the world awake; at prefent, in a city ever rent by dif-
" cord, Nero and Thrafea engage the public mind.

" The popular demagogue has his fectaries and his followers;
" a fet of men not yet, like their mafter, ambitioufly fententious,
" but, in imitation of his mien and manners, fullen, gloomy, and
" difcontented. By the formalities of their rigid difcipline they
" hope to throw difgrace on the gay and elegant manners of their
" fovereign. Your prefervation, Nero, is of no moment to
" Thrafea: he difregards your fafety; he defpifes your accom-
" plifhments. Are your affairs in a train of profperity? he is
" ftill dejected. Has any untoward event difturbed your peace
" of mind? he enjoys your diftrefs, and in fecret pampers him-
" felf with your affliction. The fame fpirit, that refufed to
" fwear on the acts of Julius Cæfar and Auguftus, denies the di-
" vinity of Poppæa. He turns religion to a jeft, and fets the
" laws at defiance. The journals of the Roman people *(c)* were
" never read by the provinces and the armies with fo much avi-
" dity, as in the prefent juncture; and the reafon is, the hiftory
" of the times is the hiftory of Thrafea's contumacy.

" If

"If the fyftem of this wife philofopher and profound poli-
"tician merits attention, let us, at once, embrace his doctrine;
"if otherwife, let us take from the friends of innovation their
"leader and their oracle. The fect, whofe precepts he affects to
"admire, has ever been proud and dogmatical, bufy, bold, and
"turbulent. It was that ftoic fchool that formed the Tuberos *(d)*
"and the Favonii; names detefted even by the old republic. And
"what is now the principle of the whole faction? To fubvert
"the fabric of a great empire they hold forth the name of liberty;
"if they fucceed, they will deftroy even liberty itfelf. Of what
"ufe can it be to Nero, that he has banifhed a Caffius, if the
"followers of Brutus are ftill allowed to flourifh, and multiply
"their numbers? Upon the whole, you have no occafion, Cæfar,
"to write to the fenate; you need not mention Thrafea to that
"affembly: leave him to our management, and the judgment of
"the fathers." Nero praifed the zeal of Coffutianus, and added
fury to a mind already bent on mifchief. To forward his villany,
he gave him for a coadjutor Eprius Marcellus, an orator of a
turbulent fpirit and overbearing eloquence.

XXIII. The profecution againft Bareas Soranus was already
in the hands of Oftorius Sabinus, a Roman knight. Soranus
was returned from his proconfular government of Afia. His
conduct in the province ftood diftinguifhed by juftice and the
rectitude of his meafures; but by the jealoufy of Nero the virtues
of the minifter were converted into crimes. He had opened the
port of Ephefus, and left unpunifhed the obftinate refiftance of
the people of Pergamus, who refufed to let Acratus *(a)*, one of
the emperor's freedmen, carry off the ftatues and pictures that
adorned their city. This meritorious conduct was an offence not
to be forgiven; but conftructive crimes were to be held forth to
the public. The heads of the accufation were, that Soranus had

contracted a clofe and intimate friendfhip with Plautus *(b)*, and had endeavoured by popular arts to incite the eaftern provinces to a revolt. To decide the fate of two upright citizens, Nero chofe a juncture favourable to his dark defign. Tiridates was on his way to Rome, to receive the diadem of Armenia from the hands of the emperor. He thought it probable, that, in the fplendour of that magnificent fcene, the horrors of domeftic cruelty would be loft : perhaps, it feemed a fair opportunity to difplay to a foreign prince the grandeur of a Roman emperor, and convince him, by the murder of two eminent citizens, that the imperial power was nothing fhort of oriental defpotifm.

XXIV. THE city went forth in crowds to meet the emperor *(a)*, and gaze at the eaftern monarch. Thrafea received orders not to appear on the occafion. A mind like his was not to be difconcerted. With his ufual fortitude he fent a memorial to the prince, requefting to know by what act of his life he had deferved fuch a mark of difpleafure. He pledged himfelf, if a fair hearing were granted, to confute his enemies, and place his innocence in the cleareft light. Nero received the memorial with eager curiofity, expecting to find that Thrafea, under the operation of fear, had defcended to the language of flattery, and tarnifhed his own honour by magnifying the glory of the prince. Stung by difappointment, he refufed to grant an audience. The fight of that illuftrious citizen, the countenance, the fpirit, and the virtue of the man, were too much to encounter. He ordered the fenate to be convened. Thrafea, in the mean time, confulted with his friends, which would be moft advifable, to enter at large into his defence, or to behave with filent indignation. They were divided in their opinions.

XXV. SOME advifed him to enter the fenate, and confront
his

his enemies in the prefence of that affembly. " Of his conftancy
" no doubt could be entertained ; they knew that nothing could
" fall from him unworthy of himfelf. Every word from his lips
" would tend to augment his glory. When danger threatened,
" to take fhelter in the fhade of obfcurity, were the act of a de-
" generate fpirit. For him, he ought to have the people round
" him to behold the fcene ; a great man advancing bravely to
" meet his fate, would be a fpectacle worthy of their applaufe.
" The fenate would hear with aftonifhment the energy of truth,
" and the fublime of virtue. Every fentiment from the mouth
" of Thrafea would rife fuperior to humanity, and found to the
" fathers as if fome god addreffed them. Even the heart of
" Nero might for once relent. Should it happen otherwife ;
" fhould his obdurate nature ftill perfift, pofterity would crown
" with immortal glory the undaunted citizen, who diftinguifhed
" himfelf from thofe unhappy victims, who bowed their necks
" to the tyrant's ftroke, and crept in filence to their graves."

XXVI. OTHERS were of a different opinion, convinced that
his beft plan would be to wait the iffue at his own houfe. They
fpoke of Thrafea himfelf and the dignity of his character in the
higheft terms, but they dreaded that his adverfaries would pour
forth a torrent of infolence and opprobrious language. " They
" defired that he would not fuffer his ear to be wounded with
" fcurrility and vile abufe. Coffutianus and Eprius Marcellus
" were not the only enemies of virtue : there were others, whofe
" brutal rage might incite them to outrage, and even violence to
" his perfon. The cruelty of Nero left none at liberty. In a
" general panic good men might follow the worft example. It
" would become the character of Thrafea to refcue from infamy
" that auguft affembly, which his prefence had fo long adorned.
" If he did not attend the meeting, the part, which, after hearing

U u 2

" Thrafea

" Thrafea in his own defence, the fathers might have acted, will
" remain problematical; and by that uncertainty the honour of
" the fenate may be faved.   To hope that Nero would blufh for
" his crimes, were to mifunderftand his character.   His unrelent-
" ing cruelty would moft probably fall on Thrafea's wife, on his
" whole family, and all that were dear to him.   For thefe rea-
" fons, an eminent citizen, who had ever fupported the honour
" of his name, and ftill flourifhed with unblemifhed integrity,
" would do well to remember who were the teachers of wifdom,
" that furnifhed the principles and the model of his conduct.
" Since he had crowded into his life all their virtues, it would be-
" come him to emulate their glory in his fall."

Arulenus Rufticus (a) affifted at this confultation.   He was, at
that time, a tribune of the people; a young man of fentiment,
eager to be in action, and warm with the love of glory.   He
offered to interpofe, by his tribunitian authority, to prevent a
decree of the fenate.   " Forbear," faid Thrafea, " and learn,
" young man, to reftrain this impetuous ardour.   By a rafh op-
" pofition you cannot fave your friend, and you may bring down
" ruin on yourfelf.   For me, I have lived my days; my courfe
" is well nigh finifhed; it now remains, that I reach the goal
" with undiminifhed honour.   As to you, my friend, you have
" but lately entered the career of civil dignities.   Life is before
" you, and you have not as yet pledged yourfelf to the public.
" Ere you take a decided part, it will behove you to confider
" well the times upon which you are fallen, and the principles
" which you mean to avow."   Having thus declared his fentiments, he gave no opinion concerning the propriety of appearing
in the fenate, but referved the queftion for his own private
meditation.

XXVII.   On

XXVII. On the following day two prætorian cohorts, under arms, furrounded the temple of Venus. A body of citizens, with fwords ill concealed beneath their gowns, invefted all the avenues. In the forum, the open fquares, and round the adjoining temples, bands of foldiers took their ftation, and through that military array the fenators were obliged to pafs, furrounded by foldiers and prætorian guards. The affembly was opened by Nero's quæftor *(a)*, with a fpeech in the name of the prince, complaining, " That the fathers" (no particular name was mentioned) " de-
" ferted the public intereft, and by their example taught the
" Roman knights to loiter away their time in floth, and inatten-
" tion to the welfare of the ftate. Nor could it be matter of
" wonder, that the fenators from the diftant provinces no longer
" attended their duty, when men of confular rank, and even of
" facerdotal dignity, thought of nothing but the embellifhment
" of their villas, and the beauty of their gardens and pleafure-
" grounds." This meffage was intended to be a weapon in the hands of the accufers, and their malice knew how to ufe it.

XXVIII. Cossutianus took the lead. Eprius Marcellus followed him, with more force and acrimony. " The common-
" wealth," he faid, " is on the brink of ruin. Certain turbulent
" fpirits rear their creft fo high, that no room is left for the
" milder virtues of the prince. The fenate for fome time paft
" has been negligent, tame, and paffive. Your lenity, coafcript
" fathers, your lenity has given encouragement to fedition. It
" is in confequence of your indulgence that Thrafea prefumes
" to trample on the laws; that his fon-in-law, Helvidius Prif-
" cus *(a)*, adopts the fame pernicious principles; that Paconius
" Agrippinus *(b)*, with the inveterate hatred towards the houfe
" of Cæfar, which he inherits from his father, declares open
" hoftility; and that Curtius Montanus *(c)*, in feditious verfes,
" fpread,

" fpreads abroad the venom of his pen. Where is Thrafea now?
" I want to fee the man of confular rank in his place; I want to
" fee the facerdotal dignitary offering up vows for the emperor;
" I want to fee the citizen taking the oaths of fidelity.   Perhaps
" that haughty fpirit towers above the laws and the religion of
" our anceftors; perhaps he means to throw off the mafk, and
" own himfelf a traitor and an enemy to his country.   Let him
" appear in this affembly; let the patriot come; let the leader
" of faction fhew himfelf; the man who fo often played the
" orator in this affembly, and took under his patronage the inve-
" terate enemies of the prince.   Let us hear his plan of govern-
" ment: what does he wifh to change? What abufes does he
" mean to reform? If he came every day with objections, the
" cavilling fpirit of the man might teafe, perplex, and embarrafs
" us; but now his fullen filence is worfe; it condemns every
" thing in the grofs.   And why all this difcontent? A fettled
" peace prevails in every quarter of the empire: does that afflict
" him? Our armies, without the effufion of Roman blood, have
" been victorious: is that the caufe of his difaffection? He
" fickens in the midft of profperity; he repines at the flourifhing
" ftate of his country; he deferts the forum; he avoids the
" theatre, and the temples of the city; he threatens to abjure
" his country, and retire into voluntary banifhment; he acknow-
" ledges none of your laws; your decrees are to him no better
" than mockery; he owns no magiftrates, and Rome to him is
" no longer Rome.   Let him therefore be cut off at once from a
" city, where he has long lived an alien; the love of his country
" banifhed from his heart, and the people odious to his fight."

XXIX. MARCELLUS delivered this invective in a ftrain of
vehemence, that gave additional terror to the natural ferocity
of a ftern and favage countenance.   His voice grew louder,

his

his features more enlarged, and his eyes flashed with fire. The
senate heard him, but with emotions unfelt before: the settled
melancholy, which that black period made habitual, gave way
to stronger feelings. They saw a band of soldiers round them,
and they debated in the midst of swords and javelins. Thrasea
was absent, but the venerable figure of the man presented itself
to every imagination. They felt for Helvidius Priscus, who was
doomed to suffer, not for imputed guilt, but because he was allied
to an innocent and virtuous citizen. What was the crime of
Agrippinus? The misfortunes of his father, cut off by the cruelty of Tiberius, rose in judgment against the son. The case of
Montanus *(a)* was thought hard and oppressive. His poetry
was a proof of genius, not of malice; and yet, for a pretended
libel on the prince, a youth of expectation was to be driven from
his country.

XXX. AMIDST the tumult and distraction which this business excited, Ostorius Sabinus, the accuser of Bareas Soranus,
entered the senate. He opened at once, and charged as a crime,
the friendship that subsisted between Soranus and Rubellius
Plautus. He added, that the whole tenour of his administration
in Asia was directed, not for the public good, but to promote his
own popularity, and to spread a spirit of sedition through the
provinces. These accusations had been long since fabricated, and
were then grown threadbare; but the prosecutor was ready with
a new allegation, which involved Servilia, the daughter of Soranus,
in her father's danger. The charge against her was, that she
had distributed sums of money among men skilled in judicial
astrology. The fact was, Servilia, with no other motives than
those of filial piety, had the imprudence, natural at her time of
life, to apply to a set of fortune-tellers, in order to satisfy her
mind about the fate of her family, and to learn whether Nero's

resentment

refentment was by any poffibility to be appeafed, **and what would** be the iffue of the bufinefs in the fenate.

She was cited to appear in the fenate before the tribunal of the confuls. On one fide ftood the aged father; on the other his daughter, in the bloom of life, not having yet completed her twentieth year, but even then in a ftate of deftitution, ftill lamenting the fate of her hufband, Annius Pollio, lately torn from her, and condemned to banifhment. She ftood in filent forrow, not daring to lift her eyes to her father, whom by her imprudent zeal fhe had involved in new misfortunes.

XXXI. The accufer preffed her with queftions. He defired to know, whether fhe had not fold her bridal ornaments, her jewels and her necklace, to fupply herfelf with money for magic facrifices? She fell proftrate on the ground, and wept in bitternefs of heart. Her forrows were too big for utterance. She embraced the altars, and rifing fuddenly, exclaimed with vehemence, " I have invoked no infernal gods; I have ufed no
" unhallowed rites, no magic, no incantations. My unhappy
" prayers afked no more than that you, Cæfar, and you, con-
" fcript fathers, would extend your protection to this beft of
" men, this moft affectionate parent. For him I fold my jewels;
" for him I difpofed of my bridal ornaments, and for him I
" gave up the garments fuited to my rank. In the fame caufe
" I was willing to facrifice my life: the blood in my veins was
" at his fervice. The men whom I confulted were all ftrangers
" to me; I had no knowledge of them. They beft can tell who
" they are, and what they profefs. The name of the prince was
" never mentioned by me but with that refpect, which I pay
" to the gods. What I did was my own act: that miferable
" man, my unhappy father, knew nothing of it. If any crime has
" been committed, he is innocent: I, and I alone am guilty."

XXXII. Soranus

XXXII. Soranus could no longer reftrain himfelf. He interrupted his daughter, crying aloud, " She was not with me " in Afia ; fhe is too young to have any knowledge of Rubellius " Plautus. In the accufation againft her hufband fhe was not " involved ; her filial piety is her only crime. Diftinguifh her " cafe from mine ; refpect the caufe of innocence, and on my " head let your worft vengeance fall. I am ready to meet my " fate." With thefe words, he rufhed to embrace his child ; fhe advanced to meet him, but the lictors interpofed to prevent the pathetic fcene. The witneffes were called in. The fathers had hitherto liftened to all that paffed, with emotions of pity ; but pity was foon converted into a ftronger paffion. The appear- ance of Publius Egnatius *(a)*, the client of Soranus, hired to give evidence againft his patron and his friend, kindled a general indignation. This man profeffed himfelf a follower of the ftoic fect. He had learned in that fchool to retail the maxims of virtue, and could teach his features to affume an air of fimplicity, while fraud and perfidy, and avarice, lay lurking at his heart. The temptation of money drew forth his hidden character, and the hypocrite ftood detected. His treachery gave a ftanding leffon to mankind, that, in the commerce of the world, it is not fufficient to guard againft open and avowed iniquity, fince the profeffors of friendfhip can, under a counterfeit refemblance of virtue, nourifh the worft of vices, and prove, in the end, the moft pernicious enemies.

XXXIII. The fame day produced a fplendid example of truth and honour in the perfon of Caffius Afclepiodotus ; a man dif- tinguifhed by his wealth, and ranked with the moft eminent inhabitants of Bithynia. Having loved and followed Soranus in his profperity, he did not defert him in the hour of diftrefs. He ftill adhered to him with unaltered friendfhip, and for his conftancy was deprived of his all, and fent into banifhment; the gods, in their juft difpenfations, permitting an example of virtue, even in ruin, to ftand in contraft to fuccefsful villainy. Thrafea, Soranus, and Servilia, were allowed to choofe their mode of dying. Helvidius Prifcus and Paconius Agrippinus were banifhed out of Italy. Montanus owed his pardon to the influence of his father, but was declared incapable of holding any public office. The profecutors were amply rewarded. Eprius Marcellus and Cof-futianus received each of them fifty thoufand fefterces. Oftorius Sabinus obtained a grant of twelve thoufand, with the ornaments of the quæftorfhip.

XXXIV. Towards the clofe of day, the confular quæftor *(a)* was fent to Thrafea, who was then amufing himfelf in his garden, attended by a number of friends, the moft illuftrious of both fexes. Demetrius *(b)*, a philofopher of the cynic fchool, was the perfon who chiefly engaged his attention. Their converfation, as was inferred from looks of earneft meaning, and from fome expreffions diftinctly heard, turned upon the immortality of the foul, and its feparation from the body. Thrafea had not heard of the decree that paffed the fenate, when his intimate friend, Domitius Cæcilianus, arrived with the unhappy tidings. The company melted into tears. Thrafea faw their generous fympathy; he heard their lamentations: but fearing that the intereft, which they took in the lot of a man doomed to deftruction, might involve them in future danger, he conjured them to retire. Arria *(c)*, his wife, infpired by the memorable example of her mother, refolved to fhare her hufband's fate. Thrafea entreated her to continue longer in life, and not deprive their daughter of the only comfort and fupport of her tender years.

XXXV. He then walked his portico, and there received the
confular

consular quæstor.   An air of satisfaction was visible in his countenance.   He had been informed that Helvidius, his son-in-law,
had met with nothing harsher than a sentence of banishment out
of Italy.   The decree of the senate, drawn up in form, being
delivered to him, he withdrew to his chamber, attended by Helvidius and Demetrius.   He there presented both his arms ; and
the veins being opened, as soon as the blood began to flow, he
desired the quæstor to draw nearer, and sprinkling the floor with
his vital drops, " Thus," he said, " let us make libation to JUPI-
" TER THE DELIVERER ! Behold, young man, a mind undaunted
" and resigned : and may the gods avert from you so severe a
" trial of your virtue ! But you are fallen on evil times, in
" which you will find it expedient to fortify your soul by exam-
" ples of unshaken constancy."   The approach of death was
slow and lingering.   As his pains increased, he raised his eyes,
and turning to Demetrius   *   *   *   *   *

THE REST OF THIS BOOK IS LOST.

BOOK
XVI.

A. U. C.
819.
A. D.
66.

APPENDIX

TO THE

SIXTEENTH BOOK

OF

THE ANNALS.

CONTENTS.

gives a loose to vice, indulges in new pleasures, and marries Sporus, the eunuch. IX. The exhausted finances of the prince supplied by draining the people. The arrogance of Helius, an imperial freedman, who directs every thing at Rome. X. Nero attempts to open a passage for the sea through the Isthmus of Corinth. For that purpose, a number of Jew prisoners sent by Vespasian to labour at the work. Vespasian appointed commander against the Jews. XI. Helius, who governs every thing at Rome, in the absence of Nero, insults the senate and the people. He writes an account to Nero of all that passes, and presses him to return to the capitol. Nero forms a design against the life of Corbulo. Arrius Varrus, an officer in Asia, sends an accusation against Corbulo. Corbulo passes into Greece, to have an interview with Nero. Corbulo compelled to dispatch himself. Nero's labours at the Isthmus of Corinth. He embarks for Italy, and arrives at Naples. He enters Rome in triumph. XII. A conspiracy discovered, and the accomplices put to death. A revolt in Gaul. Virginius Rufus defeats the insurrection of Vindex. Galba, in secret, favoured the cause of Vindex, and is much alarmed at his defeat. XIII. Nero resolves to destroy the whole senate. His designs discovered by a favourite slave. The fathers, alarmed for their own safety, prepare to counteract Nero's designs. Nero adjudged to suffer death, as an enemy to his country. XIV. Nero terrified: He is driven to despair, laments his sad condition, and, at last puts an end to his life; the last and worst of the house of Cæsar. XV. Prodigies: the sudden joy, and changeable humours of the populace. Nymphidius favours Galba's party, meaning at the same time to seize the sovereignty. He is slain. XVI. Proceedings against all the instruments of Nero's

cruelty.

7

CONTENTS.

cruelty. Galba informed of the death of Nero. He marches at the head of his army towards Italy, and begins his reign with cruelty and great effusion of blood.

These transactions passed in three years.

A. U. C.	of Christ.	Consuls.
819	66	*Suetonius Paulinus, Lucius Telesinus.*
820	67	*Fonteius Capito, Julius Rufus.*
821	68	*Silius Italicus, Galerius Trachalus.*

APPENDIX

TO THE

SIXTEENTH BOOK

OF

THE ANNALS.

I. IT is not without regret that we lose the last words of a great man at the point of death. All we know is, that Thrasea fixed his eyes on his friend Demetrius, and there Tacitus fails us. What the philosopher said, cannot now be collected from any contemporary historian. It is probable that he expired in a short time after. Seeing the vices of the age, and the savage cruelty of the reigning prince, it cannot be matter of wonder, that a man of virtue, fortified by the doctrines of the stoic school, did not think it awful to die. He was often heard to say, that he had rather lay down his life to-day, than be to-morrow ba-

VOL. II.   Y y   nished

niſhed to an iſland.   That ſentiment was applauded by the phi-loſophers *(a)* of the age.   With the ſame ſpirit he was uſed to declare his mind in converſation with his friends.   If, he ſaid, Nero intended to deſtroy no one but me, I could excuſe his flatterers; but flattery will not ſave their lives.   Since death is a debt that all muſt pay, it is better to die in freedom, than live an ignominious ſlave.   All that Nero can do, is to ſhorten my days: my memory will ſubſiſt, and men will continue to talk of me. But for the tribe of abject ſycophants, they will periſh, and be mentioned no more.   Thraſea was not more diſtinguiſhed by his unſhaken fortitude, than by the virtues of humanity.   Pliny the conſul celebrates him for an apothegm, which ſhews in the faireſt light the amiable tenderneſs of his nature.   An unforgiving diſpoſition was in his eyes not only ungenerous, but immoral; it was, therefore, his maxim *(b)*, that he, who ſuffers himſelf to hate vice, will hate mankind.   It were ſuperfluous to add any further particulars of a man ſo truly eminent.   Tacitus ſays, that by deſtroying him, Nero intended, by the ſame blow, to deſtroy virtue itſelf.   All praiſe is ſummed up in that ſhort encomium.

Soranus, and his daughter Servilia, died with equal virtue, and equal glory.   Helvidius Priſcus *(c)*, as already mentioned, was condemned to exile.   Paconius Agrippinus *(d)* met with the ſame ſeverity.   Like his friend Helvidius, he was a man of diſ-tinguiſhed virtue, and undaunted reſolution.   Being informed that his trial, though he was not cited to appear, was actually depending before the ſenate, May the gods grant me their pro-tection! ſaid he; but it is now the fifth hour, and that is the time when I uſually bathe.   His cauſe was not long in ſuſpenſe.   Be-ing informed that judgment was pronounced againſt him, he calmly aſked, What is the ſentence? Death or baniſhment? Be-

ing

ing told that it was the latter, And what have they done with my
effects? You are left in poffeffion of them. Well then, faid he,
I can dine at Aricia *(e)*. He accepted his life, and, by his calm
indifference, gained as much glory as others by the fortitude with
which they met their fate. Demetrius, the friend of Thrafea,
did not efcape the notice of Nero. The tyrant threatened inftant
execution. You may command it, faid Demetrius; you threaten
me with death, and nature threatens you *(f)*. The intrepid
firmnefs of a poor philofopher, or perhaps the meannefs of his
condition, faved his life.

II. CORNUTUS, another philofopher, who profeffed the doctrines of the Platonic fchool, had the misfortune to be confulted on
the fubject of a poem, which Nero had projected *(a)*. He fpoke
his mind with honeft freedom, and for that offence was immediately banifhed. Nor was the cruelty of the prince appeafed by
the number that fell a facrifice ; he ftill thirfted for blood ; but
happily a fcene of fplendour, then ready to be difplayed, engaged
his attention, and gave the people fome refpite from the rage of
an infatiate tyrant. Tiridates, who, with the confent of his brother Vologefes, the Parthian king, had agreed with Corbulo
to undertake a journey to Rome *(b)*, in order there to receive
the regal diadem from the hand of the emperor, was arrived in
Italy. Nero was then at Naples, and, in that city, the eaftern
prince was admitted to his prefence. The fpectacle was magnificent. It ferved at once to gratify the pride of a Roman emperor,
and for a time to footh the afflictions of the people. Tiridates
was attended by a long proceffion of officers and a military band
appointed by Corbulo. He had, befides, not lefs than three
thoufand of the Parthian nobility in his train, with his wife, and
the fons *(c)* of Vologefes, of Pacorus, and Monobazus. His

Y y 2

march

march through the provinces had no appearance of a prince subdued, and forced to submit to the will of a conqueror.   Till he entered the city of Naples all was grandeur and royal magnificence.   The act of humiliation still remained.   He was to pay homage to the emperor on his knees.   Mortifying as that circumstance was to an oriental king, Tiridates submitted to prostrate himself at Nero's feet.   Vologeses had stipulated with Corbulo, that his brother should not be compelled to deliver up his sword *(d)*; and Tiridates called it an ignominious act, beneath the dignity of the Arsacidæ.   Nothing could extort his sword. He is said to have nailed it to the scabbard.   The magnanimity, with which he refused to comply, obtained the applause of all, who beheld a scene so new and magnificent.

The court set out for Rome.   Nero thought proper to make some stay at Puteoli *(e)*, in order to entertain his royal visitor with a show of gladiators.   The spectacle was exhibited by Patrobius *(f)*, one of the emperor's freedmen, with great expence and prodigious pomp.   The genius of Nero could not lie still on such an occasion.   In his opinion it was fit that a foreign prince, and his Parthian courtiers, should know how well the emperor of Rome could sing.   Tiridates beheld the whole with mixed emotions of wonder, admiration and contempt.   The example of Nero did not tempt him to exhibit his person as a show to the people.   He scorned to descend into the arena, but did not think it beneath his dignity to call for his bow and arrow, and from the throne, where he was seated, to give a specimen of his dexterity.   He aimed at the wild beasts, and the spectators admired his address and the vigour of his arm.   Historians relate as a fact *(g)*, that two bulls were transfixed by one arrow, and died on the spot.

III. NERO

III. Nero proceeded, with a grand cavalcade, on his way to
Rome, where the moſt ſplendid preparations were made for his
reception.   The whole city was illuminated, and the houſes decorated with garlands and laurel wreaths.   The people crowded
together from all quarters, and rent the air with ſhouts and acclamations, while the emperor, with Tiridates and the Parthian
nobility in his train, made his triumphal entry.   A day was
fixed for Tiridates to receive the diadem from the hands of Nero.
Nothing could equal the pomp and ſplendour, with which that ceremony was performed (a).   On the preceding evening, the
city was again illuminated, and the ſtreets adorned with flowers.
At the dawn of day, an incredible multitude repaired to the
forum ; the tops of houſes were crowded with ſpectators, and a
ſplendid, but theatrical pomp was exhibited with laviſh expence.
The people, dreſſed in white robes, crowned with laurels, and
ranked in their ſeveral tribes, walked in proceſſion to their
reſpective ſeats.   The prætorian guards, with their ſtandards
ranged in order, and their colours flying, diſplayed their glittering arms.   Nero entered the forum in his triumphal habit.   The
whole body of the ſenate followed in his train.   He took his ſeat
on a curule chair, amidſt the ſtandards and the eagles.   In a ſhort
time after, Tiridates made his appearance.   The ſoldiers opened
their lines ; he advanced through the ranks, with his eaſtern
nobility in his train.   He approached the roſtrum, and on his
knees offered homage to Nero.   The people were not able to
contain their joy.   They ſaw the pride of an oriental king humbled at the feet of the emperor.   The majeſty of Rome filled
every imagination.   A ſhout burſt forth from the enraptured
multitude.   Tiridates was aſtoniſhed at the ſound : he ſtood at
gaze, and his heart ſhrunk within him.   Nero raiſed him from
the ground, and, having claſped him in his arms, placed the

APPENDIX
ᴛᴏ
BOOK XVI.

A. U. C.
819.
A. D.
66.

6   diadem

diadem on his head *(b)*, amidſt the repeated ſhouts and acclamations of the people.

IV. THE Parthian prince, not yet recovered from his ſurpriſe,
in the hurry and agitation of his ſpirits, addreſſed himſelf to
Nero, in ſubſtance as follows: "You ſee before you a prince
"deſcended from the line of the Arſacidæ; you behold the bro-
"ther of two kings, Vologeſes and Pacorus; and yet I own
"myſelf your ſlave. You, no leſs than *(a) Mithra*, are to me
"a god. I pay you the ſame veneration as I do to the Sun.
"Without your protection, I have no kingdom; my rights muſt
"flow from you. You are the author of my fortune; and your
"will is fate." An ancient prætor undertook to be interpreter
on the occaſion. The people, well convinced that Nero, by his
vices, had forfeited all kind of claim to ſuch reſpectful language,
received it as the homage of a king to the majeſty of the Roman
name. The ſpeech was ſufficiently mean and abject, but the
arrogance and ferocity of Nero's anſwer *(b)* exceeded every thing.
"I congratulate you on the wiſdom, that brought you thus far
"to enjoy the ſunſhine of my preſence, and my protection. The
"diadem, which your father could not leave you, nor your bro-
"thers confirm in your hand, is the gift which I beſtow. The
"kingdom of Armenia is yours: I place you on the vacant
"throne. From this day you and your brothers may learn, that
"it is mine to raiſe or depoſe the monarchs of the earth, as my
"wiſdom ſhall direct."

Such was the haughty ſtyle, in which Nero ſpoke of himſelf;
but he did not long ſupport his grandeur. The coronation being over, he adjourned to Pompey's theatre, where the ſcene
was prepared, at an enormous expence, with the moſt ſuperb

                                      decora-

decorations. The stage, and the whole inside of that noble structure, were cased *(c)* with gold. Such a profusion of wealth and magnificence had never been displayed to view. To screen the spectators from the rays of the sun, a purple canopy, inlaid with golden stars, was spread over their heads. In the centre was seen, richly embroidered, the figure of Nero in the act of driving a curricle. To the exhibitions of the theatre the pleasures of the table succeeded. The banquet *(d)* was the most sumptuous that taste and luxury could contrive. When the appetite of the guests was satisfied, the public diversions were once more resumed. Nero seized the opportunity to display his talents; and he, who a little before was master of the universe, appeared in the characters of charioteer, comedian, singer, and buffoon. He sung on the stage, and drove round the circus in his green livery *(e)*. The king of Armenia saw the prince, who talked of dealing out crowns and sceptres, warbling a tune, and managing the reins for the entertainment of his subjects. Such despicable talents, he knew, could neither form a warrior, nor a legislator. His glory, it now was evident, depended on the virtue and the genius of men very different from himself. How he found a people tame enough to obey, and general officers willing to command his armies, was matter of wonder to the Parthian prince. Struck with that idea, he could not refrain from saying to Nero, in the simplicity of his heart *(f)*, " You have in Corbulo a most " valuable slave." The drift and good sense of the observation made no impression on a frivolous mind like that of Nero. An emperor, who placed his glory in being a scenic performer, paid no attention to the merit of Corbulo. If he understood the reflection of the eastern prince, he shewed afterwards, that the only use he made of it was, to nourish a secret jealousy, and plan the ruin of an officer, whose fame in arms was too great for a tyrant to endure.

As

As foon as the diverfions of the theatre and the circus ended, Nero thought fit to open a more important fcene. He proceeded with a grand retinue to the capitol, where he entered with a branch of laurel in his hand ; and, as if he had fubdued Armenia, the charioteer and player of interludes was faluted IMPERATOR. His vanity was now amply gratified ; but vanity was not the only fpring of his actions. To be an adept in magic arts had been for fome time his predominant paffion ; and, as Tiridates brought with him in his train a number of the Parthian MAGI, he thought the opportunity fair to learn all the fecrets of an occult fcience, which he believed was not the mere illufion of mathematicians and pretended philofophers. Tiridates ftudied to ingratiate himfelf, and was proud to have the emperor of Rome for his pupil (g). By his defire, the MAGI opened all their ftores of knowledge, and Nero, with the anxiety of a guilty mind, was eager to pry into futurity. He was mafter of the Roman world, and, with the affiftance of his oriental teachers, flattered himfelf that he fhould foon be able to controul the ways of Providence, and give the law to the gods. With this view he paffed his time in clofe conference with a fet of Chaldean impoftors ; but Tiridates was not able, in return for the kingdom of Armenia, to teach his benefactor the art of holding commerce with evil fpirits. Nero found the whole to be a fyftem of fraud. Inftead of being enabled to hold a council with infernal powers, he was left to the fuggeftions of his own heart, and the advice of a pernicious crew of abandoned men and women, who were the emperor's confidential minifters, and the inftruments of every villany.

V. IT is certain that Nero's paffion for the guitar, and ftage-mufic, was not greater than his ambition to excel in magic incantations ; but though his hopes were fruftrated, he did not ceafe to entertain Tiridates with the moft lavifh profufion. An enor-

mous

mous fum *(a)* was iffued every day to the Armenian king, for
the fupport of his own grandeur, and the courtiers in his train.
At his departure a ftill larger fum was ordered, as a prefent from
the emperor; and, that he might rebuild the city of Artaxata *(b)*,
which had been levelled to the ground, a number of artificers
were added, at a vaft expence, to the retinue of the Parthian
prince, who alfo engaged a number of others to attend him, for
ftipulated wages, to his own country. The confequence of Nero's
generofity was, that the fixing of a king on the throne of Armenia, was a heavier burthen to the Romans than any of their moft
expenfive wars.

There is reafon to think, that the want of fuccefs in the attempt
to make Nero believe in the religion of the *Magi*, ferved, in fome
degree, to open the eyes of Tiridates, and remove the errors of
eaftern fuperftition. In order to vifit Rome, he had taken a wide
compafs over an immenfe tract of country, and travelled all the
way by land. The caufe of this circuitous and laborious journey
muft be referred to the fuperftition of his native country. In
the creed of the Parthian Magi, the fea was faid to be a facred
element *(c)*; and to fpit in it, or defile the purity of the waters
by the fuperfluities of the human body, was held to be profane
and impious. The defign, probably, was, by that doctrine to
prevent migration, and what at firft was policy received in time
the fanction of religion. But Tiridates, during his ftay at Rome,
fo far weeded out the prejudices of education, that he made no
fcruple to return by fea. He embarked at Brundufium *(d)*,
and, having croffed the Adriatic, arrived at the port of Dyrrachium *(e)*. From that place he purfued his voyage along the
coaft of Afia, and, being fafely landed, vifited the Roman provinces, and the moft fplendid cities on the continent. Before
he entered the confines of Armenia, Corbulo advanced to a

VOL. II.   Z z   meeting.

meeting. In his interview with the Armenian monarch, he ftill maintained that fuperior character, which he had fairly earned by his talents and his virtues. Finding an extraordinary number of artificers in the prince's train, he refolved to act with due attention to the intereft as well as the dignity of the Roman name; and with that view, having feparated fuch as were hired, he fuffered none but thofe who were a donation from Nero, to migrate to a foreign country. This behaviour gave no offence to Tiridates. He took leave of Corbulo with the higheft efteem for his many virtues; and, though he entertained no kind of perfonal refpect for Nero, he thought the regal diadem claimed a return of gratitude; and, upon that principle, as foon as the capital of Armenia was rebuilt, inftead of calling it *Artaxata*, he gave it the flattering name of *Neronia*.

VI. ROME having no war upon her hands, Nero, with airs of felf-congratulation, as if his valour had fubdued the nations, thought fit to fhut the temple of JANUS *(a)*. But that pacific difpofition did not laft long. Intoxicated by the homage which he had received from Tiridates, he wanted to renew the fame feene of fplendour and vain-glory, by the humiliation of Vologefes, the Parthian king. For that purpofe, he endeavoured, by preffing invitations, to induce that prince to undertake a journey to Rome. At length the eaftern monarch gave a decifive anfwer: " You can crofs the fea, which I hold to be a forbidden " element; come to Afia, and we will then fettle the ceremony " of our meeting." Fired with indignation by that peremptory refufal, and the tone of grandeur with which it was delivered, Nero was upon the point of declaring war, if other projects had not dazzled his imagination. He concerted his meafures, and laid plans of vaft ambition; but the caprice that dictated them yielded to the firft novelty that occurred. He intended to open

the

the temple of Janus for four wars at once *(b)*. The firft, againft
the Jews, who felt themfelves oppreffed by the avarice and rapacity of Geffius Florus, the governor of the province, and were,
at that time, in open revolt. The fecond enterprife was intended
againft the Æthiopians; the third, againft the Albanians on the
borders of the Cafpian fea; the fourth, to revenge the infult offered to him by the haughty fpirit of Vologefes. The love of
fame, whatever he did, was the infpiring motive: whether he
fent forth his armies, or drove a chariot, or fung a fong, praife
was ftill the ultimate end. If by his victorious arms the Æthiopians and Albanians could be reduced to fubjection, the glory
of enlarging the boundaries of the empire was to be the bright
reward. His exertions were, therefore, made againft the two
laft-mentioned ftates. He fent detachments forward to furvey
the country; he formed flying camps in thofe diftant regions;
he began to collect the forces of the empire; and, not content
with drawing from Britain, from Germany, and Illyricum, the
flower of his armies, he formed a new legion, compofed of men
fix feet high, and this he called the phalanx *(c)* of Alexander
the Great.

 Amidft this din of arms, and all this mighty tumult of warlike
preparations, an incident occurred of more moment to Nero than
the glory of the Roman name. A deputation arrived at Rome
from the cities of Greece, where the theatre, and poetry, and
mufic flourifhed, with orders to prefent to the emperor, from the
feveral places, the victor's crown *(d)* for minftrelfy and fong.
An opportunity fo bright and unexpected was not to be neglected. Nero was tranfported with joy: he towered above
himfelf and all competition. The deputies were admitted to his
prefence; they were careffed, invited to his table, and all other
bufinefs, however important, gave way to the elegant arts. The

APPENDIX
T O
BOOK XVI.

A. U. C.
819.
A. D.
66.

Z z 2
Greeks

Greeks were skilled in the trade of adulation. They beseeched the prince to honour them with a specimen of his talents. Nero sung to his guests; they heard, they applauded, they were thrown into ecstasies. He in his turn admired their taste; they were the only people who had music in their souls; they, and they only, had an ear for finer sound; the true masters of harmony; the judges who deserved to hear his exquisite powers. From that moment all his warlike projects vanished from his mind. He thought no more of humbling the Parthian king; the Æthiopians and Albanians might enjoy their independent state, and Vespasian might take the field against the Jews. The fame of a coachman, a minstrel, and a singer, was of greater moment. He resolved, without delay, to set out for Greece. How the administration was to be conducted during his absence, was the first consideration. That did not embarrass him long. The whole authority and all the functions of the prince were committed to Helius, one of his freedmen. That upstart minister, with Polycletus, his associate, had already enriched himself with the plunder of the public, and was now, with the whole power in his hands, to give a full display of his character. That point being settled, a weightier care still remained. An imperial charioteer, and a comedian of illustrious rank, who was to be nobly covered with Olympic dust, and to bring back laurel crowns for his victories in song and pantomime, could not undertake such an expedition without the greatest pomp. Preparations were accordingly made. The emperor seemed to be going to an important war (e). Tigellinus put himself at the head of the companions of the Augustan order, in number not less than five thousand. To these were added an incredible multitude of abandoned harlots, and the most debauched young men of the time. The whole train went forth, not in warlike array, with swords, and pikes, and javelins, but with softer instruments;

ments; with the fock and bufkin; with mufic, lutes and guitars. The retinue was fuited to the dignity of the enterprife. An idea of the fplendour and magnificence difplayed on this occafion may be eafily formed, when we are told that Nero never travelled with lefs than a thoufand baggage-waggons *(f)*; the mules all fhod with filver, and the drivers dreffed in fcarlet; his African flaves adorned with bracelets on their arms, and the horfes decorated with the richeft trappings.

APPENDIX TO BOOK XVI.

A. U. C. 819.
A. D. 64.

VII. THE confuls for this year were Fonteius Capito and Julius Rufus; but their authority was fuperfeded by Helius, the freedman, who exercifed all the powers of the imperial prerogative. This man broke loofe at once, and was foon felt as a public calamity. Pride and infolence, avarice and cruelty, the never-failing vices of thofe deteftable mifcreants, who from the dregs of the people rife above their fellow citizens, marked the conduct of this favourite freedman, and debafed the people, who fubmitted to fo vile a mafter. All degrees and ranks of men, the fenate, and the Roman knights, groaned under the iron rod of an ignoble tyrant, who confifcated their eftates, fent them into banifhment, or took away their lives at his will and pleafure. The people, who fhuddered at the prefence of the emperor, were obliged, in mifery of heart, to lament his abfence.

A. U. C. 820.
A. D. 67.

Nero, in the mean time, arrived at Caffiopœa *(b)* in the ifle of Corcyra, and there, in the temple of Jupiter Caffius *(c)*, he tuned his harp, and fung in the prefence of the people. From that place he fet fail for Greece. Being fafely landed, his firft care was, like a great officer, before he marched further into the country, to fettle the plan of his operations, in order not only to gain, but to fecure his victory. With this view, he iffued his

public

public orders, requiring that all the games *(d)*, which were cele-brated throughout Greece at ftated periods, and in different years, fhould be performed at their refpective places, during his ftay in the country; and not only fo, but that each city fhould wait for his arrival. Nor was this all: the fame of fuch as had proved victorious, and were then no more, was to be obliterated from the memory of man, that all preceding merit might be eclipfed by the luftre of a new performer. The ftatues of the deceafed were all demolifhed *(e)*. The living artifts were treated with lefs rigour. They were required to enter the lifts with their impe-rial rival, and, upon that condition, their ftatues were exempted from the general deftruction. Nero's love of fame was not a generous emulation; it was an impatience of a rival, that turned to envy, rancour, and malice. To be pronounced the firft mu-fician, and the beft tragedian, was not enough for his vaft ambi-tion; he was likewife to be the moft fkilful driver of a curricle. With that bright object in view, he had for fome years before meditated an expedition into Greece; and finding that the Olym-pic games were, in their regular courfe, to be celebrated in the fummer, in the year of Rome eight hundred and fixteen, he even then had the precaution, by a pofitive command, to defer the exhibition of that great national fpectacle till his arrival in Greece. The law, or, which was equivalent, his will and plea-fure, being announced, the people prepared for his reception. He began his tour through the country; he vifited the feveral cities, and gave himfelf a fpectacle on the public ftage. Greece had been reduced to fubjection by Flaminius, Mummius, Agrippa, and Auguftus Cæfar: and now in her turn fhe triumphed over the conqueror. She faw the emperor of Rome running from place to place in the character of a ftrolling player, a travelling mufician, and a famous coachman. He did not, however, de-pend altogether on his merit, but practifed the underhand arts,

by

by which fuccefs is often enfured. He hired a numerous party
to applaud, and diftributed bribes among the judges who were to
decide. Wherever he performed, a legion of Roman knights
was ftationed in the theatre, by their own example to excite and
animate the admiration of the multitude, and teach the Greeks
what was excellent in the arts, which they themfelves had invented, and carried to perfection. By thefe and fuch like preconcerted meafures, Nero fecured his triumph in all quarters.
Competition was invited, and at the fame time intimidated. In
one of the cities, a man well fkilled in mufic, but a bad politician, experienced the danger of contending with a powerful
rival. Zealous for the honour of his art, and proud of his own
talent, he perfifted to difpute the prize, till the lictors drove him
to the wall, and there difpatched him in the fight of the audience. Vefpafian had found it neceffary to pafs from Syria into
Greece, in order to appear among the band of courtiers, and pay
his homage to the emperor. But, unfortunately, he either had
no ear for mufic, or he did not reckon it among the accomplifhments of a prince. He heard that divine voice in a fullen mood,
or, as happened to him at Rome upon a former occafion, he fell
afleep *(f)*. For this offence, he was ordered to appear no more
in the prefence of the emperor. He retired to a fmall village,
and there, in an obfcure lurking-place, hoped to find a fhelter
from refentment. He remained for fome time in that ftate of
anxious fufpenfe, when the fates called him forth to fcenes of
future glory. The Jews were in the field with a powerful army;
they had defeated Ceftius Gallus with great flaughter, and taken
an eagle from one of the legions. The crifis was big with danger, and called for vigorous meafures. But Nero did not think that
Judæa was the field of glory. He gave the command to Vefpafian, apprehending no danger from a man of obfcure defcent, and
auftere manners, whom he was no longer willing to retain near

his

his perfon. Vefpafian departed to take upon him the command in Syria, and Nero continued his progrefs through Greece. He was received every where with public demonftrations of refpect; but the people could fcarce refrain from laughter, when they heard the found of a voice neither loud nor clear, and faw the finger rifing on his toes, in a vain endeavour to expand the notes, and ftraining his organs, till a face, naturally red, was fo inflamed as to vie with the deepeft fcarlet. Not content with the fame of an enchanting finger, he refolved to prove himfelf a great tragedian. The parts, in which he chofe to diftinguifh himfelf *(g)*, were HERCULES FURENS; ŒDIPUS, who murdered his father, and tore out his own eyes; ORESTES, poignarding his mother; and fometimes a RAVISHED SABINE, or a MATRON IN LABOUR, on the point of being delivered. When he arrived at Olympia, he found, that the celebrated games of that place confifted altogether of chariot-races, and athletic exercifes, and by confequence that no theatre had been erected. Was his darling mufic to be excluded? Rather than fuffer fuch an indignity, he ordered preparations to be made for interludes, and other dramatic performances. Not content with being blinded on the ftage; with raving like a madman, and being brought to bed like a woman; he was ftill to figure on the race-ground, and aftonifh the multitude with his dexterity in whirling round the courfe. Determined to perform wonders, and furpafs all ancient fame, he mounted a car drawn by fix horfes, but had the misfortune, in the heat of his career, to be thrown from his feat. He mounted again; but either hurt by his fall, or not able to bear the velocity of the motion, he was obliged to defcend before he reached the goal. He was, notwithftanding, declared conqueror. He contended afterwards for the prizes at the Pythian, the Nemean, and all the other games of Greece, with equal fuccefs at every place. He was proclaimed victor in all trials of fkill, and gained no lefs

than

than eighteen hundred different crowns. The honour fo obtained was always underftood to reflect a luftre on the conqueror's native country. With a view to that cuftom, the form of the proclamation *(b)* in favour of Nero was as follows: NERO CÆSAR IS VICTOR IN THE COMBAT (naming it), AND HAS WON THE CROWN FOR THE ROMAN PEOPLE, AND THE UNIVERSE, OF WHICH HE IS MASTER." Care was taken to tranfmit to Rome a regular account of all his victories. Such a career of rapid fuccefs made the people ftand at gaze. The fenate paffed a vote of thanks to the gods for fuch fignal events, and, by their decrees, fo loaded the calendar, that the year could fcarce find room for fo many rejoicing days.

VIII. NERO now conceived that he had triumphed over the arts, and, in the pride of his heart, refolved to make a progrefs through the conquered country. He took care, however, not to vifit Athens or Lacedæmon. In the former, he dreaded to approach the temple of the Eumenidæ. A mind lafhed and goaded by the whips and ftings of a guilty confcience wifhed to avoid thofe avenging deities *(a)*. He was deterred from Lacedæmon by the form of government, and the fanctity of the laws eftablifhed by Lycurgus. The place where the Eleufinian myfteries *(b)* were celebrated, was alfo forbidden ground. Murderers and parricides were excluded from thofe religious ceremonies. Nero was feized with a fit of remorfe. Bufy reflection brought to light the iniquities of his conduct; in the agitation of his fpirits, he reviewed thofe deeds of horror, which forbore to goad him, while his mind was becalmed by vanity and pleafure. Confcience may grant a truce to the guilty, but never makes a lafting peace. Diftracted by his fears, and funk in the gloom of fuperftition *(c)*, he refolved to confult the oracle at Delphi. The Pythian prieftefs warned him to beware of feventy-three years *(d)*.

He received the admonition as a certain promife of long life, not then thinking of Galba, who had reached his feventy-third year, and in a fhort time after fucceeded to the imperial dignity. The oracle pleafed him at firft by agreeable bodings, but did not continue long in his good graces. The parricide, he was told, which he had committed, placed him in the fame rank with Alcmeon and Oreftes, who had murdered their mothers. Nero kindled with indignation. He refolved that the god fhould feel his refentment, and, in his fury, disfranchifed the territory of Cirrha *(e)*, which had been appropriated to the temple, and was held to be confecrated ground. Nor did his phrenfy end here. The oracle was to be filenced, or fo profaned as to lofe its credit. With this intent, he ordered a number of men to be maffacred on the fpot; and having poured libations of their blood into the opening of the ground, from which the exhalations iffued, that were fuppofed to infpire the prieftefs with enthufiaftic fury, he clofed the orifice, and with pride and infolence left a place which had been revered for ages. After this exploit, he returned to his former luxury, and in the gratifications of vice hoped to find fome refpite from his anxious thoughts. But even vice required variety. Repetition might pall the fated appetite, and, if he did not fhew an inventive genius, the flattery of the Greeks was in danger of being exhaufted. He had made himfelf at Rome the wife of Pythagoras *(f)*; but that was become an obfolete ftory, and no longer excited wonder. He was determined, therefore, to refume his fex, and marry Sporus, the eunuch. The ceremony was performed *(g)* with great pomp and fplendour. Calvia Crifpinilla *(h)* was appointed miftrefs of the wardrobe to the emperor's wife. She adorned the bride with all the decorations of female elegance; and Tigellinus, amidft the applaufe of the aftonifhed Greeks, who, with arch fneers of ridicule, had ftill the addrefs to pay their adulation, gave away Sporus in marriage to

8

the

the emperor of Rome. It was said upon the occasion, that it
would have been well for mankind, if Nero's father had been
married to such a wife.

IX. NERO could not, in this unbounded manner, riot in vice
and folly without vast expence, and a prodigious waste of the
public treasure. To supply his prodigality, Helius the freedman, who conducted the administration at Rome, laboured hard,
by every iniquitous measure, by extortion, and cruelty, to raise
enormous sums of money. A tame and complying senate was
easily induced by the arts of the prime minister to vote an immense annual sum to be remitted to the emperor, during his absence from the capital. The rapacity of Helius was not to be
appeased. The companions of the Augustan society *(a)* had
bound themselves by a vow to erect a statue to Nero, not less
than a thousand pound weight. By that voluntary obligation
they were said to have incurred a debt, and were compelled to
advance an equivalent sum of money. No rank or station was
safe from plunder and oppression. Roman knights and senators
fell a sacrifice, and their estates were confiscated. Sulpicius Camerinus *(b)*, a man descended from an illustrious family, was put
to death for an extraordinary reason. The surname of Pythicus
had been for ages annexed to his ancestors, and was, conse-
quently, an hereditary honour. By the fertile invention of
Helius this was construed into a crime. The name might imply
a victor in the Pythian games; and when Nero, with the con-
senting voice of Greece, was declared universal conqueror, to
usurp that title was a crime of violated majesty, and an impious
sacrilege. Sulpicius and his son were put to death, and their effects were forfeited to the state. Wealth, in whatever rank, was
sure to provoke the hand of rapacity, and Rome, under the government of a presuming and arrogant freedman, was a scene of

3 A 2

plunder,

plunder, blood, and cruelty. And yet all that could be amassed by those iniquitous means, was not sufficient for the prodigality of Nero. The Greeks had flattered his vanity, and, in return, were doomed to feel the hand of oppression. The cities, which had revered him as a god, had reason in the end to execrate him as a tyrant. They saw their best and most distinguished citizens put to death, or sent into banishment, that the emperor might enjoy the spoils of their plundered property *(c)*.

X. The fame of a divine voice, and an exquisite hand on the guitar, was not sufficient for the ambition of Nero. He wished to distinguish himself by some unheard of enterprise. The grand, the vast, and almost impossible fired his imagination. He arrived at Corinth, and was there surprised to see by what a narrow isthmus the two seas were separated. Like the hero of Statius the poet, he heard the murmur of the billows, on the Ionian and the Ægean shores; *in mediis audit duo litora campis.* The project of piercing through the land, and forming a navigable canal to communicate the two seas, and render it unnecessary for mariners to sail round the Peloponnesus, struck his fancy, and fired him with ideas of immortal fame *(a)*. The Greeks opposed the design, and endeavoured to dissuade him from undertaking it. The language of superstition was, that to attempt to join what had been severed for ages, would be an impious violation of the laws of nature. Nero was not to be deterred from his purpose; religious principles were urged in vain; to conquer nature were an imperial work, and what the gods ordained, might be new modelled by his superior judgment. He knew, besides, that the attempt had been made by Demetrius Policrates, an eastern king, by Julius Cæsar and Caligula *(b)*; and to accomplish an arduous work, which those three princes had undertaken without effect, appeared to him the height of human glory. He resolved, therefore,

therefore, to begin the work without delay.   Having harangued
the prætorian foldiers, and urged every topic that could inflame
their ardour, he provided himfelf with a golden pick-axe (for
fuch hands were not to be fullied by bafer metal), and, advancing on the fhore, fung in melodious ftrains a hymn to
Neptune, Amphitrite, and all the inferior gods and goddeffes,
who allay or heave the waters of the deep.   After this ceremony, he ftruck the firft ftroke into the ground, and, with a
bafket of fand on his fhoulder, marched away in triumph, proud
of his Herculean labour.   The natives of the country faw the
frantic enterprife with mixed emotions of fear, aftonifhment,
and religious horror.   They obferved to Nero, that of the three
princes, who had conceived the fame defign, not one died a natural death.   They told him further, that, in fome places, as foon
as the axe pierced the ground, a ftream of blood gufhed from
the wound; hollow groans were heard from fubterraneous caverns, and various fpectres, emitting a feeble murmur, were feen
to glide along the coaft.   Thefe remonftrances made no impreffion.   Nero ordered his foldiers to exert their utmoft vigour;
money was levied in every quarter; cruelty and extortion went
hand in hand.   In order to procure a fufficient number of workmen, the jails in all parts of the empire were ranfacked, and
the armies in Syria and Paleftine had it in command to fend to
Corinth all the prifoners taken in battle..

The conduct of the war againft the Jewifh nation had been,
as mentioned above, committed to Vefpafian, who had already
carried his victorious arms through the province of Galilée.   The
enemy, as foon as they had intelligence that he was advancing
at the head of a powerful army, endeavoured to furprife a Roman garrifon in the city of Afcalon *(c)*, but were repulfed with
prodigious flaughter.   Not lefs than eighteen thoufand were put

to

APPENDIX
T O
BOOK XVI.

A. U. C.
820.
A. D.
67.

to the fword by the legions, who had orders to give no quarter. Vefpafian found it neceffary, againft a fierce and obftinate race, at that time for their manifold crimes devoted to deftruction, to forget the maxims of Roman clemency. It is certain that thofe merciful conquerors never fpilled fo much hoftile blood in any of their wars from the firft foundation of Rome. The city of Gadara *(d)* was taken by ftorm, and reduced to afhes. The garrifon and the whole body of the inhabitants perifhed in the flames. In the mean time, Trajan, whofe fon was afterwards emperor of Rome, was fent, at the head of the tenth legion, to fpread terror and deftruction through the country. He laid fiege to the city of Japha *(e)*, and, meeting with an obftinate refiftance, carried the works by affault. All, who were capable of bearing arms, in number not lefs than fifteen thoufand, were put to the fword. The Samaritans, who had collected their forces on Mount Garizim *(f)*, were treated with the fame feverity. Cerealis, who afterwards commanded againft Civilis, the Batavian chieftain, and alfo in Britain, had orders to march with three thoufand foot and fix hundred horfe to attack the faftneffes on the hills, and diflodge the enemy. He formed lines of circumvallation round the hill, and by a clofe blockade cut off all communication with the adjacent country. The Samaritans were reduced by famine to the laft diftrefs; yet even in that condition held out to the laft with determined obftinacy. Cerealis ordered his men to advance up the hill. The foldiers forced their way up the fteep afcent, and with refiftlefs valour foon gained the fummit. A dreadful carnage followed. Twelve thoufand of the Samaritans perifhed on the fpot. The city of Gamala *(b)* was taken by affault, and the garrifon, with all the inhabitants, put to the fword.

Vefpafian, during thefe operations, carried on the fiege of
Jotapata,

Jotapata *(i)*, the ftrongeft place in Galilee. Jofephus *(k)*, the hiftorian, had been appointed governor of the province, and he now commanded the garrifon, determined to make a vigorous defence, and hold out to the laft extremity. The particulars of the fiege are related by himfelf, and therefore need not to be here repeated. It will be fufficient to fay, that he difcharged all the duties of an able officer, by his own example, no lefs than by his fpirited exhortations, animating the foldiers, and in every part of the works exciting them to deeds of valour. The fiege lafted feven-and-forty days. In one of the approaches to the walls, Vefpafian was wounded by a lance aimed at him from the works; but he bore the pain with fuch filent fortitude, that no ill confequence followed. On the forty-feventh day of the fiege, the inhabitants ftill refufing to capitulate, the fignal was given for a general affault. Titus, at the head of a chofen band, fcaled the walls, and was the firft that entered the town. In that dreadful crifis it does not appear that Jofephus either faced the danger, or difcharged the functions of a general officer. Except the women and children, and about twelve hundred prifoners, all who were found in the town died in one general carnage. Jofephus was afterwards found concealed in a cave. Vefpafian fpared his life, and the hiftorian furvived to write an account of the fiege, intermixed, indeed, with fome romantic circum-ftances, but containing various matter for the information of pofterity. The city of Tarichæa *(l)*, which had been the re-ceptacle of a turbulent and feditious rabble from all fides of the country, was compelled, after an obftinate refiftance, to open her gates to Titus. Vefpafian ordered twelve hundred of the moft fierce incendiaries to be put to death, as a public example, and, in compliance with Nero's letters, fent fix thoufand prifoners *(m)* to work at the ifthmus of Corinth.

XI. WHILE

XI. WHILE Vespasian pursued his conquests, and, in one campaign, overran the province of Galilee, Rome was a scene of tumult and distraction. Helius reigned like a second emperor: the people called him the worst of the two. Each day produced new proofs of avarice, cruelty, and all the vices of an upstart slave. The senators began to wake from their lethargy; the clamours of the populace were loud and fierce; rage and indignation glowed in every breast; and the flame was ready to mount into a blaze. The freedman saw his danger. He dispatched letters to inform the emperor that the urgency of affairs required his presence at Rome *(a)*. But Nero's vast designs were of too much importance. His answer to the favourite was, " You ad-
" vise me to return to Rome, but whatever your reasons are,
" you ought rather to recommend a longer absence; that I may
" finish my grand undertaking, and then revisit the capital,
" crowned with immortal glory." He saw the number of labourers sent by Vespasian, and, in consideration of that timely succour, forgave the merit of that victorious general. Corbulo *(b)* had not the good fortune to be remembered with equal moderation. Tiridates had mentioned him with the praise due to his virtue, and his fame in arms. That commendation was sufficient to provoke the ingratitude of a tyrant, who beheld distinguished talents with a jealous eye, and suffered no man to be great and virtuous with impunity. Being at length determined to execute the bloody purpose, which he had for some time harboured in secret, he wrote to Corbulo in terms of great esteem and kindness, calling him his friend and benefactor, and expressing his ardent wish to have an interview with a general who had rendered such signal services to the empire. Having sent that insidious invitation, he held a private correspondence with Arrius Varus, who served in Asia; a young man of a daring spirit, in haste to rise by his crimes. To fabricate a

2

charge

charge againſt his commanding officer he knew would be the way to ingratiate himſelf with Nero. He ſent a formal accuſation, loaded with every crime that calumny could ſuggeſt. Corbulo fell into the ſnare. A mind like his, impregnated with honour and heroic fortitude, could admit no ſuſpicion of intended treachery. He embarked without any retinue, and landed at Cenchreæ, a Corinthian harbour in the Ægean Sea. Nero was there at the time, dreſſed in his pantomime garb, and ready to mount the ſtage, when the arrival of his general officer was announced. He felt the indecency of giving an audience in his comedian's dreſs to a man, whom he reſpected, while he hated him. To free himſelf from all embarraſſment, he took the ſhorteſt way, and ſent a death-warrant. Corbulo ſaw too late that honeſty is too often the dupe of the ignoble mind. He ſcorned to expoſtulate. " I have deſerved this," he ſaid, and fell upon his ſword *(e)*.

The blood of one great man could not appeaſe the cruelty of Nero. Whoever was eminent for talents, riches, or nobility of birth, was conſidered as a ſtate-criminal. In that number were the two Scribonii, Rufus and Proculus, who had lived in perfect harmony, with mutual eſteem, and true brotherly affection. Their fortunes were a joint ſtock. They aſſiſted each other in the road to honours, and both together roſe to ſtations of high authority ; one on the Upper, and the other on the Lower Rhine. While they diſcharged their reſpective duties with integrity, and unwearied zeal for the public ſervice, Pactius Africanus *(f)* was their ſecret enemy. This man had the ear of Nero, and knew how to transfuſe his own malignity into the heart of a prince too fatally prone to evil deeds. The virtues of the Scribonii were, by his artful miſrepreſentation, converted into crimes ; the happy concord, in which they lived, was a conſpiracy againſt the ſtate ;

and their fame and credit in the German armies were the means of two ambitious politicians, not the end of their actions. By conciliating the good-will of the foldiers, they hoped to overturn the government. Nero took the alarm, and, under a fpecious pretence of doing honour to the two brothers, invited them to his court. They obeyed his orders. As foon as they arrived in Greece, a new fcene was opened. An audience was refufed; they were forbid to appear in the emperor's prefence; fuborned accufations were prefented in form; and the unhappy brothers found themfelves in the fad condition of ftate-criminals. They defired to be heard in their defence. That act of juftice was denied. They knew, that, under a defpotic prince, the interval between the opening of an accufation and the cataftrophe is always fhort. They refolved not to wait the tyrant's pleafure, but to deliver themfelves with Roman fortitude from an ignominious death. They opened their veins, and expired together.

The fate of Craffus *(g)*, who derived an illuftrious lineage from Pompey the Great, and Craffus the Triumvir, may be mentioned in this place. Hiftorians have not fixed the time of his death with precifion; but it is certain that he fell a victim to the cruelty of Nero. Craffus, his father, with Scribonia, his mother, and a brother, who was named Cneius Pompeius Magnus, had been cut off by the emperor Claudius *(h)*. But the family, in the opinion of Aquileius Regulus, had not fhed blood enough. That pernicious informer knew that to be accufed, was to be condemned. He invented a charge of an atrocious nature, and Craffus fhared the fate of his murdered family. He left two brothers; the eldeft, Craffus Scribonianus; the youngeft, the unfortunate Pifo, at that time a banifhed man, but afterwards adopted by Galba *(k)*, too foon to fall from that dangerous eminence.

During

During thefe bloody tragedies, the great bufinefs of piercing the ifthmus was not neglected. The work began at a place called Lechæum *(l)*, a fea-port on the Ionian Sea. It went on with ftrenuous exertion for a number of days. A trench was dug four ftadia in length, which was computed to be a tenth part of the ifthmus. But the flame of difcord was lighted up at Rome. A ftorm was gathering in Gaul, and commotions fhook every part of the empire. In that alarming conjuncture, Helius thought fit to leave his affociate Polycletus, as his vice-gerent at Rome, and he himfelf paffed over into Greece. He met Nero at Corinth, and, by giving him, in ftriking colours, a dreadful picture of the ftate of affairs, enforced the neceffity of returning to the capital. The grand enterprife was abandoned, and the Ionian and Ægean Seas were left to flow in the direction which nature had appointed. But ftill there was an object that attracted Nero's fond regard. The time of celebrating the Ifthmian games was near at hand. His favourite paffion hurried him to the place. The pugilift and the charioteer banifhed from his mind all fear of plots and infurrections. He thought of the crowns of victory, which he had obtained in every quarter. His heart expanded with joy, with felf-congratulation, and gratitude towards a people, who had declared him matchlefs and unrivalled in all the games and exercifes throughout the country. It behoved fo great a conqueror to leave a lafting monument of munificence, and imperial grandeur. Elate with pride, and touched with generous fentiments, he refolved to give Greece her liberty. With that defign he repaired to the forum. Nor did he fuffer his gracious intention to be uttered by the public cryer. Such a gift required the accents of his own heavenly voice. He afcended the tribunal of harangues, and, having declared Greece a free country *(m)*, fet fail for Italy.

3 B 2

XII. The

XII. THE confuls next in office were Galerius Trachalus and Silius Italicus. They were both men of genius; both addicted to ftudy, and diftinguifhed by their extenfive literature. Trachalus *(a)* was an orator in great celebrity, always copious, and often fublime. Silius Italicus *(b)* had alfo diftinguifhed himfelf at the bar, but not with unblemifhed reputation. He knew that, under Nero, to be the accufer of innocence was the road to preferment; but he returned to the paths of virtue, and by his poetry, which he publifhed afterwards, tranfmitted his name to pofterity. During his confulfhip, Nero returned from Greece, to clofe the fcene of vice and folly. After a tempeftuous voyage, he arrived at Naples, where the firft difplays of his genius had been feen in their dawn *(c)*. His fame was now in its meridian luftre. The conqueror in the Olympic, the Pythian, and the Ifthmian games was to enter the city in triumph; and for this purpofe the ufual avenues were not fufficient. The occafion required fomething new and extraordinary. The cuftom in Greece was to throw down part of the city-wall *(d)*, that the conqueror in the facred games might enter through the breach. Nero ordered an opening to be made for himfelf, and entered the city in a triumphal car, drawn by fix milk-white horfes. The fplendour of the day exceeded the triumph of Flamminius *(e)* or Mummius. They had obtained victories, and fubdued a nation: but what Roman triumphed over the arts of Greece? Who, before Nero, was declared the beft charioteer, and the fineft player on the guitar? From Naples he went to Antium *(f)*, his native city, and there difplayed the fame pomp and ceremony. But Rome was the place where his pride was to appear in all its grandeur. A long proceffion led the way. His crowns of victory in the various games glittered to the eye, and infcriptions, in glaring letters, blazoned forth the fame of Nero, the firft Roman who gained the prize of theatrical talents.

Feftive

Feftive fongs, and thankfgiving hymns, were fung, not to
Jupiter *(h)*, the guardian god of Rome, but to Apollo, the deity
of fingers and harpers. The triumphal car, in which Auguftus
had been feen, was brought forth on the occafion. That
emperor, after all his victories, entered the city in triumph:
Nero fat in the fame carriage, a coachman, and a player. Auguftus was attended by Agrippa; Nero had by his fide Diodorus,
the mufician. The ftreets refounded with acclamations: Io!
Victory! Victory in the Olympic, the Pythian, and the Ifthmian
games! Io! the conqueror of Greece! Happy the people who
heard that melodious voice! Victims were flain, incenfe rofe to
heaven, and flowers *(i)* covered all the way.

APPENDIX
to
BOOK XVI.

A. U. C.
821.
A. D.
68.

Nero returned to his palace. Pomp and fplendour were at an
end; the fcenes of vanity paffed away, and he was left at leifure
to think, and to be wretched. Helius had told him that the
conjuncture was big with danger. Plots, infurrections, and con-
fpiracies filled his mind with dreadful apprehenfions. A confpiracy *(k)*, beyond all queftion, was actually formed, and ready
to break out, had it not been difcovered by a trifling accident.
It happened that one of the confpirators'*(l)*, towards the clofe of
day, paffed by the theatre. He faw, in one of the porticos, a
man loaded with fetters, and in bitternefs of heart bewailing his
unhappy lot. Upon enquiry it was found, that he was to be led
into the prefence of Nero, which he confidered as fure deftruction. The confpirator was touched with compaffion. He drew
nearer to the prifoner, and, to affuage his fears, whifpered in his
ear, " Have a good heart; live till to-morrow, and you will have
" reafon to thank me as your deliverer." Thefe were words of
comfort to a wretch, who expected inftant death. His hopes revived; fuch welcome tidings filled him with delight and wonder; but wonder was the ftrongeft emotion. The novelty of an

incident

incident fo unexpected fixed his attention. By what means was he to be delivered from impending ruin? Nothing but a dark confpiracy could bring about fuch an event. He refolved to reveal all he knew. The merit of a difcovery, made in time, would not only fecure his life, but lead on to fortune. He defired to be conducted to the prince. The confpirator was immediately feized, and put to the torture. His courage was for fome time undaunted, unfubdued. He denied the whole of the charge. But protracted mifery was too much to bear. His refolution failed. The names of his accomplices were extorted by the violence of pain, and all were condemned to fuffer. A fcene of blood was laid, and Nero's fuperftition afcribed the difcovery of the plot to the miraculous interpofition of the gods.

Having conquered his enemies, and fecured the future tranquillity of his reign, he thought it time to give a loofe to his libidinous paffions, and purfue his theatrical amufements. For this purpofe he removed to Naples, the place of perfect fecurity, and the feat of pleafure. His halcyon days were foon interrupted. A ftorm had been for fome time gathering in Gaul, and threatened at length to fhake the empire to its foundation. There was in that part of the empire, a native of the country, defcended from the kings of Aquitain, by name *(m)* Julius Vindex. His father had been raifed by Claudius to the dignity of a fenator, and the fon was made governor of a province with the rank and powers of a Roman propraetor. This man, without an army under his command, and without any refources, except what he found in his own perfonal courage, and the generous ardour of an independent fpirit, undertook to free the world from bondage. He knew that an enterprife fo bold and daring required the co-operation of the provinces of Gaul and the Roman legions. With that view, he fent difpatches to Galba *(n)*, at that time

governor

governor of the nethermoft Spain, and made him a tender of
the imperial dignity. Galba deduced his pedigree from the ancient family of the Sulpicii : his mother, by her paternal line, was
defcended from Mummius, the conqueror of Corinth, and, by
her mother's fide, from Quintus Catulus, the pride and ornament of the old republic. He was conful under Tiberius, in the
year of Rome feven hundred and eighty. He commanded in
Germany in the reign of Caligula, and, afterwards, under Claudius was proconful of Africa. His illuftrious birth, his military
fame, and high credit with the legions in every army, pointed
him out as the proper perfon to depofe a prince, whofe cruelty
made him deteftable, and whofe folly rendered even tyranny
itfelf ridiculous. Galba received the difpatches fent by Vindex
with the frigid caution of a man far advanced in life. He was
more than feventy years old, and that age is not the feafon of
ambition. To flide in quiet through the remainder of his days,
feemed to be all that he defired from fortune ; but, under that
outward calm, the fparks of a dying paffion were rekindled.
And yet the enterprife propofed to him was big with danger,
and the iffue doubtful. Prudence confpired with indolence,
and he remained filent and inactive. The governors of all the
other provinces had been, in like manner, folicited to enter into
the Gallic league : they hated Nero ; but, inftead of declaring
open hoftility, they thought it more advifable to provide for
their own fafety, by fending to Rome the letters which they had
received from Vindex. Galba fuppreffed his in filence. Nero
received the news with joy and exultation. His finances, he
faid, were well nigh exhaufted, and the forfeited eftates of the
infurgents would be ways and means. by which he intended to
fill his treafury. He confidered Galba's filence as a proof of
guilt. Without further enquiry, he confifcated all his property at
Rome, and difpatched affaffins, with orders to put him to death..

Vindex,,

APPENDIX
TO
BOOK XVI.

A. U. C.
821.
A. D.
68.

Vindex, in the mean time, exerted himfelf with unremitting vigour to roufe the people of Gaul. He went to the various cities, and lighted up the flame of war in every quarter. He called a public convention of the ftates, and harangued the affembly, in fubftance as follows *(o)*: " We live, he faid, not un-
" der laws, and civil government, but under the will of a fingle
" tyrant. Vice and cruelty lord it over mankind. The pro-
" vinces groan under the yoke of oppreffion; our houfes are
" pillaged; our wives and daughters are violated, and our rela-
" tions bafely murdered. Of all our mifery Nero is the author.
" What crime fo great that he has not dared to perpetrate? His
" mother died by his murderous hand. That horrible parricide
" makes the heart recoil; but Agrippina deferved her fate. She
" brought a monfter into the world. At length the meafure of
" his guilt is full. The eaft is up in arms; Britain in commo-
" tion; and the legions in Spain and Germany are on the eve of
" a revolt: and fhall the nations of Gaul ftand lingering in fuf-
" penfe? What confideration is there to reftrain your ardour?
" Shall the titles of Cæfar, of Auguftus, of Prince, and Imperator
" throw a falfe luftre round a man, who has difgraced his rank,
" and made majefty ridiculous? Thefe eyes, my friends, thefe
" eyes have feen him a fidler, a mountebank, and a pantomime
" actor. Inftead of his imperial titles, call him Thyeftes, Œdi-
" pus, Alcmæon, and Oreftes. Thofe names are fuited to his
" crimes. How long are we to fubmit to fuch a mafter? Our
" forefathers took the city of Rome by ftorm: and what was
" their motive? In thofe days the love of plunder was fufficient
" to provoke a war. We have a nobler caufe; the caufe of
" public liberty. It is that, my friends, it is that glorious caufe
" that now invites us. Let us obey the call, and draw the
" avenging fword. The nations round us, fired with indigna-
" tion, are ready to affert their rights. Let them not be the firft

" to

" to prove themfelves men. The enterprife has in it all that is
" dear to man, all that is great in human nature ; and fhall we
" not be the firft to feize the glorious opportunity? Let us go
" forth at once, and be the deliverers of the world."

This fpeech was received with fhouts of applaufe. The deputies, inflamed with ardour in the caufe of liberty, returned to
their refpective cities ; a warlike fpirit was kindled in the mafs of
the people ; a league was formed, and the din of arms was heard
in every part of the country. Galba was informed of all that
paffed. He alfo knew that he was profcribed by Nero, and that
his effects were fold by public auction. The tide of affairs rufhed
on with a fwell that overpowered a mind by nature indolent,
and enfeebled by age. In the number of Galba's friends Titus
Vinius was the only perfon that endeavoured to roufe his drooping fpirit. To hefitate in fuch a juncture appeared to him a pri-
vation of mind nothing fhort of madnefs. The only queftion,
he faid, was, which was moft eligible, to act in conjunction
with Vindex, or to wage war againft him? againft a man who
wifhed to depofe a tyrant, and call to the fucceffion a prince
who poffeffed the virtues of humanity? Galba faw the neceffity
of taking a decided part, but his natural irrefolution was not
eafily conquered. He wifhed to found the inclinations of the
people, and, for that purpofe, fummoned a grand council to
meet at New Carthage (p), in order, as he pretended, to fettle
the manumiffion of flaves. His friends knew that greater matters were in agitation, and, accordingly, fpread a general alarm.
On the day appointed, an incredible multitude affembled from all
parts of the country. Galba afcended the tribunal, prepared by
a well-imagined artifice to fpeak at once to the eye and the ear.
The images of the moft illuftrious of both fexes (q), who had
fallen a facrifice to Nero's cruelty, were ranged in regular order

VOL. II.   3 C   round

round the council-chamber. The silent eloquence of that pathetic scene he knew would assist the orator, and inflame the passions of his audience. He began his harangue without the usual approaches of a studied introduction. The business was of the first importance, and he rushed into it at once, with warmth and vehemence. He painted forth the horrors of Nero's reign, the acts of oppression that laid waste the provinces, and the murders that thinned the noblest families. If proofs were necessary, he looked round the hall, and behold, he said, " behold there in " glaring colours the evidence of the worst iniquity. Judge not " of Nero by my words; view him with your own eyes. Those " images inform against him. Lo! there the ghastly features of " the murdered Cæsars! You see Nero's mother, brother, and " sister! his wife, his aunt, his nearest relations! his wretched " friends! all butchered, all destroyed, by the sword, by famine, " by poison, by every villany! Direct your eyes to yonder wall; " you there behold Burrhas, Lateranus, Vestinus, Cassius, and " Lucius Vetus, with a long train of the first men in Rome! " They suffered for their talents and their virtues. Nor is this " all: think of your own native genius; call to mind the men, " born in Spain, who were the ornaments of Roman literature, " and an honour to their country. There lies Seneca (r), the " enlightened philosopher: he bleeds in a bath, and with his last " breath teaches the precepts of wisdom! Your great poet, Lu- " can, whose bosom glowed with the love of freedom, repeats " his own immortal verses, and expires: his father, Annæus " Mela, falls a victim, because he was the brother of your great " philosopher, and the father of such a son. Survey that group: " you have there Pætus Thrasea, and Barcas Soranus, who were " virtue itself. See that train of illustrious women: Sextia, Pol- " lutia, and Servilia, all led to execution. That boy is Rufinus " Crispinus (s), the son of Poppæa by her first husband; and,

" not-

" notwithftanding his tender age and innocence, they dafh him
" from a rock into the fea. Behold this youth *(t)*, whom I
" have brought before you from one of the Balearic iflands,
" where he was condemned to live in exile. He is too young
" to know the nature of a crime, or his own wretched lot. Not
" yet a citizen, and, behold! he is banifhed from his country.
" Thefe are the exploits of Nero. Vindex has undertaken to be
" the deliverer of his country. For you, and all Spain, I am
" willing to brave every danger. My commiffion is from the
" fenate, and the Roman people. I difclaim the authority of
" Nero: to me he is no longer emperor. I know that by him
" I am adjudged to death; but, if you refolve to affert your
" rights; if you make a common caufe with me in that glorious
" ftruggle, I am willing to clofe my days in your fervice."
This fpeech inflamed the multitude with uncommon ardour.
The place refounded with acclamations, and Galba was faluted
Emperor of Rome. His modefty, or his prudence, made him
decline that title. He defired to be called the general of the
fenate and the Roman people.

During thefe tranfactions, Nero remained at Naples, ftill addicted to his favourite amufements, enchanting himfelf and the
public with his harp, and chiefly intent on bringing to perfection an hydraulic organ *(u)*, on a new conftruction, which he
promifed to produce on the ftage. But that gay ferenity was
foon overcaft. Advices arrived from Spain and Gaul. In the
former, Galba had thrown off the mafk; in the latter, Vindex
was at the head of a powerful army. Nero fhuddered at the
news; indignation foon fucceeded; he threatened to punifh the
rebels with death; his frivolous paffions took their turn; he
went to fee the athletic exercifes, and tuned his guitar. In that
manner he paffed eight or ten days; no orders given; no letter

to the fenate; not a word efcaped from him; he fmothered all in fullen filence. Frefh tidings arrived from Gaul; the proclamations, which Vindex publifhed in every quarter, were delivered to him; he found himfelf called, in a ftyle of contempt, *Oenobarbus (w), and a vile comedian.* Enraged at the indignity offered to his talents, he ftarted up in a fudden fury, overturned the banqueting-table, wrote to the fenate to exert the ftrength of the empire, and, to fire them with indignation, added in pathetic terms, " Judge yourfelves, confcript fathers, judge of the info" lence of Vindex; in his own words fee the malignity of that " audacious rebel. He has dared impioufly to fay that I have a " bad voice, and play ill on the guitar." A complaint of that importance could not fail to make an impreffion on the fathers. They paffed a decree, declaring Galba a public enemy, and promifing a reward of ten millions of fefterces for the head of Vindex. The Gaul, with fuperior magnanimity, offered his own head *(x)* to whoever fhould bring him that of Nero. If he freed the world from a monfter, he fet no value on his own life; he then would die content.

Virginius Rufus, who, at that time, commanded on the Upper Rhine, had received orders to take the field againft the rebels in Gaul. Whether that officer afpired to the imperial dignity, feems to be a problem not folved by any of the hiftorians. It is certain that the legions, feeing the miferies occafioned by Nero's tyranny, and at length difgufted by the contemptible frolics of an emperor, who rendered it ridiculous to obey him, made a tender of the empire to their own general, whom they refpected for his military talents, and the virtues of moderation. Virginius declined the offer. If he nourifhed ambition in his heart, he thought it beft to fupprefs it in that juncture, and wait for future events. It belonged, he faid, to the fenate, and the fenate
only,

only, not to the legions, to difpofe of the fovereignty. Whatever were his views, he ftill retained a true Roman fpirit, and, with indignation, faw a rebel chieftain and his conquered country-men joined in a league to give an emperor to the miftrefs of the world. He refolved to collect his forces, and march in queft of the enemy. Gaul was far from acting with a fpirit of union. Internal diffenfions divided the ftates into contending factions. The Sequani (y), the Ædui, and Arverni followed the banners of Vindex. The Lingones, and the people of Rheims, accuftomed to flavery, and hating the oppofite party, declared for Nero. The cities of Vienne and Lyons, which lay conti-guous, renewed their ancient animofity; the former lifting on the fide of Vindex; the latter, with a pretended regard for their oath of fidelity, efpoufing the caufe of Nero. In that difpofition of the public mind, Virginius entered Gaul at the head of his legions, with a ftrong reinforcement of Belgic auxiliaries, and the Batavian cohorts. He proceeded by rapid marches to Ve-fontium (z), a city in league with Vindex. The inhabitants re-fufed to open their gates. Virginius pitched his camp, deter-mined to lay fiege to the place. Vindex advanced to the relief of his confederates. The two armies were in fight of each other. The Gallic chieftain, little doubting that the Roman general's opinion of Nero coincided with his own, thought it prudent, before he tried the iffue of a battle, to negociate by his deputies. He accordingly made his overtures. Various mef-fengers paffed between the two commanders, and an interview at laft took place. The refult was an agreement of fome kind, but what were the terms it is fruitlefs now to enquire. Hiftory has left us in the dark. All that can be related with certainty is, that Virginius began to withdraw his forces, and Vindex with his army made his approach to the walls of the town. The le-gions faw the motions of the enemy, and, imagining that they

meant

meant to offer battle, refolved to begin the attack.   The armies of the Upper and Lower Rhine were not enured to difcipline. Fierce, and difdaining all controul, they wanted no orders from their general.   A defperate engagement followed.   The Gauls were unprepared, but their courage braved every danger.   Both fides fought with impetuous fury; the Gauls refenting the treachery of their enemies; the Romans ftimulated by their inveterate animofity.   Blood and carnage covered all the plain. The legions cut their way with dreadful flaughter, till the Gauls, having loft no lefs than twenty thoufand of their braveft troops, and feeing inevitable deftruction on every fide, betook themfelves to flight.   Vindex exerted himfelf in every quarter of the field to prevent the maffacre: but his efforts were in vain.   He faw the flaughter of his people, and concluded that Virginius had betrayed him, and the caufe of liberty.   His enterprife defeated, and no hopes of conqueft left, he refolved not to furvive a calamity fo unexpected.   He fell upon his fword, and died on the field of battle.

Meanwhile, all Spain was in commotion.   Galba was employed in fchemes of future grandeur.   He raifed a new legion, muftered forces in all quarters, and with his utmoft art and induftry allured the different ftates to his intereft.   Cornelius Fufcus, a young man of illuftrious birth, went over to Galba, and drew with him the province of which he was governor. But the great acceffion of ftrength was from Lufitania.   Otho, who had been the favourite of Nero, and his conftant companion in all his fcenes of riot and debauchery, had been for fome years at the head of that province.   He was appointed to that ftation, as the reader may remember *(aa)*, under colour of doing him honour; but, in fact, to remove a rival, whom Nero dreaded, and to leave him at a diftance from Rome, in a ftate of honourable

banifhment.

banifhment. Otho confidered himfelf as no better than a ftate
prifoner, in a remote part of the empire. Refentment prompted
him to revenge; and ambition like his was eager to come forth
from obfcurity, and act a principal part on the great ftage of
public bufinefs. He melted down all his maffy gold and filver;
and, having converted it into coin, went with his whole treafure,
and the forces of his province, to fupport the enterprife of an
old man, who he knew, in the courfe of nature, could not long
enjoy the fupreme authority. The other governors and proprætors followed his example. The Roman empire feemed to
be transferred to Spain. Nero was at laft fenfible of his danger. He ordered the legions in Illyricum to advance by rapid
marches into Italy; he recalled the troops that had been fent
againft the Albanians to the borders of the Cafpian Sea; and he
expected the fourteenth legion, then in Britain, to come without lofs of time to his affiftance. Diftracted by the news that
filled all Italy, he forgot his hydraulic organ, and returned to
Rome, covered with confternation. His fears were foon difperfed. Letters from Virginius Rufus arrived at Rome. The
death of Vindex, and the total overthrow of his army, tranfported Nero beyond all bounds of joy. He called for his mufical inftruments; he tuned his harp, and warbled fongs of
triumph.

In Spain, the minds of men were affected in a very different
manner. Galba faw an unexpected reverfe of fortune. He
blamed his own imprudence, and accufed the folly of an old
man, who, at the clofe of life, was weak enough to liften to the
call of ambition. To try, if poffible, to retrieve his affairs, he
fent difpatches to Virginius Rufus, inviting him to a participation of councils and of future grandeur. The offer was rejected.
It was a maxim with Rufus, that the fenate and people had the

fole

fole right of creating an emperor. The civil power, he faid, in every well conftituted government, ought to be fupreme; to obey is the virtue of a foldier. Galba had no refource left. Half his cavalry fhewed themfelves alienated from his fervice, and were retained with difficulty. Dejected, hopelefs, and expecting certain deftruction from the affaffins employed by Nero, he retired to the city of Clunia *(bb)*, and there relapfed into his former indolence.

XIII. NERO was now at the fummit of his wifhes. He triumphed in the pride of his imagination over all his enemies. He had feen on his way from Naples a monumental fculpture, reprefenting a Gaul *(a)* overcome by a Roman foldier, and dragged along the ground by the hair of his head. The gods, he faid, prefented that object to him as an omen of victory, and their decree was happily fulfilled. Amidft all his frantic joy, his worft enemies were in his own breaft. His vices were undermining him with the army as well as the people. He raifed immoderate fupplies of money, and fquandered the whole with wild profufion. An occurrence happened, by which the city was thrown into a violent ferment. A fhip arrived from Alexandria, fuppofed to be loaded with corn, and, therefore, matter of joy to the populace, who dreaded a dearth of provifions. It may be eafily imagined what a turn their paffions took, when it was known that the veffel brought a freight of fand *(b)* from the banks of the Nile, to fmooth the arena for wreftlers and gladiators. The difappointment excited, at firft, a laugh of fcorn and indignation; vulgar wit and fcurrilous jefts made Nero an object of contempt; and from contempt the tranfition to hatred, rage and fury is always fure, and often inftantaneous. The public clamour was loud and violent: the people, with one voice, wifhed to be delivered from a monfter; they lamented

the

the lofs of Vindex; and the prætorian guards, who had been the fupport of a pernicious reign, began to murmur difcontent, and to fhew manifeft fymptoms of difaffection.

Nymphidius and Tigellinus *(c)*, who had often figured in fcenes of public iniquity, were joint præfects of the prætorian camp. The former, as has been mentioned, was the fon of a woman who proftituted her perfon to the flaves and freedmen of the emperor Claudius. Having recommended himfelf by his vices to the favour of Nero, he had the ambition to be thought the iffue of an intrigue between his mother, Nymphidia, and Caligula. Nymphidius and his colleague Tigellinus acted in concert, and jointly exerted their pernicious talents. They faw the difpofition of the foldiers, and, with the ingratitude of men who had raifed themfelves by their crimes, thought the opportunity fair to ftrike a ftroke of perfidy. They began by bribes to infinuate themfelves into the affections of the prætorian guards, and, when they had fufficiently prepared them for a revolt, whifpered to the fenate, that Nero was deferted on every fide; that he had not a friend left; and that, by confequence, the whole legiflative authority was in the hands of the fathers. That affembly remained for fome time in fufpenfe; timid, wavering, and irrefolute. The conjuncture was dark and gloomy. Nero was alarmed; he paufed from his pleafures, and faw that fome deep defign was in agitation. To prevent it by one bold effort, he formed a refolution to maffacre the fenate, and, after fetting fire to the city a fecond time, to let loofe his whole collection of wild beafts, to devour the people in the general confternation, and fave himfelf by flying into Egypt. This horrible fcheme was no fooner conceived than brought to light by one of his favourite eunuchs. This mifcreant had been, for fome time, fubfervient to the vices of his mafter, and lived with him in the

deareſt intimacy. From a perſon ſo beloved nothing was concealed. He was the confidential friend of the emperor, not only
in ſcenes of riot, but alſo in the moſt important councils. But
the jealouſy of an upſtart, raiſed above his baſe condition, is
eaſily alarmed. The favourite *(d)* thought himſelf ſlighted.
His pride was rouſed, and, to revenge the injury, he diſcovered
the particulars of the intended maſſacre.

A deſign ſo black and horrible raiſed the general indignation.
The fathers trembled for themſelves, but the habit of ſlavery had
debaſed their faculties. They ſaw that no time was to be loſt,
and yet could not reſolve to act with vigour. Nymphidius tried
by every means to inſpire them with zeal and courage. He had
ſeduced the prætorian guards, and, to ſecure their affections, promiſed in Galba's name, but without his authority, a reward
of thirty thouſand feſterces to each prætorian, and five thouſand
to each legionary ſoldier throughout the armies of the empire ;
a ſum ſo prodigious, that, as Plutarch obſerves, it could not be
raiſed without worſe tyranny, and more violent rapine, than had
been felt during the whole reign of Nero. The promiſe proved,
afterwards, fatal to Galba, but ſerved the purpoſes of a man,
who was bent on the ruin of Nero, and, by raiſing the military above the civil authority, intended to introduce into the
political ſyſtem, two pernicious maxims ; the firſt, that emperors
were to be created in the camp, not in the ſenate ; and, ſecondly,
that the imperial dignity was venal, to be, for the future, ſet up
to ſale, and diſpoſed of by the ſoldiers to the higheſt bidder.

Having ſettled his meaſures, and laid the plan of a revolution,
he did not as yet think it time to throw off the maſk, but, to
complete his work, choſe to proceed by fraud and diſſimulation.
He went with Tigellinus to the palace, and, with an air of deep
affliction,

affliction, informed Nero of his danger. " All," he said, " is loft ;
" the people, affembled in feditious tumults, call aloud for ven-
" geance ; the prætorian guards abandon your caufe ; and the
" fenate is ready to pronounce a dreadful judgment. You have
" only one expedient left, and that is, to make your efcape, and
" feek a retreat in Egypt." In this manner the two men, who
had been raifed from the dregs of the people, left their benefactor. In all his fcenes of vice and cruelty they had been
his chief abettors, and they now abandoned him at his utmoft
need.

Nero faw the fad reverfe of his affairs. From his armies he
could expect no fupport. The troops on their march towards
the Cafpian fea had been recalled, but a long repofe was neceffary to revive the fpirits of men well nigh exhaufted by inceffant
fatigue. The legions from Illyricum returned with alienated
minds. Scorning to difguife their fentiments, they fent a deputation to Virginius on the Upper Rhine, expreffing their ardent
defire, that he would yield to the requeft of the legions under
his command, and accept the imperial dignity. Eight Batavian
cohorts had fhewn a fpirit of difaffection, and the prætorian
guards were under the influence of Nymphidius. In this defperate fituation Nero looked round for affiftance, but he looked
in vain. He wandered through the apartments of his palace,
and all was folitude. He, who but a few days before was the
god of the fenate and the people, was now in dread of being
their victim. Confcience began to exercife her rights. Her
voice was heard ; Nero reviewed his crimes, and fhuddered with
horror and remorfe. He repeated in defpair and anguifh of
heart, a line, which, when perfonating Œdipus, he had often
declaimed on the public ftage (e): " My wife, my father, and
" my mother doom me dead." Of all his courtier-fry, and all

3 D 2

his

his inftruments of guilt, not one adhered to him in the hour of diftrefs, except Sporus, the eunuch; Phaon *(f)*, an enfranchifed flave; and Epaphroditus, his fecretary. He gave orders to the foldiers on duty, to proceed with all expedition to Oftia, and prepare a fhip, that he might embark for Egypt. The men were not willing to obey. One of them afked him in half a line *(g)* from Virgil, " Is it then fo wretched a thing to die?" He went to the Servilian gardens, carrying with him a vial of fwift-fpeeding poifon, which had been prepared by the well-known *(h)* Locufta; but his refolution failed. He returned to his chamber, and threw himfelf on his bed. The agitations of his mind allowed no reft. He ftarted up, and called for fome friendly hand to end his wretched being. That office no one was willing to perform, and he himfelf wanted fortitude. Driven to the laft defpair, and frantic with remorfe and fear, he cried out in doleful accents, " My friends defert me, and I cannot find an " enemy." He rufhed forth from his palace, as if with intent to throw himfelf into the Tiber. He changed his mind, and thought of flying into Spain, there to furrender at difcretion to the mercy of Galba. But no fhip was ready at Oftia. Various projects prefented themfelves to his mind, in quick fucceffion, increafing the tumult of his paffions, and ferving only to diftract him more. To try his powers of eloquence was another expedient that occurred to him. For that purpofe he propofed to go forth in a mourning garb to the forum, and there, by a pathetic fpeech, obtain his pardon from the people. Should their obdurate hearts remain impenetrable to the foft influence of perfuafive oratory, and refufe to reinftate their emperor in the full enjoyment of his prerogative, he had no doubt but he could, at the worft, wring from them the government of Egypt, where, in the character of praefect, he might give free fcope to his inordinate paffions. This project feemed to promife fuccefs; but a

ray

ray of reflection ſtruck him with ſudden horror. The populace, without waiting to hear the divine accents of that har-
monious voice, might break out into open ſedition, and in
their fury tear their prince limb from limb. What courſe could
he purſue? Where could he hide himſelf? He looked
round in wild deſpair, and aſked his remaining companions,
Is there no lurking-place? no ſafe receſs, where I may have
time to conſider what is to be done? Phaon, his freedman,
propoſed to conduct him to an obſcure villa *(i)*, which he
held in his poſſeſſion, at the diſtance of about four miles from
Rome.

Nero embraced the offer. There was no time to be loſt. He
went forth in all his wretchedneſs; without a ſhoe to his feet;
nothing on him but his cloſe tunic; no outſide garment; and no
imperial robe. In order to diſguiſe himſelf, he ſnatched an old
ruſty cloak, and, throwing it over his ſhoulders, covered his head,
and held a handkerchief before his face. In that condition he
mounted his horſe, ſubmitting with a daſtard ſpirit to an ignominious flight, without any attendants except Phaon, the freedman; Epaphroditus, the ſecretary; and Sporus, the eunuch,
with another, whoſe name Aurelius Victor ſays was Neophytus.
In this manner Nero paſſed the laſt of his nights. At the dawn
of day, the prætorian guards deſerted their ſtation at the palace,
and joined their comrades in the camp, where, by the influence
and direction of Nymphidius, Galba was proclaimed emperor.
The ſenate met, and, after a ſhort debate, confirmed the nomination of the prætorian guards. The time was at length arrived,
when that aſſembly could act with authority. They reſolved
to mark the day by a decree worthy of a Roman ſenate. With
one voice they declared the tyrant, who had trampled on all laws
human and divine, a public enemy *(k)*, and, by their ſentence,

condemned

condemned him to fuffer death, according to the rigour of ancient laws, and the practice of the old republic.

XIV. NERO, in the mean time, made the beft of his way towards the freedman's villa. He heard the prætorian camp ring with acclamations, and the name of Galba founded in his ear. A man at work in a field adjoining to the road, ftarted up at the found of horfemen preffing forward with expedition, and behold! he faid, " Thofe people are hot in purfuit of Nero." Another afked, " What do they fay of Nero in the city?" As they drew near to Phaon's houfe, Nero was alarmed by a fudden accident. His horfe ftarted at a dead carcafs that lay on the fide of the road; and the veil, in confequence of the violent motion, falling from his face, a veteran, who had been difmiffed from the fervice, knew his mafter, and faluted him by his name. The fear of being detected made the fugitive prince and his followers pufh forward with their utmoft fpeed. Being arrived at a fmall diftance from the houfe, they did not think it fafe to enter it in a public manner. Nero difmounted, and croffed a field overgrown with reeds (l). Phaon advifed him to lie concealed in a fand-pit, till he prepared a fubterraneous paffage into the houfe. That, faid Nero, were to bury myfelf alive. He fcooped up fome water out of a muddy ditch, and, having allayed his thirft, afked in a doleful tone, " Is that the beverage " to which Nero has been ufed?" An opening was made in the wall on one fide of the manfion, and Nero crept through it. He was conducted to a chamber, where he faw nothing but wretchednefs. In that mean room he threw himfelf on a meaner bed (m), and afked for fome nourifhment. They offered him bread; but it was fo black, that his ftomach fickened at the fight. The water was foul, but thirft obliged him to fwallow the naufeous draught. His friends faw that no hope

was

was left; they dreaded his impending ruin, and advifed him to
refcue himfelf by one manly deed from an ignominious death.
Nero fignified his affent; but he ftudied delay, fond to linger
ftill in life. Preparations for his funeral were neceffary. He
ordered a trench to be dug, fuited to the dimenfions of his
body *(n)*; a quantity of wood to be collected for the funeral
pile; and pieces of marble to be brought to form a decent covering for his grave. He bewailed his unhappy lot; tears
gufhed at intervals; he heaved a piteous figh, and faid to his
friends *(o)*, " What a mufician the world will lofe!"

During this fcene of delay and cowardice, a meffenger, according to Phaon's orders, arrived with papers from Rome.
Nero feized the packet. He read with eagernefs, and found
himfelf, not only declared a public enemy, but condemned to
fuffer death, with the rigour of ancient ufage. He afked, What
kind of death is that? and what is ancient ufage? He was told,
that, by the law of the old republic, every traitor, with his head
faftened between two ftakes, and his body entirely naked, fuffered the pains of a flow death under the lictor's rod. The fear
of that ignominious punifhment infpired Nero with a fhort-lived
paffion, which for the moment had the appearance of courage.
He drew two daggers, which he had brought with him, and, as
if meditating fome prodigious deed, tried the points of both;
then calmly replaced them in their fcabbards, faying, " The fatal
" moment is not yet come." He turned to Sporus, and requefted him to begin the funeral lamentation. " Sing the me-
" lancholy dirge; and offer the laft obfequies to your friend."
He caft his eyes around him : And why, he faid, why will not
fome one difpatch himfelf, and teach me how to die? He paufed
for a moment, and fhed a flood of tears. He ftarted up, and
cried out, in a tone of wild defpair, " Nero, this is infamy; you

2   " linger

" linger in difgrace ; this is no time for dejected paffions ; the
" moment calls for manly fortitude."

Thofe words were no fooner uttered, than he heard the found
of horfes advancing with fpeed towards the houfe. This he fignified by repeating a line from Homer *(p)*. The fact was, the
fenate had given orders, that he fhould be brought back to Rome
to undergo the judgment which they had pronounced, and the
officers, charged with that commiffion, were near at hand. Nero
feized his dagger, and ftabbed himfelf in the throat. The ftroke
was too feeble. Epaphroditus lent his affiftance, and the next
blow was a mortal wound. A centurion entered the room, and,
feeing Nero in a mangled condition, ran immediately to his affiftance, pretending that he came with a friendly hand to bind
the wound, and fave the emperor's life. Nero had not breathed
his laft. He raifed his languid eyes, and faintly faid, " You
" come too late : is this your fidelity *(q)*? He fpoke, and expired.
The ferocity of his nature was ftill vifible in his countenance.
His eyes fixed and glaring, and every feature fwelled with
warring paffions, he looked more ftern, more grim, and terrible
than ever.

Nero died in the thirty-fecond year of his age, on the eleventh
day of June, after a reign of thirteen years, feven months, and
twenty-eight days *(r)*. The news was received at Rome with
all demonftrations of joy. The populace ran wild about the
ftreets, with the cap of liberty on their heads *(s)*. The forum
founded with acclamations. Icclus, a freedman, who managed
Galba's affairs at Rome, had been thrown into prifon by Nero ;
but, on the fudden acceffion of his mafter, he was now become a
man in power and high authority. He confented that Nero's
body fhould be committed to the flames at the place where

he

he died. The funeral rites were performed without delay, and
without pomp. His remains were conveyed to the monumental
vault of the Domitian family, his paternal anceftors. The urn
was carried by two female fervants, and Acte *(t)*, the famous
concubine. The fecrecy, with which the obfequies were performed, was the caufe of fome untoward confequences, that afterwards difturbed the commonwealth. A doubt remained in
the minds of many, whether Nero had not made his efcape into
Afia or Egypt. The men, who, under a corrupt and profligate
reign, had led a life of pleafure, and were, by confequence, enamoured of Nero's vices, paid every mark of refpect to his memory, willing, at the fame time, to believe that he ftill furvived.
They raifed a tomb, and, for feveral years *(u)*, dreffed it with the
flowers of fpring and fummer. The Parthians honoured his
memory, and, being afterwards deluded by an impoftor, who
affumed the name of Nero, were ready, with the ftrength of
their nation *(w)*, to efpoufe his caufe. The race of Cæfars
ended with Nero: he was the laft, and perhaps the worft,
of that illuftrious houfe.

XV. In that age, when the public mind was overcaft with
gloomy apprehenfions and religious fear, fuperftition faw portents and prodigies *(a)* in the moft common accidents, and no
great event was fuffered to pafs without a train of awful prog-
noftics. Rivers were faid to have changed their courfe, and to
have flowed in a new direction to their fountain-head; a tree,
that had ftood for ages, coeval with the foundation of Rome,
fell fuddenly to the ground; the laurel planted by Livia, which
had fpread with fuch prodigious increafe, that in every triumph
it fupplied the Cæfars with their victorious wreaths, withered
at the root; the temple of the Cæfars being ftruck with lightning, the heads of all the ftatues tumbled down at once; and the

marble sceptre fell from the hands of Augustus.   By these and such like denunciations the will of the gods was supposed to be revealed, and the populace with frantic joy hailed the auspicious æra of returning liberty.   But no public spirit remained; every virtue was extinguished.   A people who had been taught to crouch under the yoke of bondage, thought no more of a free constitution.   With the usual inconstancy of a fickle multitude, they relapsed into their habitual servitude, and in a strain of frantic rapture began to roar for a new master.   The name of Galba echoed through the streets of Rome, and filled the prætorian camp with shouts of joy, and the warmest expressions of zeal and ardour for his service.   The prætorian guards thought of nothing but the donative promised in his name; and Nymphidius, the author of that measure, had no doubt but the soldiers, in due time, would shew themselves devoted to the man, who filled their minds with the dazzling prospect of a reward so truly great and magnificent.   The liberality was his, and the difficulty of carrying it into execution would fall on Galba.

Icelus, the favourite freedman of Galba, made it his business to see Nero's dead body, and, having enabled himself to be an eye-witness of the fact, set out for Clunia in Spain *(b)*, to inform his master, that he was raised to the imperial seat by the voice of the prætorians, and the concurrent decree of the senate. Nymphidius seized the opportunity to figure as the principal actor on the theatre of public business.   He had accomplished a great and sudden revolution, and, being high in favour with the prætorian guards, found it easy to overawe the senate, and make that tame and pliant assembly bend to his will and pleasure. The consuls, without consulting the arrogant minister, sent their dispatches to Galba, with the decree by which he was declared emperor.   This was considered by this new man as a

mark

mark of difrefpect *(c)*, and it was with difficulty that the ma-' giftrates appeafed his indignation. Flufhed with fuccefs, and proud of his exploits, he began to enlarge his views, and prepofteroufly to form fchemes of vaft ambition. Under an emperor at the age of feventy-three *(d)*, worn out with cares, and weary of public bufinefs, he flattered himfelf that he fhould be able, under the appearance of being the fecond in the ftate, to wreft into his own hands the fupreme authority; and, fhould Galba's infirmities fink under the fatigue of a long journey, he had the hardinefs to afpire to the fucceffion. Having conceived this mad project, he refolved to remove every obftacle, and, with that view, compelled Tigellinus to refign his commiffion *(e)* of prætorian præfect. A colleague, acting with himfelf in joint authority, might retard the execution of his defigns. Men of confular rank, who had commanded armies and governed provinces, did not blufh to pay their court to him. The fenate *(f)* acted with the fame fervile adulation. They crowded to his levee, and fuffered him to prefcribe the form and fubftance of every decree that paffed. The populace broke out with licentious fury, and Nymphidius, effectually to feduce the vulgar mind, encouraged the madnefs of the times. The images and ftatues of Nero were dragged through the ftreets, and dafhed to pieces. A crew of vile incendiaries fpread confternation through the city; a fcene of blood and maffacre followed *(g)*, and the innocent fell in one promifcuous carnage with the guilty. Mauricus beheld the phrenfy of the multitude with fuch inward horror, that he could not help faying in the fenate, " Let us take care that we " have not reafon to regret the lofs of Nero *(h)*."

Nymphidius foon perceived that his hopes of being the only ftatefman in power, and of governing the Roman world in the emperor's name, could not be entertained with any profpect

of

of fuccefs.   He knew by certain intellgence that Vinius, Laco, and Icelus were the men *(i)* who ftood higheft in the efteem of Galba.   The fcheme of fupplanting them was, therefore, abandoned; but it made way for a project of the moft daring ambition.   He was refolved to depofe the emperor, whom he himfelf had created, and, by another revolution, to feize the imperial dignity.   To forward this defign, he fent difpatches to Galba *(k),* ftating the danger of entering the city at a time when the whole empire was in convulfions.   Rome, he faid, was in a ferment; Clodius Macer excited a rebellion in Africa; the German armies were difaffected, and the legions in Syria and Judæa prepared to difpute with the prætorian guards the right of creating an emperor.   In the mean time a dark confpiracy was formed.   Nymphidius planned his meafures with difpatch and vigour, determined to feize the fupreme power.   He drew into his league a number of both fexes, all of great confideration, and extenfive influence.   Claudius Celfus was his intimate friend; but he faw the folly of the enterprife, and with freedom and fincerity advifed Nymphidius to defift from a wild attempt, in which he could not expect the fupport of the people or the fenate.   There is not, he faid, a fingle family in Rome, willing to give the name of Cæfar *(l)* to the fon of Nymphidia.   That remonftrance had no effect on a mind inflamed with the fever of wild ambition.   Nymphidius called a meeting of his party.   All agreed that no time was to be loft.   They refolved to ftrike the blow that very night, and to conduct Nymphidius to the prætorian camp, where they had no doubt but with one voice he would be declared emperor of Rome.   On fuch an occafion it was neceffary that the perfon raifed to that elevation fhould be prepared to addrefs the foldiers, in a fuitable ftyle.   Cingonius Varro *(m),* a corrupt and venal orator, compofed a fpeech for that purpofe, and the illiterate emperor was to grace himfelf with borrowed eloquence.

The

The defign of the confpirators was not fo well concealed, but it reached the ear of Antonius Honoratus *(n)*, a tribune in the camp, who had acquired a great military character, and was, befides, refpected for his unblemifhed honour, and unfhaken fidelity. Towards the clofe of day, he called a meeting of the prætorians, and, after laying open, in detail, all the circumftances of the plot, delivered a fpeech in fubftance as follows *(o)*: " How long, my fellow foldiers, fhall our folly, our madnefs, " or our evil genius, hurry us on from one treafon to another? " A few days only have elapfed, fince you depofed Nero. In " that bufinefs you behaved like men, who felt for the public " good. You had every provocation, and the crimes of that " flagitious tyrant juftified the act. You are recent from that " revolution, and wherefore do you want another? You de- " clared for Galba, and why now abandon him? Why with " unheard of treachery betray the emperor, whom you your- " felves created? Has he been guilty of parricide? Has he " murdered his mother, and deftroyed his wife? Has he ex- " pofed the imperial dignity to contempt and ridicule? Has he " tuned his harp on the ftage, or driven a curricle in the race? " And yet, notwithftanding all the flagitious deeds of that " hardened monfter, in fpite of all his vices, we fupported him, " blufhing indeed for his follies, and fmarting under his tyranny. " We adhered to him with fidelity; and if, in the end, we " thought fit to create another emperor, Nymphidius was the " author of that meafure. By his artifices we were taught to " believe that Nero deferted us firft, and fled to Egypt. We " concluded that he had abdicated, and, by confequence, what " we did, was an act of neceffity. And what is our defign at " prefent? What do we wifh? What do we aim at? Muft " Galba fall a facrifice to appeafe the manes of Nero? Shall a " defcendant from the family of the Servii; a relation of Quin-

" tus

" tus Catulus, and by ties of affinity connected with Livia *(p)*,
" the wife of Auguftus ; fay, my fellow foldiers, fhall fuch a
" man be depofed and murdered, to make way for the fon of
" Nymphidia ? It was his treachery, his bafe ingratitude that
" occafioned the death of Nero : let him fuffer the juftice due
" to his crime ; and let us give proof of our fidelity. Let us
" deferve the efteem of Galba, by delivering him from a
" traitor."

This fpeech made an impreffion on the foldiers. One mind,
one fentiment pervaded the whole camp ; Galba was their emperor, and they would acknowledge no other. This was followed
by a general fhout. Nymphidius heard the found, and proceeded to the camp *(q)*. Whether he thought that the acclamations of the men were in his favour, or that his prefence was
neceffary to quell an infurrection, cannot now be known. He
went attended by a numerous train, and a blaze of torches, with
the fpeech compofed for him by Cingonius Varro, ready in his
hand to be read aloud to the foldiers. The gates of the camp were
fhut, and guards were ftationed on the ramparts. Nymphidius
defired to know, by whofe order they were under arms ? The
men anfwered with one voice, We are armed in the caufe of
Galba, and we know no other emperor. Nymphidius had not
the prudence to retire from the walls. Diffimulation he thought
would cloak his defign. He commended the zeal of the prætorians, and affured them that he, and his followers, were the
avowed friends of Galba. The fentinels opened the gates.
Nymphidius entered with fome of his friends : the pafs was
immediately fecured ; and the foldiers attacked him fword in hand.
He endeavoured to fave himfelf in a tent, but was purfued, and
maffacred on the fpot. His body, on the following day, was
dragged through the camp, a fpectacle for public view. Such
was

was the end of a low-born bafe incendiary, who faw, that, in
the general profligacy of the times, the weak were the willing
dupes of the wicked.   By forming a league with the moft
abandoned, he flattered himfelf, that the loweft of mankind, who
in better times could not hope to be entrufted with the rank
of a common centurion, might boldly afpire to make himfelf
mafter of the Roman empire.

XVI. AN account of all that paffed was conveyed to Galba
with incredible fpeed.   By his order, all, who were fufpected of
taking a part in the mad projects of Nymphidius, were feized,
and, without further enquiry, or any form of trial, put to death.
Cingonius Varro, at that time conful elect, was in the number;
and, what was very extraordinary, Mithridates (a), the dethroned
king of Pontus, who had furrendered to Claudius, and from that
time lived at Rome, was hurried to execution, without being
heard in his defence.   Petronius Turpilianus (b) was another
unhappy victim.   He had been chofen by Nero to command his
armies; and, though he never went from Rome to execute his
commiffion, the very appointment was deemed a fufficient crime.
Thefe bloody executions were inaufpicious in the opening of a
new reign.   The cruelty of Nero feemed to be renewed, when
the people expected a milder government, and a regular adminiftration of law and juftice.   The fate of Turpilianus filled the
city with murmurs of difcontent.   It was known that Tigellinus
prefided at the execution; and that a man of worth and honour
fhould bleed under the eye of a detefted mifcreant, appeared to
be a continuation of the late reign, and the triumph of vice over
every virtue.

 Galba fet out from Spain, proceeding by flow marches, and ftill
wearing the military robe of a general officer, with a dagger (c)

hanging

APPENDIX TO BOOK XVI. A. U. C. 821. A. D. 68.

hanging from his neck down to his breaſt. Strong ſuſpicion, a ſenſe of injuries, and dark miſtruſt, with other paſſions unworthy of a prince, lay lurking in his heart. Before he began his journey, Obultronius Sabinus *(d)*, and Cornelius Marcellus, two governors of provinces in Spain, who had ſhewn no inclination to his party, were put to death by his order. Betuus Chilo met with the ſame fate in Gaul. Diſpatches were alſo ſent to Garrucianus, in Africa, commanding the immediate execution of Clodius Macer *(e)*, the proprætor of the province, who was known to have concerted meaſures for a revolt. It happened, however, that Calvia Criſpinilla *(f)*, the famous manager of Nero's pleaſures, arrived in Africa, and inſinuated herſelf into the ſecret councils of the governor. By her advice he formed a reſolution to eſtabliſh for himſelf a new province independent of Rome. Their ſcheme, for that purpoſe, was to lay an embargo on all ſhips loaded with corn, in order to afflict the city of Rome with all the miſeries of famine. A legion was alſo raiſed; and Macer, at the head of a conſiderable army, was on the eve of renouncing all ſubjection to Rome, when Papirius, a centurion ſent by order of Galba, gained acceſs to his preſence, and ſtabbed him to the heart.

Fonteius Capito *(g)*, who commanded the legions on the Lower Rhine, was put to death about the ſame time. It was this officer that ſent Julius Civilis *(h)* a priſoner to Rome, during the reign of Nero. The charge was without foundation, and, in time, was the fatal cauſe of the deſtructive war, in which Rome was involved by the fierce reſentment of that warlike chief. Avarice was the vice of Capito. He was in haſte to grow rich, and felt no ſcruple about the means. Ambition was laid to his charge, but an unguarded expreſſion was the only evidence againſt him. It happened that he ſat in judgment on a ſoldier, foldier accufed of a capital crime, and condemned him to fuffer death. " Know, faid the prifoner, that I appeal to Cæfar." Capito rofe, and, placing himfelf on a higher feat, told the man, " Now appeal to Cæfar: make your defence in his prefence." The foldier obeyed, and was fent to execution. This tranfaction was reported to Fabius Valens *(i)*, who commanded a legion in the Lower Germany; an officer of acknowledged ability, intrepid, active, and ambitious; eager in the purfuit of honours, and panting to fignalize himfelf by fome bold exploit. The opportunity now occurred, and he refolved to feize it. Crifpinus, a centurion *(k)*, was devoted to his fervice. In that man he found a ready affaffin, and Fonteius Capito fell a victim. The death of that commander Valens concluded would be confiderable merit with the new emperor. He loft no time, but fent an exprefs to inform Galba of what he had done, with zeal, for the fervice of his fovereign. He added, in the fame letter, that the legions on the Upper Rhine had made a tender of the empire to Virginius Rufus, who remained in fufpenfe, and, with affected delays, hefitated about his final anfwer. Galba received the news of Capito's death with fecret fatisfaction, but he thought it more prudent to connive, than openly to approve. Virginius was ftill a dangerous rival. In order to draw him away from the army, and free himfelf from all danger in that quarter, he invited him to an amicable interview, having fecretly appointed Hordeonius Flaccus to fucceed to the command of the legions. The ftratagem fucceeded. The conqueror of Vindex went to the meeting, and found himfelf the dupe of pretended friendfhip. He met with a cold reception, very different from what was due to the man who wifhed to eftablifh the civil authority, and to place the legiflative power of the ftate in the fenate only. He lived to be a fpectator of the diftractions and calamities that followed; and,

Vol. II.3 Fthat

that he was not an actor in thofe fcenes of blood and horror *(l)*, was the recompenfe of uncommon virtue.

Galba had no further reafon to be alarmed. He faw the armies of Rome willing to acquiefce, and peace in every part of the empire. He, therefore, changed his military robe for the Roman gown, and affumed the name *(m)* of Cæfar. But even in that tide of his affairs, the fimplicity of his manners fuffered no alteration. The fame frugality, the fame contempt of pomp and luxury, and the fame aufterity ftill remained. Vinius covered his table with a profufion of luxury; and Otho, who attended the cavalcade into Italy, difplayed all the magnificence of Nero's court. Galba ftill preferved his rules of ancient frugality, and condemned the vain parade *(n)* with inflexible rigour. He fhewed himfelf ready to punifh, and flow to reward. In his manners no affability, no engaging courtefy. During the whole of his march he never once endeavoured, by an act of condefcenfion, to gain the affections of the people. The army in Italy confifted, at that time, of four different claffes of men; namely, the legions, both foot and cavalry, compofed chiefly of Roman citizens; the auxiliary forces, drafted from the ftates in alliance with Rome; the body of marines, levied in the tributary cities, and confidered as flaves in the fervice of Rome; and fourthly, the gladiators, who were to fhed their blood in battle, if the occafion required, or in the circus, for the diverfion of the populace. The marines, claffed, as above, in the third divifion, were called forth by Nero, when he projected a war on the borders of the Cafpian fea, to be formed into a new legion. The men collected upon that occafion amounted to a prodigious number, and all were quartered in the city. Being informed that Galba was near at hand, they rufhed forth in a tumultuous body to the Milvian bridge, about three miles from Rome, where they befet the road, obftructed the emperor's train, and, with violent clamour, demanded a confirmation of their military rank, with an eagle to diftinguifh their legion, and an allotment of winter quarters *(o)*. Their application, they were told, was out of feafon, but might be renewed at a more convenient time and place. The anfwer was deemed evafive, and nothing fhort of an abfolute refufal. The men were fired with indignation; a mutiny enfued; they advanced fword in hand, determined to extort by force what they confidered as a legal right. Galba was not of a temper to yield to fudden emergencies. He ordered his foldiers to difperfe an infolent rabble. The cavalry rufhed on to the charge with impetuous fury, and, meeting with a feeble refiftance, cut their way with dreadful flaughter. It is faid that no lefs than feven thoufand were put to the fword. The reft fubmitted at difcretion, and were afterwards ordered to be decimated.

This tragic cataftrophe fpread a general confternation. Galba entered the city of Rome through a fcene of blood, and men expected nothing lefs than a renewal of all the cruelties of Nero's reign. He carried with him many virtues, but he had in his train Titus Vinius, Cornelius Laco, and Icelus, his freedman *(p)*; three pernicious minifters, who gained an entire afcendant over a venerable, but indolent, old man, and by their vices occafioned the dreadful calamities, which, in the following year, overwhelmed themfelves, their mafter, and the public.

APPENDIX
TO
BOOK XVI.

A. U. C.
821.
A. D.
68.

3 F 2

GENEALO-

GENEALOGICAL TABLE

OF

THE CÆSARS.

GENEALOGICAL TABLE.

1. CAIUS JULIUS CÆSAR, defcended from the illuftrious line of the Julian family, and father of Cæfar the dictator. He ferved the office of prætor. He, and his brother Lucius Cæfar, died A. U. 670. Julia, their fifter, married C. Marius, who was feven times conful.—Suetonius, Life of Jul. Cæf. f. 1, 6. Pliny the elder, book vii. f. 53. Plutarch, Life of Marius.

2. AURELIA, the wife of C. J. Cæfar, and mother of the dictator; a woman of extraordinary talents and virtue.—Plut. Life of Jul. Cæf. Tacitus, Dialogue of Oratory, f. 28.

3. CAIUS JULIUS CÆSAR, the dictator; born in the fixth confulfhip of Marius, A. U. 654; before Chrift, 100. He gained a complete victory at Pharfalia, and became emperor of Rome A. U. 706. He was killed in the capitol by Brutus, Caffius, and other confpirators, A. U. 710. The number flain in his wars is computed at 1,192,000 men. Plutarch fays that Cæfar, in his various battles, engaged no lefs than 3,000,000; that he killed 1,000,000, and took another million prifoners.— Velleius Paterculus, book ii. f. 41. Pliny, book vii. f. 25.

He was called after his death the divine Julius, DIVUS JULIUS.

4. COSSUTIA,

4. Cossutia, Julius Cæsar's first wife, of an equeftrian family, and immoderately rich.   Cæfar married her when he was young, and was foon divorced.—Suet. Life of Cæfar, f. 1.

5. Cornelia, Cæfar's fecond wife.   She was the daughter of Cinna, four times conful.   Sylla tried in vain to compel J. Cæfar to repudiate her.   He fpoke her funeral panegyric.—Suet. Life of Cæfar, f. 1, 6.   Plutarch, Life of J. Cæfar.

6. Julia, daughter of Julius Cæfar by Cornelia.   She married Servilius Cæpio, and, being divorced from him, became the wife of Pompey the Great, A. U. 695.   She died A. U. 700. Her funeral oration was fpoken by Octavius.   Honours were inftituted to her memory by Julius Cæfar.—Suet. Life of Cæfar, f. 21.

7. Cneius Pompeius Magnus, born A. U. 648.   He married Julia, Cæfar's daughter.   He entered on the public magiftracy at the age of eighteen.   He was defeated by Julius Cæfar in the battle of Pharfalia, and put to death in Ægypt, A. U. 706.—Vell. Pat. book ii. f. 29.   Plutarch, Life of Pompey.

8. A son of Pompey the Great, by Julia, the daughter of J. Cæfar.   Died A. U. 701.—Vell. Pater. book ii. f. 47.

9. A daughter of Pompey, by Julia, Cæfar's daughter. Died A. U. 701.—Plutarch, Life of J. Cæfar.

10. Pompeia, daughter of Quintus Pompeius, grand-daughter of Lucius Sylla, and third wife of Julius Cæfar, who repudiated her on account of a fuppofed intrigue with Publius Clodius.

I   Being

Being afked what was his reafon, he made anfwer, Cæfar's wife muft not only be free from guilt, but alfo from fufpicion.—Suet. Life of Cæfar, f. 6. Plutarch, Life of Cæfar.

11. CALPURNIA, daughter of L. Calpurnius Pifo, married to J. Cæfar A. U. 695. After the death of her hufband fhe fled for protection to Marc Anthony.—Suet. Life of Cæf. f. 81.

12. JULIA, fifter of Julius Cæfar, being the daughter of C. J. Cæfar the prætor, and Aurelia his wife. She was married to M. Atius Balbus.—Suet. Life of Auguftus, f. 4.

13. MARCUS ATIUS BALBUS, married Julia, the fifter of Julius Cæfar. He was grandfather to Auguftus.—Suet. Life of Aug. f. 4.

14. ATIA, daughter of M. Atius Balbus, by his wife Julia, the fifter of J. Cæfar. She married Caius Octavius, and by him was mother of Auguftus.—Suet. Life of Aug. f. 4. Tacit. Dialogue of Orators, f. 28.

15. CAIUS OCTAVIUS, hufband of Atia, the daughter of M. Atius Balbus, by Julia, fifter of Julius Cæfar. Octavius, afterwards the emperor Auguftus, was, of courfe, grand nephew to Julius Cæfar.—Suet. Life of Aug. f. 3, 4, 5.

16. OCTAVIA, daughter of Atia and Caius Octavius, and fifter to Auguftus. She was promifed in marriage to Fauftus Sylla, but married Claudius Marcellus. After his death fhe married Marc Anthony. She was a woman of exemplary virtue, and great literary accomplifhments. She died A. U. 743. Auguftus delivered her funeral panegyric.—Suet. Life of Jul. Cæf. f. 27.

17. CLAUDIUS MARCELLUS, hufband of Octavia, and brother-in-law to Auguftus. He was conful A. U. 704. Though nearly related to Cæfar the dictator, he was always an enemy to his caufe.—Suet. Life of Jul. Cæf. f. 27.

18. MARCUS MARCELLUS, fon of Octavia, the fifter of Auguftus, and, confequently, nephew to Auguftus. A youth of great expectation, highly efteemed by his uncle, and by him intended to be next in fucceffion to the imperial dignity. He died prematurely A. U. 731. Auguftus paid diftinguifhed honours to his memory, and Virgil has made him immortal.— Tacit. Annal. ii. f. 41. Annal. iii. f. 64. Virgil, Æneid vi. ver. 883.

19. POMPEIA, daughter of Sextus Pompeius, promifed in marriage to Marcus Marcellus, A. U. 715.

Julia, daughter of Auguftus by his wife Scribonia, married Marcus Marcellus, A. U. 729, two years before his death.— Dio Caffius, book xlviii.

20. MARCELLA the elder, daughter of Claudius Marcellus by his wife Octavia, and fifter to the laft-mentioned Marcellus. She was firft married to Apuleius, and afterwards to Valerius Meffala.—Suet. Life of Aug. f. 53.

21. APULEIUS, hufband of Marcella the elder. He is thought to have been the fon of Sextus Apuleius, who was conful A. U. 725.—Dio Caffius, book liv.

22. APULEIA VARILLA, daughter of Marcella the elder by her hufband Apuleius. She was alfo grand niece to Auguftus.

Being

Being condemned for adultery A. U. 770, fhe was banifhed two hundred miles from Rome.—Tacit. Annal. ii. f. 50.

23. M. Valerius Messala Barbatus, fecond hufband of Marcella the elder. He was conful A. U. 742.—Suetonius, Life of Auguftus, f. 63. Life of Claudius, f. 26.

24. M. Valerius Messala, fon of Valerius Meffala Barbatus and of Marcella the elder. He was father of the famous Meffalina.—Suet. Life of Claudius, f. 26.

25. Domitia Lepida, daughter of Antonia the younger, by her hufband Lucius Domitius Ænobarbus. She was the wife of the laft-mentioned Valerius Meffala, and mother of Meffalina; a woman of debauched and profligate manners, and a violent impetuous fpirit; in point of beauty, riches, and vice, the rival of Agrippina, Nero's mother. She was condemned to death A. U. 807.—Tacit. Annal. xi. f. 37. Annal. xii. f. 64. See Suet. Life of Claudius, f. 26. Life of Nero, f. 7.

26. Valeria Messalina, daughter of Valerius Meffala and Domitia Lepida. She was wife to the emperor Claudius; a woman of furious and till then unheard of lewdnefs. While Claudius was at Oftia, fhe had the hardinefs openly to celebrate her nuptials with Silius, and for that unparalleled crime was put to death A. U. 801.—Tacit. Annal. xi. f. 26. Suet. Life of Claudius, f. 26.

27. Marcella the younger, daughter of Claudius Marcellus and Octavia, fifter to Auguftus. She was firft married to M. Vipfanius Agrippa, and afterwards to M. Julius Antonius.

3 G 2

—Suetonius,

—Suetonius, Life of Auguſtus, ſ. 63.   Plutarch, Life of Marc Anthony.

For M. Vipsanius Agrippa, ſee No. 47.

28. The iſſue of Vipſanius Agrippa, by his firſt wife Marcella, before he was married to Julia, the daughter of Auguſtus by his wife Scribonia.—Suct. Life of Aug. ſ. 63.

29. Marcus Julius Antonius, ſon of Marc Anthony the triumvir and Fulvia his wife. He married Marcella the younger, when repudiated by Agrippa. He was conſul A. U. 744; a man of libidinous paſſions. He was put to death for his adulterous commerce with Julia, the daughter of Auguſtus. The ode of Horace, *Pindarum quiſquis ſtudet æmulari*, is addreſſed to him.—Tacit. Annal. iii. ſ. 18. Annal. iv. ſ. 44. Horace, book iv. ode 2.

30. Lucius Antonius, ſon of M. Julius Antonius by Marcella the younger. On account of his father's guilt with Julia, he was ſent in his infancy to Marſeilles, under a pretence of education, but, in fact, to a place of exile. He died A. U. 778.—Tacit. Annal. iv. ſ. 44.

31. Marc Anthony, the triumvir, ſon of Marcus Antonius the celebrated orator. He was the ſecond huſband of Octavia, ſiſter to Auguſtus, A. U. 714; but being in love with Cleopatra, he repudiated Octavia A. U. 722. After the aſſaſſination of Julius Cæſar, he ſeized the public treaſure, which was depoſited *in the temple of Ops*. He was at all times a turbulent and dangerous citizen; during the triumvirate, headlong, furious, and oppreſſive. The rage, with which he puſhed on the proſcription, rendered him deteſtable. The ſupreme power was often within his reach, but all his actions proved him unworthy

of

of that elevation. He was defeated at Actium A. U. 724.
The murder of Cicero consigned his name to eternal infamy.
By the manner of his death he effaced much of the shame that
branded his former conduct.—See Velleius Paterculus, book ii.
f. 60 and 87. Pliny the elder, book vii. f. 45. Plutarch, Life
of Anthony. Cicero, Philippic Orations.

The inscriptions of him on medals are, *Marcus Antonius,
Marci Filius, Marci Nepos, Augur, Imperator, Consul designatus
iterum et tertium, Triumvir Reipublicæ constituendæ.*

32. ANTONIA the elder, daughter of Anthony the triumvir
by Octavia sister to Augustus. She married L. Domitius Ænobarbus. She is called by Tacitus, Antonia the younger, which
makes it probable that Marc Anthony had a former daughter,
called Antonia, by his wife Fulvia.—See Tacit. Annal. iv. f. 44.
Suet. Life of Nero, f. 5. Plutarch, Life of Marc Anthony.

33. LUCIUS DOMITIUS ÆNOBARBUS, son of Cneius Domitius, one of the conspirators against Julius Cæsar, and husband
of Antonia the elder; a man of an impetuous temper, violent,
proud, extravagant, and cruel. He commanded in Germany,
and marched his army beyond the Elbe (Albis); and having penetrated farther than any Roman had done before him, he obtained the honours of a triumph. He died A. U. 778.—Suet.
Life of Nero, f. 4. Tacit. Annal. iv. f. 44.

34. CNEIUS DOMITIUS ÆNOBARBUS, son of the last-men-
tioned L. D. Ænobarbus, by Antonia the elder. He married
Agrippina, the daughter of Germanicus, A. U. 781; was conful A. U. 785. His life was a series of evil deeds. He was
the father of Nero, and was used to say, that from himself and
Agrippina

Agrippina nothing good or valuable could be born.—Suet. Life
of Nero, f. 5.   Tacit. Annal. iv. f. 75.

For AGRIPPINA, his wife, fee No. 93.

35. LUCIUS DOMITIUS NERO, the fixth Roman emperor,
fon of Cneius Domitius Ænobarbus by Agrippina the daughter
of Germanicus. She was grand-daughter to the famous Agrippa,
by Julia the daughter of Auguftus.   Nero was born 15th December, A. U. 790, the deteftable offspring of two pernicious
parents.   He was called fimply Domitius, till by the adoption
of Claudius, A. U. 803, he paffed into the Claudian family,
and took the name of Nero.   He began his reign, A. U. 807,
with fuch favourable circumftances, as, for a time, gave promife of a virtuous prince.   His enormities, afterwards, delivered
him down to the execration of pofterity.   The burning of Rome
was imputed to him.   The Chriftian religion has to boaft, that
the foe of human kind was the enemy of her moral doctrine. He
was a burthen to himfelf, and detefted by all orders of men. He
was condemned to die, *more majorum,* by a decree of the fenate.
He efcaped a public execution, and died in a daftardly manner
by his own hand, A. U. 821, A. D. 68.   By his death the race
of the Cæfars became extinct.—Suet. Life of Nero, f. 6.   Tacit.
Annal. xii. f. 25; and fee Appendix to Annals, book xvi. Pliny,
book xxii. f. 22 and 46.

The infcriptions on medals are, *Nero Claudius, Divi Claudii
Filius, Cæfar, Auguftus, Germanicus, Pontifex Maximus, Imperator, Tribunitiâ Poteftate Pater Patriæ.*

36. OCTAVIA, daughter of the emperor Claudius by Meffalina. She was born A. U. 795.   Britannicus was her bro-

                                                       ther.

ther. She was contracted to Lucius Silanus, but married to Nero A. U. 806; worthy of better times, and a better hufband. Nero repudiated her for the fake of Poppæa. She was banifhed to the ifland of Pandataria, and there put to death, A. U. 815.—Tacit. Annal. xii. f. 3, 25; and Annal. xiv. f. 60, 64. Dio Caffius, book lxi.

For BRITANNICUS, her brother, fee No. 108.

37. POPPÆA SABINA, daughter of Titus Ollius by Poppæa Sabina. She was married firft to Rufius Crifpinus; 2dly, to Marcus Salvius Otho, afterwards emperor; and at length to Nero, A. U. 815. The vices of her character refembled thofe of the emperor. He loved her tenderly, yet killed her by a kick on her womb when fhe was with child, A. U. 818. Her body was not burnt, but filled with fpices, and depofited in the monument of the Cæfars. Three years after her death, Nero dedicated a temple to her memory, with an infcription, *To Sabina the Goddefs Venus—Sabinæ Deæ Veneri.*—Tacit. Annal. xiii. f. 45; Annal. xvi. f. 6. Suet. Life of Nero, f. 35. Dio Caffius, book lxiii.

38. CLAUDIA AUGUSTA, daughter of Nero and Poppæa, born at Antium A. U. 816. She was foon after her birth dignified with the title of *Augufta*. She died within four months, to the great grief of Nero. She was canonized a goddefs by a decree of the fenate.—Tacit. Annal. xv. f. 23. Suet. Life of Nero, f. 35.

Her infcription on medals is, DIVA CLAUDIA NERONIS FILIA; *The Goddefs Claudia, Daughter of Nero.*

39. STATILIA

39. STATILIA MESSALINA, who drew her lineage through several defcents from Statilius Taurus. She was the third wife of Nero, who, to poffefs her perfon, murdered her firft hufband Atticus Veftinus A. U. 818.—Suet. Life of Nero, f. 35. Tacit. Annal. xv. f. 68.

40. DOMITIA, daughter of Antonia the elder by Lucius Ænobarbus; aunt to Nero, and the wife of Paffienus Crifpus. Nero deftroyed her by poifon A. U. 812.—Tacit. Annal. xiii. f. 19, 21. Quintilian, book vi. f. 1.

For PASSIENUS CRISPUS, fee No. 94.

41. CAIUS APPIUS JUNIUS SILANUS. He was governor of Spain. By the defire of Claudius he married Domitia Lepida, the mother of Meffalina, and was foon after put to death by order of that emperor, A. U. 795.—Dio Caffius, book lx.

42. ANTONIA the younger, fecond daughter of Anthony the triumvir by Octavia fifter to Auguftus. She married Nero Drufus, the brother of Tiberius, and was the mother of Germanicus; a woman diftinguifhed by her beauty, and no lefs by her virtue. She furvived Drufus, her hufband, many years, leading an exemplary life in a ftate of widowhood, and by the whole tenour of her conduct almoft eclipfing the luftre of her anceftors.—Pliny, book vii. f. 19. Suet. Life of Caligula, f. 1. Tacit. Annal. iii. f. 3. Annal. xi. f. 3. Plutarch, Life of Marc Anthony. Valerius Maximus, book iv. f. 3.

43. CAIUS OCTAVIUS CÆSAR, Auguftus, emperor of Rome. He was the fon of Caius Octavius by his wife Atia, who was niece to Julius Cæfar. He was born 23d September,

A. U.

A. U. 691. At the age of nineteen he took the lead in the civil wars, and, in three years after, not one of the confpirators againft Julius Cæfar (who had adopted him for his fon) furvived the fury of the deftructive fword. Sextus Pompeius was totally defeated in a naval engagement off the coaft of Sicily. Lepidus, one of the triumvirate, was difmantled of his power; and Marc Anthony was overthrown at the battle of Actium. After thofe events, Octavius was the only furviving chief of the Julian party. He became emperor of Rome A. U. C. 724.

During the whole courfe of his reign, pacific meafures were the object of his policy. Letters flourifhed, and men of genius met with encouragement. By his popular acts he gained the affections of the people, with the title of AUGUSTUS, the FATHER OF HIS COUNTRY. Scythia, Sarmatia, the Garamantes and Bactrians, India, and the people called the SERES, fubmitted to his authority, and fent their ambaffadors to fettle the terms of a general peace. At Rome, and the capital cities of the provinces, temples, orders of priefthood, facerdotal colleges, were dedicated to him, not only after his death, but, in many places, during his life. He died at Nola on the 18th of Auguft, A. U. 767. His character, ftrictly examined, was more fplendid for his policy than his virtues. He owed his elevation to the vices of Lepidus and Anthony, and the abilities of Vipfanius Agrippa; but it redounds to his praife, that, what he gained by the prudence and valour of others he was able to fupport, by a well-judged fyftem of policy, during a fpace of four-and-forty years. It was faid of him, that he found the city of Rome made with brick, and he changed it to marble. Though deified, even during his life in fome parts of the empire, he was taught by various incidents, that he was no more than man.—See Suet. Life of Auguftus. Tacit. book i. of the Annals; book xiii. f. 6. Florus, book iv.

chap. xii. Aurelius Victor, chap. i. Pliny, book vii. f. 45. Seneca, de Confolatione, 34.

Infcriptions on Ancient Medals :

Before his elevation to the fupreme power, *Octavius Cæfar, Son of the deified Julius, Imperator, Triumvir for the Purpofe of reftoring the Commonwealth, Conful, the Affertor of public Liberty.*

After his acceffion to the empire, *Cæfar, Auguftus, Son of the deified Julius Cæfar, Imperator, Conful, chief Pontiff, and, with the tribunitian Power, Father of his Country.*

After his death, *Divus Auguftus,* the deified Auguftus.

44. CLODIA, daughter of Publius Clodius, by his wife Fulvia, and daughter-in-law to Anthony the triumvir. In order to conciliate terms of peace, Auguftus married her, when fhe was yet of tender years ; but a quarrel taking place with Fulvia, her mother, Auguftus repudiated her in her virgin ftate.—Suet. Life of Aug. f. 62.

45. SCRIBONIA, fifter of Lucius Scribonius Libo, and wife of Auguftus. She had been married twice before to two men of confular rank, and by one of them, whofe name was Scipio, fhe had a daughter named Cornelia. Auguftus repudiated Scribonia A. U. 715, and Livia, in a few years afterwards, fucceeded to the embraces of the emperor of Rome.—Suet. Life of Aug. f. 63, 69. Dio, book xlviii. Propertius, book iv. eleg. 2.

46. JULIA, daughter of Auguftus, by his wife Scribonia, born A. U. 715. She was married, firft, to Marcellus; fecondly,

to Agrippa; and thirdly, to Tiberius; a woman of diffolute conduct, libidinous paffions, and abandoned infamy. On account
of her adulterous intrigues, fhe was banifhed by Auguftus to the
ifland of Pandataria A. U. 752. She was left there by Tiberius,
to pine in want and mifery. She died A. U. 767.—Pliny, book
vii. f. 45. Dio, book lv. Tacit. Annal. i. f. 53. Vell. Paterculus, book ii. f. 100.

For her firft hufband, Marcus Marcellus, fee No. 18.

47. Marcus Vipsanius Agrippa; a man of low extrac-
tion, in his manners unpolifhed, even to a degree of rufticity. For
thofe defects he made ample atonement by fuperior qualities; in
war, a great commander; and through life a man of unblemifhed
integrity. He gained fignal victories both by land and fea, and
by his brilliant fuccefs eftablifhed Auguftus on the imperial throne.
A ftranger to letters and the fine arts, he was, notwithftanding,
the friend of fcience. At a time when geographical knowledge
had made little or no progrefs, he framed a map of the world,
and prefented it to the public. Not only Rome but Italy was
adorned, under his direction, with public buildings no lefs ufe_
ful than magnificent. Auguftus, to fhew a grateful fenfe of his
fervices and his merit, raifed him to three feveral confulfhips, and
even made him his affociate in the tribunitian power. On the
death of Marcus Marcellus (fee No. 18), Auguftus chofe him for
his fon-in-law, and gave him in marriage his daughter Julia, then
a widow, A. U. 733. Agrippa, though a new man, had the art
of rifing in the world with fuperior dignity. He died A. U.
742, in the fifty-firft year of his age. Auguftus fpoke his funeral
panegyric. Tacit. Annal. i. f. 3. Pliny, book iii. f. 2; book vii.
f. 8; book xxxv. f. 4. Dio, book liv. Vell. Paterculus, book ii.
f. 96.

He was called in ancient medals, *Marcus Agrippa, Son of Lucius, Consul three times, Commander of the Fleet, and Præfect of the Sea-coast.*

48. CAIUS CÆSAR, son of Agrippa and Julia, born A. U. 734; adopted by Augustus as his son, prince of the Roman youth, and consul elect. He was prematurely cut off, on his return from Armenia, A. U. 757.—Tacit. Annal. i. f. 3. Dio, book liv.

He was married to Livia, the sister of Germanicus.—Tacit. Annal. iv. f. 40.

For LIVIA, his wife, see No. 71.

49. LUCIUS CÆSAR, son of Agrippa and Julia, brother to Caius Cæsar, born A. U. 737; adopted by Augustus into the Cæsarean family; styled prince of the Roman youth; and declared consul elect. He died at Marseilles, on his way to join the army in Spain, in the month of August, A. U. 754. Tacit. Annal. i. f. 3.

In ancient medals, both brothers are called, *Caius and Lucius Cæsars, Sons of Augustus, Consuls elect, Princes of the Roman Youth.*

50. MARCUS AGRIPPA POSTHUMUS, son of Agrippa and Julia; brother to Caius and Lucius; born after his father's death, A. U. 742. He was adopted by Augustus A. U. 757, and soon after, on account of his uncouth manners, and stupid ferocity, banished to the island of Planasia. No kind of guilt could be imputed to him; no disgraceful or flagitious action was laid to

his

his charge; and, for that reafon, Auguftus, towards the end of his life, began to relent. He intended to reftore him to his rank, and, it is faid, made a voyage to the ifle of Planafia for the purpofe of a reconciliation. Auguftus, however, did not live to carry his defign into execution. Agrippa Pofthumus was cut off by order of Tiberius, who made that murder the firft act of his reign, A. U. 767.—Dio, book liv. Velicius Paterculus, book ii. f. 104. Tacit. Annals, book i. f. 3, 6. Pliny, book vii. f. 45.

51. AGRIPPINA, daughter of Agrippa and Julia; granddaughter to Auguftus, and wife of Germanicus; a woman of noble qualities, an exalted fpirit, and unconquerable chaftity. Elate with the pride of virtue, and confcious of her illuftrious birth, fhe fcorned to bend to the arrogance of Livia, the mother of Tiberius. She was banifhed to the ifle of Pandataria, and, after fuffering every barbarous outrage from the cruelty of Tiberius, died in mifery A. U. 786.—Tacit. Annal. iv. f. 12. Annal. vi. f. 25. Annal. xiv. f. 63. See fupplement to book v. of the Annals, f. 5.

For GERMANICUS, her hufband, fee No. 81.

52. JULIA, daughter of Agrippa and Julia; fifter to Agrippina, and grand-daughter to Auguftus. She married Lucius Æmilius Paulus, and, in all kinds of excefs and vicious debauchery, diftinguifhed herfelf as the rival of her mother. In the reign of Auguftus, fhe was condemned for her adulterous practices, and banifhed to the ifle of Trimetus, A. U. 761. She died in exile A. U. 781.—Tacit. Annal. iv. f. 71.

53. LUCIUS ÆMILIUS PAULUS, fon of Paulus Æmilius
Lepidus

Lepidus and his wife Cornelia. The father was cenfor A. U.
732. Lucius the fon married Julia, the daughter of Agrippa and
Julia.—Suet. Life of Auguftus, f. 64. Dio, book liv.

54. MARCUS ÆMILIUS LEPIDUS, fon of Lucius Æmilius
Lepidus and Julia the daughter of Agrippa. He married
Drufilla, and committed adultery and inceft with her fifters. His
vices endeared him to Caligula. He was condemned for trea-
fonable practices, and put to death A. U. 792. Caligula, upon
that occafion, gave a donative to the foldiers, and dedicated to
MARS THE AVENGER three fwords, which had been prepared
by the confpirators.—Dio, book lix. Suet. Life of Caligula, f. 24
and 36. Tacit. Annal. xiv. f. 2.

55. ÆMILIA LEPIDA, the daughter of Lucius Æmilius
Paulus and Julia, the daughter of Agrippa and Julia, confequently grand-daughter to Auguftus. She was contracted to
Claudius, afterwards emperor, when he was extremely young;
and afterwards married to Junius Silanus.—Suet. Life of Claud.
f. 26. Pliny, book vii. f. 13.

56. JUNIUS SILANUS, the hufband of the laft-mentioned
Æmilia Lepida. Nothing of him can be faid with certainty;
but it is probable that he was the Marcus Silanus who was joint
conful with Lucius Norbanus Flaccus, A. U. 772.—Tacit. Annal.
ii. f. 59.

57. MARCUS JUNIUS SILANUS, fon of Junius Silanus and
Æmilia Lepida, born in the year in which Auguftus died, A. U.
767.—Pliny, book vii. f. 13. He was a man of an unblemifhed
character, but fo inactive, that Caligula called him *The Golden
Calf.*

Calf. He was proconful of Afia, and, by Nero's order, taken off by poifon, A. U. 807.—Tacit. Annal. xiii. f. 1.

58. THE wife of Marcus Junius Silanus, and the mother of Lucius Silanus Torquatus. The name is not to be found in any Hiftorian.

59. LUCIUS SILANUS TORQUATUS, fon of Marcus Junius Silanus, who was great-grandfon to Auguftus. Without being charged with any crime, obnoxious only on account of his illuftrious birth and the modefty of his youth, he was put to death by Nero, A. U. 818.—Tacit. Annal. xvi. f. 7, 8, 9.

60. LUCIUS JUNIUS SILANUS, fon of Junius Silanus and Æmilia Lepida (fee No. 55 and 56). The emperor Claudius had promifed him his daughter Octavia in marriage, A. U. 794, but foon after broke off the match, and left Silanus to choofe his mode of death, A. U. 802.—Dio, book lx. Tacit. Annal. xii. f. 3, 8.

61. JUNIUS SILANUS TORQUATUS, fon of Junius Silanus and Æmilia Lepida, who was great grand-daughter to Auguftus. A pedigree derived from the Junian family, and rendered ftill more illuftrious by his relation to Auguftus, made him obnoxious to the jealoufy of Nero. He died by that emperor's order, A. U. 817. Both he and Lucius Silanus Torquatus were cut off in the month of June, for which reafon the name was changed to that of Germanicus.—Tacit. Annal. xv. f. 35. Annal. xvi. f. 8 and 12. Dio, book lxii.

62. JUNIA CALVINA, daughter of Junius Silanus and Æmilia Lepida. She was married to Vitellius, who was afterwards.

wards emperor. Diftinguifhed by her beauty and illuftrious birth, fhe preferved an unblemifhed character, but provoked her enemies by a fierce and uncomplying fpirit. By the malice and infidious arts of Agrippina the younger, fhe was banifhed out of Italy, but recalled by Nero A. U. 812. She lived to the time of Vefpafian.—Tacit. Annal. xii. f. 4 and 8. Annal. xiv. f. 12. Suet. Life of Vefp. f. 23.

63. VITELLIUS, fon of Lucius Vitellius the cenfor and his wife Sextilia. He married Junia Calvina, and was conful A. U. 801. Upon fome diffenfion between him and his wife, a divorce took place fome time before A. U. 802.—Tacit. Annal. xi. f. 23. Annal. xii. f. 4. Suet. Life of Vitellius, f. 3 and 18.

64. LEPIDA, daughter of Junius Silanus and Æmilia Lepida. She was married to Caius Caffius, governor of Syria. An accufation alleging various crimes was fuborned againft her, but referred to the judgment of Nero, A. U. 818.—Tacit. Annal. xvi. f. 8, 9.

65. CAIUS CASSIUS, governor of Syria, and hufband of Lepida. He was celebrated for his fuperior knowledge of the laws; but being charged with having, among the images of his anceftors, the picture or ftatue of the famous CASSIUS, with an infcription, *To the Chief of Party*, he was banifhed to the ifland of Sardinia, A. U. 818.—Tacit. Annal. xii. f. 11, 12. Annal. xvi. f. 8, 9.

66. LIVIA, called alfo LIVIA DRUSILLA, and, after the death of Auguftus, JULIA AUGUSTA. She was the daughter of Livius Drufus Claudianus. Her firft hufband was Tiberius Claudius Nero: being divorced from him, fhe married Auguftus
A. U.

A. U. 716. A woman of illuftrious birth; elegant in her form and manners; of high ambition, and an overbearing fpirit. She had the fkill to manage the gentle arts of Auguftus, and the dark diffimulation of Tiberius; a complying and obliging wife, and afterwards an imperious mother. Her enmity to Germanicus and his wife Agrippina was fubtle, clofe, and unrelenting. She died A. U. 782, at the age of 86.—Velleius Pat. book ii. f. 75. Suet. Life of Tiberius, f. 3 and 4. Dio, book xlviii. Tacit. Annal. book v. f. 1.

Her infcriptions on ancient medals: *Livia Augufta, Julia, Augufta, Mother of her Country.*

After her death: *The deified Livia, Wife of the deified Auguftus, the deified Julia Augufta.*

67. TIBERIUS CLAUDIUS NERO, the firft hufband of Livia, and by her the father of Tiberius, afterwards emperor, and of Nero Claudius Drufus (for whom fee No. 79). He obtained the dignities of prætor and pontiff; a man of brilliant talents and extenfive learning. He attached himfelf to Anthony the triumvir; and after the defeat of that party, he withdrew with his wife Livia and Tiberius, then an infant about two years old, into Sicily A. U. 714. Livia fled from Auguftus, her deftined hufband, and Tiberius from his future father by adoption. Tiberius Claudius Nero made his peace with Auguftus, and refigned his wife A. U. 716. He died three years after, A. U. 719.—Vell. Pat. book ii. f. 75. Suet. Life of Tiberius, f. 4, 6. Dio, book xlvii.

68. TIBERIUS NERO, fon of Tiberius Claudius Nero by Livia his wife, born 16th November, A. U. 712; adopted by

   Auguftus

Auguſtus A. U. 757, and emperor of Rome A. U. 767. He died on the 17th of March A. U. 790, after a reign of three-and-twenty years. Julius Cæſar ſubdued his country; Auguſtus cheriſhed the conquered; and Tiberius made them crouch in bondage. He eſtabliſhed ſlavery, and deſpiſed the ſervile ſpirit of the men that ſubmitted with paſſive obedience. He hated eminent virtue, and was at the ſame time the enemy of vice. Such jarring elements have been rarely mixed in the compoſition of one man : fluctuating between good and evil, and by turns inclined to each, he did every thing by fits and ſudden ſtarts of paſſion. Before he roſe to the ſupreme power, he diſtinguiſhed himſelf by his warlike ſpirit. When maſter of the Roman world, diſſimulation was the prominent feature of his character. When he had waded far in guilt and flagitious deeds, he lay *on the torture of the mind in reſtleſs ecſtaſy.* Goaded by his con-ſcience, and alarmed by conſtant ſuſpicions, he fled from danger to the iſle of Capreæ, but could not fly from himſelf. He was often heard to utter a moſt horrible wiſh, expreſſed in a Greek verſe :

Εμῦ θανόντος γαῖα μιχθήτω πυρί.

Me mortuo terra miſceatur igni.

" At my death let the earth be involved in flames." He called Priam the happieſt of men, becauſe his kingdom periſhed with him.—Vell. Pat. book ii. ſ. 75. Tacit. in the ſix firſt Annals, *paſſim.* Pliny, book xxviii. ſ. 2.

Inſcriptions on ancient medals : *Tiberius Cæſar, Auguſtus Son of the deified Auguſtus, Imperator, Augur, Chief Pontiff, veſted with the Tribunitian Power.*

69. VIPSANIA

69. VIPSANIA AGRIPPINA, daughter of Marcus Vipſanius Agrippa by his firſt wife Pomponia, who was the granddaughter of Atticus, to whom Cicero addreſſed the well-known collection of letters. Vipſania Agrippina was firſt married to Tiberius, the emperor, but by him unwillingly repudiated during her pregnancy, to make way for a match with Julia, the daughter of Auguſtus.—Tacit. Annal. book i. ſ. 12. Suet. Life of Tiberius, ſ. 7. Dio, book liv. After her divorce, ſhe married Aſinius Gallus, the ſon of Aſinius Pollio, the conſul and celebrated orator, the favourite of Auguſtus, and, what is now of more conſequence, celebrated by Horace and Virgil. Of all the children of Agrippa, ſhe is the only one that died a natural death, A. U. 773. Tacit. Annal. book iii. ſ. 19.

For ASINIUS GALLUS, ſee Tacit. Annal. book i. ſ. 8.

70. DRUSUS CÆSAR, ſon of Tiberius by Vipſania Agrippina, who was repudiated in her pregnancy. He was born A. U. 739; a youth of a towering ſpirit, impatient of an equal, addicted to liquor, and in that vice the rival of his father. He married Livia, otherwiſe called Livilla, who was debauched by Sejanus, and drawn into a plot againſt her huſband's life. Druſus had been three times conſul, and was every day riſing to eminence in the ſtate, when Sejanus put an end to his days by poiſon, A. U. 776.—Tacit. Annal. book i. ſ. 55; book iii. ſ. 56; book iv. ſ. 3 and 8. Pliny, book xiv. ſ. 22.

Inſcriptions on ancient medals: *Druſus Cæſar Son of Tiberius, Grandſon to the deiſied Auguſtus, Pontiff, Conſul, veſted with Tribunitian Power.*

71. LIVIA, or LIVILLA, daughter of Nero Claudius Druſus

 (ſee

(fee No. 79) by his wife Antonia the younger (fee No. 42). She was fifter to Germanicus, and alfo Claudius the emperor. Her firft hufband was Caius, the fon of Agrippa: after his death fhe married Drufus, the fon of Tiberius. Sejanus fe-duced her affections from her hufband. Engaged in a courfe of adultery with that flagitious minifter, fhe hoped to rife with her paramour to the imperial dignity, and with that ambitious view confpired againft her hufband. Her guilt being afterwards fully detected, fhe was put to death by order of Tiberius (fee Supplement to Annals, book v. f. 38, 39); and by a decree of the fenate, her pictures and ftatues were all deftroyed, and her memory branded with infamy.—Suet. Life of Claudius, f. 1. Life of Tiberius, f. 62. Tacit. Annal. book iv. f. 3 and 40; book vi. f. 2. Dio, book lviii.

72. TIBERIUS, fon of Drufus Cæfar (fee No. 70) and Livilla (No. 71), grandfon to Tiberius the emperor, born with a twin-brother A. U. 772. Tiberius was fo elated with joy on that oc-cafion, that he boafted of the birth of twins, as an event which had never happened to any Roman of equal rank. Caligula deprived him of the fucceffion and his life, A. U. 790.—Tacit. Annal. book ii. f. 84. Dio, book lix.

73. THE twin-brother of Tiberius (No. 72), the fon of Dru-fus and Livia, or Livilla, died when about four years old, A. U. 776.—Tacit. Annal. book ii. f. 84; book iv. f. 15. His name is nowhere mentioned.

74. JULIA, daughter of Drufus Cæfar (No. 70) and Livia No. 71), married firft to Nero Cæfar, fon of Germanicus and Agrippina, and afterwards to Rubellius Blandus. She was cut off by the malice of Meffalina A. U. 796.—Tacit. Annal. book iii. f. 29; book vi. f. 27; book xiii. f. 19 and 32. Dio, book lx.

·For

For NERO CÆSAR, fon of Germanicus and Agrippina, the hufband of Julia, fee No. 82.

75. RUBELLIUS BLANDUS, fon of a Roman knight, and the fecond hufband of Julia, the daughter of Drufus (fee No. 70). He was married to her A. U. 786.—Tacit. Annal. book vi. f. 27. Dio, book lviii.

76. RUBELLIUS PLAUTUS, fon of Rubellius Blandus and his wife Julia. The popular voice marked him out a proper perfon to fucceed to the imperial dignity, and for that reafon he was put to death by Nero A. U. 815.—Tacit. Annal. book xiii. f. 19; book xiv. f. 22 and 58.

77. ANTISTIA POLLUTIA, daughter of Lucius Antiftius Vetus, and wife of Rubellius Plautus (No. 76). She was put to death with her father and Sextia, her mother-in-law, A. U. 818. Her crime was, that, while fhe lived, Nero confidered her and her family as a living reproach for the murder of her huf-band Rubellius Plautus.—Tacit. Annal. book xvi. f. 10 and 11.

78. A SON of Tiberius the emperor by Julia, the daughter of Auguftus (fee No. 46). He was born at Aquileia, and died in his infancy A. U. 747. His name is nowhere mentioned.—Suet. Life of Tiberius, f. 7. Dio, book lv.

79. NERO CLAUDIUS DRUSUS, fon of Tiberius Claudius Nero (fee No. 67) and Livia, afterwards married to Auguftus. Tiberius the emperor was his elder brother. He was born A. U. 716. A youth, fays Velleius Paterculus, of as many virtues as prudence can acquire, or human nature can admit. The fine ode of Horace, *Qualem Miniftrum fulminis alitem*, book iv. ode 4,
written

written in the year of Rome 743, difplays his military character in the brighteft colours. He rofe to the higheft civil offices, fuch as prætor, ædile, and conful. He commanded the Roman army in Germany, and for his victories obtained the name of GERMANICUS. He was father of the famous Germanicus by Antonia the younger (fee No. 42). He died A. U. 745; the pride of the Claudian family, and the favourite of the Roman people. Auguftus fpoke his funeral panegyric, and in his fpeech offered up a fervent prayer to the gods, that all future Cæfars might refemble him, and that his own death, whenever it fhould happen, might be equally honourable and as fincerely lamented.—Suet. Life of Claudius, f. 1. Life of Tiberius, f. 4. Dio, book lv. Valerius Maximus, book iv. f. 3, No. 3.

Infcription on ancient coins: *Nero Claudius Drufus, Germanicus, Imperator.*

For ANTONIA the younger, the wife of Drufus, fee No. 42.

80. SONS of Drufus and Antonia. They died before A. U. 745, and their names are now unknown.—Suet. Life of Claudius, f. 1.

81. GERMANICUS CÆSAR, fon of Nero Claudius Drufus (No. 79) by Antonia the younger (No. 42), the worthieft fon of the worthieft parents. Tiberius, by the command of Auguftus, adopted him A. U. 757, but afterwards, when poffeffed of the fupreme power, beheld him with a malignant eye. He died on his return from a tour in Ægypt, not without ftrong fufpicions of being poifoned by the contrivance of Livia, the mother of Tiberius, and the villany of Pifo and Plancina, A. U. 772, in the thirty-firft year of his age. The funeral ceremony was per-

formed

formed at Antioch. Germanicus fucceeded to his father in the affections of the Roman people. Of gentle manners, mild and gracious to all, he was beheld with pleafure, and heard with applaufe. Ambition, if we except the fair defire of being diftinguifhed by his virtues, had no influence on his conduct. Undebauched by pleafure, he difcharged all the duties of an upright citizen and an able officer. He commanded the Roman legions in Germany; in war victorious, and in peace moderate to the vanquifhed. Poffeffed of great accomplifhments, he was in nothing inferior to Alexander, and free from the vices of that warlike chief He was on the fide of virtue greatly his fuperior. Rome deplored his death, and with him loft all hopes of feeing the old conftitution reftored. Foreign nations paid their tribute of refpect to his memory.—Tacit. Annal. book i. f. 3, 33, 34, 42, &c.; book ii. f. 72, 73. Dio, book lv.

Infcriptions on ancient coins: *Germanicus Cæfar, Son of Tiberius Auguftus, Grandfon to the deified Auguftus, Conful.*

After his death, in the reign of his fon Caligula: *Germanicus Cæfar, Father of Cæfar Auguftus, the deified Germanicus.*

For AGRIPPINA, his wife, fee No. 51.

82. NERO CÆSAR, fon of Germanicus and Agrippina. He married Julia, daughter of Drufus the fon of Tiberius (fee No. 70), A. U. 773. By the wicked arts of Sejanus he was banifhed to the ifle of Pontia, and there put to death A. U. 784.—Tacit. Annal. book iv. f. 59, 60; book v. f. 3, 4. Suet. Life of Tiberius, f. 54. Dio, book lviii.

For JULIA, the wife of Nero Cæfar, fee No. 74.

83. DRUSUS

83. DRUSUS CÆSAR, fon of Germanicus and Agrippina, brother to Nero Cæfar and Caligula, afterwards emperor. He married Æmilia Lepida, who was induced by Sejanus to betray her hufband. Deluded himfelf by the arts of that evil minifter, he confpired againft the life of his brother, Nero Cæfar. He was imprifoned at Rome by order of Tiberius, and died in confinement A. U. 786.—Tacit. Annal. book iv. f. 60; book vi. f. 23, 24. Dio, book lviii.

Infcriptions on ancient coins: *Nero Cæfar, Drufus Cæfar, Duumviri.*

84. ÆMILIA LEPIDA, daughter of Manius Lepidus, and wife of Drufus Cæfar (No. 83). She was engaged in an adulterous commerce with Sejanus, and fuborned by that ambitious upftart to carry a clandeftine charge againft her hufband to the ear of Tiberius. Notwithftanding her crimes, fhe was protected during her father's life; but being afterwards profecuted by the race of informers, fhe put an end to her days A. U. 789.— Tacit. Annal. book iv. f. 20; book vi. f. 27, 40.

85. CAIUS CÆSAR, fon of Germanicus and Agrippina; a youth of engaging manners, and a promifing difpofition. He died prematurely in the bloom of life, much regretted by Auguftus.—Suet. Life of Caligula, f. 7 and 8.

86. CAIUS CÆSAR, better known by the name of CALIGULA, fourth emperor of Rome, the fon of Germanicus and Agrippina. He was born at Antium 31ft Auguft, in the confulfhip of Germanicus and Fonteius Capito, A. U. 765. He practifed the arts of diffimulation during the life of Tiberius, and had the fkill to conceal his real character. Having obtained the fovereign

power,

power, he threw off the mask, and shewed himself a monster of vice and cruelty. He wished with impious arrogance to be worshipped as a god, and was at the same time a tyrant of savage ferocity, the scourge of human kind. His delight in blood was so keen and ardent, that he was often heard to express his wish, *that the Roman people had but one neck, that he might at a blow destroy the whole race.* He dissipated in less than a year the whole treasure left by Tiberius, computed to be an immense sum. Nor can this be wondered at in a man who spent for one dinner a hundred thousand sesterces. Costly and effeminate in his dress, he was so extravagant as to appear in shoes composed of pearl. He was slain by Cassius Cherea, tribune of a prætorian cohort, on the fourth day of the Palatine games, A. U. 794; a man, says Seneca, designed by nature to shew what the worst vices can do in the height of power.—Seneca de Consolat. c. ix. Suet. Life of Caligula, f. 8, 37, 58. Pliny, book vii. f. 8; book xxxvii. f. 2. Tacit. Annal. book vi. f. 20.

Inscriptions on ancient coins : *Caius Cæsar Augustus Germanicus, Son of Tiberius Augustus, Grandson to Augustus, Great-Grandson to the deified Augustus, Caius Cæsar, a God and Emperor.*

As adopted son of Tiberius, he was grandson to Augustus; as the son of Germanicus, he was great-grandson.

87. CLAUDIA, daughter of M. Silanus, married to Caligula A. U. 786. She died in child-bed. Suetonius calls her JUNIA CLAUDILLA.—Tacit. Annal. book vi. f. 20. Suet. Life of Caligula, f. 12.

88. LIVIA ORESTILLA ; called by Dio, CORNELIA ORES-

TINA. She was on the point of marrying Caius Calpurnius Pifo, when Caligula, enamoured of her beauty, carried off by force, and in a few days after repudiated her.—Suet. Life of Caligula, f. 25. Dio, book lix.

89. LOLLIA PAULINA, grand-daughter of Marcus Lollius, who was tutor to Caius Cæfar, the fon of Agrippa (No. 48), and drew on himfelf a load of difgrace and obloquy on account of the prodigious prefents, which he received with a rapacious hand from the oriental princes. His daughter Lollia Paulina was married to Caligula. The emperor ravifhed her from Caius Memmius Regulus, and in a fhort time after difmiffed her from his embraces. Pliny affures us, that he faw her, not at a time of public feftivity, but at a moderate entertainment, placed at the banqueting-table, in a drefs overcharged with jewels and pearls, artfully intermixed and blended, tangled in her hair, fhining on her head, at her ears, round her neck, with rich bracelets on her arms, and her fingers loaded with rings; the whole of this laboured magnificence was not worth lefs than four hundred thoufand fefterces. Pliny adds, that this enormous difplay was not a prefent from the emperor, but all of it the wealth of her grand-father Marcus Lollius, accumulated from the fpoil of plundered provinces.—Pliny, book ix. cap. 35, f. 57. Suet. Life of Caligula, 25. Dio, book lix.

90. MILONIA CÆSONIA, daughter of Veftilia, whom Caligula married when fhe was advanced in her pregnancy, A. U. 792. In thirty days after fhe was delivered of her child. She was the wife of the worft of men, and her own vices made her worthy of fuch a connexion. Caligula was killed A. U. 794; and in a few days after Cherea, who difpatched the tyrant, ordered Cæfonia and her daughter to be put to death, that no

remains

remains of the tyrant's family fhould be fuffered to exift. She died with a degree of fortitude that would have done honour to a better character.—Suet. Life of Caligula, f. 25, 59. Dio, book lix. Pliny, book vii. f. 5.

91. JULIA DRUSILLA, daughter of Caligula and Milonia Cæfonia. Her frantic father carried her to the temples of all the goddeffes, and dedicated her to Minerva, as to the patronefs of her education. She difcovered in her infancy ftrong indications of the cruelty that branded both her parents. She fuffered death with her mother (fee No. 90).—Suet. Life of Caligula, f. 25 and 59. Dio, book lix.

92. Two fons of Germanicus and Agrippina, who died in their infancy. Their names not recorded.—Suet. Life of Caligula, f. 7 and 8.

93. AGRIPPINA, daughter of Germanicus and Agrippina, born A. U. 769. She was married three times; firft, to Cneius Domitius Ænobarbus, A. U. 781; fecondly, to Paffienus Crifpus; thirdly, to the emperor Claudius, A. U. 801. She was a woman of violent paffions, unbounded ambition, and at the fame time diftinguifhed by her literary accomplifhments. By Ænobarbus, her firft hufband, fhe was the mother of Nero, whofe name is now another word for the moft favage cruelty. Nero was born A. U. 790 (No. 35). By that execrable parricide Agrippina was barbaroufly murdered A. U. 812.—Tacit. Annal. book ii. f. 54; book iv. f. 53; book xii. f. 64; book xiv. f. 6, 7, 8. Suet. Life of Caligula, f. 7. Dio, book lx.

For CNEIUS DOMITIUS ÆNOBARBUS, her firft hufband, and the father of Nero, fee No. 34.

94. PASSIENUS

94. PASSIENUS CRISPUS, a celebrated orator, and twice conful. He was firft married to Domitia (fee No. 40), and fecondly to Agrippina. A fhrewd faying of his concerning Caligula is well known: *There never was a better flave, nor a worfe mafter.* Upon other occafions he was ufed to obferve, "*We all oppofe the door to flattery, but none of us fhut it.*"—Pliny, book xvi. c. 44, f. 91. Tacit. Annal. book vi. f. 20. Seneca, Quæft. Natural. book iv. Preface.

For CLAUDIUS, the third hufband of Agrippina, fee No. 100.

95. DRUSILLA, daughter of Germanicus and Agrippina, born A. U. 770. She was firft married to Lucius Caffius Longinus A. U. 786, and afterwards to Marcus Æmilius Lepidus. Caligula, her brother, had an inceftuous intrigue with her; and after her death, which happened A. U. 791, he canonized her for a goddefs by the name of PANTHEA. On that occafion Livius Geminius declared on his oath, that he had feen her in her afcent to heaven. For this extraordinary teftimony he was amply rewarded by Caligula.—Tacit. Annal. vi. f. 15. Suet. Life of Caligula, f. 7 and 24. Dio, book lix.

On ancient coins: *Drufilla Augufta.*

96. LUCIUS CASSIUS LONGINUS, married to Drufilla (No. 95). He was raifed to the confulfhip A. U. 783, and afterwards ftood forth the accufer of Drufus, his wife's brother (fee No. 83).—Suet. Life of Caligula, f. 24. Tacit. Annal. vi. f. 15. Dio, book lviii.

For MARCUS ÆMILIUS LEPIDUS, the fecond hufband of Drufilla, fee No. 54.

97. JULIA,

97. JULIA, daughter of Germanicus and Agrippina, called by Suetonius LIVILLA. She was born A. U. 771. Caligula, on account of her debaucheries, ordered her to be conveyed to the ifle of Pontia, A. U. 792. She was recalled in the reign of Claudius; but Meſſalina, without any crime alleged, contrived to drive her into baniſhment, and afterwards put her to death, A. U. 796.—Suet. Life of Caligula, ſ. 7 and 24. Life of Claudius, ſ. 29. Dio, book lix.

98. QUINCTILIUS VARUS, ſon of Claudia Pulchra, who was couſin to Agrippina. He married Julia (No. 97). An accuſation was framed againſt him by Domitius Afer and Dolabella, A. U. 780.—Seneca, Controv. book i. ſ. 3. Tacit. Annal. iv. ſ. 52 and 66.

99. MARCUS VINICIUS. He married Julia (No. 97) A. U. 786; was twice conful, but, by a wicked ſtratagem of Meſſalina, was deſtroyed by poiſon A. U. 799. It was to this man, in the year of his conſulſhip, that Velleius Paterculus dedicated his elegant compendium of the Roman Hiſtory; a work admired for the beauty of the ſtyle, but debaſed by the fulſome praiſe of Tiberius and Sejanus.—Tacit. Annal. vi. ſ. 15. See Supplement to Annals, v. ſ. 11. Dio, book lx.

100. TIBERIUS CLAUDIUS DRUSUS GERMANICUS, fifth emperor of Rome. He was ſon to Nero Claudius Druſus (No. 79) and Antonia the younger (No. 42); he was brother to Germanicus; born at Lyons (Lugduni) A. U. 744. He diſcovered in the firſt dawn of infancy a degree of dulneſs that bordered on ſtupidity. He grew up ſo ſluggiſh in body and mind, that Antonia his mother often declared that he was an imperfect production, ſent into the world unfiniſhed by the hand of

4. Nature.

Nature.   He fucceeded to the fupreme power A. U. 794, during the whole of his reign governed altogether by his wives or
his freedmen.   He was poifoned by the contrivance of Agrippina his wife, and died on the 13th of October, in the fixty-
fourth year of his age, and the fourteenth of his reign, A. U.
807.   After his death he was numbered among the gods.   His
deification was treated with contempt and ridicule by Seneca, in
a tract ftill extant, entitled, *Claudii Cæfari Apocolokintofis*.   The
general defign of the piece is not ill imagined; but the humour
is often coarfe, and, upon the whole, inferior to what might
have been expected from the lively genius of that entertaining
writer.   Claudius, with all the appearance of inert faculties and
an impaffive mind, devoted his time, in repofe and indolence,
to literature and the polite arts.   He was not entirely void of
tafte.   His compofitions in Greek, as well as Latin, were written
with purity and even elegance.   Two pieces of a brafs table have
been found at Lyons, on which is engraved a fpeech of Claudius,
in characters fo plainly legible, that Dotteville (in his edition of
Tacitus) has given an exact copy, faithfully compared with the
original (fee at the end of his Notes to Annals, book xii.).—Suet.
Life of Claudius, f. 2, 10, 41, 42.   Tacit. Annal. xii. f. 69.
Seneca, APOCOLOKINTOSIS.   Pliny, book xxxvi. c. 15, f. 24.

101. PLAUTIA URGULANILLA, daughter of Aulus Plautius,
who had enjoyed the fplendour of a triumph.   She was the firft
wife of the emperor Claudius, and by him repudiated on account of her licentious manners, and a fufpicion of homicide
that blackened her character.—Suet. Life of Claudius, f. 26.
Dio, book lx.

102. DRUSUS, fon of the emperor Claudius and Urgulanilla.
A match between him and the daughter of Sejanus was projected

by that ambitious favourite A. U. 773; but Drufus, as yet of tender years, loft his life by an accident. A pear, which in a playful manner he had toffed up in the air, fell into his mouth and choked him.—Suet. Life of Claudius, f. 27. Tacit. Annal. iii. f. 29.

103. CLAUDIA, daughter of Urgulanilla. She was born in lefs than five months after her mother's divorce from Claudius; and yet the emperor thought proper to difown her as his child, alleging that fhe was begot by one of his freedmen, and as fuch he ordered her to be left naked at her mother's door.—Suet. Life of Claudius, f. 27.

104. ÆLIA PETINA, daughter of Quintus Ælius Tubero, who was conful A. U. 743. She was the fecond wife of Claudius, but on fome frivolous occafion foon repudiated.—Suet. Life of Claudius, f. 26.

105. ANTONIA, daughter of the emperor Claudius and Ælia Petina. Claudius gave her away in marriage to Cneius Pompeius (fee No. 106), and afterwards to Cornelius Sylla (fee No. 107). Nero, after the death of Poppæa, propofed to marry her; and his offer being rejected, he condemned her to fuffer death, on a pretended charge of plotting againft the ftate. —Suet. Life of Claudius, f. 27. Life of Nero, f. 35. Tacit. Annal. xii. f. 68.

106. CNEIUS POMPEIUS, a youth of noble defcent, married to Antonia (No. 105) A. U. 794. He was fome time after put to death by order of Claudius.—Suet. Life of Claudius, f. 27 and 29.

107. FAUSTUS

107. FAUSTUS CORNELIUS SYLLA, of illuſtrious birth, the ſecond huſband of Antonia (No. 105). He was baniſhed by Nero into Narbon Gaul, and there put to death by aſſaſſins diſpatched from Rome, A. U. 815.—Suet. Life of Claudius, ſ. 27. Tacit. Annal. xiii. ſ. 23; xiv. ſ. 57.

For MESSALINA, the third wife of Claudius, ſee No. 26.

108. BRITANNICUS, ſon of Claudius and Meſſalina, born 12th of February, A. U. 794. By his birth, and his father's intention, who carried him in his arms and recommended him as heir apparent to the affections of the army, he was next in ſucceſſion to the ſovereignty; but by the artful policy of Agrippina, the fourth wife of Claudius, he was poſtponed to Nero, and afterwards deſtroyed by poiſon, in the fourteenth year of his age, A. U. C. 808.—Suet. Life of Claudius, ſ. 27. Tacit. Annal. xii. ſ. 25; xiii. ſ. 15 and 16.

For OCTAVIA, the ſiſter of Britannicus, ſee No. 36.

For AGRIPPINA, the mother of Nero by Domitius Ænobarbus, and afterwards the wife of Claudius, ſee No. 93.

INDEX

I N D E X

TO THE

GENEALOGICAL TABLE

OF

THE CÆSARS.

No.

Domitius Ænobarbus, father of Nero   —   —   34
Domitius Lucius Ænobarbus, hufband of Antonia the elder   33
Domitius Nero, emperor of Rome   —   —   35
Drufilla, daughter of Germanicus   —   —   95
Drufilla, daughter of Caligula, fee Julia Drufilla.
Drufus, brother of Tiberius, emperor, fee Nero Drufus
   Claudius.
Drufus, fon of Claudius, emperor   —   —   102
Drufus Cæfar, fon of Tiberius, emperor   —   —   70
Drufus Cæfar, fon of Germanicus   —   —   83
Daughter of Pompey the Great   —   —   9

Æ.

Ælia Petina, daughter of Claudius, emperor   —   104
Æmilia Lepida, wife of Drufus Cæfar   —   —   84
Æmilia Lepida, wife of Junius Silanus   —   —   55
Æmilius Paulus, hufband of Julia, the daughter of Tiberius,
   emperor   —   —   —   —   53
Æmilius Lepidus, hufband of Drufilla   —   —   54

G.

Germanicus Cæfar, fon of Nero Claudius Drufus   —   79

J.

Julia, fifter of Cæfar the dictator   —   —   12
Julia, daughter of Cæfar the dictator   —   —   6
Julia, daughter of Auguftus   —   —   46
Julia, daughter of Agrippa   —   —   —   52
Julia, daughter of Drufus Cæfar   —   —   74
Julia Drufilla, daughter of Caligula   —   —   91
Julius Cæfar, father of Cæfar the dictator   —   —   1
Julius Cæfar, the dictator   —   —   —   3
Julius Antonius, hufband of Marcella the younger   —   29
Junia Calvina, wife of Vitellius   —   —   62

O.

P.

R.

S.

I   Silanus

NOTES

NOTES

ON THE

SIX LAST BOOKS

OF

THE ANNALS.

N O T E S

ON THE

ELEVENTH BOOK

OF

T H E   A N N A L S.

Section I.

THE former part of this book, comprising no lefs than fix years, is loft, with other parts of Tacitus. Claudius fucceeded to Caligula, who was put to death by Chærea and other confpirators, on the 24th of January, A. U. C. 794. The prefent book begins abruptly in the year of Rome 800, when Claudius had reigned fix years. The very firft fentence is imperfect. The hiftorian, beyond all doubt, had been fpeaking of Meffalina and Poppæa Sabina, but neither of them is mentioned in the mutilated text. To avoid beginning with a broken paffage, the tranflator has added their names, and the fenfe will now be found complete. Valerius Afiaticus had been conful twice; the firft time, for fome months, to fupply the place of the confuls who began the year A. U. C. 796; the fecond time, in conjunction with Marcus Junius Silanus, A. U. C. 799. Suetonius, in Claud. f. 14.

(*a*) Suilius has been already mentioned, Annals, book iv. f. 31; and for the infamy of his character, fee book xiii. f. 42.

(*b*) In the tumult occafioned by the death of Caligula, when the people were wild with contending paffions, and the prætorian guards paraded the ftreets denouncing vengeance againft the confpirators, Valerius Afiaticus (according to Jofephus) rufhed forward to meet them,

Vol. II.   3 M   proclaiming

proclaiming aloud, " I wiſh the tyrant had fallen by my hand." See Seneca, De Conſtantiâ, cap. 18.

(*c*) Formerly the capital of the Allobroges ; now Vienne in Dauphiné.

Section II.

(*a*) This was agreeable to the Roman manners. What man is aſhamed, ſays Cornelius Nepos, to take his wife with him to a convivial meeting ? *Quem enim Romanorum pudet uxorem ducere in convivium ?* Corn. Nep. in Præfatione.

Section V.

(*a*) Marcus Cincius, tribune of the people, was the author of the *Cincian Law*, ſo called after his name, in the conſulſhip of Sempronius and Cethegus, A. U. C. 550. It provided againſt the receipt of gifts and preſents, but, in a courſe of time, fell into diſuſe, till Auguſtus, A. U. 732, thought fit to revive it, with an additional clauſe, by which the advocate, who pleaded for hire, was condemned to pay four times the ſum. Claudius (as may be ſeen ſ. vii.) ſoftened the rigour of the law, allowing a certain fee, and ordaining, that whoever took more ſhould be obliged to make reſtitution.

Section VIII.

(*a*) Mithridates, brother to Pharaſmanes, king of Iberia, was appointed by Tiberius to ſway the ſceptre of Armenia, A. U. C. 788. See Annals, book vi. ſ. 32. He was afterwards brought to Rome in chains, and thrown into priſon by Caligula, A. U. 793. Tacitus ſays, he had given an account of this tranſaction ; but the hiſtory of Caligula is unfortunately loſt.

(*b*) For Seleucia, ſee the Geographical Table.

(*c*) The river here intended is the Tigris. See Geographical Table.

(*d*) For the Dahæ and Hyrcani, ſee the Geographical Table.

Section IX.

(*a*) This is the ſame Cotys who has been already mentioned, as king of part of Thrace. See Annals, book iv. ſ. 67 ; and ſee the note.

Caligula

Caligula added his divifion of that country to the dominions of Rhæ-
metalces, and made Cotys king of the leffer Armenia, A. U. C. 791.

Section X.

(*a*) For the river Erinde and Sinden, fee the Geographical Table.

Section XI.

(*a*) The fecular games were exhibited by Auguftus, in the confulfhip of Caius Furnius and C. Silanus, A. U. C. 737. The famous
Carmen Sæculare of Horace has made them univerfally known. In their
firft inftitution they were to be celebrated at the end of every century;
but that regulation, as we learn from Horace, was changed to every
hundred and ten years.

> Certus undenos decies per annos
> Orbis, ut cantus referatque ludos
> Ter die clarâ, totiefque gratâ
> Nocte frequentes.

The firft fecular games were in the confulfhip of Valerius and Virginius, A. U. C. 298.

The fecond, in the confulfhip of Valerius Corvinus and Caius Pæti-
lius, A. U. C. 408.

The third, in the confulfhip of Cornelius Lentulus and Licinius
Varus, A. U. C. 518.

The fourth, in the confulfhip of Æmilius Lepidus and Lucius
Aurelius, A. U. C. 628.

The fifth, by Auguftus, as above mentioned, 737.

The fixth, by Claudius, A. U. C. 800.

Tacitus fays, Claudius differed from the computation of Auguftus;
and for an explanation of that matter he refers us to the hiftory of Domitian, who alfo gave the fecular games, A. U. C. 841. But the
hiftory of Domitian has not reached pofterity. That monfter has
efcaped the vengeance due to his crimes from the pen of Tacitus.
The difference between the calculation of Auguftus and that of Claudius appears to be a fallacy of the latter emperor. Suetonius fays, he
exhibited the fecular games, under a pretence of their having been an-

3 M 2

ticipated

ticipated by Auguftus; and yet Claudius, in his hiftory, fairly owns, *that they had been neglected before the time of Auguftus; but that emperor made an exact calculation of the time, and again brought the games to their regular order.* For this reafon, when the cryer, by order of Claudius, invited the people, in the ufual form, *to games, which no one had ever feen, and would never fee again,* the people could not refrain from laughing, as many then living had feen them in the time of Auguftus, and fome of the players, who had acted on that occafion, were now brought upon the ftage again. Suet. in Claud. f. 21.

(*b*) The *Trojan Game*, commonly afcribed to Æneas, is beautifully defcribed by Virgil, Æneid v. ver. 545. Suetonius fays it was exhibited by Julius Cæfar, when two companies, one confifting of grown up lads, and the other of boys of a leffer fize, difplayed their fkill in horfemanfhip. Suet. in Jul. Cæf. f. 39. This may account for the appearance of Britannicus and Domitius Nero, both at that time extremely young. Britannicus was born A. U. C. 794; Nero in the year 790. See the Genealogical Table, No. 108 and No. 35.

(*c*) Suetonius explains the origin of this fable. He fays, there was a report, that certain affaffins were hired by Meffalina to ftrangle Nero in his bed, in order to remove the rival of Britannicus. The men went to execute their purpofe, but were frightened by a ferpent that crept from under his pillow. This tale was occafioned by the finding of a ferpent's fkin near Nero's pillow, which, by his mother's order, he wore for fome time upon his right arm, inclofed in a golden bracelet. Suetonius, in Neron. f. 6.

Section XII.

(*a*) Silius was conful elect, as already mentioned in this book, f. 5. Juvenal fays,

> ——————————— Elige quidnam
> Suadendum effe putes, cui nubere Cæfaris uxor
> Deftinat. Optimus hic, et formofiffimus idem
> Gentis patriciæ, rapitur mifer extinguendus
> Meffalinæ oculis.   SAT. x. ver. 331.

Now

Now Silius wants thy counfel; give advice;
Wed Cæfar's wife, or die.   The choice is nice.
Her comet-eyes fhe darts on ev'ry grace,
And takes a fatal liking to his face.

DRYDEN'S JUVENAL.

Section XIII.

(*a*) Pomponius had been conful, but not in the beginning of the year, and therefore his name does not appear in the *Fafti Confulares*. Quintilian praifes his dramatic genius, and admires his tragedies. See the Dialogue concerning Oratory, f. xiii. note (*c*).

(*b*) The *Simbruine Hills*, according to Brotier and other commentators, are the hills that overlook the town, formerly called *Sublaqueum*, now *Subjaco*, about forty miles from Rome, towards the eaft, and not far from the *Sacred Cave*, now *Il Monaftero del Sacro Speco*. The waters iffuing from two fountains, known by the names of *Curtius* and *Cæruleus*, were, by the direction of Claudius, brought to Rome in canals made with great labour and vaft expence. See Pliny's Defcription, lib. xxxvi. f. 15.

Section XIV.

(*a*) The invention of letters, one of the happieft exertions of the human mind, prefents a fubject of fo curious and complicated a nature, that the difcuffion of it cannot be condenfed into a note. Plato and Cicero were fo ftruck with the wonderful artifice of alphabetical characters, as to conclude that it was not of human invention, but a preternatural gift of the immortal gods. Dr. Warburton has given a differtation on the fubject, in which profound learning and found philofophy are happily united. After him, it may be ftated, that man, being formed for fociety, foon found two ways of communicating his thoughts; namely, by founds and fignificant action. But both were tranfient. Something permanent was ftill required; fomething, by which the conceptions of the mind might be preferved and communicated at a diftance. This was done by the images of things, properly called picture writing. Senfible objects were eafily reprefented, but abftract ideas demanded further improvement. That

difficulty

difficulty was alſo conquered. Men converſant in matter wanted ſenſible images to convey the ideas formed by the operations of the underſtanding. For that purpoſe, every object, in which could be found
any kind of reſemblance or analogy, was introduced to repreſent the
inward ſentiment: as an EYE, for knowledge; a CIRCLE, for eternity.
This was the ſymbolic writing of the Ægyptians, who attended chiefly
to the animal creation, and thereby eſtabliſhed the *brute-worſhip* of their
country. The ſeveral animals and ſymbolic figures being carved on
pyramids and obeliſks, by direction of the ſacerdotal order, the art of
expreſſing ideas by analogous repreſentation was deemed ſacred, and
thence called HIEROGLYPHIC. It had, at firſt, nothing in it of
myſtery: it was dictated by the neceſſities of man in ſocial life. The
Chineſe in the eaſt had their hieroglyphics. Picture-writing was known
to the Mexicans, in a world then undiſcovered; and, accordingly,
ACOSTA tells us, that the firſt account of a Spaniſh fleet on the coaſt,
was ſent to Montezuma in delineations painted on cloth. The ſame
writer adds, things that had a bodily ſhape, were repreſented by their
proper figures; and thoſe that were inviſible, by other expreſſive characters; and thus the Mexicans wrote or painted every thing they
had occaſion to expreſs. The Peruvians made uſe of arbitrary marks.
With their knotted cords of different colours, and various ſizes, they
contrived to convey their thoughts to one another. The Chineſe proceeded from their hieroglyphics to the invention of a ſignificant mark
for every idea. It is a miſtake to ſay that they formed an alphabet, or
letters to be the ſign of ſimple ſounds. Their characters do not ſtand
for ſyllables, of which articulate words are compoſed; they expreſs
the idea, or the object itſelf; and it is ſaid that they have no leſs than
ſeventy thouſand of ſuch arbitrary characters. The confuſion that
muſt follow is obvious. Signs for WORDS, not THINGS, were ſtill the
grand deſideratum. Some happy genius (who, it is not known) aroſe in
Ægypt. He had the ſagacity to obſerve the formation of ſounds by
the human organs, and ſoon perceived that ſeveral were frequently
united to conſtitute a word. By decompounding theſe, and fixing a
mark for vowels and conſonants, which might be afterwards blended
and varied as the word required, the art of writing was reduced to ſim

plicity,

plicity, and finally eftablifhed in its prefent form. Mofes brought alphabetic letters, with the reft of his learning, from Ægypt, and was, therefore, able to reduce his books to writing. Cadmus was of Thebes in Ægypt, and paffed from Phœnicia into Greece. His native country fhews whence he derived his alphabet; though the Phœnicians were, by vulgar error, faid to be the people who invented letters, and firft taught the art of *ftopping the flying found.*

> Phœnices primi, famæ fi creditur, aufi
> Manfuram rudibus vocem fignare figuris.
>
> LUCAN, lib. iii. ver. 220.

Pliny the elder gives the honour to the Affyrians : he fays, *Literas femper arbitror fuiffe Affyrias.* Lib. vii. f. 56. It is plain, however, that he was not rightly informed. See Warburton's Divine Legation, vol. iii. page 66, &c.; and fee Memoirs of the Academy of Belles Lettres, vol. xxxii. page 212.

(*b*) Dr. Warburton fays, the Hebrew alphabet, which Mofes employed in the compofition of the Pentateuch, is confiderably fuller than that which Cadmus brought into Greece. Cadmus had only fixteen letters, and the Hebrew had two-and-twenty. Divine Legat. vol. iii. page 148. We find from Tacitus, that the Greek alphabet received confiderable additions. As to the three letters added by Claudius to the Roman alphabet, Suetonius fays, he invented three new letters, concerning which he publifhed a book, while he was yet a private citizen; and, after his elevation to the imperial feat, his authority introduced them into common ufe, and the fame were ftill extant in books, regifters, and infcriptions on buildings. See Life of Claudius, f. 41. Brotier, in his edition of Tacitus, has given, from a brafs table found at Lyons, a fpeech made by Claudius to the fenate; but in that monument of antiquity no trace appears of thofe new letters.

Section XVII.

(*a*) For an account of Flavius, the father, fee Annals, book ii. f. 9 and 10.

(*b*) See the Geographical Table.

Section XVIII.

(a) For the Chaucians, fee the Geographical Table.

(b) The countries now called *Zelande, Brabant, Flanders.* In thofe parts there were feveral canals and inlets of the fea, between the *Scheld,* the *Meufe,* and the *Rhine.*

Section XIX.

(a) For the Frifians, fee the Geographical Table: and for Lucius Apronius, fee Annals, book iv. f. 73 and 74.

Section XX.

(a) For the Mattiaci, fee the Geographical Table.

Section XXI.

(a) Some of the commentators will have this perfon to be Quintus Curtius, the hiftorian of Alexander the Great; but this opinion is without foundation. Tacitus would not omit a circumftance fo very remarkable.

(b) For Adrumetum, fee the Geographical Table.

(c) This ftory is related as a fact by the younger Pliny, lib. vii. ep. 27.

Section XXII.

(a) In the confulfhip of Fulvius Flaccus and Lucius Manlius Acidinus, A. U. C. 575, Lucius Villius, tribune of the people, preferred a *rogatio* or bill, which paffed into a law, to fettle at what age the different magiftracies might be obtained. *Eo anno rogatio primum lata eft ab L. Villio, tribuno plebis, quot annos nati quemque magiftratum peterent caperentque.* Livy, lib. xl. f. 43. The quæftorfhip was the firft office any perfon could bear in the commonwealth, and, by the new regulation, might be undertaken at the age of twenty-four or twenty-five years. Kennet's Roman Antiquities, page 115.

(b) The *Comitia Curiata* owe their original to the divifion which Romulus made of the people into thirty curiæ, ten being contained in every tribe. They anfwered, in moft refpects, to the modern divifions of cities into parifhes. Before the inftitution of the *Comitia Centuriata,*

Centuriata, or affemblies of the people in their centuries, which were in number 193, inftituted by Servius Tullius, all the great concerns of the ftate were tranfacted in the curias; fuch as the electing of magiftrates, the making or abrogating of laws, and the decifion of capital caufes. Kennet's Roman Antiquities, page 129.

Section XXIII.

(*a*) Gallia *Comata*, a general name for the whole country on this fide of the Alps. See the Geographical Table.

(*b*) For the *Veneti* and *Infubres*, fee the Geographical Table.

(*c*) Alefia was befieged by Julius Cæfar. The town, fituated on the ridge of a hill, was almoft impregnable. It could not be taken by affault. Vercingetorix commanded the garrifon. Cæfar formed his lines of circumvallation, and was obliged to fit down before the place for a confiderable time. He has left a circumftantial account of all his operations, and alfo of the fpeech of Critognatus, a leading chieftain among the Gauls, when the garrifon, preffed by famine, debated whether they fhould capitulate, or fally out in a body, and die with glory, fword in hand. Cæfar records this man's fpeech, on account of its fingular and nefarious cruelty; *propter ejus fingularem ac nefariam crudelitatem.* Critognatus oppofed all terms of accommodation. To fally out, he faid, might be called an effort of brave defpair; but it was in fact the pufillanimity of men who dreaded the hardfhips of an approaching famine. But what was the conduct of the ancient Gauls, when befieged by the Cimbri and the Teutones? Reduced to the laft diftrefs, they devoured the bodies of all who were incapable of bearing arms, and held out to the laft. That, he faid, was a glorious precedent: it deferved to be imitated, and tranfmitted to pofterity. Alefia, after an obftinate refiftance, furrendered at difcretion, and Vercingetorix was delivered up. Cæfar, De Bell. Gall. lib. vii. f. 68 to the end of 89. For Alesia, fee the Geographical Table.

Section XXIV.

(*a*) It has been mentioned, note (*b*), f. 14, that a fpeech of Claudius, engraved on a tablet of brafs, has been found at Lyons. It is fet forth at length by Brotier, in his edition of Tacitus, vol. ii. 4to. page 349, and by Dotteville, vol. iv. page 422. The speech relates to the question stated by Tacitus, namely, the admission of the Gauls into the Roman senate. The historian has not given the argument in the form and words of the original speech. He has seized the substance, and expressed it with his usual brevity, in a style suited to an emperor, of whom he says, that in his prepared speeches he never wanted elegance. *Nec in Claudio, quoties meditata differeret, elegantiam requireres.*

Section XXV.

(*a*) We read in Suetonius, that Julius Cæsar filled up the vacancies in the senate, and advanced several commoners to the rank of patricians. Suet. in Jul. Cæf. f. 41. It should seem, from what Tacitus says, that he was willing to give colour to his proceedings, and therefore acted under a law called, after Cassius the consul for part of the year, the *Cassian law.* In like manner, Augustus adopted the same measure, and carried it into execution, under the authority of a law enacted in the consulship of Lucius Sænius, who was appointed to the office towards the end of the year, and therefore does not appear in the *Fasti Consulares.*

(*b*) The number of Roman citizens mentioned in this place would be thought altogether incredible, if the estimate were to be understood to relate to the inhabitants of the capital: but the question was not, what number dwelt within the walls of the city; it extended to the whole body of the Roman people, wherever stationed.

Section XXVIII.

(*a*) This was *Mnester*, the comedian, famous for his adulterous commerce with Messalina.

Section XXIX.

(*a*) As the whole history of Caligula is lost, the part which Callistus acted in the catastrophe of that emperor is not to be found in Tacitus. Cassius Chærea was the chief conspirator. He drew into his plot a number of leading men, and among them Callistus, a freedman

man enriched by the favours of Caligula.   To apologize, in some degree, for his perfidy and ingratitude, the enfranchifed flave gave out,
that he had orders from Caligula to adminifter poifon to Claudius.
By that ftory, whether true or falfe, he varnifhed over his treachery
to his benefactor, and fecured his intereft with the next emperor.

Section XXXVI.

(a) Lateranus was nephew to Aulus Plautius, the famous general
who commanded in Britain A. U. C. 796, and fubdued the fouthern
part of the ifland.   See the Life of Agricola, f. xiv ; and f. xvii. note (d).

Section XXXVIII.

(a) Claudius contracted an inceftuous marriage with the daughter
of his brother Germanicus : Agrippina deftroyed the emperor's fon
Britannicus, and afterwards difpatched Claudius himfelf, to open the
road to empire for her fon Nero, who, it is well known, was guilty of
parricide : and Narciffus, the favourite freedman, ended his days in a
dungeon.   Annals, book xiii. f. 1.

NOTES

ON THE

TWELFTH BOOK

OF

THE ANNALS.

Section II.

(a) SUETONIUS gives an account of the wives of Claudius in regular succession. His first wife was Plautia Urgulanilla. Being in a short time divorced from her, he married Ælia Petina, descended from a father of consular rank: by her he had a daughter named Antonia; for whom see the Genealogical Table, No. 105. For Ælia Petina, see No. 104. Claudius was divorced from his second wife. He then married Messalina, and by her had a daughter, Octavia, and a son named Britannicus. Lollia Paulina, who aspired on the present occasion to the imperial bed, had been married to Caligula, and was soon divorced. See for her the Genealogical Table, No. 99. Agrippina, the successful candidate, was the daughter of Germanicus, the brother of Claudius. For her, see the Genealogical Table, No. 93; and for the whole transaction as here related by Tacitus, see Suet. in Claud. f. 26.

Section III.

(a) Domitius, the son of Agrippina, was afterwards Nero the emperor. See the Genealogical Table, No. 35.

Section XI.

(*a*) Tiberius had given two kings to the Parthians, viz. Phraates and Tiridates.   Annals, book vi. f. 31 and 32.

Section XII.

(*a*) For the Arabs, fee the Geographical Table.

Section XIII.

(*a*) A people who inhabited a part of Mefopotamia. See the Geographical Table.

(*b*) Ninos, formerly the celebrated city of *Nineve*, the capital of Affyria.   See the Geographical Table.

(*c*) This mountain, and the river *Corma*, are mentioned by Tacitus only.

Section XV.

(*a*) Mithridates mentioned in this place was defcended from the great Mithridates, who waged the long war with the Romans, called the Mithridatic War.   Claudius, in a diftribution of kingdoms among the princes bordering on the Euxine, made the defcendant of Mithridates king of Bofphorus.

(*b*) The Dandaridæ inhabited a tract of country on the Euxine fhore. See the Geographical Table.

(*c*) A people near the Palus Mæotis.   See the Geographical Table.

Section XVI.

(*a*) The Aorfians were mentioned in the former fection.   See the Geographical Table.

(*b*) For Soza, fee the Geographical Table.

(*c*) Panda, a river not well known at prefent.

Section XVII.

(*a*) See the Geographical Table.

(*b*) Taurus, a chain of mountains in Afia.   See the Geographical Table.

2

Section

Section XVIII.

(*a*) Achæmenes was grandfather to Cambyfes, and after him the Perfian kings were called ACHÆMENIDÆ.

Section XXII.

(*a*) Suetonius has given fome particulars of the marriage of Caligula with Lollia Paulina. She was in a diftant province with her hufband Memmius Regulus, in whofe confulfhip Sejanus met his fate. See Annals, v. in the Supplement, f. 32. Regulus, in the time of Caligula, had the command of the army in Syria. Lollia Paulina, his wife, accompanied him to his government. Caligula called her back to Rome, and married her; but was foon divorced. Suet. in Calig. f. 25. Pliny the elder defcribes, with indignation, the immenfe and almoft incredible wealth, which fhe difplayed in her drefs, and the laboured ornaments of her perfon at the banquet after the marriage ceremony. He fays, he faw her finking under the load of diamonds that encumbered her robe, and fparkled in her hair, her ears, on her neck, her arms and fingers. This profufion of riches was not the gift of a prodigal emperor; but the fpoil of plundered provinces, acquired by her grandfather Marcus Lollius, while he commanded the Roman legions in the eaft. The emperor of Rome exhibited the plunder he had gained by profcriptions and the murder of Roman citizens; and a woman difplayed more magnificence, than ever entered into the imagination of the CURII and FABRICII. Pliny, lib. ix. f. 35.

Section XXIII.

(*a*) Agrippa was the defcendant of Herod the Great, who was made king of Judæa by a decree of the fenate A. U. C. 714, and died in the year 750, about four years before the Chriftian æra. Agrippa, his grandfon, was thrown into prifon by Tiberius, and reftored to his kingdom by Caligula. He died A. U. C. 797. Sohemus, mentioned in the text, was defcended from Sohemus king of Ituræa, who was murdered by Herod A. U. C. 726. See Jofephus; and for Ituræa, fee the Geographical Table.

(*b*) The precinct of the city of Rome was called the POMÆIRUM, as the antiquarians fay, from *ponere mænia*. The Romans had not the *new lights* that teach the legiflators of France to make *Atheifm* the foundation of their wild democracy. After a beginning fo truly impious and deteftable, no wonder that we fee no rule of juftice, no moral rectitude, no order in their legiflative affembly, and no power in their executive council to enforce obedience to the laws. They have eftablifhed civil and religious anarchy :. rapine, murder, and every crime that fhocks humanity have been the confequence. The Romans had the good fenfe to fet out with other principles. Even in that dark age they had an idea of a fuperintending Providence, and referred every thing to the immortal Gods. The very walls of Rome were confecrated to tutelar deities, and accordingly confidered as facred. The vacant fpace on both fides of the wall was holy ground ; *quod neque habitari, neque arari fas erat*. As the city increafed, the fame religious ceremony was obferved. *In urbis incremento femper, quantum mænia proceffura erant, tantum termini hi confecrati proferebantur.* Livy, lib. i. f. 44. To enlarge the precinct of Rome was called *Jus proferendi pomærii* ; but that right was of fuch confequence, that it was allowed to none but thofe who extended the boundaries of the empire. After the inclofure of the feven hills by the kings of Rome, *feptemque una fibi muro circumdedit arces.* Sylla, the dictator, was the firft who had the honour of widening the Pomærium, A. U.C. 674. Seneca de Brevit. Vitæ, cap. xiv. Julius Cæfar, after all his victories, claimed the fame right, A. U. C. 710; and Auguftus followed his example, A. U.C. 746. Dio, lib. xliii. The number of inhabitants, when Rome was in its flourifhing ftate, Lipfius computes at four millions. Brotier has offered a more probable conjecture. He compares Paris and London with Rome ; and his numbers, on a fair calculation, are :

Paris	—	—	640,000
London	—	—	768,000
Rome	—	—	1,188,000

Brotier proceeds in his eftimate to the Chinefe empire, where he reckons two hundred million of inhabitants, whereas the number in

Europe

Europe is computed at 130 million. See Brotier's Tacitus, vol. ii. page 379, 4to edit.

Section XXV.

(a) Attus Claufus, called afterwards Appius Claudius, has been mentioned, book xi. f. 24, as the founder of the Claudian family. We are told the fame by Virgil:

> Ecce Sabinorum prifco de fanguine magnum
> Agmen agens CLAUSUS, magnique ipfe agminis inftar;
> Claudia nunc a quo diffunditur et tribus et gens
> Per Latium, poftquam in partem data Roma Sabinis.

> ÆNEID. vii. ver. 706.

Section XXVII.

(a) For an account of the Ubians, originally a people of Germany, afterwards changed into a Roman colony, fee the Manners of the Germans, f. xxviii. note (g).

(b) See the Geographical Table.

Section XXVIII.

(a) See the Geographical Table.

Section XXIX.

(a) Maroboduus being expelled from his dominions, and, under an appearance of protection, detained as a ftate prifoner at Ravenna, Vannius was made king by Drufus, the fon of Tiberius, A. U. C. 772. Annals, book ii. f. 63.

(b) Lygians, a people of Germany. See the Geographical Table.

(c) Jazyges, a people of Sarmatia. See the Geographical Table.

Section XXXI.

(a) As Tacitus's account of the fix firft years of Claudius is loft, the invafion of Britain, under the command of Aulus Plautius, has not occurred either in this book, or that which precedes it. It is, therefore, proper to mention in this place, that, from the defcent made

by

by Julius Cæsar, A. U. C. 699, and, after him, Aulus Plautius was the firſt Roman general that landed in Britain, A. U. C. 796. Veſpaſian, afterwards emperor, ſerved in that expedition. The ſouthern parts of the iſland were reduced to ſubjection. Claudius viſited his new conqueſt, and at his return, having enlarged the Roman empire, entered Rome in triumph. We now find that Oſtorius Scapula ſucceeded to Aulus Plautius. The ſequel will ſhew the ſpirit of liberty that inſpired the Britons, and the conſummate ability with which the Roman general triumphed over a fierce and warlike people. For the ſeveral officers who commanded in Britain, from this time to the arrival of Agricola, A. U. C. 831, ſee the Life of Agricola, ſ. xvii. note *(d)*. For the rivers ANTONA, now the *Avon*; SABRINA, now the *Severn*; and AUFONA, now the *Nen*; ſee the Geographical Table. Camden is of opinion that ANTONA, the *Avon*, has found its way into the text by miſtake, and that the true reading ſhould be AUFONA, the *Nen*. See Camden's Britannia, by Gibſon, 431. Camden's opinion has been followed in the tranſlation.

(*b*) The *Iceni* inhabited *Norfolk, Suffolk, Cambridgeſhire*, and *Huntingdonſhire*. See Life of Agricola, ſ. xi. note (*a*).

Section XXXII.

(*a*) The *Cangi* inhabited *Cheſhire*, and part of *Lancaſhire*, oppoſite to Ireland.

(*b*) *Brigantes*, the people inhabiting *Yorkſhire, Durham, Cumberland*, and *Weſtmoreland*.

(*c*) *Silures*; the people who occupied *Herefordſhire, Radnor, Brecknock, Monmouth*, and *Glamorgan*, and in general *South-Wales*.

(*d*) Camelodunum, now *Colcheſter*.

Section XXXIII.

(*a*) Caractacus, according to Camden, reigned in the county of *Cardigan*.

(*b*) *Ordovices*, the people of *North-Wales*.

(*c*) This ſpot, Camden ſays, was in *Shropſhire*, where the COLUNUS, now the *Cinne*, runs into the TEMDUS, now *Temd*, not far from a hill called *Caer-Carodoc*.

Section XXXV.

(*a*) This river, according to Camden, was the *Temd*.

Section XXXVI.

(*a*) Aulus Plautius, as mentioned f. xxxi. note (*a*), invaded Britain A. U. C. 796; an active and warlike chieftain in every campaign against the Romans. Tacitus is never better pleased, than when he has an opportunity of doing justice to the chiefs of foreign nations, who distinguished themselves by their virtue, their courage, and their love of liberty. See his character of Arminius, Annals, ii. f. 88. Caractacus, in like manner, is represented in the brightest colours; great in the field of battle, and not less so before the emperor Claudius, in the presence of the Roman people. Mr. Mason has formed a noble dramatic poem on the subject. He has made a fine use of Tacitus in many passages, but in none more than in the following lines, which the reader will see are a beautiful insertion from the real speech of Caractacus to the emperor Claudius:

———— Soldier, I had arms;
Had neighing steeds to whirl my iron car;
Had wealth, dominion. Dost thou wonder, Roman,
I fought to save them? What, if Cæsar aims
To lord it universal o'er the world,
Shall the world tamely crouch at Cæsar's footstool?

AULUS DIDIUS.

Read in thy fate our answer. Yet if sooner
Thy pride had yielded—

CARACTACUS.

Thank the gods, I did not.
Had it been so, the glory of thy master,
Like my misfortunes, had been short and trivial,
Oblivion's ready prey. Now, after struggling

Nine

Nine years, and that right bravely, 'gainſt a tyrant,
I am his ſlave to treat as ſeems him good.
If cruelly, 'twill be an eaſy taſk
To bow a wretch, alas! how bow'd already!
Down to the duſt: If well, his clemency,
When trick'd and varniſh'd by your gloſſing penman,
Will ſhine in honour's annals.

If Mr. Maſon has departed from the ſtrict line of hiſtorical truth, he has done it with the privilege of a poet, and his poem is enriched by the fiction. The iſle of Mona was not attacked till A. U. C. 814, when Suetonius Paulinus inveſted the place, ten years after Caractacus was led a priſoner to Rome; nor was that iſland finally reduced till the year 831. See the Life of Agricola, ſ. xviii. Virgil, it is well known, adorned his poem by bringing together Dido and Æneas. The ſame diſregard of chronology may be allowed to the author of Caractacus, ſince, by making his hero take ſanctuary among the DRUIDS in Mona, he has produced the epiſodical incidents of a beautiful piece. But why the honour of taking Caractacus priſoner, and ſending him to Rome, ſhould be transferred from OSTORIUS to AULUS DIDIUS, no good reaſon appears. Didius did not command in Britain till that event was paſſed. On the death of OSTORIUS, he was appointed go-vernor; a tame inactive officer, who did not, as we are told by Tacitus, diſtinguiſh himſelf by one warlike exploit.

Section XL.

(a) It is not to be inferred from this paſſage, that it was a general principle with the Britons not to acquieſce under a female reign. Boadicea, as will be ſeen hereafter, was queen of the Iceni; and ſhe, at the head of her army juſt going to give battle, tells the ſoldiers, " It is not the firſt time that the Britons took the field under the conduct of a woman." Book xiv. ſ. 35. The fact was, the people ſaw a warlike chief oppreſſed by his wife, and therefore reſolved to ſubmit no longer to the tyranny of a woman.

Section

Section XLII.

(*a*) Agrippina was the daughter of Germanicus, fister of Caligula, the wife of Claudius, and the mother of Nero. Racine, who has many fine infertions from Tacitus in his tragedy of Britannicus, has imitated this paffage:

Moi, fille, femme, fœur, et mere de vos maîtres.

Section XLV.

(*a*) GORNEAS, a caftle in Armenia, according to D'Anville, now called *Khorien.* For Artaxata and Tigranocerta, fee the Geographical Table. The ftory of Rhadamiftus and Zenobia, which is here related by Tacitus, furnifhed Crébillon, the celebrated French poet, a fubject for one of his beft tragedies. Pharafmanes and his fon Rhadamiftus are reprefented, with hiftorical truth, in all the colours of their guilt; the former, as acceffary to the death of his brother Mithridates; and the latter, as the murderer of his uncle. Rhadamiftus, in the end, dies by the hand of his father. In fact, he was afterwards put to death by Pharafmanes. Annals, xiii. f. 37. The Englifh tragedy of ZENOBIA deviates fo far from Tacitus, as to reprefent Rhadamiftus in an amiable light. The fable, or plot, is almoft entirely new; and the cataftrophe aims at the paffions of terror and pity, inftead of exciting horror; an emotion of the mind, to which the ftrong but fombre genius of Crébillon feems to have had a peculiar bias.

Section LIII.

(*a*) Suetonius fays that the law, of which Pallas was the firft mover, was afterwards enforced by Vefpafian, who caufed a decree to pafs, enacting that the woman, who married the flave of another perfon, fhould be deemed a flave. Suet. in Vefp. f. xi. Pliny the conful fays, that he himfelf faw, on the Tiburtine road, near the firft milestone, a monument erected to the memory of Pallas, with an infcription, importing, that the fenate voted to Pallas the prætorian ornaments, and a fum of fifteen millions of fefterces, as a reward for his fidelity, and regard for his patrons. See book vii. epift. 29. In a fubfequent letter, Pliny mentions the fame fact again. He ftates the

words

words of the inscription: *Huic senatus, ob fidem pietatemque erga patronos, ornamenta prætoria decrevit, et sestertium centies quinquegies; cujus honore contentus fuit.* Pliny adds, that he had the curiosity to infpect the decree, and he found the infcription modeft, in comparifon with the lavifh praife beftowed upon an infolent upftart by the fenate. Pallas refufed the money; and to complete the farce, the fenate voted that the emperor fhould requeft a manumitted flave to yield to the entreaty of the fathers. Pallas ftill perfifted to reject the money, profeff.ng to have a foul above the love of wealth. It was decreed, that the honours of that arrogant wretch, as well thofe which he refufed, as thofe which he accepted, fhould be infcribed on brafs, as a public and lafting monument. See the account at large, Pliny, lib. viii. epift. 6.

Section LV.

(*a*) See the Geographical Table.

Section LVI.

(*a*) For the lake *Fucinus*, and the river *Liris*, fee the Geographical Table.

(*b*) Suetonius fays, Claudius attempted the Fucine lake, as much with a view to the glory of the performance, as an expectation of advantage. He finifhed a canal three miles in length, partly by cutting through, and partly by levelling a mountain; a work of prodigious difficulty, thirty thoufand men having been employed in conftant labour for eleven years together. Suet. in Claud. f. 20.

(*c*) Brotier fays, the circumference of the lake was fix-and-twenty miles.

(*d*) Pliny the elder fays, he himfelf faw Agrippina, the wife of Claudius, at the naval fpectacle, adorned with a magnificent robe wrought in pure gold, without any intermixture of other materials. *Nos vidimus Agrippinam Claudii principis, edente eo navalis prælii fpectaculum, affidentem ei, indutam paludamento, auro textili, fine aliâ materiâ.* Pliny, lib. xxxiii. f. 19.

Section LX.

(*a*) CAIUS SEMPRONIUS GRACCHUS was the author of a law in favour of the Roman knights, A. U. C. 632. He added three hundred of the equestrian order to the same number of senators, and vested in that body all judicial authority. The *Servilian* law, introduced by QUINTUS SERVILIUS CÆPIO, in his consulship A. U. C. 648, repealed the *Sempronian* institution, and restored the jurisdiction of the senate.

Section LXI.

(*a*) See the Geographical Table.

Section LXII.

(*a*) Now *Constantinople.* See the Geographical Table.

(*b*) An obscure man of the name of Andriscus pretended to be the son of Perseus. He was found to be an impostor, and therefore called Pseudophilippus. He was defeated, and taken prisoner by Metellus, A. U. C. 606.

(*c*) Antiochus III. king of Syria, waged war against the Romans, and was conquered by Lucius Cornelius Scipio, A. U. C. 564. Perseus, king of Macedonia, was subdued by Paulus Æmilius, A. U. C. 586. Aristonicus invaded Asia, and was overthrown by Perperna, A. U. C. 623.

(*d*) The people of Cilicia fitted out a number of armed ships, and over-ran the Mediterranean. This was called the Piratic War. Marcus Antonius, son of the famous orator of that name, and father of Antony the triumvir, was sent, with extraordinary powers given to him in his commission, to clear the seas of those roving freebooters, A. U. C. 684. The war however was not brought to a conclusion. In the year 687, the same commission was given to Pompey, notwithstanding the strong opposition of Quintus Catulus, who thought that Pompey was growing too great for his country, and therefore entered his public protest against trusting the commonwealth to the hands of one man. See Velleius Paterculus, lib. ii. s. 31 ; and see Cicero, Pro Lege Manilia.

Section LXIII.

(*a*) Montesquieu makes an ingenious use of this passage: Having bestowed his encomium on the British constitution, he observes that

        Harrington,

Harrington, in his *Oceana*, has ſtrained his idea of liberty to ſo high a pitch, that it may amuſe in theory, but never can exiſt in practice. He built CHALCEDON, when he had BYZANTIUM before his eyes. Spirit of Laws, vol. i. page 324.

Section LXIV.

(*a*) Domitia Lepida is ſaid in the original to have been the daughter of the younger Antonia. But this, according to Suetonius, is a miſtake. Antony the triumvir had two daughters, each called Antonia, by Octavia, the ſiſter of Auguſtus. The eldeſt, Suetonius ſays, was married to Lucius Domitius Ænobarbus, and by him was the mother of Cneius Domitius Ænobarbus, the firſt huſband of Agrippina, and by her the father of Nero. See the Genealogical Table, No. 32, 33 and 34. Antonia the younger was married to Druſus, the brother of Tiberius, and by him was the mother of Germanicus and the emperor Claudius. See her character, Annals, iv. in the Supplement, ſ. 27; and ſee the Genealogical Table, No. 42.

Section LXVI.

(*a*) For Sinueſſa, ſee the Geographical Table. The waters of this place are recommended for their ſalubrity by Pliny the elder, lib. xxxi. ſ. 2.

Section LXIX.

(*a*) The thirteenth of October.

NOTES

ON THE

THIRTEENTH BOOK

OF

THE ANNALS.

Section I.

(*a*) THIS was Marcus Junius Silanus, the fon of Junius Silanus and Æmilia Lepida, the grand-daughter of Auguſtus. See the Genealogical Table, No. 55, 56 and 57.

(*b*) See Annals, xii. f. 57 and 65.

Section III.

(*a*) Nero's paffion for the elegant arts, had he known how to reſtrain it within due bounds, might have been not unworthy of a prince; but we ſhall ſee him in the ſequel as ridiculous for his taſte, as he was deteſtable for his vices.

Section IV.

(*a*) See the trial of Valerius Afiaticus in the apartment of Claudius, Annals, xi. f. 2.

(*b*) This ſpeech gave univerſal ſatisfaction. It was, probably, written by Seneca. While it promiſed a reign of moderation, it ſerved to give the young prince a leſſon on the true and popular arts of government. Dio tells us, that the ſenate ordered it to be engraved on a pillar of ſolid ſilver, and to be publicly read every year at the time when the conſuls entered on their magiſtracy. Dio, lib. lxi.

Section V.

(*a*) This corrupt practice, which was nothing less than open bribery, was established by law in the reign of Claudius. Annals, xi. f. 22.

Section VII.

(*a*) Agrippa was king of Judæa; Antiochus, of Commagene. See the Geographical Table.

(*b*) The Lesser Armenia was on this side of the Euphrates. See the Geographical Table. Aristobulus was the son of Herod, who formerly reigned in *Chalcis*.

(*c*) For the country called Sophene, see the Geographical Table.

Section VIII.

(*a*) See the Geographical Table.

Section XI.

(*a*) For Plautius Lateranus, see Annals, xi. f. 36.

Section XII.

(*a*) Acte was a purchased slave from Asia. Suetonius says that Nero, being at one time determined to marry her, suborned several men of consular rank to swear that she was of royal descent. Suet. in Neron. f. 28.

(*b*) Otho, afterwards emperor.

Section XIII.

(*a*) Annæus Serenus was high in the esteem and friendship of Seneca, as appears, epist. lxiii.

Section XIV.

(*a*) Pallas was the person who prevailed on Claudius to contract an incestuous marriage with his niece Agrippina. From that time his influence was beyond all bounds. Suetonius says he was the prince's treasurer: *Pallantem a rationibus*. The decree of the senate in honour of this insolent freedman has been mentioned, Annals, xii. f. 53, and

note (*a*).   Suetonius fays, that Pallas and Narciffus plundered the public with fuch violent rapacity, that Claudius at length complained of
the impoverifhed ftate of his exchequer, when it was archly faid, his
*coffers would be full enough, if his two freedmen would take him into part-
nerfhip.*   Suet. in Claud. l. 28.   The difmiffion of fuch a man from
court, and all his employments, was a fatal blow to Agrippina.   The
fpeech in which fhe gives vent to her indignation is finely imitated by
Racine, in his tragedy of Britannicus :

> Pallas n'emporte pas tout l'appui d'Agrippine ;
> Le ciel m'en laiffe affez pour venger ma ruine.
> Le fils de Claudius commence à reffentir
> Des crimes, dont je n'ai que le feul repentir.
> J'irai, n'en doutez point, le montrer à l'armée ;
> Plaindre aux yeux des foldats fon enfance opprimée ;
> Leur faire, à mon exemple, expier leur erreur,
> On verra, d'un coté, le fils d'un empereur
> Redemandant la foi jurée à fa famille ;
> Et de Germanicus on attendra la fille :
> De l'autre, l'on verra le fils d'Ænobarbus,
> Appuyé de Seneque, et du tribun Burrhus ;
> Qui tous deux, de l'exil rappellés par moi-même,
> Partagent à mes yeux l'autorité fuprême.
> De nos crimes communs je veux qu'on foit inftruit ;
> On fçaura les chemins par où je l'ai conduit.
> J'avoûrai les rumeurs les plus injurieufes :
> Je confefferai tout, exils, affaffinats,
> Poifon même . . . .

Section XV.

(*a*) The Saturnalia began on the feventeenth of December, and lafted fifteen days.   Horace fays to his flave, who wants to exercife the
equality allowed during the feftival,

> ————— Age, libertate Decembri,
> Quando ita majores voluerunt, utere ; narra.

(*b*) In

(*b*) In this play of *Who shall be King?* the boys threw dice to decide their chance. Horace alludes to this custom, when he says,

Non regna vini sortiere talis.

Lib. i. ode 4.

And again,

Roscia, dic sodes, melior lex, an puerorum
Nænia, quæ regnum rectè facientibus offert.

Lib. i.

(*c*) The commentators cite some verses of Ennius, which they suppose were sung by Britannicus on this occasion. But what they say is mere conjecture.

Section XVIII.

(*a*) They took the palaces, villas, and estates of Britannicus.

Section XXII.

(*a*) Seneca calls Balbillus the best of men, and a scholar of uncommon erudition. *Virorum optimus, in omni literarum genere rarissimus.* See Quæst. Nat. cap. iv. s. 2.

(*b*) The Romans had three ways of exterminating a man from his country; namely, *Exilium*, *Relegatio*, and *Deportatio*. The person condemned to exile lost the rights of a citizen, and forfeited all kinds of property. Sentence of relegation removed the person to a certain distance from Rome; but, if no fine was imposed, it took away no other right. *Deportation* was invented by Augustus. It was the severest kind of banishment. The person condemned was hurried away in chains, stripped of all property, and confined to some island or inhospitable place.

Section XXVII.

(*a*) The Romans had two different modes of enfranchisement, or of granting freedom to their slaves. The first was performed by the prætor, who ordered the slave to turn round, and with a switch or cane struck him on the head or back, informing him that he was thereby manumitted. The second way of granting freedom was by writing under the master's hand, or by his voluntary declaration in the

3 P 2

presence

prefence of a few friends. The moft folemn mode of manumiffion was that by the rod, called *Vindiɛ̃a :* hence Perfeus the fatirift fays, *Vindiɛ̃a poftquam meus a prætore receffi.* The perfon fo enfranchifed, obtained all the rights of a Roman citizen. The fecond form of manumiffion conveyed to the flave a degree of liberty, but did not rank him in the clafs of citizens, nor allow him to be in any cafe a legal witnefs. The confequence was, that the patron, who granted freedom by his own private act, had time to confider, whether the flave, whom he releafed, was worthy of a further favour. He might, if he thought proper, inveft him with all the rights of a citizen by the more folemn mode of manumiffion before the prætor. See Heineccius, Antiquit. Roman. Jurif. i. tit. 4 and 5.

(b) Paris the comedian was a flave belonging to Domitia, the emperor's aunt. See the Genealogical Table, No. 40. He had paid a fum of money for the degree of liberty, which her private act conferred, and ftill remained in her lift of freedmen. Afpiring above that rank, he pretended to be ingenuous by his birth, and, by confequence, intitled to all the rights of a Roman citizen; and his plea, we find, was admitted. It is faid that Domitia was obliged to repay to the pantomime actor, the money which fhe had received for his freedom.

Section XXIX.

(a) It has been already obferved, that *Ærarium* was the treafury of the public; *Fifcus,* that of the prince. Pliny the elder fays, that, in the time of the republic, when the private exchequer of the emperor was a thing unknown, the money in the treafury, A. U. C. 663, amounted to a prodigious fum. It was ftill greater when Julius Cæfar, in the beginning of the civil war, A. U. 705, made himfelf mafter of all the riches of the commonwealth. From that time the diffipation of the emperors, and the rapacity of their favourites, effectually drained the *Ærarium,* and impoverifhed the ftate.

Section XXXI.

(a) This amphitheatre was built entirely with wood. Suetonius fays it was completed within the year; and that Nero, in the public

fpectacles.

fpeƈacles which he exhibited, gave orders that none of the combatants fhould be ſlain, not even the criminals employed upon that occaſion. Suet. in Neron. ſ. 12. See Pliny, lib. xvi. ſ. 40.

(*b*) A tax on all commodities expoſed to ſale was impoſed by Auguſtus, in the conſulſhip of Metellus and Nerva, A. U. C. 755. Dio ſays it was at firſt the fiftieth penny, but we find that in time the ſum was doubled.

Seƈion XXXII.

(*a*) This was Aulus Plautius, who, in the reign of Claudius, made the firſt deſcent on Britain. See the Life of Agricola.

(*b*) Lipſius and other commentators are of opinion, that what is here called a foreign ſuperſtition, was the Chriſtian religion.

(*c*) Suetonius tells us, that Claudius put to death the two Julias, the daughters of Druſus and Germanicus, without any proof of guilt, and without ſo much as hearing them in their defence, A. U. C. 796. Suet. in Claud. ſ. 29.

Seƈion XXXIII.

(*a*) See this book, ſ. 1.

Seƈion XXXIV.

(*a*) Corvinus Meſſala was joint conſul with Auguſtus, A. U. C. 723. For more of him, ſee the Dialogue concerning Oratory.

Seƈion XXXVI.

(*a*) This mode of puniſhment was eſtabliſhed by ancient uſage. Livy relates, that the cohorts, which had loſt their colours, were obliged to remain on the outſide of the camp, without their tents, and were found in that condition by Valerius Maximus the diƈator. *Cohortes, quæ ſigna amiſerant, extra vallum ſine tentoriis deſtitutas invenit diƈator Valerius Maximus.* Livy, lib. x. ſ. 4.

Seƈion XXXVII.

(*a*) See the Geographical Table.
(*b*) For the Hyrcanians, ſee the Geographical Table.

Seƈion

Section XXXIX.

(*a*) For Trebizonde, see the Geographical Table.

(*b*) Lipsius says, this castle is mentioned by no other ancient author.

(*c*) See the Geographical Table.

(*d*) For the Araxes, see the Geographical Table.

Section XLII.

(*a*) For this man, Suillius, see Annals, iv. s. 31; Annals, xi. s. 1.

(*b*) For the Cincian law against the venality of orators, see Annals, xi. s. 5 and 7.

(*c*) This was Julia, the daughter of Germanicus. Seneca was accused of an intrigue with her, and banished by Claudius to the isle of Corsica, A. U. C. 794. He was recalled by the influence of Agrippina, Annals, xii. s. 8.

(*d*) The charge of usury, with which the memory of Seneca is loaded, rests chiefly on the authority of Dio. By that historian we are told that the philosopher had placed immense sums at interest in Britain, and, by his vexatious and unrelenting demands of payment, was the cause of insurrections among the Britons. Dio's veracity has been questioned, but the passage in Tacitus gives some colour to the charge.

Section XLIII.

(*a*) Quintus Pomponius has been mentioned before; Annals, vi. s. 18. For the death of Sabina Poppæa, see Annals, xi. s. 2.

(*b*) For the Baleares, see the Geographical Table.

Section XLIV.

(*a*) In this account of the varying passions of lovers, Tacitus seems to have had his eye on the passage in Terence:

> In amore hæc omnia insunt vitia: injuriæ,
> Suspiciones, inimicitiæ, induciæ,
> Bellum, pax rursum.   Eunuch. act. i. s. 14.

(*b*) He was sent into banishment. History, iv. s. 44.

Section XLV.

(*a*) Probably the fame who was conful A. U. C. 762.

(*b*) Her mother Poppæa has been mentioned, Annals, xi. f. 1 and 2.

(*c*) The name of the fon was Rufinus Crifpinus, who, we are told by Suetonius, was thrown into the fea by order of Nero, becaufe he was reported to act among his play-fellows the part of a general or an emperor. Suet. in Neron. f. 35. Otho, who fucceeded fo well with Poppæa, was afterwards emperor.

Section XLVII.

(*a*) See the Geographical Table.

(*b*) Brotier fays, now *Villa Belloni* and *Villa Verofpi*, near the gate called *Salara*.

Section XLVIII.

(*a*) See the Geographical Table.

Section L.

(*a*) The oppreffions exercifed by this clafs of men are often mentioned by Tacitus, Livy, and other Roman hiftorians.

Section LI.

(*a*) See Montefquieu on this fubject, Spirit of Laws, book xiii. ch. 19.

Section LII.

(*a*) Sulpicius Camerinus, with his fon, was afterwards put to death by Nero. See Appendix to the xvith book of the Annals.

Section LIII.

(*a*) Drufus, the father of Germanicus, died in Germany A. U. C. 745. He had finifhed a canal, as mentioned Annals, ii. f. 8; and to prevent the overflowings of the Rhine, which often deluged the adjacent parts of Gaul, he laid the plan of a ftrong bank, by which the waters would have been thrown into a different courfe, and difcharged into the lakes, now the *Zuyder-zee*. This great work was at length finifhed by Paulinus Pompeius.

(*b*) The

(*b*) The *Arar* is now the *Soane*. Brotier obferves, that this great undertaking, tending to communicate the Mediterranean and the Ocean, often attempted, and as often abandoned, was at length accomplifhed, to the immortal glory of Lewis XIV. That imperial work, worthy of a king, is now called the *Royal Canal*, or the Canal of *Languedoc*,

Section LIV.

(*a*) For the Frifians, fee the Geographical Table.

(*b*) Pliny the elder fays, that Pompey's theatre was large enough to hold forty thoufand men. Pliny, lib. xxxvi. f. 15.

(*c*) The Germans had no idea of any kind of public fpectacle but that which they had feen in their own country. Manners of the Germans, f. xxiv.

Section LV.

(*a*) The country into which the irruption was made, is fuppofed to be the land between *Wefel* and *Duffeldorf*. The Anfibarians, before they were expelled by the Chaucians, inhabited between the river *Amifia* (the *Ems*) and the *Rhine*.

(*b*) The revolt of the Cherufcans, in which Varus and his three legions perifhed. Annals, book i. f. 10.

(*c*) For the Chamavians, the Tubantes, and Ufipians, fee the Manners of the Germans, f. 32 and 33.

Section LVI.

(*a*) For the Bructerians and Tencterians, fee the Manners of the Germans, f. 32 and 33.

(*b*) The country on the borders of the river *Luppia*, now the *Lippe*.

Section LVII.

(*a*) See the Geographical Table.

(*b*) This was the river *Sala*, ftill known by the fame name. It difcharges itfelf into the *Albis*, now the *Elbe*.

(*c*) This method of producing falt is explained by Pliny in his Natural Hiftory, lib. xxxi. f. 7.

5

Section LVIII.

(*a*) It was supposed that under the shade of this tree Romulus and Remus were nourished by the she-wolf, as beautifully described by Virgil:

> Fecerat et viridi fœtam Mavortis in antro
> Procubuisse lupam: Geminos huic ubera circum
> Ludere pendentes pueros, et lambere matrem
> Impavidos; illam tereti cervice revulsam
> Mulcere alternos, et corpora fingere linguâ.

Æneid, lib. viii.

Rumen was an old Latin word for *mamma*, or the dug of the she-wolf: thence the tree was called RUMINALIS.

(*b*) Some of the commentators think that there is a mistake in the computation, and that it ought to be eight hundred and thirty years. The difference is not material.

NOTES

ON THE

FOURTEENTH BOOK

OF

THE ANNALS.

Section I.

(*a*) **O**THO, afterwards emperor. See book xiii. f. 45 and 46.

Section II.

(*a*) Acte has been already mentioned, Annals, xiii. f. 12.

(*b*) Marcus Æmilius Lepidus. See the Genealogical Table, No. 54.

Section III.

(*a*) See the Geographical Table.

Section IV.

(*a*) A feaft in honour of Minerva, beginning on the nineteenth of March, and continued for five days. See Ovid, Faft. lib. iii. ver. 713 and 810.

(*b*) *Bauli*, formerly the feat of Hortenfius, was famous for great plenty of fifh; hence at this day the name of *Pefchiera d'Ortenfio*.

Section V.

(*a*) The Lucrine Lake, now *Lago Lucrino*. Agrippina's villa was at *Bauli*. There is in the neighbourhood a place now called *Sepolchro d'Agrippina*.

Section IX.

(a) It is still called, as mentioned above, *Sepolchro d'Agrippina.*

(b) Marius, Pompey, and Cæsar had their villas in the neighbourhood of *Baiæ,* all built on the ridge of hills, and looking, as Seneca says, more like military works than a rural seat. *Scias non villas esse, sed castra.* Epist. 51.

Section XI.

(a) See her attempt prevented by Seneca, Annals, xiii. s. 5.

Section XII.

(a) This eclipse was the day before the kalends of May, that is, on the 30th of April, A. U. C. 812; of the Christian æra 59. See Pliny, lib. ii. s. 70.

(b) For Junia Calvina, see Annals, xii. s. 8; and the Genealogical Table, No. 62. For Calpurnia, Annals, xii. s. 22.

(c) For Lollia Paulina, see Annals, xii. s. 22.

(d) Iturius and Calvisius banished by Nero; Annals, xiii. s. 22.

(e) Silana was also banished by Nero; Annals, xiii. s. 22.

Section XIV.

(a) This was a circus begun by Caligula, and finished by Nero. The church of St. Peter is built on this spot, and the obelisk which stood there, was placed before St. Peter's, at a vast expence, by Pope Sextus V.

Section XV.

(a) We are told by Dio, that Ælia Catella, a woman of four-score, exposed herself and old age to scorn, by dancing on the stage, among the court sycophants of the time. Dio, lib. lxi.

(b) Suetonius says, that the leaders of this new society had salaries of forty thousand sesterces allowed them. In Neron. s. 20.

Section XVI.

(a) Brotier compares this poetical patchwork to the *bouts rimés,* which exercised the minor poets of France in the last century.

Section

Section XVII.

(*a*) See the Geographical Table.

(*b*) It does not appear when this man was expelled the fenate. The account of that affair is loft. It is probable that this is the Livineus Regulus, who is mentioned, Annals, iii. f. 11.

Section XVIII.

(*a*) He was afterwards reftored to his rank. Hift. i. f. 17. For the Cyrenians, fee the Geographical Table.

(*b*) This African king, according to Livy, epitome lxx. died A. U. C. 658, and left all his poffeffions to the Roman people.

Section XIX.

(*a*) Domitius Afer was a man of ambition, willing to advance his fortune by the worft of crimes. *Quoquo facinore properus clarefcere.* Annals, iv. f. 52. He is praifed by Quintilian as an orator of confiderable eloquence. See the Dialogue concerning Oratory.

Section XX.

(*a*) Suetonius informs us, that Nero was the firft that inftituted, in imitation of the Greeks, a trial of fkill in the three feveral arts of mufic, wreftling, and horfe-racing, to be performed every five years, which he called *Neronia.* In Neron. f. 12.

(*b*) This theatre has been mentioned, book xiii. f. 54. It was built A. U. C. 699.

(*c*) Among the Roman knights there were four *Decuriæ* appointed to exercife jurifdiction. Suetonius fays, that Caligula, to relieve the judges from the fatigue of bufinefs, added a fifth clafs to the former four. In Calig. f. 16.

Section XXI.

(*a*) The pantomime performers were brought to Rome from *Tufcany*, A. U. C. 390. Livy, lib. vii. f. 2.

(*b*) The people called *Thurii* inhabited part of Lucania. The fpectacle of horfe-races was invented by them, and exhibited at Rome A. U. C. 140. Livy, lib. i. f. 35.

(*c*) Lucius

(*c*) Lucius Mummius conquered Corinth, A. U. C. 608, and obtained the title of *Achaicus*.   Velleius Paterc. lib. i. f. 13.

Section XXII.

(*a*) This place received its name from its proximity to the Simbruine Lakes, and was thence called *Sublaqueum*.   Brotier fays, it is now *La Badia di Subjaco.*

(*b*) The Marcian waters were conveyed to Rome in aqueducts of great labour and expence by Ancus Marcius, one of the Roman kings. See Pliny, lib. xxxi. f. 3.

Section XXIII.

(*a*) See Annals, xiii. f. 41.
(*b*) See the Geographical Table.
(*c*) For the Mardians, fee the Geographical Table.

Section XXIV.

(*a*) For the Tauranitii, fee the Geographical Table.

Section XXV.

(*a*) The fhorteft way to Hyrcania was by the Cafpian Sea ; but, for the reafon given by Tacitus, the *Red Sea* was thought more eligible.

Section XXVI.

(*a*) Tiridates was brother to Vologefes, the Parthian king.   See Annals, xii. f. 51 ; and book xiii. f. 37 and 41.

(*b*) Archelaus was king of Cappadocia.   See Annals, ii. f. 42.

(*c*) Pharafmanes has been often mentioned as king of *Iberia* ; Polemon, king of *Pontus* ; Ariftobulus, king of *Armenia Minor* ; and Antiochus, of *Commagene.*

(*d*) See Annals, xii. f. 45.

Section XXVII.

(*a*) For Laodicea, fee the Geographical Table.

Section XXVIII.

(*a*) Suetonius fays, Nero ftruck off the fupernumerary candidates, and, to make them fome compenfation for the delay of their hopes, affigned them pofts of honour in the legions.   In Neron. f. 15.

(*b*) The fum, by way of penalty for a frivolous and vexatious appeal, was one third of the money in difpute between the parties.   The words of the law were, *Affertor, fi provocet, in ejufmodi tertiam cavere debet, quanti caufa æftimata eft.*

(*c*) The people of Mauritania.

(*d*) For an account of Vibius Crifpus, an advocate who accumulated immenfe riches, fee the Dialogue concerning Oratory, f. 8.

Section XXIX.

(*a*) Petronius Turpilianus, during his confulfhip, was the author of a law, called *Lex Petronia*, by which the mafter was no longer at liberty, at his will and pleafure, to compel any of his flaves to fight the wild beafts; but a juft ground of complaint appearing before the proper magiftrate, that mode of punifhment was enforced.. *Dominis poteftas ablata eft ad beftias depugnandas fuo arbitrio fervos tradendi. Oblato tamen judici fervo, fi jufta fit domini querela, fic pœnæ tradetur.*   Digeft. lib. xlviii. tit. 8.   Ile was alfo the author of a decree, called the *Turpilian Decree*, by which all, who began a profecution, and either haraffed the defendant by delays, or abandoned the caufe, were fubjected to heavy penalties.   Two regulations fo juft, that it is wonderful, fays. Brotier, how they efcaped the notice of Tacitus.

(*b*) For the inactivity and unwarlike fpirit of Aulus Didius, fee Annals, xii. f. 40; and Life of Agricola, f. 14.

(*c*) For the Silures, fee the Geographical Table.

(*d*) Mona, now *Anglefey*.

Section XXX.

(*a*) For an account of the Druids, fee Cæfar's Commentaries.

Section XXXI.

(*a*) Prafutagus, king of the Icenians.   See the Geographical Table.

The

The outrages committed by the Romans are ftrongly painted by the late Mr. Glover, after his mafter Tacitus.

Section XXXII.

(*a*) The world at that time was overcaft by the gloom of fuperftition. The Romans often knew how to avail themfelves of it; but the Barbarians in this inftance had the advantage.

(*b*) Houfes feemed to be inverted in the water; but the laws of optics were not confidered by the Britons.   In their minds every thing was a prognoftic.

Section XXXIII.

(*a*) London, even at that time, was the feat of trade and commerce. If it has gone on increafing for above 1700 years, till it is now become the greateft city in the world, it is becaufe induftry has been protected by a conftitution, which has improved during the whole time, and is now the wonder and the envy of furrounding nations.

(*b*) Verulanum, now *Verulam* near *St. Albans*, in *Hertfordfhire*.   The great Bacon has made the name immortal.

Section XXXV.

(*a*) Dio has put into the mouth of Boadicea, a long, a tedious, and enervate fpeech.

Section XXXVII.

(*a*) According to Camden, the camp of the fecond legion was in *Monmouthfhire*, at a place called, by the Britons, KAER LHEION, *Urbs Legionis*, the city of the legions.   The place where this battle was fought is not afcertained; but it is evident that Suetonius had collected his forces from all quarters.

Section XXXVIII.

(*a*) There is reafon to infer from a paffage in the Hiftory, book i. f. 59, that the eight auxiliary cohorts were Batavians.

Section

Section XL.

(*a*) Antonius Primus will be seen, in the History of Tacitus, acting the part of an able general.

(*b*) The man who thinks poverty the worst of evils, will not be long before he thinks honesty a ragged virtue. Seneca has left a very different maxim. *Si vis vacare animo, aut pauper sis oportet, aut pauperi similis.* Epist. xvii.

(*c*) The Cornelian law was enacted by Cornelius Sylla the dictator, who made banishment to an island the sentence to be passed on all who should suppress a true will, or forge a false one. It appears however in the History, book ii. f. 86, that Antonius was only expelled the senate.

Section XLI.

(*a*) That punishment was either *exile, relegation* to an island, or degradation from the offender's rank. *Omnes enim calumniatores exilii, vel insulæ relegatione, aut ordinis amissione puniri placuit.* See Julius Paulus, De Injuriis, leg. xi.

Section XLII.

(*a*) Slaves were in the habit of saving money in order to purchase their freedom. See the case of Paris the comedian, book xiii. f. 27. See also Seneca, epist. lxxx.

(*b*) Caius Cassius has been mentioned to his honour, book xii. f. 12.

Section XLV.

(*a*) See a decree of the senate on this subject, Annals, xiii. f. 32.

Section XLVI.

(*a*) See book xii. f. 59.

Section XLVII.

(*a*) Pliny the elder, lib. xv. f. 4, says, that the Greeks, the inventors of every kind of vice, were the first that made oil subservient to the corruption of manners, by distributing it at their public spectacles. *Usum olei ad luxuriam vertere Græci, vitiorum omnium genitores, in Gymnasiis publicando.*

Section

Section XLVIII.

(*a*) See Annals, xiii. f. 28.

(*b*) Capito was formerly accufed by the people of Cilicia, and convicted of oppreffion and extortion.   Annals, xiii. f. 33.

(*c*) The tribunitian power was affumed by Auguftus, as he faid, for the purpofe of protecting the people. *Ad tuendam plebem tribunicio jure contentum fe ferebat.*   Annals, i. f. 2.   It was, in fact, the whole executive power of the ftate vefted in one man, who could, at his will and pleafure, controul the fenate and all the magiftrates.

(*d*) By this judgment Antiftius was to fuffer *more majorum*, that is, as Suetonius explains it, to be faftened ftark naked by the neck within a forked ftick, and fcourged to death.   Suet. in Neron. f. 49.

Section XLIX.

(*a*) The fenate often decided, without calling on each member for his opinion, by *dividing the houfe* ; *per difceffionem.*   Pliny the younger defcribes the manner of doing it: You who think fo, go to that fide ; as many as are of a contrary opinion, go to this fide.   *Lex ita difceffionem fieri jubet : qui hæc fentitis in hanc partem ; qui alia omnia, in illam partem ite quâ fentitis.*   Plinius, lib. viii. ep. 14.

(*b*) This was Vitellius, afterwards emperor.

Section L.

(*a*) This man was one of the pernicious race of informers in the reign of Domitian.   Juvenal mentions him, fat. iv. ver. 123.

Section LI.

(*a*) Tigellinus rofe from obfcurity to be high in favour with Nero. He was the grand teacher of debauchery and every vice.   Juvenal has recorded him, fat. i. ver. 155.   See an account of the prodigious banquet given by this man, Annals, xv. f. 37.

Section LII.

(*a*) It is not fettled among the critics, whether Seneca did not write fome of the tragedies that bear his name.

Section LIII.

(*a*) Agrippa, in the year of Rome 731, retired to the isle of *Lesbos*, now *Metelin*.

(*b*) Mæcenas had a house and magnificent gardens near Mount Esquiline. Pliny says, that the practice of having pleasure-grounds within the walls of a city, was unknown, till Epicurus led the way at Athens. *Primus hoc instituit Athenis Epicurus, otii magister. Usque ad eum moris non fuerat in oppidis habitari rura.* Pliny, lib. xix. f. 4. The gardens of Epicurus are become proverbial.

(*c*) Seneca was a native of Spain ; born at *Corduba*, now *Cordoue*.

(*d*) Seneca had a number of villas and extensive gardens. Juvenal mentions

—— Magnos Senecæ prædivitis hortos.

SAT. x. ver. 16.

The name of one of his villas was *Nomentanum*, as appears epist. cx. where he says, *Ex Nomentano meo te saluto.*

(*e*) This confirms the account given by Dio of his immoderate riches ; but perhaps that historian exaggerates, when he imputes insurrections in Britain to the exactions of Seneca.

Section LVI.

(*a*) In the Annals, book xi. we have seen Vitellius consul for the third time.

(*b*) Volusius has been mentioned as an honest man, who acquired his wealth by honourable means, and lived to a great age. Annals, xiii. f. 30.

Section LVII.

(*a*) For Rubellius Plautus, see this book, f. 22. For Cornelius Sylla, see book xiii. f. 47.

(*b*) Rubellius Plautus was the son of Rubellius Blandus and Julia. See the Genealogical Table, No. 76.

Section LIX.

(*a*) This philosopher is praised by Pliny as an author of distinguish-

ed

ed merit.   Mufonius has been alfo much commended for his moral doctrine.

(*b*) Her father, the emperor Claudius.

Section LXI.

(*a*) This was Eucerus, a native of Alexandria, mentioned in f. lx.

Section LXII.

(*a*) For Anicetus, the murderer of Agrippina, fee this book, f. 7.

Section LXIII.

(*a*) See the Geographical Table.

(*b*) Julia, the daughter of Germanicus and Agrippina, was banifhed by the emperor Claudius, A. U. C. 794.

(*c*) The emperor Claudius her father, and her brother Britannicus, were both poifoned.   See Annals, xii. f. 67; and Annals, xiii. f. 16.

Section LXIV.

(*a*) Nero was adopted by Claudius her father, and confequently was brother to Octavia.

Section LXV.

(*a*) Doriphorus, according to Dio, was private fecretary to Nero. Pallas, the freedman of Claudius, has been often mentioned.   He was difmiffed from all his employments by Nero. See Annals, xiii. f. 14. Brotier fays that his monument was found near Rome, in the year 1720.

(*b*) For more of Pifo, fee Annals, xv. f. 48.

N O T E S

ON THE

FIFTEENTH BOOK

OF

THE ANNALS.

***

Section I.

(*a*) **TIGRANES**, defcended from the nobility of Cappadocia, was fent by Nero to afcend the throne of Armenia. Annals, xiv. f. 26.

Section IV.

(*a*) The walls were fifty cubits high, as we are told by Appian, in his Hiftory of the Mithridatic War.

(*b*) For this river, fee the Geographical Table.

Section V.

(*a*) For the city of Nifibis, fee the Geographical Table.

Section X.

(*a*) Arfamofata, a city of Armenia, near the Euphrates, now *Simfat*.

Section XII.

(*a*) He is called in the original, *Primi Pili Centurio*, that is, firft centurion. He has been mentioned, book xiii. f. 36, by the name of Pactius Orphitus.

(*b*) The civic crown for faving the life of a citizen, was often

granted

granted by the emperor; but the confular commanders had the fame power at the head of their armies.

Section XIII.

(*a*) The Roman army defeated by the Samnites, paffed under the yoke at the *Caudinæ Furcæ*, now *Forchié*, A. U. C. 183. A more terrible defeat happened afterwards at Numantia, A. U. C. 617. The place is now called *Numancia*, and the ruins of antiquity are ftill to be feen.

Section XV.

(*a*) See the Geographical Table.

(*b*) Suetonius fays exprefsly, that the legions paffed under the yoke. In Neron. f. 39.

Section XIX.

(*a*) It was a fettled rule of law, that in all elections for the magi-ftracy, or the government of provinces, the preference fhould be given to the candidate who had the greateft number of children. See Annals, ii. f. 51.

(*b*) By the law Papia Poppæa, the eftates of thofe who did not entitle themfelves to the privileges annexed to the paternal ftate, were to devolve to the public as the common parent of all. Annals, iii. f. 28.

Section XX.

(*a*) The Cincian Law againft venal advocates has been mentioned, Annals, xi. f. 5. Laws were alfo eftablifhed by Auguftus, called *Leges Juliæ*, to prevent bribery at elections. Suet. in Aug. f. 34 and 40.

(*b*) The Calpurnian Law was introduced by Lucius Calpurnius Pifo, *de pecuniis repetundis*, to compel reftitution from fuch as were convicted of extortion, A. U. C. 605, in the beginning of the third Punic war. It was followed from time to time by new decrees, but all proved ineffectual.

Section XXII.

(*a*) It was a frequent practice of the provinces, to fend a deputation to the fenate, with an addrefs of thanks to the proconfuls or prætors, who were returned to Rome, for the bleffings enjoyed by the people under their adminiftration; and this contrivance ferved to advance the fame of the men who condefcended to intrigue for applaufe, and thereby open their road to the higheft honours of the ftate. See the Panegyric of Trajan, by Pliny the conful, f. 70.

(*b*) Seneca gives an account of this earthquake, but he places it in the following year. See Quæft. Natural. queft. vi. f. 1. Pompeii is now called *Torre dell' Annunciata.* It was afterwards totally overwhelmed by the eruption of Mount Vefuvius, A. U. C. 832.

Section XXIII.

(*a*) The worfhip paid to Fortune as a goddefs is well known from Horace, lib. i. ode 35. *O Diva, gratum quæ regis Antium.* There were two goddeffes of fortune adored in that city; one, the *Happy*; the other, the *Equeftrian.*

(*b*) Nero by his father was of the Domitian family, and by adoption of the Claudian. See the Genealogical Table, No. 35.

Section XXIV.

(*a*) For more of the Parthian fuperftition, and the fcruples of Tiridates, fee the Appendix to the Annals, xvi.

Section XXV.

(*a*) Pompey was employed as commander in chief in the Piratic war, with a commiffion giving to him fupreme authority in every province to the extent of fifty miles from the fea coaft. By the decree of the fenate on that occafion, Velleius Paterculus obferves, almoft the whole Roman world was fubjected to the will of one man. *Quo fenatus confulto pæne totius orbis terrarum imperium uni viro deferebatur.* Vell. Paterc. lib. ii. f. 31. See Plutarch, Life of Pompey.

Section XXVI.

(*a*) See the Geographical Table.

(*b*) This fuperftitious ceremony is defcribed by Livy. The foldiers

were

were drawn out on an open plain, and crowned with laurel wreaths, while victims were facrificed to the god of war. The general harangued his men upon the occafion. Livy, lib. i. f. 28.

Section XXVII.

(*a*) Lucullus commanded the legions in Armenia, A. U. C. 685. See Plutarch, Life of Lucullus.

Section XXVIII.

(*a*) Tiberius Alexander was by birth one of the Jewifh nation, but an apoftate from the religion of his country. Jofephus, Jewifh Antiq. lib. xx. f. 5. The emperors frequently fent their chofen favourites to attend the general, but, in fact, to be fpies upon his conduct.

(*b*) Not yet five-and-twenty.

Section XXX.

(*a*) The night in a Roman camp was divided into four watches, each for the fpace of three hours. When the fentinels were changed, notice was given by the found of trumpet. See Hift. lib. ii. f. 29.

Section XXXI.

(*a*) Vologefes king of Parthia, and Pacorus king of Media, were brothers to Tiridates. For Ecbatana, fee the Geographical Table.

(*b*) None but perfons of high rank were admitted to embrace the governors of provinces. According to the ideas of that age, the honour was fo high, that the Parthian king thought proper to make it a preliminary article.

Section XXXII.

(*a*) The capital of the Maritime Alps was called *Ebrodunum*, now *Embrun*. See an account of the territories of the Duke of Savoy. The rights and privileges of Latium have been already mentioned, Annals, xv. f. 32.

(*b*) The *Rofcian Law*, fo called after L. Rofcius Otho, was efta-

6blifhed

bliſhed A. U. C. 685. It aſſigned fourteen rows in the theatre to the Roman knights ; but was ſilent as to the *Circus*, where the ſenators, the knights, and the commonalty were mixed in a promiſcuous concourſe. Afterwards in the conſulſhip of Cinna and Meſſala, A. U. C. 757, the ſenators and knights had a place aſſigned at the ſpectacle of the *Circus*, where they ſat apart from the *plebeians*, but without any diſtinction between their own two orders. Claudius allotted proper places for the ſenators. Suet. in Claud. ſ. 21. It remained for Nero to take care of the equeſtrian order. Suet. in Neron. ſ. 11.

(*c*) Suetonius ſays, Nero engaged four hundred ſenators, and ſix hundred Roman knights, ſome of them of fair fortune and character, to enter the liſts as gladiators, and encounter the wild beaſts. He alſo invited the veſtal virgins to ſee the wreſtlers, becauſe, as he ſaid, at Olympia the prieſteſſes of Ceres were allowed the privilege of ſeeing that diverſion. Suet. in Neron. ſ. 12. See Annals, xiv. ſ. 15 ; and notes (*a*) and (*b*). See Juvenal, ſat. vi. ver. 245 ; ſat. viii. ver. 194.

Section XXXV.

(*a*) For Silanus Torquatus, ſee the Genealogical Table, No. 61.

Section XXXVII.

(*a*) Suetonius tells us, that Nero frequently ſupped in public, either in the Field of Mars, or the Circus, attended at table by the common harlots of the city, or from Syria. When he went down the Tiber to Oſtia, or coaſted along the bay of Baiæ, booths, with all conveniencies for drinking and debauchery, were ranged on the margin of the ſea, while ladies of pleaſure ſtood like ſirens, to invite the paſſengers from their ſhips. Suet. in Neron. ſ. 27.

(*b*) The lake of Agrippa was in the gardens adjoining to his houſe, near the Pantheon.

(*c*) This platform was conſtructed by a great number of timbers faſtened together, and left to float on the water. Lucan has deſcribed ſuch a platform with a tower on it. Pharſal. lib. iv. ver. 17.

(*d*) Dio has given an account of Nero's marriage with Pythagoras,

5   and

and alſo of his taking Sporus, the eunuch, to be his wife. See Appendix to book xvi. ſ. 8.

(c) Juvenal has deſcribed this ſcene of impious proſtitution:

———— Dum ſedet illa parato
Flammeolo, Tyriuſque palam genialis in hortis
Sternitur, et ritu decies centena dabuntur
Antiquo; veniet cum ſignatoribus auſpex.

SAT. x. ver. 333.

Adorn'd with bridal pomp ſhe ſits in ſtate,
The public notaries and aruſpex wait;
The genial bed is in the garden dreſt;
The portion paid, and every rite expreſt,
Which in a Roman marriage is profeſt. }

DRYDEN'S JUVENAL.

Section XXXVIII.

(a) Suetonius relates the fire of Rome, and has no doubt of Nero's guilt. He tells us, that ſomebody repeating in converſation,

Ἐμῦ θανοντος γαῖα μιχθήτω πυρὶ,
When I am dead let fire devour the world;

Let it be, ſaid Nero, *whilſt I am living,* ἐμε ζῶντος. And accordingly, pretending to diſlike the old buildings, and the narrow winding of the ſtreets, he ſet fire to the city in ſo barefaced a manner, that ſeveral men of conſular rank met Nero's domeſtic ſervants with torches and combuſtibles, but did not dare to apprehend them. Suet. in Neron. ſ. 38. See Dio, lib. lxii.

(b) Livy obſerves, that, after the city was fired by the Gauls, it was rebuilt in cloſe, narrow, winding ſtreets. See Livy, lib. v. ſ. 55.

Section XXXIX.

(a) The gardens of Mæcenas were near Mount Eſquiline.

(b) The monuments of Agrippa were, his houſe, his gardens, his baths, and the Pantheon. The laſt remains at this day.

(c) Nero's gardens joined to the Vatican.

(d) Suetonius ſays, in expreſs terms, that Nero beheld the conflagra-

tion

tion from a tower on the top of Mæcenas's houſe, and, being highly pleaſed with ſo grand a ſight, went to his own theatre, and in his ſcenic dreſs tuned his harp, and ſung the deſtruction of Troy. Suet. in Neron. ſ. 38.

Section XLI.

(*a*) Evander was originally a native of Arcadia in Greece. The viſit of Hercules forms a beautiful epiſode in Virgil's Æneid, book viii.

(*b*) For the temple of Jupiter Stator, ſee Livy, lib. i. ſ. 12.

(*c*) The palace of Numa was on Mount Palatine, afterwards the manſion of Auguſtus, near the temple of Vesta, where the veſtal virgins watched the perpetual fire. See Horace, lib. i. ode 2.

(*d*) The fourteenth of the calends of July, or the eighteenth of June. This is confirmed by Livy, who ſays, lib. vi. ſ. 1, that the battle at *Allia* was fought on the fifteenth of the kalends ; and book v. ſ. 41, he ſays the victorious Gauls entered Rome on the following day.

Section XLII.

(*a*) According to Suetonius, Nero turned the public calamity to his own private advantage. He promiſed to remove the bodies that lay amidſt the ruins, and to clear the ground at his own expence. By that artifice he ſecured all the remaining property of the unhappy ſufferers for his own uſe. To add to his ill-gotten ſtore, he levied contributions in the provinces, and by thoſe means collected an immenſe ſum. Suet. in Neron. ſ. 38. Brotier has given an elaborate deſcription of the New Palace, vol. ii. p. 490, 4to edit.

(*b*) The Lake Avernus was in the neighbourhood of Baiæ, now *Lago Averno.*

(*c*) Now *Paludi Pontine*, in the territory of Rome.

Section XLIII.

(*a*) Strabo ſays, that by an ordinance of Auguſtus, no new built houſe was to be more than ſeventy feet high. Trajan afterwards, according to Aurelius Victor, fixed the elevation at ſixty feet. The rule preſcribed by Nero cannot now be known.

(b) We

(*b*) We are told by Suetonius, that Nero introduced a new model for building in the city, and, by porticos and piazzas before the front, contrived, in cafe of fire, to hinder the flames from fpreading. In Neron. f. 16.

(*c*) Vitruvius fays, that the Alban and Gabian ftone was not the hardeft, but it refifted fire; while the ftone from other quarries was apt, when heated, to crack, and fly off in fragments. Vitruvius, lib. ii. cap. 7.

(*d*) Brotier obferves, that by a law of the Twelve Tables, a fpace of fomething more than two feet, was to be left between all new-built houfes.

(*e*) It is known, fays Brotier, from the experience of medical people, that at Rome there are more patients, during the fummer, in the wide parts of the city, which lie open to the fun, than in the narrow places, where the inhabitants are fhaded from the intenfe heat.

Section XLIV.

(*a*) The beds, on which the gods and goddeffes were extended at all public feftivals, were called *Lectifternia*. See Livy, lib. v. f. 13.

(*b*) Brotier obferves, that the Jews, in that period of time, were guilty of great enormities; and the diftinction between them and the Chriftians not being underftood, all were confidered in the fame light, defpifed and hated by the Romans.

(*c*) This was the firft perfecution of the Chriftians. Nero, the declared enemy of human kind, waged war againft a religion, which has fince diffufed the light of truth, and humanifed the favages of Europe. It is true, as Suetonius relates, that Claudius banifhed the Jews, who were raifing feditious tumults, at the inftigation of one CHRESTUS. That name, it is almoft needlefs to obferve, cannot, at leaft ought not to be confounded with JESUS CHRIST; who, it was well known at Rome, had fuffered under Pontius Pilate, in the reign of Tiberius. CHRESTUS, Brotier obferves, was not an uncommon name among the Greeks and Romans. When the Jews were ordered by Claudius to depart from Rome, all of that nation, who profeffed themfelves follow-ers of CHRIST, were, without diftinction, included in the number. The

edict

edict of the emperor was not pointed against the Christians. Nero appears to be the first that attacked them as the professors of a new religion; and when such a man as Tacitus calls it a dangerous superstition, *exitiabilis superstitio*, it must be allowed, that, indirectly, an apology is made for Nero. But for Tacitus, who had opportunities for a fair enquiry, and ability to know and decide, what excuse can be offered? The vices of the Jews were imputed to the Christians without discrimination, and Tacitus suffered himself to be hurried away by the torrent of popular prejudice. And yet we find that his friend Pliny, during his administration in the province of Bithynia, thought and acted with moderation. The Christians were under a prosecution; Pliny, in his character of proconsular governor, was in doubt how to proceed. He wrote to the emperor Trajan on the subject; and after stating that the *real Christians were not to be forced, by any means whatever, to renounce the articles of their belief*, he proceeds to the sum total of their guilt, which he found to be as follows: They met on a stated day before it was light, and addressed themselves in a prayer or hymn to CHRIST, as to a God, binding themselves by a solemn oath, not for any wicked purpose, but never to commit any *fraud, theft*, or *adultery*; never to *falsify their word*, nor *deny a trust reposed in them*; after which, it was their custom to separate, and then re-assemble to eat their meal together, in a manner perfectly harmless and inoffensive. They desisted, says Pliny, from this custom, after my edict, issued according to your order, against the holding of any assemblies whatever. *Affirmabant hanc fuisse summam vel culpæ suæ, vel erroris, quod essent soliti stato die ante lucem convenire, carmenque Christo, quasi Deo, dicere secum invicem; seque sacramento non in scelus aliquod, obstringere, sed ne furta, ne latrocinia, ne adulteria committerent; ne fidem fallerent, ne depositum appellati abnegarent: quibus peractis morem sibi discedendi fuisse, rursusque coeundi ad capiendum cibum, promiscuum tamen, et innoxium; quod ipsum facere desiisse post edictum meum, quo secundum mandata tua hetarias esse vetueram.* Plin. lib. x. ep. 97. Such is the account of the religion, which Tacitus calls a *pernicious* superstition. Pliny adds, in the same letter, that, in order to come at the real truth, he ordered two female slaves to be put to the torture, but he could discover nothing more than a rooted and excessive superstition. Trajan,

in

in his anfwer to this letter, determines, that if Chriftians are brought before the governor, and proved to be guilty, they muft be punifhed, unlefs they renounce their errors, and invoke the gods of Rome. In that cafe they were to be pardoned, notwithftanding any former fufpicion. But the emperor fays to his minifter, " I would not have you officioufly enter into any inquiries concerning them." Pliny's letter, Mr. Melmoth obferves, is efteemed as almoft the only genuine monument of ecclefiaftical antiquity, relating to the times immediately fucceeding the apoftles, being wrote not above forty years after the death of Paul. It was preferved by the Chriftians themfelves, as a clear and unfufpicious evidence of the purity of their doctrines. It is therefore with good reafon, fays Brotier, that Tertullian, in a ftrain of exultation, declares, That the Chriftians, " for their innocence, their probity, juftice, truth, and for the living God, were burnt alive. The cruelty, ye profecutors! is all your own; the glory is ours." *Pro tantâ innocentiâ, pro tantâ probitate, pro juftitiâ, pro virtute, pro Deo vivo cremamur: Crudelitas veftra; gloria eft noftra.*

(d) The Jews, as will be feen in the Hiftory, book v. f. 5, were charged with harbouring a fullen averfion towards all mankind. It is unneceffary to vindicate the Chriftian religion from that imputation.

(e) Juvenal alludes, with his ufual indignation, to the barbarous cruelties defcribed by Tacitus. See fat. i. ver. 155.

Section XLVI.

(a) For Prænefte, fee the Geographical Table.
(b) Spartacus, a gladiator, kindled up the Servile War A. U. C. 681.
(c) For Formiæ, fee the Geographical Table.

Section XLVII.

(a) For Placentia, fee the Geographical Table.

Section L.

(a) Fenius Rufus has been mentioned to his honour, Annals, xiv. f. 51.
(b) Agrippina, Nero's murdered mother.

Section LII.

(*a*) Lucius Silanus, the son of Marcus Junius Silanus. See the Genealogical Table, No. 59.

(*b*) Caius Caffius, banished to Sardinia A. U. C. 818. See Annals, book xii. f. 11 and 12.

Section LVI.

(*a*) The weakness here imputed to Lucan, cannot be read by any man who has a refpect for genius, and the true dignity of the human character, without emotions of pity and regret. But, perhaps, without any studied comment, the cafe admits a plain and obvious apology. Two eminent men (Natalis and Scevinus) had been taken into cuftody. At *the fight of the rack their refolution failed,* and they difcovered their accomplices. Lucan knew that the fame engine of cruelty was ready for himfelf and his two friends, Quinctianus and Senecio. All three were tempted by a promife of pardon, and they endeavoured to earn it by making difcoveries. Lucan might think that his mother, a woman who boafted neither rank nor fortune, would not, among a great number of daring confpirators, be deemed an object worthy of notice; and, befides, the terrors of the rack may conquer the moft heroic mind. When the executioner appears with his torturing engines, it is no longer the moment of courage. He who in the ranks of war is ready to face every danger, may fhrink from the pangs prepared for him in a dungeon, where he muft fuffer under a villain's hand, unfeen, unpitied, unapplauded. When Felton, who ftabbed the duke of Buckingham at Portfmouth, was examined before the privy council, the Bifhop of London faid to him, *If you will not confefs, you muft go to the rack.* The man replied, If it muft be fo, I know not whom I may accufe; perhaps fome Lord at this board. Sound fenfe, fays Judge Fofter, in the mouth of an enthufiaft and a ruffian! In the fame diftrefs, the fame hurry and perturbation of fpirit, Lucan mentioned his mother. He might think that fhe was not of confequence to provoke refentment; and the event fhewed, if he thought fo, that his conclufion was right. Nero affected to forget her. She and Seneca's wife were fuffered to live. For thefe reafons, the conduct of Lucan may admit of fome extenuation; more efpecially, when he

had

had before his eyes the example of fenators, and men of confular rank. But a late writer thinks he has difcovered a better ground of defence. He denies the fact, and fays, Tacitus has *adopted a grofs calumny*, invented by Nero to *vilify the object of his envious abhorrence.* But it may be afked, if Nero framed the ftory, is it probable that a writer, who wages an inceffant war againft evil men and evil deeds, would have defcended to be the accomplice of a tyrant? Tacitus, through the whole of his narrative, has done ample juftice to all who died with glory; to Epicharis, the enfranchifed flave, who difplayed her conftancy, in defiance of the keeneft torture; to Seneca, who left an example of unfhaken virtue; to Subrius Flavius, whofe laft words to Nero were, " I hated you when you became a coachman, a comedian, and an incendiary;" to Sulpicius Afper, the centurion; and, above all, to Lucan himfelf, who died with undaunted courage, repeating a paffage from his own poem. Let it alfo be remembered, that when Lucan's father fuffered death in the following year, Tacitus fays, that the fon reflected the higheft honour on the father; *grande adjumentum claritudinis.* The writer who has treated Lucan with fo much candour, would neither adopt nor invent a calumny, to brand his name in the page of hiftory. But to conclude this long note: It is by no means probable, that Tacitus, who wrote in the reign of Trajan, not much more than thirty years after the death of Lucan, would hazard a glaring falfehood in the face of his contemporaries; and it is lefs probable, that Mr. Hayley, at the diftance of more than 1730 years, fhould be better informed than the great hiftorian, who lived at the very time of the tranfaction. See Poems, by William Hayley, Efq. vol. iii. p. 206.

Section LX.

(*a*) This was Seneca's villa, called *Nomentanum*, which he mentions, epift. cx. and alfo civ. *in Nomentanum meum fugi.*

Section LXIII.

(*a*) For his diet, fee in this book, f. 45.

Section LXIV.

(*a*) This poison was called *cicuta*. Seneca says, it made Socrates a great man: *Cicuta magnam Socratem fecit.* Epist. xiii.

Section LXVIII.

(*a*) Statilia Messalina had been Nero's third wife. See the Genealogical Table, No. 39.

Section LXX.

(*a*) The commentators point out different passages in the Pharsalia, but all depend on mere conjecture. Lipsius thinks the description of Lycidas, at the point of death, most probable.

> Ferrea dum puppi rapidos manus inserit uncos,
> Affixit Lycidam : mersus foret ille profundo,
> Sed prohibent socii, suspensaque crura retentant.
> Scinditur avulsus ; nec sicut vulnere, sanguis
> Emicuit lentus : ruptis cadit undique venis,
> Discursusque animæ diversa in membra meantis
> Interceptus aquis ; nullius vita perempti
> Est tantâ dimissâ viâ ; pars ultima trunci
> Tradidit in Letum vacuos vitalibus artus ;
> Aut tumidus quà pulmo jacet, quà viscera fervent,
> Hæserunt ibi fata diu, luctataque multùm
> Hac cum parte viri vix omnia membra tulerunt.
>
> Pharsal. lib. iii. ver. 635.

Other critics contend for the following lines :

> Sanguis erant lacrymæ ; quæcumque foramina novit
> Humor, ab his largus manat cruor ; ora redundant,
> Et patulæ nares ; sudor rubet : omnia plenis
> Membra fluunt venis : totum est pro vulnere corpus.
>
> Pharsal. ix. ver. 811.

Section

Section LXXI.

(*a*) Laurel is called by Pliny the elder, the door-keeper of the Cæsars : *Janitrix Cæsarum*. Lib. xv. f. 30.

(*b*) Virginius was a rhetorician, and the preceptor of Perseus, the satirift; as may be feen in the Life of Perseus.

(*c*) Mufonius Rufus was a teacher of philofophy. See Annals, xiv. f. 59.

Section LXXII.

(*a*) Petronius Turpilianus was conful, as mentioned, book xiv. f. 29.

(*b*) Cocceius Nerva, afterwards emperor.

(*c*) For Nymphidius, fee Appendix to Annals, xvi. f. 13 ; and fee the Hiftory, book i. f. 5.

Section LXXIII.

(*a*) Seneca, the philofopher, had two brothers; namely, Annæus Mela, the father of Lucan, and Annæus Novatus, who was afterwards adopted by Gallio, and took that name. For the death of Mela, fee Annals, xvi. f. 17.

Section LXXIV.

(*a*) The month of April was called Neronius, May Claudius, and June Germanicus. Annals, xvi. f. 12.

(*b*) For an account of Vindex, fee the Appendix to Annals, xvi. p. 374.

(*c*) Auguftus was deified by the poets, and in the provinces; but no altars were erected to him at Rome during his life.

N O T E S

ON THE

SIXTEENTH BOOK

OF

THE ANNALS.

Section I.

(*a*) THE account of Dido's flight from Tyre with the treasures of her husband Sichæus, to avoid the fury of Pygmalion, who had basely murdered his brother for the sake of his riches, is finely given by Virgil. Æneid i. ver. 347.

(*b*) The kings of Numidia, and the African princes in the neighbourhood of Carthage, were enemies to the infant state founded by Dido.

> Hinc Getulæ urbes, genus insuperabile bello,
> Et Numidæ infræni cingunt.
>
> VIRGIL, lib. iv. ver. 40.

Section II.

(*a*) The Quinquennial festival was established by Nero, A. U. C. 813. Annals, xiv. s. 20.

Section III.

(*a*) Suetonius relates the whole of this impostor's deception, and the chimerical projects of Nero in consequence of it. In Neron. s. 31.

Section IX.

(*a*) Nero did not scruple to appear upon the stage amongst other
performers,

performers, even in the fpectacles prefented by the magiftrates. He
fung tragedies mafked, the vizors of the gods and goddeffes being
formed into a refemblance of his own face. Among the reft, he acted
Canace in Labour, Oreftes the Murderer of his Mother, Œdipus blinded, and
Hercules mad. In the laft tragedy a foldier, at his poft in the theatre,
feeing the emperor bound with chains as the play required, ran to his
affiftance. Suet. in Neron. f. 21. See alfo the fame, f. 22, 23 and 24.
This ridiculous difplay of talents, beneath the dignity of a prince, is
well defcribed by Racine in his play of Britannicus :

> Pour toute ambition, pour vertu finguliere,
> Il excelle à conduire un char dans la carriere ;
> A difputer des prix indignes de fes mains,
> A fe donner lui-même en fpectacle aux Romains ;
> A venir prodiguer fa voix fur un théâtre,
> A reciter des chants qu'il veut qu'on idolatre.
>
> Act iv. fcene 4.

Racine's play was performed before Lewis XIV, who had before that
time mixed in the dance on the public ftage. The picture of Nero's
folly made the monarch fee himfelf, and from that time he refolved
never to degrade the royal character.

Section V.

(*a*) See Suetonius in Neron. f. 23.

Section VI.

(*a*) Suetonius fays, he married Poppæa twelve days after his divorce from Octavia, and, notwithftanding the vehemence of his love,
killed her with a kick when fhe was big with child, only becaufe fhe
took the liberty to chide him for returning late from the chariot-race.
He had by her a daughter, called Claudia Augufta, who died in her
infancy. Suet. in Neron. f. 35.

(*b*) The firft Romans did not burn their dead, but interred them,
according to the cuftom of other nations. Pliny the elder fays, that
the practice of committing the dead to the funeral pile, was not intro-

3 T 2

duced

duced till it was known that the bodies of foldiers, who died in foreign wars, were dug up by the enemy, and expofed to public view. And yet Plutarch, in his Life of Numa, obferves that Numa was buried, purfuant to his own exprefs injunction, directing that his body fhould not be committed to the flames; which fhews that burning was known at Rome in that early period. The cuftom of burning the dead was held in abhorrence by feveral nations, and, according to Herodotus, by the Perfians as well as the Ægyptians. Notwithftanding what Plutarch has faid, Pliny affures us, that before Sylla the dictator, the bodies of the deceafed were always interred by the Romans, and that the reafon for burning that extraordinary man, was becaufe, having dug up the body of Marius, he was afraid of being treated the fame way himfelf, and therefore ordered his remains to be confumed to afhes. Pliny, lib. vii. f. 54. The cuftom of burning at Rome ceafed under the Antonines.

(c) Befides the fpices with which the body of Poppæa was embalmed, a prodigious quantity was burnt on the occafion, infomuch that Pliny fays, all Arabia did not produce in an entire year as much as was confumed at the funeral of Poppæa. *Periti rerum affeverant* ARABIAM *non ferre tantum* THURIS ET MYRRHÆ *annuo fætu, quantum Nero princeps noviffimo Poppææ fuæ die concremaverit.* Pliny, lib. xii f. 18.

(d) For the apotheofis of Nero's daughter by Poppæa, fee Annals, xv. f. 23.

Section VII.

(a) The name of this perfon was Caffius Longinus, a lawyer far advanced in years, and blind. His crime, according to Suetonius, was, that among the bufts of his anceftors, he kept that of the famous Caffius, who ftabbed Julius Cæfar. Suet. in Neron. f. 37.

Section VIII.

(a) Lucius Silanus was fon to Marcus Junius Silanus, who was great-grandfon to Auguftus. See the Genealogical Table, No. 59. For his uncle Silanus Torquatus, fee Annals, xv. f. 35.

4

(b) For

(*b*) For Lepida, fee the Genealogical Table, No. 64.

(*c*) Marcellus Cornelius was afterwards put to death by Galba. Hift. lib. i. f. 37.

Section IX.

(*a*) Barium, a city in Apulia, now *Bari*.

Section X.

(*a*) For the death of Rubellius Plautus, fee Annals, xiv. f. 58 and 59.

(*b*) Nero and Antiftius Vetus were joint confuls, A. U. C. 808. See Annals, xiii. f. 11.

Section XII.

(*a*) For Fenius Rufus, fee Annals, xv. f. 66 and 68.

(*b*) See Annals, xv. f. 74.

(*c*) The two Torquati were, Silanus Torquatus, Annals, xv. f. 35; and Lucius Torquatus, this book, f. 9.

Section XIII.

(*a*) This was a dreadful fire, by which in one night Lugdunum (now the city of Lyons) was reduced to afhes. Seneca fays, *Una nox fuit inter urbem maximam et nullam.* See his Reflections on this Mis-fortune, epift. 91.

(*b*) The time when the people of Lyons granted a fupply to the Ro-mans cannot be afcertained. It was probably in the reign of Caligula.

Section XIV.

(*a*) Antiftius Sofianus was banifhed on account of his fatirical verfes, A. U. 815. Annals, xiv. f. 48, 49.

(*b*) For Oftorius Scapula, fee Annals, xii. f. 31; Annals, xiv. f. 48. He had commanded in Britain with great reputation.

(*c*) To give validity to a will, feven witneffes were neceffary. Digeft. lib. xxxvii. tit. De Bonorum Poffeffione.

Section XV.

(*a*) Annals, xii. f. 31.

Section

Section XVII.

(*a*) Crispinus commanded the prætorians, Annals, xi. f. 1. He was banished to Sardinia, Annals, xv. f. 71.

(*b*) For Gallio, the brother of Seneca, see Annals, xv. f. 73.

(*c*) Brotier exclaims in this place, Let the detractors from the merit of Lucan hear what Tacitus says of him, and let them blush for their malignity. That a young poet, who ended his career in the 27th year of his age, should aim in many passages of his work at ambitious ornaments, and the falfe glitter which the example of his uncle Seneca and the taste of the age encouraged, cannot be matter of wonder; but, to atone for his faults, his poem is a treasure of sentiments worthy of a Roman. Lucan taught Corneille to think, and to express his thoughts with force and dignity.

(*d*) Juvenal gives us to understand that Lucan was possessed of great riches, and might therefore seek no reward but fame:

> Contentus famâ jaceat Lucanus in hortis
> Marmoreis.   SAT. vii. ver. 79.

(*e*) The plot to which Tacitus refers, is not related with perspicuity by any historian. All that is now known is, that Cerealis was the informer, and that Sextus Paffienus, the chief of the conspiracy, with several men of rank, was put to death by order of Caligula.

Section XVIII.

(*a*) This is the writer whom Pope has celebrated in the Effay on Criticism:

> Fancy and art in gay Petronius please,
> The scholar's learning, with the courtier's ease.

The account here given of him by Tacitus, is elegant and interesting. See Plutarch, on the difference between a friend and a sycophant; and see Pliny, lib. xxxvii. f. 7.

(*b*) This was Scevinus the conspirator, for whom see Annals, xv. f. 49, 54, and 56.

Section

Section XIX.

(*a*) This defcription of Nero and his flagitious court has been fuppofed by fome critics to be the work called *Petronii Arbitri Satyricon*;
but this, it is evident, muft be a grofs miftake. The *Satyricon* is a long
work, and muft have been written at leifure. It contains nothing
that relates to the new modes of vice, or the fecret practices of Nero's
court. It glances often at the imbecility of Claudius, and prefents a
variety of mifcellaneous matter, palpably the compofition of a mind
at eafe. What was fent to Nero muft have been a fhort performance,
fuch as a man of genius might difpatch in a few hours. How fhould
the paffages, which have entitled Petronius to be ranked with the critics
of antiquity, find a place in the narrative of a dying man?

Section XXI.

(*a*) When the death of Agrippina, Nero's mother, was announced
to the fenate, and the fathers, with their ufual fpirit of adulation, were
preparing their decrees on that occafion, Thrafea rofe from his feat
and left the houfe. Annals, xiv. f. 12.

(*b*) See Annals, xiv. f. 48.

(*c*) For Coffutianus Capito, a man of infamous character, fee
Annals, xiii. f. 33.

Section XXII.

(*a*) The oath of fidelity was changed at different times At firft
it was a folemn obligation to preferve the laws. Dio relates, that on
the kalends of January, A. U. C. 712, the magiftrates fwore on the
Acts of Julius Cæfar. In procefs of time, to fwear on the Acts of the
Emperors grew into ufe; though we have feen Tiberius refufing to
admit that form of oath.

(*b*) Thrafea was forbid the prefence of the emperor, A. U. C. 816.
See book xv. f. 23. From that time, it does not appear that he entered the fenate.

(*c*) The Journals of the Roman people, called in the original
Diurna Populi Romani. Thefe were the Roman newfpapers. It is to
be regretted that no collection of thofe fugitive pieces has come down

to us. We fhould have the pleafure of feeing minutely and diftinctly *the private life of the Romans*, and the opportunity would be fair to make a comparifon between a Roman journalift and the *deer* of a modern newfpaper.

(d) Cicero, in the Oration for Muræna, gives a fketch of Tubero's character: " He was a man of illuftrious birth, a fcholar, and a profeffor of the ftoic philofophy. Being defired, at the funeral of Scipio Africanus, to lay out the couches for the farewel fupper, he chofe the vileft fort, fuch as were ufed at Carthage, and, having covered them with goat fkins, arranged in proper order a number of Samian vafes, which were earthen ware; as if he were preparing for the funeral of Diogenes the cynic, and not for that of the divine Africanus, to whofe honour Quintus Maximus, in a panegyric from the roftrum, faid, he thanked the immortal Gods that fuch a man was born a Roman citizen; for wherever Scipio lived, there by confequence would be fixed the empire of the world." Cicero adds, that Tubero, a good and upright citizen, the grandfon of Paulus Æmilius, and nephew to the deceafed Scipio, gave umbrage to the people by his perverfe wifdom, and for his goat fkins loft his election when candidate for the prætorfhip. *Atque ille, homo eruditiffimus, ac ftoicus, ftravit pelliculis hædinis lectulos punicanos, et expofuit vafa Samia; quafi vero effet Diogenes cynicus mortuus, et non divini hominis Africani mors honeftaretur; quem cum fupremo ejus die Quintus Maximus laudaret, gratias egit Diis immortalibus, quod ille vir in hac republicâ potiffimum natus effet: neceffe enim fuiffe, ibi effe terrarum imperium, ubi ille effet. Hujus in morte celebrandâ graviter tulit populus Romanus hanc* PERVERSAM SAPIENTIAM *Tuberonis; itaque homo integerrimus, civis optimus, cum effet Lucii Pauli nepos, Africani fororis filius, his* HÆDINIS PELLICULIS *præturâ dejectus eft.* Tully pro Muræna, vol. ii. p. 266, Delph. edit. Seneca, who was a profeffed ftoic, fays of that fchool, that there was no fect more benevolent, none more affectionate, and none more zealous to promote the good of fociety. *Nulla fecta benignior, leniorque eft; nulla amantior hominum, et communibus bonis attentior.* De Clementiâ, lib. ii. cap. 5. But the fame Seneca teaches the impious doctrine of fuicide. *In eum intravimus mundum,*

mundum, in quo his legibus vivitur: Placet? Pare.   Non placet? Quacum-que vis, exi.   Epift. 91.

Section XXIII.

(*a*) Acratus has been mentioned as a perfon fent into Afia, to plunder the cities of their ftatues. Annals, xv. f. 45.

(*b*) Rubellius Plautus, for whom fee Annals, xiv. f. 57 and 59.

Section XXIV.

(*a*) Nero was on his return from Campania.

Section XXVI.

(*a*) Arulenus Rufticus lived to eftablifh a great and virtuous character.   He was put to death by Domitian, A. U. C. 847, A. D. 94. See Life of Agricola, f. xi ; and note (*a*).

Section XXVII.

(*a*) The emperors had their own fpecial quæftors for the conduct of their affairs.   Auguftus was the firft that eftablifhed fuch an office. Suetonius fays, he acquainted the fenate with the fcandalous behaviour of his daughter Julia by a narrative in writing, which was read to the fathers by the quæftor.   Suet. in Aug. f. 65.

Section XXVIII.

(*a*) For more of Helvidius Prifcus, fee Hiftory, book iv. f. 5 ; and fee Life of Agricola, f. ii. and note (*b*).

(*b*) Marcus Paconius, the father of Paconius Agrippinus, was cruelly put to death by Tiberius.   See Suet. in Tib. f. 61.

(*c*) For more of Curtius Montanus, fee Hiftory, iv. f. 40 and 42.

Section XXIX.

(*a*) It is fuppofed by fome of the commentators, that the Montanus mentioned in this place is the perfon introduced by Juvenal in the deep confultation held by Domitian, about the manner of dreffing a fifh of enormous fize :

Quidnam igitur cenfes ? conciditur ? abfit ab illo
Dedecus hoc, Montanus ait, &c.

SAT. iv. ver. 130.

Section XXXII.

(*a*) Egnatius, the profeffor of the ftoic philofophy, who appears as
a witnefs againft Barcas Soranus, is mentioned by Juvenal :

Stoicus occidit Baream, delator amicum,

Difcipulumque fenex.   SAT. iii. ver. 116.

See the Hiftory, book iv. f. 10.

Section XXXIV.

(*a*) Notice has been taken, f. xxvii. note (*a*), of the imperial quæftors.   The confuls alfo had their quæftors, as we read in Dio, lib. xlviii.
where it is faid that Appius Claudius and Caius Norbanus, confuls
A. U. C. 716, had each of them two quæftors under their own immediate direction.

(*b*) Demetrius is praifed by Seneca, not merely as a philofopher,
but as a man of confummate virtue.   De Beneficiis, lib. vii. cap. 8.
In another place he calls him emphatically, not the teacher, but the
witnefs of truth.   *Non præceptor veri, fed teftis.*   Epift. xx.

(*c*) Arria, his wife, was the daughter of the celebrated Arria, who,
in the reign of Claudius, A. U. C. 795, plunged a dagger in her own
breaft, to give her hufband Cæcina Pætus an example of undaunted
courage.   See the Life of Agricola, f. ii. notes (*a*) and (*b*).

END OF THE NOTES

ON THE

SIX LAST BOOKS OF THE ANNALS.

NOTES

ON THE

APPENDIX

TO THE

SIXTEENTH BOOK

OF

THE ANNALS.

Section I.

(*a*) EPICTETUS, as we are told by Arrian, recorded the Apothegms of Thrasea, and in particular the sentiment here ascribed to him.

(*b*) Pliny the consul observes; that many, who are themselves slaves to every vice, are, notwithstanding, malicious declaimers against the errors of others; yet, surely, a lenity of disposition is of all other virtues the most becoming. The rule which ought to be most religiously observed, is, Let us be inexorable to our own failings, while we treat those of the rest of the world with tenderness, not excepting even such as forgive none but themselves, remembering always what the humane, and, therefore, the great Thrasea used to say : " He who hates vice, hates mankind." *Nostine hos, qui omnium libidinum servi, sic aliorum vitiis irascuntur, quasi invideant, et gravissimè puniunt, quos maximè imitantur ? Cum eos etiam, qui non indigent clementiâ ullius, nihil magis quam lenitas deceat. Atque ego optimum et emendatissimum existimo, qui cæteris ita ignoscit, tanquam ipse quotidie peccet ; ita peccatis abstinet, tanquam nemini*

3 U 2

ignoscat.

ignofcat. Proinde hoc domi, hoc foris, hoc in omni vitæ genere teneamus, ut nobis implacabiles fimus, excrabiles iftis etiam, qui dare veniam nifi fibi nefciunt; mandemufque memoriæ, quod vir mitiffimus, et ob hoc quoque maximus, Thrafea dicere crebro folebat: QUI VITIA ODIT, HOMINES ODIT. Plin. lib. viii. epift. 22. Mr. Melmoth, the elegant tranflator of Pliny, fays, The meaning of this maxim feems to be, that as it is difficult to feparate the action from the man, we fhould not fuffer the errors of the world to raife in us that acrimony of indignation, which, if well examined, will, perhaps, be oftener found to proceed from fome fecret principle of malice, than a juft abhorrence of vice. And, therefore, as Seneca obferves, *Satius eft publicos mores et humana vitia placidè accipere.* See Melmoth's Pliny, book viii. epift. 22.

(*c*) Helvidius Prifcus was recalled from exile, and afterwards put to death in the reign of Vefpafian. See Appendix to book v. of the Hiftory; and fee Life of Agricola, f. ii. and note (*b*).

(*d*) Paconius Agrippinus has been mentioned, Annals, xvi. f. 28.

(*e*) Thefe particulars are related by Arrian, in Epicteto, 1.

(*f*) Arrian has recorded this fact. Seneca has mentioned Demetrius with the higheft applaufe, and chiefly for the following fentiment: Nothing can be more unfortunate than the man who has never felt the ftroke of adverfity: he has had no experience of himfelf. *Nibil mihi vidétur infelicius eo, cui nibil unquam evenit adverfi: non licuit enim illi fe experire.* Seneca de Providentiâ, cap. iii.

Section II.

(*a*) Cornutus was the friend and preceptor of Perfeus the poet.

——Teneros tu fufcipis annos
Socratico, Cornute, finu.

SAT. v. ver. 36.

Crevier, in the Lives of the Emperors, tells us, that Nero intended to write the Roman Hiftory in verfe, and in four hundred books. That will be too many, faid Cornutus; nobody will read them. In anfwer, he was told, that Chryfippus had written a great many more. Yes, replied Cornutus, but the difference between the authors is very great.

He

He escaped with his life, but was banished. Crevier's Roman Emperors, vol. iv. p. 295.

(*b*) See Annals, xv. f. 29 and 30.

(*c*) Vologefes, king of Parthia, and Pacorus, king of Media, were brothers to Tiridates. Monobazus was king of the Adiabenians.

(*d*) See Annals, xv. f. 31.

(*e*) See the Geographical Table.

(*f*) For Patrobius, fee Pliny, lib. xxxv. f. 13.

(*g*) The fkill in archery, which Tiridates difplayed on the occafion, is related by Dio.

Section III.

(*a*) The appearance of Tiridates before the Roman people, and the prodigious magnificence of that public fpectacle, are defcribed by Suetonius, in Nero, f. 13.

(*b*) Suetonius, f. 13. See alfo Dio, lib. lxiii.

Section IV.

(*a*) The Sun, under the name of MITHRA, was worfhipped by the Perfians, and almoft all the eaftern nations. See Hyde, Hiftory of the Perfian Religion.

(*b*) The fpeech of Tiridates, and Nero's anfwer, are recorded by Dio Caffius, lib. lxiii.

(*c*) Pliny mentions the decorations of the Theatre, and the vaft difplay of gold for the reception of Tiridates. *Nero Pompeii Theatrum operuit auro in unum diem, quod Tiridati regi Armeniæ oftenderet.* Lib. xxxiii. f. 3. See alfo Dio Caffius, lib. lxiii.

(*d*) Dio fays, this feaft was given in Nero's golden palace; for which, fee Pliny, lib. xxxiii. f. 3.

(*e*) Rome, under the emperors, was often difturbed by the violent fpirit of theatrical factions, the leaders of which were diftinguifhed by the colour of their drefs, fuch as *white, blue, green,* and *yellow.* This is what Tacitus, in another place, has called HISTRIONALIS FAVOR. Montefquieu has confidered it as one of the caufes of the declenfion of the Roman empire. See the Dialogue concerning Oratory, f. xxix. note (*c*).

2

(*f*) Dio.

(*f*) Dio relates this remark made by Tiridates.

(*g*) Pliny the elder has given an account of Nero's paſſion for the occult ſciences, lib. xxx. ſ. 2.

Section V.

(*a*) Suetonius ſays, Nero ſpent in treating Tiridates with unparalleled magnificence, eight hundred thouſand feſterces a day; a ſum almoſt incredible! and at his departure preſented him with above a million.   Sueton. in Nero, ſ. 30.

(*b*) The deſtruction of Artaxata has been mentioned, Annals, xiii. ſ. 41.

(*c*) The ſuperſtitious veneration with which the Parthians conſidered the Sea, has been already mentioned.   Pliny ſays, *Tiridates navigare voluerat, quoniam exſpuere in maria, aliiſque mortalium neceſſitatibus violare naturam eam fas non putant*.   Lib. xxx. ſ. 2.

(*d*) See the Geographical Table.

(*e*) For Dyrrachium, ſee the Geographical Table.

Section VI.

(*a*) Suetonius ſays, Nero, having placed his laurel crown in the capitol, and being complimented with the title of Imperator, cloſed the temple of Janus.   In Nero, ſ. 13.

(*b*) Suetonius mentions his intended expedition to the Caſpian Sea, ſ. 19.

(*c*) Theſe levies of men, ſix feet high, to be called the Alexandrian phalanx, are ſtated by Suetonius, in Nero, ſ. 19.

(*d*) See Suetonius, in Nero, ſ. 22.

(*e*) Suetonius, in Nero, ſ. 30.

(*f*) Suetonius, in the place laſt cited.

Section VII.

(*a*) Helius, the freedman, is mentioned by Dio Caſſius in the character of prime miniſter during Nero's abſence from Rome.   Corneille has deſcribed a ſlave riſing to preferment, with the ſententious brevity of Tacitus:

Jamais

'Jamais un affranchi n'eft qu'un efclave infame;
Bien qu'il change d'état, il ne change point d'ame.

CINNA, act iv. scene 6.

(*b*) See the Geographical Table.

(*c*) The city of Caffiope, and the temple of Jupiter Caffius, are both mentioned by Pliny, lib. iv. f. 12.

(*d*) See Suetonius, in Nero, f. 23.

(*e*) The deftruction of the ftatues erected to the various conquerors in the public games of Greece, is mentioned by Suetonius, in Nero, f. 24.

(*f*) See Annals, book xvi. f. 5.

(*g*) Dio Caffius tells us, that when Nero performed the part of *Canace*, one of the fpectators afked, What is he doing now? A man anfwered, *He is in labour*. For a lift of the characters acted by Nero, fee Suetonius, in Nero, f. 21.

(*h*) See Crevier's Roman Emperors, Life of Nero, vol. iv. p. 304.

Section VIII.

(*a*) Suetonius fays, Nero, after the murder of his mother, was not able to bear the reproaches of his own confcience, though he had received the congratulatory addreffes of the army, the fenate, and the people; he frequently confeffed that he was haunted by his mother's ghoft following him with the whips and burning torches of the furies. *Exagitari fe maternâ fpecie, verberibus furiarum ac tædis ardentibus*. In Nero, f. 34.

(*b*) When Nero made the tour of Greece, he did not dare to attend the Eleufinian myfteries, having heard the cryer warning all impious and nefarious villains not to approach the place. Sueton. in Nero, f. 34.

(*c*) Suetonius fays, he attempted to call up his mother's ghoft, in order to appeafe and mollify her wrath. In Nero, f. 34.

(*d*) See this related by Suetonius, in Nero, f. 40.

(*e*) The territory of Cirrha was for many years annexed to the temple of Delphi: hence Lucan fays in his addrefs to Nero:

Sect.

Sed mihi jam numen ; nec fi te pectore vates
Accipiam, Cirrhæa velim fecreta moventem
Sollicitare Deum.

PHARSAL. lib. i. ver. 63.

(*f*) He became the wife of Pythagoras.   Annals, xv. f. 37.

(*g*) Chryfoftomus fays, Oration xxi, Nero offered a great reward to the perfon, who fhould change Sporus into a woman ; and there were not wanting empyrics, who promifed to accomplifh that metamorphofis.

(*h*) For more of her, fee Hiftory, i. f. 73; and fee Dio, lib. lxiii.

Section IX.

(*a*) See Crevier, Life of Nero.

(*b*) For Sulpicius Camerinus, fee Annals, xiii. f. 52 ; and fee Crevier, vol. iv. p. 310.

(*c*) Nero's diflike of every great man at Rome, joined to his rapacity, induced him, by means of his fatellites, to kill, or force them to difpatch themfelves, the richeft and moft illuftrious of thofe, who till then had efcaped his cruelty.   Crevier, vol. iv. p. 311.

Section X.

(*a*) For this attempt to penetrate the *Ifthmus* of Corinth, fee Suetonius, in Nero, f. 19 ; and Dio, lib. lxiii.

(*b*) Pliny relates this fact : *Perfodere alveo navigabili anguftias eas tentavere Demetrius rex, dictator Cæfar, Caius princeps, Domitius Nero, in faufto (ut omnium patuit exitu) incepto.*

(*c*) For Afcalon, fee the Geographical Table.

(*d*) See the Geographical Table.

(*e*) For Japha, fee the Geographical Table.

(*f*) See the Geographical Table.

(*g*) For Gamala, fee the Geographical Table.

(*h*) For the city of Jotapata, fee the Geographical Table.

(*i*) The works of Jofephus are well known.   They contain a mixture of good fenfe and credulity, of truth and fable.

(*l*) For

(*l*) For the city of Tarichæa, fee Suetonius, in Tito, f. 4; and fee the Geographical Table.

(*m*) Jofephus fays, Vefpafian fupplied Nero with fix thoufand Jews, all ftrong young men, chofen out of a vaft number of prifoners.

Section XI.

(*a*) Suetonius, in Nero, f. 23.

(*b*) For the fate of Corbulo, fee Dio, lib. lxiii.

(*e*) The tame fubmiffion with which fo many brave and eminent men received orders to die, fills the mind with aftonifhment and indignation.

(*f*) For Pactius Africanus, fee Hift. iv. f. 41.

(*g*) For the fate of Craffus, fee Crevier, vol. iv. p. 313.

(*b*) See the Hiftory, book iv. f. 42.

(*i*) For Regulus, fee Pliny the Younger, lib. i. epift. 5; and Life of Agricola, f. ii. note (*a*).

(*k*) For Pifo, adopted by Galba, fee Hiftory, i. f. 15 and 16.

(*l*) See the Geographical Table.

(*m*) Suetonius, in Nero, f. 24.

Section XII.

(*a*) Trachalus was an orator of eminence, commended by Quintilian, lib. x. cap. 1. He is alfo mentioned by Tacitus, Hiftory, i. f. 90.

(*b*) In the lift of Roman poets, whom Quintilian has criticifed, no mention is made of Silius Italicus. It is therefore probable, that his work had not appeared, when Quintilian publifhed his Inftitutes, in the reign of Domitian. Silius (like Lucan before him) undertook to make a great hiftorical event the fubject of an epic poem; but departing from the precedent left by Lucan, he has interwoven with the truth too much of fable, and what the critics call machinery. The poem, however, has many beautiful paffages. The author raifed a confiderable fortune, and was poffeffed of two villas; one that had been the property of Cicero, and the other of Virgil. He lived to the age of feventy-five, and then put an end to his days by abftinence; being inftructed in the ftoic fchool, and by the practice of the age, that

fuicide was not againſt the law of nature. Seneca, the admired philoſopher, has, among many others, the following maxim : " Live ſo, as
to welcome death ; and even if you think fit, to ſeek it. Whether it
comes to you, or you go to it, is immaterial. *Exerce te, ut mortem et
excipies, et, ſi ita res ſuadebit, arceſſas. Intereſt nihil, an illa ad nos veniat,
an ad illam nos.* Epiſt. lxix. It was not underſtood by Seneca, nor
was the light of nature ſtrong enough to inform the ſtoic ſchool, that
the life into which we are called, ought to be preſerved during the
pleaſure of the Supreme Being that gave it. Pliny the conſul gives
an account of the death of Silius Italicus. Towards the end of a long
life, he had contracted an incurable diſeaſe, and t'erefore reſolved to
cloſe the ſcene. He had practiſed at the bar in the beginning of life,
and, in Nero's time, incurred the diſgrace of being a voluntary accuſer. *Læſerat famam ſuam ſub Nerone ; credebatur ſponte accuſaſſe.* But
he afterwards, in a more retired life, retrieved his reputation. *Macu-
lam veteris induſtriæ laudabili otio abluerat.* He was a poet, but he wrote
with more care than genius. *Scribebat carmina majore curâ, quam ingenio.*
He poſſeſſed a number of villas, and had a large collection of books,
ſtatues, and pictures. He celebrated Virgil's birth-day, and viſited
his tomb near Naples, as if it were a temple. It was his glory, that
Nero periſhed in his conſulſhip, and by that event the world was delivered from a monſter. Pliny, book iii. epiſt. 7. Martial has left ſeveral epigrams in praiſe of Silius Italicus, whom, as it ſeems, he eſteemed
and loved.

(*c*) Suetonius, in Nero, ſ. 25.

(*d*) This cuſtom is recorded by Vitruvius, book ix. and Suetonius,
ſ. 25.

(*e*) Flamminius triumphed over the laſt Philip of Macedon, and
Mummius conquered Corinth.

(*f*) For Antium, ſee the Geographical Table.

(*h*) Suetonius mentions the car of Auguſtus, and the proceſſion to
the temple of Apollo, ſ. 25.

(*i*) Suetonius, ſ. 25.

(*k*) This was, probably, the conſpiracy formed by Vinicius. See
Sueton. in Nero, ſ. 36.

(l) The

(*l*) The particulars here related, are told by Plutarch, in his Essay on Garrulity.

(*m*) See Suetonius, in Nero, f. 40.

(*n*) The Hither Spain was called *Hispania Terraconensis*. In that province, Galba received letters from Vindex, requesting him to put himself at the head of mankind, the assertor of public liberty. Sueton. in Galba, f. 9.

(*o*) This speech of Vindex is recorded by Dio, lib. lxiii.

(*p*) Now *Carthagena*, in Spain.

(*q*) See Suetonius, in Galba, f. 10.

(*r*) Seneca, and his brother Annæus Mela, were born at Corduba, in Spain. Lucan, the poet, was a native of the same country.

(*s*) Rufinus Crispinus, the son of Poppæa, by her first husband. He was used, among his play-fellows, to act the part of a general, or an emperor, and for that boyish amusement was ordered to be drowned in the sea. Sueton. in Nero, f. 35.

(*t*) Suetonius says, Galba, holding a general convention at New Carthage, in Spain, under pretence of presiding at the manumission of slaves, placed around the court the statues or images of several who had fallen victims to Nero's cruelty; and in the midst of his harangue, presented to the assembly a noble youth, who had been banished to the next Balearic island (now Majorca), and was brought from his place of exile to be exhibited as an object of compassion. Sueton. in Galba, f. 10.

(*u*) Nero called a council of his favourites, and, after a short conference on the state of affairs, passed the rest of the day in shewing some musical instruments, which, on a new construction, were kept in play by the operation of water. He explained the principles of that ingenious piece of mechanism, declaring his resolution to exhibit it on the stage, if Vindex would give him leave. Sueton. in Nero, f. 41. Dio, lib. lxiii.

(*w*) Nero was the son of Domitius Ænobarbus. See the Genealogical Table. He thought it a disparagement to be called by his paternal name; but nothing enraged him so much, as to find himself railed at as a comedian and harper. Sueton. in Nero, f. 41.

3 X 2

(x) See

(*x*) See Crevier, vol. iv.   All that follows concerning Virginius Rufus, and the defeat of Vindex, is there related at large.

(*y*) For the Sequani, the Ædui, Arverni, and Lingones, fee the Geographical Table.

(*z*) For Vefontium, fee the Geographical Table.

(*aa*) Otho, afterwards emperor, was appointed governor of Lufitania, that Nero might fecure Poppæa to himfelf.   Annals, xiii. f. 46. Plutarch's Life of Galba.

(*bb*) For Clunia, fee the Geographical Table.

Section XIII.

(*a*) This incident is told by Suetonius, in Nero, f. 41.

(*b*) This cargo of fand, with the popular difcontents that followed, is ftated by Suetonius, in Nero, f. 45.   See Pliny, lib. **xxxv.** f. 13.

(*c*) For Nymphidius, fee Annals, xv. f. 72.   For Tigellinus, Annals, xiv. f. 57; and xv. f. 37.

(*d*) The wild and defperate projects conceived by Nero, in his frantic moments, and brought to light by a favourite eunuch, are recorded by Suetonius, in Nero, f. 43.

(*e*) The line in the Œdipus of Sophocles is,

Θανειν μ'ανωγε συγγαμος, μητηρ, πατηρ.

(*f*) Phaon's fidelity is mentioned by Suetonius, in Nero, f. 48.

(*g*) The paffage in Virgil,

Ufque adeone mori miferum eft?

Æneid. xii. ver. 646.

(*h*) Locufta has been mentioned, Annals, xiii. f. 15.   Suetonius fays, that Nero received a dofe of poifon from Locufta, which he carried with him into the Servilian gardens.   Not having courage to ufe it, he endeavoured to find Spicillus, the gladiator, or fome perfon, to kill him.   In that diftrefs, he cried out, *Nec amicum habeo, nec inimicum.* Sueton. in Nero, f. 47.

(*i*) Suetonius relates this fact, f. 48.   Brotier fays, Phaon's villa is now called, *La Serpentara.*

(*k*) See

(*k*) See Suetonius in Nero, f. 49. *Hoftem a fenatu judicatum, et quæri ut puniatur more majorum.* It is impoffible to read this paffage without feeling a thoufand mixed emotions. We acknowledge the juftice of the fentence; we know that vengeance was due to the perpetrator of fo many horrible crimes; and we rejoice to find that the fenate could refume its long-forgotten dignity, and act even for a day with a becoming fpirit. The interefts of humanity required that the world fhould be delivered from fuch a monfter.

The cafe is very different, when LOUIS XVI. is cited to appear before a French Convention. We fee the moft benevolent of men tried by an affembly of *affaffins*, *plunderers*, *levellers*, and ATHEISTS; by the fcum and dregs of France, mixed with the refufe of other nations. When a good and virtuous, an upright and blamelefs monarch is fentenced, contrary to every principle of truth and juftice, to fuffer as a criminal; indignation is, for the moment, loft in aftonifhment at the daring guilt of men, who have emerged from obfcurity to be the tyrants of their country; a PANDÆMONIUM of regicides! France is now left without CHURCH or KING; without law or morals; without a conftitution; and without humanity. The nations of Europe fhudder with horror at the bloody tragedy that has been acted. The virtues, which the MURDERED KING difplayed, with wonderful meeknefs, on the throne, in prifon, and on the fcaffold, are now known to the world. They will be tranfmitted to the lateft pofterity, and

> Will plead, like angels trumpet-tongued, againft
> The DEEP DAMNATION of his taking off.

But the DEMAGOGUES of France will perhaps not allow that Shakefpear is a great moral teacher: let them hear their own Boileau:

> Quoi! ce peuple aveugle en fon crime,
> Qui prenant fon roi pour victime,
> Fit du trône un théâtre affreux;
> Penfe-t-il que le Ciel, complice
> D'un fi funefte facrifice,
> N'a pour lui ni foudre ni feux?

(*l*) The

(*l*) The particulars of Nero's flight, above related, and those that follow, are told by Suetonius, in Nero, f. 48.

(*m*) He took some water out of a ditch and drank it, saying, *Hæc est Neronis decocta.* Being taken into the house, creeping on his hands and knees through a hole that was made for him, he lay on a mean bed, with a tattered coverlet thrown over it, and being both hungry and thirsty, he refused some coarse bread that was brought to him, but drank a little warm water. *Quadrupes per angustias effossæ cavernæ receptus in proximam cellam, decubuit super lectum modicellâ culcitâ et vetere pallio strato instructum. Fameque interim et siti interpellante, panem quidem sordidum oblatum aspernatus est, aquæ autem tepidæ aliquantulum bibit.* Suet. in Neron. f. 48.

(*n*) Suetonius, f. 49.

(*o*) *Qualis artifex pereo!* Suet. f. 49, where the following circumstances are related.

(*p*) The line in Homer is,

$$\text{Ιππων μ' ωκυποδων ομφι κλυπος ουατα βαλλει.}$$

(*q*) He said to the centurion, *Sero: et hæc est fides?* Those were his last words. See the description of his ghastly figure, Suet. f. 49.

(*r*) Suetonius gives the same account of his age. *Obiit secundo et trigessimo ætatis anno, die quo quondam Octaviam interemerat.* In Neron. f. 57.

(*s*) The public joy was so great, that the people ran to and fro, with caps upon their heads. *Tantumque gaudium publice præbuit, ut plebs pileata totâ urbe discurreret.* Suet. in Neron. f. 57.

(*t*) See Suetonius, f. 50.

(*u*) Suetonius says, *Non defuerunt qui per longum tempus vernis æstivisque floribus tumulum ejus ornarent.* S. 57.

(*x*) The readiness of the Parthians to assist a pretended Nero, is mentioned by Suetonius, in Nero, f. 57; and also by Tacitus, History, i. f. 2.

Section XV.

(*a*) A number of prodigies mentioned by Suetonius, in Galba, f. i. Dio, lxiii. Pliny, ii. f. 83 and 103.

(*b*) Plutarch fays he arrived in Spain on the feventh day after Nero's death. See the Life of Galba.

(*c*) Plutarch, Life of Galba.

(*d*) Galba was born in the confulfhip of Valerius Meffalinus and Cneius Lentulus, A. U. C. 751, on the ninth of the kalends of January, in a villa near Terracina. Suet. in Galba, f. 4.

(*e*) See Plutarch, Life of Galba.

(*f*) Plutarch, in Galba, gives the fame account.

(*g*) See Plutarch, Life of Galba.

(*h*) Plutarch relates this faying of Mauricus; for more of whom fee Hiftory, iv. f. 40; and Life of Agricola, f. 45.

(*i*) We read in Suetonius, that Galba was governed by three favourites; Titus Vinius, his lieutenant in Spain; Cornelius Laco, who was advanced to the command of the prætorian guards; and his freedman Icelus, who was dignified with the privilege of wearing a ring, and the name of Martianus. To thefe men Galba refigned himfelf with fuch implicit confidence, that his conduct was never confiftent; at one time frugal and rigorous; at another remifs, complying, and more lavifh than became a prince of his advanced age, who had been raifed to the imperial dignity by the voice of the people. Suet. in Galba, f. 14. For more of the three favourites, fee the Hiftory, i. f. 6 and 13.

(*k*) Plutarch, Life of Galba.

(*l*) For the origin of Nymphidius, fee Annals, xv. f. 72.

(*m*) Plutarch, Life of Galba. Cingonius Varro has already occurred, Annals, xiv. f. 45.

(*n*) For more of Honoratus, fee Plutarch, Life of Galba.

(*o*) This fpeech may be feen in Plutarch.

(*p*) See Plutarch, in Galba; though Suetonius fays, Galba was no way allied to the houfe of Cæfar. Suet. in Galba, f. 2.

( ) All thefe particulars are to be found in Plutarch.

Section XVI.

(*a*) Plutarch, Life of Galba. For Mithridates brought before the emperor Claudius, see Annals, xii. f. 21; and History, i. f. 6.

(*b*) For Petronius Turpilianus, see Annals, xv. f. 72; and History, i. f. 6.

(*c*) Suetonius, in Galba, f. 11.

(*d*) The fate of Obultronius Sabinus, Cornelius Marcellus, and Betuus Chilo, is mentioned by Tacitus, History, i. f. 37.

(*e*) For Clodius Macer, murdered in Africa, see History, i. f. 3 and 11.

(*f*) For an account of Calvia Crispinilla, see History, i. f. 72.

(*g*) Fonteius Capito, History, i. f. 7, 8, and 58.

(*h*) His name was Julius Paulus Claudius Civilis. For more of this famous Batavian chief, see History, book i. f. 59; book iv. f. 13, 14; and throughout the war, which he waged against the Romans, to the close of book v. f. 26.

(*i*) Fabius Valens contrived the murder of Fonteius Capito, in the Lower Germany, History, i. f. 7. He is mentioned often as the partisan of Vitellius. He was at last taken prisoner by Vespasian's party. History, iii. f. 43.

(*k*) This man murdered Fonteius Capito by order of Fabius Valens, and was afterwards given up by Vitellius to the resentment of the soldiers. History, i. f. 58.

(*l*) See Plutarch, Life of Galba.

(*m*) Suetonius, in Galba, f. 11.

(*n*) After a reign of luxury and dissipation, the rigid parsimony of Galba was unseasonable, and, by consequence, rendered him unpopular. Suetonius relates several instances of his avarice beneath the dignity of a prince. He adds, that soon after Galba's arrival in Rome, when he attended the performance of an Attelane Fable, as soon as the actors began the first verse of a favourite song,

Venit Io ! Simus a villa,

Here's Farmer Flatnose come from his villa, the whole audience, with

one

one voice fung the fong, repeating the firft verfe feveral times. Suet.
in Galba, f. 13.

(*o*) This cruel flaughter is told by Plutarch, Life of Galba.
(*p*) See Suetonius, in Galba, f. 14; and Hiftory, i. f. 6 and 13.

END OF NOTES

ON THE

APPENDIX.

GEOGRAPHICAL TABLE:

OR,

INDEX OF THE NAMES OF PLACES

THAT OCCUR IN THIS VOLUME.

A.

ADIABENE, a diſtrict of Aſſyria, ſo called from the river Adiaba; *Adiabeni*, the people.

ADRUMETUM, a Phœnician colony in Africa, about ſeventeen miles from Leptis Minor.

ALBA, a town of Latium in Italy, the reſidence of the Alban kings: deſtroyed by Tullus Hoſtilius.

ALBANIA, a country of Aſia, bounded on the weſt by Iberia, on the eaſt by the Caſpian Sea, on the ſouth by Armenia, and on the north by Mount Caucaſus.

ALESIA, a town in Celtic Gaul, ſituate on a hill. It was beſieged by Julius Cæſar. See his Commentaries, lib. vii. ſ. 77.

ANEMURIUM, a promontory of Cilicia, with a maritime town of the ſame name near it. See Pomponius Mela.

ANSIBARII, a people of Germany.

ANTIUM, a city of the ancient Volſci, ſituate on the Tuſcan Sea; the birth-place of Nero. Two Fortunes were worſhipped there, which Suetonius calls *Fortunæ Antiates*, and Martial, *Sorores Antii*. Horace's Ode to Fortune is well known—

O Diva gratum quæ regis Antium.
The place is now called *Capo d'Anzo*.

ANTONA, now the *Avon*. See Camden.

AORSI, a people inhabiting near the Palus Mæotis; now the eaſtern part of Tartary, between the *Neiper* and the *Don*.

APAMEA, a city of Phrygia, near the banks of the Mæander; now *Aphiom-Kara-Hiſſar*.

ARAXES, a river of Meſopotamia, which runs from north to ſouth, and falls into the Euphrates.

ARAR, or ARARIS, a river of Gaul; now the *Soane*.

ARBELA, a city of Aſſyria, famous for the battle between Alexander and Darius.

ARCADIA, an inland diſtrict in the heart of Peloponneſus; mountainous, and only fit for paſture; therefore celebrated by bucolic or paſtoral poets.

ARICIA, a town of Latium, at the foot of Mons Albanus.

ARII, a people of Aſia.

ARMENIA, a country of Aſia, having Albania and Iberia to the north; divided into the GREATER, which extends eaſtward to the Caſpian Sea; and the LESSER, to the weſt of the GREATER, and ſeparated from it by the Euphrates; now called *Turcomania*.

ARSANIAS, a river of the GREATER ARMENIA, running between Tigranocerta and Artaxata, and falling into the Euphrates.

ARVERNI, a people of Ancient Gaul, inhabiting near the *Loire*; their chief city *Arvernum*, now *Clermont*, the capital of *Auvergne*.

ASCALON, an ancient city of the Philiſtines, ſituate on the Mediterranean; now *Scalona*.

B.

BACTRIANI, a people inhabiting a part of Aſia, to the ſouth of the river *Oxus*, which runs from eaſt to weſt into the Caſpian Sea.

BAIÆ,

BAIÆ, a village of Campania, between the promontory of Misenum and Puteoli (now *Pozzuolo*), nine miles to the west of Naples.

BALEARES, a cluster of islands in the Mediterranean, of which *Majorca* and *Minorca* are the chief.

BITHYNIA, a country of Asia Minor, bounded on the north by the Euxine Sea, adjoining to Troas, over against Thrace; now *Becsangial*.

BONONIA, called by Tacitus *Bononiensis*; now *Bologna*, capital of the *Bolognese* in Italy.

BOSPHORANI; a people bordering on the Euxine; the *Tartars*.

BOSPHORUS, two straits of the sea so called; one *Busphorus Thracius*, now *the straits of Constantinople*; the other *Bosphorus Cimmerius*, now *the straits of Caffa*.

BOVILLÆ, a town of Latium, near Mount Albanus; about ten miles from Rome, on the Appian Road.

BRUNDUSIUM, a town of Calabria, with an excellent harbour, at the entrance of the Adriatic, affording a commodious passage to Greece. The Via Appia ended at this town; now *Brindisi*, in the territory of *Otranto*, in the kingdom of Naples.

BYZANTIUM, a city of Thrace, on the narrow strait that separates Europe from Asia; now *Constantinople*. See Tacitus, Annals, xii. f. 63.

C.

CALABRIA, a peninsula of Italy, between Tarentum and Brundusium.

CAMELODUNUM, said by some to be *Malden* in Essex, but by Camden, and others, *Colchester*. It was made a Roman colony under the emperor Claudius; a place of pleasure rather than of strength, adorned with splendid works; a theatre and a temple of Claudius.

CAMERIUM, a city in the territory of the Sabines; now destroyed.

CANINEFATES, a people who inhabited the lower part of Germany, the west side of *Batavia*.

- CANGI, the inhabitants of Cheshire, and part of Lancashire.

CAPUA, now *Capoa*, a city in the kingdom of Naples. It was the seat of pleasure, and the ruin of Hannibal.

CAPPADOCIA, an extensive country in Asia Minor, upon the Euxine Sea.

CASSIOPE, a town in the island of Corcyra (now *Corfou*), called at present *St. Maria di Cassopo*.

CARTHAGO, a city in Africa, the well known rival of Rome, supposed to be built by Dido seventy years after the foundation of Rome.

CARTHAGO NOVA, a town of *Hispania Tarraconensis*, or the Hither Spain; now *Carthagena*.

CATTI, inhabitants of what is now called *Hesse*, in Germany.

CENCHRIÆ, a port of Corinth, situate about ten miles towards the east; now *Kenkri*.

CHAUCI, a maritime people of Germany, between the *Ems* (Amisia) and the *Elb* (Albis).

CHALCEDON, a city of Bithynia, situate at the mouth of the Euxine, over-against Byzantium. It was called the *City of the Blind*. See Tacitus, Annals, xii. f. 63.

CHERUSCI, a great and warlike people of Ancient Germany, between the *Eib* and the *Wefer*.

CILICIA, an extensive country of the Hither Asia, with Syria to the east, and the Mediterranean to the south.

CIRRHA, a town of Phocis, near Delphi, sacred to Apollo.

CLITÆ, a people of Cilicia.

CLUNIA, a city in the Hither Spain.

COOS, an island in the Ægean Sea; now *Stan-Co*.

COMMAGENE, a district of Syria, with the Euphrates on the east, and Mount Taurus on the north.

CORCYRA, an island in the Adriatic; now *Corfou*.

CORMA, a river in Asia; mentioned by Tacitus only.

CUMÆ, a town of Campania, near Cape Misenum, famous for the cave of the Cumæan Sybil.

CYRENENSES, a people of Africa, in a part now called *the Desert of Barca*. Cyrene their capital city; now *Curin*.

D.

DAHÆ, a people of Scythia, to the south of the Caspian, with the Massagetæ

on

on the eaſt. Virgil calls them *indomitique Dahæ*.

DANDARIDÆ, a people bordering on the Euxine. Brotier ſays that ſome veſtiges of the nation, and its name, ſtill exiſt at a place called *Dandars*.

DYRRACHIUM, a town on the coaſt of Illyricum. Its port anſwered to that of Brunduſium, and the paſſage was ready and expeditious.

E.

ECBATANA, the capital of Media; now *Hamedan*.

EDESSA, a town of Meſopotamia; now *Orrhoa*, or *Orfa*.

EPHESUS, an ancient and celebrated city of Ionia in Aſia Minor; the birth-place of Heraclitus, the weeping philoſopher. It is now called *Efeſo*.

ERINDE, a river of Aſia, mentioned by Tacitus only.

EUPHRATES, a river univerſally allowed to take its riſe in Armenia Major. It divides into two branches, one running through Babylon, and the other through Seleucia. It bounds Meſopotamia on the weſt.

ÆDUI, a people of Ancient Gaul, near what is now called *Autun*, in Lower Burgundy.

ÆGEÆ, a maritime town of Cilicia; now *Aias Kala*.

ÆQUI, a people of Ancient Latium.

F.

FERENTINUM, a town of Latium; now *Ferentino*.

FERENTUM, a town of Etruria; now *Ferenti*.

FORMIÆ, a maritime town of Italy, to the ſouth-eaſt of *Cajeta*. The ruins of the place are ſtill viſible.

FRISII, a people of Ancient Germany, who inhabited what is now called *Frieſland*.

G.

GABII, a town of Latium, between Rome and Præneſte. A particular manner of tucking up the gown, adopted by the Roman conſuls when they declared war or attended a ſacrifice, was called *Cinctus Gabinus*. The place now extinct.

GALLIA, the country of Ancient Gaul, now *France*. It was divided by the Romans into *Gallia Ciſalpina*, viz. Gaul on the Italian ſide of the Alps, with the *Rubicen* for its boundary to the ſouth. It was alſo called *Gallia Togata*, from the uſe made by the inhabitants of the Roman *Toga*. It was likewiſe called *Gallia Tranſpadana* or *Ciſpadana*, with reſpect to Rome. The ſecond great diviſion of Gaul was *Gallia Tranſalpina*, or *Ulterior*, being, with reſpect to Rome, on the other ſide of the Alps. It was alſo called *Gallia Comata*, from the people wearing their hair long, which the Romans wore ſhort. The ſouthern part was GALLIA NARBONENSIS, *Narbon Gaul*, called likewiſe *Braccata*, from the uſe of *braccæ*, or breeches, which were no part of the Roman dreſs; now *Languedoc*, *Dauphiny*, and *Provence*. For the other diviſions of Gaul on this ſide of the Alps, into *Gallia Belgica*, *Celtica*, *Aquitanica*, further ſub-divided by Auguſtus, ſee the Manners of the Germans, ſ. 1, note (*a*).

GALATIA, or GALLOGRÆCIA, a country of Aſia Minor, lying between *Cappadocia*, *Pontus*, and *Paphlagonia*; now called *Chiangare*.

GALILÆA, the northern part of Canaan, or Paleſtine, bounded on the north by *Phœnicia*, on the ſouth by *Samaria*, on the eaſt by the *Jordan*, and on the weſt by the *Mediterranean*.

GARIZIM, a mountain of Samaria, famous for a temple built on it by permiſſion of Alexander the Great.

H.

HERMUNDURI, a people of Germany, in part of what is now called Upper Saxony, bounded on the north by the river *Sala*, on the eaſt by the *Elbe*, and on the ſouth by the *Danube*.

HYRCANIA, a country of the Farther Aſia, to the ſouth-eaſt of the Caſpian, with Media on the weſt, and Parthia on the ſouth; famous for its tigers. Virgil; Shakeſpear, the Hyrcanian tiger.

I.

JAPHA, a ſtrong place, both by nature and art, in the Lower Galilee, not far from *Jotapata*; now *Saphet*.

JAZYGES, a people of Sarmatia Europæa, ſituate on this ſide of the Palus Mæotis, near the territory of Maroboduus, the German king.

IBERIA, an inland country of Aſia,
2
bounded

bounded by Mount Caucafus on the north, by Albania on the eaft, by Colchis and part of Pontus on the weft, and by Armenia on the fouth. Spain was alfo called Iberia, from the river Iberus; now the *Ebro*.

ICENI, a people of Britain; now *Effex*, *Suffolk*, and *Norfolk*.

ILIUM, the famous city of Troy, at a greater diftance from the fea than what was afterwards called *Ilium Novum*.

ILLYRICUM, the country between Pannonia to the north, and the Adriatic to the fouth. It is now chiefly comprehended under *Dalmatia* and *Sclavonia*, under the refpective dominion of the Venetians and the Turks.

ISICHI, a people bordering on the Euxine, towards the eaft.

INSUBRIA, a country of Gallia Cifalpina; now the *Milanefe*.

ITURÆA, a *Transjordan* diftrict of Paleftine, now *Bacar*.

JUGANTES, faid by Camden to be the fame as the *Brigantes*; but Brotier thinks it probable that they were a diftinct people.

L.

LANGOBARDI, a people of Germany, between the *Elbe* and the *Oder*, in part of what is now called *Brandenburg*.

LAODICEA, a city of Phrygia, now *Ladik*.

LESBOS, an ifland in the Ægean Sea, near the coaft of Afia Minor; now called *Metelin*.

LECHÆUM, the weft port of Corinth, which the people ufed for their Italian trade, as they did *Cenchræ* for their eaftern or Afiatic.

LIGURIA, a part of Italy, extending from the Apennine to the Tufcan Sea, containing what is now called *Ferrara*, and the *territories of Genoa*.

LINGONES, a people of Gallia Belgica, inhabiting in and about *Langres* and *Dijon*.

LUCANIA, a country of Ancient Italy; now called the *Bafilicate*.

LUSITANIA, now the kingdom of *Portugal*, on the weft of Spain, formerly a part of it.

LYGII, an ancient people of Germany, who inhabited the country now called *Silefia*, and alfo part of *Poland*.

M.

MARDI, a people of the Farther Afia, near the Cafpian Sea.

MASSILIA, a city of Narbon Gaul; now *Marfeilles*, a port town of *Provence*.

MATTIACI, a people of Germany; *Mattium*, their capital town; now *Marpurg* in *Heffe*.

MAURITANIA, an ancient large region of Africa, extending from eaft to weft along the Mediterranean, divided by the Emperor Claudius into Cæfarienfis the eaftern part, and Tingitana the weftern, bounded by the Atlantic Ocean, the ftraits of Gibraltar, and the Mediterranean, to the north.

MEDIA, a country of the Farther Afia, terminated on the north by the Cafpian Sea, on the weft by Armenia, on the eaft by Parthia, and on the fouth by Affyria.

MELITENE, a city of Cappadocia.

MESOPOTAMIA, a large country in the middle of Afia, between the *Tigris* and *Euphrates*.

MÆOTIS PALUS, a lake of Sarmatia Europæa, ftill known by the fame name, and reaching from Crim Tartary to the mouth of the *Tanais* (the *Don*).

MILVIUS PONS, a bridge over the Tiber, at the diftance of two miles from Rome, on the *Via Flamminia*; now called *Ponte-Molle*.

MISENUM, a promontory in Campania, to the fouth-weft of *Baiæ*.

MONA, an ifland feparated from the coaft of the Ordovices by a narrow ftrait, the ancient feat of the Druids. Now the ifle of *Anglefey*.

MOSA, a large river of Gallia Belgica, which falls into the German Ocean below the *Briel*; now the *Meufe*.

MOSELLA, a river which, running through Lorrain, falls into the Rhine at *Coblentz*; now called the *Mofelle*.

N.

NARBONENSIS GALLIA, the fouthern part of Gaul, bounded by the Pyrences to the weft, the Mediterranean to the fouth, and the Alps and the Rhine to the eaft.

NEMETES, a people originally of Germany, removed to the diocefe of *Spire*, on the Rhine.

NICEPHORUS, a river of Afia that wafhes the

the walls of *Tigranocerta*, and runs into the *Tigris*; D'*Anville* says, now called *Khabour*.

NINOS, the capital of *Assyria*; called also *Nineve*.

NISIBIS, a city of Mesopotamia, at this day called *Nesbin*.

NUCERIA, a city of Campania; now *Nocera*.

NUMIDIA, a country of Africa, bounded to the north by the Mediterranean; now the eastern part of the kingdom of Algiers.

O.

ORDOVICES, a people who inhabited what we now call *Flintshire*, *Denbighshire*, *Carnarvon*, and *Marionethshire*, in North Wales.

OSTIA, a town formerly of note, at the mouth of the *Tiber*, on the south side.

P.

PALUS MÆOTIS; see Mæotis.

PANDA, a river of Asia, in the territory of the *Siraci*; not well known.

PANDATARIA, an island of the Tuscan Sea, in the Sinus Puteolanus (now *il Golfo di Napoli*), the place of banishment for illustrious exiles, viz. Julia the daughter of Augustus, *Agrippina* the wife of Germanicus, Octavia the daughter of Claudius, and many others. It is now called *L'Isle Sainte-Marie*.

PANNONIA, an extensive country of Europe, with Mœsia on the east, Noricum on the west, Dalmatia on the south, and the Danube on the north.

PARTHIA, a country of the Farther Asia, with Media on the west, Asia on the east, and Hyrcania on the north.

PLACENTIA, a town in Italy; now called *Placenza*, in the duchy of Parma.

POMPEII, a town of Campania, near Herculaneum. It was destroyed by an earthquake in the reign of Nero.

PONTUS, a country situate between the Euxine on the east, the mouth of the *Ister* to the north, and Mount Hæmus to the south.

PRÆNESTE, a town of Latium to the south-east of Rome, standing very high, and said to be a strong place. The town that succeeded it, stands low in a valley, and is called *Palestrina*.

PUTEOLI, a town of Campania, nine miles to the west of Naples; now *Pozzuolo*.

R.

REMI, a people of Gaul, who inhabited the northern part of *Champagne*; now the city of *Rheims*.

RHODANUS, a famous river of Gaul, rising on Mount Adula, not far from the head of the Rhine. After a considerable circuit it enters the *Lake of Geneva*, and in its course visits the city of Lyons, and from that place traverses a large tract of country, and falls into the Mediterranean. It is now called the *Rhone*.

RHODUS, a celebrated island in the Mediterranean, near the coast of Asia Minor, over-against *Caria*.

S.

SABRINA, now the *Severn*; a river that rises in *Montgomeryshire*, and running by *Shrewsbury*, *Worcester*, and *Glocester*, empties itself into the Bristol Channel, separating Wales from England.

SAMBULOS, a mountain in the territory of the Parthians, with the river *Corma* near it. The mountain and the river are mentioned by Tacitus only.

SAMARIA, the capital of the country of that name in Palestine; the residence of the kings of Israel, and afterwards of Herod. *Samaritans*, the name of the people. Some magnificent ruins of the place are still remaining.

SAMNITES, a people of ancient Italy, famous for their wars with Rome.

SARDINIA, an island in the Mediterranean, now belonging to the Duke of Savoy.

SELEUCIA, a city of Mesopotamia, situate at the confluence of the *Euphrates* and the *Tigris*; now called *Bagdad*.

SENONES, inhabitants of Celtic Gaul, situate on the *Sequana* (now the *Seine*); a people famous for their invasion of Italy, and taking and burning Rome A.U.C. 364.

SEQUANI, an ancient people of Belgic Gaul, inhabiting the country now called *Franche Comté*, or the *Upper Burgundy*.

SILURES, a people of Britain, situate on the *Severn* and the Bristol Channel; now *South Wales*, comprising *Glamorgan*, *Radnorshire*, *Hereford*, and *Monmouth*. See Camden.

SIMBRUINI COLLES, the Simbruine Hills,

fo called from the *Simbruina Stagna*, or lakes formed by the river *Anio*, which gave the name of Sublaqueum to the neighbouring town.

SWINDEN, a river that flows on the confines of the *Dahæ*. It is mentioned by Tacitus only. Brotier fuppofes it to be what is now called *Herirud*, or *La Riviere d'Herat*.

SINUESSA, a town of Latium on the confines of Campania, beyond the river *Liris* (now *Garigliano*). The place was much frequented for the falubrity of its waters.

SIRACI, a people of Afia, between the *Euxine* and the *Cafpian* Seas.

SOPHENE, a country between the Greater and Leffer Armenia; now called *Zoph*.

SOZA, a city of the *Dandaridæ*.

SYRACUSE, one of the nobleft cities in Sicily. The Romans took it during the fecond Punic War, on which occafion the great Archimedes loft his life. It is now deftroyed, and no remains of the place are left. *Etiam periere ruinæ*.

SYRIA, a country of the Hither Afia, between the Mediterranean and the Euphrates, fo extenfive that Paleftine, or the Holy Land, was deemed a part of Syria.

T.

TANAIS, the *Don*, a very large river in Scythia, dividing Afia from Europe. It rifes in Mufcovy, and flowing through *Crim Tartary*, runs into the *Palus Mæotis*, near the city now called Azoff, in the hands of the Turks.

TARENTUM, now Tarento, in the province of *Otranto*. The Lacedæmonians founded a colony there, and thence it was called by Horace, *Lacedæmonium Tarentum*.

TARICHÆA, a town of Galilee. It was befieged and taken by Vefpafian, who fent fix thoufand of the prifoners to affift in cutting a paffage through the Ifthmus of Corinth.

TAUNUS, a mountain of Germany, on the other fide of the Rhine; now Mount *Heyrick*, over-againft *Mentz*.

TAURI, a people inhabiting the *Taurica Chersonefus*, on the *Euxine*: The country is now called *Crim Tartary*.

TAURANNITII, a people who occupied a diftrict of *Armenia Major*, not far from *Tigranocerta*.

THURII, a people of ancient Italy, inhabiting a part of Lucania, between the rivers Crathis (now *Crate*) and Sybaris (now *Sibari*).

TIBUR, a town of Latium; now *Tivoli*.

TIGRIS, a great river of Afia, rifing in Armenia. It bounds Mefopotamia on the eaft, while the Euphrates inclofes it to the weft. It divides into two channels at Seleucia.

TIGRANOCERTA, a town of Armenia Major, built by Tigranes in the time of the Mithridatic War. The river *Nicepho- rus* wafhes one fide of the town. Brotier fays, it is now called *Sert* or *Sered*.

TRAPEZUS, a city of Afia, near the Pontic Sea; now *Trebizonde*.

TRINOBANTES, a people of Britain, who inhabited *Middlefex* and *Effex*.

TUSCULUM, a town of Latium, to the north of *Alba*, about twelve miles from Rome. It gave the name of *Tufculanum* to Cicero's villa, where that great orator wrote his Tufculan Queftions.

TYRUS, an ancient city of Phœnicia, fituate on an ifland fo near the Continent, that Alexander the Great formed it into a Peninfula, by the mole or caufey which he threw up during the fiege. See Curtius, lib. iv. f. 7.

U.

UBII, a people originally of Germany, but tranfplanted by Auguftus to the weft fide of the Rhine, under the conduct of *Agrippa*. Their capital was for a long time called *Oppidum Ubiorum*, and, at laft, changed by the emprefs Agrippina to *Co- lonia Agrippinenfis*; now *Cologne*, the capital of the Elector of that name. The *Ara Ubiorum* was an altar erected by the Ubii in honour of Auguftus; but whether it was the fame as their capital, or a different place, does not feem to be clearly afcertained.

USPE, a town in the territory of the *Siraci*; now deftroyed.

VANGIONES, originally inhabitants of Germany, but afterwards fettled in Gaul; now the *diocefe of Worms*.

VENETI, a people of Gallia Celtica, who inhabited what is now called *Vannes*, in the fouth of Brittany, and alfo a confiderable tract on the other fide of the Alps, extending from the Po along the Adriatic, to the mouth of the *Ifter*.

VXONTIUM,

Vesontium, the capital of the Sequani; now *Befançon*, the chief city of *Burgundy*.

Vienna, a city of Narbonese Gaul; now *Vienne* in *Dauphiné*.

Volsci, a powerful people of ancient Latium, extending from *Antium*, their ca-pital, to the *Upper Liris*, and the confines of *Campania*.

Z.

Zeugma, a town on the *Euphrates*, famous for a bridge over the river. See Pliny, lib. v. f. 24.

'END OF THE SECOND VOLUME..